The Highest Virtue

by Alan Stang

The Highest Virtue

by Alan Stang

Western Islands

CONTENTS

The Highest Virtue

by Alan Stang

Part I
Fyodor Voronov

I

Michael Voronov raised the mallet and brought it down with a crash. He raised it again — the heavy iron butt atop the long handle high overhead. He waited, back arched, arms raised, the mallet absolutely still — all in a single, tense, sweeping line like a drawn bow waiting to be sprung — until the pain in his arms became unendurable. Then he flexed and drove the mallet down. The butt leaped, and beneath it the metal flashed and howled.

Nothing could be seen through the windows. The countless little panes set in the rusted frames were thick with the unwashed dirt of years. It was the middle of winter, but the large factory room was steaming. The walls near the windows perspired slightly. The door of the huge furnace in the corner glowed red. From time to time someone opened it and flames leaped into the room.

Like the others, Michael worked bare to the waist, skin black with grime and streaked with sweat. Men shouted and ran from bench to bench, pointed, swore, moved equipment, spat. The mallets monotonously rose and fell. There was too much noise to talk. But he did not want to. He raised his arms and lowered them, raised and lowered, raised and lowered, enjoying the rhythm in the silence of his mind.

Somewhere outside a loud bell rang. The mallets stopped. The sound died away and the room was silent. Michael raised his mallet high and brought it down once more with all his force, making a single but reverberating explosion like a thunderclap.

He filed out with the others, washed with cold water, and began to dress.

"Hey, Voronov," said a voice.

A hand was pulling at his elbow. A familiar face was looking up. It was Kolodsky, his enormous, veiny nose waggling, his pinched features pressed around it like the buckled roots of a tree. He motioned and drew Michael aside.

"I have an opportunity for you," he whispered.

"What kind?" Michael asked.

Kolodsky handed him a card and tapped it. On it Michael read an address.

"Come at ten," Kolodsky whispered. "There's money to be made."

Michael looked dubiously at the card. Was this something serious or not? Kolodsky was strangely compelled to do everything in secret. If he ordered a meal or bought a newspaper, he made it seem as if he were arranging a plot. He could do nothing simply. In his hands, an ordinary arrangement became a conspiracy. It was as if he would like to speak openly if he could, but he could not. It was impossible. He did not know why, but he had to whisper behind his hand. So habitual, so permanent had this behavior become that Kolodsky was in effect caricaturing himself, and at the same time, he no longer noticed it. But others noticed it all the more. People raised their eyebrows at Kolodsky. They smiled. They winked, as if to say: "Oh, yes, Kolodsky. How's business? How's the plot going?" People refused to take him seriously. Their smiles and winks insinuated their opinion that Kolodsky was an inconsequential little man.

But Kolodsky pretended not to notice, and his dissimulation compounded his behavior. The secrecy grew. Kolodsky seethed secretly and steadily, recording every wink and smile, secretly preparing to retaliate. One day he would show them he was not an inconsequential little man.

So Michael looked dubiously at the card, uncertain whether it meant anything real.

"What kind of work is it?" he asked. He was interested; he wanted the money.

Kolodsky put a finger on his pinched, dry lips. The extraordinary nose above them waggled. The small eyes astride it rolled. Someone was passing in the corridor. When Kolodsky looked up, he saw that Michael was smiling. Insulted, Kolodsky thought of taking the card back. But he did not, remembering Dolgorensky, who would be displeased.

They began walking toward the factory gates. An English limousine drew up. A man got out, walked quickly to the building and went in. He was an unusually tall and muscular man which, combined with his bearing, gave a sense of extraordinary strength. It was Danilov of Danilov Agricultural Machinery, where they worked.

"Thief!" Kolodsky whispered. "Crook! Robber!"

"What do you mean?" Michael said.

"Danilov does no work, but gets most of the money. He is a leech, sucking his rubles from our hides. A thief."

4

"But he pays more than anyone else," said Michael.

"Bribes!" hissed Kolodsky. "Bribes!" He was getting excited. "We'll teach him to insult us when we take away the factory," he whispered. "This is 1910. Russia is becoming industrialized. Private ownership has run its course."

Once again, Michael smiled. Again he saw Danilov's image in his mind, massive, inexhaustible, sweeping through the gates. The idea that Kolodsky could take the factory away from him was so thoroughly ludicrous that Michael saw in it proof that what others said about Kolodsky was true: he was nothing but an inconsequential little man. Nothing he said or did could be taken seriously.

Abruptly but smoothly, Michael walked away, out of the gate and into the city. Kolodsky watched him go. He walked erectly, very erectly, as if he were marching, yet at the same time he seemed completely relaxed. There was something about his bearing Kolodsky resented, something irritating. Indeed, when they were together Kolodsky always felt insulted. Perhaps it was Michael's indifference, his aloofness, the way he kept to himself. But Michael would soon see that Kolodsky was a person of importance; that he was not an inconsequential little man at all.

Michael walked home through St. Petersburg. It was the middle of winter. A freezing wind blew in from the Neva. The city was frozen, as if carved from ice, and his patched and threadbare coat gave scant protection, so that his muscles inside it twitched in the cold. But Michael Voronov was in no hurry. As always, he took the long way around. He enjoyed the walk, and it delayed the homecoming.

He crossed the Neva, walking on the ice. It was always very quiet there, which he enjoyed. He heard only his own breathing and his footsteps crunching in the snow. The city around him seemed far away. In the distance the scant light glinted on the gold dome of the Admiralty, and the bells rang in the fortress of Peter and Paul.

He turned into the Nevsky, street of shops, power and wealth, leisure and luxury. Passersby stared at him as they always did when he strolled through the elegant parts of town, peering into the windows of expensive shops. He was a man people turned their heads to watch, not just because his presence was incongruous, but because there was an incongruity between him and his own clothes. A shopkeeper arranging a display in his window would look up into the steady, piercing eyes, smile an invitation to their owner, and then become confused by the clothes below them.

Michael Voronov did not cringe. He did not seem uneasy, as others might. He strolled slowly, browsing in the windows, his gray eyes searching and direct as though he might indeed buy something that he liked. He smiled, as if he knew some secret, as if his outworn clothes were not his own.

He turned into the yard of his tenement in the Putilovsky factory district. In the doorway of the small room not far from the entrance, Bykov the janitor snored spasmodically before a fire, drunk as usual. He had never been seen sober. A noise awoke him, and he tried to lift his eyelids to look for the disturbance. But they fell again before he found it.

The yard was full of ancient garbage: empty, rusting tin cans; broken glass; bits of old newspapers and refuse; dog droppings. A dog rooted aimlessly in the mess. The sour odor made the nostrils twitch. So did the smell of the cheap food being cooked. Michael skirted the garbage carefully and walked up in the dark, avoiding the broken steps. He stayed close to the wall; the banister was weak.

The apartment consisted of two large rooms. As he pushed open the door, he saw over his father's shoulder the wrinkled face of Misha Zabulyov. Misha was pushing a glass of vodka across the table, the brimming meniscus seesawing over the rough surface.

"Careful!" said Fyodor Pavlovitch Voronov. "Careful! Don't spill a drop."

The glass arrived intact, Misha waved to Michael and poured one for himself. He raised his glass and Voronov did the same. In a single, long swallow they threw the vodka down, some of it dribbling down their gray mustaches. Voronov wiped his mouth and licked his fingers. He did not turn around. He and Michael did not greet each other.

"That's my son, I suppose?" said Voronov, setting down the glass.

"Good evening, Michael Fyodorovitch," said Zabulyov, smiling.

Michael looked at Zabulyov, but did not answer. It was painful to engage in pleasantries in his father's presence.

"Vodka?" smiled Zabulyov. Zabulyov smiled not in response to some remark or event, but as a habitual, nervous reaction. Even when alone he always wore a smile, so it was difficult to tell when he was really amused.

"No," said Voronov. "My son does not approve." He took the bottle and refilled his glass, speaking very slowly and distinctly, carefully pronouncing each syllable. "No, my son does not believe in enjoying oneself. He has no time for spiritual matters. He is a materialist, like all of the younger generation."

Zabulyov nodded with approval and smiled, and Fyodor Voronov raised his glass.

"To the unconquerable human spirit," he said and he swallowed.

The door to the inner room opened and Michael's mother shuffled out.

She wore an ancient, faded housecoat. Her eyes were red. Her hair was askew. She did not notice Michael until she was before him, then she kissed him absently and passed, shuffling, to the old stove in the corner. Her feet were wrapped in newspapers tied with string. It was very cold even here in the apartment.

"Mother!" Michael said angrily.

Sophia Petrovna Voronova stopped short, hunching imperceptibly as for a blow.

Michael pointed at her feet. "I gave you money for overshoes yesterday."

Sophia Petrovna looked down, surprised. She shrugged. She put a finger to her lips.

"Ah, well. Ah, well," she said. "Yes, yes."

She examined the stove, sighed and shuffled out, while Voronov conspicuously ignored the incident.

Michael heard the sound of liquid being poured and turned to see Voronov filling his glass.

"Where did you get that vodka?" Michael asked, approaching.

"A man needs a little drink to entertain his friends," said Voronov in a high voice, straightening himself with dignity. He did everything very slowly, with great dignity.

Michael suddenly picked up the bottle and smashed it against the table edge. Bits of glass fell on the floor and floated across the table in a pool.

"You had no right to do that!" Voronov screeched. His eyes filled with tears of frustration. With the edge of a hand, he manipulated the disappearing pool, trying vainly to collect it. He licked his fingers, with great dignity, and spat out the bits of glass.

Zabulyov was smiling. He got up. "Well, I'll be going, Fyodor Pavlovitch."

"No!" shouted Voronov quickly, as if afraid to let him do so. He put both hands on his shoulders and forced him back into the chair.

"There's no need for you to go, Misha. No need at all." Now he spoke softly and slowly, with great dignity. "I apologize for my son."

"But, after all, my dear Fyodor Pavlovitch, if there is nothing more to drink," shrugged Zabulyov.

"Stay. We'll talk. We'll talk," said Voronov angrily.

He glanced at Michael and Michael went into the other room. Voronov got up and began to walk around, slowly, thoughtfully, with great dignity. He gesticulated and smoothed his clothes, which had been stylish twenty years before.

7

"Once again I apologize for my son, my dear Misha," began Voronov. He took long, dignified strides. "This chance, unfortunate incident once again confirms my thesis. You'll recall the point I was making when we were interrupted."

Zabulyov smiled. "No, I don't."

"There simply is no place in the world today for the man of refined feelings, my friend. Beauty, Misha. Beauty, that delicate bloom, is going out of the world, killed by the materialists with their machines. The rule of the enlightened few has been replaced by a horde of babbling rabble; yes, a horde of babbling rabble, smelly, noisy, screeching for their 'rights.' Misha, do you know when the world was at its height, when men lived as nature intended? In the middle of the monastic period, when the intelligentsia pursued its intellectual interests in an atmosphere of refined contemplation. It's my theory that everything that has happened since is a degeneration.

"That is why we must not be too hard on my son, Misha. He is not a culprit, but a victim — a victim of the coming dictatorship of the machine, a partial being without spirituality."

Zabulyov smiled and nodded, understanding nothing, obviously waiting for the next opportunity to get away. As always, this irritated Voronov, but there was nothing he could do. He needed Zabulyov to listen to his harangues.

"How inspiring it is," said Voronov, "to see how some of our young men resist; their long hair, their love of flowers, their pacifism, their sexuality — yes, their generous, honest, communal sexuality. To you, Misha, these things may be foolish, or even meaningless. But in fact they are gestures of defiance for the machine, attempts to revive the spirituality of the monastic period. Inspiring, but at the same time tragic. Pathetic, not just because they are doomed — which they are — and not because it is Michael who dooms them. But because I was born too soon to participate in the movement. Once again, as in everything else, I am cheated by fate. Yes, Misha, I too want to let my hair grow and enjoy the beautiful irresponsibility of a commune. Instead of which, as you see, I am simply a cheated, middle-aged man."

"I am sorry, Fyodor Pavlovitch," said Zabulyov. "Such a pity."

"Who can be sure of anything," sighed Voronov. "Perhaps the day of deliverance will come."

Zabulyov stretched, yawned and fell asleep. "Wake me in time," he whispered. His head hung and he began to snore.

Voronov frowned with the usual frustration. As he was fond of saying, Zabulyov had understood nothing. Why did Voronov bother to explain things to him? Zabulyov understandably enjoyed talking with a gentleman, but why did Voronov the gentleman permit it? He was a busy man. Bored and exasperated, he drummed his fingers on the table.

In the other room, Michael breathed with reluctance. The air was still and heavy, as if it had been used by generations of dead lungs. It was dark, so dark that at first he could not see. He heard a voice murmuring indistinguishable words, vague, monotonous, like the humming of a bee. Then he dimly saw Sophia Petrovna kneeling formlessly before the lighted ikon.

"Mother," he said, putting a hand on her shoulder.

She did not answer. Instead, she patted his hand to ask for silence. She pulled on his coat, pulling him down, and he resisted until he became embarrassed, yielding and kneeling next to her at last.

"Michael," she whispered. "Pray with me."

Again her recitation began, now quite close, its meaning still hidden in her voice. Michael watched her, expressionless, waiting, until she too became uncomfortable.

"Michael, this is meaningless," she whispered. "It will pass. It is necessary."

"Necessary? Why? What do you mean?"

"All of us must suffer, Michael, all, even the Tsar. We must suffer now to prepare for the great joy later. We've all sinned, Michael. Just to be human is to sin. Your father was such a good man. So full of life. So much fun. Ah, and he was so good looking in his uniform. I remember once in the country, near Voronezh, where you were born, I pointed to some cherries at the top of a tree. They were so big, and I said I'd so much like to taste them. And, do you know, he climbed to the top, to the very top, and brought them down to me. I was so afraid he would fall. If he had . . . ."

Sophia Petrovna stared into the darkness, lost, musing. She shrugged. "Happiness is not possible on earth, Michael. It's unimportant. Life is an unreal, transitory illusion. Suffering must not only be welcomed but encouraged, to enhance the genuine life to come. You do not understand this yet, I know, but you will, Michael. You must."

The light from the ikon showed only parts of her face, patches of skin hanging in the shadows. Her lips moved. Once again she was reciting, flatly, unintelligibly, her voice hanging in the air like dead leaves on a graveyard tree.

Michael rose abruptly and left the room, went to the window near the stove and looked out. In the firelight below, he saw the courtyard, covered with greasy snow like a molting coat. But he pressed his forehead to the cold glass, which was pleasantly cool. Voronov drummed on the table, and Zabulyov slumped near him, snoring. The ragged, colorless decor was uncomfortable and uninviting.

9

"Yes, Misha," said Voronov, "my son has no respect. Like so many other modern young men, he regards his poor old father with contempt — always a symptom of a degenerating society. They believe we fathers are hopelessly passé. But do I complain, Misha? Do I protest, as perhaps I should? No, Misha, not at all. The young men are right; I am hopelessly old-fashioned, as they say. I am an antique from another period, a relic of another age, the age of style, of charm and integrity. I believe in suffering in silence, Misha, not uttering a word. That is hopelessly old-fashioned, I realize — I confess, I am guilty — but anything else ishopelessly bad taste.

"I would not criticize my son, Misha, not even in private. Not one word, Misha. I would rather die."

Zabulyov was still snoring. He had not heard a word. And if he had, he would not have had the sense to be embarrassed. But Michael did have the sense and was. Why did his father go on like this? Why did he perversely enjoy pushing his own face in the muck?

"Do you believe in reincarnation, Michael?" asked Voronov.

"No."

"I didn't think you would. I do. I can't understand why we think so differently. After all, I educated you. Had it not been for me, you would not know how to read.

"I believe in it. One's life goes on endlessly in a variety of different forms. It always has and always will, which is why I am so fond of nature."

Voronov found himself fascinating. He got up and began to pace back and forth, gesticulating as always with a forefinger. His tone became declamatory.

"That is why I respect nature and all its creatures. Do you realize that even the mosquito that sucks human blood may in fact be somebody's father? Do you realize that the bee, the bee in the garden, may be a close friend? That, by the way, is what I should like to be in my next life: a bee. Yes, you may think it strange, but I'm quite serious, Michael. Consider the life of a bee. He flits, carefree and happy in the sunlight, from bud to bud sipping nectar. He doesn't have to struggle. He doesn't have to live up to anything. His life is nothing but continuous pleasure. He doesn't spend his time justifying and doubting himself. He doesn't blame himself for the absence of some nonexistent virtue, or worry about some so-called ideal.

"Indeed, how can we be sure that *homo sapiens* is of greater value than any other species? Because we think? Why should that accidental quality necessarily be the criterion? Has anyone other than humans ever believed it?"

Michael did not answer. There was no place in the apartment where he could escape. He walked out of it quickly, pursued by Voronov's voice loudly calling him back to hear more. So quickly did he go that he tripped on the

10

broken steps, so quickly that he surprised the rats feasting in the courtyard. Then he was out of the yard and into the street, walking away at the same pace.

He had participated in these conversations so many times before, unwillingly, mechanically, like an actor too long in a part. More than anything else — more than the cheap smells and the frayed furniture — they wounded him. These other things were unimportant, irrelevant, easily ignored. But this — these conversations — they were something else, something he could not name but recoiled from. Why did Voronov insist on them, insist like an alcoholic craving a drink, or as one who took pleasure in picking at a scab? Michael could hear his father's voice now, droning on and on as usual, echoing senselessly in his mind's ear.

St. Petersburg was silent, muffled by the snow, but gradually his footsteps crunched the echo out. It was cold, painfully cold, but at the same time a pleasure. The cold somehow seemed to cleanse and purify. His body moved smoothly, lean and taut. On and on he walked, at first not knowing where he was going, knowing only that he would not relent.

II

Dolgorensky looked at the others in the room and sneered covertly, his lush, feminine lips pursing slightly. So few really understood what the movement was about. So few, even Party members such as these. There was Grodsky, for instance, who unfortunately sat near him now, greasy hair hanging to his shoulders, fingernails black, the dirt brimming in his pores and crevices. An unmistakable, pungent smell rose from his body. What was it Lenin himself had said? "First we must destroy their egos, their self-respect. Only then can they be kneaded into obedient, interchangeable cells of the Party body." Dolgorensky clearly heard his voice now. Lenin was right, of course; Grodsky was worth only his willingness to have his skull cracked. But that willingness was rare and crucially important. Because of it, the campaign against "police brutality" was going well. Indeed, one of Grodsky's hands was fatly bandaged, the result of his success in the recent demonstration.

Dolgorensky passed his well-kept fingers before his face, inhaling deeply of his own perfumed scent, but its delicate, French fragrance was overcome by Grodsky's. With vindictive amusement, he noticed that the nostrils of the Smolny graduate next to Grodsky were twitching. She was washed but wore no cosmetics and her clothes were deliberately old. Yet she was still obviously a Smolny graduate and the daughter of a rich professor. Her mind had been properly prepared; she was in the movement to atone. But of course she did not understand a thing. On Grodsky's left side was the other girl, small, consumptive, also in old clothes, a genuine proletarian in rimless glasses. Dolgorensky dismissed her. She simply wanted revenge.

Across the table was Nastasya Lvovna Filipova, large, middle-aged, dressed in a tight tunic. She was so ludicrous that Dolgorensky had made her chief, which made her even more ludicrous — especially since she was entirely unaware of it. Dolgorensky did not like her. Next to her was her husband, well-dressed, with gold watch and chain, timid, liberal. Unfortunately such types were necessary until the great day.

12

There was a man about sixty in a Russian shirt hanging outside his trousers, ostentatiously belted with a piece of rope — a man obviously playing a Tolstoyan peasant, but whose hands revealed that he had never done a day's work. He was, in short, a fraud. And there was Kolodsky, scurrying nervously as always, peering out the windows, looking out the door in the usual ecstasy of conspiracy.

Not one of them, all members of the Party, knew what the Party really was. Like so many, they were simply playing at revolution — like their "explosives expert," who had blown his own hands off last week. Sometimes Dolgorensky thought only he and Lenin knew, which depressed him.

But now for the first time, he was glad. For the first time, he *wanted* a mission to fail. He did not want to free Orloff, as Lenin had ordered. He knew Lenin was right, as always, and that Orloff would be helpful in the recruitment of certain types, but he was willing to risk Lenin's anger with failure. How unusual it would be. That was why Dolgorensky had not taken charge himself.

He knew that Orloff understood less than anyone else, that he was hopelessly naive. But somehow Dolgorensky did not respond with the usual humorous contempt. He did not know why — which compounded the problem — but he regarded Orloff as a threat.

Nastasya Lvovna rapped sharply on the table. "We are behind schedule. Let us start. Comrade Dolgorensky, do you wish to speak?"

"Only to say that our street strategy is going well. Marina Nikitovna, I like your new device for the horses."

The girl with the rimless glasses nodded slightly, her mouth still a lipless crease.

"The beauty of it is that one can slash their bellies so that only the Cossacks on top of them see," Dolgorensky told her. "It makes the revolutionary truth we are telling clearer.

"As for you, Grodsky, you can wear your bandages with pride. The newspapers are filled with reports of 'police brutality.' "

Nastasya Lvovna's husband slowly shook his head. "I never realized how much preparation a spontaneous demonstration needs."

"On the other hand," said Dolgorensky, "there is a problem of finance."

Nastasya Lvovna tugged at her ear. "Collections, especially bank collections, are difficult to organize without a bomber."

"Do not play with me," said Dolgorensky. "Belsky had his accident only last week."

Nastasya Lvovna blushed like a girl, which annoyed her. "Other arrangements soon will be made, comrade, I assure you."

"They should be," said Grodsky, "and the problem centers on our woman chief."

"What's wrong with a woman chief?" snapped Marina Nikitovna.

"Woman is muck, glorious muck, to be bathed in by man," said Grodsky. "The gloriously dirty rag with which he wipes his feet."

"And you call yourself a revolutionist?" shouted Marina Nikitovna. "You're a reactionary, an Arab, practically bourgeois."

"Nevertheless," said the Smolny graduate, "men and women are different, and their physiological differences have definite psychological counterparts."

"Liar! Slut!" screamed Marina Nikitovna.

"Comrades, comrades," said the fraud who was playing Tolstoy. He wore an expression of injured regret. He held up two fingers to indicate that what he would say was religious. "Can we not discuss our problems without rancor? Is there no room in your hearts for peace and reflection? Will you not open those hearts, comrades, even just a crack, so that the universal balm of brotherly love may flow into it? Certainly our problems are complicated and real. Certainly they will be difficult to solve. But nothing, no provocation, justifies such violent abuse. Love, comrades, love alone contains the solution."

"Have you ever speculated about the actual psychology of Christ the man?" asked Grodsky. "The real, individual, historical personage. Was he a deluded and ignorant peasant? A smelly oaf? A dupe? The front man for a conspiracy of hypocritical power-seekers? Was he himself a conspirator, a cunning and ruthless agitator? Perhaps a victim of classic megalomania? Or is the truth the most prosaic choice of all: was he simply a liar?"

"Christ was no liar," said Marina Nikitovna. "To be a liar, one must first know the truth, and he was psychologically incapable of knowing it, as is well shown in the Gospels. No, Christ was definitely a Roman *agent provocateur.*"

Grodsky thrust his forefinger up his nose, grinning. "For that matter," he said, "can we even be sure of his existence? The only evidence, after all, is the Gospels. How can we be sure they are not a concoction, a joke? Certainly they do not meet Socialist standards of proof."

"That makes no difference, comrade," said Marina Nikitovna. "The question of his existence is entirely irrelevant. Even if he never existed, what we are told are his teachings have had great influence on history, influence we must evaluate and overcome. Therefore, even if he did not exist, he exists."

The Tolstoyan sat staring at his hands on the table. Without a word he jumped up and grabbed Marina Nikitovna by the neck.

"Liar! Slut!" he roared.

The Tolstoyan squeezed. Her tongue flapped out, large, brown, like an old sausage. Over and over he roared the words. Marina Nikitovna flopped like a fish held by the tail.

Grodsky laughed in falsetto. Nastasya Lvovna rapped on the table. Her husband and the Smolny graduate simply stared. Kolodsky ran nervously back and forth like a hen. Dolgorensky sat calmly as if somewhere else, his eyes just barely showing amusement and contempt. Most boring of all, he thought, were those who argued about ideology — as if ideology had something to do with the Party, as if even Party ideology were serious, as if they were fighting an ideological war. Once again, he thought unpleasantly of Orloff. So few, so few really understood.

Suddenly there was pounding on the other side of the wall. Everyone froze except Kolodsky, who scurried up and down silently, nose waggling, arms flailing, warning finger to his lips. "Comrades! Please!" he whispered. "The drunken Pole next door."

"Comrades, you are all aware of our mission," said Nastasya Lvovna as if nothing had happened. "The Central Committee itself has ordered that comrade Orloff be freed. And comrade Dolgorensky has given us the honor of the task. The best place to do it is here, now. Before comrade Orloff is sent back to Siberia.

"A diversion is necessary. An assassination has been approved. The revolutionary object will be Inspector Ogarev."

Grodsky whistled. "Of the Okhrana?"

"Exactly. I believe you know him?"

"Horrible," said the Tolstoyan. "Nothing, no provocation, could make such a thing necessary."

"Unfortunately we suffered a setback last week," said Nastasya Lvovna. "Belsky is no longer of any value without hands."

"He did not know what he was doing, anyway," said Marina Nikitovna. "It's no great loss."

"How remarkable," said the Smolny graduate. "I saw him yesterday in the charity ward. Attending to all his needs was Mme. Danilova, wife of the industrialist. She does that regularly, I'm told. Why?"

"For the same reason you have joined us," said Marina Nikitovna. "For the same reason Danilov himself contributes to the Party: guilt. Guilt for what your class has done to us. You all think you can simply buy a clean conscience. You are lucky that, at the moment, we need you.

"If only all our enemies attacked us like Telegin, the journalist."

"You have spoken the name of reaction," said Grodsky. "Have you read his series about Orloff?"

"Remarkable," said Filipov. "A remarkable adversary."

"I did not know that Danilov contributed to the party," said Grodsky.

"Oh, yes," said Marina Nikitovna. "I myself make the collections at his house. Nadia Nikolaevna is against them, of course. She buys a clean conscience with her service at the hospital. But Ivan Fyodorovitch does not work at the hospital. One can almost see the therapeutic effect of my visits, Danilov righteously handing me the rubles, as if they really meant something. Of course we do this in the servants' quarters, because I use the back door — for secrecy, Danilov tells me. But you and I know the real reason: it would be so hideously *gauche* for a member of such a trashy family as mine to mix as an equal with the daughter of a prince. Even when giving, the bourgeois take away. And their children, as you might expect, are even more rotten, if possible."

"They are getting their money's worth," said Kolodsky. "Comrade Orloff is their relative. Mme. Orlova and Mme. Danilova are sisters."

Yes, that's true, thought Dolgorensky. I had forgotten. Perhaps it will be useful some day.

Nastasya Lvovna rapped on the table. "Comrades, we have decided not to wait for the Party to replace Belsky. We cannot wait. We have decided to find someone ourselves. Nikita Sergeievitch, have you made the arrangements?"

Nodding rapidly, Kolodsky scurried up. "He is coming, comrade, but be careful. He is very difficult."

Nastasya Lvovna's ample chest swelled. "Is he!" she said. "We shall soon see."

Dolgorensky smiled inwardly. It would be all right.

There was a knock and Kolodsky scurried away and returned with Michael. No one spoke. Everyone but Kolodsky stared at him, appraising much longer than most would call insulting. Michael in turn looked from each to each, lingering with curiosity over Grodsky.

"Name?" Nastasya Lvovna finally said.

"Voronov," he said. "Now what do you want?"

Nastasya Lvovna became excited. "Your patronymic?"

"Fyodorovitch."

"And your father's?"

"Pavlovitch."

For no apparent reason, Nastasya Lvovna became agitated.

"Age?"

"Twenty." Nastasya Lvovna fell into a strange reverie.

"Kolodsky said there was money to be made," said Michael.

Marina Nikitovna nodded. "The opportunist type."

"There is," said Nastasya Lvovna, recovering. "You are familiar with explosives?"

"Yes."

"During the next week you will instruct us as thoroughly as possible in their use."

"For what purpose?"

"That does not concern you. You will simply provide us with certain technical information."

Michael looked from one to the other. He was as yet a man of limited experience, strictly limited to the factory and his books. He had never seen such people before. Even Kolodsky, whom he knew, seemed different in this setting. On each of their faces was something strange. He began to believe that what was happening was intended as a joke, which would be silly. Or was it intended to be serious, which would make it a different sort of joke?

"Exactly what technical information do you require?" he asked.

"Enough of this quibbling!" Nastasya Lvovna shouted. "I order you to cooperate in the name of the Revolution!"

"You order me?" Michael began to chuckle. So it was a joke after all, a good one. But of exactly what sort, he was not sure.

"Who are you?" he asked.

"That does not concern you either."

"Suppose I were to report all this to the police?"

"They would investigate and find nothing. You would be arrested as a fraud."

"I don't understand," said the Smolny graduate. "You are a worker. Surely you support the Revolution in your name."

"Who authorized you to act in my name?"

The Smolny graduate frowned. She had never known a worker. Indeed, this was the first she had met. And workers believed otherwise. It said so in Marx.

"You've sold out to the imperialists," said Marina Nikitovna.

Nastasya Lvovna rapped on the table. "Come, come, comrades, we're wasting valuable time." The realization that Michael not only refused to accept her authority, but was not even impressed, infuriated her.

"Tell me this," said Michael. "What is your Revolution for?"

How remarkable, thought Dolgorensky, watching unobtrusively. He is a primitive, a savage, and yet he knows more than they do.

"Absolute, irrevocable and universal annihilation," said Grodsky. "Complete destruction."

"But wouldn't that include us?" said the girl from Smolny.

"Of course," said Grodsky. "Shouldn't it?"

"What nonsense," said Nastasya Lvovna. "The dictatorship of the proletariat needs a proletariat to which to dictate."

Michael nodded. He understood. It was a nightmare. A fit of madness. On every face was the crazy proof: bizarre, inappropriate expressions. In the dim light in the tenement room, it seemed that they could not be in St. Petersburg. It seemed they could not really exist.

He turned abruptly and left the room. They heard his footsteps decisively receding down the hall.

"Just a moment!" Nastasya Lvovna called.

Kolodsky scurried after him, calling his name, shouting, but the door opened and closed and he was gone.

Dolgorensky's lush, feminine lips quivered. He felt an urge to smile, which he suppressed. Orloff would almost certainly go to Siberia. He was almost as good as aboard the train now. If only Dolgorensky could tell him why.

III

Fyodor Voronov was a victim of fate. Indeed, it was his favorite expression: "I am a victim of fate." The universe conspired against him, listening, watching, waiting for Voronov to act or even wish. Then with no effort it frustrated his act, wrecked his plans, denied his wish. That in fact was the purpose of the universe: to frustrate Fyodor Voronov. That was why it had been created, if it had been created. The universe was a large, scaly-skinned, disease-ridden, garbage-covered rodent. Voronov had often seen it at night in the darkness, grinning, waiting.

There was only one way to fight and win such a struggle — only one way to frustrate the would-be frustrator — and that was simply to refuse to act.

It had begun so long ago, in a different life, it seemed, in a small town near Voronezh. Voronov was a different person then, and yet he was the same. He had been a "promising young man." Nobody knew why, but everyone said so. Perhaps it was simply because of his good looks. Like many other "promising young men" of the time, Voronov was respectably "liberal" in politics, enough to establish him as "promising" and *avant garde,* but not enough to get him into trouble — a balance which he adjusted respectably after the assassination of Alexander II. And as a "promising young man," he had had the proper disdain for material things and wealth. Undoubtedly that explains what happened.

At that time in the town there was an heiress, the daughter of the region's richest man — and the unknowing object of the schemes of many "promising young men." She was very young, a teenager. Her father was an old widower, and there were no other known heirs to the estate — a situation which naturally caused speculation about which "promising young man" would inherit it.

Fyodor Pavlovitch Voronov was left out of this speculation. He was a "promising young man" indeed. The *most* "promising." But he was also

19

married and ineligible. His wife was a perfectly respectable girl, the daughter of a local shopkeeper. So it was quite a surprise to all when Voronov disappeared, especially when the heiress disappeared a week later. No note was found in either case. Had they disappeared together? Was this a mere coincidence? The speculation began to connect both disappearances. Other activities, such as business, fell off. The doors throbbed on their hinges with speculation. Behind them, the residents did the same. Some whispered that the missing ones had been murdered by escaped convicts.

For almost two years nothing was known. The speculation reluctantly died down. The immediacy was gone. The case became something one mentioned only to visitors.

Then word came from England that the couple was married and would very shortly begin the trip home. Again the speculation flared up. How was this possible? What were the details? Had Voronov gotten a divorce? Neither Voronov nor his new wife ever gave the answers, but they did return from England. Apparently they were really married and they moved immediately into his new father-in-law's house, where Voronov held court for those who came to pay him homage.

For those who timidly inquired, he had one word: "Love" – said with eyes looking skyward for emphasis. For those who winked or hinted about the money, he had more. "Trash!" he would say. "Senseless! Root of all evil! Unimportant in the scheme of things." He would explain that he had unfortunately been born too late for his true vocation: being a twelfth century monk. He was diffident, humble, and at the same time domineering. He had never worked at anything before. Now he was completely happy.

Once again speculation slowly subsided. The announcement was made that his present wife would have a child. His former wife and her brother quietly left town. Suddenly the last and most extraordinary revelation burst forth. His new family, the richest in the region, was ruined. His new father-in-law, the richest man, was bankrupt. There were no details. No one was able to say how it had happened. There were rumors that the elderly man was a secret gambler. But whatever the cause, the results were clear. The estate, the lands and houses, were gone. So was the jewelry. So, except for some few pieces, was the furniture. The family quickly moved into a dilapidated house in town. Voronov had a pregnant wife and an elderly father-in-law on his hands. In only three years he had been shoved even further back than where he started. The slyly grinning universe had moved a paw.

For a long time, Voronov was not seen. The speculators agreed that he was at home, hiding – which he was. He developed the habit of sitting and staring, simply sitting and staring at the wall. His wife and father-in-law gently

20

asked him what he saw, if anything, but he did not say. He would not say. He did not want anyone to know that he saw a greasy, grinning rodent.

A son, Michael Fyodorovitch, was born. After a while, Voronov ventured out, as if nothing at all had happened, as if the previous three years had not taken place. Those who remembered that they had, and had paid him homage, were cold, suddenly discovering that he had been domineering. Those who had timidly inquired about his remarriage commiserated, reminded him that, in any event, money is unimportant. Those who had winked and hinted also commiserated, reminding him of exactly the same thing with sarcasm. But most horrible whatever their attitude, he found, was the crucial necessity of pretending to believe what they said, of smiling, of shrugging, of pretending that they weren't being sarcastic at all.

The family moved to St. Petersburg where they could lose themselves. The years passed. The old man died. Michael grew. Voronov seemed to recover in a way. He no longer simply stared at the wall. He became a maudlin, philosophizing drunk, supporting the family less and less. Now he had a new word to explain his activities: "Business!" he would say to those who asked. And as always, what he meant was vague; it was impossible to discover exactly what he was busy at — except that the few remaining family possessions of any value gradually disappeared.

Michael, who was never vague, was also not a conversationalist. He took a job at Danilov Agricultural Machinery, characteristically without a word. "Degrading!" his father said. He petulantly protested that Michael had wounded his paternal pride, that no son of his could become a worker, that factory work was beneath a gentleman's son. He complained mechanically, from memory. Complained and then dismissed it from mind. A strange, tense equilibrium appeared in which Voronov earned steadily less and Michael earned more. Finally, it was wordlessly established that Michael was the family breadwinner. Voronov explained that this arrangement would end; he spoke regularly of "business," of "transactions," of "deals." But nothing of the sort ever took place.

As for his wife, she blamed herself for the results of her father's financial tragedy, gradually accepting her husband's illusion that she had cheated him. "Love," Voronov would shrug during a particularly bad period. "All for love," he would sigh. "Everything ruined." It was important to his wife to believe that, to believe that Voronov was a gentleman, to believe that she had married a gentleman. She wanted to believe that the bad periods were simply bad luck, that suffering was necessary and natural, that it was good. The years passed and Sophia Petrovna's back bowed under the guilt. She be-

left, the thing they cannot take from me, the most important thing, is the fact that I am a gentleman. Yes, a gentleman! Difficult to believe in these rags, but true! Bred and born, raised to the title. And yet you coarsely propose factory employment. For a man of my breeding and experience. Fyodor Voronov an employee in a factory! No, the thing is of course grotesque, impossible, a mockery of nature. There is such a thing, my friend — I don't know whether you are aware of it. I hope you are. I took care to instil it in you. If you are not, the blame is mine, it is another of my failures — there is such a thing, my friend, as pride. Imagine Fyodor Pavlovitch Voronov — gentleman — an employee in a factory, associating with workers, with people . . . ."

"People like me," said Michael.

"I didn't say that!" said Voronov, blushing. "I didn't mean that at all. You misinterpret me intentionally. You put words in my mouth."

Arms spread, palms up, he turned to Sophia Petrovna in mute appeal. She was as repelled by the idea as he was. Fyodor Pavlovitch Voronov — gentleman — an employee in a factory? It would reflect on her as well as him; on Sophia Petrovna Voronova — lady. It would objectify the economic bottom she had reached, make it real, make it permanent. Fyodor Pavlovitch Voronov — "gentleman" — made it possible to believe that the situation could change, that it was temporary, a strange hiatus of twenty years. To destroy the fantasy would be to admit that her life had been wasted. It would destroy hope. It would destroy her only source of pride.

"Please, Michael," she said. "Do not disturb your father."

Voronov smiled, but at the same time he was annoyed. He approved of and participated in Sophia Petrovna's fantasy, but at the same time it was a reproach, a reminder of reality. He resented it. He struggled against her wish that he conform to her idea of him. He found a perverse pleasure in hurting her. Sometimes, to do so, he deliberately played the fool.

Again he was walking with dignity around the room. "Fate has not been kind to me," he said. "Look! Look at your mother! Faded, shapeless, so pathetic. Would you believe that once she was a pretty young girl? She was. Don't worry, old girl. I won't cast you off. I'll look after you, even though your son denies me the few rubles I need."

Voronov leaned toward him over the table. "My dear friend, I guarantee that I will return it to you in a few days. And my word is as good as the Bank of England's — as you know. I appeal to you. Can you find it in you to help your old father?"

On and on Voronov's voice went, rising, falling, darting, biting, and at the same time dull, monotonous, meaningless. If only it would stop. If only it

24

were quiet. If only Michael could be left alone to study the diagrams on the page between his fingers. Perhaps the pleasure would be worth the few rubles. Without looking up, he took them from his pocket and pushed them over.

"You're a true son, a true son," Voronov's voice said.

He left the apartment. Sophia Petrovna left the room. It was quiet. With intense pleasure, Michael turned the page.

The reason Voronov so desperately wanted money was that several days earlier while walking on the Nevsky, he had been attracted by a woman and had suddenly realized that she was his former wife, Nastasya Lvovna. He had not seen her for twenty years. She had changed, of course, from a slender, young girl to a woman more than ample; but there was no doubt at all that this was she. Indeed, as he watched, she pulled at her earlobe as she always had when deep in thought, a habit about which he had teased her. She had been peering with interest into the window of a bank.

Voronov saw her face in the glass. Their eyes met, just for a moment. Then she looked away. In them, Voronov had seen the greatest change: the girlish diffidence had become domineering. The diffidence now belonged to the man with her, small, smaller than she, nervous and frail. She spoke to him shortly, shook her head and walked on — the frail little man trotting nervously in her wake.

Voronov was in a fever of curiosity. Who was this nervous little man? Did Nastasya Lvovna now live in St. Petersburg? If not, what was she doing there? Had she ever remarried? He felt a welter of long-dead emotions, emotions he had felt in his former life.

Suddenly he felt humiliation. The shock of seeing her had thrown him into reverie, but suddenly he realized that she could just as easily have seen him — recognized him in spite of the fact that he, too, had changed.

And he was wearing the usual ancient, threadbare clothes. He was down at the heels and in the mouth. He was long in the tooth, and obviously very short of everything else. He was a man who reluctantly resembled a beggar. Since his financial disaster, he had cultivated this appearance as proof of the universe's treachery toward him, as the reason it was impossible to try anything else. But suddenly he realized that for Nastasya Lvovna — for her alone — another appearance was imperative. For his former wife, whom he had left for wealth, to see him ragged as a beggar would be a highly painful defeat and an opportunity for Nastasya Lvovna to take revenge. And the look in her eyes had told him she might.

But if so, why had she walked away? Wouldn't she have stayed and been overly sympathetic? Didn't that prove that she hadn't recognized him after all? The theory seemed reasonable — she probably hadn't — but Voronov could almost hear her laughing at his defeat. Indeed, for three days he followed her, discreetly, he thought; but once again on the Nevsky, in front of the same bank, she had turned and looked quickly in his direction. Perhaps he simply seemed familiar, but she did not know why. He had to make sure. He had to prove to her that Fyodor Pavlovitch Voronov was a success.

Dressed in the style of the times with Michael's rubles, Voronov knocked on the door of her hotel room. He smiled at his cleverness in avoiding trouble at home. He had stored his new wardrobe, and changed into it, in Zabulyov's little room.

The door opened. Nastasya Lvovna stood on the sill, a quizzical expression on her face.

"Yes?" she said. "What is it, please?"

"Nastasya Lvovna, my dear," he said.

Nastasya Lvovna abruptly drew back. "I beg your pardon. What do you mean?"

Voronov hesitated, unexpectedly unsure whether the fact that she apparently did not recognize him was good or bad. He bowed.

"I am Fyodor Pavlovitch Voronov. Don't you recognize me?"

"Oh. I see. Come in," said Nastasya Lvovna. Her usually mobile face now communicated nothing, but she was glad she had already made him ill at ease.

"You do not seem at all surprised," said Voronov nervously.

She wasn't. She had indeed seen Voronov's reflection in the window the other day. The most reasonable thing to expect was that he would soon call.

"On the contrary," she said flatly. "I am dumbfounded."

She would have liked nothing better than to say she had seen him recently dressed in rags; she ached to do so, but she did not. She could imagine only one sensible explanation for his sartorial habits: that he somehow had become an Okhrana agent and had been assigned to follow her, in which case the best policy was always to feign complete ignorance.

Voronov chuckled. "Have I changed so much, then?"

"Completely," said Nastasya Lvovna. "But, as of old, your wardrobe is memorable."

Voronov laughed. He had fooled her completely. He felt relief, marred only by regret that he could not reveal it.

"I saw you walking from inside a bank the other day," he said.

Nastasya Lvovna smiled. "I see."

The thin, timid, well-dressed man he had seen her with was standing at the samovar filling a cup with tea, and Voronov looked at him interrogatively. Nastasya Lvovna blushed. Ordinarily she took pleasure in flaunting Filipov's deficiencies, but now she wanted to conceal them. For Voronov to see them would somehow demean her. She did not even want them to meet. But Filipov could not be concealed. To try to do so would only underline her embarrassment. Suddenly and involuntarily she felt mortified. Again she felt the shame and fear of being abandoned, as she had twenty-three years before. She realized with distaste that her emotion was still the same as a jilted girl's, not at all the lofty thing she thought. She wanted to hurt the man responsible.

"But perhaps you do not wish to see me," said Voronov. "Certainly I must revive what for you are unpleasant memories."

"Not at all."

"Unfortunately unpleasant. Because the truth is that, for me, those receding years are among my finest. And I do not say this to flatter you unduly. It is the truth. Indeed, I must confess it, that is why I followed you and called. Yes, to be absolutely honest, my motive is selfish, which for me, as you know, is fairly rare — perhaps too rare. Perhaps I should demand more of life. I was hoping to recall my fading youth.

"But as you will also remember, I am extraordinarily sensitive to the feelings of others. I have always cherished delicacy and refined perception. I do not need my great imaginative powers to realize the suffering experienced by a person of your fragility, a helpless girl deprived of her mate. So do not be afraid, Nastasya Lvovna. Do not hesitate. You will not offend me. I will understand perfectly. If you wish me to leave . . . ."

"Not at all," Nastasya Lvovna said shortly. "Sit down. Will you take tea?"

"Tea?"

"Or would you prefer cognac?"

"Hmm. Yes. The cognac, I think. Just a bit. I spend so much time in Italy, I have become unused to our Russian winters."

Nastasya Lvovna poured a glassful and he took it. He was already enjoying himself very much; not simply because she had not seen him the other day, but because he realized that the situation contained possibilities of profit. The suite they sat in was elegant in every respect, and the hotel was one of the best in St. Petersburg. Nastasya Lvovna, like the frail, timid man beside her, was elegantly dressed. Perhaps she would like to invest some of the money this represented. Indeed, perhaps their meeting was a sign from above, proof that he had made a monstrous mistake and should rejoin her. More and more heavily the fact weighed on him — he admitted it readily — that it was wrong for a man to leave his wife.

As for Nastasya Lvovna herself, she was extremely uncomfortable; not simply because he revived uncomfortable memories, but also because there was something crucially important she could not remember.

She pointed at the frail, timid man. "My husband. Egon Abramovitch Filipov, the worm."

So ludicrous, so incongruent, so impossible was this, that the possibility had never entered Voronov's mind. How could this frail, skimpy, timid individual be the husband of the imperious woman his former wife had become? They were like a queen bee and a drone. The revelation split Voronov's face in a wide grin.

"How shall I address you?" he asked.

"As 'worm,' of course," said Nastasya Lvovna. "That is right, is it not, Filipov?"

"Perfectly right," Filipov said.

"You see," Nastasya Lvovna said. "And this, Filipov, is Fyodor Pavlovitch Voronov, my former husband. Another worm. I believe I have mentioned him to you."

"Yes. You have," Filipov said.

"I beg your pardon," Voronov said.

"You wish to argue?" asked Nastasya Lvovna.

"I certainly do," Voronov said with rising indignation.

"I do not tolerate arguments," she said harshly. "If you wish to argue, please leave at once."

Voronov hesitated, glass raised, then laughed. "Forgive me. I understand, of course. You are still the young girl who has just been separated. You are confused, fearful, your emotions are raw, you imagine people stare at you in the street, whispering about your imagined shame. And in your confusion, pain and desperation you lash out, seeking relief, and at the same time revenge.

"I realize everything, good Nastasya Lvovna. I feel your pain. Instantly my sensitive nature responds."

Nastasya Lvovna colored, but there was nothing she could do. Somehow he dissipated and deflected everything. It was impossible to confront him with anything definite. She raised her glass.

"To the health of His Beloved Majesty, the Tsar!"

Filipov chuckled. "To our beloved Tsar!"

"How wonderful it is to hear this," said Voronov. "To hear a forthright expression of patriotism. So ennobling. Almost courageous, in fact, in view of current events. In my unhappy view, 1905 was but a prelude. The Revolution is gaining strength."

"Is it really so serious, then?" she asked.

28

"Happily, you know nothing. Women should not think of these things, dear Nastasya Lvovna. But revolutionary agents are everywhere, organized in secret groups. They have infiltrated every Russian institution. They are even able to influence our government."

"Apparently you are a student of revolution yourself."

Voronov laughed. "I hear things. I watch."

What in the world was he getting at, she wondered. More and more, the sudden reappearance of her former husband seemed strange. Was it simply a coincidence? Or was he trying to draw them out?

"And yet, I have read that a new emancipation is required," she said, "an emancipation far surpassing that of 1861, which would include not just the serfs, but all other Russian classes."

Voronov sat next to her and pressed her hands in his. "If I did not know you so well, good Nastasya Lvovna, I would be frightened by what you say. I am sure your husband, obviously a man of experience, will tell you the same."

"I am frightened already," Filipov simpered.

Voronov rose and was pacing up and down. "Nothing is more sacred than private property, my dear. I am sure that, as a person of apparent wealth, you appreciate this."

"I do indeed."

"Permit me to tell you, by the way, Nastasya Lvovna — with your permission, of course, sir — that you are even more personally attractive now, which I would have thought impossible, than you were the last time we met. Over twenty years ago, it was. I remember the date, even the hour, exactly. Let me see. But of course you find all this embarrassing. Forgive me. What was I discussing?"

"The revolutionary ferment," said Filipov.

"Correct," said Nastasya Lvovna. "The earth being turned by many boring little worms."

"Yes, the so-called 'revolutionary ferment' is precisely the work of worms," said Voronov. "Worms, thieves, loafers, weaklings. People with a fancied or magnified grievance. Natural inferiors rebelling against their natural superiors. All joined by the methods of trickery and lies to commit perhaps the foulest of all crimes: betrayal. And betrayal not just of an acquaintance, but of a fatherland — of a father. A violation of the holiest emotion. A desecration of the noblest trust.

"Yes, my friends, nothing is too severe — not Siberia, not the knout — nothing is too severe for these enemies of the Tsar."

"Telegin himself could not say it better," said Nastasya Lvovna. "In fact, his columns have contained your very phrases."

"I have the honor to be a loyal reader," said Voronov, who had once seen at a distance that prolific defender of the monarchy. "In fact, we are friends. And I can assure you he agrees that what we are seeing essentially is an attempt to destroy the father — the keystone of civilization — one of which I myself happen to be."

Suddenly Nastasya Lvovna remembered what she had forgotten, the elusiveness of which had been bothering her so. In a week-old memory she saw a young man, tall, lean, tough skin taut, standing at the table in Kolodsky's apartment. Again she heard his voice, soft and yet peremptory, and realized that this was Voronov's son — and that Michael could have been her son, but was not. The realization angered her.

"So you have children?" she asked.

"One," he said. "A son. Michael Fyodorovitch."

"A worker in some factory, no doubt."

"Certainly not!" said Voronov, bristling again. "No son of mine would ever work in a factory. Why would he want to? There is no need. In any event, I would not permit it. No, my son is a student at the Technological Institute. Soon he will be an engineer."

Nastasya Lvovna smiled. "I see." She did not know the details, of course, but at last the reason Voronov had come was clear. He was not an Okhrana agent, after all. Like her and Filipov, although for different reasons, he was trying to conceal his poverty. The mystery of his varied wardrobes was gone. He was sniffing at what he thought was her wealth.

"My friends," said Voronov, "I am blessed beyond all men. My son is an absolute paragon, a classic. But I should take some credit for that after all, should I not? In all humility, parental training and influence have some effect. Yes, my son's central purpose is to honor his father. None of this 'modern' nonsense for him."

"How boring," said Filipov. "I'm so sorry."

"And what have you been doing all these years," asked Nastasya Lvovna, "besides travelling to Italy?"

"Italy?" said Voronov. "Oh, yes, business. Business, figures, accounting, shipments and bills."

"How utterly fascinating. Perhaps you would explain it."

"As soon as I began, my dear, you would find me boring. And that is something I do not dare to be."

"Perhaps you and I can do some business," she said.

"That does sound somewhat fascinating."

He turned to Filipov. "May I ask, sir, what the nature of your profession is?"

"Printing," said Nastasya Lvovna. "Among other things."

"Fascinating," said Voronov. "Disciples of Gutenberg. Books, newspapers. In the beginning was the word. The holy *logos.*"

Nastasya Lvovna's large bosom swelled. She was manipulating him so beautifully, so delicately, so expertly, as well as she did Filipov himself. She would ruin him as she had Filipov, not for revenge, not at all, but simply because she wanted to. Men, all men — there were no exceptions — were worms. That was what the Revolution was about. She felt a strangely languorous sense of power.

IV

Michael stood on Theater Street outside the Marinsky Theater, home of the Imperial Russian Ballet. It was evening, but it was as bright as noon. Many people swirled in crowds, pushing, shouting, pointing, laughing. Carriages screeched, stopped and discharged generals, counts, princes, privy councillors, countesses, ministers, bureau heads and industrialists. From every buckle flashed a light. From every body rose fresh scent. All converged to see Karsavina.

It was real, but for Michael it was a fantasy. Where did these people come from? How did they live? Were they simply figures in a dream? He watched intently.

A long English limousine drew up. A door opened. Someone got out. Then he was being shoved roughly. Startled, angry, he turned abruptly, and found a girl staring at him, a tall girl, very pale, with abundant raven hair. She was very young, no more than sixteen. Her prominent cheekbones were haughtily high, her nose the same but not so prominent. On the ice between them lay a bag.

"Clumsy oaf!" she said. "Pick that up!"

His mouth was smiling, but his eyes were not and they steadily returned her gaze, to which she was unused. Then he bent and did as she commanded, his mouth amused, in his eyes a perfect confidence that made her feel belittled. She took the bag from him roughly.

Michael looked at the English limousine. It was his employer's. There were few such automobiles. The girl was obviously Danilov's daughter. He had never seen her. Now he appraised her boldly, insultingly, and she knew there was nothing she could do about it — nothing but ineffectually disdain his cheap clothes.

A stocky man of medium height and Michael's age sauntered up, dressed in the uniform of a cadet. On his face was a peculiar smirk.

"Is there any trouble, sister dear?" he said.

A very fat man and a beautiful, elegantly dressed woman came around the limousine.

"None at all," she said coldly.

"What is this?" said the fat man. "What's going on?"

The nostrils of the beautiful woman with him wrinkled. She drew back, slightly, in her eyes a trace of fear.

"Masha says it's nothing," smirked Stepan Ivanovitch Danilov.

The fat man's jowls twitched. He glared warningly at Michael.

"Peasant trash!" said the fat man, ushering the three others along. "A disgrace. It should not be permitted. It would not, but unfortunately I am only an inconsequential journalist."

"You are not at all inconsequential, Cyril Modestovitch," said the beautiful woman. "That is why you must not be harsh."

"You are so kind, Nadia Nikolaevna," he said, "and as usual, so right. I, Telegin, thank you."

The fat man's voice droned volubly on, but already it was receding into the general uproar. The crowd opened and closed around his party, and they were swept into the Marinsky and gone. Michael was puzzled. He understood Danilov, although they had never exchanged a word. Danilov was part of something understandable: the factory. He was there now, Michael knew, high up in the tower where Michael often saw a light. But his employer's family was something else. Only the factory, exact and obedient, was perfectly comprehensible.

His thoughts naturally led to the envelope in his pocket, which his own father had asked him to deliver. "Business, business," Voronov had said. Exactly what the business was, Michael did not know and did not care. Whatever it was, it seemed to be real. Voronov worked at it very often, and it actually brought some money into the house. So Michael was quite happy to deliver it, and now he started off to do so.

He walked briskly for some time. Then he was in an unfamiliar neighborhood, in narrow, twisted streets. He went down some steps and knocked at a door. A long time passed. Then, at last, the door opened just a crack.

"What is it?" said an unfamiliar voice.

"I have an envelope to deliver," said Michael.

"To whom?" asked the disembodied voice.

Michael gave the address on the door.

"From whom?"

Michael gave his father's name.

"Push the envelope through the door," said the voice.

Michael did so and it disappeared. He did not see so much as a finger. The door slammed and he heard footsteps receding. Again he was alone in the dark. From far behind the door came the faint sound of machinery, but he had no idea exactly what sort. He knew it would be very amusing when his father told him.

They greeted each other cordially when he got home. Indeed, the feeling between them had improved considerably, coincident with the beginning of Voronov's "business." He had repaid Michael the rubles with which he had replenished his wardrobe, with the help of which his whole appearance had changed. But his manner also had changed, in a different way; it had intensified. The wheedling had combined with the new rubles in his pocket and produced a dangerous, irritated bullying, which Michael gladly dismissed as the temporary exaggeration of someone returning to self-respect. For different reasons, relations between them had become very warm.

As usual, Voronov was sitting at the table with Zabulyov. He rose carefully, balancing a brimming glass of vodka, and greeted Michael with half an embrace.

"Ah, dear friend," he said, "did everything go well?"

"Yes," said Michael, "the envelope has been delivered."

"Splendid!" said Voronov. "There, Misha. You see? You had no right in the past to criticize my son."

"What do you mean?" asked Zabulyov, suddenly nervous.

"Come, come, Misha, this makes no sense. You are being insincere, which as you know is one thing I cannot bear."

"I am sorry, Fedya, but I do not understand."

"And, by the way, who authorized you to call me that? In the future you will address me as Fyodor Pavlovitch."

"Certainly, Fyodor Pavlovitch. Whatever you say."

"I was saying that I must authoritatively inform you that I heartily disapprove and reject your attitude. Yes, Misha, to loll about all day and waste oneself in boring, unproductive activity, or rather inactivity — and you must admit that is an accurate description of your activities — yes, it's hopeless, my friend, and can only lead to hopelessness, as I am sure you will agree."

"I do, Fedya. For instance, I cannot reach the bottle. Look. My fingers fall far short. Slide it over, will you, please?"

"Application, Misha," said Voronov, doing so. "The answer is application. Take my son Michael here. He applies himself. In that lies the whole difference between you. But of course, he has had the benefit of my diligent, parental influence. Yes, my dear friend, you should take this advice to heart. Believe me, it is given in a spirit of constructive impartiality."

"Sure, Fedya. I believe you. And you are quite right."

"Why don't you go to the factory with Michael tomorrow? I'm sure he'd recommend you. Wouldn't you, Michael, my dear friend?"

"Of course."

Zabulyov vigorously shook his head. "It can't be done, Fedya. You forget. I am hopelessly disabled. A victim of alcoholism. Look." Zabulyov quickly filled a glass, gulped it down and filled another. "You see? Some of us must depend upon Capitalists like yourself."

Voronov's lips quivered, but he smiled. "You are right of course, Misha, but you misunderstand. Certainly you are welcome to drink my vodka. Certainly you are welcome to eat my food. My home is open to you, as you know. No, Misha, I make my suggestion not for financial, but for therapeutic reasons. Honest factory work would probably produce a cure."

"Impossible, Fedya. My health would not permit."

The door to the other room opened and Sophia Petrovna shuffled in, preoccupied and unaware.

"Sophia Petrovna!" said Voronov abruptly and with great formality.

A startled Sophia Petrovna shuffled to the table, eyes narrowing as if trying to focus.

"Tea," said Voronov, gesturing at the samovar which stood before him in easy reach. He watched her appraisingly as she poured. "Tell me, Sophia Petrovna, what is wrong?" he asked.

"Wrong? What do you mean, Fedya?" Her voice quivered.

"There, Misha," he said. "Do you see? A lesson. Look, Misha, and be warned. Application is the only answer."

*   *   *

Several days passed, days on which Kolodsky did not report for work. No one had seen him. In a few days more, if no one saw him, it would be said he had "disappeared." The foreman had tried without success to replace him, and then stopped when his absence made no difference in productivity. Just before he vanished, he had called Michael a "traitor to his class."

It was evening. Michael left the factory and looked up. As usual, the light was high in the tower. Danilov was at work. And Michael had things to do, too. He walked to the bookshop and went in.

"We're just closing," said the girl at the counter.

"That's all right," said Michael. "I know what I want."

The book was still in its place on the shelf and he slid a forefinger along its page tops, tilted and removed it, riffling through the heavy paper, already studying the diagrams.

He peeled off the necessary rubles and put them down. He already knew the price. He had long wanted this book.

"Which way do you walk?" the girl asked.

"That way," he said, pointing down the Nevsky.

"I do, too," she said. "Wait a moment."

"All right."

As they walked along the Nevsky it began to snow and the traffic beside them became indistinct. As usual, his mind filled with smokestacks and smoke, with whirring machinery and railroad cars. Again he saw the light in the tower.

They did not speak. It was quiet except for the horses clopping by, followed by the metallic creak of trolleys. She had seen him at the store before and wanted to know his name but could not ask him, because she could not tell him hers. After the last beating, she had left her husband in Moscow — the husband her father had carefully picked out. She knew they were both looking for her now. She was afraid that Michael would question her, like everyone else. But Michael said nothing, and she relaxed.

They were already entering the unfamiliar neighborhood, and Michael felt in his pocket for the envelope containing more of Voronov's "business." They were at the top of the small flight of stairs, and went down. Michael knocked on the door as before. It was dark. The snow had stopped and a wind rose. As before, he waited a long time, but realized at last that no one was coming. He knocked again and waited, finally knocked noisily again. The door creaked. It was ajar. He pushed it open easily and they went in.

They were in a very dark corridor, along the length of which were several doors. He opened the first, and in the dim light saw a completely empty room. The next three doors were locked. The last faced him at the end of the hall. Beside him, the girl shuddered.

"I'm frightened," she whispered.

Michael opened the final door. He struck a match and found a lamp. They were in a very large room, the contents of which had been completely wrecked. The doors of a big closet hung askew. In it were some dishes, and before it lay the smashed remains of others. A desk stood on its end, the drawers open. Near it was a table, right side up, with a half-eaten plate of food on it, and in the far corner were the remains of a printing press and the large hammers used to destroy it. Sheets of paper were scattered all around.

"What is this place?" asked the girl. "Where are we?"

"I don't know," said Michael.

36

"You don't know?"

He picked up several sheets of paper. All were the same. All were blank. The girl's breath came in piercing bursts. "Perhaps I should go."

"Perhaps you should."

The girl half-ran from the room, along the corridor and up the stairs. As she did so, Michael saw some papers covered with figures and a description of some incomprehensible financial dealings, all written in his father's familiar hand. There was no mistaking the florid, theatrical script. For the first time in his life he felt fear, uncontrollable fear, squeezing all breath from his lungs. What, indeed, was happening here? What business was his father in?

He folded the papers, put them in his coat and left. The street was deserted. It was cold. A high wind blew scraps of refuse. He walked slowly, wanting to run. At last there were some people in the streets. He bought a newspaper and got on a trolley. He began to read: "Attempted Assassination of Okhrana Official. Part of Plot to Free Peter Sergeievitch Orloff. Foiled Owing to Vigilance of Police Officer. Chief of Police Promises Repressive Measures."

He read the story:

> Dynamiters yesterday attempted to take the life of Okhrana official Sergei Dmitrievitch Ogarev only a few minutes after he left the Admiralty and an important conference with naval authorities. According to the police, Inspector Ogarev, long a popular member of Petersburg smart society, was saved only by the quick action of a police officer and a happy oversight on the part of the conspirators.
>
> Apparently one of the conspirators threw a bomb into the Inspector's carriage window, whereupon Mme. Ogareva, who was with him, threw it back into the street. Simultaneously, an alert police officer, one Officer Khodolyubov, began firing at the bomb thrower, who ran around a corner with some others and disappeared. Whether he was wounded and how many others are actually involved is not known at this time. But witnesses describe him as a 'modern' type, with long, greasy hair, and as being hygienically offensive.
>
> The whole affair was made ludicrous by the fact that the bomb did not detonate, and was found by police to be defective.
>
> "Nevertheless," said a government spokesman, "a serious breach of legality has been committed, and no stone

will be unturned in a search for the perpetrators. In fact, we are already in close pursuit. An attempt upon a member of His Majesty's government, is an attempt upon His Majesty himself."

Horrifying though the attempt could have been, it was apparently a diversionary part of a plot to free Peter Sergei-evitch Orloff, disgraced former Army officer and Bolshevik leader now being returned to Siberia.

Officer Khodolyubov is to be personally commended tomorrow at the Winter Palace by His Imperial Majesty. The Inspector himself is conducting the investigation.

Again he felt the fear. But it was worse. It was apprehension. It was dread. And at the same time, he was confused. He did not know what to think. He did not know what had happened. He did not know whether anything had happened. Should he feel simply the natural fascination of someone knowing more about a story than appears in the newspaper, and amusement at the recollection of the schemers at the meeting? Or should he believe that what he had seen, which obviously involved his father, had something to do with what he had just read — and feel fear? Perhaps the only connection was the coincidence that he had seen and read them at the same time. Perhaps the wreckage in the basement was just the result of a robbery, and the owners had gone to the police. But perhaps it wasn't. He did not know. He could not know until he talked with his father. And so these emotions competed blindly to be felt, with the result that he felt a painful uneasiness — and the weight of the envelope and papers in his pocket.

The trolley stopped and he got off, walked to the house and climbed the stairs. His father was not at home. Sophia Petrovna was asleep in the other room, but there was no point in waking her. She would know nothing. His father would come soon enough.

Michael greedily unwrapped the book, touched the binding and began to read, studying the various diagrams of machinery, of cams and pulleys, shafts and pistons, usually enough to keep him rapt. But now he could not concentrate. He read, and reread, several paragraphs. He reexamined several cams.

Far below in the lobby he heard a distant clatter. There was some kind of commotion, but it died away. The clock ticked. The fire crackled, embers silvery, very low but very hot.

Then he heard someone coming up the stairs, already passing the second floor. Was it Voronov or not? He could not tell. Recently his father's gait had changed. But the sound seemed too definite, too peremptory. Indeed, now it was at the third floor landing, where Voronov always caught his breath, but the footsteps did not even hesitate. They were loud, very loud — there was almost an echo. Michael realized there was more than one man.

Then they were just outside the door. Michael stared at it. Their footsteps died away. He heard them whisper, and for a long time there was nothing. Whoever they were, they were simply waiting.

Then there were three blows on the door, not quick raps made with knuckles, but deliberate blows, made with a fist. Michael waited a moment, staring at the door as if it held the meaning. Then he went to it and opened it.

Three men stood on the sill, one in plainclothes, the others in uniforms. The plainclothesman's left fist was raised, just about to knock again. In his right hand was a pistol. He looked steadily into Michael's eyes and slowly lowered his fist, still staring.

"Michael Voronov?" he said coldly.

"Yes."

"You are under arrest."

He entered the room, followed by the others, and gestured. The others methodically began to search.

"What are you doing?" Michael asked.

"Isn't that obvious? We're searching your apartment."

The other man smiled. "Your memory will be refreshed at the station. Until we are finished you will stand where you are."

"And the charge?"

"I see. Of course you know nothing."

"No."

The other man laughed. "It will be explained."

The door to the other room opened and Sophia Petrovna came out, hands to her face, hunted eyes staring through her fingers.

"What has happened, Michael?" she whispered.

He did not answer. No one paid her the slightest attention. She went to the table and sat down. Instantly she was up, a hand still on her face, the other tentatively reaching for Michael.

"Michael, what have you done?" she whispered.

In his confusion, Michael felt one unadulterated emotion: embarrassment. Why must she always behave like this, even before strangers? Indeed, his embarrassment intensified when the other man smirked.

"Forgive me, madame," said the other man. "He does not know."

"Mother! Please!" said Michael. "Go inside."

The men in uniform came out of the other room.

"Well?" said the plainclothesman.

"Nothing," said one.

"Michael!" said Sophia Petrovna. "Confess! Ask forgiveness!"

Again he did not answer, and the other man smirked. He gestured with the pistol. "All right. Let's go."

Michael looked into the muzzle of the gun. The rim caught the light, but inside it was dark. And it faced the exact center of his chest.

"All right," he said.

Sophia Petrovna was suddenly calm. She sat again at the table and closed her eyes, hands clasped under her chin. She began to rock back and forth.

"Forgive him," she whispered. "Persuade him to confess."

But Michael and the others were already out the door. Other doors opened, slightly. In the gloom of the stairwell, eyes in shadowy faces stood in narrow shafts of light.

"I knew it!" whispered a voice. "I expected it. It had to be."

"Yes," said another. "Always putting on airs."

The smell of sour cabbage was in the air. The doors closed and it was gone.

"Look out for that damned broken step," said the plainclothesman. "We have to bring him in alive."

"Michael!" screamed Sophia Petrovna from above. "What will your father say?"

V

Michael sat in a room in the police station, drumming with exasperation on a table. Everything would be all right. He knew that. But so far they had told him nothing, not even what he was accused of. And the interminable waiting was beginning to annoy him. He was not used to it. How long had he been alone in the room? He did not know; there was no clock. The uncertainty made him nervous.

A door opened and a smallish man entered, elegantly dressed, wearing a Vandyke, carrying a bulging leather briefcase. He sat at the table and offered Michael a cigarette.

"No," said Michael.

"Suit yourself," said the other, lighting one himself.

From an inner pocket, he took a pince-nez and put it on. His chin rose, the beard on it pointing like an accusing finger, and he obviously and carefully began to stare.

"How fascinating it is to study a man," he said, "really to study a man closely. You for instance, Voronov. I see you look away."

"That is because you are playing some game."

"You are wrong, Voronov. And you are unfair. I am Inspector Ogarev, in charge of your case. I am sincerely interested."

"Then why don't you tell me what I am accused of?"

"Please, Voronov, we are both professionals. Must we participate in this charade? Won't you feel as embarrassed and amateurish as I shall?"

"I insist," said Michael.

"You disappoint me." Ogarev shrugged. He drew a sheaf of papers from his briefcase. "But since you do, I shall play my part. You are accused of trying to murder Inspector Sergei Dmitrievitch Ogarev — me. Surely you won't insist that I read the date and place. You are accused of operating an illegal printing press. You are accused of committing several bank robberies. Really, Voronov, this is beneath us both."

"It isn't true," said Michael. "It is so untrue that I begin to think you know it."

"Now you surprise me," Ogarev said. "This was the point, as you know, for you to take credit for these achievements. To denounce me, scream, perhaps even spit. You disappoint me again, Voronov."

"I am telling you the truth," Michael said.

"Voronov, listen to me, I'll be frank. We're both obviously intelligent men. Believe me, I am not at all angry that you tried to kill me. I am not a vengeful man. I have grandchildren. I have no desire to retaliate. I *expect* people to try to kill me — as a matter of course. And perhaps one day they will.

"It is true, of course, that I kept you waiting several hours. I did that to produce in you the nervousness you now feel. I tell you this because we are being frank. But I could have pretended to torture someone next door. I am sure that, as a professional, you are familiar with that trick. I could have used others, but I did not because we are being frank, are we not?

"You see, Voronov, I am not a bad man. This is difficult for you to believe, but it is the truth. I did not enter this profession because I enjoy sending men to prison. I don't. I abhor any type of cruelty. Anyone will tell you that. What I enjoy is simply the puzzle, the investigation — and the intellectual thrill of finding the solution. That is why I stared at you: to see whether you satisfy my theory of you. And you do. Isn't it remarkable? Of course, I also did it to make you nervous, to weaken your resistance. That is perfectly true. We are being frank. Look, Voronov, look. Here is proof of what I say."

Ogarev's forefinger tapped a newspaper and Michael picked it up. " 'By Cyril Modestovitch Telegin,' " he read. " 'The Inspector and I are close personal friends. We were together only last week at another party given by Nadia Nikolaevna Danilova, wife of the owner of Danilov Agricultural Machinery, in honor of her daughter who is a student at the Imperial School of Ballet. He is the mildest, most tolerant of men, much respected by liberal Russians. The attack on him must not go unchallenged. The people must demand that the government change its way. The criminals must be found at once and punished. No leniency should be shown.' "

Again Michael heard Telegin's voice as he had heard it the other night: "Peasant trash!"

"Do you see?" said Ogarev. "Do you see how I am loved? No, Voronov, the truth is very simple. Isn't it always? I am simply a dull, timid, unimaginative bureaucrat trying to do his job — the type you so unjustly hate. Perhaps you should reconsider, Voronov. It is important to me. I like you,

42

personally, man to man. That is why I am telling you all this, an extraordinary departure from procedure. Surely you understand. You, too, are loved — but of course by different people. Look! Look at this! It occurs to me you haven't seen it."

Now Ogarev was handing him a single sheet of paper. "People of Petersburg!" Michael read. "Our leader is in the hands of the Okhrana, captured during the attempt to liquidate Ogarev the pig. His revolutionary, fraternal duty is clear. He is sworn to reveal nothing. If he does, it will be proof of Okhrana torture.

"The fight against the enemies of humanity — such as Ogarev and Bloody Nicholas — goes on. Long live the Revolution!"

"This is insane," said Michael.

"Isn't it!" Ogarev said. "You see? There is something we agree on. Let us begin with our agreement that this is insane."

"But anybody can print anything he likes. This doesn't prove a thing."

"Such a waste of time," said Ogarev. "Really, this is silly."

He rapped on the table, the door opened and a uniformed police officer came in.

"Khodolyubov!" said Ogarev.

"Yes, excellency," said the policeman.

"Have you ever seen this man before?"

"Yes, excellency."

"When?"

"Exactly two days ago."

"And what were the circumstances, Khodolyubov?"

"He is the man who threw the bomb into your carriage, excellency."

"You are sure?"

Khodolyubov squinted nearsightedly. "He is the man."

Michael felt himself struggling in a net, becoming more and more enmeshed. It was Grodsky who had thrown the bomb, he knew. The newspaper description bore this out. But the fact that he had actually met with Grodsky and the others, even though he had immediately rejected their proposal and walked out, produced in him a natural feeling of disadvantage. Ogarev would never believe the truth. He could not name Grodsky without implicating himself. There was nothing he could do about this nearsighted policeman who was hiding his defect even from himself.

"Thank you," said Ogarev. "You may go."

Khodolyubov did so and Ogarev spread his hands. "You see, comrade Voronov? It's a childish waste of time. Look. Let's be frank. I mean you no harm. All I ask is your cooperation. Perhaps I could use my small influence with the courts. Your conviction could be arranged as a political, rather than as a criminal. You could ride through Siberia in a cart. In the camp, you would have certain privileges. The politicals have a separate room."

On and on went Ogarev's voice. The words blended into a single sound which finally could not be understood. The Vandyke punctuated whatever he was saying.

"I don't know anything. I'm telling you the truth," Michael said over and over.

Again Ogarev drew a sheaf of papers from his briefcase. "Perhaps you can remember these. These are the work sheets we found in your pocket. And these, almost identical, are the ones we found last night at your headquarters, where we were waiting when you came in. Perhaps you would like to tell me what they mean. What is the significance of these various figures?"

Again Michael was looking at his father's handwriting, at the calculations he did not understand on the sheets of paper he had found in the wrecked room near the printing press. At last he had a definite answer: his father was involved after all. Indeed, it was because of his father that he had been arrested. His father's "business" was revolution. Michael was calm, but he felt himself whirling.

"I don't know what they mean," he said.

Ogarev colored. "I am sorry, comrade Voronov. You have made me angry, which is a bad thing. You have made me lose my temper, which is a victory. I tell you this because we are being frank. Apparently you have decided that you do not want my help — which hurts me. You have only been pretending to be frank. But it is a small victory, Voronov. True, I am a humane man; I proved that. But apparently you do not know that there is nothing in the world more dangerous than an even slightly offended bureaucrat."

Again Ogarev rapped on the table and the door opened. "Bring him in," he said. "Perhaps this is the way." The door closed. Ogarev lit another cigarette. "Really, it's a pity you won't try one."

The door opened again and Voronov came in, dressed in his most expensive clothes. He looked at them both. His lips quivered. "Michael," he said. But he did not advance into the room.

"Come in, come in," said Ogarev, waving. "Take a seat."

"I have come to negotiate my son's release," said Voronov.

"Of course you have, Fyodor Pavlovitch," said Ogarev. "Here. First have a cigarette."

Voronov took one and sat down. Ogarev lit it and leaned back, staring at Voronov as at Michael.

"I so enjoy studying people," he said. "Don't you?"

"Most assuredly," Voronov said.

"For instance, my study of you says you are a reasonable man."

"Reason is my god," said Voronov.

Ogarev smiled. "Do you read Voltaire?"

"I have come to negotiate the release of my son."

"Of course you have," said Ogarev. "And I am glad you are so reasonable. Your god is what your son needs most."

Voronov looked at Michael and felt a rush of love — intense, blinding, enveloping, protective — a love he had never felt for him before. For years Michael's mere presence had been an unsaid reproach, an accusation, a reminder of what Voronov was and was not. But now Michael had been arrested and was in the hands of the police, and Voronov felt the oppression lift. Michael had gotten himself into trouble. Poor Michael needed his father's help.

"Michael," he said, "whatever you have done, I . . . ."

He touched Michael's arm, but withdrew his hand as from a hot stove. Michael was tense, stiff, a solid but quivering object. His large gray eyes stared into Voronov's. And Voronov felt an unaccountable disappointment. Somewhere in his face he felt a tic.

"My son is innocent!" he said loudly. "He has done nothing."

"Of course," Ogarev said genially. "No one ever does. Crime is a fiction invented by police. We bureaucrats must justify our jobs."

"And of what, exactly, is my son accused?"

Ogarev consulted his papers. "Of leading a revolutionary cell, to be exact. Of operating an illegal printing press. Of attempting to murder me, Ogarev. I presume you do know who I am?"

Voronov did not know what to think. It seemed that whatever he decided, everything always changed. He wanted to get up, to walk, to talk, to overpower Ogarev verbally as he did Zabulyov at home. But he was not at home, and Ogarev was most definitely not Zabulyov.

"Michael," he whispered, "is there any truth in this?"

Michael's large gray eyes stared strangely. "None."

"This is preposterous!" Voronov said. He jumped up. He began to walk up and down. "Surely there must be some joke. I hope so. You are looking at a man of affairs, Inspector, a man engaged in private business. And I promise you I shall not abandon my son. I shall do whatever needs to be done."

"Good," said Ogarev. "We understand each other."

Voronov was at the other end of the room. When he returned, Ogarev handed him the badly printed sheet which ended, "Long live the

45

Revolution!" and Voronov read it. His hands shook. In the stillness of the room, they heard the rustling of the paper.

"Michael," he whispered, mouth almost too dry to speak.

Ogarev rapped on the table again, again the door opened and a girl came in. It was the same girl Michael had met at the bookstore. Her eyes were puffy. Her face was streaked. When she saw him she clasped her hands and came forward slowly.

"Please," she said. "Tell them I had nothing to do with it."

Michael turned to Ogarev. "And who is this?"

Ogarev smiled. "You don't even know her name, I suppose."

"No."

"It's true," said the girl. "And I don't know his."

Ogarev turned to Voronov and shrugged. "Straight from the Moscow Art Theater. Do you see?" He turned to the girl. "Shall I introduce you? Anna Andreevna Kursamina, Michael Fyodorovitch Voronov.

"It is perfectly possible, my dear Fyodor Pavlovitch, that her story is true. Perhaps the fact that we saw her with your son at his printing press means nothing. But we have no way of knowing this without your son's cooperation."

Their words slashed into Michael's mind. Ogarev was right. Michael could easily clear the girl, but the only way to do so was to involve his father, which, no matter what happened, he could not do. He knew only that he had to keep still.

But Anna Andreevna stood imploringly before him. And Michael felt outrage strangely mixed with guilt.

"You may go," Ogarev told her. But she fell to her knees before Michael, "Please," she said, "I have done nothing to harm you. You don't even know me. You have only to say a few words to release me. Why don't you? Don't you realize what will happen to me?"

Ogarev rapped on the table, the door opened and she was gone. "Such a pity," said Ogarev. "So young. So full of life."

The tic made Voronov's entire jowl jump. He put a hand to his cheek to keep it still. He looked at Michael, but his son's face was like a death mask.

"Have another cigarette," said Ogarev.

"Thank you. I shall."

"Isn't it remarkable, Fyodor Pavlovitch, isn't it remarkable how many offspring of respectable businessmen go wrong? Prudent, industrious businessmen like yourself."

"It is."

"All over Russia lately, we find sons and daughters of businessmen throwing bombs. Children of prudent, industrious businessmen like yourself."

"Yes. I have noticed. Luckily . . . ."

"Why, Fyodor Pavlovitch? Explain it to me."

"I am sorry. I really don't know."

Ogarev's small but clear eyes darted. His Vandyke hopped as if recording their words. He lit Voronov's cigarette and shrugged.

"I'll be frank, Fyodor Pavlovitch. Luckily we're reasonable men. And sincerity is one of the things I prize most. Don't you?"

"Most assuredly."

"I like you, Fyodor Pavlovitch. You do not surprise me." Ogarev took some vodka from a drawer, set out two glasses and poured. "Have some vodka, Fyodor Pavlovitch."

"No, I couldn't. I don't drink."

"Nonsense!" said Ogarev. "We are being sincere. I am a faceless bureaucrat doing his job, and you are a father fighting for his son. We are reasonable men, we are being sincere, and we are both men of experience and affairs . . . . What did you say was your profession, Fyodor Pavlovitch?"

"Private business."

"Yes. Forgive me. I forgot. What were we talking about?"

"Sincerity."

"Yes, we were. We have so much in common. How unfortunate that the circumstances necessarily make us foes."

"Yes," said Voronov sadly. He took the vodka and drank.

"And how difficult it is so often to accept the truth. Your loyalty to your son is touching, Fyodor Pavlovitch. Truly, I admire it. I encourage it. Keep fighting me, by all means, as you reluctantly have. Family loyalty is the cement of the Empire. But you cannot help your son until you recognize the truth, which is that your son has been doing what I say he has.

"The humiliation, the shock and outrage will pass. Believe me, Fyodor Pavlovitch, I am familiar with these cases. Orloff, for instance, whom your son foolishly tried to free, is a former officer of the Grand Duchess's Hussars and a member, formerly, of one of our best families — the brother-in-law of your son's employer, in fact. And then you will realize, as did Orloff's family, that you are not alone. And most important, that you are not to blame; that you are the victim of a strange disease whose symptoms include ingratitude shown by offspring to the parents who gave them life."

Voronov sobbed. The vodka had begun to loosen his emotions, and so had Ogarev's last remarks.

"I've tried so hard to be a good father," he sobbed.

Ogarev smiled. "Of course you have. But it isn't easy."

"It isn't easy," Voronov sobbed. "Especially if you insist on being punctilious, like me. It isn't necessary, I know — but it is worth it. We are talking, after all, about my own flesh and blood. Every sacrifice is a reward."

"Will you take my advice, Fyodor Pavlovitch?" said Ogarev.

"Anything!" said Voronov. "Anything you say. Whatever you think will help my son."

"Your son does not have your broad experience, Fyodor Pavlovitch. I tried to gain his confidence, but could not. He would not let me help him. He does not have your sophistication and depth. Perhaps, if he cooperates, I could arrange his conviction as a political. He would ride through Siberia like a gentleman, in a cart. He would have privileges. He would be quartered separately, with the other politicals. Like the politicals, he would do no work. But he refuses to honor my sincerity and good nature.

"Do you see, Fyodor Pavlovitch, why I called you here? Perhaps you, his father, can bring him to reason. Perhaps your sincerity and wisdom, combined with the fact of your paternity . . . ."

"Let me try, Sergei Dmitrievitch, let me try."

"I am going to leave you two alone," said Ogarev. "You will be more at ease. Do not hurry. There is plenty of time. Gently exert your parental influence. Here is pen and ink. All you need write is the names of the others and their addresses, if known."

Ogarev unfolded some sheets of paper. "Oh, yes, as a businessman you may be interested. We must know the exact meaning of these figures. To what do they refer? What do they measure? No doubt something to do with your son's bank robberies, but what? And we must know the name of the author."

Voronov looked down at his own handwriting. The columns of figures, the notes and calculations were as he remembered them. So was the paper itself and the way it folded. There was no mistake. He looked down, but he could not look up. He could not bear to see the others' faces. He felt an eerie, disjointed fear. At last he realized what Michael was involved in — realized that he, himself, had caused his son's arrest, that he, Voronov, should be in Michael's place.

Voronov looked at Ogarev and wondered. Would he believe the simple truth that Voronov knew nothing, always had known and always would know nothing? That he knew only now that he was involved in something illegal? Voronov looked at Ogarev and saw the answer. He had not believed the truth about the son. Why would he believe the truth about the father?

In a very short time, Ogarev would decide that Voronov was avoiding his son and would wonder why. Voronov forced himself to look and saw a hallucination. He knew it was a hallucination, knew it clearly, but the knowledge did not make the experience less intense. He knew the room was lit, but it grew dark. Everything — Ogarev, the incriminating papers and Michael's face — faded away. And at the same time, Michael's eyes grew bigger and brighter until at last they hung before him, disembodied in space.

Does he know? The question filled Voronov's mind, leaving room for nothing else. Over and over it asked itself, underlined by a sound which was probably his heartbeat, like the nonsense statements with which passengers accompany the clacking of their train. But it was not nonsense. It was as deathly grim as could be. *Did* Michael know? So much depended on the answer.

And Voronov decided that Michael probably didn't know. Michael had seen him working several times at home, but had never paid any attention. Voronov had never left any papers around. And he had always sent the work in a safely sealed envelope. Michael had never seen it, and would not recognize it now. Besides, it was just calculations, not handwriting.

Perhaps, after all, Michael knew nothing and had no idea that his father's "business" was his son's crime. Voronov did not know why, but it was crucially important for him to believe this. Why had Nastasya Lvovna done this? What role had his calculations unwittingly played in her crimes? Only that morning, he had learned that she and her husband had left their hotel. Now he understood why. But where had they gone?

But the room was still dark and his son's eyes remained, standing before him like two brightly lit globes. Why must he insist on staring impassively like that? Voronov felt the desire to run, for hours, for days — to run endlessly until he dropped. The tic in his jowl would not stop. It seemed that he had lost control of his face. If only there were something he could do to help Michael. If only he could help his son!

Ogarev turned to go. "Well, I'll leave you."

"Wait!" said Voronov, catching his sleeve, gray with the looming horror of being left alone with Michael.

"You heard my son say he is innocent," he said. "Did you think I would take your word before his? Did you imagine that I would talk with him in private to confirm your theory of his guilt? You mistake me completely, Sergei Dmitrievitch, I am glad to tell you. I have not lovingly raised a son to compromise him by falling for this cheap police trick. You are looking at a man who prizes loyalty before all else. And I warn you, I shall be satisfied with nothing less than complete exoneration."

He moved toward the door, voice barely under control. Michael's impassive eyes followed him.

"Michael, do not say a thing," he said. "I must write letters, make inquiries, see people in the Ministry. Have confidence. I shall not fail. A monstrous, criminal mistake has been made."

Voronov opened the door and ran out.

"Mercurial, isn't he?" Ogarev said. "So unlike you, comrade Voronov. But it is genuinely touching to see how much he loves you."

VI

Voronov's elbow was in a puddle of vodka, and the puddle was growing. He was filling his glass with more than it could hold. But he did not notice. He did not want to notice. His mind was a blank. And it took all his attention to keep it that way.

He was tired. For three days he had been to offices, seen people and asked questions — and had been told that procedure was inviolable and nothing could be done. He expected this; he knew that there was no point at all in making these visits, but he had told Michael he would. They gave him the spurious impression he was accomplishing something. And, for the same reason, he had gone back to Nastasya Lvovna's hotel and had been told twice more that she had left without a word.

Now there was nothing else he could think of doing. Moreover, the incident had brought his "business" to a halt, Nastasya Lvovna paid him no more money, and his remaining funds were quickly dwindling. If only there were something he could do to help his son.

At last he stopped pouring and tears came to his eyes. "Look, Misha," he said. "Now see what I have done."

"Yes," said Zabulyov. "Now it never can be drunk. You are guilty, Fyodor Pavlovitch. Guilty."

"Yes," said Voronov. "I am guilty. I am. Guilty." The word gave Voronov a strange pleasure to say.

"Such a waste," said Zabulyov.

"Yes."

"Take your son. To think that he could do such a thing."

"My son is not guilty, as I told you before. He is not guilty and I am. I am guilty and he is not."

"I am sorry, Fyodor Pavlovitch, I am just a stupid peasant. I turn my glass upside down."

"No, Misha, no. What you said was meant well. Take my son, for instance. What he does is meant well. What I do is always meant well. Always. But however something is meant, it must always go badly because we are victims, victims of fate.

"A bad bargain, Misha, necessarily bad. Always it is the same. It's the nature of human life, my dear friend. Time passes, one's clothes fray, one gets flabby and bald. Look, Misha, look, I am losing my hair.

"Is it worth it, I sometimes wonder? Should I have bothered to have a son? Should I have devoted so much care to his rearing — well-meant care — knowing that he would be taken as he has been, capriciously, for no reason, by life? If only there were something I could do for him, Misha."

"Why don't you tell the authorities that you did what he is accused of? Sacrifice yourself."

"No, Misha. I thought of that. They would not believe me."

"Luckily there is always vodka," said Zabulyov.

The door to the apartment opened and Sophia Petrovna came in, taking the thick scarf from her head.

"Did you see him?" asked Voronov.

"Yes," she said.

"What did he say?"

"Nothing. It's as if he is waiting. But he didn't say for what."

"Did he ask for me?"

"No. But you should have come. He wants you to come. I know it. Perhaps he is waiting for you."

"Impossible. I could not do it. The emotional stress of seeing my son there is just too great."

"Fedya, I have a premonition. Our son is doomed."

"Nonsense. Don't imagine things. There is still time."

"I see it clearly. We are being punished. It is the vengeance of God. At least come with me to church."

Voronov hit the table. "Must you constantly bicker?"

A movement at the door caught his eye, and he looked to see a folded sheet of paper sliding under it. He went to the door, opened it and went out into the hall. No one was there. At least, he saw no one. He picked up the piece of paper and unfolded it. There was no salutation and no signature, only the words: "Go to Riga."

Was this more of Nastasya Lvovna's "business?" What train was he supposed to take? Where was he supposed to go in Riga? Whom was he supposed to see? Did the note have to do with his son?

The next train left in two hours and Voronov was on it. As during his visits to the various bureaus, he felt better. The mere movement created the illusion that he was acting. It delayed the time when he would have to think. He leaned back against the seat and sighed. I am indeed a victim of fate, he thought.

He stood on the platform in Riga, perplexed. It was deserted. The other passengers had long since gone. Steam rose silently from a locomotive. Ahead in the darkness, a train shunted tracks. He walked up and down wondering what to do next.

Then he felt a hand at his elbow, and was looking down at an upturned face. The prominent nose on it waggled cautiously. The small mouth under it began to grin. It was Kolodsky.

"Voronov?" asked Kolodsky with impudence.

"Yes," said Voronov, backing away.

"This way," said Kolodsky, already moving.

"Where?" asked Voronov, out of breath. But the strange little man did not answer, except for a satisfied, feline leer.

A cab was waiting and they got in. Without a command it began to move. It was late and Voronov saw only a rare pedestrian. Some men stood at a corner, warming their hands around a bonfire. At another, a couple of policemen did the same. The cab made an intricate series of turns, once even reversing itself. Voronov was already lost. And all the while, Kolodsky silently stared, hugely enjoying a secret joke.

"Are you taking me to see about my son?" Voronov asked.

"It's a pleasure to see a man so well dressed."

"I am in business."

"Business," mused Kolodsky. "Of what sort?"

"Look here," said Voronov. "I will not be interrogated."

Kolodsky shrugged. "Suit yourself." Again he simply stared and smirked. The cab silently crossed the snow.

Then they were at a door. Kolodsky rapped a signal and it opened. They were in a small, bare room. A man lounged on a bench. It was Dolgorensky. His lush, feminine lips were pursing quizzically. And Nastasya Lvovna sat writing at a table. She had changed. No longer was she the feminine person he had seen in her hotel room. Now she wore a leather jacket, trousers and boots.

"Nastya!" said Voronov. "A horrible mistake has been made."

Nastasya Lvovna did not answer. She did not look up. With the heel of her pen she pointed to a chair before her table.

"But, Nastya . . . ."

Nastasya Lvovna did not speak or move. Her pen still pointed at the

"Certainly not!" said Nastasya Lvovna. "It was Kolodsky's idea. We needed an expert and Kolodsky here worked with him."

Perhaps Michael was not so innocent after all. Why had he not told his father this?

"There is a way to free your son," said Nastasya Lvovna. "Only one way. That is why I brought you here."

Voronov trembled. "Tell me. I would be so grateful."

"Simply give yourself up," said Nastasya Lvovna.

"Give myself up?"

"Surely the possibility has occurred to you. Or has it? Go to Ogarev and tell him the truth. You should. Your son is innocent, is he not?"

"They would not believe me," said Voronov.

"Convince them," said Nastasya Lvovna.

"Of course, that could create a problem," said Dolgorensky. "You would not want to create a problem."

"No," said Voronov. "Certainly not."

"If you do it," said Dolgorensky, "you must do it properly. Your son has not talked. We have ways of knowing that. But if you do it, Ogarev will ask you the same questions. And unlike your son, you will have no one to protect. That could be inconvenient for us. Do you see?"

"Yes."

"Have you ever seen one of these?" asked Dolgorensky. He had been slowly burnishing a Luger and held it up. "Remarkable piece of machinery, don't you think? Amazing, really. Such engineering. Only the Germans could have produced it. Notice how everything fits together so well."

"I see."

"Look at this round. Imagine what that could do to a man. Makes quite a hole in a chest. Do you see?"

"Yes. Yes."

"Kolodsky!"

"Yes?"

"Escort our guest back to the station."

Still trying to think of something to say, Voronov was pushed out of the room. A hand propelled him down the corridor. Again he was in the cab and it was moving. Kolodsky was near him, grinning as before. Dazed, he realized that nothing had been accomplished.

On the platform in Petersburg, he saw a tall man, far away and moving further. It was Michael's employer, Danilov. Perhaps Danilov would be willing to help. It was generally agreed that he treated his workers better than anybody else.

Voronov pushed through the crowd and began to run. The tall man had already left the station. But it was difficult to make any headway in the crowd. His movements became somewhat hysterical. He smashed his knee on something projecting from the wall. At last he was past the crowd, gasping, running after the man ahead.

"Please," he wheezed. "May I speak with you?"

"Of course."

"Please. I am sorry. My son . . . ."

"Yes?"

Voronov saw that the man was not Danilov after all.

"Pardon me," he gasped. "A mistake."

The other man frowned and walked away. Voronov extended some fingers and fell against a wall. He could not breathe. His head was whirling. And the mind inside it was whirling, too.

VII

It was late. The clock ticked, slowly but loudly — like his own footsteps approaching the future, Voronov mused. Behind its glass door, the moving pendulum caught the light. He had only to use a forefinger to stop it, but its mates everywhere would show the truth.

He listened. Nothing moved throughout the house. He looked through the window. Nothing was in the street. The night was white, white and still, like a winding sheet in the silence of a tomb.

It was cold. He stood over the fire warming his hands. It was low, dying, shimmering in a haze. Here and there a knot cracked. He stirred the embers and they glowed, but it was as if the poker were disturbing someone's bones. He shuddered. Death everywhere, he thought. In every corner. Death warming me; fire is the color of blood. No chance for the living. Why?

That morning, in a few hours, Michael would be tried. And Voronov saw his son's face looking up at him, the face of a small boy looking at his father. On it, Voronov saw admiration. He felt a twinge of remorse, which quickly became anger. Such foolishness, he thought. Such dangerous nonsense. As if there had ever been a reason for admiration! It is a father's protective responsibility to prove the emotion false, to warn his son against hypocrisy. There is no reason to admire anyone.

And yet, I have always allowed him to push me, Voronov thought. Because of my love. In that sense I have failed. I confess it. I am guilty. I played the part he wrote for me. It was his insistence that I put on airs that made all of this happen. He made me a hypocrite. Playing upon my weakness, my solicitude for his immaturity, he made it impossible for me to teach him the lesson he needed. Had he left me alone, let me sit here quietly with Zabulyov, not insisted I put on airs and go into business, not do something to admire, none of this would have happened. He's arrogant; I don't like to admit it, but that fishwife downstairs — what's her name? — she's right: he is arrogant. So now he gets what he deserves. He brought it on himself. Now he will be forced to learn the lesson he would not let me teach him. I have a right to be angry. I resent his attitude.

Again Voronov saw the small room in the police station, and Michael in it. Why had Michael said nothing, his face frozen? Why had he simply stared at Voronov?

Because he knows! thought Voronov. He knows the truth and is trying to torture me. That is why he doesn't accuse and attack me. That is why he waits. He is deliberately trying to prolong my suffering. He will wait until the last moment, at the trial, and then he will expose me. He enjoys it!

Voronov nevertheless flushed painfully with guilt. His face tingled. He shrugged. It doesn't really matter, he thought. Life is short. Death is long. Death is the only thing that matters. Life is just a futile interlude between two types of nothingness. It makes no difference who lives or dies. It makes no difference which one of us is condemned. Any gesture either of us may make is meaningless. Whatever I do, it won't mean a thing.

Voronov stood at the window, rubbing his hands, listening to the oppressive stillness as before. Now he could not even hear the clock, but he knew that the pendulum was still moving senselessly. Somewhere in the house, a woman began to cry. Below, a bent old man carrying a sack trudged past. Soon I shall be an old man myself, Voronov thought. Old and helpless, and it will not matter.

Again Voronov stirred the dying fire. A knot cracked. The complaining embers sent up sparks. I'm a fraud, he thought. I've never been anything else. Everything I've done is a fraud. And now at last I have betrayed my son. Tomorrow is the last day of my life, he thought. I'm a failure. My whole life — wasted, nothing. Nastasya Lvovna was perfectly right.

For what seemed the first time in his life, Voronov saw clearly. He felt no fear. And he saw that he must save his son. A plan was already in his mind. In a few hours, at the trial, in the midst of the proceedings, he would stand, confess, and exonerate Michael. He saw himself standing at the rail of the gallery, and saying to the prosecutor in a low voice, "I shall be at home — with my son — when you wish to see me." In great detail, he saw the shock of the audience, the confusion of the officials, the consternation of the prosecutor. He already could hear the shouting and applause. Nastasya Lvovna would be there, he knew, and he saw himself looking at her in challenge. Then he would turn and walk out slowly, paying no attention to the uproar.

Voronov straightened and stood erect, chin raised, stomach in, like a soldier on parade, as he would stand in court tomorrow. He smiled. The warmth of returning virtue suffused him and bore him up. And the theatricality of the plan appealed to him.

Suddenly he seized the mantelpiece, frozen by horror. A word Ogarev had said was now in his mind, only one, and the word was "Siberia." Now he saw naked aborigines and wolves. He was plodding across the tundra, a wind like a knife slashing at his face. And then he was crawling blindly in a mine, mouth dusty, covered with sweat.

His lips quivered. His body shook. Limp with terror, he clung to the mantelpiece.

"No!" he said aloud. "No!" Again he stood erect. In a minute, the terror began to subside, and he put what Ogarev had said from his mind.

Tomorrow, he thought. Tomorrow in court I shall be redeemed.

* * *

Khodolyubov leaned as far as he could over the railing and peered. He had a clear view but he squinted, bobbing his head, as if Michael were far away or some obstruction were between them. He longed for the spectacles he wore only in secret.

"Well," said the prosecutor, "come, come, Khodolyubov."

"Yes," said Khodolyubov with certainty, "that is the man."

"What happened then?"

"He threw the bomb."

"You saw this, Khodolyubov?"

"Yes."

"Step down."

Khodolyubov squinted again and did so, but Michael paid him no attention. From the beginning of the session he had ignored the proceedings, staring upward instead at a point in the gallery.

"What was your general opinion of the defendant?"

"He was a bad one, your honor," said the fishwife from downstairs. "I didn't like him."

"Why not?"

"He was very close. He always kept to himself. Lord knows what he did with his time. All of us wondered, and rightly, I now see. It's a wonder we weren't killed in our beds. And I didn't like his manner, your honor. Too good for us common people, he thinks he is. As if he isn't one himself."

At a nearby table, Ogarev was pleased, more pleased than he had expected to be. Everything was arranged. Michael Voronov would be condemned as an ordinary criminal rather than as a political.

60

And Nastasya Lvovna sat in the audience, unobtrusive for a change. She, too, was pleased, but at the same time disappointed.

"What is your name?" the prosecutor asked.

"Anna Andreevna Kursamina."

"And did you see the defendant on the night of January twenty-third?"

"Yes."

"What were the circumstances?"

"He took me to a printing plant. It had been wrecked."

"Step down," said the prosecutor.

But Anna Andreevna did not move. She had been promised a minimum sentence if she cooperated and talked, but since she did not know anything, she could not.

"Please," she said. "Please . . . . "

Ogarev gestured and an attendant led her away. Again Michael felt the unaccustomed emotion of guilt. But as always he did not look. His eyes were fixed on the gallery. He was waiting.

The prosecutor raised his arm and pointed. "And I therefore demand the severest penalty. The facts have incontrovertibly been proved. Justice demands that the defendant be made an example. For we are dealing here not only with a criminal act — that, in itself, would be a serious offense — but with a criminal act which in reality was an attack on His Imperial Majesty, on Russian civilization itself.

"Such ingrates and criminals, who look back to 1905 with nostalgia, must be brought by swift and merciless retribution to realize such a thing can never happen again. I therefore demand — "

"Stop! Stop! Wait!"

The prosecutor's arm paused in midgesture. The room was silent. His arm fell. Everyone began to talk at once. The prosecutor and the officials, Ogarev, Nastasya Lvovna, and the rest of the audience, all craned their necks, shuffled their feet, and peered around the room, wondering at the interruption, searching for its source. "Who was that?" said voices. "What did he say?" "Please shut up!"

Voronov stood at the front of the gallery.

Gradually the noise abated. No one spoke. No one moved. Once again the room was silent. Michael rose in his box and smiled, watching Voronov as he had from the beginning.

And Voronov looked down at his son. They looked at each other as if they were alone. Voronov seemed startled, surprised at himself. His hands were on the railing, knuckles like eight white knobs on a limb. He opened his mouth.

"I . . . . "

Everyone in the room leaned forward involuntarily. A rattling sound came from Voronov's throat. His face contorted. The sound increased. His brain struggled to think the first word, his lips laboriously attempted to shape the sound, but he could not speak. He knew exactly what it was he wanted to say, he had prepared it carefully, even memorized it, corrected it to make it clear, but now, because of some breakdown, he was unable to say it. He was like a racing motor with barely disengaged gears.

Voronov looked from Michael to Nastasya Lvovna and to Ogarev. He looked again at Michael, and could not look away. He struggled on in the silence, rattling, for one minute. For two. The combined desire of everyone in the room to help him say it — whatever it was — became almost tangible. Then the dramatic climax had passed, and with it the audience's satisfaction. The tension abated, and Voronov's struggle became merely embarrassing and annoying.

The prosecutor had a good record of convictions. That was why he had been chosen for this case: the evidence, after all, was not airtight. He had a reputation for a remarkably quick mind. He had no idea what this interruption was about, but now he raised his arm again and pointed at Voronov.

"Yes," he shouted, "and there you see a living example, human documentation of my argument. A father, an honest, industrious Russian father, laboring with the support and comfort of his family as his only goal, brought to the intensity of suffering you see before you by the criminal, irresponsible actions of an ungrateful son. A son who refuses to show any contrition or apology, who arrogantly clings to silence. And in spite of this the father rises, as in heroic legend, trying vainly to protect his son — the son who has brought his father this humiliation!"

"He's right, the prosecutor is right," said voices. "The younger generation!" "Ingrate!"

The sound in Voronov's throat had stopped, but Michael's eyes were still upon him and Voronov could not bear the pain. He turned, blindly, arms flailing, and went out. On his back he felt friendly pats; in his ears, encouraging words. Someone warmly squeezed his arm. A woman pointed, whispering to a child.

At last he was in the street, again blissfully anonymous. A crowd of pedestrians swept him away. Faces and lights appeared before him in a haze. He was semi-conscious, but he had to keep moving.

He found himself inside a church. It was dark. A strand of light fell in beads on the floor. Ikons hung on the walls. Shrines were in the recesses.

Innumerable unintelligible voices whispered. Mystery pervaded the air, penetrated the mind, permeated the body.

Voronov knelt and put his forehead to the floor. The stone was cold and strangely soothing.

"The sins of the fathers," he mumbled. "The sins of the fathers." His words joined the other whispers.

He felt a strong hand on his shoulder. He looked up. It was a priest. The priest smiled. He did not speak, but in his face Voronov saw reassuring spiritual force. He began to cry, spasmodically. He kissed the priest's robe. He felt the strong hand tighten on his shoulder.

Unexpectedly his crushing guilt began to lift. In its stead he felt relief. He wondered why he had not been to church for years. He resolved to go again more often. And he did.

Indeed, Sophia Petrovna often said later that that that was the one blessing of their misfortune.

*   *   *

It was an ideal day on which to die. Thick, dirty clouds covered the sun. It was damp, too damp to rain. A veil of mist joined the earth and sky. The marshy earth was bare, punctuated only by a struggling bush and a stagnant, viscid pond. Beside the tracks was a rotting shed, splotched with mold, slats green like the sea, its rusty door hanging open, unmoved by any breeze.

Michael sat very still in the motionless train. When he moved, he was reminded of the chains. What annoyed him was not so much the chafing at his ankles, but the noise. Experienced convicts could move in perfect silence, but he of course had had no experience.

He looked up. Far above, a hawk stood against the sky, moving his wings very slightly as if floating. Suddenly the hawk dived, straight and far down, almost plunging into the earth before he flew up. He resumed his lazy position as before, luxuriating as the air itself supported him, as if there were no need to move.

My life, which is now ending, thought Michael.

There was a lurch and his chains jangled. One of the other prisoners sighed. The train slowly began to move. The hawk receded and disappeared.

Michael Voronov sped eastward into the unknown.

Part II

Peter
Orloff

VIII

Peter Sergeievitch Orloff looked up at the sky. It was spring, the worst season of the year. In the winter just past, as always, they had been deadened by ice. In the summer to come, as always, would come the heat and mosquitoes. Without a horsehair net there was no defense. And the heat would scald and crack his feet. In those seasons, the prison camp was easier to take. But in spring he, too, thawed like the earth and his dormant feelings reawakened. He remembered a favorite restaurant in St. Petersburg; the section of Moscow he called home. If only he could sit at his favorite table or walk at this moment through the streets. But most of all he wanted his wife Katya, who, like the wives of most politicals, lived in the nearby town. The fact that she visited regularly only made his desire keener. He loved his wife more than anything else, including himself. More than anything — except the Revolution.

It was 1914. It had been the same for seven years. Soon he would be forty years old.

There was a breeze, pleasantly warm and at the same time cool. A bird nearby flushed and flew. On the other side of the hill was the river. Some other prisoners were atop the hill and pointing. Still others drifted over and did the same. Orloff climbed the hill.

He saw a young girl on the other side of the river. Her hair was long and very blonde. She wore a white blouse and full peasant skirt. She was probably the daughter of one of the exiles in the town. Orloff waited for the usual obscenity, but none came. The men were hushed. Apparently they sensed the same thing he did. The girl was walking slowly. She was alone, absorbed, not even noticing the watching men. She was doing exactly as she wished. She was free.

Like the others, Orloff drank in the sight. It was beautiful, but it was also painful. He wished he had not seen it. Yet he had expected it as he climbed the hill.

Someone was near him. A hand touched his sleeve. "Such a pity we can't do the same," said Yellin. "Monstrous! Keeping human beings penned in like this."

Orloff closed his eyes. Yellin had destroyed the mood. Yellin had roughly returned him to reality. If only Yellin had not been the one to do it. There was a grotesque quality to his statement that hurt Orloff all the more.

Nikolai Semyonovitch Yellin had served ten years at hard labor, during the first six of which he complained that he had been wrongly imprisoned and described what he would do when released. At last the day came. The gates opened and closed. Yellin stood alone on the plain. Westward, beyond the horizon, was Russia. To the east, much closer, was Vladivostok. And he had the right to do as he liked. He was free.

Yellin saw this vastness and suddenly was afraid. He considered these possibilities and was terrified. He shrank against the fence of the stockade. Behind him was a life in which everything was decided for him. Ahead, nothing definite could be known. Yellin did not know what to do.

He went into town and began to drink and to tell everyone who would listen how happy he was. But he could not bear to leave the town. He did not yet admit it, but he felt nostalgic about the prison. He had made so many friends there; in fact he knew nobody else. And Savitsky, the prison governor, provided the necessities of life. The routine was bearable, secure. There was something to be said for the prison existence.

He went to Savitsky and asked to be resentenced, but Savitsky ordered Yellin thrown out. So Yellin returned to town and drank all he could. Then, one cold night, he cut somebody's throat. The police found him asleep with his feet on the table.

Yellin got his wish and was returned to the prison, not even knowing how pleased he was. Time passed, the terror of his free interlude faded, and gradually Yellin's earlier personality returned. He began to complain about prison life and about how monstrous it was to keep human beings penned. He talked about the joys of freedom and what he would do when released. But unknown to himself and most of the others, he was inwardly at peace. He had forgotten why he happened to be there.

This was why Orloff usually wanted to smash a fist in his face. But he did not. He did not even say anything in response to Yellin's remark. He needed Yellin for the escape.

He opened his eyes. The girl was gone.

Then Prishkin, the sergeant, gave the order and the prisoners moved off toward the sheds and the wool-cleaning machines. The chains connecting his ankles weighed thirteen pounds, but in seven years he had learned to move silently. Like the others, he had tied the leather strap in the center of the connecting chain to his belt. Even now the ankle irons chafed the skin, even through the leather of his slippers. He wore a long, gray gown, on the back of which — according to regulations — the yellow hard-labor square was sewn. According to regulations, the right side of his head was shaved.

Hours passed. Inside the shed the machines were roaring. The heat was fierce. An itching patina of sweat stood on his face. He could feel it even between his toes. But he had no clean sleeve with which to wipe it. His eyes prickled as if punctured by needles. A fine, gray dust hung in the air like a sequined curtain sparkling in the dim light, filling the nose and mouth and pores. Shadowy men felt their ways through it, as if walking on the ocean floor, gesticulating and shouting in near pantomime. Almost nothing could be heard but the roar of the machines. Next to him, Yellin was coughing uncontrollably. That was the first sign. Just yesterday another man had finally coughed his last.

But this was where Orloff wanted to be. The work — the real work — was going very well, painfully, slowly, but better than expected. Sometimes it seemed that the tunnel did not grow at all, but the proof was the sacks of dirt they removed. It would go even better if they had the proper tools, but he could not risk attracting any more attention. For the same reason, he signalled to Yellin to do up the sacks. The day was almost over.

The tunnel was at the back of the big room behind one of the machines. When finished, it would be long. But it was dug along the shortest route: under Savitsky's house and beyond the walls. The guards never nosed about. They, too, hated the dust and came in only when they had to. In fact, the hole could not be seen even when uncovered, except from up close. Several other men made up his and Yellin's work. The politicals helping him had again chosen Orloff to make the attempt, because his escape would most embarrass the authorities. And at the end of the day, Yellin carried out the sacks of dirt under his gown. None of the guards ever searched Yellin. That was why Orloff needed him. Why should they? They thought of Yellin not as a real prisoner but as a joke. Who could suspect Yellin of a plot?

That was why Yellin was so eager to cooperate. Nobody took him seriously, which he resented. He did not like being a joke. He did not like being a false prisoner. But now he was participating in, indeed was vital to, something very serious: helping a dangerous Bolshevik to escape. And he would not have to escape himself. The situation, for Yellin, was perfect.

There were many risks: the guards for some reason might search Yellin after all, they might find the tunnel entrance, or discover Orloff's absence during the day. But the plan was the best that could be made.

69

Yellin had already adjusted the sacks under his gown. In a few minutes the day would end and the men would file out. He pointed to himself and nodded to show that he was ready. Then Mitka Dubin appeared in the passageway at the far end of the big room and started toward them. Orloff bent and quickly concealed the hole. He motioned to Yellin, who pretended to adjust his chains. Although the hole was well-hidden, they knelt shoulder to shoulder before it.

Mitka hurried toward them, searching and excitable, waving his arms. He stopped. He was shouting something through the dust. "The new man . . . the rods . . . regulations . . . ."

Orloff strained to hear. "What? What?"

But Mitka Dubin could no longer wait. There was no time to be lost. He was already hurrying to someone else. Here was another of the chances they had to take. Dubin was a type found in all penal institutions: the lawyer. He had studied and memorized all the laws and regulations. Asked why he was in prison, he would not name the crime, but would cite the number of the governing law — recite it like a court official. Asked, for example, about Orloff he would say simply, "Paragraph 102." He had once become convinced that the soup did not contain the prescribed sixty grams of boiled meat and complained. Savitsky had convinced him that it did.

But, unlike other "lawyers," Mitka did not learn the regulations to outwit the authorities. He did not learn the regulations to circumvent them. He learned the regulations to enforce them. Nothing made Mitka happier than the fulfillment of a regulation. The regulations had an unusual power for Mitka. Not only was there no question for which they did not have the answer, not only did they infinitely regulate the activities of men, but — Mitka believed — they *caused* the activities of men. He believed that the regulations were the reality of which the men they moved were merely the reflection, that he and the others owed their existence to the regulations. He had long ago forgotten that one can live without regulations; that he himself had done so once. Had he remembered, he would have been frightened. As in Yellin's case, there would have been disaster had he been sent into the world.

So Mitka made it his business to see that the regulations were obeyed. Everywhere in the compound, he would suddenly appear: his head on the long, bony body turning quickly, the eyes twitching; anxiously stooping, peering and searching; hurrying, always hurrying on to the next point and the next; assuring himself that all the regulations were intact. When Mitka stopped to talk, he did not stay long. Quickly, abruptly, he said what he had to say, listening, waiting, moving from foot to foot, and then he was off to the next checkpoint, where a crisis might be taking shape.

Indeed, Mitka thought of himself as an unofficial official. He was a sincere and forceful defender of the throne. It was a regulation. Some who attacked it in his presence were attacked in return. The politicals talked pleasantries until he went away. It was mildly surprising to see his gray gown and chains. And when Mitka discovered an infraction, he would report it to Golovin, the head warder, and they would confer. Mitka was Golovin's unofficial legal adjutant. Much of what he reported, Golovin would have been unable to find out. Had Mitka found the tunnel, he would have reported it immediately. It would not have occurred to him what the tunnel meant. He would have reported it only because the regulations did not specify a tunnel. If they had specified a tunnel, he would have been delighted to find one.

Lately, Mitka was even more nervous about the matter of his handcuffs. Under a twenty-year sentence, he had been ordered handcuffed for four — pursuant to regulations. The end of the fourth year was now approaching and soon Golovin would remove them — pursuant to regulations. Mitka Dubin counted the days.

Yellin and Orloff were glad to see him go. The day had ended. The men were moving out. The machines had stopped, but the noise hung in the air. Yellin and Orloff filed out into the fading sunlight, squinting while their eyes focussed. Then the noise faded and they heard excited voices. They were marched not to the barracks, but to positions in the yard.

The talking stopped. Michael Voronov and two guards were coming across the yard to the low stone table in the center. Still a few yards away, Michael shook the guards off, went to the table, and lay on it face down, after which they tied him to it.

This was what Mitka had been talking about; it was an infraction of the regulations.

The top of the table was depressed to fit the body. There were gouges at the sides and one end for the arms and legs. The setting sun blazed on the stone and Michael's back. Orloff's mouth was dry and burning. The stillness and expectancy were unendurable.

A door opened, and the men shuddered almost audibly. Golovin came slowly across the yard with some rods. He had been standing just inside the door for several minutes. He knew that expectation was often worse than reality, so he had waited, savoring the men's impatience. They knew this; he had done the same thing many times. But against their own wills, they became tense and terrified.

Golovin looked at the bare back and smiled. A piece of straw was on it. He removed it. He chose a rod, cut the air with it, and then chose another. He knew everyone knew that there was nothing wrong with the first, but it heightened the tension all the same. His arm rose. The end of the raised rod disappeared in the sun, like the tip of a poker glowing in a fire.

Then the rod descended and bit into the bare back. Michael's body noticeably went taut. And at the same time, with an almost audible sigh, the men relaxed. What came would still be bad, but for them the worst was over. The rod rose and fell, again and again.

"Who is he?" asked Orloff.

"I don't know," Yellin said.

"A troublemaker transferred from Irkutsk," said another.

Mitka scurried up. "His name is Michael Voronov," he said. "He refused to greet his honor and to take off his cap."

The name was perfectly familiar to Orloff. He had read four years earlier that Michael had led the band that tried to free him.

"This is monstrous," said Yellin. "It should not be permitted."

"If only he would take off his cap," said Mitka. "Why would anyone refuse to do that?"

"Regulations, Mitka?" somebody asked.

"I just don't understand," Mitka said. "Look, I take my cap off. It doesn't mean a thing." Mitka took his cap off.

"What will you Communists do for the prisons?" asked Yellin.

"After a while, we won't need them," Orloff said.

"Next time he'll know better," Mitka said.

Orloff said, "I don't take mine off."

"You're a political," said Mitka.

"Here's five rubles that say he'll howl," said someone.

"And here are five that think otherwise," said Orloff.

The rod slowly rose and fell. Golovin heard the guard count thirty. Soon the prisoner would begin to beg. There was nothing like the rods to teach a man a lesson. But no sound came from Michael's lips. The skin on his back turned white and puffy. Then the skin turned red and burst. Bits of it rose on the rod and fell. Blood rose in the gouges and overflowed. The guard called fifty, but still he made no sound. Golovin was getting exasperated and tired. He threw the rod away and chose another. Again his arm rose and fell. All was quiet, except for the slashing of the rod. The event had become boring. Golovin wanted to finish as quickly as he could. It was not the usual success.

At last it was over. Golovin's arm fell. The guards untied the prisoner and raised him from the table. He leaned against it briefly, then shook them loose as before. Slowly, very slowly, he pulled himself erect. Then he moved off stiffly to the infirmary. His raw back hung in strips. Behind him was a trail of blood. No one moved. No one spoke. The men before him stared in wonder as he approached. He did not pause. He did not veer. He did not look down. His shadow fell across them and they got out of the way. He disappeared around a corner.

Orloff opened his hand. "You lose," he said.

IX

There was nothing in the world Golovin hated more than Orloff. There was nothing about him Golovin did not hate. He realized this once more as he looked at Katerina Nikolaevna, Orloff's wife. They were so much alike. Indeed, her arrogant posture now was the feminine counterpart of Orloff's. Golovin did not hate Katerina Nikolaevna — not at all. She was a woman, a beautiful woman. But everything she did reminded Golovin of her husband Orloff.

Golovin had not said so, of course, but it was because of Orloff that he had mixed the politicals with the common criminals. He had claimed that the government would approve, as part of the reaction to 1905. The politicals had traditionally been kept separate and given their own cell, in deference to the belief that their crimes were of a different sort. They had vehemently complained when Golovin made the change. Some had even gone to pieces. It was because of Orloff that Golovin had forced the politicals to work. He did not know that work was just what Orloff wanted.

There were so many reasons for Golovin to hate Orloff. Golovin had come from the slums of Odessa. No one had ever given Golovin a chance. But Orloff came from the right family and had gone to the right school. He had been an officer in the Grand Duchess's Hussars. His so-called Revolution was a game, a game for which working people had no time. It was no wonder that he had such a woman as this.

Golovin walked slowly around Katya, inspecting. On her arm was a basket of food for her husband. When Orloff got the contents, he would divide them among the men. That was another reason to hate him. Indeed, Orloff was the recognized leader of the men, even of the ordinary criminals. He settled disputes. Other convicts came to him for advice. Orloff had won without even trying what Golovin could not win by force.

He walked completely around Katya and faced her again. She was

74

smiling and looked directly at him — exactly as Orloff always did. That was another thing to hate: the fact that Orloff did not hate him, the fact that Orloff was not afraid. For Golovin this was a subtle insult, compounded by his certainty that, although Orloff knew it rankled, he did not care.

When Orloff had been recaptured after his escape, Golovin — according to regulations — had chained him to a wheelbarrow for a year. But, as always, Orloff had shown no hate. As always, he had smiled, almost as if in reassurance. There seemed to be no way he could be hurt.

Indeed, in addition to the baskets, Savitsky even allowed Orloff to wear the silk underwear which Katya brought. And one did not need a Mitka Dubin to know that underwear should be coarse. Savitsky had even ordered that Orloff be allowed to come to his apartment regularly to talk. Golovin had thought of complaining to the governor of the province, or even to Petersburg, but that might start more trouble than it was worth.

Golovin laughed falsely and immediately resented having done so. "Any knives or pistols, Katerina Nikolaevna? Any bombs or files today?"

Katya smiled. "Not today."

A scarf covered Katya's basket and Golovin slowly drew it off. It was silk and he enjoyed its feel. It was as if he were removing a part of Katya's clothing. Inside the basket were various delicacies for Orloff, which he enjoyed tossing around. But his satisfaction was incomplete. He could do nothing about Savitsky's order that Orloff should receive them. And some of them were things that Golovin could not afford. Even here in prison, Orloff had so much of what he wanted. He was merely playing at revolution. Golovin was the real victim of the system.

Reluctantly, he finished his examination of the basket. "Today is not the day," he said.

"No."

That was another thing she and Orloff had in common. They smiled and answered Golovin as though he were not there. They did not treat him personally, nor even with dislike.

"May I ask you a question?" Golovin asked. "You have been here many years and will be here many more. We both know that your Revolution will never come. You have given up your comfort for nothing. Why? Why is a woman like you doing all this?"

"Because of a man like you, Victor Karpovitch."

Katya looked directly at him, still smiling, but as if he did not really exist.

He flushed. "All right," he said. And Katya left the room.

That night, as was his habit, he sat in Savitsky's study, listening to

Savitsky and Orloff talk. Yaacov Trofimovitch Savitsky, the prison governor, was perfectly happy in his job. He would have had no other. He liked being a prison governor. It gave him an unusual chance to do good. It also made him a celebrity in town. But Yaacov Trofimovitch was homesick. He came from faraway Tsaritsyn and had never felt at home in this small town near Lake Baikal. He was not married and had no friends here. He wanted the company of someone who could remind him of Russia, and who could participate in the spirited conversations he missed — an ability which in that neighborhood was exceedingly rare.

So Savitsky regularly invited Orloff to his study to talk. Orloff's qualifications were perfect. Savitsky enjoyed their meetings very much. Savitsky thought of Orloff as a highly challenging case, which was exactly what Orloff thought of Savitsky. Changing the other's mind would have been a big victory for either.

And this, perhaps more than anything, particularly annoyed Golovin. Why should Orloff, a convict, have this privilege? A convict who had once escaped and been chained to a wheelbarrow! He complained to Savitsky without success, having to be satisfied with sitting in the room during the conversations — for "purposes of safety," he said. He sensed and resented his imperfect understanding of what was said.

"I wish to complain," said Orloff.

"I am sorry," said Savitsky. "Where have we failed?"

"You already know, Yaacov Trofimovitch. I refer to this evening's whipping because a man refused to lift his cap."

Savitsky smiled and smoothed his mustache. He took off his rimless glasses and rubbed his prominent, watery eyes.

"You misunderstand," he said. "The culprit is your false assumption that physical punishment is bad. You do not wish to associate it with an intellectual like yourself. Another demonstration of the senseless contradictions of your Marx. A symptom of spurious guilt for your action at the Winter Palace in 1905. You are unaware that your order to shoot was good."

Golovin smiled. Everything about his superior filled him with contempt. Yaacov Trofimovitch talked too much and always justified himself.

"But the severity of the punishment!" said Orloff. "For such a so-called crime!"

"A knowledge of how to lift his cap is something the prisoner needs at home. In later years, he will come to thank us. He will realize what you do not: the metaphysical necessity for complete and rigid discipline. As a good Bolshevik, you should know that now."

"Are you confident you are not concealing a simple desire to inflict pain? Even your orangutan here is more honest that that."

Golovin scowled, not knowing whether to be pleased.

"I expected you to say that," Savitsky smiled. "It is typical Marxist pseudo-psychology. Whether or not it is true is completely unimportant. It may be true, but so what? Nothing matters but the proper preparation for the world to come. The head and brain on our neck become a skull. Passing worms crawl through our eyes. The body is transitory, almost an illusion. But we are dead the longest time."

"I expected you to say that," said Orloff, "and of course it means nothing. Once we are dead we don't know a thing."

"You do not believe in God, of course."

"Certainly not."

"That is like the tail not believing in the dog."

"Isn't that analogy blasphemous, Yaacov Trofimovitch?"

"Probably, but God will understand the context."

"Prove God," said Orloff.

"I don't need to," said Savitsky. "God cannot be proven. My proof of God is the fact that you cannot disprove Him."

"A logical fallacy," said Orloff. "A negative cannot be proved. A negative is something for which no proof exists."

"Logic in this case is, by definition, illogical."

"What is the moon made of?" asked Orloff.

"I don't know," said Savitsky.

"The moon is made of ripe green cheese."

"Nonsense."

"My proof is the fact that you cannot disprove it."

"Logic in this case is, by definition, illogical."

What nonsense was all this? Golovin wondered. When he had Savitsky's job, things would be different. If only the government knew its own mind. If only it did not fearfully insist on restraints, justifying itself as Savitsky always did.

"Apparently we are at an impasse," Orloff said.

"We are," said Savitsky, "and your admission of defeat is the bridge we will use to cross it. You are doomed, you know. Your so-called science cannot win. Man is not as perfectible as you think. You are deceiving yourself. You do not like to admit that you are as base as the rest of us, but you are. And, after a while, you will. You will see that you have been fighting reality, which is most unscientific. And then, one evening, you will sue for pardon."

This was what Savitsky wanted more than anything else. Orloff was his most important subject and, as a political, could sue for pardon and be released — if only he recanted his revolutionary philosophy. It would be a great victory for Savitsky. He thought of Orloff as a problem to be solved.

Several days passed. It was morning. Golovin was inspecting a new prisoner in the guard room, a procedure he much enjoyed. As usual, he walked round and round the man in silence. Already he could see a slight movement at his lips. He routinely described at length the many prison regulations, and what the man who did not cooperate completely might expect.

"Don't even bother to think about complaining," he said. He poked the man in the chest. "Remember! You are not a man. You're a convict! And I am your chief, your god and your Tsar!"

Golovin drew back and studied the man's face. "Do you see?"

"Y-y-yes," stuttered the prisoner, as if startled, as if trying to say the words too fast.

"What are you?" asked Golovin.

"I am s-sorry. I d-do not understand."

"I just told you. You are not a man."

"I am not a man. I'm a convict."

"Good. And me? What am I?"

"You are my chief, my god and my Tsar."

Golovin walked from the guard room to the barracks. He felt good. The new prisoner had changed his mood. Golovin would remember to treat him fairly well. Inside the barracks he opened the first door, and forty voices boomed at once.

"Good morning, your honor. I hope you are well," they said.

He heard the rustling of many caps in hands pulling them off heads. He nodded and smiled and started down the line. It was all so natural. All these men wished him well. All so eagerly deferred to him. He liked them. Nevertheless there was a vague feeling of tension in the room, which he disregarded. He knew each of these men so well. And with a word, he controlled them all.

Suddenly, Golovin's face went white. The blood left it as if sucked away. Michael Voronov stood before him, cap set firmly on his head. Golovin knew it was unnecessary to wonder whether Michael had voiced the greeting. His thin lips appeared to be tightly shut. His face was taut. Their glances met and, unlike the others, Michael did not look away. Indeed his deep-set eyes stared coldly. And in them, Golovin saw a pure and intense hatred, of a purity and intensity he had never seen before — even in that forsaken place.

Golovin was startled. He had completely forgotten about Michael. How could he have been released from the infirmary so soon? It seemed that he actually wanted to come back. Golovin was startled — and he was afraid.

Ordinarily, he welcomed and even encouraged such hostility. He liked it. He preferred it to Orloff's infuriating indifference. In a way, it was a compliment. But now he involuntarily drew back. What he felt was not a powerful emotion; it was as if something in him had fluttered for a moment, something cold and shiny like the tip of a rat's tail. He had never felt anything like it before, not even as a child in the slums of Odessa. Perhaps the cause was the total incongruity of the situation. For here, Golovin had all the power and Michael had none. And yet in Michael's eyes, Golovin saw a strange confidence; a glittering, predatory, penetrating quality. An almost tangible hatred rushed silently toward him.

The big, dusty room was strangely quiet. All eyes were on Golovin to see what he would do. Had the men already seen his fear? The fear was replaced by a frenzy of rage, and then by the desire to knock Michael down and crush him. But at the same moment, he knew he could not do that. He thought of the rods. But the man had just come from the infirmary. Surely the doctor would not give his permission so soon, especially since Golovin and the doctor did not get along. And if Golovin ignored the doctor, and Voronov died? In the glittering eyes, Golovin saw the certainty that it made no difference to their owner what happened. And, with equal certainty, he knew that Voronov would never lift his cap.

Golovin chuckled and poked Michael in the chest. "You do not lift your cap, comrade," he said.

"No."

"I am sorry, comrade. I have not made it fully clear. But we cannot wait until your back is healed to do so."

Golovin chuckled again and slowly walked out.

X

Michael sat alone in the sun against the palings. The pressure against his back was good; it eased the pain temporarily. But before long, he knew, Golovin would punish him again. The yard was full of prisoners, but no one approached him. Michael had silently indicated that no one should. And no one wanted to. He was a difficult man to know. The other prisoners were uncomfortable around him.

He had already been in prison for four years. He had spent some time at the Petersburg House of Detention and then at Irkutsk, where he had knocked down a guard and been whipped. He kept to himself and had made no friends. In Irkutsk, he had received a letter from his father, telling him his mother had been killed in a fall down the stairwell, a fall caused by the bad step and weak banister. Voronov wrote that he had returned to religion and felt better, and recommended that Michael do the same. Shortly thereafter, he sent Michael a copy of the Bible.

Michael heard footsteps. He saw a shadow. A hand descended with a package of cigarettes. He took one, the hand rose and returned with a match. It was Orloff. "May I?" he said, already starting to sit down.

Michael chuckled. "Suit yourself."

Orloff extended his hand again, but Michael did not take it.

"You are not hospitable," Orloff said.

"No," said Michael.

"That is a mistake."

"Why?"

"You don't know yet whether I can do anything for you."

Michael chuckled again. "That's all right. People have done things for me before."

"You are Michael Voronov."

"That's right."

"I am Peter Orloff."

"That's the trouble with hospitality. It collects people."

"You are bitter. I am sorry. I owe you a debt."

"You are misinformed, comrade. You owe me nothing. I did not lead the attempt to free you, as you have read. In fact, I knew nothing about it. Your friends arranged for me to be framed."

"You are not a Party member, then?"

"Of course not."

"That doubles the debt."

"Just give me another cigarette."

The setting sun's rays fell across their shackled feet. Bent-headed prisoners slowly crossed the yard. Mitka Dubin hurried by, whispered to a guard, and was gone.

"The law of causality is a remarkable thing," said Orloff. "The stone dropped in the pond makes waves to the shore. A decision I made almost ten years ago, when you were just a child, causes you to be here now. We had never met, we had never heard of each other, but you were sailing on the pond. I dropped the stone and years later the waves reached you."

"How so?"

"I was an officer in the Grand Duchess's Hussars. It was 1905. We were sent to the Winter Palace. A crowd carrying crucifixes and ikons approached. The Grand Duke Vladimir gave the order to fire.

"My closest friend and I looked at each other. How well I remember that single look. Everything around us seemed to disappear. But the priest and his women and children were still advancing. And we in turn gave the order the Grand Duke had given us. The rifles cracked. The advancing people stopped.

"Later, I joined the Revolution and the Party. My closest friend did not. Today he is the colonel commanding the regiment. And you and I are here in chains."

"Your cosmic guilt is egotistical for a Party man."

"How?"

"A man guilty of everything has the power to commit everything."

Orloff smiled. "Perhaps you are right. I want many things. I want my wife. Have you ever loved a woman?"

"No."

"Imagine that you did and saw her often, but could only touch her hand."

"It's good to know you want something," Michael said. "The man who says he doesn't is a fraud. The man who says he does is only a fool. Those are the only two kinds of people. Your guilt is unnecessary. Not only do you owe me nothing, but I owe you. I'm glad all this has happened. It has taught me the truth. Now I know what life really is."

"Then you don't believe that loyalty and honor are possible?"

"Now you are talking like a fraud again. Or is it like a fool? Does anything really make a difference? No, those things are inventions used to deceive those still as naive as I was. Used by the inventors to deceive themselves. One believes in them at first, of course. All of us do. And later some of us find the truth. Shouldn't it be taught at first, instead of the nonsense that ruins so many lives? That is the revolution you should be fighting."

"Now it's my turn to smile," said Orloff. "Would it anger you to know that you sound exactly like Savitsky?"

"Not at all. He is sensible. We are very much alike. In fact, I would like his job. The only difference between us is these." Michael raised his leg irons with the centerpiece and let them fall.

What bothered Orloff even more than Michael's words was his manner. It should have been appropriately violent, even brutal. Instead, he talked calmly — even genially — with a smile, as if there were no need to convince.

"You are wrong, you know," Orloff said. "Both of you. We are going to prove that. The Revolution *will* make a basic change in man. And one day you will tell me I am right. Remember."

Michael shook his head. "You are doomed. I am sorry."

"All social problems are caused by economic conditions. Economic conditions cause the evils you complain about. Economic conditions determine man's behavior. Man is not responsible for these evils. He is a victim. When his conditions are changed — scientifically — his behavior will change, too. That is why our Party alone can do the job. Only we Bolsheviks will apply science to society. Take your own trouble, for instance. How did it start?"

"I don't know, exactly. My father needed money."

"You see! Economic conditions betrayed you. Your father was not responsible. You are not responsible. That is why I can listen to you and Savitsky so calmly. That is why I can smile. Because you are both victims."

Michael pointed across the yard. "And he?"

He was pointing to Golovin, who was just mounting a horse. As he did so, the gates opened, and he galloped through them to town. Then the gates closed and the scene was as before.

"He, too," said Orloff.

"He's a son of a bitch."

"He *is* a son of a bitch. But why? Because he cannot speak for himself.

Because when he tries, what you hear is the Odessa slums."

"And after the Revolution?"

"He will be rehabilitated. You will see. We will take the Odessa slums out of Golovin."

"Yes. I have heard all this. It is amusing as a theory. But surely you do not apply it in real life? You couldn't. Somewhere, somebody is responsible for something."

A man came up softly, twisting his cap. "Petya," he said, "may I speak with you?"

"Of course," said Orloff. "Talk, Plotkin."

Plotkin looked at Michael and down at his cap.

"Go ahead," said Orloff. "It's all right."

"I have decided to sue for pardon," he said, without looking up.

"Yes."

"You knew?"

"I have been watching."

"I have not heard from my wife for months, Petya. And I have a child I have never seen. I have been here for seven years, Petya."

"Yes. I know."

Plotkin's hands shook. He dropped his cap. He picked up some soil, sniffed it, and sifted it out through his fingers.

"What rotten soil," he said. "Good only to plant corpses."

"Perhaps one day you will make it yield," said Orloff.

"Remember that bank on Fonarny Pereulok we robbed?"

"Yes," said Orloff. "Very clearly."

Plotkin chuckled. "One million rubles. Quite a haul."

"Yes."

"The Party made good use of that."

"It did."

Plotkin waited for Orloff to say something, something specific, but he did not.

"Well, I'll be going," Plotkin said.

"All right," Orloff said. "Goodbye."

Plotkin rose and turned to go. "Why don't you say what you're really thinking?" he blurted.

"If you know what I'm thinking, there's no need to say it."

Head bowed, Plotkin shuffled off across the yard.

"So much for your Revolution," said Michael. "There's a sensible man. Why don't *you* sue for pardon, comrade?"

Orloff smiled. "Why don't you?"

"I can't. I'm not a political."

Michael, too, rose and walked off across the yard. Orloff could not let him go like that. He felt the need to prove something to Michael. More than anything else, he had to pay his debt. Somehow he had to get Michael assigned to the wool-cleaning machines.

*　　　*　　　*

Golovin eagerly knocked on the door. It was always such a pleasure to choose a woman. Already he was debating with himself which he would chose now. As usual, he favored the Pole. She was so stupid. But inside, he saw a new girl, which was unusual in that forsaken town. She was a small, finely boned girl, and he chose her.

"Take off your clothes," he said when they were alone.

She did so, slowly, without expression, and Golovin circled her as if inspecting a new prisoner. He could not help it.

"You are thin," he said.

"Yes."

"What is your name?"

"Anna Andreevna Kursamina."

She spoke as if this nude interrogation were quite normal, as if telling a boring story she had told many times before.

"Your name is familiar," he said. "Where do you come from?"

"From prison."

"The offense?"

"Paragraph 102."

Golovin smiled. It was unusual to find a political in a brothel; in fact, he never had. He knew he was going to enjoy himself.

"Why are you here?" he asked.

"I haven't the money to go home."

"Such behavior for a political?"

"Yes," she said. "I am a political. I was convicted with Michael Voronov."

The unexpected name caused him to start. His mood changed. The girl had ruined his evening. He had been putting the incident of the morning from his mind, and now it was back. And he had to do something about it very soon. If he didn't, his absolute authority would be diminished. Golovin stood silently, thinking of the compound.

Then his mood changed again. Suddenly he had realized what he should do. He could not understand why he had not realized it before. Direct methods like the rods would do no good in this case. Voronov required indirection and a policy of attrition. He needed wearing down like a knife on a sharpener's wheel. At first, he would get sharper; then he would slowly disappear. Already Golovin saw the deterioration of the lungs and the weakening of the eyes. Then would come the faint but ever-present taste of blood. And then the coughing, the hemorrhages, and the pleading. In the end, Voronov would beg like the others. Golovin wondered whether he would be kind. He recalled having seen Voronov and Orloff together. How appropriate! They had so much in common. They were the same type.

Golovin undressed. Tomorrow he would order Voronov to the wool-cleaning machines.

XI

Michael tried to draw a deep breath, but could not. The air in the tunnel was even worse than in the big room. And its walls were only slightly wider than his shoulders. His head was in a burning vise. Burning, dirty sweat filled his eyes. There was no point in trying to wipe them, but he did anyway.

Again he raised the chisel and drove it into the hard earth. A few crumbs fell to his knees in reward. Again and again he drove the chisel home. The new pile of earth at his knees was growing. The rhythm reminded him of his work years before at Danilov's.

He put the chisel down and handed the earth back. Behind him, Orloff quickly filled the sacks. They could not be sure exactly where they were; the din of the machines was already far behind. But Orloff calculated that they still had a healthy piece to go.

Again Michael drove the chisel into the earth. The chisel hit a rock and Orloff's warning hand tapped Michael's foot. He dropped the chisel and grappled with the rock. Orloff felt Yellin immediately behind him.

"It's time to go," Yellin said, backing out.

Orloff tapped Michael's foot again.

"All right," said Michael. "I'll just get this one rock."

"Come on," said Orloff. "We'll get it tomorrow."

"Wait," said Michael, tugging. "It's coming now."

The earth let go and the rock fell to the ground. Michael grinned and they began to crawl out. The machines behind them were slowing to a halt. They had already been in the tunnel too long. Orloff saw Yellin's legs at the tunnel mouth. Then they were standing back in the machinery room. The men were about to leave. Dust hung in the perpetual half-light. Everything seemed routine and normal.

Except that they were looking into the puzzled, fearful eyes of Mitka Dubin. And he was looking into theirs.

Mitka's small head bobbed on the end of his long neck. His mouth made a little circle. He looked from Orloff to Michael, to Yellin, to the tunnel. Thousands of regulations flashed through Mitka's mind. Nobody moved; the three prisoners because they were simply too startled, Mitka because he had not yet reached the regulation which governed such events.

Then everyone moved at once. Yellin and Michael reached for Mitka, Orloff reached for Yellin and Michael, and Mitka ran off, realizing that a tunnel was against regulations. Orloff and Michael struggled until Mitka disappeared in the dust. Then, as usual, Orloff concealed the tunnel.

"Why are you doing that?" Michael asked. "It's over."

"Not necessarily," said Orloff. "We'll know soon enough."

"No," said Yellin. "He will tell Golovin. It's the wheelbarrow for all of us for a year."

"Don't tell me why you stopped me," Michael shrugged. "I already know. You feel sorry for Dubin — as for everyone else. He was born to a family of brutes and was raised in the slums. He can't be blamed for what he does. He's a victim of economic conditions."

"So close," murmured Yellin. "We came so close." His voice cracked, but he did not actually mind at all. Now he could say that his escape had been prevented.

"It was my fault," said Michael. "Go ahead. Say it."

Orloff smiled. "What good would it do? You don't know what you're doing. I feel as sorry for you as for Mitka."

Several days passed, days on which they did no work on the tunnel. There would have been no point. They were waiting for Mitka to report and for Golovin to discover it. Once, in the yard, Golovin had passed them too slowly, pointedly smiling at them as if sharing some secret. But nothing happened and they did not know why.

They did not know that Mitka was waiting. The day had been approaching on which — according to regulations — his handcuffs should be removed. And Mitka was waiting until then to report the tunnel. That would prove how he had obeyed the regulations. If he told Golovin now, it might seem that he was trying to persuade him to remove them sooner than the regulations specified. But if he waited, it would prove that he loved the regulations for themselves; that he had no other motive. It would be like an exchange of courtesies between two government officials. Already Mitka heard himself saying, "I must make a report."

At last the day came and Mitka went to Golovin. Even more nervous than usual, he extended his hands, cuffs jingling, and announced that — according to regulations — they must now be removed.

"Hurry, your honor, please," he said. "I must make a report."

Golovin never had understood Mitka. Why was he always running about, jingling and shaking, making investigations and reports? It was almost as if Mitka were more zealous about the regulations than Golovin, which was impossible. The only thing Golovin could be absolutely sure of was that there was no need to consult the records. If Mitka said that the time had arrived when — according to the regulations — his handcuffs should be removed, then it was time to take them off. And the day was ending; Golovin was eager to get to town.

"All right," he said. "Come."

They started off to the guardroom when the idea came to him. It was so amusing that it brought him, smiling, to a stop. Suppose he did not remove the handcuffs. What would Mitka Dubin do? Whatever it was, it would have to be unusual, considering Mitka. Possibly, it would even explain his extraordinary personality. The case wasn't at all like Voronov's; Golovin wanted no revenge. He did not even dislike Mitka. In fact, he actually liked and enjoyed Mitka. He just wanted to annoy him. He could not help being flattered by Mitka's perpetual fawning. What appealed to him about the idea was simply the question it posed. What, indeed, *would* happen? It would be like a scientific experiment. And just thinking about it already gave him a great deal of pleasure. It was not until later that he realized it had been a stroke of genius.

By the time they entered the guardroom, his mind was made up. The only problem was that the magisterial face he now showed Mitka was difficult to maintain. Behind it, an irrepressible gaiety was trying to break out.

Mitka was seething like a kettle on the boil. He was not used to withholding information so long. More than anything else in the world, he wanted to tell Golovin about the violation of the regulations in the wall behind the wool-cleaning machines.

Golovin tapped Mitka's chest. "I have been considering your case with the greatest care, Dubin. With the greatest care."

"My case?"

"The truth is, Dubin, I am surprised. You are the last man here I would have expected to commit infractions."

Mitka grew very still. "Infractions, your honor?"

"Especially infractions of such a sort."

"But your honor," said Mitka, "I . . . ."

Golovin put his face close to Mitka's. "Come, come," he growled, "don't play the fool. Violations of the regulations. *The regulations.*" Again he tapped Mitka meaningfully on the chest.

A glistening, sticky sheet of sweat covered Mitka's face. He began to shake. He could barely speak.

"But your honor," he whispered, "there have been no violations. The regulations are intact, your honor, I assure you."

"What's this?" boomed Golovin. "You're calling me a liar?"

"No!" wheezed Mitka. "No, your honor, never. A specific prohibition . . . . It would be a violation."

Golovin reflectively stroked his chin. "The only thing left to be decided is the punishment."

"But your honor," Mitka moaned. "Which regulations do you mean?"

"What do you take me for?" Golovin roared. "Do you want to make it worse?"

Mitka's eyes bulged. The small head on his long neck lolled crazily. His arms flapped as if his body were no longer under his control.

"Oh, your honor," he moaned. "Oh . . . I . . . if only . . . but I take the greatest care, your honor. How could it have happened? Was it at night when I was asleep? Yes, that must have been it: when I was asleep. Was that when it happened, your honor?"

"All right!" Golovin shouted. "That's enough! Shut up! For now we'll leave the handcuffs on, while I consider your case further. But let me warn you of one thing: take care that it doesn't happen again. All right, back to the barracks now. Go ahead."

Mitka's eyes were wide with horror. "Oh," he said. "Oh." He fled in a crooked line, like a bird with a broken wing.

Golovin felt a murmur of conscience, faint, unrecognizable. After all, he liked Mitka. And this was just a piece of good fun. Surely Mitka, his "deputy" and "informant," would not deny him that. Golovin smiled. That Mitka! The sight of him rushing around like that! It would be interesting to see what Mitka did next. Nothing definite could be predicted about such a personality.

And Golovin was right. What happened next was fascinating. At first Mitka continued to rush about, even more irritable and frenetic than usual. It was as if Mitka were conscientiously trying to do what he considered his duty, while in the path of an irresistible force. It was as if the thing, whatever it was, were trying to seize Mitka, and succeeding — no matter how fast he ran or how hard he tried to get away. Mitka developed the habit of looking back over his shoulder as he ran, as if trying to keep ahead of something. "What is it, Mitka?" others asked. "What do you see?"

Others stopped Mitka with surprise. "Still got the cuffs on?" they would ask. "What's this about? What about the regulations?"

At this, Mitka would turn white and run off. Everyone wondered about this new quirk in Mitka, but no one could explain it. The men smiled. Mitka was an unfortunate, but he was also amusing. And Golovin roared. This was better than almost anything.

At last there was no more reason to run. The thing was no longer a threat to be escaped. It no longer pursued Mitka; it had become Mitka, taken possession of him completely. Hour after hour he unsuccessfully tried to remember the numbers and the wording of the specific regulations he had insulted. He could think of nothing but his own sins. He was no longer worried about others committing violations, but about himself. The thing had happened before, quite by accident and even without his knowledge. So it was reasonable to fear that it might happen again. An instant of inattention was all it would need.

So Mitka no longer rushed about the compound. Now he sat in his barracks in his place on the top shelf, with his back against the wall. He did not move; the slightest gesture might lead to something dangerous. He did not eat; it was too complicated. There were too many chances for mistakes. But the most dangerous thing of all, of course, was sleep; hours of inattention during which anything could happen. Mitka had no doubt that he had committed the earlier violation while sleeping. He could not afford to relax for a minute. During the night, men would awaken to see Mitka sitting against the wall, inflamed eyes burning in the dark, head cocked, neck craned, listening, listening for what he did not know.

The men got worried. These new quirks of Mitka's were no longer amusing. But no one understood. It was as if some favorite house pet were dying. They asked him what was wrong and begged him to eat. To which Mitka would carefully put his finger to his lips. "Ssh," he would whisper. "Watch me. Watch me." The men reported the matter to Golovin, who almost did not trust himself to investigate. Indeed, as he stood before Mitka he almost lost control. For days he would chortle, put a finger to his lips and whisper, "Watch me. Watch me."

So Mitka remained in his place on the shelf. He heard voices, saw faces and felt hands on his sleeves. But he did not move. He smiled slyly through his stained and broken teeth. His birdlike, emaciated face was crafty. I won't fall for it, he thought. This is Mitka Dubin and I know the regulations. Imagine trying to fool Mitka Dubin. He knew that the others were trying to trick him into a violation.

It could not last. There had to be an end even to Mitka's valor. On the fifth morning, he appeared in the yard, absolutely calm. No longer was he nervous. No longer did he peer. So unlike himself was he that the others simply stared.

Suddenly Mitka began to shake. He grabbed his head as if it might come off. The pain in it was intolerable. He would do anything to stop it. "Friends!" he shouted. "Victor Karpovitch! You're right. A violation! I have committed a violation!"

Not far away was a thick stone wall. Mitka Dubin lowered his head, ran as fast as he could and smashed his head against it. There was a crunch, and at the same time a wet sound, as when a foot is withdrawn from mud. The pain in Mitka's head had stopped.

Some of the men crossed themselves. Even Golovin was transfixed.

"What did Mitka mean, your honor?" asked Yellin after a time. "What was he guilty of?"

"I don't know," said Golovin. "His imagination. Crazy fool!"

Mitka lay in a lump at the wall. Above him, what appeared to be bits of brain and bone stuck to it. Golovin felt an unaccustomed reluctance to approach.

"All right, what are you staring at?" he said angrily. "You three men. Clean this up!"

Golovin felt a twinge of regret. He was sorry, genuinely sorry for poor Mitka. He had liked Mitka. He hadn't wanted or expected his joke to end like this. How amusing Mitka had been. And, at the same time, how pathetic. Why, one could hardly imagine Mitka doing injury to a mosquito, much less committing a crime or a violation. Yet he had screamed that he was guilty — but of what? What on earth could Mitka have meant? Mitka wasn't guilty, not even of one thing. And yet there he was, lying against the wall, dead. Poor Mitka. Poor, pathetic Mitka. The thing shouldn't have ended like this. It shouldn't have. Golovin felt the unaccustomed emotion of guilt. And Orloff was looking at him queerly from across the yard.

Late that afternoon they buried Mitka. Golovin read the service himself, with feeling. But it did no good. Even the day seemed to share his mood. Golovin went to his room, poured a vodka and then another. His mood changed. Again he saw the humor in what had happened. Mitka on the shelf. Mitka with his handcuffs. And Mitka rushing back and forth. Mitka stooping, poking and peering.

Golovin put his finger to his lips. "Watch me!" he said aloud.

That Mitka! What right had he to spoil such a good joke? It was almost as if Mitka had done it deliberately to accuse Golovin. Why, yes, of course; that's why he did it, Golovin thought. That's why he smashed his head against the wall. He did it to insult me, to spit in my face. Why, the son of a bitch, that shrimp, that runt! And him pretending all the time to be my helper. I was too easy with him. He deserved what he got — and more. I won't let him ruin such a good piece of fun.

Golovin remembered Mitka's last report. He chuckled. Poor Mitka never got to make it. Probably found a hole in the wall, Golovin thought. Violation of the regulations. Paragraphs such and such, numbers this and that. That Mitka!

Golovin felt good. His experiment had turned out well.

XII

After the death of Mitka, Orloff and Michael resumed work on the tunnel. They could not be sure what to do about it. They could not be sure that Golovin was not toying with them. But just as it would have been pointless to continue after the discovery, so now, after the suicide, there was no reason not to resume. Day after day, they laboriously filled the bags. Day after day, Yellin emptied and returned them. And because there was so much they did not know, they worked even harder and made even more progress than before. They were now doing the last and most delicate part of the digging: under Savitsky's house and beyond.

One afternoon Savitsky invited Orloff to his house, which was unusual. They had always met at night. Indeed, Orloff had never seen Savitsky so excited.

"An event of extraordinary importance has occurred," Savitsky said. "I assume you are aware of what I mean?"

"Certainly," said Orloff. "You mean the death of Mitka Dubin."

"You misunderstand," said Savitsky. "That was an event of extraordinary unimportance. No, Peter Sergeievitch, I refer to the assassination of the Archduke Franz Ferdinand in Sarajevo, apparently by a Serbian nationalist of sorts.

"There will be a war. A world war. The Austro-Hungarian Empire can not and will not tolerate this offense. Russia will be drawn in on the side of the Slavs."

"That is good."

"You approve?"

"Yes."

"Isn't that interesting," said Savitsky. "We agree."

"The war will expose the ruling class. It will destroy the monarchy. People will get tired. Russia will be free."

93

"No," said Savitsky, "you are wrong. The monarchy will not only survive, it will triumph. The war will bring people together. It will provide the needed reason for sacrifice."

"Your idea of sacrifice is really self-indulgence."

"Is that the position of the Party?" Savitsky said.

"The Party's position is my position."

Savitsky smiled. He took some cognac from a drawer and filled a glass. The mouth of the bottle stood ready over another glass. He looked at Orloff, but Orloff shook his head. "You still refuse to drink with me?" Savitsky said.

"I do not drink with my enemies," said Orloff.

"But I am not responsible. Have you forgotten? My attitudes have been determined by my class."

"You will be my enemy until you are rehabilitated."

This was the part Golovin resented most. Savitsky was willing to drink with Orloff, a criminal, but had never offered Golovin a glass. He behaved as if Golovin were not in the room, which was humiliating. Savitsky and Golovin were on the same side of the law, but Savitsky and Orloff belonged to the same class, which was more important. Golovin was sure they were slyly laughing at him.

"Why do you speak of freedom and yet allow the Party to enslave you?" asked Savitsky.

Orloff chuckled. "No one is forced to join."

"You don't understand," said Savitsky. "I do not criticize the fact. I applaud it. That is the only redeeming thing about your Party. Surely you realize that the most dangerous and unnatural condition for man is freedom. Freedom means choices, independence, movement. And nothing in the world is more terrifying to man. Freedom is unnatural, you see. That is why man escapes its oppression whenever he can. The real enemies of humanity are the impractical theorists like yourself. Man deserves to remain in the slavery he craves.

"That is why I chose my profession, you see. Nothing in the world is more soothing than a prison. Only here is life truly sane. As you know, I must retire soon, to my regret."

"Where will you go?"

"To Petersburg. You could go, too."

"Could I? How?"

"Peter Sergeievitch, I'll be frank with you. I feel drawn to you, as you know. You are a problem to be solved, which bothers me. I have spent my life in various prisons helping inmates become aware, helping them realize that prison is good. But you are the only man I have never understood. And you will not explain. Your friend Voronov, for instance, is a pane of glass. He is in violent opposition. In time, he will learn. But you, Peter Sergeievitch, you are mild, calm, happy.

"Perhaps you would be more receptive outside. Why don't you sue for pardon, Peter Sergeievitch? A simple declaration of loyalty to His Majesty would be enough. Perhaps it would help you crush your pride, which I assure you is the cause of your problem."

Golovin leaned forward, trying to look bored. The conversation at last had become somewhat interesting.

At that moment, Orloff heard a sound. It was a faint sound, but he could not tell whether it was the result of something done softly and nearby, or something done loudly from afar. It sounded like a tapping, but as he listened it changed. Now it was a scraping, and then it seemed that something was being smashed. It was impossible that either of the others could not hear it. Indeed, Golovin's head appeared to be cocked.

Suddenly Orloff realized what the sound was. Somewhere nearby, Michael was digging, dusty face streaked with sweat, eyes narrowed, jaw set. He was hacking away at the wall in a frenzy. And so absorbed was he, that he had forgotten about the noise. It was impossible for anyone in the room not to hear it, and Orloff knew that in a moment the others would. He had no time to think. Savitsky stood before him, rubbing at his chin.

Orloff got up, walked to the window and came back. For years he had walked in the heavy chains silently. Now he made noise. It was important not to arouse suspicion by making too much.

"I believe I will have some cognac after all," he said.

"Splendid! Splendid!" Savitsky said. He filled a glass quickly, before Orloff's mood changed. "To Russia!" he shouted, and they both drank.

"Extraordinary!" said Savitsky. "Such a surprise."

Orloff listened closely. Between their voices he heard the sound again. He knew that Michael would be at it for the rest of the afternoon. If only there were an easy way to warn him. If only he had stopped when Orloff had been called away.

Again Orloff walked to the window and back. He began to walk in a circle around the room, making as much noise as he dared. He wanted simply to drop the center chain, but it would have been too obvious.

Below in the tunnel, Michael did not know the time. He did not need to. Yellin would warn him when to quit. But the work was harder than usual. He had to fill the sacks himself. Why had Orloff been called away? Suppose Golovin already knew about the tunnel. Suppose he were only waiting for them to finish. With even more ferocity, Michael attacked the earth.

"I must tell you something, and it is not an easy thing to say," said Orloff. "My wife, as you know, lives in town."

"I have seen Katerina Nikolaevna in various shops."

"I miss my wife, Yaacov Trofimovitch. Terribly. But perhaps, as a bachelor, you do not understand."

"We bachelors are not immune from human emotion."

"I have come to realize that this is more important than any theory. May I have another?" Orloff put his glass down and continued walking as Savitsky filled it. He could not stop. The noise was now even louder than before.

"Yaacov Trofimovitch!" said Orloff. "I have decided to sue for pardon!"

Orloff's statement put Golovin in a turmoil. He could not decide whether it was good or bad. On one hand it meant that Orloff was abasing himself in a silly, incomprehensible way known only to intellectuals. But on the other, it meant that he would be allowed to leave the camp.

"Incredible!" said Savitsky. "The solution was right under my nose. Isn't it incredible, Peter Sergeievitch, how often a solution is right under one's nose?"

Orloff listened again. The sound had stopped.

XIII

The day was ending. The machines ground to a halt. Orloff and Michael sat with their backs against the tunnel walls, listening. Each stared at the other's eyes. They had already said goodbye to Yellin and the others, and now came the first test. It was unlikely but possible that the guards would notice they were missing. Close by, Yellin began to sing — the signal that all was clear so far. There were receding footsteps, the big door closed heavily and all was still. Both men exhaled slowly. In the dust and darkness, the guards as usual had been unable to count. And at bedcheck they would look into the rooms, but would not enter. So Orloff's and Michael's absence would not be noticed until morning. All they had to do now was wait.

They moved to the end of the tunnel and sat. The digging needed a few minutes more work, which prudence had told them to leave for later. They looked up. A thin shaft of sunlight came through the hole, and Orloff put his hands into it. The fine hairs behind his knuckles caught the light. He moved still closer and the light caught his face.

"What route do you propose?" asked Michael.

"There are three possibilities: west to Irkutsk and through the woods, generally the way we came; the other way, to Vladivostok; or across the Amur and into China. The first is impossible, as I know to my regret."

"That's the way you went the first time."

"Yes."

"How far did you get?"

"Just this side of Baikal, in the mountains. A Buriat hunting party found me."

"Buriats? Not the guards?"

"The seventy-five-ruble bounty is a lot of money out here."

"Interesting," said Michael. "I'm just a common criminal. My bounty's only thirty-five. I'll be more than twice as hard to catch."

"You don't know the Buriats. That's not the way they think."

"How do they think? Is all this explained in Marx?"

"Yes, it is. They are totally victimized by their conditions. They don't know what they're doing. They can't behave any other way."

"They probably just don't know which side you're on."

"They don't know which side they're on themselves."

"And the Bolsheviks will change that."

"By changing the conditions."

"We were discussing the route."

"That's right. We were. So much for the first possibility. The second is also out. They'd telegraph ahead and be waiting for us. Not a chance."

"Gershuni made it."

"Luck. They've been more alert since. They've even taken a few off Japanese steamers in the harbor."

"Which narrows the choice considerably . . . ."

"To the third. We'll be all right if we can make Urga."

The shaft of sunlight vanished as if snuffed out. Their glances locked. They felt their mouths go dry.

"No, let's wait a bit," said Orloff. "Let's not be hasty."

Behind and above them a beam creaked. Dust fell.

"Savitsky," said Orloff. "I still don't know why neither of them heard you."

"Don't give up. He may join us yet."

Orloff thought of Katya. They would be together soon. He could see her now in his imagination quite clearly. She sat at her dressing table, brushing her long hair. If they were together now, he would take it in his hands.

"What will you do?" he asked.

"I don't know," said Michael. "It doesn't matter."

"Then why don't you simply serve out your term?"

Michael smiled. "What will you do?"

"The Party, of course. There will be lots to do now that Russia is at war."

"Yes. I heard about it. I'm glad. War is good."

"We probably will never meet again after we separate."

"Probably not," Michael said. "What I want to know is why you picked me. You knew I hadn't really tried to break you out. I'm not a Party member. I don't agree with you. So why?"

"I wanted to prove something. I don't think I have yet. If we do meet again, perhaps you will tell me. You see, human life is possible. You don't think so, but it is."

98

The sun set. The moon rose. Their faces were pale, cool, calm.

"It's time we were leaving," said Michael.

"Yes. The time has come."

They began to scoop away the loose dirt. A small hole opened above them and they stopped for a minute to look at the moon. Michael reached toward it with a silvery hand.

Suddenly they shrank against the earth and froze. Someone was walking quite nearby, walking slowly, as if strolling. They could hear his heels descend with a crunch. Fine sand fell on them gently from the surface. They stared up at the moon, which filled the hole like an eye. And Michael felt his hand close on a rock.

The hole was still no bigger than a man's fist and probably looked like an animal's burrow on the surface. Whoever was walking might see it and pass by. The footsteps retreated, seemed to hesitate, and then returned slowly. Closer and closer they crunched in the loamy earth. Something passed quickly across the moon and then a cascade of earth descended. It was impossible to see through such a small hole in that dust.

The footsteps retreated, were faint and then vanished. All was again still. The moon shone calmly as before. But a long time passed and still they did not move, until Michael dropped the rock.

Then the footsteps returned as before, slowly, calmly, in no hurry at all. Closer and closer they came again. Michael's scarred back arched like a bow. A fresh cascade of dust descended. The footsteps became louder and louder. Something black crossed the moon. The footsteps exploded directly overhead.

Suddenly there was a shout and an avalanche of earth rushed in. There was a thud and Orloff was thrown against the tunnel walls. At last the dust settled, and the light returned.

Golovin lay between them, looking up shaken and amazed, peering through the dust, still unable to see.

"What is all this?" he said in a shaking voice.

"Well, well, well," said Michael. "Well, well, well."

"Who is that?" said Golovin, rubbing his eyes.

Michael took off his cap. "Good evening, your honor. I hope you are well."

Golovin still could not see who it was. He saw only a silhouette in the dim light. The voice was insulting. But the words were obsequious. Golovin began to feel reassured.

"Help me up, you fool," he said. "Don't just stand there."

"Don't talk," said Michael softly. "Don't even breathe."

99

Golovin could not have talked had he wished to. He had just realized whose voice it was.

"Out for a stroll, your honor?" said Michael. "I, too, love to walk. Once I did a lot of it in Petersburg. There's nothing more interesting than a walk on the Nevsky. Don't you agree? Of course, I don't do it much any more. Perhaps I should. What do you think?"

"I . . . I . . . ."

Michael began to chuckle, softly, musically. He took out a knife and tried the blade. "Well?" he said to Orloff, with a mocking smile. "Will you do it, or shall I?"

Orloff did not answer. His eyes stared through Michael into the night. His face was expressionless, like a monk's in a cathedral. In the pale, silvery light, he looked like a statue.

"Good," said Michael. "I've never killed a man before. I can't understand how that can be. Why is it, do you think, your honor?"

Golovin's lower lip began to twitch. He sighed. For the first time, he noticed Orloff.

"Excellency!" he whispered. "Please! Help me!"

"The important thing," said Michael, "is that you know why you must be killed. That is something a man should be told."

A soft but hysterical whine came from Golovin.

"I could say it's because we can't take you and can't leave you," said Michael. "That's true. You would understand it. You would even agree. But it doesn't go far enough. No, Victor Karpovitch, the truth is that you simply need killing. You need it!"

Michael showed Golovin the knife. The blade caught the light. "Can you imagine what that will do to your insides?" Michael asked. "Peter Sergeievitch will tell you that I will surely twist it. Ask him. Peter Sergeievitch will tell you how bad I am. Why, a thing like that will gut a man like a chicken. The intestines will probably come out on the point."

Michael took Golovin's pistol. "I could say I can't shoot you because of the noise. That's true, too, but it also doesn't go far enough." He put the blade against Golovin's neck. "The point is that this is what you need!"

Golovin lost control completely. His body violently shook and twitched. "Please," he said apologetically, pulling timorously at Orloff's gown, "don't kill me. Please don't kill me. I have always obeyed. I have always done what I was told. Excellency! Please! They are trying to hurt me!"

Golovin's voice meandered on. Once again he was a child in Odessa.

Again Michael smiled strangely at Orloff. "How sad his childhood must have been." He raised the knife.

But Orloff's hand was around his wrist. "Wait," he said. He spoke softly, but his hand was like a vise.

"For what?" said Michael, through his mocking smile.

Orloff's face was wet with sweat. Golovin's words had had a strong effect. He *had* always obeyed, *had* always done what he was told. He, too, was a victim, *as Orloff had said*. He had never known what he was doing. He did not know now. He had never had a choice. He was a victim of economic conditions. Golovin deserved not punishment, but pity. The Revolution would rehabilitate him — resurrect him, in fact. Conditions would change and so would Golovin. To kill him now would simply be murder. It would prove that Michael was right — that Socialist theory was impractical. That Orloff did not really believe it himself. It would betray the ideal. It would be hypocrisy. It would make irrevocable Michael's spiritual death.

What did Orloff's personal desires mean in the face of all this?

"You cannot do this," Orloff said.

"You are mistaken, comrade," said Michael. But he could not free his hand from Orloff's grip.

Golovin was between them, crying on the ground. "Please," he mumbled. "Please don't hurt me."

"You cannot do it," Orloff said. "It would be like killing an epileptic in a hospital."

"This epileptic chained you to a wheelbarrow."

"Epileptics do such things."

"If he gets the chance, he will do it again."

"No, your honor, never," Golovin whispered.

There was nothing in the world Orloff wanted more at the moment than to kill Golovin, quickly, quietly, and to escape. But that was exactly why he could not do so. It would be too personal, which made him suspicious. He had learned to suspect personal decisions. The motive usually turned out to be detestable. He could have killed someone he did not know more easily.

Their faces were close. Each could feel the other's breath. Yet they were separated by an immeasurable gulf. Orloff still held Michael's wrist. And the blade still flashed in Michael's hand.

"Well?" said Michael. "We can't go and leave him here alive."

"No," said Orloff. "We can't do that."

"Shall we sit here all night, or just give up now?"

"No," said Orloff. "We can't do that either."

"Stand aside, or I'll kill you both."

"You go," said Orloff.

"Alone?"

"Alone."

"And you?"

"I'll just sit here all night with Golovin."

"What?"

"You go alone, or you don't go at all."

"All right."

"And you will take a note to my wife."

"All right."

"Give me a piece of paper," Orloff said to Golovin.

But Golovin did not answer. He still had not recovered his mind. Orloff looked through his pockets and found paper and a pencil, wrote a message and handed it to Michael. They stared at each other. Then Michael turned to the wall of the excavation.

"Remember!" said Orloff. "West to Irkutsk."

Michael smiled. "Yes. To Irkutsk." He was on the face of the plain, looking down.

"And remember what you have seen here," said Orloff.

"You're a fool," said Michael. He turned and was gone.

Orloff listened to his fading footsteps. He wanted to call after him, to ask him to wait. The words formed on his lips and he said them soundlessly. Then the footsteps were gone. All was still.

Golovin was crawling at Orloff's feet. "Thank you," he whispered. "Thank you. Thank you."

Suddenly, Orloff remembered something. He took a handful of Golovin's tunic, lifted and pressed him against the wall.

"Why did Mitka kill himself?" he said.

"I don't know," Golovin wheezed.

Orloff took a bigger handful. "Why did Mitka kill himself?"

"It wasn't my fault. It was a joke. I only told him he had committed a violation."

Orloff threw him against the other wall. He fell. Blood gushed strongly from his nose.

"We have a long time," said Orloff. "It will be interesting to see whether I can keep myself from killing you. Perhaps you can persuade me not to."

"Please!" said Golovin. "Please! I promise . . . ."

"Don't talk," said Orloff. "Don't say a word."

He reached as far out of the excavation as he could and scooped up a handful of earth. He pressed it to his face. It was cool and pungent, bursting with life. He inhaled the thick aroma deeply. He closed his fist so tightly that it shook. "Katya!" he said. He opened his hand. It was wet with blood.

XIV

Golovin lay half awake in the semi-darkness. His mind was blank. He remembered and thought nothing. The unaccustomed and unsettling question of whether it was morning or evening presented itself. Through the high window, he could see that the day could go either way. He had gone to bed an hour or so after dawn, so it could not be morning. What he saw then was twilight. The thought of waking at night disturbed him. He had not done such a thing in years.

But the ordinary sounds of evening were missing. It was quiet. Could it be that it was dawn after all, a new dawn? That he had slept through the entire day? This possibility disturbed him, too; disturbed him even more than the other. The uncertainty itself was annoying. Something was out of control. He moved slightly and grunted with pain. His whole body was twisted and stiff.

The rising sun filled his window. So it was morning after all. He had slept for twenty-four hours. He had never done such a thing before. It scared him. This small lapse, meaningless in itself, might be an indication of something more serious.

Then the details of his nightmare came back. But it had not been a nightmare. It was real. He felt a spasm of humiliation. He saw himself again: him, Golovin, crawling, trembling, pleading for his life; him, Golovin, who rightly took pride in his courage. It was he who had somehow gone out of control. Pain as from a blow jolted him stiff. His skin was violently itching everywhere. He felt himself spinning uncontrollably across the plain, whirling in no particular direction. He curled his toes and dug his fingers into the sheet to hold on.

Golovin felt fear; a fear without specific cause. He had to do something immediately to control it. Perhaps movement, activity, was what he needed. He dressed quickly and went to the door. It was already a bright day. He heard voices. The men were walking in the yard. He put his hand on the knob and suddenly, as if stopped by the contact, he stiffened. Once again, his skin violently itched. He began to choke. He could not breathe. Suppose . . . ! A frenzy of shame covered him like a burning shroud. Suppose the men knew! Suppose Orloff had told them! By the time the guards had found them yesterday morning, he had recovered himself at least outwardly, so that it seemed to his credit that he had merely been taken by surprise and overcome. Orloff, after all, had taken his gun. But suppose . . . .

Golovin visibly began to shake. He visualized himself in the yard, going about his duties, and the men lifting their caps and saying the greeting as before. But all along they were smirking at him covertly, whispering about him behind their hands, addressing him deferentially but with just a hint of sarcasm — enough to be noticed, too slight to challenge. Enjoying this discovery about him. Him! Golovin! He felt himself itching, covered with sweat. The thing was unbearable. He went to the window and looked out. Everything was as usual. The men were on their way to work. He could tell nothing.

He stood again at the door and felt a chill. He knew he must go out. He had to! He opened the door slowly and went down the corridor, stood at the front door and collected himself. Then he stepped outside and slowly crossed the yard to the guard room. As usual, men got out of his way. Caps lifted. "Good morning, your honor, I hope you are well," voices said. Golovin nodded magisterially, as always — magisterially but woodenly. It seemed . . . . No, no, everything was all right.

Indeed, Orloff was already in solitary. Soon Golovin would chain him to a wheelbarrow. That was the regulation. Mitka would approve. And the lunatic Voronov would soon be captured. Men were as thick as a fish net near Irkutsk. Golovin was already wondering about the punishment. Something special would have to be devised.

As for his momentary lapse, anyone surprised like that, alone and at night — and threatened with death — anyone would behave as he had. It was natural. It was human. Anyone who wouldn't was probably abnormal. And begging for his life had been natural and human, too. Indeed, it was clever! He was alive. Had he not begged for his life he would be dead. The fact that the men he had begged were beneath him was irrelevant. The fact that, in the same situation, they would not have done the same only proved that they were not human.

Golovin entered the guard room in a good humor. But inside, he saw Prishkin, the sergeant, on whose face was a strange smile. He did not like Prishkin. He knew that Prishkin wanted his job.

"Savitsky wants to see you at once," said Prishkin.

"About what?" Golovin asked.

Prishkin spread his hands, but his smile widened. His lips contorted as if trying to suppress it without success.

In his office, Savitsky waved Golovin to a chair. He handed him some cognac, which had never happened before.

"An unfortunate situation has developed," he said. "I assume you know to what I refer?"

"The escape."

"More than the escape," Savitsky said. "You see, Victor Karpovitch, Orloff is a famous man. There will be rumors. There will be investigations. Stories will begin to appear in the newspapers. Which means that someone must be found to take the blame. If the person chosen was at fault, so much the better. But whether he was or was not is totally irrelevant. Do you see the problem, Victor Karpovitch?"

"I do, Yaacov Trofimovitch, and you are right."

"I am glad to hear you say that," said Savitsky. "But do you see all the details? Soon a complaint will be coming from Petersburg, perhaps from His Majesty himself. Through a web of department heads and privy councillors, it will reach the governor. Through another such web it will come to me. And this will put me in a nasty position. It will mean that I must either choose or be chosen. If no one is chosen quickly, His Majesty may choose a minister to blame. The minister would choose a privy councillor, who would choose the governor, who would choose me. After all, I *am* prison governor. That is why I have decided to choose, rather than be chosen. To choose quickly, before the trouble even starts."

Golovin refilled his glass and drank. Savitsky was treating him as an equal, which he enjoyed.

"You are wise, Yaacov Trofimovitch. I would do the same."

"The unanimity of our opinions astounds me. Tell me, Victor Karpovitch, whom would you select?"

Golovin smiled. "Why not Orloff?"

"You misunderstand," Savitsky said. "The individual chosen must have some authority."

"Then why not Prishkin?"

"Good!" said Savitsky. "But he doesn't have enough. A man of Orloff's caliber needs more."

Golovin put all his intelligence to work. A look of baffled concentration was on his face.

"Don't you see?" said Savitsky. "I have chosen you."

"Me?"

"Don't you see how perfect you are? You are the officer in charge of the guards. It was because of your laxity that the escape was made."

"That isn't true!"

"Of course not. So what?"

Savitsky looked at his watch. "You have all day. Unfortunately this will ruin your career. But there is no excuse for such laxity, is there? You are being dismissed from the service, Victor Karpovitch. I am sorry. Get your things together and be gone by evening."

"You can't do this!" Golovin said.

Savitsky filled Golovin's glass again. "I've talked with the governor. It's all arranged. Prishkin will take your place."

"Prishkin is a fool."

"Isn't he? Such a pity."

Golovin put his hands to his face. "Why are you doing this?"

"Please!" said Savitsky. "Let's not spoil our talk."

"What will I do?" Golovin moaned. "Without the service?"

"The question occurred to me," said Savitsky. "It is interesting to speculate."

Golovin found himself in a daze in the hall. He did not know where to go. He did not know what to do.

He developed the idea that he had to see Orloff. He did not know why, but this desire had the strength of a compulsion. He went to the cell and ordered it thrown open.

"Why do you hate me?" he said when he was inside.

"I don't hate you."

"You do. You feel contempt."

"I don't feel anything for you at all, Victor Karpovitch."

"I have been dismissed from the service," Golovin said.

"I see."

"You are not surprised?"

"No."

"Why?"

"That is how the system works. You are another victim of the system, Victor Karpovitch."

Suddenly Golovin began to cry. Orloff's words had unlocked him like a key.

"You're right," he sobbed. "I am a victim. The system has chosen me as the scapegoat. After all these years, I am being thrown out. With nothing. Thrown out like a piece of garbage."

"Yes."

106

"I have never had a chance. Never. Nowhere. Not here. Not in Odessa. Always the *barins* crowd me out."

"You begin to understand what I have been talking about."

"Yes, yes! I do!" said Golovin.

Orloff felt a triumphant emotion. He had been right after all. Here was the proof. If only Michael were here to see it.

"It is still not too late to join us," Orloff said.

Golovin was pounding violently on the door. "I have to get out before the men come back," he said.

The guard opened the door and he went to his room to pack. He had to leave the camp before the prisoners finished work. Afterward, they would be in the yard and would see him. And under no circumstances could he permit that to happen. By now, they certainly knew what had happened. And nothing in the world would be more horrible than their eyes upon him when he left. He had been their tsar, but now they knew he was nothing.

His things needed only a few minutes to collect. There was so little, some clothing, an old suitcase, an obscene picture. The room was already bare — as if Golovin had never used it, as if he had never been in the service, as if there were no such person as Victor Karpovitch Golovin. And perhaps there wasn't. Who was Victor Karpovitch Golovin now? Where would he go? What would he do? He was afraid. And in his pockets he found only a few rubles.

He left the room, went down the corridor and opened the front door. No one was there. It was still. He began walking across the yard to the gate. In his old civilian clothes he looked different, smaller. With his battered old suitcase he looked pathetic.

Then Golovin heard laughter. He turned. Quite nearby, a prisoner was staring and laughing at Golovin boldly. Golovin was dumbfounded; how dare a prisoner behave like this? Indeed, the prisoner raised his arm, still laughing, and pointed. Golovin realized that he could do nothing. He turned and there was more laughter, more prisoners, more pointing. Every prisoner in the compound was there, following him on either side as he approached the gate, pointing, laughing. Their voices joined in an unbearable sound.

Golovin began to run and so did they. The suitcase got in his way and he fell. The suitcase broke completely, spilling its contents. There was a shout of laughter even louder than before. The prisoners elbowed each other and slapped their sides. Golovin crawled about clumsily retrieving his old clothes. He got to his feet and ran to the gate, pressing his things to his chest. The gate was closed and he kicked it.

"Let me out!" he sobbed. "Let me out!"

Prishkin was standing near him, but he did not move. There was a sly smile on Prishkin's face. On his shoulders were Golovin's insignia of rank.

"Your papers, please!" Prishkin said.

"What do you mean?" said Golovin.

"All prisoners to be released must have the proper papers."

"What are you talking about, Prishkin? It's me."

Prishkin smiled even more broadly. "Excuse me, Victor Karpovitch. I did not recognize you."

At last Prishkin opened the gate and Golovin staggered out. Again he began to run. The only thing in the world he wanted to do was escape — escape those pointing fingers and that laughter. He wanted to hide so that no one could ever see him again, so that no one could ever laugh and point.

The laughter followed him well into the woods. He fell heavily beneath a tree. His head whirled. His skin felt seared. The utter humiliation of his experience ate painfully at his face.

Orloff was responsible, Golovin knew. He was as sure of this as he had ever been of anything. Orloff had humiliated him at the mouth of the tunnel. Now he had arranged for everyone to laugh. He had probably laughed louder than anyone else. He had always treated Golovin with contempt. He had only been pretending to be sorry for him.

The fact occurred to him that Orloff had saved his life and that he himself had thanked Orloff for it. The lunatic Voronov would certainly have killed him. But hadn't Orloff, too, said that he wanted to kill Golovin? And by restraining Voronov, hadn't he protected himself from the consequences of killing an official?

Golovin's lips shook. He wanted to hurt Orloff, hurt him badly — so badly that he would never recover. But how? Even had Golovin not been dismissed, he would have been able to do nothing. The rods and the wheelbarrow meant nothing to Orloff.

Then the idea occurred to him. It was so simple. He would enjoy it so much. He had been wanting to do it for such a long time.

XV

Katya was depressed. She was lonely. She had no friends in this forgotten town. She had been there so long. And only three days earlier, Michael had brought her husband's message. "Patience," she had read.

"What does this mean?" she had asked.

"I escaped," said Michael.

"Who are you?"

"Convict Voronov."

"And my husband?"

"He did not escape."

"Why not? Is he hurt?"

"No."

"I don't understand."

"Your husband is a fool."

Katya became angry. "What happened?" she demanded.

"Golovin found us. Your husband wouldn't let me kill him. Golovin begged. Your husband fell for it. He stayed with Golovin so I could get away."

"My husband sacrificed himself for Golovin?"

"That's right."

Her anger at Michael was replaced by resentment for her husband. This was so like him. And Katya was not a revolutionist, but a wife. She was not opposed to her husband's Party work. She had always willingly helped him with it. But it was not something she would have done alone. She would have been just as happy — happier — had Orloff never become involved. Indeed, he always put the Revolution before either of them.

"You surprise me," said Michael.

"Do I? How so?"

"You are supposed to be pleased by this humanitarian gesture."

"Am I?"

"Of course. It is a lesson in Marxism."

"You are a Party member, of course?"

"Definitely not."

"What do you mean?"

"The Party is a fraud. Your husband is a fraud. You and I are frauds, too."

To her great surprise, Katya began to cry. She tried to stop, but could not. Her shoulders shook. She could not catch her breath. She was humiliated because she had lost control, especially before a stranger.

"Get out!" she said. "Get out! Go!"

Michael felt the beginnings of sympathy, which he suppressed. Katya really had surprised him. But sympathy was part of the fraud he had mentioned. It was sympathy which had ruined Michael himself. No one could be trusted. One should not get enmeshed in someone else's life. Sooner or later, it always meant betrayal. Michael had already made that mistake once. He would not make it again.

"As you can see, I am a fool, too," said Katya.

"Yes."

"How lucky for you that you are not."

"Yes."

And Michael was gone. Once again, Katya was alone. Days passed. She sat at her dressing table brushing her hair. Her emotions had not yet subsided into the dormant state she preferred. Nothing hurt more than wanting something which she was denied. Hell was being unable to act. Hell was a forgotten town like this.

Her sister's face appeared in her mind. She saw Nadia Nikolaevna at one of the parties she loved to give, surrounded by music, champagne and food. But Petersburg was so impossibly far away.

Then in the mirror she saw Golovin. He was leaning against the wall behind her, on his face a humorless grin. Katya looked at him and was afraid. She did not turn around. Slowly she kept moving the brush. "What are you doing here?" she said.

"I am watching you brush your hair, Katerina Nikolaevna. Isn't that obvious?"

Katya did not answer. Golovin's humorless grin broadened.

"You do not stop," he said. "You don't even turn. That is good. You are not afraid."

"Should I be afraid, Victor Karpovitch?"

Golovin chuckled. "Certainly not."

110

"What are you doing here? How did you get in?"

Golovin began to walk around the room. "Charming," he said. "You should have invited me here before this."

"I haven't invited you."

"Haven't you? Perhaps you do not remember." Golovin sat on the sofa and put his feet on a chair.

"What do you want?" said Katya.

"A terrible thing has happened, Katerina Nikolaevna. Your husband, Peter Sergeievitch, has tried to escape. Now do you see my wisdom in looking through your things? Perhaps in the future you will be more gracious when I do it. I say, 'in the future,' Katerina Nikolaevna, because your husband was caught. By me. I am sorry."

"There is no need for you to tell me this," said Katya.

"I am glad to do it," Golovin said. "But I *am* sorry. You see, Katerina Nikolaevna, your husband behaved badly. He broke down. I could have shot him, but he pleaded with me. It was pathetic, Katya. You should thank me. I believe you will."

Now it was Katya's turn to laugh. She did so with amusement, staring boldly into his eyes. So fierce was her laugh that he knew she knew the truth. And the feeling of impotent rage returned.

"Voronov was here," he said. "He told you everything."

"Yes," Katya said. "Quite graphically."

Golovin shouted, in great pain. With the back of his hand, he hit Katya across the mouth. She reeled across the room into a table, grasping at the table cloth. She fell and the cloth came, too. Several plates fell to the floor, shattering. Blood poured from her nose. On her cheek was a bruise made by Golovin's large ring.

Golovin sat down and lit a cigarette. "You see, Katya. You see I am going to teach you both a lesson. Later you will thank me."

"You will be dismissed from the service," Katya stammered.

"I have already been dismissed. Didn't Voronov tell you that? No, that's right, he wouldn't know. But it's true. Peter Sergeievitch has beaten me in everything. Except in this. He can't do anything about this. He's in solitary. And this will more than make up for the rest. You will see."

Katya rose to her feet and staggered toward the door, but Golovin got up, too. He took her by the wrist, used it as a handle and again threw her against the wall. She fell to her knees. The long sleeve of her blouse was ripped.

She got up again and her hand closed on something hard. She went at Golovin with it, but he sidestepped, again caught her wrist and swung her arm behind her back. She gasped. Her arm suddenly was burning with pain. The heavy object fell to the floor. Again Golovin knocked her down. Her left eye began to swell.

"I begin to wonder whether your invitation was sincere," said Golovin. He opened a bottle of vodka he had brought, took a long drink and extended it to Katya. "Drink?"

"I did not invite you," Katya said.

"You said that before. And I explained that you didn't remember. You are a lonely woman, Katya. You long for my company."

"Get out," said Katya. "Leave me alone."

She got up and leaned unsteadily against the wall. There was blood on her face. Her eye was closing.

"You misunderstood," Golovin said. He went to her. "Your blouse is ripped. Let me help." He took a handful of her blouse and ripped it off. It tore easily. A sweet, female scent sprang out. A film of sweat was on her neck. Her arms and shoulders were completely bare.

"What beautiful arms you have, Katya," he said. "I never really noticed before. You shouldn't keep yourself so secret."

She did not answer. In the silence of the room, he heard her stays creak. He took her arms, and Katya spat wetly into his face.

Golovin roared. With a palm on her chest he shoved Katya across the room, into another table. A samovar was on it, along with some glasses and cups. The edge of the table cut into Katya's thigh. She fell, the dishes shattering all around her. The samovar fell also. Boiling water began pouring out.

Katya screamed and crawled away. But the boiling water seemed to follow. Her foot was on fire. She screamed again and again.

"Stop it!" said Golovin. "You will annoy me."

He took a long swig from the bottle and than another. Katya was still. She had passed out. And he wanted her to be awake and aware. He wanted her to know everything that happened. To know. To remember. And especially, to be able to relate everything afterwards.

He turned her over and took her slipper off. Her foot was swollen and splotched with red. He began to kiss her roughly. She revived instantly and fought, silently, furiously, with all her remaining strength. Fingernails clawed at Golovin's face. A fist punched him on the forehead. But he liked it. The fact that she fought meant that the end would affect her greatly. If she did not fight, the end would mean nothing. So he opposed her, but only slightly, so that she would lose strength very slowly.

At last Katya had no strength left. Her eye was closed. Her thigh ached. Her face was bloody. Her foot burned. But she was conscious. She was aware.

112

Golovin took her clothes off. He turned her back and forth and removed her skirt. With the soles of her feet against his chest, he removed her stockings, rolling them up very slowly. But he could not figure out her corset.

Katya felt a strange lassitude. She wanted to continue fighting, but could not. She could not lift her arms. She could not move.

Golovin took out a knife, cut the strings, and tore the corset off. Then Katya was completely naked.

She crawled away, got up and leaned unsteadily against the wall. Golovin cut her clothes into bits. The idea occurred to her to wrap herself in a curtain, but she dismissed it. One could not be embarrassed before Golovin.

Golovin sat on the sofa and poured a drink. There was no hurry. He had plenty of time. He wanted to enjoy this as long as he could. He studied the naked woman before him.

"You surprise me, Katya," he said. "You really do. I had a long speech prepared and now it's useless. You've ruined it. And I was looking forward to it so much.

"I had planned to tell you that you are just like other people, basically. That you are no different from the sluts down the street. That you have no reason to hoist your nose.

"But I was wrong, Katya. You tricked me. Now I understand. You have good reason to hoist your nose. You are magnificent. Whatever possessed you to hide such beauty?

"Perhaps that is why you mistakenly believe you are better than I am. It *is* a mistake, Katya. You are wrong. You aren't any better than anyone else. That part of my speech holds good. That is what I am going to prove."

Golovin noticed that Katya's hair was still not undone. Something in it still held it up. It annoyed him. It was as if she were partially clothed.

"Take whatever that is out of your hair," he said.

But Katya did not move or answer. He got up, went to her and did it himself. Her thick blonde hair cascaded and caught the light. So did the film of sweat on her neck. Her lips were wet. Her arms were full. Her breasts gently rose and fell. They were large, yet they stood erect.

"Such a pleasant surprise," Golovin said.

But a combination of defiance and pride was in her eyes. It told Golovin that he could not win, that nothing he might do could beat her. What she needed was complete humiliation, an insult she could not forget.

Golovin knocked her to the floor and slowly forced her knees apart. Katya felt boots and coarse cloth along her legs, a buckle on her stomach, button and straps against her chest. There was no point in fighting any more.

She could not. And fighting was exactly what Golovin wanted.

Then a pain like a surgeon's incision cut through her. She tried to scream, but could not. And the pain came again and again.

"Do you see how right I was?" Golovin said. "You aren't any better than I am at all. Look at yourself! See what you are doing! And with me, with Golovin, trash under your nose. Don't you see how it proves my point?"

Golovin moved roughly and the pain came again. Katya's body burned. Her ears rang. Her skin was hot. She could not move. After a time, she fainted. Hours passed. It was well after midnight. When she revived, Golovin was sitting quietly, staring at her.

"You will visit your husband soon," he said. "You must tell him everything. Everything! After all I have done for you, you owe me that. It is more important than anything else."

"Is it, Victor Karpovitch?" Katya said. She began to laugh hysterically. She had realized the reason for what had happened. And at the same moment, Golovin realized that she would not tell her husband, that nothing in the world could induce her to do so. It meant that she would cheat him of the victory he deserved. She was already laughing to show him her victory.

He ordered her to stop laughing, but Katya continued as if she had not heard. "Hit me, Victor Karpovitch," she said. "Go ahead."

Golovin felt his face go red. "No, you're right. There is no need to tell him." He got up, got the knife and turned her over with a foot. "I'll tell him myself," Golovin said.

He held her to the floor tightly and, as she screamed, he carved his initials across her buttocks. The letters immediately filled with blood.

"VKG," he said. "He will know."

He brought the bottle of vodka over. "Drink!" he said, and forced the contents down her throat.

He rolled Katya in a small rug, carried her outside to his horse and threw her across the saddle. Then he swung into the saddle and rode slowly out of town. It was very late. The streets were empty, and if anyone had seen him, they would remember only a man they did not recognize in civilian clothes who, for some reason, had been riding with a rolled-up rug across his horse. Inside it, Katya could not move. It made no difference; she had again passed out.

When morning came, he was already far out of town. He dismounted and put the rug on the ground, unrolled it, shoved Katya off, rerolled it and put it back across the horse. Then he remounted and rode off. Katya lay still, just off the road where they would find her.

He regretted only that he could not stay to tell them all. But he and she and Orloff would know.

114

Part III

Ivan Danilov

KHANNA

XVI

Maria Ivanovna Danilova stood in the wings of the Imperial Marinsky Theater watching the prima at downstage center, whirling and flashing, fire and ice. Maria knew that subdued but animated voices were around her, arguing, explaining, accusing, denying. Tata Beresova whispered eagerly in her ear. But Maria dismissed the voices from her thoughts. She wanted to be alone, completely alone. It was as if she were about to enter a cathedral. As if she were still a child, waiting for her mother in the portico of St. Issac's, peering inside with awe, half afraid to go in. To speak now would be unthinkable; it would shatter the tension of the moment.

She examined herself carefully to make sure her costume was in order. She heard Tata's voice rise and fall excitedly behind her. Then the music seemed to hesitate. Suddenly it rose to a crescendo, filling her body as if she herself were some instrument. She flushed as always, unable to contain her excitement. The cymbals crashed. The timpani thundered. The horns called — summoning her.

Maria Danilova rose on her points. She raised her arms. She flashed through the wing and burst upon the stage.

Then she was flying. Up to the sun. Without fear. Without effort. Light, majestic. She hesitated at her apogee, defiant, reaching higher. Then she dove in a long arc and rose again.

It was what she had known she was born for ever since she saw her first ballet at the age of eight.

The *pas de quatre* was over and Maria and Tata rejoined the line. The music rose to one crescendo and then another. The prima did a pirouette and then an *arabesque penchée.* Maria envied her, but only a little. She knew that one day she, too, would be a prima. Then the timpani announced the finale. Maria flashed into the wings and returned to earth. The curtain fell. The performance was over.

"You make a beautiful swan," said Vasya Lopatkin.

"Thank you, Vasya," Maria smiled.

Dancers, stagehands, friends ran around them. Everyone shouted, and no one understood a thing. A path opened before the prima, who came from the first wing for the last time.

"Masha, I've enlisted," said Lopatkin, with a slight flourish.

"Enlisted?" said Maria. "But why, Vasya? There was no need. You could just as well have remained at the Institute."

"I'm in your brother's regiment. I leave in three days."

Maria could not visualize Lopatkin in uniform, especially not in uniform in a trench. He was shy, studious, even ineffectual. He had a youthful awkwardness, too. In kissing a lady's hand, he would be likely to get one of her fingers in his eye.

But Lopatkin kissed Maria's hand gallantly now. "Try to understand, Masha," he said. "Try! I can no longer stay here while the others are out there fighting . . . and dying. It's almost as if — I know it isn't so — but I feel it's as if everyone's eyes were on me in the street, staring at me, prodding me, asking, 'And you? And you?'

"What can I answer, Masha? 'There's no need? I know your husband, father and son are dead or captured, but I am a student at the Institute and there's no need?' No, no, Masha. It's impossible, impossible. I must go. Now. It's a sacred duty."

"You should not worry about what other people think."

"But I do."

"You don't! You don't care what *I* think."

"What nonsense, Masha! How can you say that?"

"I don't stare at you in the street, Vasya."

"No, you don't. But that doesn't matter, Masha. You're a woman. You couldn't understand."

"That's true," said Maria. "I am a woman. I don't understand. I also don't know what the war is about. I know what they *say* it's about; they say it's about lots of things. But at the same time, I know it isn't about those things at all."

"The war is an opportunity, Masha. A chance for heroic deeds."

"What nonsense, Vasya! How silly!"

"It will make me worthy of you, Masha. You will see. Perhaps I will be lucky enough to get a chance for a Cross."

"Vasya, don't claim you have done this for me."

"Certainly not! You are a woman. You could not understand."

Lopatkin was in love with Maria, but knew they were destined to remain merely friends. Nevertheless, he acted otherwise and refused to admit it. He loved her as if she were a figure in a painting — which was partly why they were destined to remain friends. Lopatkin was really in love with his emotion; Maria only gave it substance.

Tata joined them, hands to her mouth. "You've really put Crispina in a state," she whispered with delight. "She says you deliberately made her lose her balance."

"But I didn't!" said Maria. "Why on earth would I?"

"Of course you didn't," chirped Tata. "So what?"

Maria did not participate in the rivalries, gossip, jealousies and feuds which perpetually erupted in the company. Neither did Tata. The difference between them was that Maria ignored them while Tata enjoyed them immensely. "So and so has hired a claque," Tata would whisper happily in her ear. "Her rival, such and such, has complained to Platon Sergeievitch."

"What does Crispina have against me?" asked Maria.

"She's afraid you'll get the parts she wants," Tata said.

"Will you come to the soldiers' benefit tonight?" asked Lopatkin.

"But Vasya, surely you haven't forgotten my mother's party," said Maria. "Tata is coming, too."

"Yes, I remember. I had deliberately forgotten," said Lopatkin. "You see? A party in honor of your brother, a winner of the Cross of St. George, while I . . . . It will be such an honor to serve with him."

Tata clapped her hands. "Vasya, have you . . . ?"

"Yes," said Maria wryly. "Vasya has joined Stepan's regiment."

"How wonderful!" said Tata. "How marvelous! The truth is, Vasya, I had been wondering . . . ."

Lopatkin turned to Maria and shrugged. "You see?"

"Oh, how I envy you," Tata said. "How I wish women could fight too."

"What nonsense!" said Lopatkin. "Women in the trenches! Your place is here, maintaining the serene excellence of Russian culture, the envy of the world."

"I had a letter from Stepan last week," said Tata. "He didn't mention the war at all."

"How typically noble," said Lopatkin. "Your fiancé is trying to spare you."

Crispina's face severed the conversation. "Why did you put me off balance, Danilova?"

"You know that I did not, Vera Karpovna," Maria said softly.

"If I were vindictive — which I'm not — I'd report you to Platon Sergeievitch. You'd be fined ten rubles for malexecution."

"Report me then, Vera Karpovna."

"You aristocrats think you can trample everyone underfoot, don't you?" said Crispina. "But some of us will not allow it. I got where I am without a father's influence!"

Maria flushed.

"You'd better go, Vera Karpovna," said Tata with delight.

"Luckily for you, I am not a vindictive person," said Crispina. She glared at them all and then stalked off.

"There's no understanding women," Lopatkin said. "The female is by nature devious and incomprehensible, a creature of mystery. It's well known that they cannot even understand each other."

"Ignore her," said Tata. "The professors say it's a matter of glands. The truth is, though, I would enjoy seeing you two in a good fight. You're too aloof, Masha. Natalia Stepanovna is right."

"Come, Masha," said Lopatkin. "Let's go to the Wandering Dog."

"No, Vasya. I must go to Platon Sergeievitch and then to Natalia Stepanovna. We'll see each other tonight."

They talked a bit more and then parted, and Maria went to see Platon Sergeievitch.

"Ah, the little Danilova," he said as usual, advancing with arms wide. Platon Sergeievitch always greeted his female dancers in this way. They were all "little," even though he was usually smaller than they were. At his age, even a prima was little.

"And how is your health, my dear?" said Platon Sergeievitch, looking up at the little Danilova.

"Platon Sergeievitch! Have you any reason to be dissatisfied with my work? Tell me, please."

Platon Sergeievitch gestured, alarmed. "Why, by no means, my dear. How could you think such a thing?"

"Yes, so you say, yet you've given me no parts."

"Ah. Yes. But there is the problem of your health. You must conserve your energy, little one."

"My health? What do you mean, Platon Sergeievitch?"

The old man squeezed and clapped her hand. "Yes, you would never speak of it yourself. You are brave, like the young men. Like your brother. You, too, deserve a medal."

Too surprised to speak, Maria simply stared. He was humoring her about something, but she could not guess what. He shook a finger, trying to make it a joke.

"Yes, you should thank heaven," Platon Sergeievitch said angrily.

"Instead of berating a poor old man, you should thank heaven that you have such a friend as the little Crispina. Such solicitude in our little family is regrettably all too rare." Platon Sergeievitch bowed his head, pretending to be hurt.

"But what has she told you?" Maria asked.

"Come, little one, come," said Platon Sergeievitch, pressing her hand. "There's nothing to fear. There's no reason to be embarrassed. Many have been slightly consumptive and recovered completely. It is important only to conserve one's energy."

Maria shook her fists. "Bitch! Bitch!"

"Stop that at once!" said Platon Sergeievitch, now genuinely angry. "Where in the world have you learned such language?"

*   *   *

"Very well, you spoke at last with Platon Sergeievitch," Natalia Stepanovna said later. "At last, thank heaven, you condescend to consider mundane matters." Her majestic bosom rose accusingly. "Now at last, perhaps, you will take my advice and . . . ."

"No, Natalia Stepanovna, please. I've told you. No."

The older woman's majestic bosom rose again. Natalia Stepanovna was indignant, even angry. There was much more to a successful career than a mere knowledge of choreography. There were so many people to be influenced or flattered. There was so many others to be avoided or rapped on the knuckles. And there were groups it was important to set upon other groups. Indeed, it was a war, a war sometimes more complicated than the one in the trenches. One could not even always be certain who the enemy was, or who maintained the balance of power at any given moment. It was all so delicate, so complicated, that a girl of Maria's youth and inexperience could not hope to understand it without the assistance of a virtuoso like herself. But Natalia Stepanovna enjoyed all these machinations. If she had been a man, she would have been a general.

And yet Maria was not only apathetic in this regard, she refused to cooperate with Natalia Stepanovna's efforts. "All that's unimportant," Maria had often said.

"All right, all right," said Natalia Stepanovna. "Must you always bother me so? We won't discuss it now. Here, come, show me how you will tie your ribbons.

"Ah, ha! As I thought! Just as I thought! That's not the way. The knot must be on the outside of the ankle. And take care to moisten it with spit or it may come undone."

Natalia Stepanovna believed that the faults that continually appeared in her students' executions were the work of some diabolical force bent on affronting her by insinuating them into a performance. Hiding themselves from her in practice, they would spring triumphantly forth on the stage, labelled "Natalia Stepanovna." It was almost as if the dancer herself were not responsible. Or was she? Were the mistakes a conspiracy to mock Natalia Stepanovna? Either way, the best thing was to trick them into the open during lessons. Approaching casually, she would suddenly catch the dancer off guard, point a finger and spring before the flaw could disappear.

"You're young," said Natalia Stepanovna. "So young. That's your problem, Masha. Perhaps you will grow out of it if you do not make me lose my temper. How old are you?"

"Twenty," said Maria. "Same as yesterday, Natalia Stepanovna."

"Incredible!" said the older woman. "Impossible! No one is twenty! You have your whole career before you Masha, if you listen to me. Oh, how I envy you — but not entirely! I have my new pleasure: food. Yes, food! Does that sound gluttonous to you, Masha?"

"No."

"Do you realize that during my entire career I didn't eat? Twenty-five years without food, Masha! Oh, Yes, of course, a nibble of this, a bite of that. Enough to prevent them from burying me. Enough to sustain a mouse in a state of torpor. But never the joy, the serenity of a completely full stomach. They tortured me, Masha. They would not let me eat. Everywhere I went, they sent someone to watch me. Is that conceivable to you, Masha? Can you imagine it? Compared with it, my treatment of you — which you unjustly criticize — is that of a mother for her baby.

"And my dreams! Fragrant, sugary, dripping with butter. Bulging with éclairs. Bursting with cream. Such agony! Don't worry, Masha, it's a problem you'll never have; you're thin. In fact, you're skinny. You're too skinny. You don't eat enough, do you? Tell me."

"I do. I do. I assure you, Natalia Stepanova."

"Ah, the pleasure of a good restaurant. The pleasure! I could tell you of nights at Félicien. One night the Grand Duke Nicholas Alexandrovitch — His Imperial Majesty himself — together with the other Grand Dukes and some others . . . . Well, never mind. It would do you no harm, none at all, I assure you."

"Please, Natalia Stepanovna. No more schemes." Maria jumped up and tightly embraced her teacher.

122

"All right," said the older woman, making herself appear angry. "That's enough. Don't try to ingratiate yourself. If only you could be so charming when necessary. You aren't. I know that. But you could pretend."

Natalia Stepanovna threw up her hands. "Ah, the difficulty of launching a career with an empty head. That's your trouble, Masha, you have an empty head. Do you wish to remain a coryphée? You are satisfied, perhaps, with your 720 rubles? You do not wish ever to be a prima? Of course, your initial success was impressive. But the precocity has worn off. How can you hope to succeed if you insist on antagonizing the critics? You refuse to have supper with them. Do you know that they regard you — I have spoken with them — they regard you as aloof, as a condescending snob? And of course, they are correct, aren't they? You *are* a condescending snob. You're a spoiled brat. There, it's out. Stop smiling at once!"

"I am trying, Natalia Stepanovna."

"Telegin, for instance, is one of the most influential journalists in Petrograd. Such a patriot! And he adores you, follows you passionately — but you snub him. Why? It's outrageous! Tell me!" Natalia Stepanovna had worked herself into a fervor. Telegin was a ripe fruit pleading to be picked. It was imperative that Maria pick him, and yet she refused to do so. The facts were so obvious. Why would she not see?

"It's because of your childish principles, isn't it?" said Natalia Stepanovna. "Restaurants are wicked, isn't that right? You think you will be abducted, isn't that it?

"If only I might be," said Maria.

"Do not joke," said Natalia Stepanovna. "You're a regular little prig it's not enough that you spent eight years locked up in school like a nun. But these are modern times, Masha. This is 1916. Women are emancipating themselves at last.

"True, Cyril Modestovitch is not the most attractive of men. He, too, likes to eat. But does he deserve such rudeness because of it? And he has attractive qualities, Masha: his French — so musical, and his manners — so perfect. Besides, this is *business*. We are speaking of your career. It would be such a coup if you condescended to enslave him. And all you need do is have supper, nothing more. Ask your father. It's business. He would understand."

"I would not bother my father with such nonsense."

Natalia Stepanovna threw up her hands. "Well, it doesn't matter. You are a stone wall. But I have taken my own measures, as I knew I must. I have spoken with your mother, Masha, who has twice your sense. Cyril Modestovitch will be at her party tonight."

"Natalia Stepanovna! Please tell me you are joking!"

"Did you think I would be stopped by a silly child, Masha? Ah, you haven't the talent of a Kshessinska. That is clear."

"Natalia Stepanovna!"

"Do not attempt to argue. I hear nothing. Must you waste all our time with talk? Are you a politician? Perhaps you are Kerensky? Or are you a dancer, after all? Come, show me how you will take a call. Show me!

"Ah, ha, as I thought! Just as I thought!" Bosom heaving, Natalia Stepanovna pointed. "Are you a horse? Are you a plough horse? Tell me, Masha, I want to know. Should we harness you to one of your father's pieces of equipment? Or are you perhaps Isadora Duncan? Ugh! That horrid woman! You'll want to take your shoes off next.

"A dancer must never walk on flat feet. You trip lightly to the center, like so; curtsey to the right — Imperial box; curtsey to the left — director; two steps forward, semi-round curtsey to the parterre. Now you raise your eyes, smile and curtsey to the gallery. Come, show me, Masha. Yes, that's it. Exactly!"

XVII

"It's a scandal, a disgrace!" said Cyril Modestovitch Telegin. He shook his fist at the windows as if the perpetrators were just outside. "The cream of the nation dying in the trenches, the country prostrate, and here is Petrograd full of profiteers. It's criminal! It's treason! Something should be done!"

He pushed the last of a canapé inside his bulging cheek. As usual, crumbs stood on ledges of the vest over his large stomach, and he brushed them away angrily, sprinkling Rakov the lawyer. Rakov smiled and slowly drew away. Telegin glared for emphasis at the others, and in particular at his host, Ivan Fyodorovitch Danilov, who was an industrialist but not a profiteer. This Telegin already knew, which was why he had made the remark.

The others were impressed. He could see that on their faces. People were always impressed by a journalist. How stupid! But Danilov was not impressed. He was not listening. As usual, the party and people were boring. He wished he were still in his office at work. He was here only because his wife had reminded him that the party's purpose was to honor Stepan. He watched Nadia Nikolaevna now as she flitted from group to group, light flashing on the silk of her gown. She was not boring. He would have preferred that they be alone.

His daughter and Tata were standing at the side table. Tata, as always, was whispering and gesticulating. Maria, as always, was steadily eating. Yet she always looked so underfed. Why?

"Why not expose the facts in your column?" asked Rakov.

Telegin smiled. "Apparently you misunderstand modern publicity, counsellor. That would only demoralize our troops."

"Only when they are thoroughly demoralized will we have peace."

"That, my dear sir, is what the Bolsheviks want."

"Hurrah for the Bolsheviks, in that case. Do I scandalize you, Ivan Fyodorovitch?" asked Rakov.

Few people knew Danilov contributed to the Party. "Not at all," Danilov said. "All of us want peace."

"Can you tell us anything for publication about the incredible shortage of rifles?" asked Telegin.

"No," said Danilov, "I don't make rifles. And my schedule is kept."

"I, too, applaud what is happening," said Yaacov Trofimovitch Savitsky, a prison governor recently retired after service in Siberia. "But for an entirely different reason. Russia is undergoing a necessary purge. The war is to our country as the emetic is to the patient. The suffering will return Russia to health. The laxity which caused the problem will be thrown up. Don't you agree, Ivan Fyodorovitch?"

"Probably not," said Danilov. "What did you say?"

Bondarchuk, the retired general, chuckled. "You're right, it's nonsense. We ought to avoid it. What we need is discipline. The army's gone soft. Do you know the shelling stops at six and then they sit down to tea — just like a pack of office workers? Do you call that a war? It's a maneuver. Now, when I was in Bulgaria against the Turks . . . ."

"What's needed," Telegin interrupted, "is for the 'Imperial adviser' to be shipped back to Siberia immediately."

"It's wrong of you to condemn Rasputin," said Savitsky. "He is a man of God. He must be excused."

"Why?" asked Danilov.

"I agree most emphatically, Ivan Fyodorovitch," Telegin said. "His behavior is inexcusable! It provides opportunities for Lenin."

"Probably," said Danilov wryly. The agreement left a sour taste in his mouth. He did not like Telegin. Why was he here?

A slender man with lush, feminine lips was near them. It was Dolgorensky, posing as a "businessman." Dolgorensky could tell them about the rifles.

"Excuse me," he said, "but I disagree. Lenin is inconsequential. There is nothing to fear."

"Let us hope so," Telegin said. "The war must be fought to a typically glorious conclusion."

Actually, the war was irritating Telegin more and more. Everything had so expanded that his own position appeared to have shrunk. What did a journalist matter in such a mess? Telegin genuinely resented the profiteers — not because they were wrong, but because they were successful. Yet his own position demanded that he publicly applaud the war. He could not understand why Danilov had not joined them. Telegin had investigated and found that he had not.

"But Stepan refused," Nadia Nikolaevna said to Lopatkin elsewhere in

126

the large room. "Against the orders of his colonel, he recrossed the bridge under fire and brought the others out alone. And only one was an officer. It's an expression of his democratic views. Stepan carried one poor boy the whole way."

"I only hope I can emulate him slightly," Lopatkin said.

"He's to be decorated by His Imperial Majesty himself," said Nadia Nikolaevna. "Imagine it!"

Always a highly volatile personality, Nadia Nikolaevna was intoxicated by the music, the dancing and the conversation. But now her mood changed. Her face darkened slightly. "Vasya, promise me you'll tell him he's done quite enough. He's to stay indoors and keep warm. You don't know him; he's so terribly impulsive — like me."

Nadia Nikolaevna recalled her experience of the day before when, during her voluntary duty at the hospital, she had fainted at the sight of a particularly unpleasant wound, and the doctor had angrily ordered her from the room. A small chink had appeared in the wall of publicity; she had seen the war as it really was.

"Yes, of course," Lopatkin said.

"Good. Thank you," she said, reassured. "You must stop by before you go, Vasya. I have some things you might deliver to Stepan."

Through the alcove, near the orchestra, she saw the Princess Moldawsky, and rustled off to repeat the story of her son's exploit.

"Mark my words," Savitsky was saying. "When the soul is tarnished, the hand will tremble."

Telegin repeated the remark aloud. How surprising! It would make an appropriate warning for his readers.

"And this is particularly true today," Savitsky said. "Not the slightest reverence for art or beauty. The heart shrivels at the insidious consequences of materialism. The intellectual climate of our youth has gone."

"Some changes must be made," Rakov said. "Society is not static. There is need for improvement."

"And you liberals believe you have the only answer."

"The only answer," said Rakov, "is a bit of socialism. The acquisitive and communal instincts must be returned to proper balance — if we are to avoid the holocaust which is already so near."

"I beg your pardon," said Bondarchuk. "I know to what you allude, and I can assure you that the monarchy was never stronger."

"What do you think, Khlebanov?" Rakov asked Dolgorensky.

Dolgorensky smiled. "I couldn't agree with all of you more. People worry too much today."

Telegin was no longer listening. Across the room, under a portrait of her mother by Repin, he had just seen Maria leaning against the wall, tall, austere, dressed in black. The only other color he had ever seen her wear was white, on stage at the Marinsky. She was so like her father, a person of extremes. Like him, she was aloof and did not talk very much. She could be alone even in a crowd, as they both were now. Was that why Telegin felt drawn to her, as he had never been drawn to anyone else? He could not be sure. A few years ago he had been invited very often to this house, and then for a reason he did not know, he had not been invited until now. He did not know this invitation was the work of Natalia Stepanovna. Then, Maria had been nothing but a gawky child. Now, of course, she was a beautiful woman. The only thing that had not changed was her manner: arrogant, contemptuous, mocking, pampered. So typical of a person without experience, he thought. So like the cloistered person she was. Could that be the reason he was looking for? He did not know. Was it that she had ignored his invitations, that she obviously did not care about the influence he had? Or was it simply that he wanted to bring knowledge to her ignorance? He was sure only that he wanted his pudgy fingers on her flesh, wanted to feel her naked body next to his.

Only too glad to fulfill her promise to Natalia Stepanovna, Nadia Niko-laevna approached and took his arm. If her husband complained about his presence, she could use her promise as an excuse. After all, perhaps it would help Masha's career! She had never understood her husband's hostility to Telegin and his insistence that Telegin not be invited to their house. His corpulence should not be criticized, but pitied. And Maria was simply a disobedient child, as Natalia Stepanovna had rightly said.

"Come, Cyril Modestovitch," she said. "Let me take you to Masha. I know you have much of professional interest to discuss."

"Permit me to say, madame, that your daughter is a balletomane's delight."

"You are so courtly, Cyril Modestovitch."

Maria saw them coming and went to Lopatkin, who stood with Tata at the side table rooting through the canapés.

"Vasya, stop eating!" she said. "Dance with me."

He could not replace his canapé, since she had already pulled him away, and he could not eat it since he was already chewing, so he quickly put it in his pocket and put his arms around Maria.

But Nadia Nikolaevna's hand was already on his arm. "Vasya, come! There is someone you must meet. Look, Masha, I've brought you Cyril Modestovitch. He says you are a balletomane's delight." Then she was gone with Lopatkin in tow.

"Your mother tells the truth," said Telegin. "I say that in my columns."

"I have not read your columns lately, Cyril Modestovitch."

Telegin shook a finger in mock reproof. "The truth is, Maria Ivanovna, that you have been avoiding me. Why?"

"Yes, I have been avoiding you. I don't like you," she laughed.

Telegin smiled with genuine delight. Perhaps this was why she attracted him so. What other woman would say something like that? All the others simply mouthed the usual meaningless endearments. But Maria not only said it, she said it so easily, without a trace of the belligerence which would conceal fear. Indeed, she smiled, slightly but mockingly. Her chin was raised. Her eyes stared into his. And her perfectly black hair shone in the light.

"Splendid!" he said. "And why not?"

"I'm not quite sure. Probably because you would ooze if squeezed."

"An interesting theory. Squeeze me and see."

"I'd better not. It would ruin the party."

"Perhaps you would amplify your theory over supper some night."

"Thank you, Cyril Modestovitch. No."

They were standing at the sideboard and Telegin began to eat, slowly, delicately, but incessantly, jowls quivering as he chewed, his highly mobile lips working very hard. Again he brushed the crumbs from his vest. With a bulk like his, he naturally wore clothes badly, as if they had been made for someone else. His tailor believed Telegin's body changed between the measurements and the fitting. Ordinarily this annoyed Telegin, but now he liked it. Maria's contempt made him glad to be so fat. Indeed, his voluminous stomach was near her now.

"I believe you will change your mind," he said. "You and I will become good friends. You don't know this yet, but you desire me passionately. That is the reason for your contempt. You don't know yet that you are trying to fight it."

Maria laughed. "I may win."

"Until then I shall be content to admire you in your tutu. You have very beautiful legs, Maria Ivanovna," Telegin winked.

For the first time, he had said something that rankled her. Of course, she knew he had been watching all the time. But now that he said so, it annoyed her. It was as if, in a large audience, he was nevertheless spying.

At last, he thought. At last I have drawn blood. She is such a thorough fraud. Telegin took a canapé and smiled.

"Perhaps you would say something for publication about the war."

"I never say anything about the war. I know nothing about it and don't want to know."

"Yes, it is tiresome, isn't it? So dirty. So mundane. Such a rude intrusion for people of the theater. But surely you have something to say about your brother."

Stepan's face appeared in her mind. "I have not seen my brother in a long time. I am glad he rescued all those men."

"Touching," said Telegin. "May I write that down? I have not seen your brother myself for years. I doubt that I would know him."

Elsewhere in the ballroom, Nadia Nikolaevna asked Savitsky to follow, and they went into Danilov's study.

"Well," she said, "tell me about my sister, Madame Orlova."

"Your sister?"

"Peter Sergeievitch Orloff is my brother-in-law. I believe he was under your administration."

The color left Savitsky's face. He had known but had not realized this. He had not realized why he was invited. He looked at the door. It was too late to escape.

"I am puzzled, Yaacov Trofimovitch. Worried. My sister's letters have changed. They are vague; she mentions nothing. You have seen her, I'm sure. Tell me how she is."

Savitsky stammered. "I'm sorry."

"Please, Yaacov Trofimovitch, you frighten me."

"Excuse me. I am sorry. It is embarrassing to discuss."

"Embarrassing?" said Nadia Nikolaevna. "What can you mean?"

"Your sister was found outside town one day — drunk."

"Drunk?" Nadia Nikolaevna fell into a chair. "Surely this is some joke, Yaacov Trofimovitch?"

"I wish it were," Savitsky said.

"But my sister does not drink," said Nadia Nikolaevna. "She tasted vodka once and spat it out."

"I believe it," said Savitsky. "It is so unlike her. But you do not know the reality of a small Siberian town — the cold, the mosquitoes, the horrifying boredom, so trying in particular for a Moscow lady alone. The mind is strange. Perhaps . . . ."

"I know exactly," said Nadia Nikolaevna. "My husband was born not far from Krasnoyarsk."

"Of course, there were extenuating factors," said Savitsky. "Katerina Nikolaevna was also found naked — and beaten."

Nadia Nikolaevna shuddered and covered her face as if the humiliation were her own. "Oh, how horrible! My poor, poor sister!"

"Perhaps this means she was attacked by a criminal . . . ."

"Of course it does. What else could it mean?"

"She may have been simply the victim of a robbery. Her clothes may have been stolen, the alcohol forced down her throat."

"But why? Why would a robber force vodka down her throat? And why was she found not at home, but outside town?"

Savitsky shrugged. "She would tell the police nothing. The exact reasons have never been found."

Nadia Nikolaevna touched her hair. Her hands fluttered like birds in a trap. She did not know what to do with them.

"And my brother-in-law?" she asked, and immediately regretted it. She resented Orloff. She always had. He was responsible for her sister's wasted life. His sympathy apparently only extended to others. And yet Nadia Nikolaevna had repeatedly been unable to dissuade her own husband from contributing to Orloff's Party. She shuddered as she always did when thinking of Orloff, shuddered as if threatened by something incomprehensible.

"He is in prison. Such a waste."

"He belongs there," she said. "Were it not for my sister, I would be glad he had been caught."

"A tragic situation," said Savitsky. "I was forced to dismiss a loyal officer from the service. A career ruined. If I may say so, your brother-in-law's humanitarianism is misplaced."

Nadia Nikolaevna nodded. "I have often thought that."

"For instance, your brother-in-law was caught trying to escape, and another man with him did escape that night. Yet Peter Sergeievitch refused to tell us the facts we needed to catch this man, even though I promised leniency. Perhaps you remember him: a Michael Voronov. He worked at one time for your husband at the factory."

"Yes, I do remember. It was some years ago."

"Violent. Dangerous. A mental case. Perhaps, a few days later, he was involved in your sister's misfortune. We considered the possibility, although one cannot imagine a motive. But we do not know. He has never been found."

"Yes, yes, thank you, Yaacov Trofimovitch." Nadia Nikolaevna rose. She could not go on. They were speaking of an unreal but painful world. As an antidote, she needed the reality she heard faintly through the doors.

She opened them. The music and voices flowed in. Before her was the reassuring swelter of lights and colors and dancing feet. This was the gay, dependable, real world in which Voronovs could not exist.

She did not see Dolgorensky, who stood quite near. She did not know him. Indeed, someone else had brought him to the party. Like Nadia

Nikolaevna, Dolgorensky was smiling, but for a different reason. He was thinking how amusing it was that none of the others knew that soon they would all be his.

In the center of the room, Maria flashed round and round, leaning far back on Lopatkin's arm, laughing. People, perfume, voices and music flashed past. The bald head of the violinist appeared and disappeared like a bobbing, yellow globe as Maria whirled by. Everything merged into a mosaic of pleasure.

They went out on the balcony and looked at the city. It was quiet. Lights here and there hung in the night. New snow lay white, still untrodden. There was no sign of anything wrong. Then the cathedral bells of Peter and Paul chimed, "God Save the Tsar." It was midnight.

"I've never been so happy," said Maria.

"Promise me if you ever need something you'll tell me."

"All right."

"Promise!"

"Yes, I promise. Thank you, Vasya. But you see, when I was a child, I told myself exactly what life is, and now I find it's just as I thought. I need nothing, Vasya, not a thing. I have everything I could ever want. Isn't that wonderful and amazing, Vasya?"

"Yes," said Lopatkin without conviction. He had just discovered the canapé in his pocket.

"It must last forever," said Maria. "Will it, Vasya? Do you think it will last forever?"

Lopatkin smiled. "Forever and ever," he said.

XVIII

In the headquarters at Mohilev, in a large room, a man sat at a table piled high with papers. It was a long table. It was elegant. It was imposing. And before it, on foot, another man rooted nervously through the pile, and, speaking quickly and excitably, as if afraid he might not be allowed to finish, deferentially presented one exhibit after another for the other's perusal. Still and impassive, the other stared without response as if waiting to be convinced, as if weighing, judging, and comparing what he saw. And this encouraged the speaker, who eagerly pressed on, enthusiastic but restrained, persuasive but deferential.

He had good reason to be deferential. The man seated across the table was the Tsar of Astrakhan, King of Poland, Hereditary Lord and Master of the Provinces of Armenia and Circassia, Lord of Turkestan, Grand Duke of Finland, descendant of Peter and Catherine the Great and Defender of the Orthodox Church, master of almost two hundred million souls, Commander-in-Chief of the Russian Armies, Nicholas II, Tsar of all the Russias.

"Don't bother me," said the Tsar of all the Russias. "Please, please, don't bother me!"

He was a perfectly ordinary little man. Elsewhere, in other circumstances, he would not have been noticed. But he was here, now, and he was Tsar of all the Russias.

"But, Your Majesty," said the speaker with a tinge of exasperation which he angrily and fearfully hurried to suppress. He darted for another paper.

The Tsar of all the Russias took the bridge of the Imperial nose between thumb and forefinger, and sighed. It was so difficult, so annoying, so horribly exasperating, to be the Tsar of all the Russias, and at the moment to be as well Commander-in-Chief of the Russian Armies. No one else understood. No one else could. There was only one Tsar of all the Russias. There were so many questions, discussions, and calculations, so many people always pulling

133

at his sleeve, darting and springing at him hour after hour, biting, snapping, and yelping like terriers, demanding and pleading, pleading for the impossible: a decision. A decision was impossible because it would imply that the maker believed at least to some extent that it might lead to success, and the Tsar of all the Russias, unlike the others, unlike the relatively unsophisticated fellow before him now, had long since realized that success was impossible; that, faced with the hostile, terrifying, incomprehensible thing that is existence, life was impossible, even for a Tsar. Especially for a Tsar! He sighed, the prisoner of his own majesty. Why could no one else understand?

Of course, there were things in his strange prison he enjoyed, advantages, luxuries, things he deserved because he was himself, because he was Tsar of all the Russias. But, for the rest, the trick was to remain still, still as death, not to move, not even to wet one's lips, hoping that life — which had yellow teeth and bad breath — would pass by. All that really mattered was to look after one's comfort, to ensure that one had fresh linen, that the food was properly prepared, and that the servants were prompt — among other things. That was what was really important. If people were interested in his welfare, as they claimed, if they weren't just the grasping schemers he secretly knew they were, why didn't they put more effort into his linen? Why was it so difficult to get proper food? What else was the point of being Tsar of all the Russias?

With a fixed smile to show benign mastery, the Tsar of all the Russias now applied the tactic. It was necessary only to conserve himself until the other tired. Eventually, the painful voice would run down. But the other — whoever he was — did not tire. Endlessly his voice sprang on, sharp, penetrating, painful, relentless, grating against the Imperial skin, hurling hot, stinging darts of words fruitlessly but irritatingly at the Great Wall of China that was the Tsar's consciousness. Some, with greater charge and trajectory, lodged like burning sabers in his brain, disconnected and meaningless, incomprehensible. "Third Army . . . Eighth Army . . . Brusilov assures us . . . Rumania's entry into the war . . . . "

The Tsar of all the Russias brightened. Both Imperial eyebrows arched. Rumania! He was reminded of the only witticism he had ever been heard to utter: "Rumania isn't a nation; it's a profession." His smile widened. The remark had nicely retained its charm.

But his enjoyment had been a mistake. Somehow the voice had been encouraged. How stupid! It rose noticeably, compounding the pain. On and on it swept without pause. Papers appeared before him, were tapped, brandished, rustled, folded, were withdrawn and replaced by other papers. The annoyance of it, the irritation, the boredom! That was it: the boredom, the horrible, horrible boredom! Why must he be here at headquarters? Why

134

could he not be in his garden at Tsarskoe? Why had he taken the command, voluntarily subjected himself to all this boredom? Could not these schemers run the war themselves?

The face of the Grand Duke Nicholas Nikolaevitch appeared before him; Nicholas Nikolaevitch, the former Commander-in-Chief, whose popularity, whose competence, at least, had evoked in professional circles a satisfaction, an eminence, which rightly should go to the Tsar of all the Russias; an eminence which vaguely nibbled at the edges of his majesty. He was punctilious as a clerk on that particular subject. He had to be. Otherwise the schemers would destroy him. He had had to replace Nicholas Nikolaevitch.

Indeed, now he recalled the faint, distant bitterness he had felt long ago as a child, a last, fleeting sign of life indicating at least a mild dissatisfaction with the way the world was arranged. Now even the bitterness had gone, like cinders blown away by a breath. All that remained was the horrible boredom.

The memory nevertheless provoked him to act. He leaned forward, over the papers. Like a fly in a pot of jam, his will struggled tenuously toward the words. And the words lashed, bit and burned him. "Southwestern front . . . offensive . . . time most opportune . . . Brusilov insists . . . General Alexeiev . . . . " He studied the table. A forefinger stood erect on a map. Slowly, stealthily, it marched back and forth across the Bug, among the Carpathians, into the Hungarian plain, arching, curling, twisting, tapping. The finger rose. A fist descended and smote Rumania. The voice charged, bugling, irresistible. The fist smote Rumania again and disappeared. The finger returned. Now it was accompanied by another finger, on which was a fairly ornate ring. The fingers warily circled each other, charged, signalled and withdrew. What did it all mean? He struggled to understand but could not. He saw lines, circles, dots, and calculations, all meaningless. And the voice now spoke smoothly of batteries and rifles, of emplacements, divisions, corps, and armies.

And suddenly, as if through a chink, he caught a fleeting glimpse of the meaning. These marks, these circles and dots, these lines, were men, men exactly like himself, men kneeling, shooting, praying, marching, bleeding, and dying, men in bunkers, trenches, and mud holes, men watching, crawling, sitting, and waiting, every one of them waiting for him, for the decision of the Tsar of all the Russias.

The Tsar of all the Russias sighed. Singed and terrified, his tattered will sank again into its jampot. He fell back against his chair. The effort had been too much. The chink disappeared. All was again meaningless. Again he saw nothing but lines, circles, dots, and the inexorable forefinger. And still the sadistic voice charged on.

Some step must after all be taken. Even the Great Wall of China could not much longer withstand such a barrage. Mortar fell in chunks which broke. The bricks buckled. Through them he saw light. Something alien appeared in his mind and he regarded it warily, not knowing but that it might be still another affliction. Then he happily recognized what it was: an idea. He leaned forward and smiled.

"I don't say yes, and I don't say no," said the Commander-in-Chief. "Bring it up at the next meeting of the Council of War."

Rigid with suspense, Nicholas smiled vaguely, fearfully waiting in a trench of his own. Would that work? Was it enough? Yes, the forefinger hesitated and then withdrew. The map was whirled away like a tablecloth. Sated, at least temporarily, the voice receded, fired a parting salvo and was gone. Who had it been, actually? Some general? The Commander-in-Chief smiled, pleased with his tactics. He adjusted his uniform and went to the door.

Suddenly another voice was rushing up, higher than the other, even more unpleasant. Another fist came into view, another paper. More words: "A message from the front, Your Majesty. Urgent!"

Alert and wary, Nicholas bristled. The danger was clear. It was urgent, indeed! He acted — quickly, decisively.

"Later! Later!" he said.

He waved imperiously with just the right touch of annoyance. Voice, fist, and paper vanished. Still another tactical victory!

Just beyond the door, he heard whispers. He opened the door and it stopped. He stood for a moment on the sill, savoring the knowledge of his efficacy. Then, relieved and smiling after his ordeal, already enjoying his Imperial reward, the Tsar of all the Russias majestically sailed forth, like a stately ship, through the reverent sea of upturned faces.

XIX

Maria and her father sat playing chess. She pondered the board but could think of nothing. Her castles were gone and she was about to lose her queen — as usual.

"Papa, why is it that you are the only one I cannot beat?"

"That's easy. Because I taught you."

"Obviously you didn't teach me everything."

"Certainly not."

"Is that fair?"

"It is wise."

"I always beat Stepan. Then he refused to play."

"Yes."

"Did you teach him less than you did me?"

"No." He had her king in check. "Well, did you enjoy the party?"

"Yes, but I detest the people. Is that a contradiction?"

"Yes. Did you invite Telegin?"

"Certainly not. I am insulted that you ask. The culprit as usual was Natalia Stepanovna. And as usual mama was her dupe."

The door opened. It was the maid, face covered with outrage and contempt. Danilov knew immediately that Marina Nikitovna had arrived. Like many servants, the maid was stricter about class lines than her employer. She felt contempt for Marina Nikitovna. She was outraged that Danilov allowed her in the house, even through the servants' entrance, and that he gave her money she was using to destroy the Tsar. Whenever she came, the maid wore these opinions on her face. A man like her employer should know better!

"Your visitor is here, sir," said the maid briskly.

"Show her in," said Danilov and went to get the money.

The maid was not alone in her dislike. They had never discussed it — they could not — but she knew that Nadia Nikolaevna felt the same way.

Danilov had never mentioned it to his son. Maria knew about it, but she neither understood nor cared.

Danilov gave his money to the Party for a different reason than Orloff had for giving it his life. The president of Danilov Agricultural Machinery had not been forced into something shocking like his brother- in-law. He had not been ordered to shoot anyone down. He had not been shocked into feeling guilt. He had done nothing to feel guilty about. And he did not feel sorry for anyone. There was no need to. Everyone was as free as he to work. No, he contributed in the hope of personal advantage. He wanted more freedom for himself. In recent years the government had become more and more oppressive, bigger, more and more total. Bureaucrats had multiplied like germs in a wound. And the infection had touched everything private, seizing, regulating, complicating, prying. Every transaction included some bureaucrat's long nose. To do anything at all required written permission from some third assistant privy councillor at the end of a long hall. Indeed, the bureaucrats were currently using the war as their *raison d'être*, with the usual result that the war they said needed them so much was becoming increasingly more difficult to fight. Soldiers short of rifles waited in the woods until others who had them in nearby trenches were killed. There were shortages of other important equipment. And Danilov had found it more and more difficult to get raw material to fill the orders for that equipment to which he had devoted most of his production. It was criminal that he had to waste time getting papers signed by bureaucrats who didn't know what he was doing and didn't care, people he wouldn't have hired to wash a floor. It was so bad that it almost seemed planned, as if the inefficiency were sabotage and the confusion hid intent. Could the Germans have infiltrated the government? Was Rasputin a German agent as the rumor said? It would be so much better for Russia and for himself, Danilov thought, if a thorough change in the system were made, if the government were made as small as possible. Exactly what change he wanted, he did not know. But he wanted to run his life and business alone. It was not long ago that he had come from nowhere in Siberia, with nothing but the five fingers on each of his hands and the will to work.

He had heard that after the Revolution the government would "wither away."

He had not actually read Marx himself. He had picked up a volume once and tried; it had been too impossibly pedantic and boring. He could not find the science the revolutionists said they had found, which appealed to him as it did to Orloff. But the government *was* oppressive, as Marx said. As the Revolution said, it *should* wither away.

The maid returned with a dour expression and showed Marina

Nikitovna into the room. She had not changed. Her hair was drawn back in a tight bun, her lips were pressed together and she wore rimless glasses. As always, her clothes were worn. She was in good health, but still appeared ill.

Maria's eyes flickered with disdain. She extended a hand. "I am Maria Ivanovna Danilova."

Marina Nikitovna did not take it. "I know who you are."

"Is anything wrong?"

"Why do you ask?"

"You seem strangely nervous."

"Certainly not!" said Marina Nikitovna.

But Marina Nikitovna *was* strangely nervous. Everything was going well. Dolgorensky had told her that only the night before. The campaign to sabotage war production was a success. Even such necessaries as rifles were short. The war had become endless and could not be won. It was demoralizing Russia as they had hoped. And Marina Nikitovna had visited Danilov once a month for years, taking his money and treating him with veiled contempt, and very much enjoying herself.

But his daughter made her ill at ease. Perhaps it was simply that Maria was a woman, a reason Marina Nikitovna would never admit. Such bourgeois nonsense did not concern her. Yet, Maria's clothes were so painfully well cut. Why should that be, just because she was the daughter of an industrialist? Marina Nikitovna was not the daughter of an industrialist. Luckily she did not care. But her clothes were not well cut. And Maria was clearly a supercilious snob.

Marina Nikitovna became conscious of herself. Her mouth got dry. Her skin got hot. The mortifying realization that she was blushing overcame her, and she tried to stop, which only made it worse. She had been unable to compete with other women, convincing herself that she didn't want to — but she did. The realization made her angry. She wanted to hurt Maria, the cause.

"You are a member of the Imperial ballet," she said.

"Yes," said Maria.

Marina Nikitovna nodded. "A dancer. Of course."

"You find that amusing?"

"Yes."

"Why?"

"Don't you know? The time is coming when all must work. All! Such frivolity will be stamped out, like everything else without social value. All parasitism and exploitation will be erased, completely expunged, ripped out by the roots. There will be no mercy. There will be no compromise. Everyone will be called to account."

"You shouldn't puff like that," said Maria. "It makes you look like a toad."

Marina Nikitovna pretended not to be offended. But Maria's body shone with health. Marina Nikitovna's was an offense even to herself.

"You have always had everything you wanted," she said.

"Yes," said Maria. "I'm lucky."

"What you have is stolen. Don't you know that? Taken from the workers. And it must be returned."

"How stupid!" said Maria. "Do you really believe that?"

Marina Nikitovna smiled too warmly, her eyes gleamed much too much. "No," she said softly, "you are mistaken. Your father is the stupid one."

She resembled a small pile of old clothes. On top of it, her dark, narrow face bore a sheen, a sickly patina of yellow sweat.

"There will be no room for expropriators or parasites. All will be ripped out, trampled, erased. Do you think your father will escape?"

Maria shook with disbelief. "But my father gives you money!"

"He is trying to buy himself off with a few rubles. He is trying to buy insurance. But the Party does not sell insurance. The money is not even his to give. He is a silly, stupid fool."

With the back of her hand, Maria hit the smaller woman on the mouth. The mark of Maria's hand was on her face.

Marina Nikitovna chuckled weakly. "The funny thing is that when you tell your stupid father what I've said, he won't believe you."

Maria abruptly left the room. Marina Nikitovna was right; Danilov would refuse to believe her. He refused to believe ill of people. He would say Maria had misunderstood and would call her a child.

Her father was coming down the hall with the money. "What's the matter?" he said. "What happened?"

Maria shook her head. "Nothing."

He went in. Marina Nikitovna stood calmly by the table.

"What happened?" he said, studying the mark on her face.

"Stupid, really," said Marina Nikitovna. "I tripped over my own feet and fell. We were discussing the weather. That's what it was, I guess. It's spring."

As usual, Marina Nikitovna was obsequious, which annoyed him. He hated obsequiousness. Her manner reminded him somehow of Telegin's. You think you are better than I am, it said, but see how meaningless is your belief when I exaggerate it by fawning to the point of ridicule.

Marina Nikitovna knew he knew and thought all this, which encouraged her to behave even more the way she did. Both knew he could not mention it. She would innocently deny it.

"So clumsy, your honor," Marina Nikitovna said.

As usual, there was just too much emphasis in her tone. Danilov searched for something he could be sure of. But all these things were too vague, too indefinite. Danilov had a distaste for the indefinite. And he could not ask Masha again. She was just an inexperienced child.

"All right," he said. He gave Marina Nikitovna the money.

"Thank you, sir." She curtseyed slightly and walked out.

As soon as she had gone, Nadia Nikolaevna appeared. She had been supervising the removal of the double windows.

"I heard a noise," Nadia Nikolaevna said.

"Masha and that girl," said Danilov. "Perhaps I shouldn't have left them alone. Masha is just a child."

"She is woman enough to recognize trash. Why do you allow that horrid person in the house? Why give her money?"

"That is one of my favorite subjects: because of the bureaucracy, because of the war, because of what you see every day in the hospital, because the one thing Russia needs is less government. Forget the girl, Nadia. She is unimportant. Something is obviously wrong with her. Think instead of your sister and brother-in-law."

Nadia Nikolaevna flushed. "That's just it. I am."

But the subject was just too painful to discuss. She went to her daughter's room and found her reading.

"Tell me what happened, Masha," she demanded.

"Yes, mama. It's nothing. Marina was insolent. I slapped her."

Nadia Nikolaevna clapped her hands to her mouth. "So willful, so rude, Masha. You must apologize."

"No."

"Masha, why do you do such things? You will make yourself unfeminine! What will the young men think? What would Stepan say?" Nadia Nikolaevna smiled, pleased with her inspiration. "Yes, what would your heroic brother say?"

XX

"You bastard!" said Stepan Ivanovitch Danilov. "You deceitful, back-biting bastard!"

"But I couldn't help it, Stepan," said Belkin. "There was nothing I could do, believe me." Belkin's soft face trembled.

"I couldn't help it," Stepan mimicked. As if in answer, a finger of dust descended from the dugout ceiling and touched the back of Stepan's neck. "You bastard!"

"But Stepan . . . ."

"Oh, shut up." Stepan moved away in the narrow dugout, but the dusty finger followed as he knew it would. "And for this I crawled 500 yards through the wire for you. For this! I should have left you. The Austrians would have finished you off.

"But, no, you would have sat out the war in a plush prison camp. That would be just like you. While I was bleeding, you would have eaten Viennese cream."

Belkin's face trembled at the finale of what he had assumed to be their friendship. "But Stepan," he pleaded.

"All right!" said Stepan. "Stop whining. It's done."

"But he knew already, Stepan! He confronted me! I swear it! The dates, the amounts. He knew everything! It was someone else who told him. And you know he replaced me even before he called me in."

"Yes, that's true. Now Lopatkin is doing the accounts. Who was it, then? Was it Lopatkin?"

"I don't know."

They both fell silent. Stepan drummed on his boot. The smoky light rose and fell in the chilly draft. As usual, it was impossible to feel dry.

"You shouldn't have done it, Stepan," said Belkin. "You shouldn't have taken all that money."

142

"What's that?" Stepan got up quickly. "What?"

Belkin flushed and began to stammer. His chubby features twitched. Stepan's stocky figure was before him, wearing its habitual expression of angry petulance. Each knew and appreciated his part. In exchange for Belkin's submission, Stepan extended a tentative friendship. But Belkin suffered periodically from rebellion, which he sometimes could not suppress. And Stepan enjoyed this. He was curious. He enjoyed prodding Belkin, searching for his limits.

Stepan smiled with mock astonishment. "If you really thought that, you wouldn't have given me the money. You were doing the accounts. You should have refused. Why didn't you, if you are really my friend? You're the one responsible for this mess. Admit it!"

"But what's the point?" said a voice just outside.

"I don't know," said another.

A hand drew back the ragged flap and Crestin-Galkov, the new officer, entered, followed by Lopatkin and a cold gust of rain.

"What's the point of being in the Grand Duchess's Hussars if we have to muck about here in the trenches?" Crestin-Galkov asked them all. "It just doesn't make sense."

Lopatkin shrugged. "Someone has to hold the position."

"Of course," said Crestin-Galkov, "but why us? Why the Grand Duchess's Hussars? Doesn't the Russian Army have infantry? It doesn't make sense. Our mounts will lose their tone."

He spoke with puzzlement and at the same time with authority, as if arguing at a meeting of the general staff. His clothes were wet and he shivered and looked resentfully at his muddy boots.

Stepan smiled, his good humor partially restored. There was nothing he liked better than a discomfiting joke. "Not quite what you expected, is it? Nothing like the Champ de Mars."

Crestin-Galkov stiffened, stung. That was exactly what he had been thinking. It was nothing remotely like a colorful Imperial Review on the Champ de Mars in the spring — lances flashing, tunics spotless, boots polished, women shrieking. Here in the dugout, all that seemed unreal.

"Not at all," he said hastily, meaning to disagree.

"You learn quickly," grinned Stepan.

"Not at all. You misunderstand. Your remark is irrelevant." He sat on the bench and pointed at Stepan. "Improper disposition of forces. Waste of invaluable skill and training. Those are the crucial issues here."

Crestin-Galkov was a schoolteacher and most at ease when explaining something. But here at the front, he missed the attention and obedience that usually greeted his remarks. A volunteer of forty, he did not want to appear unsophisticated before these younger men, especially before Danilov, who would soon be decorated by the Tsar.

"I admire your zeal," Stepan said. "Of course, you'll get used to a lot worse before it's all over."

"Nothing to fear," Crestin-Galkov smiled smugly.

"What's worse, of course," said Stepan, "is the boredom. Worse even than the filth and bad rations. You've had a taste of that. Perhaps one of your brother officers will betray you. It happens all the time. Or you may simply be shot, like your predecessor."

"His predecessor took a bayonet," said Belkin.

Stepan snapped his fingers. "You're right. I forgot. Smack in the gut. That's where it hurts the most, you know."

Crestin-Galkov waved it away. "Worth it all if there's a chance for a Cross."

Stepan sneered. "Yes, of course. The Cross. Worth anything, isn't it, Belkin?"

"You'll soon have your chance, Yevgeny Andreievitch," said Belkin quickly. "Spring is here and the offensives will begin."

Crestin-Galkov waved with deprecation. "I am satisfied only with the chance to do my duty. I stand firm in spite of the rumors from the capital."

"It may not be as easy as you think," said Stepan.

"Oh? Difficult fellows are they, the Germans?" Crestin-Galkov drew back the flap and peered toward the river, just across which were the forward enemy positions. But nothing could be seen through the dark, heavy mist.

"Those aren't Germans, they're Austrians," said Stepan. "Didn't you know? Nothing but a crowd of pastries. Whipped cream soldiers filled with fudge. But this time, I assure you, you'll see the real thing."

"What's the point of all this talk?" said Lopatkin. "One isn't here to win a Cross. One's here because it's necessary and one does the best he can. That's all there is to it. The rest makes no sense."

"I disagree with you most emphatically, sir," Crestin-Galkov said, bristling. "Imperial recognition for valor. Most commendable. The soldier's purpose." He looked at Stepan for approval, but Stepan was staring intently at Lopatkin, trying to confirm his certainty that it was he who had exposed him. He saw nothing. Lopatkin was thinking that the war was not what he had expected. He had been in the dugout much longer than Crestin-Galkov.

"They say the Germans have wooden floors, electricity and women," Crestin-Galkov said wistfully.

"Quite true," Stepan said. "There you have a people that knows how to treat an officer. That's the way to conduct a war. Their food is shipped in from Berlin. They even have intermissions for sauerkraut. Did you know that?"

"No."

"Neither did I," Belkin said.

"While we are up to our bottoms in muck," Stepan said.

"He's joking," said Lopatkin. "Stepan loves jokes."

"Nevertheless," said Crestin-Galkov lamely. For once he did not know what to say. He could not make Stepan out. Every time he was about to do so, Stepan said something confusing. His conversation was characteristic of the general mood, but Crestin-Galkov did not expect it of a member of the Order of St. George.

The flap opened and Spassky, the colonel's adjutant, came in. He was in his middle twenties. A black patch covered an eye.

"Gentlemen," he said curtly. He turned to Crestin-Galkov. "Yevgeny Andreievitch, you're to report to the telephone officer."

"The telephone officer?" said Crestin-Galkov. "Why?" His face furrowed. Everything puzzled him.

"Never ask questions in the army," said Stepan. "You may get answers."

"At once," said Spassky mildly. "Orders."

"Of course," said Crestin-Galkov. "At once." He put on his cap, opened the flap and went out.

Spassky turned to Stepan, mouth tight with contempt. "And you're to report to Alexander Maximovitch in ten minutes." Spassky's nose quivered with disdain. He looked with reluctant curiosity at Belkin, who smiled nervously and got up to examine the lamp.

Stepan chuckled. "Ah, a lecture from the righteous."

Spassky turned to go. He drew back the flap, then changed his mind and took Lopatkin's hand.

"You're to be congratulated, Vasili Ignatievitch," he said. "Permit me to express my appreciation. Your discovery of the shortage, I need not tell you . . . ." Lopatkin was getting embarrassed but Spassky went on. He enjoyed emotion, and he was talking as much to Stepan as Lopatkin. He wanted Stepan to hear his words but could not bear to speak directly. "Luckily we still have the price of a pair of boots. You've saved the regiment from bankruptcy. One can be satisfied now that the accounts are in good hands."

"Please, Igor Sergeievitch," said Lopatkin. "Anyone given the accounts would have done the same. It was simply duty."

Spassky pressed Lopatkin's hand, feeling for him a kinship that offset his dislike of Lopatkin's absent-mindedness. "Yes," said Spassky. "Yes, of course."

Spassky drew back the flap, admitting a cloud of mist, and went out. The lamp faded and flared up. Belkin stood up ostentatiously and shook himself.

"I think I'll . . . ."

"No, no, stay," said Stepan, drawing him back to the bench. "Let's hear what else our proper gentleman has to say. He's a regular little archangel. Perhaps we can give him another chance to advance his career."

"You're so wrong, Stepan," Lopatkin said. "Do you think that's why I reported the shortage?"

"Certainly not!" Stepan chuckled. "Did I give that impression? You reported the shortage because you're an archangel. You had to. It *will* advance your career, but that is accidental."

"Why did you do it, Stepan? The regimental funds. Absent without leave papers. And you're a professional officer, not some draftee. Don't you realize what this will do to your family? I can't understand it."

"I can't understand it!" Stepan mimicked. He had always been a very good mimic. "I can't understand it! I simply can't! Of course you can't understand it, you ass. You're stuffed to the ears with goodness. You're an ass. I did it for a bit of fun, that's why!"

"His Majesty was to decorate you himself," said Lopatkin.

"Yes, isn't that funny? For saving *him*." Stepan stuck a finger in Belkin's face. "I went to all that trouble so that he wouldn't be replaced, and then our honored colonel replaces him anyway. The joke's on me, isn't it? You must laugh doing the accounts. You should. There's nothing better than a practical joke. Life itself is a practical joke. Did you know that? The St. George ribbon you're all jabbering about is just a rag. And 'His Majesty' is just a silly little man like you."

Belkin blushed and covered his face, mortified to hear that Stepan had saved him for that reason. Against all the evidence, he still insisted they were friends.

"You have ruined your career," Lopatkin said. "You're no better than the revolutionaries."

"Perhaps they have the right idea," said Stepan. "Shall I tell you something? You disgust me. Always mouthing these proverbs, this jabber; honor, duty, country, the reputation of the regiment, the conduct of an officer. Don't you know what a joke all that is? You remind me of my sister. Yes, you do. Everything so important, always so important. Mustn't do this, can't do that, shouldn't do thus and so. Imbecilic! Revolting! You're both spoiled rotten. You make me sick, the both of you."

146

"I enjoy the reference to Maria Ivanovna," said Lopatkin.

"Of course you do. You've probably been sleeping with her."

"I beg your pardon!" said Lopatkin. He jumped up, banging his head against the beam.

"Well, why not?" said Stepan. "That's what you're after, isn't it? We all are. Proceed at will; you have my brotherly blessing."

"Stepan Ivanovitch!" said Lopatkin. "Listen to me. I insist . . . ."

"You hear, Ilya?" Stepan chuckled. "Our archangel insists. Is that proper behavior for an archangel? Hmmmm . . . ."

But Belkin was now embarrassed as well as humiliated. He did not look up. "Your sister, Stepan," he said. "After all."

"You, too?" said Stepan. "Why, I *am* surprised. Do you know my sister, Ilya?"

"No," said Belkin. "But she is your sister."

"Yes, she is. Isn't that amusing? The baby of the family. Coddled. Spoiled. I can't understand how we could be so closely related. Perhaps one of you gentlemen could explain it to me. Surely it violates Mendel's laws!

"She is so dishonest, you see. She puts on airs. She hoists her nose. She won't admit she's rotten like the rest of us."

"She isn't," said Lopatkin.

Stepan ignored him. "Stupid, isn't it? Funny. Insulting. Easy when you have been spoiled. I'd like to see her up against it; alone, helpless, not spoiled at all, crawling blindly through the muck. It would do her good. After all, what's a brother for? I'd like to see the expression on her face."

Stepan took Lopatkin's arm. "Perhaps you could join her, Vasili Ignatievitch. Now you and I have a score to settle."

"It would be better for you, Stepan, if you tried to reform."

"No, Vasya, you are wrong. I am right, you will see. Trust me. Later you will agree. And I shall enjoy settling it so much."

"I am sorry for you," said Lopatkin.

"Of course you are. We have our score. You feel guilty. But after I settle it, you won't feel sorry any more. Not for me, at least. Remember this, Vasya. You will see."

"You yourself have forgotten too much."

Stepan went out of the dugout and walked along the trench toward the colonel's hut. As if at a signal, the mist turned to rain. Large, cold, penetrating drops churned up the mud like bullets. Stepan was soaked almost immediately, but not surprised. Indeed, in a perverse way, he enjoyed it. It confirmed his view of the universe. The purpose of the universe was to frustrate him; to ruin his plans and defeat his hopes, to deride, hurt and humiliate him. If Stepan tried a door, it would lock as he turned the knob. If he kicked the door — as he would — he would break his toe. Indeed, the universe had been created for that reason — not by God, but by a bald little man with a big head and narrow, hooded, Mongolian eyes. Or was the little man God, after all? If so, it was a good joke. Stepan saw him clearly now. As always, the bald little man was laughing.

It would be so good to shut his mouth, but Stepan could not. Indeed, the little man made all the rules, a violation of which brought a definite penalty. Stepan nevertheless broke them regularly, not because he expected success — he knew that was impossible — but simply as a challenge. As a demonstration that the little man was not supreme. Stepan's protest was a victory of a sort.

Yet, when the penalty inevitably arrived, Stepan was surprised, surprised and further infuriated as at a fresh insult. His resentment grew, feeding itself. And he hated reality even more.

Now he had to answer for his latest slap in reality's face. His boots sank in the mud. His feet were wet. As always, Stepan was surprised and indignant, angry at being subjected to this. But as always, there was not the slightest reason for surprise. A shortage had been discovered. He, through Belkin, had been found responsible, and now the colonel demanded an explanation. That was one of the little man's rules; and what could be more logical? It was almost like a law in physics describing the behavior of a particular type of matter: If you embezzle money, someone asks questions. Yet Stepan felt the usual resentment. There was no need for the lecture he now had to hear. It would make the colonel feel good and that was all. Only a few thousand rubles were involved. Why all the fuss? No one ever gave Stepan a chance. The little man wanted to humiliate him even more.

Stepan remembered crawling through the wire. That was the biggest joke of all. He had dragged Belkin back to the trench to prevent his replacement as clerk by someone who would discover the shortage — and later discovered that the colonel already knew. And now Stepan would lose the medal he had won. Perhaps he would be expelled from the army. The little man was rubbing Stepan's nose in the mess, as if he were a disobedient puppy.

What would he say? Why had he taken the money and gone to Warsaw? Why had he gone without leave papers? There was the boredom, of course. The hideous, suffocating, unbearable boredom. Others had gone mad. But no, that explanation was no good. The colonel had not taken any money and had not gone mad. Stepan sneered. He knew what to expect. Already he could see the colonel before him, slow, stiff, immovable. Stuffed with honor, duty, and loyalty. Reeking with the "reputation of the regiment," soon to be tarnished.

148

It reminded Stepan of his father. Why must there be this hypocrisy and pretense? Why must there be this nonsensical talk? Everyone knew what everyone wanted. Why would no one else admit it?

The word "loan" vaguely came to mind. Yes, that was it! The colonel had misunderstood. It was unthinkable that Stepan would steal the regimental funds. He had simply borrowed the money and meant to replace it. It would have been replaced with no one the wiser had it not just then been discovered. In fact, Stepan would replace it now. Yes, that was it! That and the necessity of asking for the colonel's mercy. Stepan stopped, revolted, and then brightened. Perhaps he would be successful and outsmart the grinning little man this time.

Inside the hut, Alexander Maximovitch Borishevsky, colonel of the line, hero of Mukden and member of the Order of St. George, sat at a table stacked with military odds and ends. Spassky bent over him. Both studied a sheet of paper.

Borishevsky shook his head. "It's a disgrace. A disgrace."

"Indeed it is, Alexander Maximovitch," said Spassky. "How could it have happened . . . ?"

Borishevsky picked up the paper and read aloud, " 'Peace without contributions or annexations,' " then threw the paper down. "Damned agitators! How the devil did that get among the men?"

"I don't know, your excellency," Spassky said.

"Not that it could do any damage here. Not *my* men. Still . . . ." He tapped the paper. "You're still looking for the man?"

"Everywhere, your excellency. Don't worry, he'll be found."

"What do they hope to achieve, these fools with their pieces of paper and printing presses? What's the point?" Borishevsky massaged his temples. He had a headache. He was tired. "A thing like this comes at the worst time, what with the men bored, morale at a low ebb. I must admit . . . ." Borishevsky turned to the younger man. "Yes, I myself feel some sympathy for this language. Does that shock you? It does, I see."

Spassky turned away embarrassed. "I must confess, your excellency . . . ."

"Think," said Borishevsky. "Remember the lesson of Mukden. Of course you were still a schoolboy then, but surely you discussed it in tactics. And what was this lesson of Mukden? Do you remember? Trench warfare was a serious mistake. All agreed. And now, of course, here we are again in the trenches. In the trenches — and without boots, shells and rifles. And I'm expected to send unarmed men against the Austrians. Unarmed men, Spassky. No, this is not war. This is a scandal. This is duckshooting." Borishevsky thought angrily of his men. "Like ducks in a barrel on a fairground.

"And there's no need to search for the cause." Like all other line officers, he knew who was to blame. "Staff college careerists!" He said it like a curse. To them the regiment — each man — was nothing but a number on a slip of paper. What could they know of the war from behind their desks, far away?

"True, your excellency, true," said Spassky, wincing at the inescapable truth of what had been said. "Still, supplies are arriving. And, in spite of everything, there are the Germans. If necessary, we must fight with rocks."

Borishevsky snorted. "The Germans. Yes. We're *surrounded* by Germans. The Empress is a German. One wonders who the enemy really is."

Spassky went white. "Pardon me, your excellency."

Borishevsky became severe. "Yes, yes. All right."

Sometimes Borishevsky found Spassky annoying, as he did now. He was so moralistic and easily outraged. He had so little experience and understanding. He did not know life. He was so naive. He reminded Borishevsky of himself as a youth. How thick, how stupid he had been. The younger man would have to learn how wrong he was, besides which, Borishevsky wanted to tell someone what he thought, and there are few to whom the commander of a regiment can speak plainly. He felt a surge of affection for the younger man, which manifested itself, in masculine fashion, in brusque raillery.

"All right," said Borishevsky. Again he picked up the sheet of propaganda. "Where did you find this, by the way?"

"Prokurov, excellency. He had collected a handful and was about to . . . about to . . . ."

Borishevsky chuckled. "Best use in the world for them. Trust Prokurov. Orderly!" he shouted. "Orderly! Where the devil . . . ?"

A huge form thrust itself officiously into the hut. Completely bald and with a large mustache, the man was so big that he could not stand erect under the low roof. Hunching over like a headwaiter, head shining in the light, he saluted Borishevsky with a flourish.

"Prokurov, your honor," he boomed. "Reporting for duty drunk."

"Drunk, is it?" said Borishevsky. "Hm. Grounds for court martial."

"Justly so, your honor," Prokurov boomed.

"Unfortunate," said Borishevsky. "You'll probably be shot."

"Justly so, your honor," Prokurov bellowed. "To be expected." Prokurov wore an expression of approval, as if they were speaking of someone else, someone whose inexcusable behavior he disdained, and in whose punishment he would eagerly collaborate.

150

"Adjutant," said Borishevsky in a judicial tone. "Draw up orders for court martial. To be forwarded at once to division."

Spassky sighed and began to scratch the matter out on a piece of paper. Borishevsky sat sternly at his table. Satisfied, but still indignant, Prokurov stood hunched before him. Both enjoyed the business enormously. They always did. Prokurov had started it, Borishevsky could not remember how. It was necessary to Prokurov's strict sense of decorum. To Prokurov, the expectation of imminent death was less intolerable than that either man might not behave as he should. But both did behave as they should, with the easy authority of experienced repertory actors in a familiar scene.

Spassky sighed again, making his disapproval plain. As usual, Borishevsky looked at him with reproach. Spassky was too young to have a sense of humor. He was always too serious.

But Spassky believed the farce was dangerous to the dignity of this man he idolized. Why did Borishevsky participate in it? He and Prokurov had been together for twenty years. There was no chance at all that he would permit Prokurov to be executed. He and Prokurov were playing with the regulations. Indeed, seventeen identical demands for Prokurov's execution were mouldering in the table drawer.

With the usual success the farce ended, to the satisfaction of the principals. Spassky filed the paper on top of its seventeen predecessors. Borishevsky again picked up the sheet of propaganda.

"Prokurov. This paper, where did you get it? How did it come into the camp?"

Prokurov knew everything and could find anything. He lowered his head to the document and beamed.

"Ah, yes, your honor. A small gentleman was kind enough to distribute them. A new service from the center, no doubt, and very practical indeed, if I may say so. It isn't easy to find proper paper. But, look, your honor, folded in half this just fits the palm of the hand." He laughed.

"A small gentleman?" Borishevsky asked.

"Indeed, your honor. A small gentleman with a big nose."

"And is this small gentleman still anywhere about?"

"Indeed, your honor, the little *barin* is somewhere among the men, distributing the papers and encouraging them. Most thoughtful on the part of the center, if I may say so."

Borishevsky grinned wryly. "Most thoughtful indeed. Find him, Prokurov. Bring him here."

"At once, your honor!" Prokurov bellowed. "You will want to congratulate him." He turned to go and then came back. "I have the honor to announce a duck for your honor's pleasure."

"You found a duck here, Prokurov? How?"

The bald, shining head shook slowly in mild reproof. Prokurov laid a finger along his nose. "Trust Prokurov," he whispered.

His eye fell on the sheet of propaganda. He brightened. "The little gentleman is right, if I may say so. We have no need of Contributions. It's hot enough to roast the devil and so far away. I'm told they even torture Christians."

"What's that, Prokurov? What do you mean?" said Borishevsky. He and Spassky exchanged puzzled looks.

"Contributions, your honor," Prokurov said. "The city of Contributions. That's what the gentleman said we're fighting for."

"St. Nicholas!" said Borishevsky. "That's Constantinople, you devil. Constantinople, the capitol of Turkey. It has nothing at all to do with contributions."

"Ah," said Prokurov. "Constantinople. I see. Where then, your honor, if I may inquire, is Annexations?"

"Get out, you devil!" Borishevsky roared.

"At once, your honor!" Prokurov bellowed, and left.

"That devil Prokurov," said Borishevsky. "Sometimes I regret having taught him to read."

Spassky was about to reply and then stiffened. Someone else had come in the door and snapped to attention at the table.

"Danilov, excellency," said Stepan, saluting smartly. "Reporting as ordered."

"Danilov, yes," said Borishevsky wryly. He looked up and then away quickly, and then looked through his papers until Spassky placed the proper ones before him. "Danilov," Borishevsky said again. Once again, he was in a bad mood. Prokurov had diverted him temporarily from the annoying discovery that an agitator was loose among the men. But the Danilov matter was even more annoying. Borishevsky looked at Stepan with irritation and surprise. Like Prokurov, he demanded that people behave as they should. When they did not, he turned away with distaste, as from an embarrassing accident which should not be discussed. He wanted to do so now, but of course he could not. The agitator at least was an avowed enemy, like the Germans, but this problem concerned an officer in Borishevsky's regiment. Borishevsky rustled the papers too much. He felt humiliated. How stupidly like Spassky he himself still was.

"There's no point in small talk, Stepan Ivanovitch," he said. "We're concerned here with an embezzlement of regimental funds. There is also the matter of the leave papers. Less important, but still very serious in itself."

"With your permission, your excellency," Stepan said softly. "I prefer to think of the money as a loan."

"A loan?" said Borishevsky angrily. "What sort of loan?"

"Perhaps I was fooling myself," said Stepan. "It was stupid, I know. The worst possible judgment." Spassky's face was a mask of indignation. What a pleasure it would be to smash it. "I meant to repay the money, of course," said Stepan. "I still do."

"You will replace it. To be sure."

" 'The shortage will never be discovered,' Belkin said. 'Take it,' he told me. 'No one will ever know.' I believed him. I was stupid. There is absolutely no excuse."

Borishevsky's voice softened. "Why did you save Belkin?"

Stepan shrugged. "He is my friend."

Borishevsky shook his head. "Still, I cannot understand why. Embezzlement of regimental funds. Forgery of leave papers. An officer of the Imperial Russian Army. Why?"

How characteristically stupid, Stepan thought. He had done it because he wanted to. Wasn't that obvious?

"And a Danilov, too," Borishevsky said. "It's incomprehensible. I know your father well."

"Yes," said Stepan dully, annoyed. There could be no doubt what his father would say.

"And as you know, his brother-in-law — your uncle Orloff — and I were at the academy together."

"Yes," said Stepan. "I remember him only vaguely."

"My closest friend," said Borishevsky. "Tragic. Another example of wasted youth. Unfortunate for him and for the family."

"Yes."

"How is Peter Sergeievitch? Do you know?"

"No, excellency. I am sorry I don't." Stepan felt a growing confidence. The conversation was clearly going his way. "Perhaps I could find out, if you like."

Borishevsky was extremely uncomfortable. He wanted to believe what Stepan said. It would be difficult to do, but he wanted to excuse him. Perhaps his crimes had just been pranks after all. Borishevsky himself had committed his share.

"All right," he said brusquely. "Let's not lose the thread." He looked through his papers. "The sum in question is . . ." Spassky put his finger under the right figure. "You owe the regiment eight thousand rubles. Eight thousand rubles! The two of you must have lived like Tartars. What the devil did you do in Warsaw?

"Let's see, it took you two weeks to spend it, so you and Belkin have two weeks to replace it. This time, of course, you'll have proper leave papers. I hope you will succeed. Spassky has already drawn up the orders for court martial. Here they are. They need only my signature and they will be forwarded to division if you do not return in two weeks with the money. Do you understand, Stepan Ivanovitch?"

Stepan covered his face to conceal the smirk he could not suppress. "Perfectly, excellency. I am overcome."

"As for your decoration . . . ."

Stepan shook his head. "I understand that, too. It's lost. I'm glad. It would be wrong."

Borishevsky felt the same. Danilov did not deserve membership in the Order of St. George. As a member himself, Borishevsky recoiled. But too many arrangements had already been made. The Cross was to be presented at an Imperial review. Borishevsky wished he had known earlier that it was Stepan who had taken the money. But he had not known. If he acted now, there would be an investigation, there would be a scandal. The Tsar himself might be displeased. His displeasure would touch the regiment and its commander. Borishevsky's enemies at staff would question his judgment. His promotion to general would be delayed.

Also, it had been some time since one of his men had won a Cross. The Cross would set them an example. The Imperial review would be inspiring. It would be good for the regiment, for morale. And Stepan seemed sufficiently chastened. He had learned. He would replace the money. His crime would be erased. There was no need to bring more grief to his family.

"Nonsense," said Borishevsky. "The Cross is yours. When you return with the money, we'll say no more about it."

Borishevsky could feel Spassky stiffen at his side.

"I'm overcome," said Stepan. "I don't know what to say. I don't deserve your generosity."

"All right," said Borishevsky. "Dismissed."

Stepan saluted smartly and was gone. Borishevsky bent again to his papers, hoping Spassky's indignation would disappear.

But Spassky could not contain himself. "It's a disgrace, excellency!" he burst out, frightened by his own manner. "A disgrace! An insult to the regiment and to you. Excellency — please. Reconsider. This man is to be decorated by the Emperor himself. To conceal his crime is to participate in it.

154

It's scandalous. It's a deliberate deception and degradation of His Majesty . . . . "

Spassky suddenly interrupted himself. He went white, then snapped to attention. "I am insubordinate, excellency. That is inexcusable too. Please place me under arrest."

Borishevsky suppressed a smile. "Consider, Igor," he began. "Which would make the greater scandal: to suppress the incident or to advertise it? Which would most damage the regiment and embarrass the Emperor? Advertisement is the answer. The Emperor plans to inspect us and would have to cancel those plans.

"Now as to the crime itself. Serious, true, but not irrevocable. The damage can be undone. The money can be repaid. It will be. And consider the circumstances. They are no excuse, but it is easy to understand that after being planted here for useless months, particularly at the height of one's youth . . . . You're too serious, Igor, far too serious. Many others might have done the same.

"And consider the last and most important argument. The act for which he is to be decorated was actually performed, was it not? Stepan Ivanovitch did in fact bring Belkin back to our lines under heavy fire. And that is why he is being given the Cross."

Spassky said nothing. He was not satisfied but could think of nothing to say.

"Why ruin him?" said Borishevsky, as if to himself. "He'll replace the money and the experience will be a lesson. His career will be saved. There is much good in Stepan Ivanovitch."

Borishevsky went to the door and looked out. He thought again of Orloff, his old friend. There was another life irrevocably ruined, ruined in this case because of its virtues — however misguided — which only made it worse. The shooting at the Winter Palace had been a horror, yes. But it had been provoked by the revolutionaries. Orloff should not have ruined his career over it. Where was he now? Would they ever meet again? Borishevsky felt a twinge of hopeless regret, the same thing he felt for the present. Everywhere there was an atmosphere of slackness and disintegration. Not just the usual tedium of the endless winter stalemate, but something else, something more, something physically oppressive which he tried to throw off. It was spring, supplies were arriving, and soon the offensives would begin. He looked forward to them. Perhaps they were the remedy. But as if mocking him, the feeling intensified. He could not shake it loose.

Stepan, however, had never felt better. He had staged an absolutely brilliant coup. Just the right combination of upright youth misguided by its own enthusiasm, and apologetic submission to the colonel's will. Altogether a success. Stepan felt a surge of confidence and health.

As if in agreement and approval, the sky began to clear. The rain stopped. It would be a pleasant night. Stepan thought of Borishevsky and his adjutant. It had been too easy. They were so much alike. Such people always failed, stifled by their hypocrisy. They were weaklings hiding behind meaningless ideas, no match for a man with a clear view of reality. And Stepan was such a man. Stepan Danilov knew what he wanted. Slowly he climbed the hill toward the big tree, his sense of well-being entirely restored. The moon came out, cold and clear, like a large pearl on a velvet cloth. It reminded him of his Cross. Even the Cross had been saved. And soon the spring offensives would begin. He looked forward to them. Stepan was not a coward.

Of course there was the matter of the eight thousand rubles. A large sum. A new problem. But Stepan did not allow it to upset him. He never thought very far ahead. As always, the mere fact that he wanted them was proof that the eight thousand rubles would come. Perhaps he could wangle them from his father; he, too, was like Borishevsky. Or from his mother; she had never been able to refuse him anything. He felt a certain warmth for her, mixed with pity. And there were other possibilities. Telegin, for instance. His mother had recently written that Telegin had developed a passion for his sister. Stepan smiled at the thought of Telegin's pudgy features, his shapeless body, his thick fingers. How terribly, terribly droll.

Stepan Ivanovitch laughed out loud. He had realized for the first time that his misdemeanor had earned him two weeks' leave. He thought again with contempt of Borishevsky, who lacked the courage of his beliefs. He, Stepan, better deserved the colonel's epaulets. Had he been colonel, he would have had a thief shot.

As he was walking through the trees, he saw the dark figures of several men. From beyond them came a voice, an agitated voice, high, sharp, speaking very quickly.

"Why do you fight the Germans?" the voice was saying. "Why? Tell me. Why do you freeze and die?"

"It's the will of the Little Father," said another.

"Yes," said others. "Sure. Why else?"

"They told me I was definitely going to be shot," said a gravelly voice, "either at home by them, or here by the Germans. So here I am. And they were right. The Germans shot me. Here. Look. Look at this leg."

"If only we had decent boots," said another.

"Comrades!" shouted the nervous voice. Over the heads and shoulders of the men before him, Stepan saw two small, raised fists. "The Germans are not your enemies — but your brothers!"

"Our brothers?" the men murmured. "The Germans? That's crazy."

"Think, comrades," said the voice. "Before you ever came here, at home in your villages, what did you have against the Germans? Were you angry with them? Had a German ever done anything to you? Who among you had ever seen a German?"

"It's true," the men buzzed. "I'd never laid eyes on one."

"I still haven't seen one," said a boy.

"Were they angry with you?" asked the voice. "Had they any reason? Had any of you ever done anything to a German?"

"No. No. That's a fact."

The fists shot up. "Well then, comrades. Why are you here?"

"We don't know!" the men shouted. "Tell us. Why?"

"It's the will of the Little Father," someone said again.

"Bloody Nicholas is what he is!" the gravelly voice barked.

"Comrades!" The voice rose to a crescendo. "You are here because of the expropriators. Because of the exploiters."

"What? Who?" said the men, confused. "Exploitators?"

"And who might they be?" said the gravelly voice. "Just put their necks between my mitts."

"I know them," said an old man. "They're a regiment of Turks."

The voice fell. Now it was soft. "Comrades," it said patiently, "the exploiters are the Capitalists. The exploiters are the greedy Petrograd industrialists. The exploiters are the fat businessmen of Moscow. In collusion with their German partners, they decided to make more business by ordering their lackeys, Willy and Nicholas, to start a war. To make more rubles and marks from your flesh and blood.

"Comrades, the German people are not your enemies. Your enemies are their masters, the German industrialists. Your enemies are our own masters, the Russian industrialists. While you are freezing here in the trenches with your bottoms caked with mud, your enemies are sitting in the Nevsky surrounded by tarts, their faces full of whipped cream paid for with your blood."

"It's true!" said indignant voices. "They're laughing at us. The Germans are suffering just as much as we are."

"Comrades!" the voice shouted. "You've been duped!"

"Here, what's all this?" Stepan bellowed from the dark. "What's going on here?" He shoved the men aside and pushed roughly to the front. All was suddenly silent under the trees. The only sound was the spent rain dripping from the leaves. No one moved. It was as if all had vanished or were suspended. And facing Stepan in a small patch of light was Kolodsky. But Stepan had never met him. He had visited his father's factory only twice.

Kolodsky slowly extended his nose, and Stepan stared at it, too puzzled to think. It was red and blue and veiny. It did a little dance, gesticulating at him. And Kolodsky's little eyes peered at Stepan around it. It was as if the nose had past and future, wife, children, and a will of its own, as if Kolodsky were an unimportant excrescence upon it. He crouched, alert and nervous like a setter on the point, staring at Stepan, trying to see. But he could not see. Like the others, Stepan was in the shadows. To Kolodsky he was just a voice.

Then Kolodsky turned and was gone at once in the darkness and the trees. The spell was broken. Stepan came alive. He stepped forward, but the muddy ground was treacherous underfoot. He slipped and fell against a tree trunk. The men milled about, nervous and confused, and he grabbed the nearest and shoved them roughly.

"Here! You!" he said. "Go after him. Catch that man. Bring him back." The men moved off, muttering and reluctant.

Stepan pushed another man. "Go after him!" he yelled.

But this man did not move. Indeed, his body did not yield. It was as if Stepan had pushed a tree.

"I said go after him!" Stepan yelled.

Still the man did not move. It was as if Stepan did not exist. He peered at him through the darkness but could not see. He raised his arm, about to strike. He was a tall man, tall and lean with a hatchet face, pale as ice in the white light. Stepan squinted up into his eyes. Cold and bright, they held neither fear nor anger, neither curiosity nor explanation. They were completely expressionless. They were the eyes of Michael Voronov.

After his escape, Michael had slowly made his way back to Russia. With the outbreak of the war, he had sought out the Russian army and the front. It had not been long before he came across the frozen body of a fallen Russian soldier, formerly a peasant. Michael had taken the corpse's uniform and papers, assuming the dead man's place in the battle. He liked the army; it was a good place to hide. And above all, he liked the war. It made sense. So little else made sense anymore.

He, too, had been watching Kolodsky from the shadows. He had not seen Kolodsky since the incident in Petrograd that had caused his own arrest. Watching him now aroused painful memories. But he felt no anger for Kolodsky. After all, Kolodsky had not caused it. Yet Michael remained in the shadows, and it had not suited Kolodsky to expose him. They had just exchanged quick glances of recognition.

158

Stepan slowly lowered his arm, which instantly made him angry. "Name?" he said shortly.

"Marchenko," said Michael.

Stepan's mouth pursed with annoyance, which he realized with exasperation was visible. "Marchenko, your honor," Stepan snapped.

Michael smiled, coldly. "You are mistaken," he said. "I am not an officer."

Stepan snorted. The man had deliberately misunderstood. Stepan looked again into the cold eyes. "The reason is obvious, comrade Marchenko," he said. Stepan smiled and turned away, unsuccessfully trying to ignore the fact that his sarcasm was unsatisfying.

"Well then, you devils!" he shouted at the men. "Back to your posts! Is this how you repay His Majesty for the chance to defend him? Have you nothing better to do than entertain a filthy agitator? Have you no loyalty? Have you no honor?"

XXI

"Masha, look!" said Tata. "Look at this shoe. Shreds! Just four days and nothing but shreds!" She held out a torn toe shoe. "Look! Disgusting!"

Maria turned it over. "Yes. It's finished."

"It's dead," said Tata. "I don't finish a shoe. I kill it. Ugh! Disgusting! So unfeminine! Can it be me, do you think? My feet?" Tata examined her feet. "No, nothing unusual. No."

"It proves you are working hard," said Maria.

"Disgusting! Ugh! Hideous!"

"I'm so hungry," said Maria. "Aren't you?"

"Let's go to the Wandering Dog."

"No. Come home with me, why don't you?"

"All right. Your parents will be pleased with your good luck."

Maria started. Vera Crispina stood before her, fighting back tears. Her lips parted. She tried to speak. "I wanted that part," she said at last. "You knew how much I wanted it."

"Yes, Vera Karpovna," said Maria. "So did I."

"It's easy for you," said Crispina. "You've always had everything you ever wanted."

"So what?" Tata said.

"But Vera Karpovna," said Maria, "you know I did not cheat. I *earned* the part."

"That has nothing to do with it," said Vera Karpovna. "It's that you've always had everything, even in school. Favors from the headmistress. Forgiveness for misbehavior. Presents from home. Always. You've never had to struggle for anything. You don't know what it means. You've never suffered. You've never gone without . . . ."

"Stop it," cried Tata mockingly. "Please, I'm going to cry."

"You may laugh if you wish, but this does not concern you, Tatiana Petrovna," said Crispina. "You're as empty-headed as she is spoiled." She pointed at Maria. "Things will change. Some day you will be alone. You cannot always depend on your father."

Crispina hoisted her chin and walked out.

"Ugh!" said Tata. "Disgusting!"

"But why does she act this way?"

"Because women are so childish. So petty. Vasya is right, you know — we *are* devious. Men don't behave like Crispina. They make beautiful speeches in adorable tight breeches about poetry and honor. And then they kill each other cleanly through the gut. Men don't act; they *know* who their enemies are. But women — women are scheming, deceitful creatures. We're betrayers, that's what we are. Betrayers."

"The marvel is that she's so unfair."

"Pity her, Masha. She isn't responsible for what she says. She's annoyed that she can't do thirty-two *fouettés* as easily as you. Besides, her father was a convict escaped from Akatui. He helped himself to her mother one night in a field and forgot to leave his name."

"Ugh!" said Maria. "Disgusting!"

"There! You see? I'm being disgusting," said Tata. "Now I'm playing the woman. So are you. We can't help it, Masha. We can't be blamed. It's the glands, according to the professors. Try it, Masha! Try it! Give in!"

"Ugh! Disgusting!"

"Face it, Masha. Don't be childish. You're not disgusting enough to be feminine. Men will think you strange. Besides which, you have no choice. It's glands. Destiny!"

They left the building and walked past its yellow facade and down Theatre Street. The sun flashed on the three bronze horses atop the Alexander Theatre.

"I suppose it's best to ignore her," Maria sighed.

"Ignore whom?"

"But somehow I can't. I'm afraid of her. She frightens me. There's an air about Crispina that's, well, almost brutal. And why should I know about suffering? Why should anyone? There can't be any value in it. If there were, it wouldn't be suffering."

"They say it's very rewarding," said Tata. "Builds character, if you do it right. You're not supposed to complain too much. Cyrano, for instance. He suffers beautifully."

"I couldn't bear it. I'd die."

"If you hate it so much, why do you torture poor Vasya?" Tata laughed.

"I don't torture him. He does it to himself."

"By the way, have you heard from him lately?"

"I've just received a letter. He says that he and Stepan get on very well."

"They would, of course. They're both so idealistic. I've had a letter from Stepan. He's been given two weeks' leave."

"I didn't know." Maria brightened at the possibility of seeing her brother again.

"Yes," said Tata. "He says he's deserting his command of the Southwestern front because he can't go on without another sight of me. You see? Aren't they wonderful, the darlings?"

"Ugh! Disgusting!" Maria said.

XXII

Ivan Danilov looked at his son with unpleasant emotions. He did not like his son. He could have phrased that differently, he knew, but that was what he would have meant. He simply did not like him. Had they not been related, he would have avoided Stepan. He wanted to avoid him now. But he could not. Blood alone kept them together.

"What is the attitude of the men?" he asked. "Is their morale good?" This was something Danilov really wanted to know. But it was also a neutral subject, which was comfortable. He did not like to discuss personal things with Stepan.

Stepan, as always, felt the tension too. His father really was serious about the war. He really believed it was some sort of "cause." Or was it, as the agitator had said, that his father was making lots of money?

"Ready for anything," Stepan said. "We've been short of supplies, of course, which is discouraging. But a Russian soldier will fight bare-handed. You will see in a few weeks when we cross the Carpathians. We'll make dessert of those chocolate soldiers."

"Yes, yes," Danilov said shortly. As always, Stepan's cavalier attitude annoyed him. "What shortages are there?" he asked.

"Boots and rifles, among other things. We can't run and we can't shoot. They say you industrialists are making a fortune."

"Do they?"

"Yes. Are you?"

"What do you tell them, Stepan?"

"I always tell them I hope it's true."

Danilov frowned. "I'll look into the matter again. Perhaps it's simple German sabotage. What does Alexander Maximovitch say?"

"He doesn't say anything, to my knowledge."

"Is he well?"

"Yes."

"That is good."

"Yes. Our colonel is one of my favorite people."

Was there a note of sarcasm in his tone? Danilov could not be sure — which annoyed him.

"It's easy to see why," said Danilov. "I'm told two-week leaves are scarce even for members of the Order of St. George."

Stepan chuckled. "Yes. Aren't they."

There was a long silence. Danilov tapped on the desk. It was getting dark, and he reluctantly turned up the light. He breathed deeply. The mild air smelled pleasantly of spring. Stepan stirred and they looked at each other.

"This question of the money," said Danilov.

"Oh," said Stepan. "Then mother mentioned it?"

"She did. After all, eight thousand rubles is a large sum."

"I'm sorry. I wanted to avoid bothering you."

"What, actually, is the money for?"

Stepan rose and chuckled again. "This is why I didn't come to you. It's embarrassing, you see. A gambling debt. That's the painfully honest truth. Stupid, I know, but there it is. There isn't much else to do out there. You can't imagine how tedious and boring it is. Not what the women think it is at all. Most of it is just waiting. Waiting and cards."

"Yet many do not pile up eight thousand ruble debts."

Stepan chuckled. "They are luckier."

"And to whom do you owe it?"

"To Belkin. That's why he's here. He has an amazing talent for cards."

"Does he?" said Danilov. "Belkin. I see."

"It's a debt of honor," Stepan said.

"Perhaps you should have embezzled it. Then it wouldn't be a debt of honor. There'd be no need to pay it back. Honor is the determinant here, don't you agree?"

Stepan was even more alert. The remark was covertly sarcastic — so unlike his father.

"What do you mean?" Stepan asked, suspiciously.

"Only what I said. What do *you* mean?" Danilov smiled. There was a vindictive pleasure in using Stepan's own tactics against him.

"You know, don't you?" Stepan said.

"Know what? What do you think I know?"

"Who told you?"

"I don't understand."

"It was Belkin, wasn't it? Belkin again."

"Tell me what I'm supposed to understand. Say it."

"All right! I'll say it. I took the money. I took the money. I took the money. That's what you want to hear, isn't it?"

"Yes."

"Did Belkin also say the money was a loan?"

"A loan? No. The word was not used."

"So it was Belkin. Of course. He is scheming against me. Trying to divide father and son. I suppose he didn't tell you that he persuaded me to take the money?"

"And the leave papers?"

"There is no point in having money in a trench."

Resentment was boiling beneath Stepan's thin skin. Why must he undergo this interrogation — and pretend to like it? Was it worth a lousy eight thousand rubles?

"No, there isn't," said Danilov. He shook his head. "I'm sorry. You have a problem."

"Yes. I do. I made a stupid mistake."

"I can't imagine how you're going to solve it."

Shock appeared on Stepan's face. "But surely you're going to give me the money. It would be a loan. I would pay it back in time. You're my father. I need your help."

"What you need is eight thousand rubles."

"Please."

Stepan stared at his father, at the deep creases descending from the corners of his mouth, the high cheekbones, the hard eyes. It was his own face. The same and yet not the same. As if Stepan were a bad imitation made from a faulty mold. The purpose on Danilov's face was petulance on Stepan's.

Appraising and pitiless, the eyes looked at Stepan now.

"No," said Danilov.

"But you're my father," said Stepan. "You cannot refuse me."

"I am your father, yes. That is what puzzles me. But I can and do refuse you. About that I have no doubt."

"But my commission's at stake, my decoration, my career."

"You should have spent more time at the plant," said Danilov. "Perhaps you would understand. For instance, I insert a pulley here and produce a result there. I raise this gear and lower that piston. That causes other results. A cause for every result and a result for every cause. It's a very simple lesson, really. At the plant you would have seen it quickly.

"You must see it now instead. Imagine that you have pulled a certain lever and now certain things will happen. If they don't, you know there was something wrong with the lever. If they weren't supposed to, you know there would be no lever there. But the lever is there, and it is working perfectly. I want you to see that. Perhaps you will be more careful at the next lever."

"It's funny," said Stepan. "If there's one thing I can't bear, it's moralizing. And yet nothing in the world gives you more pleasure."

His father looked at him pitilessly.

"All right. All right. The truth is you don't believe that guff about your machinery at all. You couldn't. Nobody could believe such stupid junk. The truth has nothing to do with principle. There's no such thing. But I'm the one who's willing to say so. You just don't *want* to help me. You never have. Everything you ever gave me you gave grudgingly. If you had had the courage, you would have given me nothing.

"It's true, isn't it? There's no need to answer. You'd give money to anyone rather than to me. You resent me. You always have. Your own son comes last. You hate me so much you will even take the coming scandal. Is that why you give thousands to the Bolsheviks? To ruin my inheritance? Yes, that's right. I know about it. Thousands to that pack of trash and not a ruble for me. And not very logical, speaking of your gears. Here I am, a glorious but penniless Russian hero, freezing in the trenches, defending Russia, *while you are paying people to persuade our men to surrender.*"

"They are educating for peace. They are sincere."

"Ha!" laughed Stepan. "That's a lever you're pulling that will also have a result. But it may not be the result you expect. I'd like to see the Bolsheviks succeed. I'd like to see the factory taken. I have nothing to lose; I know *I* won't get it. You'll probably give it to someone else.

"Yes, I'd like to see you poor. Poor like me and needing help. If that happens, please come to me. We can moralize together. Perhaps I could pull some levers. You and Masha would enjoy it."

"Do not mention your sister in this conversation."

"Why not? Don't you give her all the money she asks for?"

"She doesn't ask for any. Besides, she is a child — not a lieutenant of Hussars."

"You've never given me anything without forcing me to work. You've made me beg. You enjoy it. But you've always given Masha everything she wants. Why? I'm curious. You've indulged her, encouraged her, spoiled her rotten. It's no wonder she carries her nose so high. You've been giving her what should be my due. Admit it, all she has to do is smile at you, and the spoiled bitch . . . ."

Danilov went white. "Are you crazy? Shut your mouth."

Stepan chuckled. "Still more principle?" He leaned across the desk. He was like a train, a train out of control and approaching a curve. He knew that he should stop but he could not. It was as if he were watching himself, mesmerized.

"Come," he said. "Tell me. All this principle. There must be a reason, there's always a reason. You say so yourself. You're helping yourself to government money like all the others. Or perhaps your equipment is defective. Or are you diverting the supplies we're short of at the front? Is that it? Tell me. I don't condemn you. On the contrary, why should you be any better than anyone else? Tell me — one thief to another."

Danilov hit him hard across the mouth. Stepan fell against the nearby wall, the marks of his father's fingers on his cheek. They stared at each other, shocked for different reasons. The door flew open and Nadia Nikolaevna ran into the room.

"What's this?" she screamed. "Fighting? Father and son? Incredible! Impossible! Please! Please! Ivan, how could you? Stepan is upset." Nadia Nikolaevna fell into a chair. "Oh, my heart. I'm going to faint. Stepan, dear. Help me to my room."

Stepan smiled. "Certainly, mother. I'm so sorry." He helped her out and closed the door. Danilov was alone. He turned off the light and sat in the dark. It was soothing. His hand still tingled and he rubbed it calm. He tried to understand, but he could not. He did not want to. Stepan wasn't at all like a piece of machinery at the factory. Danilov had done everything reasonable to produce a certain result, and instead had gotten a different product. It was as if he had pulled a lever to operate machinery that did one thing, and the machinery had decided to do something else. But that never happened and could never happen at the factory. Why was it so different here? Why was Stepan what he was? Was there a reason? Or was it simply Stepan's choice?

He thought of Orloff, his brother-in-law. Still rotting in Siberia. Denied release under the amnesty. There was a ruined life he could understand, a man ruined not by his faults but by his virtues. But Stepan apparently had no virtues. Why? It was incomprehensible. There seemed to be no reason for what he did.

Danilov looked out the window. He could see nothing. It was dark. It was dark throughout Russia. Lately he had sensed a brittleness around him, a strange malaise, an inability to move. And at the same time he sensed that there was movement indeed, an eerie fluttering, as if something prehistoric were preparing for flight. It was definite but vague, pervasive but intangible. In a way he was not sure of, it was related to his son.

Danilov slowly rubbed his temples. He was very tired. Momentarily, he felt old. The world was whirling off its axis, smashing everything to bits. No sense anywhere. Supplies were short, as Stepan said. And what there was was defective. The temper at the front was bad. Money disappeared. Profits grew, yet profiteers multiplied. He threw them out of his office every day. And prices were rising. Here in Petrograd there was an incomprehensible shortage of food. People were complaining.

Who profits from all this? he wondered. Who? Someone had to. Logic said so. If no one were profiting, it wouldn't be happening. But who in the world was it? Who?

XXIII

Cyril Modestovitch Telegin raised his glass. It had been a wonderful dinner. A wonderful dinner! Some of it still stood in the folds of his vest and Cyril Modestovitch brushed it away. He began to debate with himself agreeably. Did he prefer Donon's? Or perhaps the Morskaya? Difficult. A man should not be expected to choose. So many subtleties and shades of excellence were involved. And then, of course, there was the Cuba. An entirely new dimension. All previous calculations ruined. Telegin sighed. The problem was insoluble. Luckily, a man did not have to decide. There they all were for the blessed, the brilliant and the strong. They softened the pain of being unable to dine in Paris.

Yes, a wonderful dinner. *Délicieux.* Not a fault. And perhaps later a tart for dessert. Telegin reached with effort across his desk, took a Havana cigar from the inlaid case and rolled it pleasurably across his tongue. Delightful! Its blue smoke rose languorously in the still air of his study.

Cyril Modestovitch raised his glass. The rings on his pudgy fingers tinkled against it musically. Nose at its brim, he inhaled the bouquet. He studied the amber richness of its contents. He took a sip without swallowing, as one should, pursed his fleshy lips with care and slowly worked the wine under his tongue and throughout his mouth, at last reluctantly letting it slide down while inhaling its aroma. Cyril Modestovitch smiled and nodded. *Tout à fait superbe. Le mieux.* Incomparable. Incomparable!

Cyril Modestovitch set the glass near his typewriter and returned to work, writing as always boldly and surely: "Brothers, the Holy Russian land suffers today under her greatest trial and torment. Her cup runneth over — not with the wine of plenty, but with the bitter nectar of violence. Outraged Russian hearts cry out for justice.

"And yet voices are heard, few but influential, counselling compromise, even urging surrender. Pathetic voices — yes, Russian voices — whisper defeatist slogans. Moral saboteurs distribute propaganda to our men.

"Brothers! Can we then excuse the bestiality of the enemy? Should we endorse German rapacity? Can we make ourselves accessories to Wilhelm's greed?

"No! The word thunders proudly through the land. Millions of true Russian voices cry out, condemning the complacent, embarrassing the timid, demanding but one thing — sacrifice!"

Cyril Modestovitch read it through slowly. How beautifully clear and direct. How brave. How admirably modest and intelligent. And the mellifluous, alliterative cadence of it. So sonorous, stirring and inspiring. But now, at the end, Cyril Modestovitch frowned, surprised. No, no, it's not right. There's a weakness. Another would have been satisfied, even pleased, but Cyril Modestovitch was a craftsman, an artist. And there was a weakness. Something was wrong. The last line needed more weight.

Telegin took a pen and scratched it out. Something ... hmm .... He wrote again: "The bleeding, wounded hearts of our Russian mothers cry out. Hundreds, millions. They rise as one. To condemn the complacent and berate the timid. To point trembling, bereaved fingers in silent reproach. To demand but one thing and one thing only. To demand what is owed — what they and their sons have already fully given. To demand that which is holiest: sacrifice!"

Cyril Modestovitch threw down his pen. Style! Entirely a matter of style! Either it's there, or it isn't. He chuckled and praised himself. It was there!

His valet came in and announced two visitors. Officers, one Danilov and a Belkin.

"Danilov?" said Telegin, puzzled. "An officer? Ah, yes. Of course. The son. Of course, Yevgeny, show them in. Ah, Stepan Ivanovitch, welcome! An honor. So thoroughly pleased. We have not seen each other for years. Come, sit down. You'll join me, of course, *pour un verre du vin*?" Telegin already was filling two glasses. He handed one to Stepan. "Impeccable bouquet. And your friend?" He looked at Belkin quizzically, handing him the other glass.

"Ilya Platonovitch Belkin," said Stepan. "Also of the Grand Duchess's Hussars."

"Cyril Modestovitch Telegin at your service. And an honor to say so, gentlemen, I assure you. One can only admire and envy the brave Russian men with courage enough — with luck enough — to offer their breasts to the enemy in the service of His Majesty."

"You embarrass us, Cyril Modestovitch," said Stepan. He smiled. He had never known Telegin very well. And when they had last met, Stepan was still a boy. Now he realized that Telegin was a fraud. Stepan had been worried but now he relaxed. He knew that he and Telegin would get on. It was always so annoying, so risky, to deal with someone who was not a fraud. One never could be sure what to expect. There was always the danger that, in the midst of delicate negotiations, such a person mught suffer an attack of nobility. But with a fraud one could feel secure. A fraud was reliable. One could depend on him. Stepan was pleased, so pleased that he overlooked his revulsion for Telegin's sensuality. Sensuality repelled him; it was a sign of weakness.

"You embarrass us," said Stepan, "and yet we understand. And if I may say so without demeaning you, Cyril Modestovitch — I am sure you, too, will understand — your thoughts are only what one expects of any true Russian patriot. Don't you think so, Ilya?"

"I certainly do," Belkin said.

"Embarrass us, therefore, if you must."

"How kind you are," Telegin said. He chuckled. Stepan had surprised him. How clever his remark was.

"Indeed," said Stepan. "Your sincerity affects us. We are touched. Aren't we, Ilya?"

"We are."

"There are several vacancies in the regiment right now. Tragic losses. Dead, of course. German lances in the guts. I would consider it an honor . . . ."

Telegin quickly raised a hand. "Gracious, gentlemen. Kind indeed." He sighed. "If only nature had made it possible. Unfortunately . . . . " Telegin caressed his voluminous belly. "Unfortunately it isn't, as you see. Nature has cheated me, gentlemen. One is sad to be unable at such a time to hurl one's all . . . . Gentlemen, it takes everything I have to avoid self-pity. Sometimes, I must confess, I fail." He lowered his head.

"Please," said Stepan. "You make us feel guilty. Doesn't he, Ilya?"

"He does."

Telegin raised a finger. "Yes, gentlemen, I must confess — for in such terrible and heroic times, only perfect truth, though painful, does justice to events — am I not correct, Ilya?"

"You are."

"I must confess that when I look at you, you honest Russian heroes nobly covered with the blood of the barbarians, I involuntarily ask myself: Am I worthy? Do I deserve . . . ? Perhaps you did not know how much we suffer here.

"But, gentlemen, let me assure you your sympathy, though appreciated, is unnecessary. I cannot take it. It would be stealing. Save it for our maimed

Russian heroes on the line. I realize that even were I as slender as either of you two athletes, my place would be here. Yes, I too have my duty as a member of the intelligentsia. Not as demanding and glorious as your own — I am quick to add — but necessary, valuable, quite important. May I remind you, gentlemen — I know you will appreciate the spirit in which I do so — may I remind you that Balzac completed what Napoleon began. Yes, my friends, the pen and the sword." Telegin handed his manuscript to Stepan. "For tomorrow's editions."

Belkin leaned over Stepan's shoulder and both began to read. While they did so, Telegin studied Stepan with surprise. With mild irritation Telegin visualized Stepan's father, saw him stiffening, frowning, forehead wrinkling, the deep creases descending from the corners of his mouth. He thought of Maria Ivanovna. Masha. Telegin saw her head go slowly back, the eyelids arrogantly descend half way. The large, veiled but clear black eyes. The nostrils fluttering. The long, contemptuous look down her nose. Was that what drew Telegin so?

Unlike them both, Stepan sat before him perfectly at ease. Had Telegin missed something? It was theoretically possible, of course, but how? As usual, Telegin had made himself appear ridiculous, expecting to elicit from Stepan the usual response, expecting Stepan to indicate that he thought Telegin was a mere fool. But Stepan had not made the usual response. He had not indicated anything at all. Telegin was puzzled.

He liked people to think he was a fool, to patronize him. He looked like a fool; slow, dull, impossibly fat. People did not take a fat man seriously. But he was not a fool. Behind his simpering, apparent sloth and inflated manner were will and mind as big as his bulk.

It was possible, of course, for Telegin to eat less. He could have denied himself and become thin. The smiles, jokes and condescension would have ended. But Telegin refused to deny himself. He refused to be denied anything. It would have been painful. It would have meant capitulating to the ideas of real fools. And that Telegin also refused to do. Years ago, even as a child, he had begun to caricature their ideas, to express his contempt for them by making himself grotesque, to get even fatter; to create a fat man for the thin man to hide behind.

When Telegin met someone, he would play the fat man, play the fool, flaunt his creation, overplay his part. If, as usual, the other did not perceive the truth — if he laughed — Telegin laughed, too. The other did not know that Telegin's small, piggish eyes were laughing at him. That he, not Telegin, was the real fool. And Telegin did not tell him. The secret knowledge was a pleasure. It gave Telegin a kind of power. Indeed, people trusted a fat man and let down their guard. A fat man got what he wanted much more easily. People freely gave him what another had to take.

It has been said that inside every fat man is a thin man trying to get out. The thin man inside Telegin was pleased to be there.

In the rare event that someone else noticed this, he did not confirm it. Anyone perceptive enough to make the discovery knew that to reveal it would spoil the game. The rare brother spirit would not point a finger and say smugly, "Cyril Modestovitch, I expose you. You are in reality a thin man." He knew that Telegin would riposte by feigning ignorance and claiming to be a fool. No, the good player simply communicated subtly that he knew this. And Telegin returned with equal subtlety that they understood each other. The art lay in sending the message without making it absolutely clear.

This was the game to which Telegin now introduced Stepan, not with enthusiasm or anticipation — those who could play even passably were rare — but simply as a matter of course. It was a formality, a habit. He knew only that Stepan had just won the Cross of St. George, and that he was the son of Danilov and the brother of Maria, both of whom were fools. Yet now, Cyril Modestovitch wondered whether he was wrong. Had there been, after all, some sign? Some thrust so subtle, so expert, that even he, Cyril Modestovitch, had failed to notice it? Could it be in fact that he himself, Cyril Modestovitch, was also being tested?

Cyril Modestovitch grimaced. Preposterous! Stupid! Nevertheless, there was something. He could not see what. Something . . . . While the others read, he looked at them and wondered.

Then Stepan looked up with an arch, sly smile, conspiratorial and at the same time congratulatory. Telegin returned it and Stepan read some more.

What a refreshing surprise, thought Telegin. Remarkable. So unlike the others who were so stiff and impossibly serious, so unaware of what life is really all about, so totally unable to play the game. Danilov, Nadia Nikolaevna, Masha. Impossible! Useless! Except Masha, of course, with her thick hair and long, slender legs.

Stepan returned the manuscript and paused, as if to prepare Telegin for his opinion. Interesting, thought Cyril Modestovitch. Interesting move. Definitely not a beginner.

"Lofty," said Stepan. "Religious. It has a certain ring."

Telegin smiled. A bit naive. Still, Stepan played well. He would profit by seeing how it should be done.

Telegin raised a deprecatory hand. "Gentlemen, I think I may say with confidence, with gratitude, and I must confess, not without pride, that my pen has never wavered. It never will." Telegin looked at Stepan intently. Message received.

"Most lofty indeed!" said Belkin. "Admirable! Stepan's right."

Telegin seemed startled, as if surprised Belkin was still there, and with a grimace dismissed him from further consideration. He was a fool!

"In fact," said Stepan, pointing an admonitory finger, "and Ilya will agree, I am sure" — Belkin was already nodding vigorously — "in fact, Cyril Modestovitch, your work, these sentiments, are of considerably greater importance than you so modestly are willing to admit. Greater, without doubt, than our own earnest but inconsequential efforts. We reject your protests without appeal. They do you honor and at the same time cheat you. We can easily recall the many miserable, lonely evenings lightened by your wit, constantly inspiring us, spurring us on. Just the other night, in fact . . . do you remember, Ilya?"

"I do."

"Gentlemen, I apologize in advance for using a cliché — who can improve upon the simple truth — but the fact is that man does not live by bread alone. There are spiritual values for which he hungers. There are eternal verities. Lack of them can cause death of the soul. And so, my dear Cyril Modestovitch, we stand knowingly, willingly, gratefully in your debt. As a member of the heroic Russian intelligentsia in these difficult times, you recall us to our better natures and our Holy Cause. I look at you and am proud to be Russian."

"Hear, hear!" Belkin said.

Telegin nodded, in a reverie of admiration. The man was a genuine artist, a genius. Such style! Such expression! A mélange of melodious sounds. Cyril Modestovitch felt himself stirred as by a passage from Dowson, or perhaps from Pierre Louÿs, his favorite. This was not to say that Stepan was derivative. He wasn't. His genius was unique. Aside from his own, Telegin could compare it with no other.

"Gentlemen, you are too kind," Telegin said. "And I must admit that your praise, your sincere praise — and I speak as a man to whom sincerity is holy, a man unwillingly surrounded by flatterers and hypocrites, than whom there is no one I more detest . . . ."

Stepan grinned. "I do, too."

". . . your sincere appreciation falls like manna through my soul. Hm. 'Manna through my soul.' Interesting."

"Poetic," said Belkin.

"I agree," Stepan said.

"Yes, my friends, literary creation is a lonely thing. A strain. The Muse is hard to satisfy — a creative burden I eagerly accept. And yet, like everyone

174

else, I need encouragement. I need to know that my small labors actually bear fruit. And, gentlemen, if you will permit me a metaphor, your deeds are that fruit — ripe, wholesome, thoroughly Russian."

"Rest assured, Cyril Modestovitch," said Belkin. "We are devoted readers. You are an inspiration to us all."

Telegin squeezed his shoulder. "So kind. So generous. To be admitted into the fraternity, so to speak, into the regiment. To be allowed to consider my work, too, as a kind of service. For I realize that whatever applause comes to me is meant — and should be meant — for the holy message I am lucky enough to convey. I think of myself, my friends, as a kind of mirror or prism, meant to reflect and focus the spirit of the Motherland.

"That is why, as you see, I call for sacrifice. Russia needs it. It will purify her soul. That is why I willingly accept her suffering. What can be more ennobling than suffering?"

"True," said Stepan. "I had not realized."

"I hadn't either," Belkin said.

"But forgive me," said Telegin. "I have been monopolizing the conversation. And I hold you equally responsible, Stepan Ivanovitch. One rarely finds so sympathetic a personality as yours, able to appreciate intellectual subtlety. When one does, the surprise and pleasure are too great. You have made me sin, Stepan. You have turned me into a conversational profiteer, if I may allude to another defect of our unfortunate Russian character.

"Of course, your estimable father is an exception. We see in him, do we not, everything an industrialist should be."

"He is an example to us all," said Stepan.

There had been a note of hesitation in his voice. And at the same time, too much solemnity. Hm, thought Cyril Modestovitch. Peculiar. Somewhat vague. Adequate in a beginner, but Stepan was not a beginner. Stepan was a proven master.

"He is indeed!" said Belkin with vehemence. He knew Stepan was aware that his father had been told the truth. Danilov had not asked for it. Belkin had simply blurted it out. As Stepan had said himself, Belkin was weak. He had been unable to withhold it and at the same time be Danilov's guest. He knew that Stepan would say something about it. But so far, he had not.

"It is good to hear you say so," said Telegin.

Stepan watched with pleasure as Telegin performed — darting, turning, backing and sidestepping. It was a beautiful thing to see. Stepan anticipated the coming struggle with almost as much pleasure as the victory he already knew to be assured.

"Do you know what I am thinking, Cyril Modestovitch?" said Stepan. "I am relieved. Profoundly. Yes, that's right. We have not seen each other for so many years that until now I knew you less in friendship than by reputation, an error I intend to correct, you may be sure. I had formed an idea of the type of person you are. I hoped. That is why I'm here tonight. But until tonight, I could not be positive."

What on earth? thought Cyril Modestovitch. Some new tack, entirely unexpected. But what in the world . . . ? His skin tingled. His eyes darted at Stepan's but could detect no sign.

Stepan leaned forward earnestly. "My dear friend, Cyril — may I call you that? — you have my profoundest gratitude and admiration for having proven me right."

Telegin waved a hand. "It's nothing. Nothing." He felt uneasy, which diluted his appreciation of Stepan's artistry. He did not know what was happening. This had never happened before.

"In fact," said Stepan mildly, and at the same time with authority, "it is for these very reasons that I come before you now; my father's well-known excellence and irreproachable character, and my certainty that a brother spirit like your own could not fail to appreciate them fully. Cyril, my dear friend, I place myself entirely in your hands."

Telegin smiled in answer. It was almost more than he could manage. Could it be possible that he had missed the cue? That he, whose perception made even the most sensitive barometer faulty, who could read with ease a faded hieroglyph — was it possible that he had overlooked a fairly obvious sign? He, Cyril Modestovitch? It was impossible, of course! Laughable. Ludicrous. The fact that it could even occur to him was annoying. And yet something was wrong. It was as if he had rubbed a magic lamp of his own creation only to find that its genie not only pleased himself but actually pulled Telegin's nose.

Telegin coughed. "I'm afraid I . . . ."

Stepan's face was quite near his. The manner on it was youthful and sincere, confident, with an air of genial conspiracy, as if he were about to reveal a secret that Telegin needed to know.

"Cyril, my dear friend," Stepan said, "I . . . the matter is difficult to mention, even to a friend with a nature as sympathetic as your own. But things are best said straight out, aren't they? Cyril, my dear friend, I've come to you for a loan."

"A loan?" Telegin repeated the words mechanically. His body slowly began to contract, as if within an invisible shell. The thing was impossible. It was out of control. He stared at Stepan without comprehension. It was as if

176

he, Telegin, the originator of the art, the world's foremost living authority, had patiently cultivated a promising student and was suddenly beaten by him. It was impossible. It could not happen. But it *had* happened. Puzzled and uneasy, Cyril Modestovitch searched hastily through his reservoir of technique.

"A delicate matter," Stepan said. "Concerns a woman, of course. Pathetic. Naturally I can say no more of the lady in question. But I knew, my dear friend, that to you I would not have to."

"Of course," said Telegin, a bit abstractly. "Understood."

"The fact is," said Stepan, "that I have always been able to regard my father as my closest friend, a friend in whom I have always confided, no matter what. But your quick intuition has, of course, already told you that in this unfortunate case such a luxury is regrettably impossible. Impossible because of the very qualities, the very excellence, you so properly applaud. My father's delicacy is too great, his nobility too fine, to be exposed unnecessarily to such an unpleasant matter. And your beautiful appreciation of that fact evokes my profoundest gratitude, I assure you.

"My friend, it is this rare appreciation of my father's qualities, and those of the rest of my family, that led me to see in you a kindred spirit and brings me to you now in the hope that you may extend it to me as well. I must congratulate myself for being so beautifully right about you."

"You should," said Telegin. He was beginning to get the point. "I do admire the rest of your family so."

"I am told, for instance, that you admire my sister."

Telegin chuckled. "You are told correctly. I do."

"What a coincidence that I should come to you for a loan."

"Isn't it."

"And yet I hesitated — *c'est vrai* — to bring the matter to you. The amount involved is so small, so *petite*, that I feared you might laugh, which I could not bear. We aren't overpaid in the Grand Duchess's Hussars, are we, Ilya?"

"That's the truth!" Belkin said.

"But we are proud! The truth is, Cyril Modestovitch, I already regret having come here. Perhaps we should forget the whole thing, with mutual good feelings."

Telegin grinned. "Don't be silly! What are friends for? You should congratulate yourself again. Our transaction will be conducted with the greatest dignity. You will see. Come, my friend, name a sum. I will be insulted if you don't." Telegin was already moving toward his desk.

"Kind," said Stepan. "So kind. So generous. So kind, in fact, that I believe I must refuse. Our friendship is too important. I refuse to risk it."

"But, my dear fellow, don't be stupid!" Telegin crowed. "A few meaningless rubles. Laughable. Ridiculous. Not worth our valuable time to mention. Come, come, *je t'implore.*" Telegin shook a warning finger. "I warn you, I may become offended after all. I am hurt, Stepan. I confess it, hurt. My admiration for your tact may well be overcome by your refusal to take me into your confidence. Please, my friend."

Stepan shook his head. "Such grace. Such delicacy. You overwhelm me, my dear Cyril. You leave me no retreat. I surrender. Here, I gladly hand you my saber." The imaginary blade lay on Stepan's upturned, extended palms. "To be beaten by you is a victory in itself. True friendship is so rare. So rare — some never see it — that if it comes, one must seize it with both hands. *N'est-ce pas*? It would be stupid, as you say, to reject your friendship because of misplaced pride — over a paltry eight thousand rubles."

"Eight thousand?" Telegin's voice sprang up like a flushed duck, and it was only by the rarest marksmanship that he shot it down.

". . . an encouraging, an inspiring gesture in these times of avariciousness," Stepan was saying.

"Yes, an act of magnanimity," said Belkin. "It is an honor to know you, Cyril Modestovitch."

"Eight thousand," said Telegin mechanically.

Stepan smiled. "Yes."

Swine! Bastard! Whoreson! Could it be possible? Yes, there sat Belkin, the amebic cretin whose relationship to Stepan and presence here had been so puzzling, gazing at Telegin fawnlike, with admiration. The perfect witness, already impatient to advertise his generosity. It could not be withdrawn. There could be no doubt. Painful though it was, the fact must be faced squarely, without hesitation. He, Telegin, the master of the art, was trapped. He, Telegin! It defied all logic.

The amount really didn't matter, as money. Telegin had plenty. People gave it to him. The money was a symbol of something more important; a measurement of their respective artistry. No, the problem was in esthetics, not finance. Had the amount been smaller, it would have been largesse, which Telegin would have distributed in the manner of the Louis XIV he knew himself to be. It would have meant victory, victory over an exciting opponent. But this — Stepan's boldness, the brilliance of his tactics — this was defeat. Defeat, furthermore, which the rules of the game demanded Telegin represent as his own victory.

Defeat? No. It had to be admitted this was rout, utter irreversible rout. It was impossible. It had never happened before. But it was happening now.

Telegin's mind was spinning out of control. Far below, he felt the thin man stir in his secret place, stretch, and then rise through his psychology, level after level, silent, eager, waiting for the summons. Telegin shuddered and, with effort, pressed him back. That way lay disaster, an even greater defeat — the admission that he had lost. The thin man sulked and descended slowly, flicking petulantly with saber tip at Telegin's insides.

Telegin reached into his drawer and began to peel off bills like layers of his own skin. Stepan watched him, impudently. Brilliant, he told himself. Can't possibly be faulted. He winked at Telegin — to convey the fact. Telegin knew it, he was sure, but Stepan did not want to take a chance.

Telegin stared at him sourly in return. He had underestimated Stepan. That had been his mistake. He had allowed his pleasure in so rare a game to distract him. Yet he realized that he was in the presence of a genius. He felt what Plato must have felt when confronted with Aristotle.

Yes, it was in fact a family of genius. Danilov, a genius at industry, at engineering; Maria — yes, she too had genius, a genius which had only begun to flower. Of what sort, exactly, he was not sure, but it was there. Yes. Masha, hmmmm . . . . The thought of her dissipated the irritation of the disaster, turned it on its side, so that, though the same, it was different, no longer a disaster at all. Telegin felt again the usual anticipation. He smiled. Yes, Masha. So young, so aloof, arrogant actually, so desirable. She had a quality . . . so difficult to describe. Perhaps it was a small thing, a habit, perhaps, one of those unconscious characteristics of which she herself was unaware, and which set a woman off, made all the difference, drew a man without his knowing why. In this, as in everything else, Telegin was a connoisseur. The timbre of a woman's voice. The way she smiled. But in this case . . . . Hmmm. Perhaps it was her carriage, the provoking way she tilted her head. Or was it the way she walked? So peculiar in a young girl, so uncharacteristic, not tripping or mincing in the manner that was fashionable, but with unembellished strides, almost like a man. Her long legs, of course. Yes, Masha.

And here was the honored brother, another genius, a hero, soon to be a member of the Order of St. George. Eight thousand rubles. Hmmm. Cyril Modestovitch castigated himself silently but severely for his involuntary stinginess, his lapse of patriotism. True, it had been involuntary, momentary, a blameless omission, but Cyril Modestovitch was strict with himself. The loan — or rather, the gift — was not merely an annoying duty, to be borne with unwilling resignation, but a pleasure, an honor. One should want to give it and compete for the privilege. It was an investment; it was, yes — dare he say it? — an investment in the future of the Motherland. As for the dividends, what could matter but the Cause? Who could be so petty as to demand notarized stock certificates when Russia was the property? And who, faced with the always surprising, endlessly revolving kaleidoscope that is human life, could even attempt to predict the future? Who indeed?

Renewed well-being surged through Cyril Modestovitch. His mood had completely changed. Again he felt gay, relaxed, powerful. From far below he heard even the thin man chortling. Cyril Modestovitch was expressing his own genius, his ability to make profit from a situation that to another might seem a total loss. He congratulated himself. He continued counting the money, but with pleasure, as if a woman were inside it. He chuckled, at which Stepan started, instantly alert, the master as always, expecting some further move. He chuckled again. A feeling of warmth for Stepan came over him.

But wait! Telegin's hand hesitated and then resumed, more slowly than before. There was still the crucial matter of the game. His renewed well-being brought with it renewed ambition. Cyril Modestovitch was not only a genius and an optimist, but a perfectionist in all things. Could he allow the matter to remain as it was? And was it, in fact, so hopeless? One campaign, after all, did not make a war. What would von Clausewitz say? War is merely the continuation of policy. No, no; true but inappropriate. Hm. Let us see. Faced with annihilation, one must retreat. And the cleverest retreat is, of course, not a retreat at all, but rather a planned withdrawal to a prepared position.

The cleverest retreat, in fact, is actually an advance. An attack! A riposte was already taking shape in Telegin's mind, an attack by a squadron with the effect of a corps, bringing victory with it whatever Stepan did. So brilliant was it that Telegin trembled, frightened by delight. At last he finished and pressed the bills into Stepan's hand. In each other's eyes they saw a mutual respect and admiration.

Telegin quickly raised a finger. "No. No. Not a word. Please! I see that you are about to embarrass me again. Not a word, Stepan. I insist. We'll say no more about it. The matter is closed." He tapped Stepan's hand. "Count it now. Be sure it is right."

"That is unnecessary, Cyril Modestovitch, I am sure."

"Nonsense," said Telegin. "We are doing business. I insist."

Telegin turned away, almost obviously, and began to arrange his drawer. He could hear the bills crinkle as Stepan riffled throught them. His fingers shook so that he had to press them against the desk. He felt a desire to shout and suppressed it. The delightful suspense was almost unbearable.

Stepan smiled. The trap was so ludicrously childish it was offensive. What did Telegin take him for?

"But, Cyril, my dear friend," he said feigning confusion, "you've made a mistake after all. There are ten thousand here." He held out the money as if the victim of some hoax.

Telegin barely suppressed a snicker. He would almost have preferred the other choice . . . but no; too much to ask for. Still, no matter. The result would be the same.

His face turned red, just the right shade. He got flustered. "I beg your pardon," he whispered, as if writhing in guilt. "I had hoped to avoid . . . I realized, that is to say, I intuited, that a gentleman of your tact and breeding would underestimate his needs, would hesitate . . . I am demoralized by the fear that you may be offended . . . and after all, only another two thousand. Who can say what extra expenses you will incur? I beg you to accept as a favor to me. Please don't mention it. Don't say a word. I realize how embarrassing it is for a gentleman to ask for a loan. Now it is my turn to be embarrassed. The blame is entirely mine, my friend. And yet, perhaps you will understand and forgive the typical clumsiness of the fat man. It has its psychological counterpart, you see." He pressed Stepan's arm. "My friend, I place myself entirely in your hands."

"You shouldn't," said Stepan. "I release you. Your motive shines unblemished through your protests. I accept, of course, humbled by your grandeur."

In his eyes a trace of irritation vanished quickly — but not so quickly as to escape Telegin's stethoscopic perception.

"Such breeding," said Telegin. "Such generosity. And such an honor to be of service to our young Napoleon." Telegin chuckled. They were on the plain of Waterloo. "Yes," said Cyril Modestovitch, the Iron Duke, "it again demonstrates beautifully the simple, basic principle of my entire philosophy. Truth, Stepan. Sincerity. Honor. So lamentably rare. So beautiful. And are these things not essential to the friendship you spoke of before? To the innocent trust, the mutual assistance, exchanged by two harmonious spirits? How indeed could human affairs advance otherwise?"

"True," said Stepan. "So beautifully true."

"Yes," said Belkin.

"Reassuring to hear from a man destined without doubt to play a large part in the future of Russia," said Stepan.

"Yes," said Belkin.

"In fact," said Stepan, "I would be honored if we were related."

"Related?" said Telegin. "What do you mean?"

"Come, come, you wily one," Stepan said. "Your feeling for my sister is public knowledge."

"Can I keep nothing from you at all?" said Telegin with mock horror.

181

"Is nothing safe?"

"Luckily, I now can endorse you without fear."

"I am overcome, Stepan Ivanovitch."

"But be careful, I warn you. My sister is priceless. I shall protect her virtue and reputation to the end."

"Priceless indeed!" said Telegin gaily. "We agree again. What harmony of spirit! What endless discoveries! Stepan, my dear sir, ours is a friendship that will be described in books.

"Gentlemen, I was about to go out as you arrived. Why don't you join me? We'll drive down the Nevsky. Perhaps we may find some suitable entertainment."

"Your mind is working with the beautiful precision of a Swiss watch," said Stepan.

"Isn't it!" said Telegin. "Splendid! Yevgeny," he shouted. "My coat!"

XXIV

It was warm. The air was strangely thick and heavy, as if the spring night were pregnant with summer. All of Petrograd was in the streets. Yet the city was still. Only the soldiers, lounging in bunches, reminded one of the war.

"Brave Russian lads," said Telegin.

"Indeed," said Belkin.

"It is sad to realize that they will soon be dead."

"Perhaps they won't."

"Do they realize it, do you think?"

"Don't be silly," Stepan said. "If they did, no one could get them to the front."

"That's what I thought," said Telegin.

"You're both too morose," said Belkin. "It isn't that bad."

"I have made myself sad," said Telegin, "but I enjoy it. Sadness is good. It reduces the guilt."

"Guilt?"

"In the face of all this, I am haunted by the question of whether I am entitled to my small pleasures. Small, true — I eagerly submit in my own defense — but pleasures nevertheless. Please, my friends, reassure me."

"You shouldn't need it," Belkin said. "Your guilt is wrong. The fact that you feel it is proof of that."

"He's right," said Stepan. "Aren't you, Belkin?"

"Yes."

"You're humoring me," said Cyril Modestovitch. "I deserve better. I want the truth."

"You're wrong," said Belkin. "You deserve as much as any of us. More! Tell him, Stepan. Aren't I right?"

"No," said Stepan, "you are humoring him."

"He's joking," said Belkin. "He likes to do that."

"I don't know," said Telegin. "You sound convincing enough, yet . . . . "

He and Stepan exchanged a grin. They both were in the best of spirits.

"Since you are lucky enough to be here," said Belkin, "what possible harm . . . ?"

"Yes, yes," said Telegin shortly. His mood had changed. The thing was getting boring. But Belkin did not know that. Still he droned on. He lacked the others' faultless sense of timing.

The reins snapped and the carriage lurched forward. There were shouts. Pedestrians jumped to escape the horse.

"What is so rare as a night in June?" shouted Telegin.

"What, indeed!" Stepan said.

The cab stopped and they stood in front of a small house. Telegin paid the driver and danced about. "Come, gentlemen," he said. "Let us dally well." They were inside and walking up the stairs. "But please let me warn you to maintain your decorum. This is not an ordinary place. I would not insult you. You will see. Combined with which there is my admiration and reverence for woman."

"Trust us," said Stepan.

"Ah," said Telegin as the door opened. "Marfa, friend, confidant, colleague."

Marfa wore, as always, a severe expression and was dressed entirely in black. She liked to give an impression of respectability, as if she were dealing in high finance. Or in funerals. Or in anything rather than women. Dignified and austere, she spoke with circumspection compounded with euphemisms. Her house was always very still. She ran it like a convent. Never had the police complained. Marfa Mironovna was a great lady.

All of this was nevertheless not appreciated, at least not in the way Marfa intended. She knew that her girls talked about her endlessly. As for her clients, they treated her with hilarity and took great pleasure in baiting her, which was one of the reasons for her success. But Marfa did not become offended. That was beneath her. Unless the offense were too severe, she simply refused to admit its existence. That was why she liked Telegin. He behaved with great courtliness; he did not treat her like a whore.

Telegin kissed her hand. "Marfa, my dear friend."

She did not realize that Telegin treated her with great courtliness *because* she was a whore. A retired whore, true. An executive. But a whore nevertheless. Like the others, Telegin found her funny. But he appreciated her, characteristically, in a subtler way. She was a fountain of pleasure.

"I have the honor to present two representative Russian heroes," said Telegin.

Marfa put a hand to her breast. "Poor boys. So sad. I want to cry. So terribly, beautifully young." She patted Stepan's cheek. "You deserve some refined, fastidious entertainment."

"Yes," Stepan smiled. "Perhaps some vodka, too?"

"Vodka?" said Marfa. "But my dear, young man, surely you'll remember. The law. Ever since the war . . . ."

"No vodka?" said Stepan. "What kind of nonsense . . . ?"

"And a good thing it is, too. The restraint is our patriotic duty. A small sacrifice compared with your own."

"Patriotic duty?" said Stepan with indignation. "Law? What kind of nonsense is this? This *is* a whorehouse, isn't it?"

Marfa recoiled with distaste. She had misjudged him. "Oh, Cyril Modestovitch, oooh . . . ."

Stepan pounded on the table. "Vodka now," he shouted. "At once!" He was enjoying himself immensely.

Telegin patted his shoulder. "Yes, yes, my dear fellow, *tout de suite.*" He enjoyed Stepan's move, but was nevertheless slightly alarmed. It was as if the thin man within him had escaped and stood before him now. He envied Stepan. He was always thin.

"I won't be silenced!" Stepan roared.

"Stepan, really," Belkin said.

Telegin took Marfa aside. "Try to understand," he whispered. "A difficult case. Fresh from the front. Nerves. The slightest thing sets him off. Deserves our pity.

"And yet, completely reliable. Perfect discretion, both of them. Perhaps a bottle for medicinal purposes. Trust me."

He hurried Marfa to the door. She went out and returned almost at once followed by a girl who carried glasses and a bottle on a tray.

"Ah, Sonya," said Telegin.

"Hmpf! Law indeed!" said Stepan. "No vodka."

Sonya distributed the glasses, opened a bottle and poured. Telegin rolled a bill into a tight cylinder and with the tip of his little finger pushed it smoothly between her rounded breasts.

Stepan raised a glass. "To you and to me."

"To us," said Belkin.

"To Russia," said Telegin.

An hour passed with much exalted conversation and several bottles.

"The time has come," said Telegin at last. "Don't you agree?"

"Yes," said the others.

"Good. It's unanimous. Sonya for me. Shall we see what else . . . ?"

Marfa took the cue. "May I recommend a Circassian?" she asked Telegin. "Absolutely unspoiled, I guarantee."

"A Circassian. Hm. Interesting."

"Interesting indeed," Stepan said.

"And unspoiled. How thoroughly exciting."

"On the contrary," said Stepan. "That's what I call boring."

"On the other hand," said Telegin, "she is probably quite wild. Bunch of savages."

"Now that is exciting," said Stepan. "We disagree again."

"On the contrary," said Marfa, "she is surprisingly refined. Remember, Cyril Modestovitch, you are in *my* house."

"True," said Telegin. "Quite true."

"Unfortunately, she does not speak Russian."

"Interesting," said Telegin. "Barbarous, but interesting."

"Fascinating, in fact," Stepan said.

"Yes," said Telegin, "I would tend to agree. In fact . . . ."

"In fact, just the thing for Belkin," said Stepan. "He likes to get right to business. Don't you?"

"A little talk does no harm," said Belkin.

"Exactly what I was about to suggest," said Telegin. "No nonsense about him. I saw that at once."

"Yes," said Belkin. "You're right. That's true."

"Of course it is," Stepan said.

"Yes, my dear, come," said Marfa, drawing Belkin into the corridor. She liked him. He did not make remarks. He was a real gentlemen, unlike so much of this modern trash.

"The corner room!" Telegin whispered. "Do you hear?"

He got up quickly as soon as they had gone. "Quick, now! Hurry!" he said. "This man puzzles me."

"Where are we going?" Stepan asked.

"Hurry. Come. I must know," said Telegin. They went quickly down the corridor and into a small room, and pressed their eyes to two small holes. They were looking through the fireplace into the next room at Belkin and the Circassian.

"What a fascinating idea," Stepan said.

"Isn't it?"

"You realize, of course, Cyril Modestovitch," said Marfa behind them, "the observation holes . . . ."

"Of course," said Telegin. "Include it in the bill."

The girl was small, and dark, and excitable. She playfully

helped Belkin remove his clothes, babbling in an unknown tongue.

"I wonder," Telegin whispered. "He seems an absolute slug."

"I have wondered, too," said Stepan.

"But wait!" Telegin clapped Stepan's shoulder in excitement. "Why, who could have believed . . . . The man is magnificent."

He turned to Stepan with mock confusion. "Inexplicable. Impossible. How can it be? Such a marvel wedded to such a psychology. Why, it defies . . . so inappropriate, so wrong, so terribly unjust. But, most of all, such a hideous waste."

They separated, laughing hysterically. Telegin took Sonya off. Marfa took Stepan to a room.

Hours passed. It was late. Stepan lay on the bed. The girl sat in a chair, smoking. She was Anna Andreevna Kursamina. Not long before, she had finally returned to Russia. But she had been gone so many years, she no longer knew anyone. She had approached her parents, but they had rebuffed her as they had years before, after her arrest. It was embarrassing for a prominent family to have a convict in its midst. Anna Andreenva realized that there had been no real reason to return. Returning had been a goal and there had been no satisfaction in it. It was empty. Anna Andreevna felt even more dazed than before. And gradually she had drifted back to the only thing she knew.

Stepan watched her. Her face was young, clear and smooth. She annoyed him.

"Where do you come from?" Stepan asked.

"From here. From Petersburg," said Anna Andreevna.

"We've called it Petrograd since the war began."

"Yes, that's true. I've been away."

"Where?"

"In Siberia."

"Why?"

"In prison."

"How did it happen?"

"Let's forget it. It makes no difference now."

Anna Andreevna's face was blank. Her mouth opened. The words came out. But it was as if she were totally incapable of emotion; as if she were a mechanical contrivance, not a person.

Stepan smiled. His opinion had changed. Anna Andreevna's face no longer annoyed him. Indeed, he felt comfortable. He could be himself. If he wanted to yawn and scratch, he could do so. He could do whatever he liked. His engagement to Tata was advantageous, of course. She would be a famous dancer. It would help his career. But he resented Tata. With her he could not be himself. She was another like his father, like his colonel, like Maria. And Stepan resented them all.

"Come here," he laughed.

XXV

Borishevsky looked out the window. It was a perfect day, cool and dry. He inhaled it deeply, with pleasure, and at the same time with reserve, for he knew that it would end badly and that nothing could be done. The back door opened and Spassky came in. In his eyes, Borishevsky saw the same pleasure but not the same reserve. That was the difference between them. Spassky did not know that the day would end badly.

Borishevsky dug quickly into the piles of paper on the table, and found something appropriate just in time to forestall conversation.

"Just finish this up, will you?" he said.

"Of course," said Spassky.

Borishevsky turned abruptly and left the room. He had been avoiding Spassky all morning because of the difference between them. Like Spassky, he wanted the day to end well — that was his incurable romanticism — but he refused to discuss it, knowing it could not. Talk would only produce more suffering. There was no reason for it and no profit in it and nothing to be done. That was the important thing to remember: The day would end the way it had to end and nothing could be done.

Crestin-Galkov and Lopatkin, immaculate in dress uniforms, sat unobtrusively in a corner of the sun porch, drinking and smoking.

"Paraguay," said Crestin-Galkov.

"Uruguay," said Lopatkin.

"Paraguay!"

"Uruguay!"

"But, Vasya, you don't understand," said Crestin-Galkov. "Please, I insist. Paraguay!"

"Excuse me, I'm sorry," said Lopatkin. "All right, then, Paraguay it is."

"Uruguay!"

Borishevsky shook his head. This was Prokurov's doing. Prokurov again.

The man was incorrigible. Everywhere it was possible to do so, Prokurov had built a still. Borishevsky had given up destroying them. They seemed to mate and reproduce. Perhaps he should have Spassky draw up another spurious order for court-martial.

He went outside, mounted and moved slowly up the road, posting lightly to the trot. It really was a splendid day. There was not a cloud but it was cool. The sun flashed through the birches. Birds wheeled in and out. Water fell on rocks nearby. The horse broke without command into a canter and tried to run, as if eager to see it all. Like Spassky, he did not know that it would end badly. Borishevsky let him go. He sympathized with their point of view, even though it stemmed from ignorance. His would have been the same, were it not for his wide experience. He, too, would have liked to enjoy the day without reserve, but the day would end badly and nothing could be done. He pulled out his watch. Only two more hours.

A squadron of hussars came out of the crossroad, already on their way to the field, jaunty, arrogant, burnished and bright.

"Health to your honor!" they boomed as one like cannon.

Borishevsky flushed and returned their salute, as always glowing with pride. It was stupid, he knew, naive, unworldly, but he could not help it. At least, unlike Spassky, he knew it was stupid. He sat and watched as the men passed. No infection there, he told himself. The heart is sound, sound as ever. All the rest was unimportant. But his mood predictably shaded slowly to regret, as he realized more clearly than ever that the day would end badly and that nothing could be done.

Late in the afternoon, drawn up by squadrons in the sun, the men covered the field like banks of poppies. They were in full dress, they were hot and had already been in formation for almost two hours, but they were only slightly restless. The expectation they all felt had in fact not nearly reached its height, the point beyond which it would curdle into boredom. They were very still. They rarely spoke, and then abruptly, as if afraid of distracting themselves. The only real sounds were the puzzled conversation of some reconnoitering birds and the reflective stamping of the horses.

Borishevsky's horse bent to take his lunch and Borishevsky pulled him up. His tail swished languidly, like a woman's dress. Without turning his head, Borishevsky looked at Spassky. He looked calm, even uninterested, but Borishevsky knew that he shared the mood, shared it to excess. He himself shared it. His romanticism really was incurable, he thought wryly. In the face of all his own warnings, he himself felt the same expectation. He castigated himself, but mildly. He knew that in this case he would be disappointed, but that his ability to feel this expectation was sound.

There was a stir among the men and he looked up. Just at the horizon, a ball of smoke stood on a thin stem like an exclamation point. There was a puff of wind and it became a question mark. Then the head of the train rose to view and rushed toward them. A wave of excitement rolled through the ranks. Officers turned to reexamine their squadrons. Then the train screeched to a halt in a cloud of steam. Some officers got off and there was animated conversation. Fingers rose and pointed in various directions. Borishevsky bent to greet an old friend, who explained the delay and asked about the state of his regiment. Borishevsky told him. Men shouted and hurried up and down. Some whispering generals studied a watch. Then the conversation and movement gradually died away and again there was a stillness, even more complete, uncomfortable this time because it was not just an absence of movement but a hostility to movement, in which everyone breathed furtively, almost with apology. All eyes were on the train.

At last the door opened and a man stood on the platform. He hesitated and then descended slowly. He extended a foot. He stepped completely down. Yes, it was he, the Tsar of all the Russias. A spontaneous roar of approval came from the men. But Spassky, who began, did not finish. He petered out. The man before him was a small man, stiff, uncomfortable, hesitant, apologetic. Spassky stared at him, unable to understand.

It has been such a wonderful day, thought Borishevsky. A perfect day. Such a pity. A cloud passed across the sun and he looked up. It was the only cloud in the sky. Such a waste! If only the day did not have to end badly. He knew that Spassky was looking at him but he avoided his eyes.

Now an officer was coming from the ranks. It was Stepan, Stepan Danilov. In fact, now Stepan was standing before the Tsar of all the Russias, and the Tsar was placing the white cross around his neck; the Cross of St. George that made him a Knight of the Order of St. George. Spassky, in his anticipation, had forgotten about all this. He had not been lucky, like Stepan. So far, he had had no chance for a Cross. Now Stepan and the Tsar were talking, talking in a relaxed, conversational way, intimately, as if exchanging secrets, smiling at each other. The Tsar embraced Stepan and kissed him on both cheeks. Then they smiled some more and talked some more.

Spassky stared at them in disbelief. Something was wrong, very wrong, so wrong that it threatened everything Spassky believed. If it were not soon set right, what he believed would be destroyed. Yet the trouble was subtle. He could not understand what it was. Hurt and astonished, nervous, afraid, he stared at Borishevsky, pleading for an explanation, for some word, even a look; at the same time afraid to get one. But Borishevsky rigidly avoided his gaze. At the moment, he felt dislike and antagonism for Spassky. Spassky wasn't stupid. Why could he not realize that nothing could be done?

Stepan returned at last to the ranks and the Tsar stood alone before the regiment. It was still. The Tsar burrowed with his toe in the soft earth and abstractly examined his boot as if he had forgotten where he was or was thinking of something else. He inspected his tunic with satisfaction. How crucially important a good tailor was. To his annoyance, he saw an insect on the sleeve. The Tsar brushed the offender away. The silence was intense, magnified by the size of the field, by the undeviating concentration of the men, magnified even by the whispering of the birds and the restrained shuffling of the horses, as if the universe were astonished that so much life could be held in abeyance by one man.

But the moment would soon be lost. The point was fast approaching beyond which the mood would dissipate if something were not done. A general with a sense of theater was in fact already walking cautiously toward the Imperial presence.

The Tsar of all the Russias raised his head. He leaned forward. In his eyes there was a light, clear, unmistakable. The Tsar of all the Russias was going to speak. As if drawn involuntarily by a single, master hand, the regiment came off its cantles like one man. Yes, thought Borishevsky, yes, yes.

The Tsar of all the Russias studied them, veterans of Galicia, of Warsaw, veterans of Mukden, veterans, even, of 1878, all willingly in the palm of his hand. The Tsar of all the Russias had only to close his fingers. He smiled, shyly, sweetly, preoccupied. He leaned forward. He pulled at his mustache, once, twice, quickly, mechanically. His mouth faintly began to work. In his eyes, the light wavered, flickered, and went out; as if it had been the reflection of the night light of a passing ship, which he, like the others, like castaways, had been glad and surprised to see, but which had now sunk irrevocably below the horizon. His shoulders sank slightly with it. His head fell. Once again he examined his boot. As if released by a spring, the men fell back in their saddles.

Pity, thought the Tsar of all the Russias. Pity. They would never know. It had been a brilliant remark, highly inspirational. He could not remember it, but there could be no doubt. He shrugged with regret, sorry for them. He wanted to leave. This was getting unpleasant. He wanted to be back inside the train. As if somehow aware of this, a cloak of generals surrounded him and the Tsar of all the Russias moved off with strange dignity, like a single being with many arms and legs. He approached the train. The generals guided him noisily, darting in and out like tug boats around an ocean liner. Then the Tsar of all the Russias was aboard, there was a shout, a hiss of steam, a roar, and the Imperial train was again plunging forward imperially.

192

There was another silence, complete, impenetrable. They were alone and motionless on the plain. I really am an incurable romanticist, thought Borishevsky. Incurable. A damned fool. The men waited behind him but he did not move. He did not want to look at them. He did not want to see their faces. The sun faded like a candle snuffed out. He looked up. As he did so it began to rain, not the usual, annoying cloudburst, but a thin, penetrating, undramatic drizzle. The sky was strangely full of clouds. He smiled wryly. All right, he thought. Enough. I get the point.

He turned to the regiment. At the expression on Spassky's face, he felt renewed dislike and hostility. Added to all the rest was Spassky's hurt incomprehension of why he was so distant. He, too, thought Borishevsky. Hopeless.

"Dismiss the men," said Borishevsky shortly. He turned at once and moved slowly up the road. Behind him he heard Spassky's shout and the men wheeling in squadrons. They did not speak. They were not intoxicated as they should be, nor even jaunty as they had been. They stepped out smartly, heads erect, sabers clanking, trying to sustain the old arrogance, but without success. They felt embarrassed, embarrassed and frustrated. They felt a vague resentment but were not exactly sure why. Only the proper tongue could give it voice.

Borishevsky violently applied his spurs. His horse bucked and galloped on. It had been a splendid day, a perfect day, but it had ended badly and nothing could be done.

XXVI

It was dark. The night was clear, but there was very little moon. Far across the woods, the pinkish smoke of the Austrian cannon sprang in bouquets over the treetops and disintegrated. The reports followed, dull, distant, seemingly harmless, as if they had nothing to do with the shells. The woods below them seethed with life. The Russian Army was retreating all along the line. The plains of Hungary and the promise of Prussian graves were farther away than ever. The squadron moved through the flashing birch.

"Nonsense!" Prokurov was whispering. "Without meaning, totally. I ignore, I ignore deliberately and completely, with a laugh. Ha ha. I laugh."

"Yes," said the other man, "but . . . ."

Prokurov raised a hand. "Our strategy is simple, outrageously so. Even you will understand. We will withdraw cleverly to the Urals, and when we get there, the enemy's pursuing army will have dwindled in Napoleonic fashion to a single German and a single Austrian. The Austrian will surrender, according to custom. The German we will kill. Armistice, peace treaty, end of war, medals, and home to your faithless obscenity of a wife. Simplicity itself. Unfortunately, you can't read. The entire plan has been worked out minutely by Brusilov at Corps."

"My faithless obscenity of a wife will be glad to hear this."

At the head of the squadron, Stepan turned in the saddle and glared. He could not understand how Prokurov could be perpetually drunk and still function. Prokurov rolled his eyes knowledgeably, trying to convey that nothing was wrong, that he and his companion had merely been discussing strategy.

The trees thinned out. They had come to the road at the edge of the village. They turned in and moved slowly along its shoulder. An endless army of refugees faced them, crawling to the east. Children perched with delight on furniture in ancient carts. Men swore and shouted. Women screamed.

Thousands of wooden wheels creaked. A man with a long, slender neck and a tiny head was running spasmodically up and down, peering like an ostrich into the oncoming horde.

"Dunya!" he shouted. "Dunya! Oh! They'll cut off her ears!"

"Worse," Stepan laughed.

The man grabbed his bridle and ran alongside, his head rising, falling, dodging, weaving. "Please, your honor, they'll cut off her ears. I know it! Find her. Stop them. Please!"

Stepan took a foot from a stirrup and pushed him loose. "Move on. It's too late. Her ears are gone."

Prokurov frowned. He did not like Stepan. "No grace," he said loudly. "The man is ungenerous. Nothing to fear, brother," he called as he drew abreast. "They'll not pay any attention to her ears."

But the man had not heard. He was running back and forth again, nervous and birdlike. "Dunya!" he called. "Dunya! Oh!"

Now they were moving through the village, horseshoes clattering on the stones. Faces appeared in windows, shouting. Here the barrage seemed strangely close. Fingers fluttered and pointed in signs, as if everyone were deaf and mute. People came out of doorways dragging sacks full of household silver, much of it not their own. From an open window on the ground floor the head of a dead Jew, still wearing his cap, hung crazily over the street, hands nailed neatly to the sill. Someone had taken time to avenge the Crucifixion.

Then they were out of the village and the noise stopped so abruptly that they could still hear it for several minutes. They turned off the road and struck again into the trees. They stopped. A man was at the head of the squadron, shouting something, pointing. An Austrian patrol was ahead in the woods.

Stepan rose in the irons. "Lava formation," he whispered. "Pass the word." The squadron fanned out and they moved forward warily into the darkness. There was a metallic hiss as they drew their sabers, then silence. The men were tense, alert, sharp. A long time passed. They were almost out of the woods. They began to relax, breathing deeply. They saw nothing. Either the warning had been a mistake or the Austrians had gone. One after the other, they sheathed their sabers.

Then it became lighter and they saw the Austrians just ahead in a clearing. The squadron stopped and Stepan looked them over. There were six men and an officer. They were talking. The officer pointed to a map and then pointed off through the trees. The men nodded. Stepan strained his ears and caught a few phrases here and there. *"Recht . . . ein hundert*

195

links . . . fünfzig kilometres . . . ja, natürlich. " The officer returned the map to its case. Stepan raised his lance. Now was the time, before they could remount. Prokurov drew his saber. The officer jumped into the saddle at the sound and whirled his horse, looking for the source. The others did the same. But Stepan was already shouting "Charge!" and the gigantic Prokurov was plunging past on his tall horse, saber whirling, like a being from legend.

Prokurov bellowed. His arm flashed at the nearest man and caught him between neck and shoulder. The man fell back over the cantle, dead. From every side the squadron converged. The remaining six Austrians and the clearing disappeared. All were roaring. Flashing arms rose and fell. The Austrian officer's horse burst out at the near side and cantered off into the woods. Stepan circled the crowd and saw the officer just crawling out. He got to his feet and began to run for the trees on the far side. Stepan dug his spurs in and aimed his lance. Face wild, the officer looked back. He had almost reached the trees. Stepan leaned well forward, shouting to his horse. In another step the officer would reach the trees, but in that same step Stepan would be upon him.

Suddenly they were together at the edge of the clearing, the officer turned, at bay, and Stepan lanced him hard against a tree.

Stepan flashed past into the woods, whirled as soon as he could and came back. The officer was impaled through the stomach against the trunk, back pressed tight against it, fingers fluttering feebly, vainly trying to grasp the lance.

Stepan dismounted and rubbed his chin. He took the officer's map case. "I really don't think you need this now."

The officer was young, very young, and seemed suddenly to have shrunk, which made him appear even younger. He opened his mouth but could not speak. Blood streamed out from each corner.

Stepan pulled hard at the lance while the Austrian's hands fluttered vainly. There was no result. Stepan again pulled the lance with all his strength. It did not give, not even a bit. Behind him, the noise was dying down. The battle was over. All the other Austrians were dead.

"Hans," said Stepan, "I apologize for having to leave you here like this, but we must be getting on and — as you see — nothing can be done."

The Austrian turned his head, opened his mouth again and spat a gob of blood full into Stepan's face. Stepan raised a hand, enraged, then lowered it. The others were watching. He wanted to smash the Austrian's mouth but thought better of it. Instead, he wiped his own with his sleeve.

"You're running out of that stuff," he said. He mounted and rode quickly away. "Form up, boys," he shouted. "Move on. To the bridge!"

The bridge had to be held until the order for its destruction. Why it could not be destroyed at once was a mystery, since all the Russian troops who could had already withdrawn across it and there was no hope of a reversal. But orders were orders and could not be questioned. That was the definition of an order. The charges were already placed, so there was nothing to do but wait. Only Belkin and Lopatkin were still on the other side with a handful of men at the top of the hill commanding the bridge. Stepan, at the bank, could barely see them. He was glad he had not drawn that duty.

He drew his pad from his tunic and scribbled a note. He must tell the others he had arrived. As he folded it, he wondered whom to send. There was Prokurov, of course. A good choice. By giving Prokurov dirty duty, he could feel he was annoying Borishevsky. But Marchenko was even better.

"Marchenko!" Stepan called into the trees. From the corner of his eye, he saw the small figures on the hill across the river begin to wave. That had been a mistake; his enthusiasm had exposed him. The note was no longer necessary. Yet he knew that he would send it. He enjoyed making work, annoying and dangerous work, for Marchenko. He did not want to be denied the pleasure. Marchenko needed it, as human shoulders need a load. Stepan ignored the two barely visible figures. And a heavy fog was rising from the still water, totally obscuring the other bank.

Stepan smiled. "Marchenko!" he called again.

Michael came out of the trees and rode toward him slowly, as always when responding to Stepan's command. It was as if he were satisfying not the order but his own curiosity. As always, his face was opaque, expressionless, the eyes cold, in the plunging corners of the mouth a suggestion of contempt, a definite warning in the hawklike nose. And at the same time, he seemed slightly amused. As always, he said nothing. He sat far back and waited, patiently, almost negligently, not at all impressed. He's one of those dirty Bolsheviks, thought Stepan.

Stepan waited for the customary greeting, for the two simple words, "your honor." He had never before realized how important they were. He would not admit it, but he resented the readiness with which Marchenko greeted Lopatkin. He would not admit it because he resented his resentment; it fed upon itself. He was furious to realize that his emotions were being dictated, with his acquiescence, by the actions of an insignificant private. It was almost as if Stepan were the private and Marchenko the officer, making Stepan wait on him. All this was clear and intolerable, but Stepan could do nothing. The thing induced in him a growing combination of fury and curiosity, fury at his impotence, curiosity at its cause, which at times was almost unbearable. He struggled to conceal it, feigning disinterest, knowing that to make Marchenko aware of it would be even more unbearable. But at the same time he suspected unwillingly what was most unbearable of all: that Marchenko thought him too unimportant to evoke interest.

He looked at Marchenko now, sitting patiently relaxed, blankly returning Stepan's look. And Stepan realized that there was nothing he could do. Damn the man! He was incomprehensible. He could not be understood. Stepan could not even find what he was after. In his eyes Stepan saw no challenge, no antagonism, no desire for battle. In them he saw nothing, nothing but the act of observation, as if from the upper end of a microscope.

Stepan looked across the river. He held out the paper.

"You'll find two officers on the hill on the other side. Deliver this note."

Michael took the note and smiled.

"At once, your honor," Michael said. From anyone else, the words would have been thoroughly satisfying. They were said mildly, automatically, respectfully. Yet they somehow sounded like an insult. Stepan studied his face, but found in it no indication of how this effect was produced. It was clear, but at the same time elusive. It made him uneasy.

As at their first meeting, he wanted to strike this man. And Michael hesitated, almost eager. The smile was still on his face — a strange calm, a strange serenity, a suggestion of something dangerous. Stepan's desire dissipated quickly and he put it from his mind, to forestall the painful sense of impotence he knew so well. Michael turned, pushed the note inside his tunic, squeezed his horse and disappeared in the mist over the bridge. Stepan swore softly. If only he could discover what Marchenko was after. The man's impenetrability was infuriating. He was impossible to deal with, far more difficult than Borishevsky or his own father, both of whom were troublesome but transparent. Stepan shrugged and told himself that Marchenko was best ignored, knowing at the same time that this was impossible.

It was quiet. He imagined he could hear the horses grazing in the woods. There was a lull in the barrage and nothing could be seen. The war had momentarily stopped. Stepan lit a cigarette and looked at his watch by the dying match. It was very late. He dozed in the saddle, trying to get what rest he could. It would be a long time before they slept again. It had been a terrible day, an impossible day, and now it was ending badly. Again he heard the endless barrage, saw the confusion, relived the skirmishing and the retreat. Again he saw the pink smoke of the Austrian shell, heard the explosions of the 4.2's, and from behind a wall a Russian battery commander's shout: "Ready, lads. Eighty. Fuse eighty." All merged into a single, vast uproar. A noisy swirl of horses and men, of dazed refugees going nowhere and colliding on a road littered with all sorts of dead. The Southwestern front was crumbling. The eagerly awaited, long-prepared offensive was a failure. The Germans had turned it into an offensive of their own.

Stepan swayed, dizzy with exhaustion. Names and faces flashed through his mind and were gone, like the retreating army of which he was a part. No wonder, he thought. No boots, no rifles, no supplies. Damned speculators and their Capitalism. His father's face appeared before him. Brusilov, he thought. Alexeiev. The Emperor.

Galloping hoofbeats plunged through his semi-sleep. Stepan tried to shut them out, couldn't, and tried to incorporate them in his meanderings to make them illusory. Still they came on, louder and louder, until he had to admit they were real. Someone was coming up the road fast on his side of the river. He backed off the road under a tree and drew his pistol. The sound rose and then receded, as if an invisible rider had already passed. Then a horse sprang ghostlike from the mist and Stepan shouted. It was a courier from regiment with a message from Borishevsky.

The Germans were already crossing downriver in force and pouring through the thin line. The raw flanks of the entire army were in danger. The line had to be shortened. There was no hope of a counterattack. The bridge had therefore lost all value. Stepan was to blow it at once and withdraw.

As Stepan finished reading, the barrage resumed, slow, steady, insanely deliberate. He wheeled his horse. His mouth was already opening to shout, to order someone over the bridge for the others. Indeed, he shouted across the bridge — it was no longer necessary to fear detection. But there was no answer. The barrage made it impossible to hear.

Then the idea came to him and he hesitated, smiling as its deliciousness dawned. It was so impossibly amusing, such a joke. And there was nothing Stepan loved better than a joke. Belkin, Lopatkin and Marchenko would like it, too. Wasn't it remarkable that the three men with whom he had scores to settle were on the other side? He looked again at Borishevsky's orders to make sure they were signed. They were. That would solve any problems later. He put a finger under the phrase "at once." He grinned. Orders were orders. They could not be clearer. He saw himself standing sadly before Borishevsky, bravely bearing the fact that he had been forced to abandon his friends. He chuckled. Perhaps as the finishing touch he would complain.

Stepan carefully buttoned the orders in a pocket and rode into the trees.

"Prokurov," he whispered. "We're moving out. Take the men at once and I'll follow."

"And the others?" said Prokurov.

199

Stepan adopted a look of resignation. "The others must do the best they can."

"Let me cross," said Prokurov. "All I need is a few minutes."

Stepan shook his head. "Impossible! Too great a risk. The Germans are already crossing in force."

"But they'll be captured, maybe killed."

"Don't you think I know that, you fool!" Stepan flashed. "Be glad the responsibility isn't yours. Now go."

Prokurov did not argue. It was an unusual situation and he did not have all the facts. To wait a few minutes might indeed be dangerous, and the squadron mattered more than any few men. Besides, he was outranked. Prokurov passed the order and the men began moving off along the road.

Stepan dragged the firing box as far as it would go into the trees. He lit a cigarette and savored the moment. The mist still completely obscured the far bank. The three men on it were looking the other way, of course, watching for the forward German columns. They would be so perfectly surprised. This was a joke of the sort one could enjoy for years. What fool was it who said war is hell? The only flaw was that he could not see their reactions — their surprise, their shock, their fear and confusion. That, after all, was the whole point of the joke. Surely it would force some reaction even from Marchenko. Stepan felt somewhat cheated, like the creator of a masterpiece denied his applause. He wanted to hear the others curse him.

He stubbed out the cigarette and caressed the plunger. Such a joke! He pushed the plunger very hard. Nothing happened at first. Then the bridge sprang up like an animal surprised. There was a rapid series of small bursts, then a single blast. A flaming cloud lit up the mist. A shower of blazing bits and pieces rose and fell like a holiday sight. Then there was a long hiss and the scalded ruins settled into the river. The powerful current bore chunks of it away. Its stumps protruded like maimed fingers from each bank. The light faded and went out. Once again it was very dark.

A shout came from the other side. Someone was calling. Stepan leaned forward, stiff with concentration, but could not make out who it was. The voice wavered, fighting to keep calm. He could not place it. Then he realized it was Belkin. It would be. That damned Marchenko! Still, it was such an incomparable joke. And again the voice came, hysteria nibbling nervously at its edges. Stepan squeezed his arm to keep from crying out. The joke was unbearable. It was too funny. He turned his horse and trotted after the retreating squadron, feeling perfectly satisfied and serene.

It had been a terrible day, an impossible day, but it had ended well.

XXVII

Nicholas pored for the hundredth time through the litter of dispatches and reports on the desk. They fluttered as he did so, clutching at his sleeve, like reptilian fingers slimy to the touch. Nicholas shuddered with fear and repugnance. They were trying to pull him into a swamp. And yet he plunged in, goaded by these emotions. He chose a crumpled paper, uncurled it and read. He understood the words but not the meaning. He felt the usual hopelessness and dread. He read it again, made no progress, and felt the same emotion, and then threw it back into the morass. It was gone. He chose another, dealt with it in the same way, and then another, propelling them in a counterclockwise direction, trying to pretend he was directing events; but to his irritation they reappeared unchanged to prove he wasn't. The morass seemed to grow, to spread, to deepen. Shifting and heaving, it was impossible to contain.

It represented the rising tide of reality. It lapped at his ankles and bit at his calves, making a wet, sucking sound, fondling Nicholas almost in appraisal, as a cat plays with a mouse it plans to eat. Nicholas shuddered, repelled; he wanted to escape. And at the same time, he felt attracted, irresistibly drawn, as if involuntarily he would throw himself in. What a relief it would be to surrender and sink. How good it would be to submerge and dissolve. But in still another contradiction, his desire was more horrifying than anything else. He pulled quickly at his moustache and fell back in the big chair. There was no way out. He was trapped. Every way he turned was wrong. Reality had always been the same and could be nothing else — illogical, unreliable, shapeless and dangerous, impossible to master or predict. So unlike the dependable satisfactions of one's own whim and the absolute monarchy of one's own imagination.

There one could be king, even Tsar!

Nicholas stiffened. Just beyond the tall doors there was a noise — or was there? He rose. Yes, there was a voice, a familiar voice. It was she. Nicholas braced himself against the desk and stood erect. He pulled at his moustache and held his breath. Soon the tall doors would burst open. Alexandra would stand on the sill. But the voice rose and fell, rose again and disappeared. It had been another false alarm.

Nicholas sagged. His chest collapsed. Why must he be subjected to this? He had done nothing. He was innocent. To his dismay, he felt a twinge of anger for Alexandra, and this was instantly replaced by fear.

He sank again into the chair and fingered the reports. The situation was critical, so critical that a few facts had somehow lodged in the Imperial consciousness. It was late in 1916. Transport was deteriorating steadily. The number of available locomotives was infinitesimal, and few new ones were being produced. Everything seemed to be falling apart. It was as if someone were deliberately sabotaging the war. And even more important, and more dangerous, prices were rising and food was scarce. People in the cities were beginning to starve. Here in his hand, in fact, was the report of a food riot. It was all the fault of those damned farmers, of course. They could deliver the food if they wanted to. Why wouldn't they?

Something decisive would have to be done; in fact, something Imperial. Nicholas had already replaced Prime Minister Sturmer with Trepov without consulting Alexandra, and this had made the Tsarina nervous. She was worried. She thought it might be bad for "Gregory, our Friend." She complained that Trepov might not like him.

And this in turn made Nicholas nervous. He felt guilty. He too was worried, afraid this might be bad for him, afraid that Alexandra in turn might not like *him*.

And now Trepov wanted to dismiss doddering old Protopopov, Minister of the Interior and a prize disciple of Rasputin's. No successor could like "Gregory, our Friend," as much as Protopopov. Yet Nicholas had turned the matter over, and from every aspect it was obvious that Trepov was right. Protopopov had to go. It was unthinkable that someone so incompetent could be Minister of the Interior, especially in times like these. It was not enough to like Rasputin. People would begin to laugh at Nicholas. They were probably already doing so.

Impossible. Trepov is right. Protopopov must go. Nicholas drew himself up, as he did always when reviewing a decision, and as always fought down panic at the realization that he had made one. A sense of dread squeezed his chest. He knew without being told that Alexandra was already on her way to change his mind.

Nicholas burrowed once again through the reports. They were impossible

202

to understand, of course; everything was; reality was; but he was at least making the attempt.

Again there was a noise, this time the sound of approaching horses. Again Nicholas rose and stiffened. Impossible. Trepov is right. Protopopov must go. The words fled through his mind like a terrified refrain. Now an automobile came to a halt. Doors opened and closed and he heard voices. A psychological electricity seemed to seep into the room. Nicholas stood erect and braced himself against his desk. Inside his well-tailored tunic, he swelled his chest.

Impossible. Trepov is right. Protopopov must go.

A parade of his ancestors passed before him in review: Michael Romanov, Peter the Great, Catherine the Great, Nicholas I, his namesake. A voice echoed, booming irresistibly: You are Tsar, Tsar of all the Russias.

Nicholas pulled quickly at his moustache. "Of course I am," he said aloud. "I, Nicholas Alexandrovitch Romanov, am Tsar of all the Russias."

The Tsar of all the Russias waited, eyes inward, mind prepared, on his blank face a smile. The doors opened.

Alexandra stood on the sill, maternal, imperial, perspiring with love. She was not a big woman, but seemed to be. She stood quite still, watching, weighing. Soon she would spread her wings and swoop.

In her eyes was the thing that had always frightened Nicholas: will, purpose, desire. Nicholas had never understood what it was. Alexandra replaced it at once with tears. Her mouth quivered to indicate suffering. She spread her hands to indicate helplessness. And she waited a moment to heighten the effect.

Her hands rose and covered her face. "Oh, Nicky," she wailed. "Poor, poor Nicky."

The Tsar of all the Russias braced. He was concentrating. He knew he needed to remember just one thing. He said it now, even before Alexandra announced why she was here. "Impossible. Trepov is right. Protopopov must go."

Then she swooped, crossing the room with one flap, and like a hawk on a chicken came to light on his chest.

"Oh, Nicky, Nicky, poor, poor Nicky."

"Impossible! Out of the question! It is as good as done."

"Poor, sweet Nicky."

The Tsar of all the Russias stood like a rock.

Alexandra held him close, so close. She caressed his cheek and lips with her own. All around him he smelled her scent. She put an arm around his neck. She put another around his waist. With a third arm, she rubbed his back. And with another arm she curled his hair.

They were in love, you see. In fact, theirs was a love that would go down in history.

"Impossible. Trepov is right. Protopopov must go."

What! What was this? Alexandra drew back. What in the world? The Tsar of all the Russias making a decision? But everyone knew that Nicky did not make decisions. It was stupid, illogical, uncharacteristic. Who was this man? Slightly frightened, Alexandra peered out at him like an Eskimo, from the igloo of her psychology. Hm, yes, the same hair, the same nose, the same coloring, the same clothes; there could be no doubt; it was he, Nicky, poor, sweet Nicky. But what then was the explanation? What did this mean?

Alexandra hung on tightly with all her arms. She looked over his shoulder at the morass on his desk, but saw nothing. She was hurt, shocked, dumbfounded, afraid. Like a trooper in a trench attacked by a new weapon, she pressed herself flat, trying to hide.

"Poor Nicky. Poor, poor Nicky."

"Out of the question."

Alexandra's voice became hollow. Her confidence was rapidly draining away. She was disoriented. But she decided to proceed as usual, not bravely, but because the usual was so habitual, she did not know what else to do. She would have been afraid to do anything else.

"Nicky, Nicky, think, think. This may be bad for Gregory, our Friend. Protopopov admires and understands him. But what if he is replaced by someone who does not? Think, Nicky, think. The danger is great."

"Impossible," said Nicky. Nicky knew he would be all right, if only he thought of nothing and periodically said this word.

Alexandra's eyes watered even more. Her mouth shook. Her shoulders quivered. "Nicky, I am just a woman, a stupid, weak, insignificant woman. I am helpless. I know that. I can do nothing alone. Only you can help me, Nicky — and you must. You alone are strong enough. I know that this is not your decision. You are surrounded by intriguers here. They are trying to force this on you. You, yourself, want to keep Protopopov, don't you, sweet, strong Nicky? You know how useful he is to Gregory. You must fight them, Nicky. You must be strong."

"Absolutely impossible. Out of the question."

Alexandra fell heavily into a chair. She drew a handkerchief from a sleeve and dabbed her eyes. Her hands shook. The new situation was too much, too incomprehensible. "Oh, Nicky, please, don't abuse me. I am weak. You are strong. Aren't you ashamed? You know how much I have

204

suffered. My nursing, my work at the hospital, is my only joy."

Nicky sighed. "True. I know."

Alexandra felt a tiny thrill. "Oh, Nicky, you know I do my best."

The Tsar of all the Russias bowed his head. "Of course you do."

Alexandra was not sure why, but she felt returning confidence. She rose and embraced Nicholas again. "Darling," she whispered, "you know I do nothing for myself."

"True," said Nicholas. "Beautifully, beautifully true."

The Tsarina's voice breathed unselfishly in his ear. "In fact, never, never have I done anything for myself. You know that, Nicky. I never will."

Nicholas slowly began to relax. He felt himself sinking, sinking with relief into a soothing sea. Tears of joy were plopping on his face. "All true," he said. "Beautiful, so beautiful."

Alexandra flushed with pleasure. The fact that the Tsar was speaking freely somehow seemed encouraging. She grabbed his tunic in her two fists. "Tell me, Nicky," she cried accusingly, "when have I ever done anything for myself? Tell me, Nicky, please. When?"

Nicholas instantly came to her defense. Face still streaming, he embraced her. "Never. Never in your life have you done anything for yourself. I'll tell them all." The Tsar of all the Russias shook his head. "Never." She was right, as always, painfully right. She was so pure, so perfect, so much better than he. He was unworthy of her. He always had been. How dare he make such trouble for her.

Alexandra smiled and pressed him close. She was crying too. She could literally feel their souls unite. There was a mystical bump and they were one. "I do all this only for our son, Nicky, our poor son. Surely you must know that, Nicky. Have we not the right to think as parents, like any others? Won't you think of our poor son, Nicky? Won't you have pity on a poor Russian mother?"

Instantly Nicholas felt a flash of guilt. "I do think of him," he cried. "I do think of him."

Alexandra's mouth shook. She spread her hands. "But, Nicky, you know that Gregory, our Friend, is the only one who can help him, yet you have allowed these intriguers who surround you to persuade you to dismiss Protopopov, who is so helpful to Gregory. Oh, Nicky, Nicky, I am weak, helpless, I am only a woman — and you refuse to be strong."

Nicholas trembled. Alexandra's logic whirled in his brain. As always, nothing was clear. Or was it? He pulled at his moustache. "You are so fine."

Suddenly Alexandra was on her knees, a finger raised. She had located the trouble. "I'm so happy," she whispered. "I have located the trouble. Tell me, darling, before you made this decision did you use Gregory's comb?"

The Tsar of all the Russias blushed. He pulled at his moustache. He was a gentleman, and gentlemen do not lie. "Hmpf," he mumbled. "You see . . . . "

"There you are!" Alexandra shrieked. She felt humble. She knew she was involved in something holy. Her face shone. Her mouth fell, lips pouting in reproof. "Oh, Nicky, Nicky, you know Gregory told you to stroke your hair with the comb before important decisions. It's been blessed. It has the power to influence events. Your decision cannot count without it. Oh, Nicky, Nicky, I am just a poor, weak woman, helpless, defenseless; alone I can do nothing. Will you not be strong, Nicky, for your son — for Russia?"

The Tsarina was pulling Nicholas down. "Come, Nicky, let us pray. Let us pray for Russia and our son."

Everything swirled as always in his brain. Protopopov, life, and reality flashed by. Nicholas could not seem to focus, he pulled at his moustache. Why? Why, oh, why must this be? How could it happen? He had always been as quiet and still as possible. Why, then, did life always teem with such problems? It was not his fault that he was Tsar of all the Russias. He did not want it. He never had. It was not his fault he had been born. If only he could sit down to his dominoes, with nothing to think of but playing the game, or walk in his rose garden at Tsarskoe. That was all he wanted. Was it such a crime?

Alexandra was pulling at him, dragging him down. "Pray, Nicky, pray. Please. Come down."

Yes, perhaps Alexandra was right. Perhaps it was prayer he needed. Perhaps prayer would bring relief. Perhaps it would help him blot everything out, revoke logic and the law of cause and effect.

He bent his knee and began to descend when suddenly the voice in his mind spoke again. Nicholas Alexandrovitch Romanov, it said.

Nicholas started and froze in a crouch. "Why . . . what? Who?"

You are Tsar of all the Russias!

His vision cleared. The whirling stopped. Everything was still, calm and intelligible. Before him was the massive figure of Peter the Great. Peter the Great was pointing at Nicholas.

You are Tsar of all the Russias!

"Yes," said Nicholas. "I am."

Everything was clear. Nicholas stood at attention, as if he, the Emperor, were being inspected. His chest swelled inside his tunic.

"Impossible!" he said. "Trepov is right. Protopopov must go."

Alexandra was pulling at his sleeve. "But, Nicky, remember, you are Tsar. You are Tsar of all the Russias."

"Impossible; out of the question. I am Tsar of all the Russias."

Alexandra embraced his legs, sobbing. "Oh, Nicky, Nicky, you must be strong."

Nicky smiled, perfectly confident. "Impossible. Absolutely out of the question."

"Please, Nicky."

There was a knock at the door and Nicholas started. "Who is that?" he called. "What do you want?"

The door opened. Someone was coming across the floor. A sheaf of paper was placed in his hands. Nicholas stared at it but did not understand. What's this? he wondered. What in the world . . . ? Nothing but a sheaf of paper. And the intruder had already gone. On every page were words and paragraphs, but no meaning. What in the world . . . ?

Nicholas saw the word "dispatch." He remembered. Oh, yes, there was a war on. How amusing. He had forgotten all about it.

Several days passed. Nicholas Alexandrovitch Romanov, Tsar of all the Russias and of Poland, Grand Duke of Finland, Defender of the Orthodox Church and descendant of Peter the Great and of Catherine, stood at a window. It was a perfect day, clear and crisp, and through him flowed a corresponding feeling of well-being. Once again he unfolded Alexandra's note and reread it with pleasure:

"I am fully convinced that great and beautiful times are coming for your reign and Russia. Only keep up your spirits, let no talks or letters pull you down — let them pass by as something unclean and quickly to be forgotten. Show to all that you are the master and your will shall be obeyed — the time of great indulgence and gentleness is over — now comes your reign of will and power, and they shall be made to bow down before you and listen to your orders."

Nicholas sighed. It was nice to be master and have his will obeyed. It was nice to have people bow down and listen to his orders. And it was nice to be strong, very nice. He was glad he had been strong enough to refuse to dismiss Protopopov, against the advice of the petty intriguers who surrounded him. It was slanderous to say that Protopopov was incompetent. It was jealous gossip. He was not incompetent. Nicholas needed him.

The Tsar of all the Russias and of Poland, Grand Duke of Finland and so on, smiled. Yes, the time of great indulgence and gentleness is over. Now comes my reign of will and power.

Nicholas debated about whether to answer Alexandra now or after his walk. From his tunic he drew Rasputin's comb and slowly, meditatively, stroked his hair. He smiled. Yes, yes. All was clear. He sat at his desk and composed a telegram:

"Have arrived safely. A lovely clear day. Two degrees of frost. Thank you once more for dear letter. Hope you are feeling well."

He went to the door to have it sent. And suddenly a wave of anxiety pressed him flat, completely without cause, or so it seemed. He dropped the telegram. With both hands he seized a chair, as if afraid he would be swept away. He could not breathe. A dry heat burned his skin.

When will it end? he wondered. When will it all end?

And suddenly, as in an inspiration, he knew.

"It will never end," he said aloud. "It will go on always. It will never, never, never, never end."

XXVIII

In a small room over a shoemaker's shop in the Spiegelgasse in Zurich, a small man sat at a desk. He was a little man, an unimpressive little man, undistinguished, insignificant, a mild little man; almost microscopic, in fact. It could be said in fact that he had only a small toehold on existence. His rumpled and ill-fitting clothes hung slack. His shoulders sagged. The wispy beard on his flat, Mongolian face was sparse. The only thing big about him was his bald head, which shone.

Yet, at the same time, he was an interesting little man, a fascinating little man. For in all his adult life, he had fully experienced only one emotion: envy. He did so now, as he sat at his desk over his article. In fact, envy, allied with hate, was the motive power behind his article. It was so infuriating, so hateful, to be just one man — that is, one unimpressive, insignificant, meaningless little man. It called for some revenge against the universe. Why in the world did you have to be what you were? Everything and everybody was something specific, something definite. That was the problem. That was *why* he was a meaningless little man. He wouldn't be, if he weren't forced to be what he was.

Those who knew him would have been surprised, of course. He was so unselfish, so completely without ego. He seemed so to *enjoy* being a meaningless little man. He seemed to *like* ill-fitting clothes. He even joked about it. He made fun of himself. He loved a little joke. He did not love a big joke; he was, after all, a little man. And he was very fond of children. He was kind to his wife.

His resentment was his secret, his alone. Like Aesop's fox, he knew that he was sour, not the grapes.

But now as he worked on his article his motive power seemed to fail. His pen faltered. He put it down. Deep within, he heard a tiny voice: You are a meaningless little man. You have always been a meaningless little man. You always will be a meaningless little man. The idea that you could ever be anything else but a meaningless little man is senseless, hopeless, laughable, ridiculous.

The meaningless little man sighed. He massaged his sloping Mongolian forehead. I can't go on, he thought. It's hopeless. Absolutely impossible. Out of the question. I'm a meaningless little man.

The meaningless little man looked at his wife. She was of course a meaningless little woman. Dumpy and shapeless, she slept in her chair. She was snoring. She made an unpleasant, porcine noise. Her mouth hung open, sucking air. The meaningless little man could not concentrate.

The meaningless little man felt a surge of hatred, exactly for what he did not know. Encouraged, he picked up his pen, but then the hatred was gone and he threw it down. He sighed. He put a finger in his collar and worked it around. It was hot, so hot. It was impossible to breathe. There was very little air in the room. He looked at the one window. What a pleasure it would be to throw it open, all the way. Was even this too much to ask? True, he was a meaningless little man, but all he wanted was some fresh air. Did he not deserve to breathe?

But he did not open the window. He knew that if he did, the smell of the sausage factory below would nauseate him.

When will it end, he wondered? When will it all end?

And suddenly, as by an inspiration, he knew.

"It will never end," he said aloud. "It will go on always. It will never, never, never, never end."

He looked at the calendar on his desk. It was March the eighth, 1917.

The meaningless little man sighed. Deep within, he felt again the nasty stirrings of his secret wish, his ambition, the real goal of all his work. It skittered through his stomach on lots of little legs, evil-smelling, small, greasy. It had a long nose and little whiskers. It was gray. It was very friendly. He could feel it rub against his stomach.

He shuddered. The thing repelled him but at the same time he was drawn. He wanted it passionately. He could not help himself. He wanted to embrace it, to bite it, to plunge into the sticky wetness where it stood. Even the thought of it gave him great relief.

As always, he tried to name it, to identify it, to say what his secret desire was. But as always, he could not. The words seemed within easy reach, as if he already knew them, but when he reached for them they were gone. His secret wish remained a secret.

The meaningless little man looked down. Across the floor there came a bug, plump, juicy, obviously a patron of the sausage factory just back from lunch. It was a very interesting bug. The meaningless little man got interested. He placed the length of his shoe before it and watched.

The bug stopped. It extended its antennae and waved them around, sizing up the little man's foot. Then it turned sharply and scurried away.

The meaningless little man smiled. It was a very interesting bug. He placed his shoe before it again. Again it waved its antennae and was gone.

The meaningless little man was fascinated. What a fascinating little game! Such a pleasure! His hooded little eyes began to twinkle. His mouth grinned. His nose puckered. At such times, he could be such a jolly meaningless little man. He raised his foot and placed it, raised and placed it, raised and placed, raised and placed. Such fun!

The bug began to get hysterical. It rushed back, forth, and around on its small square of floor without plan or reason. Then it did so very slowly. Then it stood still, antennae quivering, thwarted, indecisive, disoriented, a rare example of a neurotic bug.

The meaningless little man was thoroughly absorbed. It was remarkable. The interesting question occurred to him: What in the world could the bug think? Did the bug know what was going on? Did the bug really understand why there was no escape — and why there could be no escape? The meaningless little man hoped that the bug did. He was sure it did. He would be so disappointed if it didn't.

But all good things must come to an end — *especially* good things. The meaningless little man was again getting bored. He was getting tired. Besides, it was time the bug was taught a lasting lesson. The meaningless little man realized it was necessary that the bug understand, really understand — deep in its guts — what the whole affair was really about. The bug must be made to know.

The meaningless little man raised his shoe and pressed it slowly down on the bug. It was like stepping into something wet and sticky. There was a pop. A dark green liquid rushed from beneath his shoe. An unpleasant smell filled the room, overpowering even the sausage casings. The meaningless little man smiled. It had been a good lesson. There could be no doubt that the bug understood.

The meaningless little man raised his foot. There was a sucking sound, as if the bug was reluctant to let go. With the blade of a knife, the meaningless little man scraped the remains from the bottom of his shoe.

Lenin sighed.

He felt a great sorrow for humanity.

211

Part IV

Stepan Danilov

XXIX

Maria fell to the floor in the big mirrored room at Natalia Stepanovna's. Painfully she got to her feet and again threw herself down. She rose, rubbing her forearm. Just below the elbow was a big bruise. She had always bruised easily. Her ears still rang; she had knocked her head a few falls ago. Natalia Stepanovna was dissatisfied with her falls. "Over and over, again and again," Natalia Stepanovna had ordered. "Until you reach perfection."

The door opened. It was Natalia Stepanovna's servant. He had a finger to his lips and carried a mug.

"Here, your honor," he said. "Try it."

"What is it?" asked Maria.

"Beer," he whispered. "Delicious."

Edouard Andreievitch liked to bring Maria little treats. He felt sorry for her. He had no idea why Natalia Stepanovna was making her fall down, no idea what ballet was about. He believed Maria was being abused — which, of course, she was. He wanted to defend her. She seemed fragile, breakable, no match for the titanic Natalia Stepanovna.

Maria eagerly took the mug. She had never drunk beer. She wanted to see what it was like. Besides, this falling down was thirsty work. She put the mug to her lips. Over it, she saw Edouard Andreievitch beaming. The door opened. Natalia Stepanovna was already swooping down, snatching the mug from Maria's hands.

"Here," said Natalia Stepanovna, "what's all this?" Natalia Stepanovna puckered her nose. "Ugh. How repellent. Edouard Andreievitch, must you tempt Maria Ivanovna with such a coarse drink?"

In answer, she saw only Edouard Andreievitch's back, just disappearing through the other door. She shook her fist. "Coward! Devil!" She threw up her hands. "As for you, you loafer, are you a dancer? Or perhaps you are a beer drinker! Which is it to be? I leave you for ten minutes and already you are drinking beer."

"Terrible, Natalia Stepanovna. Outrageous."

"If I go out again, I shall probably come back to find you drunk."

"Probably," said Maria, "after what we have seen. Something comes over me, Natalia Stepanovna. You must watch me."

Natalia Stepanovna smiled, mollified. She did not realize Maria was being impertinent. She assumed, as always, that she was terrified. "Quite right," she said. "I shall, you may be sure. If only you were sensible, Masha, like your father." She sat on the chaise longue. "All right. Show me." Natalia Stepanovna drank the beer. As Edouard Andreievitch had promised, it was very good.

Maria again threw herself down. Instantly, Natalia Stepanovna clapped herself on the forehead and was on her feet. "Can it be possible?" she complained to the universe at large. "Can it be possible! Are you a dancer? Or are you perhaps a hippopotamus? Perhaps you are simply a horse, Masha! Why am I cursed with such clumsiness? What have I done?"

"I am sorry, Natalia Stepanovna."

"It doesn't help."

Maria knew that Natalia Stepanovna did not like to abuse her. She felt it was her duty. Maria did not know that Natalia Stepanovna felt it was her duty because she saw that Maria would one day be a great dancer, and therefore not the slightest sloppiness could be allowed to escape. Maria loved this. She loved the strictest discipline, the hardest routine. She loved to test herself against it, to hurl herself into it. She seemed fragile, and she was. But at the same time she had a strong will. This was part of the reason she would be a great dancer. And at the same time, it was the cause of what Natalia Stepanovna complained about now. Maria was hurling herself violently to the floor.

"Are you a piece of shrapnel, child?" complained Natalia Stepanovna. "Are you shot from a cannon? Are you trying to damage my floor?" She spread her arms. Her majestic body filled with joy. "You are an artist. You are a dancer. You are love. You are beauty. You are Giselle and you are dying. Slowly, languidly, you wave an arm. You shed tears. You sink slowly, gracefully, gracefully, gracefully, into the waiting arms of eternity." Natalia Stepanovna's face was shining. "Do you see, child? Do you see?"

"Yes, Natalia Stepanovna. "

Natalia Stepanovna seized her arm. "What's this? What's this bruise? Are you trying to destroy yourself? And you don't tell me. You say nothing."

Natalia Stepanovna was furious. Another addition to Maria's long criminal career! Maria began to apologize, but Natalia Stepanovna would not

216

hear it. She rushed to the door. "Edouard Andreievitch! Edouard Andrei-evitch! What has that devil gotten into now?"

Edouard Andreievitch's white-fringed head appeared at the other door. "More beer?" he grinned.

Natalia Stepanovna made a face. "It was hideous, Edouard Andreievitch, as you know. And please bring a mattress for Maria Ivanovna. She has hurt herself." When he had gone, she waved Maria into a chair. "Come, Masha, sit while we are waiting. Rest.

"Tell me, Masha, what are your opinions about marriage?"

What was this? Maria was suspicious. "I don't know, Natalia Stepanovna," she said. "I haven't thought about it. I have no plans. And my work takes up so much . . . ."

Natalia Stepanovna took her hand. "Child, take the advice of your old teacher who loves you: never marry. A dancer should not marry, especially a prima. And you are going to be a prima, my darling — that is, of course, if you take the advice of your old teacher who loves you.

"No, my dear, it's no good. A dancer must be free. Free! She cannot be running home to cook. There can be no husband to demand her time. She must be free to think, to dream, to dance, to create. And marriage means the death of love. You will see.

"No, darling, take my advice. You must have affairs. Wonderful, glorious, exotic affairs — with lovers of all types and flavors." Natalia Stepanovna was on her feet. Her face shone. Her voice rose, carrying her away. "Glorious affairs. Lovers at your feet, promising, pleading. Roses in your dressing room."

"How wonderful."

"Look at Kshessinska. If only you weren't such a little prude. Ah, such glorious affairs. I could tell you, Masha. I could tell you . . . ."

Natalia Stepanovna whirled and pointed. "Tell me, Masha, have you had an affair yet? One small affair?"

"No, Natalia Stepanovna. I apologize."

"How old are you, Masha?"

"Twenty-one."

"Twenty-one! But that's impossible! Almost a middle-aged woman and not one affair. It's outrageous, Masha. It's not healthy. Do you want to be preserved in a museum?"

"I am sorry, Natalia Stepanovna. I know I'm behaving badly."

Natalia Stepanovna brightened. "Perhaps we can pick someone nice for you. Let me see. Hmm."

Maria stiffened. What was all this? Another of Natalia Stepanovna's schemes?

"Preferably someone who can advance your career. Always mix business with pleasure, Masha. It saves so much time."

There could be no doubt. Maria tensed for what she knew was coming.

"There is dear, sweet Cyril Modestovitch, for instance," said Natalia Stepanovna cautiously.

There it was. Telegin again. Again! The color rushed to Maria's cheeks. It had been no surprise, but still she was flustered. She jumped to her feet. She was furious. She could imagine no circumstance so pressing, no reason so demanding as to make it worthwhile to touch Telegin. She could not bear even to be near him. Why must her career be perpetually involved with politics? She could not bear politics.

"Stop it, Natalia Stepanovna! Please! It's disgusting."

Natalia Stepanovna became haughty. "What's this? Impudence?"

Immediately Maria was subdued. She sat down. "Forgive me, Natalia Stepanovna." She did not really take them seriously, but she could not help worrying about Natalia Stepanovna's periodic refusals to teach.

Natalia Stepanovna marched up and down. "I see. I understand. You refuse to help me do anything to advance your career. You have decided deliberately to work against me. Your technique is passable — barely passable, I should add. Without my struggles you could barely walk. And you know your parts, after a fashion, but still you refuse to understand the real intricacies of the art. The most influential journalist in Petrograd could be your willing slave, throw himself at your feet . . . . "

Maria smiled. The thought of Telegin at her feet was funny.

"Go ahead. Laugh at me. Make me a joke."

"I'm not laughing at you, Natalia Stepanovna."

"Masha, you have been several times in Kshessinska's house. Where do you think it came from — and why? Tell me. Because she can do thirty-two *fouettés?*"

Natalia Stepanovna had always been jealous of Kshessinska. There had been a battle between them for years. Natalia Stepanovna hoped to win it for good with Maria's success.

"No," she said. "I see. I understand. You refuse to profit from the advice of your teacher who loves you. You would rather destroy your career by remaining celibate."

Natalia Stepanovna sheathed her claws. Her manner changed. She was soggy with sympathy.

"Look, for instance, at your poor friend Tata. Pining away for her lost fiancé. Look, Masha. Only engaged and already there is grief. No, Masha, it's bad luck. A dancer should not marry." Natalia Stepanovna sighed. "How long has your brother been missing?"

"I don't know. Several months."

"Such a waste. So sweet, so terribly charming, so perfectly open and sincere."

Maria made a face. Natalia Stepanovna had such a weakness for men. True, Stepan for some reason *was* attractive to women. Maria had tried without success to ask Tata why. She recalled Stepan's last visit a year past. She did not know why, but they had grown apart in spirit. There had been something about Stepan's manner, the expression on his face. He had seemed always to be watching her. His general conversation had been sarcastic.

"Perhaps he will turn up," said Natalia Stepanovna.

"We have not yet lost hope," sighed Maria.

"So sad," said Natalia Stepanovna. "And so characteristic. Isn't it always the heroes who are lost?"

The door opened. Edouard Andreievitch staggered in with the mattress.

Natalia Stepanovna wiped her eyes. "All right. All right. Come. Show me."

Maria stood before the mattress. She was an artist, a dancer, love, beauty. She was Giselle and she was dying. Slowly, languidly, she waved an arm. She shed tears. She sank slowly, gracefully, gracefully, gracefully, into the waiting arms of eternity . . . . It was much nicer with a mattress.

Natalia Stepanovna seemed hesitantly pleased. "Hm. Yes. Perhaps. Again."

Maria did it all again.

Natalia Stepanovna clapped her hands and jumped up. "Yes, that's it. Perfect! Exactly! At last you begin to understand.

"All right. Enough. Go home, Masha. You've driven me sufficiently mad for one day." She was still slightly hurt. She wanted to sulk. "Show me your fingernails." She took Maria's hand. "No, they're too long. Cut them. You'll claw your partner."

"Yes, Natalia Stepanovna."

"What will you do tomorrow morning?"

"I'm not sure, Natalia Stepanovna. It's so lovely. I think perhaps I'll take a walk."

Natalia Stepanovna clapped her cheek. Her paws tingled. Her claws unsheathed. The stiff, tawny fur on her neck stood erect. "A walk indeed! Hmpf! You'll do no such thing! You'll lie down and concentrate on your part. Feet up and put on light-colored stockings. They're more restful. Walk indeed! Such nonsense!"

219

There was a knock. The door opened. Ivan Danilov burst into the room.

The claws retracted. The stiff, tawny fur on her neck fell back. Natalia Stepanovna was a lady in distress. "Ivan Fyodorovitch, I appeal to you," she said, not all surprised. "An important appearance in *Corsair* tomorrow, and would you believe it, she wants to take a walk."

Natalia Stepanovna began to pout. She was helpless, so helpless. It was terrible, horrible. How lucky it was that Danilov had come.

"Is anything wrong?" asked Maria, alarmed. Her father rarely came here. He was strangely agitated.

"A walk, you say?" Danilov said. "Terrible. Unheard of. Out of the question!"

"But, papa . . . ."

Danilov was delighted. "Hmpf! Walk indeed!"

Deep in her throat, Natalia Stepanovna began to purr. She did not know that Danilov knew she was a lioness.

"Dear Natalia Stepanovna," he said. "I am fully aware of your terrible struggle. We all are. We know the true nature of what you must deal with. Be assured that we are fully aware of her criminal activities." He clasped her hand. "Leave it to me."

Maria stamped her foot. "But, papa . . . ."

Natalia Stepanovna sat back in victorious satisfaction.

"Is the lesson over, Natalia Stepanovna?" Danilov asked.

"It is, Ivan Fyodorovitch. I could not go on."

"All right, Masha," he said. "Let's go."

"But what has happened?"

"Nicholas has abdicated. The monarchy is no more. The Revolution is here at last."

"The Revolution?" Maria said, wondering.

Natalia Stepanovna started. "What sort of nonsense is this? Revolution? In Russia? The devils! How dare they? They must be arrested and punished at once." She rushed to the window and peered out. Nothing could be seen but a few sauntering men. Natalia Stepanovna shook a fist. "You devils. You devils."

"But what does it mean, papa?" said Maria.

"It means that at last we can make sense of our situation."

At that moment, they distinctly heard a volley of shots. It seemed quite near. Distant voices began to shout.

"My God!" said Natalia Stepanovna in fear and horror. The day's events had been too much. "Masha," she whispered, and held Maria close. Consumed by this new mood, she began to cry.

Maria petted her. "There, there, Natalia Stepanovna, it's nothing. You know it."

Natalia Stepanovna abruptly stood erect. "That's enough! Stop it! What utter nonsense! All right, Ivan Fyodorovitch, take her. Lock her up. Watch her. Make her practice."

Danilov and Maria left the apartment, walked a few minutes through the streets and were swept away. A frantic mob was coming down the Nevsky, jostling, shoving and mauling each other, all shouting, spattered with red. Many carried banners: *No Annexations and No Reparations, Peace, Down With Alexandra, Down With the Bourgeoisie,* down with this . . . down with that, down, down. A band of children held a banner of their own: *Down With the Parental Yoke.*

With Maria in tow, Danilov pushed through. The sidewalk was packed. A little man with a goatee and his shirt hanging out was shouting: "Freedom, freedom." The main current of pedestrians swirled around innumerable islands of debate.

"Yes, true, but the composition of the government . . . ."

"I assure you that the question of the land . . . ."

"Capitalism must be swept into the dust bin."

"Believe me, the Bolsheviki have no chance."

Everyone poked everyone else in the chest. Everyone argued. Everyone talked. In all of Russia, only one thing could not be found: an official. One of the biggest, most powerful bureaucracies in history had disappeared. Russians hurried to talk, like champagne bubbles following a cork. There was no time to lose. A moment of silence was a moment of waste. It was important to operate one's jaws, if only for the exercise.

"What is happening? What is it?" Maria asked, dazed.

"The workers are assembling on the Viborg side. They are holding elections by a show of hands."

"The Volinski regiment has executed its C.O.!" a man shouted.

"Hooray."

"And the Pavlovsky?"

"What about the Semionovsky Guards?"

Two small old women were muttering and gesticulating.

"Keep your Revolution. What about the price of tea? Two hundred kopecks a pound — when you can get it. Why, it's gone up forty kopecks since the war started."

"Yes, and look at black bread. Eight kopecks."

"Look at them, the loafers. Marching all day. Here, what will you loafers do about the prices?"

221

A gang of soldiers wearing red neckerchiefs was pointing.

"Here, you, take off them epaulets — and be quick."

A small, stocky officer drew erect and spat. On his tunic was the black-and-orange ribbon of St. George.

"Stop that!" the soldiers shouted. "Take off them epaulets. We'll teach you to insult the people's power." They drew near in a body, fists clenched, working each other up to the necessary courage. Their mouths opened. A barrage of sunflower seeds shot forth. People protested. The officer spat again.

Suddenly, there was a volley of shots far down on the Nevsky. People screamed and began to run. Looking easily over their heads, Danilov saw barricades and patches of red. There was shooting opposite the Anichkov Palace.

Danilov held Maria close. She could see nothing. People were running into each other in all directions. A soldier came at them, and with a large hand Danilov pushed him aside.

"What is happening, papa?" she asked. "I can't see."

There was another volley, this one quite near. The crowd rushed about like wild horses.

"Run!" someone yelled. "It's the Cossacks."

"No, the Cossacks are with us. They refused to fire."

"It's the police."

"Look! One of them's up there."

On a nearby roof, a blue-coated figure was crawling toward a machine gun.

"Kill him!" cried a high voice. "Kill the police!"

"Yes!" yelled others. "Kill the police!"

Danilov whirled. The high voice was familiar. And not far away was a little man with a big nose. It was Kolodsky, his former employee. They had not seen each other for years. Kolodsky's mouth curled in a smirk. His eyes stared mockingly at Danilov.

"Kill the brutal lackeys of the Capitalists!" he yelled.

There was a shot. The blue-coated figure on the roof fell. The crowd pushed about even more. Danilov looked closely, but Kolodsky had disappeared.

"To the Fontanka!" someone shouted, and the crowd moved off.

"Yes, to headquarters!" yelled someone else. The soldiers unleashed another deluge of seeds.

Now a big man with a pince-nez was running up and bellowing, "No, no, to the Taurida. To the Taurida!"

"He's right," said voices. "To the Taurida."

222

"Yes, yes. To the Duma!"

The crowd surged off, sweeping Danilov and his daughter along. Others standing on the banks were sucked in as the mob whirled by. The current rose. It was impossible to hear. It was impossible to see. A broad red banner flew in their eyes.

Suddenly there was silence and the torrent stopped. They looked up. They were before the Taurida. Just overhead on a balcony, a man in a tunic shouted and waved.

"You are the first revolutionary guard."

The crowd roared.

"Freedom! Democracy! The Russian Soul!"

The crowd roared again. They loved it.

The man on the balcony beat his chest. "The sobs and pleas of the Motherland . . . ."

He raised his arms. He lifted his face. Tears of joy streamed from his eyes. He could barely go on.

The crowd howled. They loved it. It was great.

The man on the balcony was approaching his peak. His chest was heaving like a bellows. His eyes flashed, his hair flew. His forefinger rose high, reached its apogee, and then with a thrust impaled the crowd.

"Which of you," he roared, "is prepared to defend the Revolution? Which of you will stand to the end against the Capitalists?"

The crowd was still, muted, chastened. The challenge was too demanding, the responsibility too great. Then they were shouting and waving, trying to catch his eye.

"I, comrade, I. Count on me."

"Long live the Revolution."

He raised his arms. Instantly the crowd was still. He controlled them completely.

He extended his hands. His voice shook in the grip of "The Cause."

"Comrades!" he bellowed. "Freedom, purity, victory, glory . . . ."

The crowd roared. They were going wild.

"Comrades, I must leave you," he said. "I am overcome." The door behind him opened and he was gone.

"What will happen now?" Maria asked. "What does it mean?"

Danilov was asking himself the same question. What *did* the events of the day mean? What, exactly? Why were so many shouting anti-Capitalist slogans? He had always dismissed them as meaningless rhetoric. But now, hearing them in the streets, he felt threatened.

His reverie was interrupted; he returned to the present. Someone was shouting. He had lost Maria. Some sailors were before him wearing red ribbons. Obviously Bolsheviks from Kronstadt.

"Stop that struggling," a rough voice said. "Give us a kiss, you little *boorzhui.*"

"Don't waste your time," said another. "She's too skinny."

One of the sailors held Maria's wrists. Another's arm was around her waist. She was struggling.

Danilov roared. The sailors looked up. They saw a furious, hulking bear of a man, thundering down upon them. His mouth curled. His neck bulged with rage.

The nearest sailor opened his mouth to shout. He was too late. A heavy fist exploded in his face. The second sailor was already down. A third raised his arm and was instantly smashed in the stomach. He twitched on the ground, gasping for breath.

The first sailor sat stupidly on the ground, blank and dribbling, still wondering where he was. A peculiar noise came from his mouth. There were shouts and running. From far off came the sounds of scattered shots. Maria had fallen to the ground. Danilov picked her up, quickly, easily. She was very light.

But another sailor was upon them, short, stocky and drunk. He hit Danilov hard on the back, and pulled Maria roughly away.

"Here, *boorzhui,* let go!" he bellowed. "We want your tart, and I tell you we'll have her!"

Danilov whirled. The little sailor looked into a harsh face, eyes cold, cheekbones high, teeth prominent, mouth tight. He also looked into the barrel of a gun. The mouth smiled. The barrel blazed. The little sailor's face exploded.

Another sailor was coming up, waving a knife. Again the tall man smiled faintly, distant, detached, slightly amused. Again he fired, slowly, carefully. The knife clattered on the cobblestones as the second sailor fell across the first.

A woman screamed. An elderly man was on hands and knees, squinting and blindly feeling the ground. More and more sailors were rushing up.

"What happened? Who is it?" someone shouted.

"It's Polovtsev."

"It's the cadets."

"No, it's him! The big one!"

"Get him!"

Danilov half dragged, half carried Maria. Head and shoulders easily visible above the rest, he ran through the crowd like a great stag in the bush.

224

The sailors' shouts were falling far behind. "Get him, somebody. Stop that man."

They were shooting wildly. He could hear the bullets zing and whistle. Quite nearby, someone gasped and fell. The crowd thundered off in a stampede.

Still running madly, Danilov turned into a side street. It was dark. There were only a few people.

"Papa, it's all right now," Maria whispered.

There was another volley. As if in answer, shots were heard from every direction. The whole city seemed about to explode. Sweating heavily, breathing hard, Danilov ran on, still dragging Maria. She had thought she was in better physical condition than he, yet she could not keep up with him.

"Please, papa, stop," she whispered. "I can't breathe."

At last they leaned against a wall.

"You eat too much, Masha," he said between gasps.

"You've never told me that before," she said, gasping too. "Just last week you said I don't eat enough."

"I was wrong last week. You're positively fat." He laughed weakly.

"Papa, that's not true. It's a terrible thing to say."

"True. It is. But since you flirt with sailors . . . . "

"Papa! Stop! That isn't funny."

"It is possible that I can be persuaded not to tell Natalia Stepanova of your latest exploit. But I doubt it. Any suggestions?"

"Please, papa. Be serious. You know she'd make a fuss."

But their gaiety was false. It could not be sustained. As their laughter petered out, so did their conversation.

Their mood was somber as they walked away. They could not shake off a growing sense of foreboding. It was probably just the result of the day's events, Danilov thought.

"There's nothing to worry about," he told himself. "I've financed this thing for years."

XXX

Danilov stood at his desk in his office and slowly packed his personal mementoes: pens, a letter opener, a paper weight, an ash tray. Memories flooded his mind. In the top drawer were some personal letters from friends. He folded them and began to put them away.

The door opened and Kolodsky briskly entered, nose twitching, searching the air.

"No!" he said, pointing. "You may take no papers. You have been told."

Danilov put the letters down. Kolodsky's nose dove at them and began to sniff. They were very pleasing. There were some interesting odors.

"I know that," said Danilov. "But, you see, these papers are only . . . ."

Kolodsky stared at him with the dead eyes of a mole. "Perhaps you would like to spend a few days with us, eh?" said Kolodsky. "At the Gorokhovaia."

Kolodsky howled. He slapped a thigh. He had to admit, in fact, that he had recently become a very witty fellow. Ever since he joined the Cheka. Many people told him so, especially those he came to search. He had never fully realized it before.

Danilov stared at him, perplexed. As he had so many years before, he wondered what Kolodsky was. Danilov remembered having seen him agitating in the streets several months before. He knew Kolodsky was a Bolshevik — but the knowledge added nothing. He simply could not imagine what made Kolodsky run. It was impossible to tell anything about him without a microscope.

"They are only some personal letters," said Danilov, "of no use to you."

Kolodsky's nose jiggled. He jumped up and down. He, Kolodsky, was frustrating his former employer, ordering him around, actually kicking him out of his factory. Kolodsky was in a fairyland made real.

226

His nose wiggled and darted at Danilov. "But there's no such thing, Ivan Fyodorovitch," he said. "The personal no longer exists. Don't you see? It's all ours. All. Even you are ours. Or should I say *especially* you?"

Again Kolodsky slapped his thigh and howled. His wit had become painfully sharp. He remembered another witticism and told it now. " 'Who has been nothing, shall be all.' " It was his favorite quotation. He began to hum the *Internationale* softly. It was his favorite song.

"Suppose you are less than nothing," said Danilov. "What then?"

"Less than nothing?" Kolodsky was puzzled. The quotation had never been greeted like this before. Something was wrong. "What do you mean?"

Danilov smiled. The Revolution had its moments. Perhaps there would be others. But someone was coming down the hall. Danilov heard squeaking shoes. Kolodsky scurried to the door and opened it. A stocky figure stood on the sill. At the top, on a thick neck, a small walnut head appraised the room. Small eyes stared with suspicion. It was a very unusual personage. It was well dressed, but with a strange effect, as if a bear had been stuffed into an evening suit. It was dangerous and at the same time comical, almost clownish.

The unusual figure entered the room, suspicious, distant, head nodding critically, eyes searing everything in appraisal. Its mouth opened and sounds came out.

"Hm . . . yes . . . of course . . . I see."

Danilov was truly startled. What in the world . . . ?

"You have the honor to be addressing comrade Volkov," said Kolodsky, "your successor as factory manager of the People's Agricultural Machinery Works."

With the mention of the name, Danilov recognized the man. Volkov had until recently been his night watchman. Could it be possible? A night watchman had been chosen to run the factory?

Danilov stared. "Volkov . . . ? The night watchman . . . ?"

Volkov came forward, slowly, critically, mouth disdainful, covered with hauteur. Unlike Danilov, who always wore work clothes at the plant, Volkov was dressed like a gentleman. He walked with his hands clasped behind his back, as Danilov always did when solving a problem.

He thrust himself up toward Danilov's face. "You wish to argue?" Volkov said.

Danilov smiled. "Not at all."

"That is good," said Kolodsky. "Comrade Marchenko himself made the choice."

Volkov walked suspiciously around the room and removed his gloves. "Hm," he said. "Yes . . . of course . . . I see." He saw everything. He understood everything, even before it was there. He saw into your very soul. "It's small," he said. "Too small. But it will have to do." He looked knowingly at Danilov. "I am here, of course, to obfuscate the machinations."

"I beg your pardon?"

"I said I am here, of course, to obfuscate the machinations. You wish to argue?"

"Certainly not. You're here, of course, to obfuscate the machinations. Nothing in the world could be more obvious."

For the first time, Volkov smiled. He sat at the desk. He opened a drawer and removed a file, opened the file and looked through it. He knew that when you sat at the desk you looked through a file. He had seen Danilov do it many times, through the glass door of his office, late at night after the others had gone.

But it was a disappointment. It was boring. All he found was sheets of paper covered with numbers. He could not understand them. They made no sense. Comrade Volkov threw the file down.

"Naturally, citizen Danilov," he said, "I intend to introduce many alternative factors into the concepts of machination. Inferior bourgeois methods will be replaced."

"It goes without saying, comrade Volkov," said Danilov. "I have long been aware that you bear within you the seeds of great obfuscation."

Volkov smiled knowingly at Kolodsky. He put his feet upon the desk. To his surprise, his hostility for Danilov disappeared.

"You are wondering why all this is happening," he said.

"I do have some questions," said Danilov.

"You are familiar, citizen Danilov, with the lessons of our great teacher, Marx?"

Kolodsky stiffened. The conversation had become important.

"No," said Danilov. "Unfortunately, I am not."

Volkov raised a finger. "All value is the product of labor."

Danilov was startled, at a loss. "Why, that makes sense!"

"Exactly. And that is exactly why we do not need you. Instead of allowing the factory owner who does nothing to throw them the pit, the workers who create everything have decided to take the whole peach. Because, of course, as the science of Marxism teaches, there is no economic reason for profit.

"Don't you see, citizen Danilov? You're a biological holdover, a curiosity, a fossil. You're an anachronism."

Danilov rubbed his chin. "I see."

Volkov pointed. "I know what you are thinking: 'I contributed heavily to your treasury, comrade Volkov, long before October — when it was dangerous. You owe me something, comrade Volkov. I deserve different treatment. The factory is mine. I did not steal it.' This is what you are thinking, citizen Danilov, is it not?"

"It had crossed my mind."

"I warn you," said Kolodsky. "Do not insult the people's power. I will stand for no more provocation."

Volkov smiled. "Like all anachronisms you are quite naive, citizen Danilov. The facts you have cited, like yourself, are irrelevant. Try to understand. There is nothing personal involved. I hold nothing against you. I like you, in fact. What is machinating here is history, is biology, is physiology, is science. What you alone — a puny atom — have done is irrelevant. You are a bourgeois. That is all we must know. It's a question of blood."

"I see," said Danilov. "May I go?"

"Of course."

Danilov realized painfully that he would never enter his office again. He walked slowly to the door and turned the knob.

Volkov called after him, "All property is theft — stolen from its rightful owners, the people."

Danilov opened the door of what had once been his office and walked away slowly through what had once been his machines. He was somber. He felt eerily disoriented, as if he were attending his own funeral. But the corpse was still very much alive. The machines whirred. He felt them going underfoot. They were unconscious, automatic — they did not know that they were dead. What he felt was their version of a death rattle.

Workmen came out to the center aisle as he passed. They bowed their heads and removed their caps.

"We are sorry, Ivan Fyodorovitch," one said.

"God bless you," said another.

"We have done nothing," said a third.

Danilov nodded. "I know. I know."

An old man came from the crowd at the gate and took his sleeve. "We have not been paid, your honor. Please. Forty kopecks for a biscuit. Eggs, three rubles. Butter, fifty. How are we to eat?"

"All property is theft," said Danilov, "stolen from its rightful owners, the people."

The old man's face furrowed. "All property is theft?"

"The people are now the owners," said Danilov. "Go to them."

The old man began to whine and pulled his sleeve again. "But, your honor, we did not complain. We did not turn you out. We were satisfied. We simply want our pay."

"Yes, yes," said the others.

"Please, your honor," said the old man. "The prices. How are we to eat? Forty kopecks for one rotten biscuit."

Danilov could not answer. He could not talk. He had to escape the painful loathing. He pushed through the shouting men, through the gate. Volkov's voice boomed out behind him.

"All right, you loafers, back to your work. You act as if you own the place."

At last Danilov was outside. The gate clanged. He looked up. Kolodsky's small face was grinning from his office window. Just above, on the building's facade, the tall, bold letters of his name had been replaced. The factory was now "People's Agricultural Machinery." The messily painted new letters dribbled down the brick.

Danilov tramped slowly away over the snow. It was knee-deep. The streets had not been cleared in weeks. It was cold. He pulled his coat close. Its frayed edges were unpleasant to touch. It was three in the afternoon and just getting dark. He was reluctant to go home. This was the worst time of the day. There would be no electric lights until six. And he knew that, as always, they would sit in the light of their one candle and discuss food. But there was nowhere else to go.

Almost reflexively, his large hand closed over the bread ration in his pocket. It fitted easily in his palm. He tried to save it as long as possible every day, but no matter how late he ate it, he always went to bed hungry. An eighth of a pound, the bourgeois ration, did not go very far — especially for a man of his size. He could not control his hand. Almost spasmodically, he tore a small piece off, took it from his pocket and put it in his mouth. Perhaps he would just have this small piece now. But, as he should have known, it was a mistake. Instantly, his stomach sprang savagely awake, pleading, wheedling, demanding more. Every cell in his body was unpleasantly alive, clamoring, complaining. And he chewed slowly, mechanically, literally in pain — knowing that his hunger could not be satisfied, and that the pain would not stop.

Spasmodically, he ripped off another piece and another. He surrendered completely and brought the remaining bread out, ripped and tore at it, wolfing it down. He had known that once he began he would lose control. He searched his hands for any overlooked crumbs. There weren't any. The bread was gone and he was hungrier than before. His body had become a painful burden, a ball and chain which he had to drag around.

The last crumb was now at the back of his mouth and he fondled it as long as he could with his tongue. Then it was gone. Already he was thinking, against his will, of when he would eat next. He vividly saw the communal dining room: the rotten millet, the frozen potatoes, the large vat of watery soup, the old fish heads, the dirt, the surly attendants. The thought made him nauseated. That was good; he could begin to think of something besides food.

He put out an arm and leaned against a wall. Slowly his strength returned. His hunger subsided. It was there, all around him, ready to flare up. But for the moment, at least, it was somnolent, slightly pacified. The attack was over.

Some tattered posters were on the wall: *All Power to the Soviets. Down With the Bourgeois Ministers. Power to the People. Peace, Land, Bread.*

Again Danilov felt intense loathing, not just for Dolgorensky, not just for the Reds, not just for their hypocrisy. Now he felt intense loathing for himself. Like so many others, he had subsidized all this. What right had he to complain about it now? Danilov's face blazed with shame. Was there some fatal weakness in his thinking? Again he visualized the girl who used to come for his contribution. He had seen her just last week. Now she worked for an important commissar. What was her name? Yes, Marina Nikitovna. He remembered Maria's complaints about her and how he had ignored them. But Maria had been right; the Bolshevik talk about freedom had been bunk. Danilov flushed with humiliation. Why had he refused to see this? It was painful to admit, but duped by a few dishonest slogans, he had financed his own destruction.

It had happened so quickly after the February Revolution. The Kerensky Offensive had failed miserably. Crime, anarchy and demoralization had spread. The Bolsheviks had grown in power and then seized the government. And Danilov had approved. Unlike Kerensky, the Bolsheviks were serious. The Bolsheviks would "do things in a businesslike way."

And now the Bolsheviks had evicted Danilov, their supporter. It was early in 1918. Other industrialists still had their places. Danilov considered going to Marchenko to protest, but it was useless. One did not see comrade Marchenko, and protests had no effect. He had protested when the new government had ordered all users of safe-deposit boxes to report to their banks with their keys, opened the boxes, and confiscated what they found.

"Long Live the Constituent Assembly," Danilov read on another wall. Only a short time before, as a member, he had sat on the floor of the Constituent Assembly — which had been dispersed with machine guns by Lenin's Red Guard. During the Kerensky regime, Lenin had demanded that the Assembly be convened.

Danilov shrugged wryly and tramped on through the snow. How completely everything had changed. Nothing meant what it had meant before.

Lenin had urged that local governments — now become soviets — be formed to decentralize the Tsarist dictatorship and destroy it; and then had formed "Committees of the Poor" — composed of the drunkest, laziest, dirtiest crooks in town — which destroyed the local governments and recentralized the power.

That was probably dialectical materialism, Danilov thought. Or was it? Why had he not found out before?

Orloff, his brother-in-law, came to Danilov's mind. How things had changed. Only a short time before, Danilov had been an industrialist and Orloff a hard-labor convict. Now Danilov was a starving outcast and Orloff a Red Army general. Stories about him appeared regularly in the Communist press.

Danilov was home at last. He turned in at the rear entrance and climbed the greasy stairs. Pursuant to a decision of the House Committee, he and his family, as "former persons," were not allowed to use the front. It was very quiet. A dead smell rose from below. Sanitation had disappeared, and their new neighbors disposed of their garbage by throwing it down the stair well. Even the walls seemed to be greasy. Danilov climbed slowly, already salivating, involuntarily anticipating the painful conversation about food. Nadia Nikolaevna would talk about Stepan, of course. And there would be the nightly waiting — for the screeching brakes and the boots coming up the stairs.

Pursuant to a decision of the House Committee, they were living in what had been two small storage rooms at the rear of their apartment. Before they moved in, Danilov had almost forgotten they were there. The other rooms were now occupied by formerly "underprivileged masses," pursuant to a decision of the House Committee. Everything was done or was not done pursuant to a decision of the House Committee. It was to the House Committee that Nadia Nikolaevna had unsuccessfully complained, after Danilov had refused to do so. According to regulations, each citizen in the Socialist paradise was to have sixteen square yards of living space and, according to Nadia's measurements, her family had less.

Maria and Nadia Nikolaevna sat at the table. It was barely lit by a single candle. It was still too early for the electric light. Danilov heard other people moving about in the other rooms. He could not get used to strangers living in his home.

Nadia Nikolaevna's hands fluttered like birds in a trap. She pulled at a handkerchief. She did not look up.

"Well?" she said. "Is it over?"

"Yes," said Danilov. "I am now unemployed."

"Good," said Maria. "Now we're all Capitalist loafers."

Maria, too, was unemployed. Crispina had finally had her revenge. She had been elected chairman of the company's Artists' Committee and ordered Maria expelled. Tata had quit the company in protest.

"Please, Masha, please!" Nadia Nikolaevna said crossly. She could not bear the slightest humor. She bowed her head. Her fingers fluttered, kneading her handkerchief.

Danilov was filled with horror at the sight. Once again he had been wrong. He had always expected that, under stress, his wife would be strong and his daughter would need coddling. But in the current situation, the reverse was true. Nadia Nikolaevna was like champagne in a bottle without a cork; it was still champagne, but the bubbles had gone. It was not a lack of character. And it was not a lack of courage. It was simply that she had been made for a different life.

Danilov shuddered with unaccustomed impotence. The situation was impossible. Nothing could be done.

There was a long silence. Everyone unsuccessfully sought for something to say. Danilov put his hands in his pockets for warmth, and to his surprise discovered still another crumb of his bread ration for the day. Automatically, without thinking, he put it in his mouth and began to chew. As always, the puny pleasure was not worth the intense pain. The simple act of eating had been transformed. For a moment, he regretted not having offered the crumb to Nadia Nikolaevna and Maria, even though they had already finished theirs. They were staring at him wordlessly in the wavering light, mesmerized, trans-fixed, hypnotized, studying every detail of the operation of his mouth. But he realized that to do so would have been a mistake. They did not know that they were staring. They did not know what they were doing. They, too, were in the grip of a reflex. Had he offered the crumb, as he often had in the past, they would have started, as if suddenly awakened, and rejected it with cries of protest. They all had played through the scene many times.

Danilov forced the crumb down and the clock struck. It was one of the many things they still had left. They had been lucky; they had been raided only once.

"Well, it's nearly time to dine," he told Maria. It was one of their many jokes. They called the communal kitchens, where the Bolsheviks handed out the food, "restaurants," and described what they did in them as "dining."

Maria laughed, a laugh without irony. She had not yet been touched psychologically and spiritually by the Bolshevik coup. She refused to be touched. That was why, unlike Danilov's, her laugh contained no bitterness.

She refused to admit there was cause to be bitter. She refused to admit that what appeared to be happening was really happening. It was real enough, of course, she knew. But it was not reality. It wasn't the thing known as "real life." It was "reality" of an unusual and strictly limited sort. It was a piece of bad theater on which, after a time, the curtain would fall.

"Yes," she said. "Perhaps there will be a nice fish head."

"It wouldn't surprise me," said Danilov.

"I love a nice fish head."

"So do I. There's nothing in the world I like better."

"But suppose there isn't, papa. It's happened before."

"Perhaps there'll be a nice frozen potato."

"I love a nice frozen potato."

"So do I. There's nothing in the world I like better."

"Perhaps there'll be soup."

"I hope so," said Danilov. "I like greasy, hot water."

"So do I."

"Our tastes coincide."

"Yes," said Maria.

"Have you ever wondered who eats the actual fish?"

"What do you mean?" asked Maria.

"The fish to which the heads belong. Fish heads, like all other heads, are originally always attached to bodies. That is why we call them heads. Didn't you know that, Masha?"

"Papa, please! You don't mean there is more to a fish than just the head?"

"Of course there is. Otherwise a fish head would be called something else." They laughed.

As usual in their hopeless situation, the conversation turned nostalgic. They began to compare the various excellences of their favorite restaurants, here in Petrograd, and in Moscow: Donon's, the Cuba, this one and that one.

"Oh, yes, and the whipped cream, papa. And the sticky sweet buns."

"Yes, and the roast beef. Those juicy, thick slabs."

"With those huge gravy boats."

"Yes, I had almost forgotten."

"And the beautiful linen, papa. Don't forget that."

Once again their senses came alive. Heavy tables buckling with food passed before them in the dim light — roast meats, fruit, eggs, sugary desserts, chefs all in white and waiters like generals. They began to salivate. They got dizzy. Their heads spun in a welter of tastes, colors and smells.

"Stop it!" said Nadia Nikolaevna. "Stop it! Stop it! Stop it! Stop it!"

234

She pounded the table with the flats of her hands. "Must you both continue this senseless charade night after night?"

But she knew as well as they did that the answer was "yes." Night after night, no matter where the conversation started, it somehow always arrived at food.

The door opened without a knock and Anna Andreevna Kursamina sauntered in. "What's going on in here?" she said. "Why all the noise?" She was munching on exactly the sort of bun Maria had just described.

Anna Andreevna had come far from her days in the bordello. In fact, she who had been nothing now was all. She was chairman of the House Committee, and had the Danilovs' bedroom all to herself, which she owed to the fact that she was now the mistress of comrade Marchenko, Kolodsky's Chekist boss.

Anna Andreevna had changed. Now she was a Bolshevik. They had treated her very well for having been involved, however accidentally, in the scheme to free Orloff. She no longer blamed them for her imprisonment. As they taught, she now blamed the system. Her bitterness had permeated and hardened her completely. But now, as a practicing Bolshevik, she was in charge. The parents who had disowned her after her arrest had recently come to visit, ragged, pleading for help, nervously hoping for reconciliation. Anna Andreevna had coldly sent them away, taking great pleasure in berating them for seeking special favors. Her bitterness intensified. Her revulsion increased.

Indeed, the only thing that had not changed was the story of her arrest. Over and over she referred to it and repeated it to the same people. She was innocent. She had been betrayed. Michael Voronov, Danilov's former employee, could have said the word to free her but did not. It was an essential, underlying theme of her psychology — like everyone else's talk about food — just below the surface, waiting to break out. The others knew the story by heart.

"Damn, it's cold in here," she said. "How can you bear it?"

It was not a stupid blunder. She knew very well that they had no wood. These provoking remarks were one of her specialties.

Nobody answered. The presence of this woman who had commandeered their apartment, who walked on their floors and handled their things, was intolerable. They stared at her with frustration, with aversion and contempt, and with complete attention on the sugared bun she was eating.

"God, this is good!" she said. "You really should try one." Her mouth opened and another piece of the bun disappeared.

"We lost citizen Koroshin," she said. "Did you know? The man downstairs. Died this morning. Or at least, we think so. Stiff as a board he was when we found him." Now she was carefully licking the sugar from each finger. "Pitiful," she said. "Makes your heart bleed, doesn't it? Of course, it wasn't the cold that killed him. But you know that." She finished licking and brushed her fingers together. A barely noticeable twitch developed in Nadia Nikolaevna's left eyelid.

"It's a fascinating thing, this process of starvation," Anna Andreevna said. "I was reading about it just the other day. I love to read. I was working in a book store when I was betrayed. Have I told you that?

"What was I saying? Oh, yes, starvation. I was reading about it. It seems the horrible pain doesn't last forever. No, after a while there's a sort of numbness, a stupor, a kind of trance which apparently doesn't bother one a bit. The only problem then is the swollen limbs. Of course, no two cases are exactly alike. Take Koroshin, for instance . . . ."

Koroshin had been a very old man who lived alone with no one to help him. By refusing him food and wood, Anna Andreevna had as good as killed him. Maria wanted to scream this at her. She looked at her mother. Nadia Nikolaevna's lower lip began to tremble. Anna Andreevna saw it, too.

"Something occurs to me, Nadia Nikolaevna," she said. "You're a bourgeoise. Let's do some business. Business is what you understand, isn't it? You clean up my rooms and I'll see what I can do about some food."

Danilov rose.

"Wait, Ivan," said Nadia Nikolaevna nervously. "Please." Her lower lip was out of control.

"Get out of here at once," said Danilov.

Anna Andreevna was slightly frightened, which annoyed her. She knew there was nothing whatever to fear. She put on a face of hurt surprise.

"But I'm only trying to help. After all, I am chairman of the House Committee. If you insist on being rude, perhaps I should consult comrade Marchenko."

"To hell with your House Committee and to hell with your comrade Marchenko," Danilov roared. "May he die slowly with a bullet in the belly."

Anna Andreevna could not help it. She was scared. Danilov was absolutely without fear. Anna Andreevna feared that her face would lose its haughty look.

Maria lost control. "Didn't you hear what he said?" she screamed. "Get out at once."

Anna Andreevna shook her head. "All right. I'm going. You don't need to shout. Now do you see what I've been talking about? It's stupid to help a neighbor. One only gets abuse."

The door closed and she was gone. The three Danilovs looked at each other, embarrassed, revolted, frustrated, angry. They tried to get themselves under control. They did not speak. There was nothing to be said. What had happened was all explained by one word: "Revolution."

"Ivan, I have cleaned house before," said Nadia Nikolaevna softly after a time, bent low over her handkerchief. "I'm cleaning now. Perhaps if Anna Andreevna will really give us food . . . ."

"No," said Danilov. "Do not mention it again."

"Is all this really happening?" she said. "Are we all really alive? Are these people really human, like us?"

"One wonders," said Danilov.

"Everything upside down," she said. "Everything backwards. Tsar gone, country gone, Stepan gone, our house gone."

"We don't know for sure about Stepan," he said. "He may be in an Austrian prison camp, in which case he's doing quite a bit better than we are."

Nadia Nikolaevna shook her head. "No, no, even if he is alive, the Cheka has him. I know it."

"Nonsense, Nadia. What would the Cheka want with Stepan? If he is alive he is simply an unimportant former lieutenant."

"No, Ivan, he is a member of the Order of St. George. He is a bourgeois like us."

"Wait, mama," said Maria. "He'll turn up. You'll see."

But Nadia Nikolaevna was not impressed. "No, no, he's gone."

The conversation petered out. Soon they would go to the "restaurant" to "dine," perhaps on a nice fish head or frozen potato. Then they would sit at home in the dark, listening, waiting, wondering who would be arrested next.

XXXI

It was the worst of times, but it was not also, like the French Revolution according to Dickens, the best of times. The Bolsheviks had systematically shattered the country in order to seize it, but now they did not know how to put it back together. They had confiscated all property, of course, and outlawed trade. The factories did not produce what the farmers had been promised in exchange for their crops. The farmers stopped going to market. The Bolsheviks forcibly confiscated the crops, and the farmers stopped planting.

Whether one ate or starved had become a matter of politics, of class, of the category of one's ration card, of whether or not one received extra rations as a student or an employee of this or that Soviet bureau.

Tata Beresova and Maria were aboard a train moving north to Petrograd. It was cold, frigid in fact, even though they sat on warm straw in the middle of a freight car packed with people. The smell of stale bodies hung in the air. The ride was long and they could not see out the door to judge their progress. Hour after hour the wheels barely turned, little faster than a man could walk. But Tata and Maria were contented. It had been a good day. Like many of the millions who enjoyed no extra rations, they made regular trips to the surrounding towns, which were teeming with speculators who, for the right price, could supply anything. The Communists had been unable to stamp out trade and speculating completely. It was absolutely the only way "former persons" like themselves could eat.

Now they huddled nervously around their loot: some eggs, bread, a bottle of milk, some sausages. Tata had even managed to corral a bit of wood. She had torn down part of somebody's old fence. The fence was now unnecessary. There were no more animals to contain. The wood would be more valuable at home in Petrograd, where people needing fuel were tearing buildings down. The girls had set aside portions for their parents and could not bear waiting to devour their own. But they were completely surrounded. They knew that most of the others were nervously concealing food of their own, waiting just as painfully to devour it. But they knew it would be a mistake to bring anything edible into view.

"I can't bear it," whispered Tata.

"I can't either," said Maria, "but we'd better wait."

Sitting against the wall not far away, an overgrown boy in a ragged army overcoat stared at them lazily. His expression was blank, without comprehension. His mouth hung open in a stupid grin. Next to him, someone was engaging in the national sport of spitting sunflower seeds. They fell in a row at Tata's feet, and there was no room to pull her feet away.

"Have you ever seen such louts?" she asked in French.

An indescribably ragged old man looked up and shook his head in warning. He, too, was a "former person." The car was full of every conceivable sort of being, dressed in every inconceivable sort of way. Many of them were going nowhere in particular. They were simply travelling, like driftwood on a tide. And all talking, talking, talking.

"In fact," said a voice, "the Bolsheviks will succeed only because they are dealing with Russians. For three hundred years we have been waiting to talk. That is why we now form committees and go to meetings. Ask yourself, do any of these committees or any of these meetings have any real purpose? Have you ever seen them accomplish a thing? Of course you haven't. Their sole purpose is to make a forum for talk. The Bolsheviks would never succeed if they were dealing with Englishmen or Swedes. Look at me, for instance. I'm a classic example. As you can see, I am incapable of being silent. I am simply compelled to talk, talk, talk, forced to babble on and on . . . ."

There were cries of "Shut him up!" Throw him out!" and "Quiet!"' '

"I can't help it," he said. "I'm Russian. Don't you see?"

"Then we had them surrounded," a calm voice was saying with satisfaction. "First we pulled off their epaulets . . . ."

Tata was reminded of Stepan, her fiancé. Tata still insisted that Stepan was alive. But with the passage of time she believed it less. No, she finally admitted, Stepan had gone for good. First the Bolos had pulled off his epaulets. Then . . . .

The cold and hunger, the intolerable boredom, the interminable trip all pointed a single way. "Stepan is dead, Masha," she said. "I know it."

"Yes," said Maria. "I have long thought so."

"He can't be an Austrian prisoner. We would have heard."

"No," said Maria. "The Bolos got him."

"First they pulled off his epaulets. He wouldn't have done it himself. He was so proud. You knew that. You were his sister. Then . . . ."

"Just think," said Maria, eager to change the subject. "If you hadn't quit the company, you wouldn't be on this train now. You'd be a certified Soviet performer, with extra rations."

"And I'd feel guilty. They'd stick in my throat."

"You shouldn't have done it," said Maria. "It's every man for himself. It was stupid to quit on my account."

"Don't overly flatter yourself. There was more to it than that."

"You disillusion me, Tata. I am hurt."

"You never danced for the new proletarian audiences. Crispina had already had you fired. You never suffered their obscene gestures and remarks, their noise and smell, their sunflower seeds. For the first time, I somehow felt indecently dressed."

"You're a snob, Tata."

"Yes," she laughed. "So are you."

There was an edge in Tata's voice. Maria had raised a sensitive subject. The revolutionary audience *had* repelled Tata. But, as Maria had said, she had quit the company mainly because Crispina had expelled Maria. And now, after several weeks of searching painfully for food, Tata slightly resented Maria. She felt guilty for this, and resented her slightly more.

"I can't stand it," said Tata in French after a time. "Not another minute. I refuse."

"Wait, Tata. Please," said Maria.

"Being right next to it is torture. I shall faint."

Tata raised her shawl, silently unwrapped the end of the sausage, and with their heads together they inhaled the intoxicating smell.

The shawl was suddenly whirled away. Before them stood the seed spitter, pointing and gesticulating. "Look at this, will you comrades!" he bawled. "The *barinyas* have got themselves a sausage."

Behind him was the stupid boy, grinning incessantly. His expression had not changed.

"Give it here," said the seed spitter, advancing. "You know damned well speculation is illegal."

The girls were already on their feet. "Don't you touch us, you ape!" Tata yelled.

Maria was gathering up their goods, and the seed spitter became enraged. "Look at this, comrades. They've got a whole pile of stuff. While us honest workmen are too weak to work, the *boorzhui* are speculating with food that belongs to us."

240

"Ain't that always the way," said a voice. "Damned oppressors."

"Go on!" said Tata. "You never worked a day in your life."

"Give us those sausages!" the seed spitter bellowed. "We're honest workmen. They belong to us."

At that moment, the train lurched and came to a dead stop. People rose and fell and were thrown against the walls.

"What's happening?" asked somebody.

"Where are we?"

"I don't know."

Somebody threw the door open. It was still quite bright. They appeared to be somewhere near Gatchina. They were stopped on a curve and far ahead, just where the train disappeared, Maria and Tata saw a band of men in the snow.

"It's a search detachment!" someone shouted.

"It's the Cheka!"

A tremor of fear passed through the car. The men in the snow were working their way back, turning people out of the train.

"Oh, my God!" said Tata. "It is."

The car came alive with movement, everyone futilely wondering what to do with the groceries he had hidden in his clothes, which the Chekists would now confiscate.

"What shall we do?" said Tata.

"Get off!" said Maria, shoving her. "Get off the train."

"But why, Masha? Are you sure?"

Maria shoved her hard and followed her through the door. They both were on hands and knees in the snow. They got up with difficulty, encumbered as they were. They were quickly behind a drift, barely out of sight of the men down the line.

"Run," said Maria. And they began to do so.

The noise behind them fell away. The dominant sounds now were their own breathing and the soft crunch of the snow underfoot. If only they could reach the trees at the bottom of the incline.

But then there was a shout. "Look at the *boorzhui!*"

"Stop those lousy speculators!" the seed spitter yelled.

Behind them, they heard the thuds of three others jumping off the train, and the crunch of running feet added to their own.

"Come back with that stuff, you thieving wenches!" someone called.

The girls were running well, as well as possible. Tata already had reached the first trees. But the men behind were quickly gaining. Maria did not turn around, but she could hear heavy footsteps and breathing almost as loud as her own. Another minute and she would be caught. She was gasping. She knew that in any moment her lungs would burst. Then she herself was at the trees, and at that moment she was hit very hard from the rear. She fell in the snow and heard Tata scream.

Hands turned her over roughly, tearing and pulling, searching the folds of her clothes for food. Her packages were gone. The breath had been pressed out of her. Her mouth and eyes were full of snow. The seed spitter was on top of her, pressing her flat, his face very close to hers. Some unspat seeds still clung to his lips. He was laughing. His teeth were crooked and brown. Maria recovered her breath and began to fight, silently, furiously and futilely. Tata was both swearing and crying nearby. She, too, was struggling without effect.

Someone shouted. There was a different sort of crunch, the sound of bone encountering a fist. Then suddenly, the seed spitter was gone, abruptly and completely, as if plucked away by an invisible force. Maria sat up. Tata was already coming toward her. Only a few feet away, the seed spitter lay still. Somebody else lay further back in the trees. And the stupid boy with the grin was running up the incline to the train.

Someone stood before her, looking down. Maria looked up, but she could see nothing. He was standing against the sun, his silhouette glowing at the edges. He was tall. She could see only that his profile was like the blade of an ax. Then he moved so that Maria could see his face.

It was Michael Voronov.

He wore an old Austrian army overcoat without insignia, a Russian cap and Russian boots. His face was expressionless. His prominent teeth were slightly exposed. His steel gray eyes looked down at Maria, calm, distant, uninquisitive, uninterested, simply recording and cataloging the necessary facts.

Despite the cold, Maria unaccountably felt hot. She was sure her face had become very red, as if she had done something to be embarrassed about. She felt that her skin was unusually sensitive, as if each cell, pore and hair were operating independently, painfully recording the slightest impression. It was a fleeting notion, and it quickly passed.

The seed spitter was now conscious. His lips were free of seeds. They had been washed away by blood. The left side of his face was swollen and he staggered into the gully at the bottom of the incline leading to the train.

"I'll see you again, you rotten crook!" he shouted.

Michael took two steps toward him and he turned, and began crawling quickly up the incline.

"Thank you so much," said Tata, coming up. "What luck."

Michael did not answer. A trace of disdain crossed his face, too faint to be noticed. He took a large sack from inside his overcoat and silently began picking up the groceries.

"Oh, no," said Tata. "Please. You've already been too kind. Let us do that."

She picked up the milk bottle. It had not broken. Michael took it and put it in the sack. He picked up the other groceries and put them all in his sack. Then he threw the sack across his back.

"What are you doing?" Tata asked.

"Isn't that obvious?" said Michael. "I'm robbing you."

"But, then, you're no better than they are," said Tata.

"That's right."

"You're a bandit, too."

"Correct. Trust no one and rely on no one."

"You've done this only to get the food yourself."

"Yes." He hefted the sack. "You made quite a haul."

"We didn't steal it!" said Maria angrily. "We bought it. We aren't thieves."

Again the expression of disdain crossed his face, and this time Maria saw it there. It annoyed her; she was usually the one to be disdainful.

"Of course you are," he said. "We all are. Don't you know that? Buying and selling food is illegal. When you bought this stuff, you were stealing it from the state."

"That's nonsense," said Maria, annoyed by his certainty.

"Of course it is, but please don't make a speech. There's nothing I like less."

"I won't," said Maria. "Just give the food back."

"No," said Michael. "You'll make one anyway. I know your type. Seething with rectitude. You live to make speeches but you don't know a thing."

Maria flushed. Such a thing had never been said to her before. She wanted to reply with something devastating, but could not.

They heard distant but excited voices. The Chekists were coming down the line.

"They'll be here before long," said Michael. "We'd better get scarce. There's a hut two or three *versts* straight back in these trees. And there's enough here for the three of us. You may as well come along."

"But some of that is for our parents," said Tata.

The remark irritated him even more than the others. "It's rotten with search parties between here and Petrograd today. You'd never get through. Not with a crumb. In fact, the thief I just dealt with is telling the Chekists about it now, so that they can steal from me what I just stole from you. The only question is which particular thieves will get the prizes — the Chekists or the three of us."

"No," said Tata. "We're not going."

Michael shrugged. "Suit yourselves." He turned and started off through the trees.

"Wait!" said Maria. She pulled Tata angrily along. He was right, of course. The Chekists would be along at any moment, and that would mean questions and papers and possibly arrest. Indeed, the Chekists had already taken food from them several times. It was important to get away at once.

Michael did not answer. He did not turn or even slow down. It was another demonstration of his inviolable calm, his perfect certainty, the fact that she seemed to be making no impression.

He moved quickly and easily through the trees with the sack. Freed of its weight, the girls nevertheless had to work to keep up. They glared at his tall form, always just ahead, moving effortlessly and erectly in the Austrian overcoat.

He had picked the coat up in an Austrian prison camp. He had been trapped on the wrong side of the river and captured soon after Stepan had blown the bridge. He knew that Stepan had done it deliberately, not for any particular reason or result, but simply because he had thought it funny. Stepan, he knew, was a great one for jokes. And Michael knew, calmly and surely, that when next they met he would kill Stepan with the same emotion with which one finishes a fly.

He had escaped some months before at the end of 1917, between the Bolshevik takeover and the treaty of Brest-Litovsk. He had had no particular complaint about the prison: indeed, it had compared very favorably with the Russian variety he was used to; the service was better and there was a better clientele. It had been more comfortable, in fact, than the trench life that preceded it. But Michael still found it impossible to adapt himself to prison life. He realized that this difficulty limited his chances of success in organized society.

Now, like many others, he had become a bandit. One had no choice. One took what one could. That was the only way to stay alive. And Michael liked this arrangement. It corresponded to the way he felt. It was clean. It was honest; that is, without hypocrisy. It wasn't falsely solicitous or sentimental. It recognized that in real life there are only two sorts of people: the victims and the victimizers, the givers and the takers, the betrayers and the betrayed.

That was why he so admired the Bolsheviks. They, of course, were the biggest crooks of all. Time after time he had decided to join them, feeling that he already belonged. Perhaps one day he really would. After all, he had been imprisoned for political reasons by the Tsar. He would be welcomed. He was someone who had "suffered before October for the Revolution," as the Bolsheviks would put it.

But at the same time, Michael felt repelled as intensely as he was attracted to them. The Bolsheviks didn't steal honestly. And they made too many speeches. They insisted they were committing robbery for the victim's own good. Even a small-time crook — like himself, he thought — readily admits he steals just because he wants the prize. That was honorable. It was clean. Michael remembered Orloff, who was also very fond of speeches. They all were. And so were these girls, although they were on the other side. Especially the tall, solemn one. She, too, was bursting with speeches. It was apparently an unfortunate, universal problem.

They were soon at the hut. Wedged among the trees against a hill and almost covered with snow, it was difficult to see. They went in and sat down. There was no fire, but it was surprisingly warm inside. Michael emptied the sack and spread the food out on it. No one spoke. No one could. They all began to salivate, simply savoring the sight.

Then with exaggerated slowness, as if afraid they would lose control, they each picked up a sausage. As they bit into the greasy meat, their taste buds came alive with a painful shock. It was wonderful not to have to take infinitesimal mouthfuls to prolong the meal, to be able to eat as much as one liked. Maria and Tata wolfed down large chunks of meat. They were hungrier than Michael. They had not eaten as recently. Now they ate with uncharacteristic noisiness, interspersed with exclamations. Maria felt dizzy. She was sure she would be sick.

Michael threw back his head, closed his eyes and drank some milk. It was ice cold. It was ecstasy. It was something one could be sure of. Then, breathing hard, they all collapsed on the dirt floor. Eating like that was not easy work, especially when one was out of practice.

"I'm going to be sick," said Tata. "I feel it."

"Go outside if you're going to make a mess," said Michael.

"Ugh!" said Tata. "Must you be so crude?"

"Obviously he doesn't know any better," said Maria.

Michael chuckled. "You'll have to polish off the rest. The Chekists may find us. We must destroy the evidence."

"Oh, no. Impossible!" said Maria.

"Mercy!" said Tata. "Please! I can't!"

"I'll bury it, then. The snow will keep it fresh."

He gathered up the remaining food, went outside and buried it beneath the snow. When he came back, streams of milk were still running from the corners of his mouth. He blotted them up with the end of his sleeve.

"It's difficult to imagine," said Maria, "but in normal times people eat like that as a matter of course. They're doing it right now in England and America."

"Yes," said Tata. "Isn't it fantastic?"

"But these *are* normal times," Michael said gently. "Perfectly normal."

He shook his head, as if puzzled that they did not understand. He knew that the smaller girl could not. She was the sort that grapples violently with life without ever really knowing what it was about. She was intelligent enough, but she lacked the necessary fineness of mind. But the other one, the tall, skinny girl with the voluminous black hair, she did have the ability to understand. But she refused. Like so many others, she was a naive little prig, annoyingly self-righteous, belabored by ideals. She smugly denied the existence of real life. Still, she had a certain quality. Her face seemed familiar, as if Michael had always known her — or wanted to. He was sorry that she refused to understand. This would certainly cause her grief. Indeed, it was always far worse later for those who had the ability to understand but at first refused, than for those who simply could not understand at all.

"And England and America do not exist," he said.

"That's nonsense," said Tata. "Of course they do."

Maria lost her temper. Why was he so smug? She wanted to hurt him, to shake his composure. He refused to understand. And he had said he was a thief and robbed them. But at the same time, he did not look like one. It was as if he were somehow trying to be evil, without success. She could not make him out. To her annoyance, she felt drawn to him. He had a certain quality.

"Why are you so bitter?" Maria flashed. "You and your Revolution have robbed us. You and your fellow peasants have everything you want."

"You're confused," said Michael. "And at the same time, you are right. I'm not bitter in the least. One shouldn't be. Bitterness means that one is unhappy with the way things are, that one feels wronged and wishes things were otherwise, that one believes things *should* be otherwise. But they shouldn't. Sooner or later you will see that that is true."

He spoke as always flatly and surely, as if contradiction were not only impossible but inconceivable. It was infuriating. Maria felt like an insect fluttering in a web.

"But it isn't," she said, exasperated. "Bolshevism isn't normal. It couldn't be. Very soon we'll wake up and find that Lenin wasn't real. This horrible nightmare we're dreaming will be over. But until that time we should ignore him."

"That's right," said Tata.

Michael chuckled. "It's very embarrassing," he said, "but the truth is that years ago I believed such nonsense myself."

"It's true," said Maria. "You should believe it now."

"But, you see, Lenin *is* real. He *does* exist. And he won't disappear. If he were to disappear — he and his entire band — it wouldn't make a particle of difference now. That's the lesson you should learn. And you will learn it. But you should learn it quickly. Because the longer you wait, the more painful it will be.

"Perhaps, on second thought, that would be best. You will learn it well, indelibly. Forget everything I've said. Ignore it."

Michael was disappointed. She was so hopelessly naive. On one side or the other, these types were all the same. They all needed a good lesson — a lesson in reality — to cure their painfully stupid hypocrisy. His eyes narrowed, his nostrils flared and the corners of his expressive mouth drew down. His axelike face became remote and cruel.

"I already have, peasant!" said Maria. "Please don't waste your solicitude on me. Perhaps you should join the Bolsheviks. That's where you belong."

Suddenly, Michael remembered who she was. It was the disdain with which she pronounced the word "peasant." When had he last seen her? . . . 1910? A completely different universe. The same contempt had been in her voice then. It was in front of the Imperial Theater on Theater Street. She had been with her brother, Stepan Ivanovitch . . . .

"The last time we met . . . ."

"We have never met, peasant! We never will."

". . . was in nineteen ten. A different world, of course. You were even skinnier, if possible. But you were the same stupidly condescending, spoiled brat you are now."

Maria blushed and became even more furious. "Come, Tata," she said. "Let's go." She got up, but Tata did not follow. She was beginning to enjoy the conversation, although she was annoyed by the fact that she seemed to be left out.

"It was in front of the Imperial Theater on Theater Street," said Michael.

"Yes," said Tata. "It would have been."

"You were getting out of a carriage. You were with your mother. Telegin was there."

"Yes," said Tata. "Her admirer."

"And there was your brother, Stepan Ivanovitch. Yes. We two also met again."

"Where?"

"At the front. In the same regiment. The Grand Duchess's Hussars."

"He was my fiancé," said Tata. "Stepan is dead."

Maria saw genuine regret on Michael's face, genuine but strange. It was the expression of a wolf denied his prey.

"Are you sure?" Michael said softly.

"Yes," said Tata. "He was lost in the 1916 offensive."

"I'm sorry," said Michael. "That really is a shame. I've been looking forward to the pleasure of meeting him again."

The girls shuddered. There was something about his face; the eyes slit, the skin taut, the lips barely restraining the teeth.

"Why?" asked Tata.

Michael smiled. "The usual reason. To discuss old times."

"Do you know Vasili Lopatkin?"

"Yes."

"Where is he now?"

"I don't know. He was in the Austrian camp when I escaped."

"What is your name?"

"Michael Voronov."

Anna Andreevna had been talking about him just that morning. And Maria remembered her father mentioning his name years ago. She did not remember the incident at the theater, but she felt she knew him fairly well.

"You have been playing with us," said Maria. "You are a Bolshevik after all."

"Is he?" asked Tata.

"Comrade Voronov is an important revolutionary hero. He spent years in prison because of his beliefs."

"Is that true?" asked Tata.

"Perfectly," said Michael.

"How horrible!" said Tata. "You *have* been playing with us. You didn't rob us because you were hungry. You did it simply to see us suffer."

"Stop whining," said Michael. "You begin to annoy me."

"You are part of the Chekist detachment at the train."

"Now you bore me," Michael said.

"Come, Masha," said Tata. "You are right. Let us go."

Was Tata right? Was he a member of the search detachment? Was he really laughing at them with a typically perverse, Bolshevik sense of humor? Maria was repelled. She wanted to hurt him. She wanted to prove what a peasant he was. And at the same time, to her annoyance, she was attracted to him.

"Perhaps we can do some business," said Maria.

"Is that so?" Michael smiled.

"We have many things at home to sell. They will buy a lot of food. But it isn't easy to get it safely home. You aren't the first grinning Bolshevik thief we've met. You won't be the last."

Michael grinned. "I hope you're wrong. It's been such a pleasure robbing you."

"You, on the contrary, have nothing to sell — except your stupid peasant strength. If you were to see us safely home, we would be sure of something — and so would you. You would eat much more than you do now. That should appeal to your peasant mentality."

"Masha, have you gone crazy?" said Tata. "You can make no such arrangement."

"It does," said Michael. "But, if I am a Chekist, why shouldn't I rob your apartment and sell your things myself?"

Maria had already thought of that. He would meet Anna Andreevna, who was howling for his scalp. She would denounce him to her lover, Comrade Marchenko. Michael would get what he deserved.

"Nothing," said Maria. "Nothing would have prevented you if I hadn't said a word. Besides which, you're a peasant. You're too lazy, too stupid."

"That's true," said Michael. "I had forgotten."

"Masha, do not include me in this deal," said Tata. "You are being stupid." Tata was furious. The other two were talking as if she somehow were not there.

"So, in a sense, I would be your personal bodyguard," said Michael, smiling.

"Yes."

"Instead of stealing food from you, I would be joining you to steal it from the state, which stole it from someone else."

"That's right, peasant."

"Interesting," said Michael. "A good idea. I like it."

"I am leaving," said Tata. "I won't hear any more."

Tata was unsuccessfully blinking back her tears. She pulled the door open roughly and tramped away in the snow.

"Wait!" called Maria.

"No!" Tata called. "I don't want to see you."

Michael smiled. "Your little friend is stupid, too."

"No, she isn't. She will see the sense."

"No, she won't. She's as stuffed with talk as you."

"Where shall we meet?"

"Meet me here," Michael said.

Maria went out without another word, and Michael watched as she struggled after Tata. It was getting dark. He could hear nothing but his own breathing and the girls' diminishing footsteps.

Michael shook his head. It really was a shame.

XXXII

It was hot. The hall was filled, huge though it was, with greater and lesser benefactors of humanity. In fact, it was about to burst. There was no room to fall down. Belly to belly and rump to rump, they shook their fists, pointed, and roared, announcing their right to prescribe "for the people." After all, they were so much more intelligent than the people, so much better educated, so much better fed. They deserved their power. The people did not.

And they let each other and the people know it. The walls shook. The noise was intense. Nobody could hear anybody else.

Now someone was on the podium, shouting and waving. He withdrew. The noise abruptly stopped, and then began again even louder as Lenin slowly took his place. He had come a long way from the room over the sausage factory in Zurich. He savored that fact for a moment as he looked around. Now that the Tsarist tyrants had been deposed, Russia was free to progress under his direction. Before him waved a field of raised, clenched fists, like Venus fly traps digesting their prey.

The large bald dome between his ears rotated slowly on the end of his neck. His small, porcine eyes peered. His body relaxed in his ill-fitting suit. The clamor rose to a crescendo and went beyond. Very soon it was over his head. He was swept along like a chip on the crest of a flood, completely helpless. And at the same time, he felt vast, enormous and limitless, as if he contained everyone in the room, the room itself, the building and the Kremlin, Moscow, Russia and the world. He felt in fact that he had become the universe, and that everything in it was subject to his will.

Suddenly he realized what his secret ambition had been all along, and at the same moment it was fulfilled. He tilted his broad, Mongolian face, the better to let the cheering beat down upon it. His fleshy lips parted in a smile.

At last, he thought. Victory. I do not exist!

XXXIII

It was the spring of 1918 and the world was awakening from a fearful winter. Water trickled everywhere. The earth had begun to thaw. And once again, Michael and Maria were returning to the hut. They had been meeting almost daily for months. Tata had refused to join them, as Michael had guessed she would, and she had avoided Maria completely for weeks. Even on their way home the night they had met Michael, Tata had refused to speak. She felt that Maria had somehow betrayed both her and Stepan.

Michael opened the door and they went in. They were both disappointed. It had been a bad day; they were returning to the hut without a crumb of food. Search parties of Chekists were roaming the area as part of the continual Bolshevik campaign to eradicate speculation and, momentarily, the speculators had retreated to their hiding places. Tomorrow they would be back — with milk and eggs and sausages and cheese that had originally been taken from the farmers for distribution to the people by the Food Trust. But now as Michael and Maria returned, their hands were empty. There was no reason for Michael to escort her back to Petrograd.

Yet they did not want to part. Although they refused to admit it, Michael and Maria had formed a bond. Although they were radically different, something had grown between them which, although they would not call it love, made them both a little stronger. Across the boundaries of psychological warfare, they had somehow touched each other.

"How hungry are you?" asked Maria, sitting down.

"Very."

"I mean exactly."

"I'm four slices of roast beef and six eggs hungry."

"That's very hungry."

"Yes."

"We'll eat like kings when this is over."

"And in the interim?" asked Michael, irritated as always by the remark.

"We'll do what we are doing now."

"Being stupid, in other words."

"You're trying to hurt me again. I can tell."

"Yes, but like the Bolsheviks I am doing it for your own good."

"I suspected that. Please tell me when to thank you."

"Why continue this fruitless nonsense? You should rejoin your company. That's the smart thing to do. As a 'Soviet artist' you'd get a hefty ration."

"I don't want to. I couldn't if I did. The chairman of the Artists' Committee has always hated me."

"Join another company. Change your name. Commissar sons of industrialists do it every day."

"I would never do that!" flashed Maria. "That would be treachery."

"I'd do it," said Michael.

"Of course. You're a peasant!"

"Think of all the food you could bring your parents."

"They would rather go hungry."

"But you would rather they didn't."

"I would not dance for you peasants. We are basically different, you see. It isn't just a matter of cleaning your ears."

"That's bourgeois arrogance, isn't it?"

"That's right."

"I thought so."

"Perhaps I could become some commissar's mistress. That happens every day, too."

"Does it?"

"Of course. Wouldn't that please you?"

"What difference would that make?"

"None, I suppose. Or would it?"

"Certainly not."

"That's good to know. Perhaps I'll do it."

"Go ahead. Now you're being smart."

"You really are a peasant."

"That's right. I am. And you're a rotten, spoiled little brat."

"That's right, I am. Rotten to the core."

"Insufferable."

"You seem to be suffering fairly well." Maria's arrogant nose rose still higher. "And by the way, there is no need to take such an interest in my welfare."

253

She stood quite near him, looking up. On her face was a challenging, disdainful smile, her large black eyes mocking and fearless. Michael chuckled softly and Maria shuddered. The sound was somehow very painful. Once again her skin was very sensitive, as if it had a consciousness of its own.

With a large hand, he took her arm. The flesh of her arm swelled around his thumb and caught the light. It was a perfectly ordinary effect, of course, and he had seen it many times. But now it struck him as highly unusual. Her skin always seemed so fragile and thin, as if at any moment it might burst.

He reached behind her neck, his fingers invading her thatch of hair, took a handful, and pulled her head back. She turned it slowly and bit his forearm, with all the energy in her jaws, and pressed as hard as she could while he watched. She released him and they both examined her work. Blood slowly filled the indentations. Then Maria looked at him again, her expression as always mocking and fearless.

Michael chuckled once again. Again he took her hair and forced her head back. Then he crushed his lips on hers, roughly, brutally, painfully. She struggled, but he easily forced her to her knees. She tried to get up, but he pressed her back. She fought intensely and without a sound. But Michael did not rush, deliberately delaying what they both knew would be the outcome. He held her lightly, while her struggles drained her strength. And then, finally, it was gone. She could not move. She had only enough strength to smile. She had never before been mastered and was glad it could be done. Since she was completely self-confident, she could surrender completely, as she had psychologically surrendered to him so often; and she surrendered completely now.

Hours passed. They did not speak. They did not need to. Their hands remained entwined, framed in a square of frail sunlight cascading through the window to the floor. They heard water running nearby. The pleasant smell of grass was faintly in the air. It was almost possible to believe that Lenin and the Revolution did not exist.

"You're right," Maria whispered. "I am a spoiled brat."

"Yes, you are. And I am a peasant."

"No, you're not. You have a noble nature."

"No. I am a peasant."

"All right. You win. You're still a peasant."

"And you are still a perfectly spoiled brat."

" 'Perfectly' is the word for it. Beautifully spoiled."

The square of sunlight on the floor went out. It was getting dark. They went outside. It was time to go.

"Suppose I'm pregnant," said Maria.

"Suppose you are."

"What shall I do?"

"Most pregnant women have babies."

"Is that supposed to be a joke?"

"Yes."

"It isn't."

"Then why are you laughing?"

"I'm not laughing."

"Then straighten your face."

"What's happened to us means nothing," said Maria. "Isn't that right?"

"Perfectly," said Michael. "Doesn't mean a thing."

"It's merely biological."

"Correct."

"It would be stupid to think otherwise."

"Yes. It would."

The sun had set. Maria felt a chill. "I'd better go."

"Yes," Michael said curtly. "You'd better."

"Goodnight, peasant."

"Goodnight, brat."

At the top of the hill, Maria turned and waved. Michael did not respond, and then she was gone. It was important to emphasize that there was nothing between them, that what had happened didn't mean a thing. It didn't, but now he felt painfully sad whenever she left him. What a pity it was, he thought. What a shame. He walked off through the woods and tried to shake the feeling off.

Suddenly, three armed men in uniform blocked his way. One stepped forward.

"You are under arrest."

XXXIV

Peter Orloff did not like paperwork. He never had. But as he now sat at his desk, he was able to concentrate completely, which almost made the paperwork pleasant. Orloff was a happy man. His life's ambition had been satisfied. His years in prison had been worthwhile.

He had been released in late November, 1917. The entire local soviet had come from the town. There had been a celebration. Orloff had become an overnight hero. Savitsky's successor as prison governor had become a criminal. It had not been easy for Orloff to persuade the other prisoners not to lynch him. And since that day, Orloff had lived in permanent exaltation. Not long before, he had finally returned to Moscow, where Trotsky had appointed him a general in the Red Army then being organized. Orloff was working on the job now, in his small office on the long military train.

Only one thing was wrong, but it was very serious. Katya had been refusing to sleep with him. They did not fight, or even argue. Their relationship was good. Katya seemed happy. She did not refuse defiantly, or to get her way in something else. She was sorry about it, even apologetic. It was as if the problem were somehow not in her control; as if she wanted to sleep with her husband, but could not.

And she could not talk about it, either. Time after time, Orloff had painfully brought the subject up, but Katya would blush and become agitated almost to the point of hysteria. She could not discuss it, but she could not bear to be touched.

Orloff wondered — was the problem related to the incredible fact that Katya had been found drunk and naked outside town? It had to be, but what was the cause? He flushed with humiliation. The incident had caused the area's biggest scandal in years. Luckily it had not pursued them to Moscow. Had Katya been unable to endure the town's loneliness? Or had some unknown individual been involved? Such behavior was so unlike Katya, but

256

she could not discuss it. She refused to admit the incident had even occurred.

Orloff looked out the window. It was dark. He could see nothing. The train had stood for hours on the open plain for no apparent reason. The locomotive probably needed repairs. From Vladivostok to Minsk, the railway system was disintegrating. Breakdowns had become so common that he no longer bothered to inquire. He knew the railroads would recover as the economy was reorganized along Socialist lines. That was as clear as a geo- metric proof.

Some of his men boarded the coach, the train lurched and started at last. He returned to his work, but their heavy boots came down the passage and into the room.

"Excuse me, excellency," said a voice.

As usual, the word "excellency" annoyed him. Why did so many men refuse to learn that that antiquated title had no place here, that both generals and corporals were comrades in the Red Army? It was another Capitalist hangover that would gradually fade away. That was why there was no need to mention it now. The historical process would inevitably take its course.

"What is your name?" Orloff asked.

"Suslov, comrade general."

"Can you read?"

"No."

Another Capitalist hangover that would eventually fade away. Yet Orloff was annoyed a bit more. His adjutant had been killed ten days before, and Orloff could not find a proper replacement. In a few years everyone would be able to read, but Orloff could not wait that long.

"Well? What is it?" Orloff asked.

"Another prisoner, comrade general. Suspicion of speculation."

Why must these things follow one another so closely? Now Orloff was really depressed. Of course people were speculating; they were starving. This problem, too, would be solved by Socialist reorganization. There would soon be abundance such as the world had never seen. But meanwhile they were starving, and the law had to be enforced. Only in that way could the food on hand be distributed fairly. If only the Chekists would not enforce it so harshly. Orloff knew that this was Dolgorensky's fault. Orloff had never liked Dolgorensky. Dolgorensky was not a true Bolshevik, a scientist, an engineer. Dolgorensky enjoyed being harsh.

Orloff bent over his paperwork again. "All right," he said. "Bring him in."

Suslov's boots left and returned with others. There was a silence. Orloff heard a sharp intake of breath.

"Good evening, your honor," said a familiar voice. "I hope you are well."

Orloff looked up. It was Michael Voronov. They had not seen each other for years; not since Golovin had found them outside the prison wall and Michael had escaped. It was as if Michael were a visitor from another world. Orloff felt a combination of pleasure and fear. Perhaps Michael knew what had happened to Katya. Orloff wanted to know, but was afraid to learn the truth.

"Sit down," he said. "Leave us," he told the others. He went to the samovar and drew hot water for tea.

"So you're a speculator these days," he said.

"Yes," said Michael. "It's a childhood ambition."

Orloff pointed to the sideboard, on which was some food. "If you are hungry, eat."

"I'll do that. I'm starved."

"What have you been doing?"

"Speculating. As you know."

"And before that?"

"Before that I did some soldiering."

"In whose army?"

"Ours, of course. Why do you ask?"

"You're a cynic. You believe in nothing. I had to ask."

"You're right," Michael chuckled.

"But why?" asked Orloff. "Wasn't that risky?"

"No," said Michael. "I changed my name."

"I see. An old revolutionary tradition. But that wasn't what I meant. Why would you fight for a cause? That would violate your principles."

"You're right, it would — if I had any. But there's no better place than the army to hide."

"What was your outfit?"

Michael told him.

"Then you must know Borishevsky."

"Of course. He was the colonel."

"We were students at the academy together. Intelligence tells us he is fighting with Kornilov in the South."

"I'm sorry, but not surprised. He believes in something, too."

"But what a waste. Is he a good officer?"

"He is. The best. I liked serving under him. In fact, I liked being a soldier and being in the war. War is good. It's clean. It's honest. Lies are told about it, of course, but not on the front line. Unfortunately, it's occasionally interrupted by peace."

258

Orloff smiled. "It's good to hear you say that. I need an adjutant. The job is yours."

"A general's adjutant? I don't have the rank."

"You don't need it," said Orloff. "This is the *Red* Army. There's no room for general staff careerism here. A man finds his place strictly by ability. As I remember it, you can read?"

"Yes."

"Good! You're my adjutant."

"Why do you need an adjutant just now?"

"My last was killed ten days ago."

"That's too bad."

"Yes."

"But suppose I refuse."

"Suit yourself. You'll rot in a cell."

"I see."

"Good."

"Perhaps you are right. The class struggle is the one thing that makes sense in your theory."

"You *are* making progress," said Orloff. "As I said years ago, one day you will tell me you understand."

"I doubt it."

"I am sorry you will be disappointed when the class struggle ends."

"Will it end?"

"Yes, when society is properly arranged. It will end simply because there will no longer be classes. Man himself will have been modified. There will no longer be war. There will no longer be any reason to struggle. Cooperation will become the highest virtue."

Michael stared at him. "How depressing."

"Does your Austrian overcoat mean you were captured?"

"Yes."

"Were you released after Brest-Litovsk?"

"I escaped. By the way, your nephew was an officer in our regiment."

"Stepan Danilov? Yes, I knew but had forgotten. We have not seen each other for years. I would not know him if he walked in right now."

"He won't. He's dead."

"I'm sorry."

"So am I."

"What happened?"

"He was killed in the retreat of '16."

Orloff still had not seen Stepan's family. He had hesitated to do so after his return to Russia. Family relationships today did not mean much, but politics meant a great deal. Katya had even hesitated to see her sister.

"As my adjutant," Orloff said, "when we get back to Petrograd you will convey my regrets to the family. The news will upset my wife. Stepan was a favorite of hers."

There was a long silence, painful to Orloff. He was not sure how to proceed. He wanted to learn whether Michael knew anything about Katya, without telling him anything.

"She has been upset enough for years," he said hesitantly.

He looked closely at Michael, but Michael's face was blank. He had not been listening. He did not remember Katya. He was thinking of Maria, whom he did remember. The turning train wheels contained her voice, her laugh.

He looked at the window, but it was now completely black. He could not tell where they were or why.

XXXV

Nicholas awoke with a headache. It was stuffy in the room. Should he open a window? He could not decide. He wanted more air but at the same time preferred not to move. He thoroughly kneaded his eyeballs between thumb and forefinger. But it did no good. In fact, now there was a foreign object in his right eye. He stopped kneading it. Must be careful not to embed the object in the cornea. He had read that somewhere.

Suddenly he realized that this was one of those nights when, for a few seconds on awaking, he couldn't remember who he was or where. As always, Nicholas was terrified. He concentrated. Who was he? Where was he? Suppose on some such night the answers did not come. But tonight the answers came immediately. He was Tsar of all Russias, of course, and now he was in Ekaterinburg. Ekaterinburg. Such a nice little town. And he was living in such a nice little house. He thought with pleasure of his daily routine: reading, gardening, sitting with Alexandra and the children. It really was so much nicer than constantly having to think about the government. He had never imagined how nice it could be. Why had nobody ever told him?

He became aware of a dull, steady pounding in the distance, and just as he was beginning to wonder what it was, the door opened and Yurovsky stuck his head in.

"Time to get dressed," Yurovsky snickered.

He closed the door, then reopened it immediately and quickly added the words "Your Majesty," obviously pretending to be worried about forgetting them. He snickered again, and again shut the door.

That Yurovsky! Nicholas could not figure him out. All the way from Petrograd, he was. But he certainly had acceptable manners, unlike the local Ekaterinburg oafs. Not court manners, of course, but he was careful to address Nicholas properly. He really knew how to treat the Tsar of all the Russias. He probably had been specially selected for the job. Good manners were so important, more important than anything else.

Nicholas swung his feet to the floor and began to dress. How nice it was to have someone to tell him what to do. How efficient. It saved so much time. It was so nice not always to have to wonder. And it was only the fact that he was Tsar of all the Russias that made it possible. How lucky he was!

From out of the darkness, the wheedling voice of Alexandra came. "Nicky, why must we get dressed? It's not even dawn. I'm so tired. Please find out."

"What? Why? Oh. Hm." Nicholas pulled reflectively at his beard.

Alexandra went to the door and looked out. Yurovsky was coming back down the hall. She did not like him. She never had.

"Why must we get dressed?" she asked.

"But you *must* get dressed," said Yurovsky. He was agitated. He had just come from the grand duchesses. "The Czechs are advancing. That's their artillery shelling the town." Yurovsky once again was calm. He snickered. "You must go to the cellar where it is safe, Your Majesty."

Alexandra shut the door. "Brute!" she said. Yurovsky's manner was so insolent.

The dull booming was in fact noticeably closer. Nicholas imagined he could already see the Czechs. He had heard of their Captain Gaida. The monarchy had been overthrown and there was a civil war. And the eastern front was now here at Ekaterinburg in the Urals.

Suddenly, a band of anxiety squeezed his chest. Suppose the Czechs took the town and took him away from the Bolsheviks. Nicholas would be sent to Kolchak in Omsk, or perhaps to Denikin and the other generals in the South. Once again, he would be forced to take control of the government. Once again, he would have to think and plan — decide about troops, ammunition, and tactics.

It could not be! Such a thing must not be allowed to happen. It was so nice the way it was. He had to cooperate in every way with Yurovsky.

The booming was even closer. He thought he could hear some damage being done.

"Hurry!" he said. "To the cellar!"

Everyone was dressed and in the hall. Nicholas led the way, carrying the Tsarevitch, followed by Alexandra, Anastasia, and the other grand duchesses.

The cellar was bare, with whitewashed walls. There was no place to sit down. The family milled about uncertainly. The girls chattered. The Tsarevitch was still asleep.

Alexandra touched his arm. "Nicky, there are no chairs. I'm tired."

Nicholas was listening, but not to her. The Czech artillery seemed almost overhead. He imagined he heard Gaida shouting commands. He strained his ears, almost on his toes, trying to hear.

"Sh," he said. "Sh. Please."

A shell landed quite nearby. There was a roar. Something fell. The Tsarevitch woke up and rubbed his eyes. One of the grand duchesses began to cry.

Alexandra pulled his sleeve. "Nicky, please, I am so tired. My feet hurt. Find a chair."

"What? Oh. Hm. Yes." Nicholas put the Tsarevitch down and pulled nervously at his beard.

Suddenly, Alexandra stiffened and sucked in breath. Nicholas peered around the room. Yurovsky was standing at the other end, at the entrance to the stairs, with a stupid grin. Behind him were six or seven soldiers, staring and smirking, and digging their elbows into each other's ribs.

"There are no chairs," Nicholas said.

Alexandra grabbed his arm. She had suddenly realized what was going to happen. "Nicky, you are Tsar of all the Russias. Tell them, Nicky. Tell them."

Nicholas pulled furtively at his beard. "Of course. Of course." He stepped forward and drew erect. "Well, gentlemen, my children, that's true, you see. That is to say, I am Tsar of all the Russias. Bring a chair. Please."

Yurovsky shifted his cigarette with his tongue, and spoke to his men over his shoulder from the side of this mouth. "Boys, he says he's Tsar of all the Russias."

There was a roar. It was so funny they had to hang on to each other to keep their feet. It was priceless.

"Tell him I'm Queen Victoria!" someone shouted.

It was the funniest thing they had every heard. They were helpless.

Yurovsky grinned like a Cheshire cat. His eyes shone with a feline glare. "But, of course, you're right, aren't you, Your Majesty?" he said. "You *are* Tsar of all he Russias." He flicked away his cigarette and spat on the floor.

Then Yurovsky drew his pistol.

XXXVI

It was autumn of 1918. Michael and Maria sat under a tree. They had not seen each other for months. Maria had looked for him at the hut without success. Without his protection, she had been robbed several times. And things had been getting even worse since the recent assassination of Uritsky and the attempt on Lenin. The Communists had announced that they would take nationwide revenge.

But Maria was not hungry. She had just eaten. Indeed, she had already hidden some food in her clothing for her parents. And now Michael wore the uniform of the Red Army.

"So you've become a Bolshevik, after all," said Maria.

"You so often said I should."

"Don't blame it on me."

"I don't. Why don't you look at me?"

"I don't want to," said Maria.

Maria had often said he should join the Bolsheviks, but now that he had, she somehow felt betrayed.

"Your uncle sends his regards," said Michael.

"I don't accept them. My uncle is a Communist."

"That's why he's ordered me to go to your house."

Maria bristled. "What do you mean?"

"I'm to give his sympathy to your parents about Stepan."

Maria felt a combination of panic and fear. Michael must not be allowed to do that. Anna Andreevna would see him and complain to Marchenko, her lover, who would then take revenge on Michael despite Michael's new Red Army uniform. The Cheka was supreme. It could not be stopped. And Anna Andreevna had been talking violently about Michael just that morning.

"That won't be necessary," said Maria. "I'll convey it."

Michael smiled. "I have my order. I'm your uncle's adjutant. I have no choice."

"No!" said Maria. "Is that clear enough?"

"Perfectly," said Michael.

"Don't you know why?"

"Why don't you tell me?"

"Because you're a peasant. The fact that you've finally become a Bolshevik proves it. I don't want a stupid peasant in my home."

She was saying the first thing that came to her mind, excitably and irritably, as if out of control.

"I meet you *because* you're a dirty, stupid peasant. You're thoroughly swinish. That's what I want. I want you to make me swinish, too, because that's what your kind is making the world. But you must keep your distance. Don't get too familiar. Remember your place. You are a stupid peasant. I don't want you in my home with my parents. Our relationship is strictly business."

Her mind was whirling. She knew only that she had to prevent Michael from coming to her home. But her tongue did not believe her words. She was about to cry. Michael must not see her cry. It was a sign of weakness.

"I'm going now," she said. "Good night."

"Good night, brat."

"Good night, peasant."

She turned abruptly and walked away, the tears already on her cheeks, face burning, eyes blind. In a moment she was gone and Michael was alone.

His face was burning, too. Maria's words had made him flinch. He was still flinching. But why? She had talked and was behaving exactly as he had urged. Why was he complaining now? The answer was no doubt stupid, but he did not know what it was. And he did not care, he told himself. He was *not* complaining. He was glad Maria had said what she had.

Maria laboriously returned to Petrograd. She was almost home, at a corner, crossing a street. In the middle of the intersection, a wagon had been overturned. Sacks of grain and other supplies were strewn around it. Shabby people were struggling, trying to set the wagon right. Maria stopped, startled, staring at it. Her food was safely concealed in her clothes, but the sight of food made everyone nervous lately. One hushed before it as in a church.

Suddenly, someone was grabbing her arm. A face was near hers, and a rough voice.

"Get over there, *boorzhui!*" it said. "Right that wagon! Load those sacks!"

The speaker wore a Red Army uniform. He had recognized Maria as a "former person" despite her old clothes. Maria had temporarily been nationalized. The officer pushed her roughly and Maria was in the street. Too numb to argue, she joined the others.

"What happened?" she asked.

"A government automobile hit it," someone said. "Damned Chekists!"

"They don't give a damn," said somebody else.

Pushing and heaving, they righted the wagon, and began loading it with the sacks. A man lay in the street nearby, groaning and bleeding.

"Whose are these?" asked Maria.

"Comrade Marchenko's," said the other. "Who else's?"

"All right," said the officer. "Get on with it. Hurry up!"

They worked on in silence for more than two hours. Then the officer released them and they parted without a word.

Maria walked the block or so to her house and went in. The summer's heat had gone, in fact there was the beginning of a chill, but here in the stairwell it was as hot as the dead of July. She paused on the landing to catch her breath, but that only made it worse. The air was heavy, thick, almost visible.

Suddenly she felt dizzy. There was a pain in her head. She put a hand against the wall and some plaster fell to the floor. There was a squeak in the darkness and something scurried off. She looked at her hand. There was nothing on it, but she rubbed it carefully on her coat. The front entrance to the house was in no better condition, but she would have preferred it to these back stairs.

She climbed another flight and sat on the landing. She had no strength left. She could not go on. On the other hand, here she could not breathe. She rose and climbed the rest of the way.

When she came into the room, the first thing she noticed, as always, was her mother's hands fluttering helplessly at the handkerchief in her lap. It was something Maria could not get used to. She wanted to shout and scream at her mother. She was convinced for no reason it would do some good. Nadia Nikolaevna had changed so completely that Maria often had to concentrate to remember that she was the same person. The frightening thing was that she was.

Now Nadia Nikolaevna looked up uncertainly, and her mouth weakly began to work. "Masha, Masha . . . ."

Her voice dwindled off. Her mouth was still working but nothing came out. Face falling, head bowed, she returned to her handkerchief.

Maria realized that something more than usual was wrong. She advanced cautiously into the room. "What is it, mama? What has happened?" she asked, afraid that Nadia Nikolaevna would tell her.

266

Telegin rose from a chair and Maria saw him for the first time. On his face was a perfect expression of sympathy.

"Masha, Masha," Nadia Nikolaevna said again.

"What has happened?" Maria asked.

The hands fluttered. "Masha, your father . . . ."

"What? What?" She could no longer disguise the terror in her voice.

Telegin clicked his tongue sympathetically and shook his head.

"Arrested," said Nadia Nikolaevna. "Gone."

"But . . . ."

"Cyril Modestovitch was kind enough . . . ."

"I came at once," Telegin said.

The room was whirling. Maria could not move. Always before, in such situations, she had depended on her father who always knew what to do — but now it was her father who needed the help. She looked quickly at her mother, but Nadia Nikolaevna only looked back. And on her face there was a plea.

Maria realized that she was completely alone. An unspoken agreement had passed between the women that Maria was now the head of what remained of the family. She would have to do what was necessary to get her father released. But what? The palace coup engineered by Lenin had finally begun to touch her for the first time — really touch her. She could no longer pretend by bravado that life was just another tragic romance like the ones she had performed in on stage at the Marinsky. Now, for the first time, she was face to face with life, *real* life. Or rather, with the vicious and senseless thing Michael had told her real life was.

She was angry. And she was afraid. Suppose she was unable to help him. Suppose she had been completely wrong about life! Suppose Michael was right, after all!

"Maria, my dear," said Cyril Modestovitch. He smiled, but in view of the occasion was careful to color the smile with a tinge of sadness. He was delighted. Here was exactly the same person who had attracted him before. But why? What did she have? Telegin was not sure, but he wanted to own her.

His voice brought Maria back into the room and she recoiled. Telegin was a basic element of "real life."

"What happened?" Maria asked.

She had not seen Telegin for more than two years. Not since her mother's party in Stepan's honor early in 1916. It was more like two light years, of course. The world they knew — the real world — had completely been destroyed. Yet Telegin, unlike Nadia Nikolaevna, unaccountably had not changed at all, not in the slightest respect she could see. He was dressed as well, or rather as expensively, as always, and seemed exactly as healthy and well-fed. Indeed, he had not lost a pound. Beneath his expensive overcoat, his imperialistic waistline swelled as before. In the present context, his appearance was strangely obscene.

"It is my fond hope that you will permit me to be of service, dear Maria Ivanovna," said Telegin. "I have established certain connections with the authorities. Perhaps, if I ask . . . ."

"No!" said Maria shortly. "No!" She flushed.

"Masha, please!" said Nadia Nikolaevna, kneading her handkerchief. "Cyril Modestovitch is trying to help."

Telegin raised a hand. "Do not chastise her. Please! Maria Ivanovna is upset. She will only feel worse."

He hunched his shoulders, spread his hands and smiled to show Maria how solicitous he was.

"What happened?" Maria asked coldly.

"It is my sad duty to report that your dear father — and my dear friend — Ivan Fyodorovitch has been arrested for counterrevolutionary activities."

"Nonsense!" said Maria. "He's done nothing. It's a lie!"

Telegin put a fingertip against a temple. "Is that so? I see. That, of course, will come in handy. I'm so glad to hear it. One can never be quite sure."

"Yes one can," said Maria.

"You can prove that?"

"Of course."

"How?"

"He has not left the house."

"The Chekists were here," said Nadia Nikolaevna. "They took him. They said nothing."

"It is also my sad duty to report that Ivan Fyodorovitch has been injured, but only slightly," said Telegin. "The automobile collided with a wagon at the corner quite near here."

"What?" Maria exclaimed. "The wagon?"

This time his remark took her out of the room, and she clearly saw her father lying somewhere in the dirt, broken, bloody and unable to move.

"But how do you happen to know all this?"

Telegin was having a marvelous time. Such delightful perception! Such intelligence! Telegin produced a self-deprecating smile.

"As I said, dear Maria Ivanovna, I have established certain connections among the authorities. It is not impossible that they would be willing to intercede for Ivan Fyodorovitch."

Maria sat down. "We don't deserve this. We have done nothing."

"Such a pity," said Telegin. "One individual commits an act, and it profoundly affects thousands the individual has not met."

"What does that mean?" Maria asked.

"If only the Kaplan woman had not made that criminal attempt on our great leader, Vladimir Ilyitch."

Maria's mind reeled in confusion. "What?" she said softly. "Lenin – 'our great leader'?"

"Certainly it is true that the guilty class, the Capitalist class, must be punished," he said, "but in revolution, mistakes and excesses are made. How tragic it is, Masha, that one has been made in your father's case."

For the first time, Maria noticed a piece of red bunting in his lapel. "Please leave us, Cyril Modestovitch," she said. "We won't need your help."

"Masha, please!" said Nadia Nikolaevna. "Do not insult our guest! Excuse her, Cyril Modestovitch, please."

Telegin was delighted. It was so interesting to watch her struggle like a fish on a line. And it was so satisfying to play the line so expertly. It would greatly heighten the pleasure of taking her. He congratulated himself. He had not realized he was such a sportsman.

"Have you forgotten Stepan so soon, mama?" asked Maria. "What would he say now about a turncoat?"

Telegin colored, slightly shaken. Nadia Nikolaevna did not answer. She looked down quickly and returned to her handkerchief.

"A man studies, thinks and learns," said Telegin, once again completely in control. "New experiences come rushing in, enlarging one's ideas, demonstrating the spiritual rewards of serving humanity. Yes, the days of selfishness are over, ladies. I am happy. I mean that sincerely. The curse of ego has gone from my mind."

He seemed to be playing with her, daring her, saying the most ridiculous things he could. There was a diamond ring on one of his little fingers, and he took it off and held it out to Maria. "Do you like it?" he said. "I just picked it up."

"It's beautiful," said Nadia Nikolaevna, her eyes reflecting the shine in the diamond. "You will enjoy it."

Maria put a hand over her mouth in horror at her mother's naivete. Telegin could not remember when he had enjoyed himself more.

Maria opened the door. "Good night, Cyril Modestovitch."

Telegin started as if surprised. "Yes, of course. You must be tired. How stupid of me. I have kept you up." He took a large sausage from a pocket and put it on the table. "Here. Please say nothing. I am glad to be of service.

Giving is its own reward."

Nadia Nikolaevna spasmodically kissed his hand. "Thank you, Cyril Modestovitch, dear friend." She was already cutting through the sausage with a knife. A drop of saliva was on her lower lip.

"Get out, for God's sake!" Maria said, immediately regretting it. Her anger was a confession that he could manipulate her emotions.

Telegin was delighted. "I'm so sorry you don't feel well, Masha. Eat some sausage. You'll feel better."

Maria closed the door. Nadia Nikolaevna did not look up. She was already wolfing down large chunks of sausage.

XXXVII

"Real life" was exactly what Maria dreaded — dull, petty, senseless and vicious. Shielded by her career and family, she had been able to avoid it, until now. Now she was hurled headlong into it. Now, for the first time, "real life" could deny her something she really wanted. She had no choice. She was finally vulnerable.

The first problem was to find out exactly where her father was. This was not easy. Arrests were not recorded alphabetically in a handy file. People simply disappeared without reason into the Bolshevik machine, and reappeared the same way — if they *did* reappear. While inside, they did not exist and no one knew a thing. Maria had already been to various government offices, and had been greeted with a combination of fear, surprise, confusion and contempt. Various index fingers had descended down various lists — but her father's name had so far not appeared. And she had been to the Spalernaia prison, where, she had been assured, her father had never set foot. On the next Sunday afternoon at the regular visiting hour, she returned to the prison with a box of food, along with the lucky people who knew that their friends and relatives were there. But she was once again assured that her father was not there. And everywhere she asked questions, there were people doing the same, trying to find out where somebody was, trying to find out whether someone still existed.

She had not gone to see Michael again. She did not want to get him involved. She was afraid he would come to her home, after all, and that Anna Andreevna would report him to Marchenko. She was afraid that if she asked him, he would help look for her father, and get reported for that.

Now she had found her way to the office of a commissar named Dolgorensky. For four hours she waited, while people with documents hurried back and forth. No one paid attention to her. Her clothes were properly old and ragged. Then a finger beckoned and she followed it inside.

To her surprise, Dolgorensky rose. Such a thing had not happened for so long. It was so totally at variance with the current social scene. But so was Dolgorensky himself. He was completely happy. Indeed, he was smiling. He looked not a day older than he had years before. At the moment, he was slightly annoyed. He had just read an article in *Pravda,* hailing Orloff's leadership in the Red Army.

"You won't mind, I hope, if I eat while we talk?" he asked.

Dolgorensky was holding a linen napkin. On the table before him, steam rose from various dishes.

"No," said Maria in a mechanical voice.

"Thank you," he said. "We are so busy here."

On one plate sat part of a wheel of cheese. On another, a bright yellow slab of butter. Maria had not seen any for months. There was an elegant china serving dish piled with slices of meat, a pitcher of milk, bread, and sugar. It was amazing such things still existed. Yet Dolgorensky seemed unimpressed, as if they were the most plentiful and unimportant things in the world.

Dolgorensky sat down and pushed something into his mouth with an elegant forefinger. Between his teeth, Maria saw the last of a descending tomato. A tomato! It could not be! She began to salivate against her will. She could not stop. Her taste buds awoke with a burst of pain. She could show none of this. She had to conceal it all. Dolgorensky would have loved nothing better than to see her crawl. But the sights and smells whirled in her brain and made her dizzy.

"Cigarette?" Dolgorensky was saying.

"What?"

"Would you like a cigarette?"

Maria had never smoked and did not know how. But she had to have something to put in her mouth. She took one. It was an English cigarette. Could there really be such a place? Was Michael right? Dolgorensky lit it and she cautiously drew in and out, imitating what she had seen.

"You've changed," said Dolgorensky.

"Have we met?"

"I have seen you dance and have been in your home. I have also met your father. He was a contributor to the Party for years."

"Yes. He believed the Revolution was meant to benefit us all."

Dolgorensky shook his head. "Did he? Too bad!"

"His property was taken, and now he's been arrested."

"I see."

"That's why I'm here. He deserves better."

272

Dolgorensky cut some cheese and chewed it carefully. "Exquisite. Really exquisite. I don't suppose you see any of this?"

"No."

"Pity. You'd like it." Dolgorensky cut another slice and with the elegant forefinger pushed it into his mouth. "Exquisite."

The smell of the cheese reached Maria. She drew in too much smoke and coughed it out. Dolgorensky poured some water and handed her the glass.

"So you think that because your father has contributed to the Party, he now deserves something in return."

"Of course."

Dolgorensky elegantly blotted his lips. "Pity. Someone has made you the victim of a monstrous misunderstanding." He shook his head. "You see, we and we alone — the Party — determine who deserves what, if anything at all. And your father made his ... 'contributions,' to use your misnomer, simply to protect himself after what he saw would be our inevitable victory."

"That's not true."

"He is what we in the Party call a 'useful idiot.' "

Burning words rushed to Maria's lips. She pressed them tight and held the words back. It was an unusual experience; in fact, she could not remember ever having done that before. She was surprised that she did it so well. It was clearly part of the thing called "real life" — grimy, vicious, petty and dull. She carefully pushed the water glass out of reach.

"So the point," Dolgorensky was saying, "is that all along the people really owned the property your father claimed to be contributing. He was able to make the claim only because of the criminal basis of the former society. And, therefore, he didn't really contribute anything at all, did he?"

"No," said Maria, in a metallic voice.

Dolgorensky smiled. "Splendid. You understand." He pushed another tomato home. "So to be exact, you are not here in any way to demand payment of some imaginary claim. You are here to beg, to plead, aren't you? You are here to ask the Party for mercy."

"Yes. I am here to beg and plead for mercy."

"Splendid! But you see, my dear Mademoiselle Danilova, the truth is that the Party does not deal in mercy. We deal only in justice."

"But he's not guilty," said Maria. "He's done nothing."

Dolgorensky chuckled. "Is that so? I'm puzzled."

"Puzzled?"

"Yes. If he isn't guilty, why was he arrested?"

"I don't understand."

"You must try. You are implying that the Party has made a mistake, which is impossible. His guilt will be established to your satisfaction by the interrogation."

"How can that be? My father's done nothing."

"An unimportant problem. Do not worry. Soviet interrogation consists in convincing the malefactor of what he has done. Your conception of guilt is quite naive. Archaic, in fact. I'm surprised. Guilt is objectively established not essentially by what one does, but by what one is. If what one is is bad for the Party, one is guilty. And your father happens to be an industrialist."

The door opened and an elderly woman brought in a samovar and left. Dolgorensky was going to have tea, real tea. Surely such a thing could no longer exist.

Dolgorensky filled a glass, sipped and nodded. It was good. "Of course," he said, "it is not impossible that a token of your appreciation could lead me to take an interest in your case. One never can be sure."

"You mean . . . a bribe?" Now it was Maria's turn to smile. A bribe was something she understood.

Dolgorensky grimaced. "Is there really no bottom to your misunderstanding? The term 'bribe' implies that one is paying for a service. An illegal service. It implies a business transaction between equals. But in the first place, illegality is determined only by the Party, and in the second, you are to me as a cockroach is to a god — speaking metaphorically, of course."

"I am to you — metaphorically — as a cockroach is to a god."

"So what we are really discussing here, aren't we . . . ?"

"Yes."

Dolgorensky smiled. She understood. ". . . is an offering, a supplication, not to me but to the Party. Because no part of me exists apart from the Party. I am giving you a chance to learn a valuable lesson, a lesson which would be good for your soul — if you had one. But of course, you don't."

"Thank you," said Maria. "How much do you want?"

Dolgorensky drew a bottle of cognac from a drawer, filled a glass and tossed it down. He was not in the least interested in a bribe. Indeed, the very idea was silly. But he was annoyed about Orloff, who was getting good publicity. He, Dolgorensky, had been getting none. *Pravda* did not print articles about him. He had been discussing this just the other day with Marchenko. Yet, he grudgingly admitted that the Cheka's activities were best not known. Indeed, *Pravda* was right to publicize the Red Army. It was objectively correct — at the moment — to glamorize Orloff.

Still, Dolgorensky resented it. And Maria was Orloff's niece. He could not hurt Orloff at the moment, but he could hurt her. And nothing would do that like disappointment. He would make Maria work; she would raise the bribe — and then he would refuse to accept it. He had ordered her father arrested for the same reason.

"That's difficult to say," said Dolgorensky. "I'm such a moody creature. One never can be sure what mood I may be in. You'll simply have to try your luck."

"But we have lost everything. There is nothing I can do."

"Pity," said Dolgorensky. "You must be very sad. And now I suggest you leave me before my mood changes."

Maria rose. "All right. I'll get what you want."

"Splendid!" said Dolgorensky.

"May I ask you one question?"

"Of course."

"I am not being impertinent, believe me. I sincerely want to know. Why is it that while people are trying to survive on fish heads and literally dying in the streets — the very people you claim to represent — why is it that you and your Party allow yourselves to sit here surrounded by delicacies? I really want to know that."

Dolgorensky considered for some time. "A good question. A necessary question. Not formulated perfectly, but it shows that you are making progress. I am happy to tell you. You deserve to know.

"You see, we are artists, artists of revolution, scientists of revolution. We are the bearers of a great idea. We must be insulated against picayune daily cares."

"But what is the idea? I want to know."

"This brings us to the problem of your faulty formulation. The term 'represent' implies that our power comes from the people, an idea so stupid that the Americans deserve it. We do not represent the people. We control, use, and direct the people.

"Smelly, stupid, obstinate man is obsolescent. We are constructing an entirely new man. So new he may in fact be a separate species, replacing current, stupid man as inevitably as Cro-Magnon did Neanderthal. He will be a man without emotion, without personality, without privacy or self, without the slightest desire for them — without desire itself — a man perfectly conditioned for service.

"In order to do this, we must use what we have. We must use smelly, obstinate man. We must rip out the weeds in order to plant grass. We must destroy in order to create. We must reach deep within the man we have — reach to the core and do what is necessary. We will rip out his intestines, length over length, his liver, his kidneys, his heart and lungs, and rearrange them, if necessary, to reach the goal. But most important, we will penetrate his thick skull and replace the soggy mess he calls his brain. How important in all this, do you think, is the one microbe who is your father?"

Maria's ears were ringing strangely. Dolgorensky's voice seemed very far away. As he had said, this was something completely new. It was not simply insane. That term, as Dolgorensky would say, implied the existence of sanity with which to compare it. But this — this was something which could not be compared.

"But your slogans," she said weakly. " 'All power to the people!' 'Land, peace, bread.' What do they mean? Don't you really want these things?"

For the first time, Dolgorensky laughed. "Certainly not. They don't mean a thing. The problem is that obsolescent man is unable to understand anything else. You, apparently, have the same problem. So does your father. When you do understand — all of you — the Revolution will be complete.

"In fact, that is why, in your case, I have prescribed a supplication. You will struggle against it and deny it, but it will help you begin to understand. The only real problem in Russia today is a lack of understanding. If enough people understood, the civil war would end. Do you see?"

"I think so."

"You are perceptive. An unusual quality. That is good. Tell me, what, in your opinion, is the greatest joy?"

"I don't know, comrade. Please. I'll go now."

"Not yet. I insist. Imagine yourself into my mind. Think!"

"All right. Women."

"Good God, no!" Dolgorensky's lush, feminine lips were pursed. "Perhaps I was wrong. For a woman, you're unobservant. Try again."

"No. I'm going."

"Please!" Dolgorensky was excited, losing control. It was as if he, the all powerful, were begging the powerless for a favor. "Ask me whether money is the greatest joy," he said.

"All right," said Maria wearily. "Is money the greatest joy?"

"No," he said, smiling. "Money is almost unimportant. Greed for it is almost childish. Now ask me about power."

"Is it power?"

"No. But you are getting close. You are going in the right direction." Dolgorensky was strangely stimulated. He was breathing in shallow, spasmodic bursts. A humorless grin was on his face. "The greatest joy consists of smiling at a man, befriending him, getting him to take one into his confidence — and then, while he is revealing himself in perfect trust, plunging a knife deep into his back. This is the greatest joy. Do you see?"

276

There was a knock, the door opened, and another man in uniform stood on the sill.

"Ah," said Dolgorensky. He looked at his watch. "Excuse me."

He took out a pistol and several rounds of ammunition and, with great concentration, began filling the chamber.

XXXVIII

It was too late to do anything more that night, but the next morning she was up at dawn and went immediately to work. What remained of the silver was still where Danilov had hidden it, high in the wall behind a tall chest. She decided to take it on the second trip, when there would be more protective noise in the other rooms. Now she turned instead to their clothing and chose everything of value, leaving only what was worthless and absolutely necessary. It would soon be getting cold again, and she shuddered involuntarily at the memory of the previous winter, when every dawn revealed the night's frozen bodies.

Nadia Nikolaevna was asleep in her chair, the handkerchief in her lap, her hands thankfully still at last. For the first time, Maria noticed that they had become knobby and lined — the same hands which as late as a year earlier had been beautiful enough to inspire comment. The muscles in her face were also relaxed, which made it possible to see a trace of the person she had been, but no more than a trace.

At the moment, Nadia Nikolaevna was wearing a valuable fur boa. It was one of her favorite things; in earlier times — when reality had existed — she had often chosen it for duty on cold nights. But it was no longer a necessity. And it would bring a good price. Maria stood before her, wondering how to get it away.

She reached out to see whether she could slip it from around her mother's neck, and at that moment Nadia Nikolaevna opened her eyes. There was nothing in them. They simply stared without comprehension at Maria. Without hesitation, Maria continued the movement of her hand, but instead of touching the boa, she caressed her mother's face. She flushed with humiliation. She felt almost as if she had been caught stealing. And she had not meant the caress she was now giving. It was a fraud. She was repelled to notice the ease with which she dissembled.

278

Nadia Nikolaevna stretched and drew the boa closer. Recognition came into her eyes. "Good morning, my dear," she said, smiling sweetly. She took Maria's offending hand and pressed it to her lips.

Maria shuddered and studied her closely. Was this some subtle irony and reproof? But no, Nadia Nikolaevna was perfectly sincere. She really had been asleep during Maria's apprenticeship at theft.

Nadia Nikolaevna stretched again. "I feel so well, Masha. So very well, I think I'll read and have some tea. I feel in the mood for a good French novel."

Once again, the night had worked a change in her mother's behavior. But what exactly was it? It was subtle, impossible to know. Now Nadia Nikolaevna did not fidget and play with her handkerchief. Her hands lay calm and still in her lap. The worried agitation was gone from her voice. Now she spoke with the old assurance. There was even a hint of her former authority. She sat with regal ease in her chair. She was once again the original Nadia Nikolaevna — but she was different. Her spirit had changed. The old effervescence and alertness were gone. Now she was placid, bovine in a way. It was as if a small but crucial part had been removed from her brain.

"Mama, are you sure you are feeling well?" Maria asked.

"Of course I am, Masha! What do you mean? Haven't I said so?" Now there was a trace of annoyance in her voice. Then it was gone and she again became placid, even complacent. "Come, Masha. Join me. Here's my glass. Pour."

It was as if they were reaching out to each other, trying to touch, but Nadia Nikolaevna was slowly drifting away into the sea.

"No, mama, thank you, I must go," Maria said. She could not wait, and she could not take the boa now.

Nadia Nikolaevna pouted. "That's it," she said. "Ignore me. I'm only your mother. I understand."

"I'm not ignoring you, mama," said Maria.

"You are. I'm useless. You don't need me any more. Why don't you admit it, Masha? Be honest. I don't want your charity. I'm not a child."

"Of course you're not, mama. Who said you were?"

"That's it. Insult me. I'm only your mother."

She had not mentioned her husband once, as if she had forgotten all about him. A book was in her hands and she bent abruptly to it, as if doing so would somehow make Maria disappear.

Maria quickly took her package and left. She had to escape. There was nothing more to say. She could do nothing about what was happening to her mother. It was a splendid day, crisp and clear. In spite of the weight of her package, she enjoyed the long walk to the Alexandrovsky market. The reassuring thought occurred to her that her father — wherever he might be — was enjoying the day, too. The Chekists could not control the weather.

The market was crowded and business was good. She sold what she had and went back for the silver. Then again she made the long trip across town to the market, as unobtrusively as possible. The streets were teeming with beggars and others with nowhere to go, but there was very little traffic. Cabs were viewed with suspicion as a hangover from Capitalism. And any horse foolish enough to venture out ran the risk of being eaten.

Now the market was so crowded it was impossible to walk. It was hot. She set the silver out and a middle-aged, overfed, overdressed woman was upon it. She was apparently the wife of some sort of commissar, accompanied by a young man in a Red Army uniform.

"What's dis junk?" asked the woman, examining a spoon.

"Silver," said Maria.

"I know dat," said the woman.

"Then why did you ask?"

The woman sneered and studied a knife. "I suppose you know dat selling on da private market not legal?" Her Russian was atrocious. Maria suspected she was a German. She herself spoke German well, but she responded in Russian of the same quality.

"Oh, *ja*," Maria said brightly. "But I don't let it worry me none."

The woman snorted and smiled with intimacy. "I suppose you steal all dis."

"Oh, no, *Gnädige Fräu*," said Maria with mock indignation. "I took it from my mistress. The new Tsar, comrade Vladimir Ilyitch, said it was mine all along. I never thought of dat before. But you're a *boorzhui*, ain't you? You better not complain."

The woman flushed redder than the band on her arm. "Begging your pardon. Dere ain't no bourgeois blood in me at all. I come entirely from working people."

The woman had felt reproved and was on the defensive. As soon as the bargaining began, she agreed to Maria's high price. "Always charge what someone is willing to pay," Danilov had said. The woman knew she had lost. She gestured to the silver, the boy in uniform gathered it up, and they were gone.

Maria had her father's ransom. Deep in her pocket, where no one could see, she squeezed the coins and bills, and began to work her way through the crowd. The shouting and pointing, threats and fights would go on all day, but her job was done and Dolgorensky would be waiting. Her fingernails dug

280

painfully into the heel of her hand. Some yards away, through the haggling fingers and shaking fists, she thought she was a familiar face. Was it . . . ?

Then, far away across the square, she saw crowds and automobiles pouring in from the side streets. People were running.

"It's a search party!" someone yelled.

"It's the Chekists!"

"Run!"

Maria shook with fear and outrage. Was there no safe place? Was there nowhere one could trade and be free?

The crowd dissolved as if blown to bits. Arms, heads and people disappeared, stooping, falling, kneeling, rising, collecting their wares as best they could.

Maria was running full out with the others, her hand in her pocket, her fingernails drawing blood. Over her shoulder, she saw the automobiles bearing down, and the long bayonets of the Chekist troops. Her ears rang. She could not hear a thing. It was almost as if the others had disappeared, or she had, and she were running alone in a soundless dimension.

She looked again and saw that she was indeed running alone. The others had been scattered and left behind. One of the cars was already very close, and inside it she saw some smiling faces. It was almost as if, for some reason, they had singled her out.

The streets leading out of the square were also quite close. If she could reach them perhaps she would be safe. But she was gasping. It was impossible to force even another whisper of air into her lungs.

A blow to the back of the head literally launched her into the air and then smashed her to the ground. She rolled with a jolt against the wheel of a standing wagon. Pain chewed up her arm into her shoulder and her neck. The taste of blood appeared in her mouth. For a few seconds, she lost consciousness.

Someone was pulling roughly at her coat, and she came awake flailing at him wildly. It was a little man, a strange little man with an unusually large nose, and he was very much enjoying what he was doing. It was Kolodsky. Maria did not know him. But Kolodsky knew who she was. That was why he was enjoying himself so much. Her father had employed him years ago.

She pushed her hand quickly into her pocket. The money was there. Her hand closed convulsively around it, making a fist of dirt and blood. She rose to one knee and tried to get up, but at the same time, Kolodsky merrily pulled her fist out.

"What have you got there?" he said. "Let's see."

Maria hit him squarely and painfully on the ear. He slapped her hard across the mouth. The marks of his fingers could be seen clearly. Then he shoved her back against the wheel and one by one unpeeled her fingers.

"So!" he screeched. "The fruits of speculation!" He had heard that phrase somewhere. He liked it. "A crime against the state. Comrade Marchenko will be angry."

Maria's ravished hand hung limp. Kolodsky was transferring the money to his own pocket.

"I am not going to arrest you, citizen," he said. "You are lucky. My orders are to be generous today. Perhaps tomorrow my orders will change. Who knows? It's amusing to speculate."

His laugh dissolved in the hoots of the others.

"Nothing's too bad for these *boorzhui*," someone said.

"Next time you won't be so lucky, bitch!"

Maria heard the car door slam, there was a smell of gas, and the car roared away. The ransom was gone. Her hand was empty. Her father was no closer to freedom than before. In her dazed and bloody condition, it seemed as if, impossibly, the raid and the little man, everything, had been arranged, just to produce that result.

Now someone was gently lifting her and talking. "My dear lady, how beautifully fortunate that I happened to pass by."

Maria could not see. "What?" she said. "What?" She sniffed. There was the odor of good cologne.

"What a beautiful coincidence," said the voice. "I refer, of course, to our meeting here."

He was holding her erect. Her head fell forward on his chest. She could not hold it up.

"They took the money," Maria said.

"But, my dear lady, how fortunate that I am here. Permit me to advance you the necessary sum."

"They took the money."

"Yes, of course, my dear Masha. They took the money. I understand. But, as I say, I am going to advance it."

Suddenly Maria realized that she had no idea who was talking to her. "What?" she said. "Who is that?" She blinked and squinted. The daylight was painfully bright. Her eyesight returned. She was talking to Telegin. His was the familiar face she had seen.

She drew back, startled. "What? Cyril Modestovitch?"

Telegin smiled. A gold tooth glistened. "Your servant, Madamoiselle. *Enchanté*." He took her ravished hand and kissed it.

"No," said Maria. She took it back. Without thinking, she rubbed it on her coat. "I don't want your help. Leave me alone."

Telegin chuckled, not at all rebuffed. "You hurt me, Masha. I'm a sensitive man. But my admiration for you drives me on." He shook a finger. "I predict you will change your mind."

She turned and walked with difficulty to the side street and out of the square. Telegin watched her. He did not follow. Interesting, he thought. Such a fascinating experiment. He congratulated himself once again for having thought of it. How clever he had been to suggest it to Marchenko. She was getting further away and then finally out of sight. But he knew that he controlled her movements as a playwright does a character's. How pleasurable that was. It was his greatest work, a masterpiece in the midst of these unesthetic times.

Telegin smiled broadly. His tooth gleamed again. The Revolution was beautiful, as comrade Lenin had said.

XXXIX

Nadia Nikolaevna stood at the small kerosene stove, stirring some barley. Pinched and bent, her posture announced that she was no longer capable of indignation. She could no longer be outraged. She had given up. With the passage of time, she remembered her former life less, as if it had been a dream and she had awakened long ago. The present nightmare seemed normal, anything else unreal. The only important thing was the struggle to survive.

Maria shuddered. Her mother seemed dead — dead but still walking, breathing and eating. She talked, even read, but her soul had gone. Nadia Nikolaevna had been destroyed by "real life." Maria would never let that happen to herself. Her former life had been real and was normal. Communism was transitory and wrong. Life, human life, was natural and possible and, somewhere in the world, was being lived properly. That was why she had to find her father. She had to do anything to arrange his release.

But, for the moment, she had no more ideas. She had seen Dolgorensky again, of course. She wouldn't have been able to rest had she not. And he had refused, as she had expected, even to say where her father was. But now Maria had no idea what to do. Should she risk seeing Michael and asking for his help? Suppose that only succeeded in making trouble for him? On the other hand, it would be pleasant in the "little hut."

It was now a few days after the incident at the Alexandrovsky market. She felt much better. The swelling on the side of her head had gone down. If only her mother would talk as she used to. Her silence was painful. When she did speak, it was always to complain. She had no interest in anything else.

Maria thought of Telegin, as she often had during the last few days. Strange that he happened to be at the Alexandrovsky at the time. And why, in the midst of all this suffering, was he prosperous enough to lend money?

Suddenly a paralyzing thought was in her mind: Suppose Telegin could, as he had said, help her father. Didn't his mysterious wealth and influence prove at least that it was possible? Maria tried to put the idea from her mind and flushed painfully with guilt. Hadn't she sworn to do whatever was necessary? Wouldn't her father do the same if their positions were reversed? Shouldn't she at least find out what Telegin could do?

A wave of fear crushed her against her chair, fear of everything and nothing, the most terrifying kind. There had to be a way to get the job done. But she could think of nothing else and there was no one to consult.

There was a knock at the door and both women froze. One always froze when there was a knock at the door. It was a reflex. Nadia Nikolaevna accepted that. Maria did not accept it. She was outraged. The fact that she had frozen was insane. She went to the door and opened it.

It was Tata Beresova.

Months had passed since they had last met. Tata had changed. No longer was she thin and underfed. Now she was rosy with health — almost plump. She seemed incongruous in the room with the other two women. They were irritated, in fact. Not psychologically, not because of jealousy, but physiologically — because her robust presence in this small space threatened to overload their sharpened senses. Her annoying physical exuberance was out of place in their dingy room.

And at the same time she was diffident, afraid of her reception, which compounded the incongruity and irritated the others even more. She stood just inside the door and smiled uncertainly.

"Come in, Tata," said Maria, angry at her own irritation.

Tata did so hesitantly, presenting a small bag. "Just a few things I thought you might like."

Nadia Nikolaevna did not say a word. She sprang from her chair with an agility Maria thought she had lost and pulled the bag from Tata's hands. Her eyes had not left it since Tata had come in. Tears overflowed them as she pulled out a sausage, a real sausage. Its smell, thick and pungent, seemed to permeate the entire room, providing nourishment all by itself.

They ate. Maria forced herself to do so slowly, chewing each mouthful more than was necessary. This was very painful. Eating had always been, and should be, such a pleasure. Nadia Nikolaevna, however, ate very quickly, biting off a much larger piece than she could chew and then biting off another before she had finished. She pushed it in to make room and licked her fingers and rooted in the bag to see what else was there. It was a very noisy process on which she concentrated completely. She still had not acknowledged Tata's presence in the room.

Tata looked down at her hands and then quickly about, embarrassed, blushing, trying to find something to look at or think of something to say.

Maria touched her arm. "It's all right, Tata."

Tata flushed even more and jumped up. "I'll make some tea."

"All right."

Nadia Nikolaevna could not talk. Her mouth was still full. She pointed nervously at the empty, tarnished samovar.

Even the tea was real, not the usual Soviet issue. It was so pleasant just to hold the glass in one's hands and, with one's nose at the brim, inhale the steam and the aroma.

Now Tata herself was irritated. Why didn't Maria openly notice her prosperity? Why didn't she ask about it and criticize? Tata knew Maria was doing so silently. She lit a cigarette and began to smoke, which was also something new. Still another incongruity was the fact that the cigarette, unlike everything else, was the spurious Soviet variety.

Maria smiled as the unpleasant odor of the *mahorka* filled the room. "What's that stuff?"

"I could get nothing else, of course," Tata snapped. Instantly, she was sorry. "I'm so nervous."

"Aren't we all?"

"Thank you, Masha. It is good of you to welcome me."

"Nonsense, Tata. All friends fight. 'We're women. We can't help it.' Remember?"

"Yes. Thank you, Masha. We *are* good friends."

"Yes."

"We've had so many good times."

"Yes."

"Such good times. Remember the summer in the country when we were little girls and picked wild strawberries, and we took off everything but our hats? And your neighbor, what was his name — God, he was awful! — complained to your father?"

"Yes."

"And your father was so amused, and your neighbor was so angry. And you, Nadia Nikolaevna, were so thoroughly scandalized."

"Was I?" said Nadia Nikolaevna. " I don't remember."

"Such fun," said Tata. "So amusing. Ha, ha, ha . . . ."

Tata softly began to cry, her head bowed, the tears falling silently on the hands in her lap. "Masha, I've returned to the company. I am now officially a Soviet artist."

"I see."

"My brother was ill. He was dying. There was nothing else to do."

"Yes."

"Now it's your turn to despise me. Go ahead."

"No, Tata. I have also lost a brother, remember? One does what one must."

But that statement, calculated to soothe, surprisingly did exactly the reverse. Tata gasped.

"Oh, Masha, if you knew . . . ."

"Knew what, Tata?"

"One has no choice."

"No."

"They've made everything so grubby and small."

"Yes."

Tata took her hand. "Thank you. You are a real friend."

Head bowed, Nadia Nikolaevna worked at her handkerchief. Her voice was nervous, wheedling and soft. "Masha, if Tatiana Lvovna could rejoin the company for her brother — Tata, you are so good, so fine — perhaps you as well, Masha . . . ."

Maria's eyes narrowed to slits, as did her lips. She tossed her head. Her chin rose. "Never would I dance before those people. Never!"

Tata blushed Soviet red and looked away. "It's just as well," she said. "Crispina is still the chairman of our committee. She would not admit you."

Maria sneered. "A soviet! In a ballet company!"

Tata smiled cynically. "That's Communism. Everything is political. And Vera Karpovna has the best proletarian background."

There was an uncomfortable silence. Tata sighed. "Natalia Stepanovna is coaching me. It was the only way I could keep her alive."

Maria's former teacher appeared vividly in her mind, the room they worked in, her servant Edouard Andreievitch and his beer. Maria had not seen any of them for months.

There was a knock at the door and the three women froze. Tata, an official Soviet artist, was not immune to the reflex. Maria got up and opened it. "Well?"

An elderly, diffident man came in. "Please excuse me. I live downstairs. I'm the new chairman of the House Committee. This is very embarrassing, but I must inspect your rooms."

"Why?" asked Maria.

"I don't know. I'm sorry. They told me to. Probably because doing it is so horribly painful."

"Yes," said Maria. "That is the Bolshevik style. But what happened to Anna Andreevna?"

The elderly man shrugged.

The door swung wide and crashed against the wall. Anna Andreevna herself came in. She pointed at Maria. "You've done this."

"What do you mean?" Maria asked.

"Don't play dumb, you bitch!" she said. Her mouth was shaking. Her eyes were red. "My boy friend, Marchenko, has kicked me out! He's tired of me. He's found some slut. I have to leave. She's moving in." She pointed at Tata. "Is that the bitch?"

Tata also began to shake. All the color left her face. She rose and put a hand on her heart. "I'll go now, Masha. I'll come back later. I'm very sorry about your father."

"What do you mean?" Maria asked, puzzled. "I didn't mention my father. How did you know?"

"Oh . . . yes," said Tata, confused. "Vasya told me."

"Vasya is alive? In Petrograd?"

"Yes."

"Why didn't you say so, Tata?"

"I'm sorry."

"Why hasn't Vasya come to see me?"

She had last seen Lopatkin two years ago, in the former world. There had been a party. Once again, Maria saw the lights, smelled the food, heard the music. There was a beautiful woman there, her mother. So long ago, ages, an eternity. The memories returned with painful intensity.

She and Vasya had stood on the balcony in the snow. What was it Vasya had said? "Promise me if you ever need anything you'll tell me." Again, she heard him saying that. For the first time in days, Maria felt hope. Vasya now would honor his pledge. He would locate her father and have him set free.

"Tata, where is Vasya?" she asked. "Where?"

*   *   *

In a small room in an old hotel in the Slaviansky Bazaar district, citizen Vasili Ignatievitch Lopatkin sat on the bed. He wore the remains of his old uniform, the coat now stripped of its buttons and the hated epaulets. It was such a pleasure to see him again, not simply because they were old friends but because he was a reminder of years ago. He was living proof of the reality which would reappear as soon as the unreal and impossible present ended.

"It's good to see you, Vasya," she said.

"Yes, yes!" he said. "Of course it is. Thanks. Please sit down. I'll find a chair. Let me see . . . ."

Maria laughed aloud with delight. It was the same old Vasya, as preoccupied as ever. "But why haven't you been to see me?"

"How did you find me?" Lopatkin asked shortly. No, this was something new. This was not his usual confused preoccupation. It was as if he were angry at her presence and, at the same time, embarrassed. Something was clearly making him uncomfortable.

"Tata told me," said Maria. "Is anything wrong?"

Lopatkin made a face. "Tata. Of course."

"Why haven't you been to see me?"

He shrugged. "The Cheka."

Nothing more needed saying on the subject. It had been covered. It was closed. "Cheka" was a word containing dictionaries of meanings, which answered every question asked.

"My father, too . . . ."

"Yes. I've seen him."

"You've seen him?" Maria was instantly at his side, pulling at his coat. At last, after weeks of failures, the mystery would be solved. "Where, Vasya? Is he well?"

Lopatkin shrugged. "For the time being."

"What do you mean?"

"I don't know. Perhaps I mean something. Perhaps I don't. One can't be sure of anything, you see. Someone disappears, reappears, is shot or is transferred, and there is no way of knowing why or who made the decision. That's because no one made a decision at all. These things happen by themselves. It's like being a fly trapped in a web."

"Vasya, I want your help. That's why I'm here. Where is my father? Help me get him released."

Lopatkin shook his head. "You don't understand, Masha. One doesn't get anyone released. If the person in question is to be released, the machine— at the right time and when it decides to do so — will spit him out, or maybe it won't. There's no way in the world to interfere. So it's best just to sit and make no noise and wait until whatever will happen happens."

It was strange. Lopatkin was not cynical. He was not bitter. In fact, he said all this softly, completely without emotion. It was as if he had been pressed emotionally flat. His attitude was similar to Nadia Niko-laevna's.

"What has happened, Vasya?" Maria asked. "You told me to tell you if I needed your help — you made me promise, remember — and I need it now. You know my father. You admire him. And you served with my poor brother at the front."

Lopatkin began to shake, as if he had a chill. He reached under the mattress, drew out some vodka, and drank, long and noisily. This, too, was new.

"Your brother is dead," Lopatkin said harshly.

"Yes," said Maria. "That's what we thought. Did you see it?"

"Yes." He drank again.

"How did it happen?"

"Your brother died a hero, Masha," Lopatkin said. "You can be sure of that. He sacrificed himself so the rest of us could escape from an Austrian prison. He deserved another Cross."

There was a strange, uncharacteristic quality in Lopatkin's speech. It was nervous, loud, clipped, tense, as if his words held back hysteria. But the quality was too vague to define.

"So you see, Vasya, with my brother gone, only my father is left. And Stepan would want you to do what you could."

"Oh, God!" said Lopatkin. "Stop it! Go home! Please, Masha! That's the best thing to do."

Maria became unusually calm. "Vasya, if you are too cowardly to give me any help at all, just tell me where he is and the name of the official in charge."

Lopatkin swallowed again. His mind was swimming.

"All right," he said. "Perhaps you're right. There's no point to this. I'm being stupid. He is with the Petrograd Cheka."

"In the Gorokhovaya?"

"Yes."

"How do you know?"

"He is there. We were there together."

"Why hasn't he been transferred to one of the prisons?"

"Because the Chekist in charge of his case is Marchenko."

"Marchenko? But I know of him! His mistress has our apartment!"

"Not any more. He's kicked her out."

"Yes. That's right. She just told us so. But . . . ."

"His new mistress is our former friend Tata."

Maria said nothing. Tata's behavior suddenly became clear. Poor Tata! She had been unable to tell Maria the truth. She was suffering so. It was she who would move in to replace Anna Andreevna. She had hoped to assuage her guilt by paying Maria a visit, and had only succeeded in feeling worse,

290

which was senseless. As Tata had said, she had no choice. This was comrade Marchenko's doing.

"Go to the Gorokhovaya, Masha. See Marchenko. You will not get what you want, but you will learn something everyone has to know. You will learn what Communism is really about — not what they say it is, but what it really is. Go, Masha!"

"Thank you, Vasya," Maria said. At last the waiting and uncertainty were over. At last she had the facts she needed. She knew that somehow she would arrange her father's release.

XL

Orloff was ill at ease as he waited in the small room at Number Two Gorokhovaya. He knew the horrors happening there were part of a necessary evil, necessary as an unpleasant treatment is often necessary to fight a disease. The disease in this case was the previous Capitalist economic system. The Cheka was the treatment, and health would be restored in the form of the Socialist utopia. Russia was undergoing a necessary purification, necessary but temporary. It would soon come to an end. But now the new regime was surrounded by enemies and fighting for its life.

Yet, what necessarily happened at Number Two Gorokhovaya repelled him. He was ill at ease. It was messy. He would have much preferred to settle the entire matter exclusively in clean, open, military fashion. He knew that was impossible, but that was how he felt. He hated secrecy and deviousness. He did not like police work. There was such a difference between it and the army life he loved. The difference was a matter of psychology, of style. He was glad he did not have to be a Chekist.

Perhaps that was what made him so uncomfortable. The difference was that the Chekists he knew were delighted to be Chekists. They enjoyed their necessary but evil work. They enjoyed the work more than the goal they were working to protect. There was Dolgorensky, for instance, whom Orloff had never liked. A perfect Communist, but something was wrong. Perhaps it was Dolgorensky's annoying effeminacy.

The door opened. Dolgorensky stuck his head in. "Ah, Peter Sergeie-vitch, my dear friend," he said. "I was curious and I didn't know it was you. Our clients are not often visited by Red Army generals. You are here to see . . . ?"

"Danilov," said Orloff stiffly.

"Your brother-in-law. Of course!"

"I am here as a representative of the Food Trust."

292

"How fortunate for your brother-in-law that they sent you."

"They believe I can persuade him to accept a proposal."

"Clever." Dolgorensky smiled sulkily. He knew that this was true. Orloff would give his own relative less advantage than anyone else. "His daughter, your niece, came to see me not long ago. Unfortunately I could not permit a visit. And Marchenko agreed. But for you, Peter Sergeievitch, a Red Army general . . . ."

Dolgorensky suddenly became aware that Danilov, who had just come in, was standing behind him, and he felt an uncomfortable twinge of fear. There was no reason for it, as far as Dolgorensky knew. Danilov was, after all, only a prisoner. But that made the emotion particularly annoying. It was as if Danilov nevertheless could dominate him simply by exercising his will. There was a hidden confidence about him that Dolgorensky disliked. Perhaps it was that he was completely unafraid of Dolgorensky.

Dolgorensky's emotion was replaced by anger, which showed itself on his pursed lips. He smiled at Orloff. "Prisoner Danilov is delivered, comrade general," he said, and went out. Just behind him, down the corridor, went the two Chekist guards.

Orloff closed the door. There was a long silence. "How long has it been?" he said.

"I don't know. Since you were sent away."

"Nineteen seven. Almost twelve years, now. A long time. A different world."

"We visited Katya in Krasnoyarsk one year."

"I know."

"How is Katya?"

"Very well. And Nadia?"

"I don't know. I have not seen her for some time."

"Yes," said Orloff. "Of course."

"Now I suppose you will want to know about Maria."

"Yes."

"As far as I know, Maria is well."

"And your son?"

"He was lost in the retreat of '16."

"I'm sorry," said Orloff. "That was a totally senseless war."

"Yes. It was."

"But it was good for profits."

"No," said Danilov. "I am out of business. It was good for you Communists. You took all the profits. That is why the war against you makes sense."

"If Stepan were alive, he would be fighting us," said Orloff.

"Yes," said Danilov. "We have discussed our families. What shall we discuss now? Or is it time for you to tell me why you are here?"

"I'm sorry," said Orloff. "I'm as uncomfortable as you are."

"No," Danilov said, "you aren't."

"Until recently I was more uncomfortable."

"But you didn't give any money to the Tsar."

They became aware of a scuffling in the corridor. It became louder, peaked, and then quickly receded in a flurry of boots and mutterings. A door slammed. All was again quiet.

Orloff took out a paper. "Ivan, I have here an offer from the chairman of the Soviet Food Trust."

"What sort of offer?"

"There is an unusual shortage of agricultural machinery. Food is scarce, as you know. There have been many cases of death by starvation. You are needed again to help run the factory."

"Which factory is that, Petya?"

"Yours, of course. Danilov Agricultural Machinery."

"Strange, I've never heard of it. But why? What's the point?"

"Our Socialist managers have not yet had the opportunity to acquire the necessary skills. The transition will take considerable time. Every Soviet enterprise has made arrangements with bourgeois specialists. The Food Trust wants to make one with you. You would be well paid, Ivan. You would be free. And, most important, you would be of value to the Socialist reconstruction."

Danilov began to chuckle. It was funny. He shook his head.

"What is the joke?" Orloff said shortly. He was annoyed.

"The Socialist reconstruction should find it interesting, Petya. What does the sudden importance of my services do to the labor theory of value?"

Orloff became more uncomfortable. He had never been able to penetrate the incomprehensible morass of *Das Kapital*. Leave the economics to the economists, he thought. He was a soldier.

"Ivan, I urge you to accept this offer."

"No, Petya. I don't want to participate in the Socialist reconstruction. I won't cooperate with you because you have stolen my property. You're a thief."

Orloff colored. No one had ever dared tell him that before. "You are mistaken, Ivan. Why must you persist in clinging to an outmoded myth? Private property itself is theft. You fail to see the perfect justice of Socialism."

294

"They really have taken you in, Petya, haven't they? I mean, the people really running the show. I know how that happens. They took me in for years. I realized that only a few years too late.

"Remember when I began to contribute to the Party? I became interested, as you will recall, because of your arrest and conviction. The Party, I was told, would eliminate injustice. I'm amazed now to remember that I believed that for years. I've questioned my intelligence, even my sanity. Haven't you questioned yours, Petya? We both know that the Party's purpose is to capitalize on injustice — and that the result is the most monstrous injustice ever committed."

Orloff was more uncomfortable than ever. Danilov's conversation sounded something like his talks with another prisoner, years ago in Siberia. But Michael was now Orloff's adjutant and Orloff patronized him slightly. He knew that Michael would eventually understand. Danilov, although he was a prisoner now, was Orloff's equal. Orloff could not shrug his criticisms off as easily. Danilov was forcing Orloff to think — and Orloff didn't want to think about these things. He did not have an analytical mind. Furthermore, he resented Danilov's introduction of the personal factor into the conversation. He mistrusted the personal factor. It always cheapened whatever it touched. The value of any activity was enhanced to the extent that the personal factor had been eliminated. And as Orloff had feared, Danilov was trying to establish some sort of personal claim. The personal factor had intruded itself.

"I won't discuss it," said Orloff. "Ivan, I urge you as strongly as possible to accept this offer. It's important!"

"Why, Petya?"

"It would be of great value to the Party. You are needed."

But Orloff knew that that wasn't the entire truth. The offer had been the idea of the Food Trust, as he had said. The commissar of the Food Trust himself had asked Orloff to make it. But Orloff wanted his brother-in-law to accept it because he liked him. He could not deny the personal factor.

"Here I am merely a prisoner," said Danilov. "There I would be a slave."

"Your case is to be disposed of in the next few days," Orloff said. "You know that I cannot interfere with Soviet justice. The decision must be made by the authorities in charge. I would like to see comrade Marchenko about it. But I won't."

"If only you would understand," said Orloff.

"That's what *I* was about to say." He smiled vaguely.

Both men rose. They were enemies — albeit reluctant enemies. They still admired each other. That had not changed.

"It's strange," said Danilov, "that we are forced to be enemies."

"Yes."

"Why is that, Petya?"

"I don't know."

"I ask one thing," said Danilov. "Not because I am your brother-in-law, nor because Masha is your niece, but because I do deserve some reward — don't I? — for my contributions to the Party. Masha does not have the strength of my wife. She is naive, without experience, still a child. And she is completely without politics; though, of course, as my daughter her blood is slightly bad. I ask for your word that you will do what you can to protect her."

"Yes," said Orloff. "I will do what I can."

XLI

The Gorokhovaya was a difficult place to visit. Puzzled glances followed Maria as she entered. Conversations stopped. There was a hush. She asked someone a question. His eyes widened and he walked away. It was dark. Muffled sounds came from various rooms, as if people inside were whispering and moving with great stealth. A pair of eyes stared at her from around a door post. She turned and the eyes disappeared. No one knew a thing. No one spoke. It was impossible to learn where anything was. There was nothing but the vagueness of a nightmare.

She walked up a flight of stairs and down a corridor. At last she was in a very small room. A little man sat at a desk — a little man with a big nose. She still did not know his name, but it was Kolodsky, of course — the same little man who had robbed her not long before in the Alexandrovsky. Maria stood before him paralyzed with dread, her face averted as much as was safe, trying subtly to cover her mouth. Was there any explanation for this amazing coincidence, she wondered?

But Kolodsky appeared not to remember. He drummed his fingers on the newspaper he had been reading and smiled. He got up and came around the desk where Maria towered over him. She looked down warily, as his nose began to work. It was red, pitted, mottled and veiny. It flitted in and out, waggling, vibrating, extending and retracting, efficiently conveying important sensory information to his brain.

"Hm, yes," Kolodsky sniffled, through the small aperture beneath his nose. "Yes. *Boorzhui.* Name?"

"Danilova, comrade. I wish to see comrade Marchenko."

Kolodsky chuckled. His nostrils wagged. "You are mistaken, Danilova. No one *wishes* to see comrade Marchenko." It was a good joke. Kolodsky laughed and pounded his fist on the desk.

"I do."

Kolodsky abruptly went back behind the desk, sat down again and began to read. "Wonderful!" he said periodically. "Great!" It became obvious that he was deliberately ignoring her. Did this mean he recognized her after all? Was he worried? Was his behavior part of some monstrous joke?

Suddenly he looked up. He pointed at Maria. "Danilov Agricultural Machinery!" he said.

"Yes," said Maria, inwardly cringing. Her head fell. It was like being castigated by Natalia Stepanovna at ballet practice years ago.

"I worked for your father! I was a wage-slave!"

"Oh." A more articulate answer rose to her lips, but she did not say it. It was pointless. There was no adequate answer to a remark so stupid. This was not just a stupid departure from a context of sense. This was stupidity gone crazy; stupidity in charge.

"Wait here!" he said, and was abruptly up again. He was having a good time. It was so good to put them in their place. The daughter of the man — and the man himself — who years ago had humiliated and exploited Kolodsky by employing him in such a menial position. It was just as the *Internationale* had promised. Kolodsky had been nothing and now he was all. His little pigeon chest swelled. He chuckled. Danilov had had a son, an officer lost in the 1916 campaign. Such a pity! Kolodsky had been cheated of the chance to put the son in his place, too.

Kolodsky disappeared through the inner door, was back immediately and returned to his newspaper, mumbling periodically, his waggling nose taking in the news. Nearby in another office, a telephone rang. "Yes, comrade chief. By all means, comrade chief." There were other, stranger noises, mysterious and indistinguishable. Doors opened and closed. There was muttering and whispering, labored breathing. And yet somehow the room and the building itself was enveloped in a stillness, as if inside some sort of vacuum.

A nondescript, young man came running in. "Good news!" he shouted. "Germany is ours! The German Soviet Republic has been declared. The English comrades have presented an ultimatum to King George."

"Wonderful!" cried Kolodsky. He rose.

"Two divisions of Americans have revolted in New York. They refused to fire on starving workers and are marching on Washington. Wilson has fled. He's going to resign."

"Great!"

The nondescript young man was already out the door. Maria heard him running down the hall. Kolodsky himself scurried from wall to wall, chuckling and snuffling, in a fever without purpose.

He stopped before Maria. "Yes, yes?" he said. "What do you want?"

298

"Citizen Danilova, comrade, to see comrade Marchenko." She spoke softly, keeping her temper with an effort.

"My God, you *boorzhui* are thick!" said Kolodsky. "Go through that door!"

Maria opened the door and went in. The room was large and well furnished, but it was so dark she could barely see. There was only one lamp, on the desk, but it cast a dim light, and little more came in through the small window. A man in a military tunic, his back to her, was looking out.

She shut the door but the sound got no answer, and she stood in silence with growing exasperation. Another Bolshevik psychological experiment! Was she supposed to start talking or simply to wait? A long time passed. The man did not stir. She did not want to make a mistake, but the waiting became intolerable.

"Comrade Marchenko," she began cautiously, "thank you for seeing me. I know you are busy with the Socialist reconstruction." She stopped abruptly. She was trying very hard, but it was so difficult to utter such nonsense without sounding sarcastic.

"I am here to ask about my father," she continued. "Ivan Fyodorovitch Danilov, a Soviet citizen. He has been arrested by accident . . . ." Maria related the details of the arrest, explained why it had been a mistake, said that her father should be released and that not only had he never participated in anti-Soviet activities, he had contributed regularly to the Party treasury when it was unpopular to do so.

Marchenko waved her into silence without turning around. A long time passed. He was very obviously playing with her. Then he slowly turned around and came into the light.

It was Stepan.

Maria felt no shock, no surprise. She felt nothing, as with a wound which is far too painful to feel. Her mind was drained, suspended, disoriented. She knew what she saw, but could not comprehend it. She put a hand against the wall to keep her balance. Fear, wonder, horror and relief collided painfully in her reeling consciousness. But which emotion was correct? What should she feel? What should she think, seeing her dead brother resurrected as a uniformed Chekist in charge of their father's case?

Gradually, relief drove out the others. She surrendered to it. It flowed luxuriously through her body, like the comfort of mulled wine. She was right to feel relief. It was the only choice. Her search had ended successfully at last. Her brother was alive and would now release their father. Nothing else was of any importance. Indeed, the thing was ending better than could have been imagined.

She stepped forward tentatively with a nervous smile. "Stepan?" she called softly. "Stepan?"

There was absolutely no expression on Stepan's face. "You don't make sense," he said. "What is your name?"

"It's me, Stepan. Masha, Maria Ivanovna, your sister. Have I changed so much?"

Stepan's mouth opened again. His lips moved. She saw his tongue darting in and out. She heard words. "You are mistaken, citizen," said Stepan. "I have no sister. My name is Pavel Vladimirovitch Marchenko."

"Stepan, please . . . ." She stared at him. Could there be some mistake? Was he someone else? No, there was Stepan's face, his military haircut, his strong bearing. It was definitely Stepan. Suddenly she began to cry. She tried to press the tears back, unsuccessfully.

"Formerly a soldier in the Grand Duchess's Hussars," said Stepan.

"Stop it, stop it!" screamed Maria. "I realize you have rejected your own name to win favor with the Party, but your joke is not funny and we are absolutely alone. Stop this grisly charade at once!"

Stepan took a *mahorka* cigarette from a jade box and lit it. Somehow he still preferred the cheap tobacco to any other. "This is highly irregular, citizen. Why are you here?"

"You're moving your mistress into our apartment," she said.

"That's true," said Stepan. "She needs a place to live."

"You've arrested your own father. Are you mad?"

"I'm quite sane, thank you. Citizen Danilov is being reeducated. He needs it. His arrest was ordered by the Food Trust and comrade Dolgorensky."

What it all meant, she did not know. But she was beginning to understand that she was facing an evil she had never before dreamt possible.

She sank to her knees. Suddenly she was very, very tired. "Stepan, please, I beg you," she said. "Our father is here and needs your help. I know you are in charge of his case, and you *must* help him now. Why won't you answer me? Tell me, Stepan, please! You are carrying this joke too far."

Maria was dizzy. Her head began to whirl. She was too tired even to stay on her knees. She prostrated herself before him, her face to the floor, her head between the polished columns of his boots, the palms of her hands clutching at his heels.

"Please, Stepan," she whimpered. "Papa needs your help."

A smile appeared for the first time on Stepan's charming, proletarian, well-fed face. A feeling of omnipotence came over him; the spiritually satisfying ability to tell people what to do, the right to issue orders and have

300

them obeyed. I control them all, he thought. I can squeeze them in my fists. I can squeeze them until they ooze like mush between my fingers.

Stepan had taken as his own the name of the man he had left on the wrong side of the river more than two years before. He had joined the Bolsheviks, who would obviously beat the Whites. What a beautiful way to even the score. He had needed Marchenko's obvious proletarian background and had taken it. Stepan had had nothing but successes since, proving that Communism was indeed superior to the system it had replaced — a system in which Stepan had had nothing but failures.

But this, this was by far his greatest success. This was priceless. It was even better than Telegin had promised, well worth the small risk of showing Maria who he was. There was nothing she could do about it. Who would believe her? Once again Stepan marvelled at Telegin's artistry. Who else could have conceived so subtle a scheme? Who else had the humor to use Kolodsky for the job at the market? Who else had the artistry not to rush, the ability to savor, to gradually press Maria not just to her knees but absolutely flat? Telegin had thought of Stepan's cooperation as his own reward, his reward for the loan Stepan had needed years before. But Stepan was enjoying the reward even more than Telegin was. How amusing it would be to see Maria with Telegin. She would be so humiliated. Telegin was so repulsive.

Indeed, what Stepan was doing was simply playing a joke. He loved a joke. He always had. And this was such a splendid little joke. It played itself. He wasn't doing anything wrong. As Stepan had said, he had not arranged the arrest. That, in fact, had been the work of the Food Trust. Stepan was simply using the arrest. Surely Maria and his father would not deny him a little fun. And the joke was not only splendid but necessary. Maria and his father needed it. Capitalist abundance had made them smug.

Once again, Stepan recalled with pleasure his fear that Orloff would come to him to discuss the case, or that his father might accept Orloff's offer — and then his certain knowledge that neither would happen. It was amusing to realize that the reason it wouldn't happen was because of the characters of these two men: his father would refuse to compromise and his uncle would not do anything which he considered self-serving. How alike they both were in so many ways.

Stepan looked down at Maria and spoke. "What you are hinting at, citizen Danilova, would be a serious violation of revolutionary morality, an inexcusable insult to Socialist justice. You are asking for favoritism. You are asking me to violate my principles. I am insulted. I could very well lock you up. Perhaps I should. If I were a harsh man, I would. But I'm going to give you another chance. We'll simply assume that you became confused."

301

He pulled her to her feet. She was completely limp, as if every bone in her body had carefully been broken.

"Please, Stepan," she whispered. "Please."

He hurried her to the door and thrust her out into the waiting room.

"Kolodsky!" he shouted.

Kolodsky leaped up. "Yes, comrade Marchenko?"

"Put this girl out of the building!" said Stepan. "Keep her out! It's your fault she was able to get this far."

Kolodsky grabbed Maria. "At once!"

He hurried her down the corridor. What would happen in Kolodsky's pea-brain, Stepan wondered, if he knew who "Marchenko" really was. Stepan recalled his fear on first seeing Kolodsky in this building. Would he remember seeing Stepan in an officer's uniform one night at the front? But he hadn't. Stepan had stood deep in the shadows.

And now Kolodsky was pulling Maria along, nose waggling, mouth grinning, enjoying this chance to irritate the world which had made him such an inconsequential little man. It brought back old times. Why comrade Marchenko was playing these tricks on the daughter of Kolodsky's old employer, he did not know. But they revived the necessity for the type of secrecy Kolodsky so loved. Kolodsky did not like to think about it — it was so illogical — but the Bolshevik victory he had furthered for years had brought him an unexpected dissatisfaction. For years, he had delightedly schemed to seize the government — and now he *was* the government. True, there still were innumerable opportunities for scheming — more, in fact — but it was scheming of a different sort. It had a different quality. Now its purpose was not to seize the government, but to maintain the *status quo*. It lacked the satisfactions of the scheming of old. Kolodsky had been feeling strangely disappointed. He liked nothing better than to complain about the *status quo*, but now, as a part of it, he could not.

That was why he so enjoyed Marchenko's little game. Maria revived the excitement of the vanished great days. Kolodsky rushed her along the corridor, down the stairs as Marchenko had ordered, and pushed her into the street.

The weather had turned bad. It was snowing thick, heavy, wet flakes. It was still early in the morning, but it was very dark. Maria could not see. She staggered away blindly, without turning around, without any idea where she was going. Her mind was numb. The only thing she knew was that this was surely as bad as "real life" could be, that at last it could get no worse. "Real life" had now done to her everything it could possibly do. Slowly, unemotionally, she had been pressed deeper and deeper into it — deeper and

302

deeper and then absolutely flat. This was surely the bottom. For the first time, she felt the hopeless victim of events. She was beginning to understand what "real life" was all about. She had no more ideals. She surrendered. She was through.

The numbness slowly dissipated and her emotions conflicted painfully. She felt revolted as she realized that Lopatkin had been right. The visit *had* taught her what Communism was. Communism is what is happening to me, she thought. Communism is "real life."

Communism had happened to Tata. Now Maria fully understood her visit. She pitied Tata as she pitied Vasya. Communism had happened to Vasya, too. He had known the truth all along. He had been Stepan's prisoner and had tried to protect her from him. Poor Vasya! How he had shaken.

Communism was what was happening to her mother and father.

Communism was Stepan. He was not the person she remembered so many years ago. Or was he? She had never known him very well. Was he, as he said, not her brother after all? Could her brother really be playing such a monstrous joke? Why was Stepan really doing this? It was quite common in these days, she knew, for sons to deny their bourgeois fathers and change their names to get ahead. Sons did that all the time. Indeed, fathers encouraged them. Otherwise they would be refused admission to the army and the universities. But this — this was something else. And Stepan enjoyed it.

Maria staggered blindly through the snow. She squinted, but she could not see. If only she could lie down in it and go to sleep. Where was she going? What would she do?

Now a face was descending toward hers through the snow, a familiar face, but it was difficult to see.

"Masha?" said a voice. "Is that you?"

"What?" Maria asked. "Who is it?"

A hand appeared and caressed her cheek. A face glistened with snow and she recognized her uncle, Peter Orloff.

"Uncle?" she asked.

"Yes."

What was she supposed to feel this time? Again she felt nothing. She was looking at her uncle and her mind simply recorded the fact. The fact that she had not seen him for years meant nothing. She knew he was a Bolshevik. She did not care.

"I've seen your father," he said after a time.

"My father was arrested."

"Yes. I know."

"Nothing can be done."

"Come. I'll take you home."

He took her arm. He led. She followed. Now he was opening a door and putting her into an automobile. She had not been in an automobile for more than a year. Her father's, and all others, had been drafted by the government. People usually rode in one only on the way to the Cheka, where they were now.

Her uncle climbed in beside her and sat down. The door closed. The automobile started.

"Masha, do you remember my *troika?*" he said.

"Yes."

"Your aunt held you on her lap. You were still a child. You screamed. I couldn't tell whether you were happy or afraid. I yelled to the horses. Your aunt laughed. We flew across the snow."

"Yes."

"You won't scream now?"

"No, uncle. I won't scream."

Maria looked at him. As she had expected, he wore the uniform of a Red Army general. She knew that nothing could be done.

XLII

The door opened as Maria reached for the knob, and Telegin was smiling and beckoning them inside. For a moment she hesitated, vexed not just because he was there again, but because he was letting her into her own apartment — as if *he* lived there. Why? Her mother was well aware of her opinion. Why did she insist on encouraging this man?

Nadia Nikolaevna was coming from behind him. "Masha, Cyril Modesto-vitch has wonderful news . . . ." She sounded almost her former self, but her voice stopped dead when she saw Orloff's uniform. It had stopped many a conversation before.

"It's all right, Nadia," said Orloff, slightly annoyed. Her fear was obviously a hangover from the previous regime. He had expected it. That was why he had been reluctant to come.

"It's Peter Sergeievitch, mama," said Maria. "Don't you recognize him?"

"Oh." The color slowly returned to her face. "Please," she said. "Come in. Come in."

"Come in by all means, my dear fellow," Telegin chuckled. "We are all loyal Communists here."

Maria grimaced. "Uncle, this is Cyril Modestovitch Telegin, a loyal Communist."

"Delighted, my dear fellow," Telegin said. "Such a pleasure. We have all heard so much about you, of course."

Orloff nodded stiffly as he took off his cap. He remembered Telegin very well. This "loyal Communist" was the same man who, as a loyal monarchist, had written articles denouncing Orloff after his arrest. Did he seriously believe that Orloff had forgotten? Why was he pretending to be Orloff's friend?

Still, he was a Party member now, as he had said. Indeed, Orloff had heard that, just as in the old regime, Telegin had established influential new friendships.

Orloff shrugged. He was only a soldier. His business was war. Someone else decided who should and should not be admitted to the Party.

"And how goes it with our glorious Red Army, my dear comrade general?" asked Telegin, with enough of a hint of theatricality to make the matter seem ridiculous. He loved playing the innocent while others were unnerved. It was such an unassailable position.

"It goes well," said Orloff stiffly. Guile was not a method he knew. His emotions were travelling across his craggy face. He wanted to give them voice, but he could not. He knew he could not trust Telegin.

Telegin noted with amusement that he himself was the only person in the room who was at ease. Indeed, there was a definite tension which everyone else regretted. Nadia Nikolaevna, for instance, was genuinely glad to see her brother-in-law for the first time in years, but his Red Army uniform caused her a certain anxiety. And Orloff, who was just as glad to see her, was aware of her feelings, which made him uncomfortable. Unlike Kolodsky, he had not become a Communist to inspire fear.

Yet there was nothing either of them could do. The simplest and most ordinary events and activities, such as getting a letter or taking a walk, which in normal times had been too commonplace to mention, now took on an inflated significance. Would the act violate some bureaucrat's decree — a decree which might be issued after the act had been committed? Was it an offense to "Socialist morality," whatever that was? Might it annoy someone in authority? There was, in fact, no way of knowing the answers to such questions, no way of knowing what would produce a visit from the Cheka.

Nadia Nikolaevna, for instance, regretted having said that Telegin had good news. She was reluctant to mention this good news in front of Orloff. She shouldn't have been. The good news was in no way a violation of "Socialist morality." But she was succumbing involuntarily to the fact that, because it was impossible to know what "Socialist morality" permitted, any act might become a violation of "law."

"Such a long time, Peter Sergeievitch," Nadia Nikolaevna said. "So long."

"Yes, a long time," he said, remembering that he and Danilov had recently said the same thing.

"You are well, Peter Sergeievitch?"

"Yes. And you?"

Nadia Nikolaevna bowed and shook her head. Tears fell on her hands, which fluttered as usual at the handkerchief in her lap. "Not good, Peter Sergeievitch. The rations . . . . "

Orloff stiffened involuntarily. He hoped she was not going to ask for some favor. It would be a violation of his principles – his Socialist principles – to accede, a thing he took pride in never having done. And the problem was getting worse the more influential he became. More and more he was suspicious of friends and relatives, of personal relationships. They were dangerous. For instance, he genuinely wanted to help Danilov – but that was exactly why he could not. His actions would be clouded by personal motive – which had caused the world's troubles in the first place.

On the small, rickety table were half a large sausage and some eggs in a basket. Orloff pointed at them. "But this?"

"An exception," said Nadia Nikolaevna. She waved at Telegin. "Cyril Modestovitch was kind enough . . . ."

Telegin waved, theatrically. "You shouldn't, Nadia Nikolaevna. I embarrass so easily. Generosity should be selfless, known but to God."

"God?" said Orloff.

"The commissar of commissars. I am speaking metaphorically, of course."

Orloff felt a growing revulsion and contempt. It was impossible that Telegin could belong to the Party – but he did. "We are all going through a necessary purification, Nadia," Orloff said.

"Is *that* what it is!" Maria snapped.

"My sentiments exactly, my dear comrade general," said Telegin. "A formulation with which no loyal Communist can disagree. We must purify the last traces of selfishness and greed." Telegin opened a silver cigarette case and lit an English cigarette.

"Apparently you two have something basic in common, uncle," said Maria.

"We do," said Telegin. "Our implacable hatred for selfishness and greed. Our implacable concern for the poor and oppressed. Am I not right, my dear comrade general?"

"Some of us need more purification than others," interjected Maria.

Telegin smiled. "Permit me to show you my good news, my dear."

"How is my sister, Peter Sergeievitch?" Nadia Nikolaevna said quickly. "Is she well? Why haven't you brought her?"

"Katya is in Moscow," Orloff said. "My adjutant and I are here for a short time with comrade Trotsky."

Nadia Nikolaevna wanted to keep the conversation away from the good news. She also wanted to learn any news of her sister. It was possible that Orloff did not know what Savitsky said had happened to Katya, and Nadia Nikolaevna did not want to tell him. But Orloff did not want to talk about Katya. Their marriage problem was too painful.

"Your adjutant," said Maria. "Is he a Communist?"

"My adjutant is a cynic. He believes in nothing. He worked at one time for your father and was betrayed by his own. We spent some time together in Siberia. Perhaps you remember his name — Voronov."

"Betrayed, did you say?"

"Yes." Orloff told her the story. He had gotten it from Marina Nikitovna and the others. Characteristically, Michael had told him nothing.

"Tragic," Telegin said. "Really touching. There is nothing I admire more than loyalty."

"Then surely you will remember him, Cyril Modestovitch," said Orloff. He could not call Telegin comrade. "You wrote some articles denouncing him — for 'plotting an insult to our beloved Tsar,' I think you said."

Telegin rubbed his chin. "Hm. Let me see. Yes, I think you're right. Lyrical pieces. Full of imagery. The same sort of things I wrote about you."

Orloff could barely suppress his annoyance. The impudence of the man was almost intolerable.

Such an interesting family, thought Telegin. Orloff, unlike his nephew Stepan, was very difficult to figure out. He did not play the game, not at all. He said the usual nonsense about selfishness and greed, but what was his real motive? What was he after? A man with unknown motives was not only fascinating, he was also dangerous.

"Perhaps we should wait no longer to give Masha the good news," said Telegin. "It would be too cruel."

"Later, Cyril Modestovitch, please!" said Nadia Nikolaevna. "Let us not waste Peter Sergeievitch's time with our personal problems."

Ignoring her, Telegin turned expectantly to Maria, waiting for her to ask what his good news was. He guessed that she would not, which was the basic reason he found her so irresistible: she treated him with complete and open contempt.

He took a folded paper from under a glass on the table and held it toward her almost like a treat with which one entices a pet. "A letter from your father, Masha," he said.

A curious little smile was on his face. The letter swung back and forth between his fingers. Maria hesitated for a moment, then took it roughly, which Telegin considered a minor victory — and it was. It was a letter from her father, all right. A note really, addressed to her and her mother in his own handwriting. Its meaning was not in the few inconsequential lines, but rather in the fact that her father was alive and able to compose them. At last after all these months, there was finally something tangible. She crinkled it slightly and rubbed it between her fingers.

"Where did you get this?" she asked, curtly.

"Friends, Masha. Sympathetic officials. Don't burden yourself with the details. You're too sensitive, too feminine. After all, it is the purpose of Communism to assist the unfortunate. Am I right, comrade general? I am not very strong on theory."

"But from whom?" Maria asked. "Who gave it to you?"

"I have established a friendship with comrade Marchenko."

"Marchenko?" Maria stared hard at Telegin.

Telegin smiled and returned her look. He knew! His smile was bland and friendly, the smile of the fat man he appeared to be. But his eyes were challenging, hard and quizzical, the eyes of the lean and hungry man he was inside. Remarkable, he thought. His scheme had barely begun to function and already it was producing incomparable pleasure. At last he had solved the puzzle of Maria.

"Remarkable fellow," he said, holding her gaze. "Splendid, really. Such understanding. So *en rapport*. And, of course, a Communist's Communist, you will be glad to hear. In fact, just as 'the Cheka is the pride and joy of the Communist Party,' to quote comrade Zinoviev's glorious remark, so Marchenko is the pride and joy of the Cheka."

Telegin held Maria's gaze in silence and then abruptly turned to Orloff. "Do you know him?"

"No."

"Tell me, Cyril Modestovitch," said Maria, "do you know Marchenko well?"

"Quite well," he smiled. "In fact, I have had the honor of working with him very closely. Marchenko is the ideal Soviet Man, the 'pride and joy,' the goal of the science of Marxism-Leninism. That is why I am so inspired that he has generously agreed to visit our nurseries as part of our program to inspire youth. You did know, I suppose, that I am assistant to comrade Lunacharsky, commissar of Education and Culture? Yes, I remember so well the theme of the material I composed for comrade Marchenko: 'Join the Fight, Dear Children — and Then Fight On! Defend Our Glorious Revolution!' Do you like it? Marchenko spoke so effectively, Masha, so sincerely. You would be inspired to see the way he has with youth."

Telegin looked at her closely. He smiled. The thin man's eyes shone in his chubby face. He turned abruptly to Nadia Nikolaevna.

"You really should let me introduce you," he said. "After all, he is the one who made this letter possible. He has done so much for Ivan Fyodorovitch."

Nadia Nikolaevna looked at Maria and then at Orloff. "I don't know . . . ." Her voice trailed off.

Telegin smiled at Maria with the smile of a conspirator. Stepan's secret was the first thing they had ever shared. Maria involuntarily had become part of the plot. He and Stepan were working together. Everything that had happened to her was part of their plan, part of some monumentally bad joke. The robbery in the market, the little man with the big nose, her father's arrest itself had carefully been arranged by Telegin and "Marchenko."

In her eyes, fixed on Telegin's, a warning appeared. She took her mother's hand. "Mama, I have definite news of Stepan."

"Stepan?" said Nadia Nikolaevna, as if unfamiliar with the name. Telegin turned, abruptly.

"He is definitely dead," Maria said to Telegin. Her mother must be denied the truth: it would kill her.

"Yes," said Nadia Nikolaevna. "I know."

Telegin replaced his smile with the appropriate shade of grief. Such a pleasure, he thought. Remarkable! Such a bold move. So Masha *can* play, after all.

"You see, Cyril Modestovitch?" said Nadia Nikolaevna. "You were wrong."

"Yes," said Telegin. "I'm sorry." The grief was gone. The conspiratorial smile was back. "I have been insisting to your mother that Stepan is alive."

"Wishful thinking," said Maria, coldly.

"Yes, no doubt. Such a pity! A heroic officer in the service of a doomed and evil cause. Tragic. He could have played such a useful part in our great Socialist reconstruction."

Nadia Nikolaevna nodded. "Yes. He was so noble."

A question occurred to him. His eyes shone with excitement. In the folds of his face were beads of sweat. "But how do you know?" he asked her. "Are you sure?"

Maria said smoothly, "I've seen my old friend Vasya, Vasya Lopatkin. You remember him, mama. They were in the same regiment."

Nadia Nikolaevna nodded and squeezed Telegin's hand. "How lucky we are to have your friendship, Cyril Modestovitch. Masha, isn't that right?"

"What about my father?" Maria asked.

Orloff had been uncomfortable when he came in and was now very tense. The conversation had become painfully personal. Indeed, Maria might ask him the same question. He wanted to leave, but he was trapped. Luckily, the others seemed to ignore him.

"I don't know," said Telegin. "His case will be settled soon."

"What are the possibilities?"

"The usual. Labor camp. Or death."

Nadia Nikolaevna gasped.

"And release?" asked Maria.

"I'm sorry. Not in this case."

"Is it possible that he might be sent to a comfortable place to live out his days?"

"Of course it is, Masha. As you have read in your Voltaire, all things are possible in 'this best of all possible worlds.' "

"Except release."

"Correct."

"How could the next best thing be arranged?"

Telegin's conspiratorial smile was there again. His porcine eyes glowed like lamps behind curtains of fat.

"I have been giving the matter considerable thought, Masha. I really have," he said.

"And the result?"

"There *is* a solution. It would allow me to use my growing influence to best advantage. I don't know why I never thought of it before. If I were to give you the protection of my name, Masha . . . . If we were married . . . . "

Nadia Nikolaevna began to cry, soundlessly, and at the same time she smiled. "You are so kind, Cyril Modestovitch. Thank you. You have my permission of course. Masha will be so happy! Thank you."

Telegin grinned broadly. How remarkable it was, how fascinating, to see her thrash and struggle as he slowly drew her in, his hook deep in the tissue of the heart. Such a satisfying study in psychology. And at the same time, such a dramatic demonstration of his own artistic powers. It was as if he were carving and shaping a tableau, not from marble or clay, but out of humanity itself.

His excitement spilled over and demanded physical release. He cut a piece of sausage and began to chew, carefully, fastidiously, lips pursed. He held the meat delicately between his thumb and forefinger, an artist in this as in everything else. As usual some bits rolled down his chest and lodged on his vest. He brushed them away with expert disdain. He drew a flask of vodka from his coat and drank.

Maria heard her voice as from a distance. It was cold. "How would I know of my father's condition?"

Telegin picked up Danilov's letter. "It has already been arranged, Masha. You will continue to get his letters."

"Through Comrade Marchenko?"

"Yes."

"Masha, why do you hesitate?" said Nadia Nikolaevna. "What can you be thinking? Of course Cyril Modestovitch will look after his father-in-law. Excuse her, Cyril Modestovitch, she is too overjoyed to be sensible."

Telegin grinned. "That's what I thought."

Maria went to the window and pressed her forehead against the glass. It was cold and very soothing to her feverish skin. At last she understood the events of recent months. They had all been parts of Stepan's and Telegin's joke. But why did Telegin want her so? Certainly he was aware that she held him in contempt. What was there about her for which he would go to so much trouble? Was it revenge, or physical attraction? Or was it something deeper?

The situation he was arranging for her had been dramatized many times. It was a cliché. Indeed, it had become very common. Innumerable "Soviet secretaries" could tell the same story. "Soviet artist" Tata could. Perhaps his motive was simply to make her common, to bring her down to everyone else's level.

She imagined she could hear the walls moving in on her. Already there was only a little room left. She had to press herself against them. Soon they would crush against her, pressing her to death.

She was tired. The refreshing coolness on her forehead showed how tired she really was. She had tried everything she could think of just to get to see her father — and she had failed. Her failure had been planned. Her efforts had been wasted. Stepan and Telegin had been playing with her all along.

What more could be expected of her? Hadn't she done enough? A blast of guilt made her shudder. Her face blazed painfully with shame.

"Be honest at least!" she told Telegin. "Stop this pretense! Admit your joke!"

Telegin's eyes flashed. The lips pursed. The open hands spread imploringly.

"What can you mean?" he said. "My only motive is love."

"Of course it is!" said Nadia Nikolaevna.

The grinding of the walls made it difficult to hear. It was painful to stand in the remaining space. There was no room left. Telegin would not compromise. She had no choice. Perhaps she should let go. She would no longer have to struggle.

She heard Michael's voice. What had he said? "I'm sorry. That really is a shame. I've been looking forward to the pleasure of meeting him again." Michael had served with Stepan. What had he meant? "To discuss old times," Michael had said. Perhaps Stepan owed him a favor. Perhaps

Michael could persuade Stepan to help. She had to see him.

She said to Orloff, "Where is your adjutant now?"

"At regional Army headquarters," he said, startled.

She turned abruptly, went out the door and down the stairs. Orloff and Nadia Nikolaevna called from above. Telegin did not, which meant, she knew, that he was sure he didn't have to. In the dark of the stairwell she saw his face even now, eyebrows raised, lips pursed, supercilious and smug. She had to get away from it. She had to run.

She left the house, walked for a while and found the building. She found Michael inside almost at once. They sat on a wooden bench in a hall.

She hesitated for a few moments. If he gave the wrong answer, he must not suspect the truth. Maria forced herself to wait, with idle chatter.

"I've seen Vasya Lopatkin," she said at last. "Vasya assures us my brother is dead."

"Oh."

"You once said you wanted to see my brother again."

"Yes."

"Why?"

"Your brother is dead. Forget it."

"I want to know!"

Michael was puzzled. She was acting as if this useless knowledge were important. Perhaps he should tell her: it would widen the breach between them. It was no good to get too close to someone in the real world.

"All right," he said. "I wanted to see your brother again so that I could kill him. That's why I'm so sorry he's dead."

Michael told her the story of the joke Stepan had played on them at the front. And Maria knew that what he told her was true. It was so perfectly characteristic of Stepan. He always enjoyed a good joke. He still did. She heard phrases and clauses of Michael's narration. "The river . . . the charges . . . . Then he blew the bridge . . . . " The rest she understood from his tone and the hatred in his voice. His words pierced her skin like burning arrows. He did not know they sentenced her to death.

"And you were never discovered as a Siberian escapee?"

"I changed my name. I called myself Marchenko then."

It was an arrow in her heart. With that one name everything became clear. Stepan, for his part, believed that Michael was dead. He had taken the name Michael was using. He did not know it was a second-hand alias. In the new proletarian society, Stepan was pretending to be Michael. Michael would be the last man on earth he would want to see alive. Michael could expose him. Stepan would have him killed.

She could not ask Michael to intercede. She could not even mention the matter to him. Indeed, it was important that Michael be kept far away. Her love could only be expressed as hate. The more she felt the first, the more she had to show the latter. The arrow is barbed, she thought. It cannot be withdrawn. It has torn up the tissue. I am dead.

"Why did you ask?"

"I just wondered," she said. "I had no reason."

She rose abruptly. "Goodbye, peasant."

"Goodbye, brat."

She turned stiffly and left the building. She felt nothing, which was appropriate — for a corpse.

XLIII

Telegin and Maria sat at a table. Maria had finished eating. He had not. As usual, he ate with great gusto. As usual, the residue lay on the ledges of his vest.

They were in a restaurant reserved for Party members. The food was plentiful and fairly good. But this did not mean what it would have meant in England, for instance. It was not a sign of corruption and decay. Indeed, it was good. It was necessary. It was scientific. It took food and energy to remake the world. Guiding the inevitable steps of history was not easy. The fact that the beneficiaries of the Revolution — the People — were starving, was irrelevant. It was unfortunate, but scientifically, they deserved no better. They were peasants — illiterate, sick, smelly peasants — scientifically incapable of Revolution.

Only healthy, wealthy intellectuals could successfully protest against poverty, ignorance, and disease. Peasants were too poor, too sick, and too stupid.

Telegin's jaw was operating well. His jowls jounced. Bits of food were on his lips, which smacked; and the bits fell onto his vest. He looked approvingly at Maria. She was well-dressed. A commissar's wife should be. That was science. If a commissar's wife weren't, the commissar would get depressed. He would be unable to guide the inevitable steps of history. And Maria was well-fed. She had regained her former health. This too was science. Telegin must not become depressed. It would be a violation of the public interest.

"You think me disgusting, don't you," he said.

"Yes, Cyril Modestovitch. Anything you say."

Telegin laughed. He loved her contempt. Maria was as satisfactory as he had expected. Telegin was a completely happy man.

"Would you like a dessert, Masha?" he asked.

"I don't know, Cyril Modestovitch. Would I?"

"Yes. You would."

"I'd like a dessert."

"You're so beautifully submissive, Masha."

"What kind of dessert would I like?"

Telegin laughed again. He loved it. He snapped his fingers and the waiter came over. Telegin ordered the dessert she would like. He took out an envelope and held it up.

"This month's letter," he said.

Maria flushed. Telegin pointed. "Masha, look out! Your face! An emotion!"

She snatched the letter with annoyance and put it in her pocket. She would wait to read it until she was alone. She kept her hand on it. It proved her father was alive. She looked away, and saw Michael coming toward them through the tables. They had not seen each other for some time. Maria had wanted never to see him again; it would be too painful.

But Michael felt otherwise. He had been trying to find Maria for months. He had gone to the old Danilov apartment, where someone named Tata Beresova said Maria had moved. He did not know that she and her mother were living with Telegin, as beneficiaries of the Soviet science of housing. Telegin's new apartment was luxurious and spacious. He, his wife, and his mother-in-law had far more than the sixteen square yards of living space guaranteed each Soviet citizen. Yet the government, unusually, had moved nobody else in. It was unfortunate that throughout the city, families of workers were living in single rooms, but it was a scientific fact that without space and luxury, Telegin could not help them.

Michael had reached their table. On his face was a smile, mocking as always, ready to be withdrawn, as an animal in a jungle is always ready to flee; but much less mocking than usual. Maria felt intense dislike for him. She wished he would go. She wanted to annoy him, to hurt him — at least to remove his sickening smile.

She, too, smiled, as sweetly as she could. "Cyril Modestovitch," she said, "this is Michael Fyodorovitch Voronov, a hero of the Revolution and my uncle's adjutant. Perhaps you remember him. Your articles helped to send him to prison in 1910."

Michael's smile abruptly disappeared. The jungle animal had fled.

"Yes, of course," said Telegin, perfectly at ease. "Forgive me, my dear fellow. I did not recognize you. You have matured. Such a pleasure to see you again."

Telegin ostentatiously extended his hand. Michael ignored it. "Is anything wrong?" asked Telegin, slightly too solicitous.

316

He was amused. He was delighted that Maria was playing the game, but surely she could not think that amateurish gambits such as this would unnerve him in the least. He waited blandly for the inevitable signs that her gambit had boomeranged.

"And this, Michael Fyodorovitch," she said, "this is Cyril Modestovitch Telegin — my husband."

She looked at Michael closely. There was no expression whatever on his face.

"As you see," she said, "I have taken your advice."

Michael carefully inspected Telegin, the small diamond ring on his little finger, his silk ascot, his stickpin, the jowls overhanging his collar, the inflated figure in the expensive, ill-fitting clothes, in his hand a glass of liqueur, on his face a self-satisfied smile.

"Yes," said Michael. "You certainly have."

Beneath his impassive face was growing rage. But why? What Maria had said was true. She *had* taken his advice. A look at Telegin made that clear. Be smart, Michael had told her many times. Avoid sentiment. Trust no one. Take what you can get. Why then should he be so angry? It was illogical. He had given her the advice as a sort of psychological insurance, to armor himself against the possibility that she might do what he advised, and now that she had — like everyone else — his insurance turned out to be worthless.

Maria patted Telegin's paunch. "Isn't my husband charming?"

Telegin himself was slightly on edge. Voronov was a fool. He played clumsily. He had no talent whatever for the game. Something was happening now, but what?

"You are, Cyril Modestovitch," said Michael, smiling again. "She's right." His voice sounded strangely like Telegin's. And his smile now was uncharacteristically ingratiating. "Heartiest congratulations, my dear girl. Congratulations indeed."

Maria literally shook with hatred. With all her strength, and to her own surprise, she slapped Michael across the face, as if trying to obliterate him, so hard that it seemed she had broken something in her hand.

But aside from the imprint of her fingers on his cheek, his face showed nothing. Its expression did not change. He turned to the still perplexed Telegin.

"And congratulations to you, my dear Cyril Modestovitch."

Part V
Maria Danilova

XLIV

Borishevsky leaned back on the cantle, the palm of his hand on his horse's rump, and inhaled the scent of the early spring buds. It was a clear day, although a little chilly — exactly what he liked. The rain of the last few days had stopped. The regiment was moving north along a river. From the rear of the column, he saw the buckles shining on Prokurov's huge form at the front. Prokurov bellowed and the men began to sing, the words bobbing back on the breeze:

> Keep step, Kornilov's men!
> Kornilov is with us here.
> He'll save our motherland
> And ne'er betray her people.

A year had passed since the commander-in-chief's death in the first assault on Ekaterinodar, yet the men were still singing it with gusto. It was remarkable. Indeed, ever since the Bolshevik coup, time had had a different quality, a different measurement. It was as if a day took a week to pass, as if an event of the year before were already a decade old. The Volunteer Army under Kornilov had left Rostov to the Reds under Antonov on February 9, 1918, escaping over the Don into the Kuban. They marched on Ekaterinodar with no bandages or spare clothes, one day's rations, eight pieces of artillery, six hundred shells and thirty-five hundred men — and fought a Red army of two hundred thousand. Kornilov had been killed on April thirteenth. Borishevsky had been talking with him minutes before. He had just left the hut when the shell hit. There was nothing he could do but watch. It was too late. He remembered all these events precisely, but as if he had read them in some military history, as if he himself had not seen them and made them.

Borishevsky felt a surge of eagerness. He had always been on the losing side, with Kuropatkin at Mukden in 1905 and during the recent war. But now he knew his luck would change. The Volunteers would retake Moscow — and Russia. He knew this because through every encounter and every defeat, he had managed to keep the regiment together. The mere existence of the regiment was proof that the current lunacy would pass. True, it was not really a regiment at the moment. It was a mere handful of troops. But that, in a way, confirmed his hope. The regiment was still the same identifiable Grand Duchess's Hussars. As far as he knew, there were few other such outfits. Many of the men had been in it for years.

Borishevsky spurred his horse, startling Spassky, still his adjutant, who was lost in his own thoughts beside him. He rode ahead along the line, followed by a booming "Health to your honor!"

Far away, on their stomachs among the rocks on the next ridge, Orloff and Michael watched him through their glasses, neither mentioning his fleeting thought that the rider was familiar.

"How many do you make out?" asked Orloff.

"Less than a squadron."

Orloff's finger ran over a map. "Could these be part of Shkuro's horsemen?"

"Shall I order the men to prepare to attack?"

"We can't attack," said Orloff, looking again through his glasses. "You forget the wounded."

"No, I don't."

Orloff put down his glasses. His voice was cool. "Surely you don't mean we should expose them and our position to cavalry when we are so immobile?"

Michael shrugged. He did not answer. They bellied back down the ridge, mounted and rejoined the column.

Neither of them said so, each for his own reasons, but the bond between them which had begun years ago in Siberia as a slender thread was growing into a powerful hawser. Each saw in the other his own ruthlessness. And at the same time, each was repelled by the other's motives for ruthlessness: Michael by Orloff's radical ideals, which allegedly had caused the so-called Revolution; Orloff by Michael's thoroughly cynical attitude toward life. Orloff knew, as he had told him years before, that sooner or later Michael's attitude would change. He ignored Michael's contempt for his ideals. Michael, he knew, was convalescing after an illness, the Capitalism of the former society. He still had no interest whatever in Communism — or in Tsarism either, for that matter. Indeed, he only loved being a soldier. The war for

322

Michael was an end in itself. No one fought the war with more intensity. He could just as well have fought for the Whites. His only worry was that the war might end.

And this, too, Orloff knew would change. Man and society were perfectible. In Communism, man would work joyfully for the pure joy of the work. Who could want more? Michael would see that honor was possible.

They reached the head of the column. The men were waiting. Orloff raised his arm. Far in the rear, they heard short but muffled noises. They wheeled and rode back along the column, one on each side. A nurse stood near the hospital wagons, staring, numb.

"What is it?" said Orloff.

She could not answer. She pointed to the wagons and he dismounted to have a look. Blood was dripping from the sides of one, pinging into the muddy puddle in which the wheel stood. An orderly was climbing out.

The orderly, too, was in a state of shock. "Comrade general," he said, "the wounded have committed suicide so we can attack."

Orloff pulled back the flap and looked in. He lowered his head. Once again reality had confirmed the rightness of what he believed and what he did. Could anyone dare intrude personal wishes or cynicism in the face of such as this?

"Now there's no reason not to attack," Michael said, flatly. As usual, he was unimpressed, emotionless. Orloff wanted to drag him to the wagon and force him to look.

Michael dismounted and ordered the guns positioned along the ridge. The men crouched behind them, waiting. Snatches of song came from below: "Keep step, Kornilov's men . . . . He'll save our motherland . . . . " The Whites had heard nothing.

Michael remounted. "Fire!" he roared.

The artillery boomed, recoiled and boomed again. A barrage fell among the Volunteers. Smoke rose. The Red cavalry swept down the ridge.

The Volunteers were milling about, not yet sure where the enemy was. Prokurov was bellowing. A shell landed in a knot at the center of the column, sending chunks of horses and men into the air. Prokurov was spattered with a sheet of blood. Borishevsky pulled at Spassky's sleeve and pointed to a copse of trees. Spassky nodded and gave the order to Prokurov.

"At once, your honor!" Prokurov bellowed. He wheeled, saber whirling, and rode up the line. "Into the trees!" he roared.

It was just barely possible to see. A wall of shells was coming down. A wall of dust was going up. A shell fell quite near, and Borishevsky could hear nothing. Soundless shapes flitted by; men, horses, guns, all in an eerie

323

pantomime. Then his hearing returned, along with the ringing he expected. He made his way toward the trees, where they could regroup. Ahead, a horse was down. A man was under it, head sticking out, eyes and mouth wide open.

Suddenly, he noticed Spassky's absence. Borishevsky turned, and went back, finding Spassky near what remained of his horse. His left side from shoulder to thigh was bloody and mangled. The top of Spassky's face was gone. Borishevsky could not see his eyes. He folded him over his saddle and rode quickly to the trees.

The Reds had already turned the Volunteers' flank and a few stood in his way. He drew his pistol, fired carefully and emptied two saddles. Quite near but unseen, Prokurov bellowed, his saber whistled, there was a gurgle and a sigh and a body hit the ground. Then they were into the trees and on their feet.

The Reds withdrew. The smoke dissipated. Once again it was a crisp, clear day. Borishevsky lowered Spassky to the ground and examined the wound. The left arm was gone below the elbow, leaving a mangled stump in a dripping, shredded sleeve. Undoubtedly there were also internal injuries. Spassky's remaining eye was gone. He was blind. Borishevsky saw only raw meat. To survive, Spassky needed a doctor. And the Reds alone had one.

We must surrender, Borishevsky thought. I myself will take the white flag out. And as he thought this, he realized how impossible it was. Would he permit Spassky to surrender if their positions were reversed? It would be an insult. Ever after, each would feel guilt in the other's presence.

Spassky tugged feebly at Borishevsky's tunic. Bubbles of blood came out of Spassky's mouth. His lips were moving and Borishevsky bent to hear.

"Alexander Maximovitch?" Spassky whispered.

"Yes."

"Do not surrender."

"No."

"Attack!"

Spassky's mouth moved slowly. More bubbles of blood came out. Only moments ago, his face had still been pink, boyish and unlined, the face of a cornet on his first patrol. Now . . . . With his remaining hand, he drew his pistol.

"Alexander Maximovitch?"

"Yes."

"Goodbye."

"Goodbye."

"Russia lives."

"She does."

He put the pistol to his head and fired. Borishevsky held him. Spassky was dead.

There was a boom and a whistle and a shell fell in the trees. The Red artillery had begun a new barrage. Earth sprang up. Green tree limbs twisted and tore. A tree fell, crashing against others. A man screamed. Others tried to lift the tree and pull him out. The Volunteers were surrounded on three sides. On the fourth was an impassable wall of rock. The Reds apparently meant to stand clear and shell the trees flat.

The bodies of men and horses covered the ground. Six or seven wounded sat senseless under a tree. The Volunteers had lost all their guns. Borishevsky was now examining the twisted, blackened wreckage of his army. Prokurov and the elderly bugler were the only ones left. They could not answer the barrage. Their rifles were useless. The Reds were out of range. But they could not stay where they were, simply waiting to be pulverized. The most sensible thing to do was surrender. There was, in fact, no other choice.

"Prokurov!" said Borishevsky.

"Your honor!" Prokurov bellowed.

"Prepare to charge!"

Prokurov's seven yellow teeth shone. "At once, your honor!"

They sat in a row, close together. The bugler held the bugle to his lips, adorned with the black and orange ribbons of St. George. There was a lull in the barrage. Borishevsky looked up. The leaves were waving in front of the sun. It was mild and clear, still a perfect day. It was a good day on which to die. He would die with the certainty that life would go on. From his scabbard he drew the gold sword of St. George, inscribed with the words, "For Bravery."

"For Russia," said Borishevsky.

Prokurov bellowed. The bugle sounded, haughty and gay. Orloff stiffened. "Here they come," he whispered to Michael.

"Ready," Michael called to the gunners.

The men stirred. A horse whinnied. In the stillness, they heard hoofbeats.

Three riders burst out of the trees into the sun and started across the field. Three riders and that was all. The sight was so startling that Orloff, Michael and the gunners hesitated, thinking for a moment there were more behind them. Then Orloff nodded, Michael gave the order and the guns boomed.

One of the riders was the man both Orloff and Michael had thought familiar. But he was still rather far away. Some shrapnel emptied the bugler's saddle. His horse galloped on with the others. Then there was a roar, smoke, and the large man with the saber simply disappeared along with his horse, leaving no proof that either had ever existed. The explosion caused the familiar rider's horse to rear, but he drove him on. Another shell landed and the horse stumbled. But the rider again spurred him up. He was beginning to get close.

Suddenly, Orloff realized that the man approaching across the field was Borishevsky, whom he had not seen for over twelve years. At the same moment, Michael realized the man was his former colonel.

"Hold your fire!" Orloff shouted. The firing stopped and he stepped out in front of the guns. "Alexander Maximovitch!" he shouted. "Alyosha! It's I, Orloff!"

Borishevsky changed direction and headed straight for him.

"Alyosha!" Orloff shouted. "It's not too late. Join us!"

Borishevsky gave no indication that he recognized Orloff or had heard him, but continued to gallop toward him at full speed. Nothing could be heard but his advancing hoofbeats, underscoring the eeriness of a large, silent and motionless army of men being attacked by a cavalry force of one.

Borishevsky was now very close. "Alyosha, please!" Orloff shouted. "We can come to an agreement. The people need you."

Borishevsky thundered on and raised his arm. The sword of St. George flashed in the sun.

"Shoot, you bastards!" he roared. "Shoot!"

Orloff nodded. He understood. He raised his pistol reluctantly and fired. The sword of St. George fell to the ground. Borishevsky went back over the cantle and down. A spur caught in a stirrup. The horse turned, dragging him along in front of the silent row of men as if in some strange travesty of an inspection, and then turned again, dragging the body back into the trees.

Michael shook his head. "The fool!"

"Shut up!" said Orloff. He picked up the sword. It was broken.

XLV

The Princess Lobanovsky sat still and erect at the edge of the bench. She was very young, no more than sixteen, and she was very pretty. But her face was blank. It was impossible to tell what she was thinking, or if she was thinking anything at all. Indeed, her eyes were wide open, but it was impossible to tell whether or not she knew what was happening. An ancient toothless woman sat next to her on the bench.

"Well?" said Orloff.

The Princess Lobanovsky did not answer or even give any indication that she had heard.

The old woman spread her hands, palms upward. "You see?"

"Princess, can you hear me?" he asked. But again there was no response. What had happened to her mind? What was she thinking? What did her staring eyes see?

"And you?" Orloff asked the old woman.

"Oh, yes," she said, "I know them well, I do." She got up and shuffled down the row of six men who stood at attention before the desk, peering up into each of their faces. "Yes," she said. "It's them, all right."

"Well?" he said. "Is this the truth?"

"Sure it is, comrade," said the man on the end, "and so what? We're heroes of the Revolution, ain't we? We deserve some fun. Ain't that right?" He playfully elbowed the next man's ribs.

"Right," said the next man, belligerently.

"Besides, so what if she's a princess? She's a *boorzhui,* ain't she? And all property must be expropriated because 'all property is theft.' That's Socialism, comrade. We expropriated a piece of her property."

They all roared with delight at this masterful application of Socialist theory.

Orloff turned to Michael. "Shoot them."

The laughing stopped as if severed with a knife. The theorist's jocularity changed to bravado. "Now look here, comrade . . . ." He spat some sunflower seeds on the floor.

"The next seed you spit, you will remove with your tongue," Orloff said. "Comrade Voronov, carry out the order."

The jokers began to realize that it wasn't really a joke after all, that in fact it was very serious. The theorist's tone changed again.

"Comrade, please, we're honest workmen."

Michael motioned to the two soldiers at the door, and the three of them pushed and shoved the six out.

"That's all. I'm sorry," Orloff said to the old woman. She got up, and with a hand on her elbow propelled the princess out, still in her strange trance.

The townspeople were aroused. Even in this time of division, they had taken the princess' side, even though she was a bourgeoise, demanding death for her assailants. The reason was probably her youth. And her father, they said, had been a very kind landlord, which proved once again that an evil system can somehow produce a good man.

Indeed, the isolated crime committed here against the Princess Lobanovsky was normal procedure elsewhere, along with robbery. But under no circumstances would Orloff tolerate such excesses in his own area. That was why they rarely happened. His attitude was well-known — especially his attitude toward the vicious crime of rape. It was a hangover from Capitalism, of course, and would soon be wiped out. If only this damnable war would end so he could devote all his energy to the great Socialist reconstruction!

Michael's voice came from outside, and then a rifle volley. So much for the local Committee of the Poor, Orloff thought. Would there be trouble from the Center? Or would they simply appoint another? Why were the committees always composed not of workers and farmers, but of the drunkest and dirtiest scum of the villages, who were given the power to hire and fire, set work loads and conduct the grain requisitions? Why, in fact, were they necessary at all? They simply replaced the local soviet, which could do these chores at least as well. Perhaps that was why the townspeople had been so aroused. Perhaps their concern for the princess had been insincere, not a violation of their class loyalty after all. Perhaps they were motivated by the cause of all evil: self-interest.

Orloff shrugged. Theory is not my department, he thought. They know what they are doing at the Center.

For the next few weeks things were calm. Orloff made sure his men minded their business, and the townspeople eagerly minded theirs. As usual, he received their requests and complaints. With the permission given by the local soviet soon after the Bolshevik coup, the Princess Lobanovsky and her old woman continued living in the part of her house that the deceased Committee of the Poor had not torn down. Then orders came from Voronezh that, until further notice, Orloff would handle the requisitions himself. He immediately assigned Michael to the task.

Michael went from barn to barn and found nothing. He knew he would find nothing. Had he found anything at all, he would have been surprised. There were only the farmers, faces blank and solemn, but smiling in a peculiar way, and the pitchforks innocently on their shoulders. Could they really believe at the Center that a farmer would voluntarily produce and deliver grain without payment? Could Orloff? It was impossible to penetrate the peculiar Communist mentality. Could this monumental ignorance simply be the result of stupidity? Or was it part of some idiotic joke? Indeed, there was the feeling of charade as farmer after farmer smilingly explained that he had produced only enough for his own appetite, and that nothing remained to ship into the cities. Michael had recently heard that in a town outside Moscow, a local Party secretary had been found murdered, his mouth stuffed with food cards. Michael was careful not to let the farmers get behind him.

Orloff called the farmers together and made a speech about Socialist morality and Socialist justice. It did not go well. The same blank, solemn, impenetrable faces stared up — as they had at Michael — probably wondering whether Orloff was equally mad. Once again, Michael realized that Orloff believed what he was saying. Michael had known this, of course, but he was never really convinced. Every proof of it came as a new surprise.

Some days later a train arrived from the south on its way to Moscow and Petrograd, and those same blank, solemn faces were volubly at the station, briskly selling the grain and other edibles they had never produced and then carefully hidden. They did not disperse as Michael worked his way through them. They were not alarmed. Indeed, they greeted him with knowledgeable, sarcastic smiles. Inside the private coach before which they were gathered, Michael found Kolodsky doing a land-office business.

"Get off! You can't do that!" he said, as Michael climbed aboard.

"Can't I?"

Kolodsky's nose waggled. There was something familiar about the scent. "Michael Fyodorovitch!" he said at last.

"I'll wait," said Michael. "Go right ahead."

The coach was loaded to the roof with food. Hams, cheeses, chickens and caviar, baskets of eggs and bottles of wine and innumerable other delicacies covered every surface. Obviously it had been collected at many other stations. And as Michael watched, more came in. Hands handed it up from below, and withdrew with the money Kolodsky took from a wallet. The hands gesticulated. Their owners shouted prices. Kolodsky shouted prices down.

"I'll be right back," said Michael. He climbed down and was gone for a few minutes.

"We've read so much about you," Kolodsky said when he came back. *"Pravda* describes all your battles. The way you and comrade Orloff destroyed Borishevsky was great. His regiment had been insulting us for months. You see, Michael Fyodorovitch? I was right. The Party was the place for you all along."

Michael chuckled. "You haven't changed. You're still a funny little man, Kolodsky."

"You don't hold me responsible for what happened, I hope. After all, Michael Fyodorovitch, almost ten years . . . ."

"Not at all," said Michael. "You did well. You saved your scrawny, shrivelled hide. We need more men like you in the Party."

Kolodsky was uneasy. He had never understood Michael's sense of humor. Then he decided his remark was a compliment.

"Thank you," he said. "Coming from you, that has meaning."

"What is all this?" asked Michael, pointing at the groceries. "You're a good Party man. You know that buying and selling are strictly forbidden violations of Socialist morality. Don't tell me you're a speculator now."

Kolodsky's pigeon breast swelled. "I beg your pardon. I am an official of the Extraordinary Commission. And this is official Party business, authorized by comrade Marchenko himself." He drew some papers from a pocket and handed them over.

They were all in order. All the necessary papers were there, covered with all the necessary seals, stamps and information. Michael studied Marchenko's signature. It seemed genuine. He had seen it before. It looked very different, of course, from Michael's version when he had used the name.

"Do you know comrade Marchenko?" he asked.

Kolodsky's pigeon breast swelled again. "I do indeed, Michael Fyodorovitch. He is my superior. Proletarian through and through. Yes, the Cheka is the pride and joy of the Communist Party, and comrade Marchenko is the pride and joy of the Cheka, as comrade Telegin likes to say."

"Telegin? Do you know him, too?"

"I'll say," said Kolodsky. "I've really come up in the world. You'd be surprised. There's a real Communist."

"I'd even call him the prototype of the New Soviet Man."

"We work together closely," said Kolodsky excitedly, but in a lower tone. "With Marchenko. These trips, for instance. I've come up in the world, Michael Fyodorovitch. You'd be surprised."

Michael was inspecting some wine nonchalantly, pretending to read the labels, inhaling the heavy aroma of the cheese.

"In fact, comrade Telegin lives near here," said Kolodsky.

Michael looked up. "And his wife?"

Kolodsky smiled broadly. "Amazing change. Perfect example of Soviet reconstruction. I wouldn't have believed it, had I not seen it with my own eyes. She's the daughter of your old exploiter, in fact – Danilov. An uppity bourgeoise bitch, she was. But what else could you expect, with a Capitalist father like that. Then Marchenko went to work on her. Gave her the psychological treatment, he did. Now she works right along with us. Once a month, on my way south, I deliver Marchenko's instructions. She's proof that with enough hard work it's even possible to overcome bad blood. She was lucky. Comrade Marchenko took special interest in her case. And her husband is very close to comrade Lunacharsky."

"So they live near here?"

"Not far. Staying at her father's old house, they are, through arrangements by comrades Marchenko and Telegin. It pays to know the right people, eh, Michael Fyodorovitch?"

Michael smashed the neck off a bottle and drank. Kolodsky became strangely nervous. "Please!" The train jolted and began to move. Kolodsky brightened. "You'd better get off."

But Michael did not move, except to slice some cheese from a wheel. He drank again. "It's good," he said. "Thanks. There's nothing I like better than wine and cheese. Or is there? I don't know. What does the Party say? It's French, isn't it? I'm sure of that. I can't read the label. It's good to be ignorant."

"But we're moving."

"I'm aware of that. The train is changing tracks."

"Why? That doesn't happen here."

"Say, this cheese is really good."

Kolodsky's nose shuddered with fear. He had never been able to understand Michael. "Please, Michael Fyodorovitch! What are you doing?"

"You see, you and your Marchenko are raping Socialist morality by stealing all this stuff from the State. No. Please. Don't interrupt. I don't complain that because of you people are starving. That would be bourgeois. It is good they are starving. Their bellies will teach them a practical lesson in Socialism. It's good that you are stealing. It's socialistic, which I like. But the

State can do more harm with this stuff than you. Besides, I have my orders. I never question orders. The crazier the orders are, the better."

"But my papers are in order."

"Of course they are. So what?"

"There is a Chekist detachment on the train."

"Isn't there always? That's all right."

The train jolted to a halt, went back some way and jolted to a halt again. Kolodsky ran to the window and looked out. They were on a siding. Their car, which was the last in line, was already being uncoupled. Several soldiers already stood around it.

Kolodsky pounded on the sill with frustration and began to cry. "You've tricked me! You've tricked me!"

"Of course. I'm a Communist. Why are you surprised, Kolodsky? You're a Communist too."

"I'll lose my post," Kolodsky wailed.

"No, you won't. You know the right people. It pays to know the right people. Now you'd better go. You'll miss your train."

"You don't know how to treat an old comrade," said Kolodsky.

"Oh yes, I do."

"I'm sorry you took the rap, Michael Fyodorovitch."

"Of course you are."

Kolodsky climbed down. The train was already moving and he ran for it and climbed aboard. His small head protruded from a window, peering back, nose trying to catch the scent. The train picked up speed, turned a curve and was gone.

Michael put more cheese and another bottle of wine in a basket, added some sausages and eggs, left the car himself and mounted.

"Let no one near here," he told a soldier.

"No, comrade adjutant. No one."

Michael squeezed his horse and rode off. A ragged group of refugees sat at the edge of the platform among their belongings, intently watching the progress of his basket.

"Look here!" he called.

Some of them rose and looked at him hopefully. They were at the point in starvation at which one still feels hungry and tries to find food. Michael lobbed an egg into their midst. In the ensuing struggle it naturally broke in a clutching hand, oozing down the sleeve on an arm. He lobbed another, which spattered on a shirt, and then another and another. The refugees were pushing, shoving and kicking each other, vainly trying to catch these fragile bits of food. And at the same time, they tried vainly to lick the egg from their own and each other's clothing.

Michael chuckled. It was like a scene from a burlesque comedy. "Compliments of the Communist Party!" he called. Behind him, the soldiers held themselves and howled. That adjutant! What a sense of humor!

But the refugees were all much too busy to hear. The fools! They didn't understand. They didn't understand anything! They would die without ever having understood anything. They resembled nothing so much as insects on a dunghill. But that is what people really are, Michael thought, aren't they?

He spurred his horse and started back to headquarters. He was eager to hear how Orloff, another fool, would explain Kolodsky's trip. An exception which is magnified by the greatness of the rule, he heard Orloff's voice say clearly. An irrelevant exception which time will overcome.

Three days later, while Katya, Orloff and Michael were eating, orders arrived explaining that Denikin was advancing all along the line and directing Orloff and his units to advance and stop him — but not before burning the town for its general refusal to cooperate with the requisitions.

"You'll alert the men," Orloff said dryly. "We'll move in the morning." Michael rose to go, but Orloff pressed him back. "Not now. Later. There's time." Perhaps if they simply kept talking, they could prevent Katya from speaking. She was getting ready, Orloff could see. He knew that she was planning what to say. She had become maudlin during the last years in Siberia, and now was even more so. No longer did she see things rationally — like a Communist — as she had before. She had become nervous and emotional.

"But, surely, Petya, their refusal is easy to understand," she said, as he had expected. "The manufactured goods they were promised have not been delivered."

"They haven't been produced," Michael said.

"Your sympathy is touching!" she said with sarcasm.

She had been hostile to Michael ever since they had met again. Why did Petya insist on befriending him? Michael did not know that she associated him with Siberia and Golovin — with what Golovin had done to her there. Indeed, she still felt a violent anger toward her husband whenever she remembered it. She remembered awakening and being found outside town, being covered with an overcoat and taken home in a wagon, the sly looks, the humiliation. She remembered every detail. She could not forget. And it was Petya's fault. This feeling manifested itself now in her inability to sleep with him. Inability was the right word. She wanted to, but she could not. She refused even to let him see her undress. He would see Golovin's initials blazing on her skin. She knew that Orloff was right, was always right, had always been a good Communist; that his behavior toward Golovin had proved some good Communist point. That was why she admired him so much. Yet there was nothing she could do about it. Her inability was there. She knew her husband was right and was suffering, and she felt guilt. She was wrong to have expected him to put her before the Party. But she could not say so. She was even unable to stop feeling the anger toward him, and this naturally compounded her guilt. The real cause of the trouble, it occurred to her, was Michael. After all, he had been the beneficiary of her husband's act. Golovin would not have humiliated her had her husband escaped alone. It was Michael, not her husband, toward whom she should feel resentment.

"The lack of manufactured goods is the work of Capitalist wreckers," said Orloff. "It will be corrected. Meanwhile there is nothing to discuss."

He made a deliberate effort to be pleasant, concealing the anger he felt toward Katya for her refusal to yield.

"This will not be as popular as the executions," said Michael.

"I know that," said Orloff. "It can't be helped."

"Executions?" said Katya.

"A few weeks ago," Orloff said. "You were in Moscow."

"What happened?"

"Some 'honest workmen' attacked the Princess Lobanovsky," said Michael.

"Attacked?"

"Raped!"

"Petya, you executed someone for rape?"

"Yes."

Katya's head shook and fell into her hands. She began to sob, loudly, painfully. Her shoulders heaved. A lock of her fine, blonde hair came undone.

"What is wrong?" asked Orloff.

She shook her head. "Nothing."

Her hair caught the light. Orloff softened. He wanted to touch it. But he did not. To do so would arouse him, and that would be bad. He stiffened. Why did Katya persist in behaving like this? What caused these painful conversations? What caused the gulf opening between them? The answer was uncommunistic, he knew. Some violation of Socialist principles, somehow the work of Capitalist wreckers, but he could not put his finger on it. This nonsense about "female psychology" was exactly that: nonsense — another Capitalist hangover. Every *homo sapiens* had the same psychology. The difference between the sexes was anatomical — nothing more.

"The destruction of the town is strategically necessary," he said. "Denikin, I am sure, would love to find the town intact. Your trouble, Katya, is that you forget the social and political context. You forget that there is more at stake here than one little town. You are too emotional and not reflective enough. The same qualities that led you into the movement are now causing your mistake."

She shook her head again. "No, I'm too reflective." She looked up at Michael. "Must you gawk?"

"Good night," said Michael. He got up and went out.

"Your adjutant is insolent," said Katya.

Before dawn the next morning they were already well under way. Columns of men, guns and wagons were moving south. Michael and the men he had chosen were moving through the town with torches. The townspeople, too, were on the move. Somehow they had heard what was going to happen. Their remaining belongings were already packed in bundles. They were about to become part of the homeless army of refugees. Their faces were blank, past all thought and emotion, as if they had become automatons to which things simply happened. They had no interest in finding out why.

Michael chose the Lobanovsky house for himself. It was at the edge of town on a low hill. By the time he reached it, the town was burning well, brightening the early morning sky. It was a large old house, the kind which had been added to over many, many years. Generations had been born in it, lived in it, died in it. Yet it could be destroyed in minutes. Michael smashed a window and threw a torch inside. He rode to the rear of the house and did the same. The fire was already blazing. It was unnecessary to dismount.

Suddenly somebody was pulling on his boot. It was the old Lobanovsky woman. She was shouting, but he could not hear a word. She pointed to the house, he looked up and in an upstairs window saw the princess, not afraid or angry in the least, simply looking out as if this were a normal morning. He rose in the stirrups and shouted, furious, but there was no indication she had heard him.

He jumped from his horse and ran into the unfamiliar house, with difficulty found the stairs and the proper room, and pulled the princess roughly by the arm. She did not protest. Apparently, she simply stayed where she had been put last. He carried her out easily, but the halls were almost solid with smoke. It took a long time to find the stairs. Flames shot out and disappeared. The noise was deafening. Wood popped and pieces of the house were already falling.

Coughing and staggering, he finally found his way out and set the princess down. Her dress began to burn. He knocked her down and put it out.

He walked clear to get some good air and was immediately smashed to the ground. An intense pain shot from his heel up through his leg to the thigh.

He awoke to find Orloff pulling him from under some debris. "What happened?" Orloff asked.

"I don't know."

"Can you ride?"

"Of course."

He got to his feet and looked around. "The princess?"

"Apparently they're gone."

Michael took a step and promptly fell down. His leg was a cylinder of pain cruelly attached to his body.

Orloff pulled off his boot and examined it. The leg was broken. He got Michael to one foot and into the saddle as gently as he could. "The war is over for you for a while," he said.

"No," said Michael. "I'll be all right."

"I'll have to leave you. You say my niece and her husband are at her father's old house?"

"Yes, but . . . ."

"You'll go there."

"It pays to know the right people," said Michael.

"Do you know them?"

"We've met."

"I'm told they've become good Communists. Perhaps they can straighten your politics as well as your leg."

XLVI

It was a time of travel — of incredible travel, of impossible travel, of dedicated and ferocious travel by people who did not know where they were going or why. Some travelled from city to country to find food. Others did the opposite for the same reason. And still others simply travelled — for no reason at all.

Telegin and Maria were among those who had travelled from the city. Telegin's mysterious and powerful influence made it unnecessary that they join the battle for food. They had eaten well in Petrograd, as well as she ever had before the Bolshevik coup. Indeed, she had completely lost her concave appearance and now resembled exactly what she was: the prosperous, well-fed wife of a commissar. Furthermore, Telegin regularly travelled to Moscow, Petrograd and elsewhere. But she did not wonder where he went, what he did, or why he was so enormously influential. She did not care. She had made a deal. On her side, she would stay here — or wherever else she was told to stay. And in return, Kolodsky would deliver the letter from her father once each month.

So she stayed. The letter was vital. It was her only solace. The fact of its existence meant more than the few words her father had written.

Whatever was necessary, she would have done — and had done — to get the letter. All her father's letters — each representing a month she had spent with Telegin — were neatly filed in a drawer in her bedroom.

Whatever Telegin suggested, she did. Whatever Telegin said, she agreed with. Whatever Telegin denounced, she denounced. She behaved like what she was — a slave. Submissive, selfless, obedient. But at the same time, she was sarcastic, which Telegin enjoyed. Her sarcasm was a sign of rebellion, which proved he controlled her, proved Maria was his slave. She regretted this. She tried to stop. She wanted to be a slave calmly, coldly, because she had no other choice. But she could not. Her sarcasm welled up irrepressibly. To her it

337

meant that she was still her own property, still whole within. It proved to her that Telegin did not own her soul.

She no longer thought of Stepan. It was no longer necessary to convince herself that her brother was dead. Now she believed it. The man named comrade Marchenko was someone she did not know, someone born as comrade Marchenko. Comrade Marchenko was simply the man through whom she received the letter delivered by Kolodsky, that amusing, repulsive little man who had once worked for her father.

Maria understood and accepted all that. It was "real life." What annoyed her now more than anything else was her mother's attitude and behavior. Nadia Nikolaevna treated Telegin with respect, with timidity. She was even obsequious to indicate her belief that he was their benefactor, which Telegin hugely enjoyed, too. It was another joke on Maria, more proof of his total control. There was nothing she could do about this, either, which he alluded to subtly in her mother's presence. There were few things he loved better than communicating with someone in the presence of another who remained ignorant. It was one of many proofs of his creative power.

To Maria's horror, Nadia Nikolaevna had even sent a letter of appreciation once to Marchenko. Telegin had found it particularly amusing. Luckily, there was no answer. She had much to be thankful for. Nadia Nikolaevna, like Maria, was once again well-fed, although she looked slightly worn. Only her personality had permanently changed. The nostalgia had gone. She was placid, bovine. The effervescence had not returned. The champagne was flat.

Still, thought Maria, there was a pleasure in being there, even when Telegin was at home. It was more than the pleasure of being once again in her country house, every foot of which she knew as well as her own body — which reminded her of childhood joys. It was the great pleasure of stillness, of quiet, of being alone. Isolated in the country as it was, the house created the illusion that nothing else was real; that it was an oasis in a desert, or an island in a sea — a sea or desert of death or madness.

Into this deceptively placid country routine, her uncle had introduced Michael, the convalescent. Now his leg needs straightening as much as his ideas, Orloff had said. She had wondered about him, of course, since they had last met in Petrograd. But time and her new situation had made those questions less frequent. Indeed, she had tried to put him from her mind.

Now, here he was, living in the same house, at least for a time, interrupting its deceptive calm simply by being there, re-arousing in Maria all the emotions she thought she had suppressed. Indeed, he did so deliberately. He mocked her by imitating Telegin in a way Telegin hugely enjoyed. In the evening, on the porch where they all gathered, Michael and Telegin talked endlessly, both for Maria's benefit. As she propped up Michael's leg or got something he could not reach — as a part of the job as nurse to which Orloff had assigned her, which she would ordinarily have enjoyed — Michael watched her carefully and smiled, which made her nervous. Being near him was upsetting. She tried to pretend it wasn't, to ignore it. For different reasons they were both playing parts. They all were. Only Nadia Nikolaevna did not act.

"It is so good to have you here, Michael Fyodorovitch," said Telegin one night. "I have always admired you so much."

"Of course you have," said Michael. "Except when you haven't."

"True," said Telegin, chuckling. "That covers all the possibilities. You have a logical mind. I like that. My admiration is sound. Permit me to share some good news with you. Maria Ivanovna is going to have a child."

Michael smiled. "How charming! How beautifully old-fashioned! Congratulations, Cyril Modestovitch, my friend."

Nadia Nikolaevna blotted her eyes. "Yes, it is wonderful. In the midst of all this . . . ."

Telegin was delighted. He beamed. Maria's pregnancy was even more proof of his control over her. Maria was not delighted. She did not beam. She had told Telegin about it only to prevent the pleasure he eventually would have had in discovering it himself.

"Let's not be premature," said Maria. "We can't be sure what species it will be."

"*Touché!*" said Telegin, even more delighted. It was such a luxury to see Maria struggle.

"Masha, please!" said Nadia Nikolaevna, scandalized.

"Perhaps the result will be the New Soviet Man comrade Trotsky talks about," said Michael. "The truth is, my dear Maria Ivanovna, the truth is that I had noticed a subtle change in your figure, a change from the slender promise of girlhood to the full, rounded solidity of womanhood."

"True," said Telegin. "Nicely put."

"You should take all the credit, Cyril Modestovitch."

"I do."

Maria blushed, she hoped invisibly, and winced. Michael's personal reference was embarrassing and painful.

"Imagine, Maria Ivanovna!" said Michael. "In your body a seed is growing which with your maternal nourishment — and your guiding influence, my dear Cyril Modestovitch — will eventually develop into a perfect Communist."

"I understand that you yourself have become quite a Communist," she said angrily.

"Quite right!" said Michael. "Like Cyril Modestovitch, I am delighted to be a member of the Communist Party."

"How long will it take to uplift your fellow peasants?"

Michael smiled. They were talking only to each other. "You misunderstand, my dear Maria Ivanovna. You've got me and the Party wrong. I didn't join to uplift my fellow peasants or anyone else. Anyone who joins for that reason is a fool. Like Cyril Modestovitch, I became a member because the Party is the most stupid, petty, brutal and mindless organization I know. Which means, of course, that it is the most honest and realistic organization I know. More than any other, the Party knows what life is all about.

"Of course, it is also the most hypocritical and pompous organization on earth. It isn't perfect. What is? As you indicated, we members must endure a lot of nonsense about 'land, bread, freedom' and the 'liberation of the masses.' But, of course, no one really believes that. It's a stupid pretense the peasants enjoy, and the Party pleasures of killing and stealing are well worth it.

"It is true, I am the first to admit, that it would be even more satisfying simply to tell people, 'Look, we are Communists, which means that we're here to kill you and rob you simply because we want to,' instead of saying that we are doing it for their own good, but you must admit that is a rather minor detail.

"In fact, as I talk it becomes clear that aside from that one rather minor detail, Communism is an absolutely perfect system. One can't even imagine any way to improve it. That's why Ilyitch doesn't. Don't you agree, my dear Cyril Modestovitch?"

"Ha! My dear fellow . . . ." The conversation had taken a peculiar turn. Was Voronov joking? He wore a smile, and yet . . . . It was always so difficult to grasp what he was thinking, really thinking; what he was really after. It made Telegin nervous.

"I agree completely," said Maria. "Cyril Modestovitch, do you mean to deny that Communism is perfect?"

"Certainly not!"

"There you are!" said Michael. "We have so much in common."

"Yes," said Maria.

"Don't you agree, Cyril Modestovitch?"

"Of course he does," Maria said.

"Good," said Michael. "We're all nothing but contemptible thieves and liars. All of us. Some try to hide it, but it's true. Communism proves it. That's why it's so great. You, for instance, Cyril Modestovitch. You're nothing but a contemptible thief and liar. Don't you agree?"

"Certainly he does," said Maria, enjoying herself for the first time in years.

"Masha, please!" said Nadia Nikolaevna. "Cyril Modestovitch was very kind to take us in. More than kind. He is a remarkable person. He married beneath himself. You should be grateful. He could just as easily have chosen the daughter of a worker. You have no right to make such remarks. Forgive her, Cyril Modestovitch. She does not understand."

Why must her mother abase herself like that? It was embarrassing and humiliating even to hear.

"True," said Telegin. "But her confusion is so charming."

"Let's take a hypothetical example," said Michael. "Suppose for a moment, Cyril Modestovitch, that I decided to take your wife. Before Communism there would have been a lot of sneaking and nonsense. Innumerable niceties. But today — in the beautiful simplicity of Communism — I would simply take her. No fuss and bother."

"After all," said Maria brightly, "I belong to the State."

"Of course, I would have to tell you I was doing it for your own good. That's true. That is a nicety. We've mentioned that. But it's unimportant. Doesn't your husband agree?"

"He does," Masha said.

"Really, comrade Voronov!" said Nadia Nikolaevna.

For a moment, Telegin did not answer. Then he laughed shrilly, almost in falsetto. Voronov was joking, after all. He must be!

Michael joined him. Maria was amused but did not. Lately her emotions could get out of control too easily. Laughter so often turned to tears.

"You see, Nadia Nikolaevna, you are making a mistake," said Michael. "The only thing wrong here is that you are still suffering from bourgeois morality. You are horrified because dear Cyril Modestovitch and your daughter are speculators — making a fortune while others die — and because their boss is a Chekist, who is 'fighting speculation.' But you're wrong. These things should be encouraged, not denounced. Any Communist knows that. Am I right, Cyril Modestovitch?"

"Quite right!" Telegin roared.

"The trouble is you still believe you're better than everybody else."

"No!" shrieked Nadia Nikolaevna. "I don't!"

"Perhaps a self-criticism session . . . ."

"I'm not even as good."

"You say so. That's easy. But can you prove it?"

Telegin beamed. He liked Michael very much. As Michael had said, they

341

had so much in common. In fact, they seemed to agree so well. "He's right," Telegin said. "You can't."

Maria did not speak. She had become depressed. In her pocket was the latest letter from her father. Her hand was on it now. She did not want to suffer in silence. If only she could hand Michael the letter and tell him the story. If only she could hand him the letter without a word. Would he understand, would he sympathize, after what his own father had done?

There was no point wondering. Michael would ask questions. She could not answer. It would be dangerous. She had Telegin's promise not to mention the matter. But he would love nothing better, she knew, than for it to be accidentally revealed. No, she had no choice but to continue the sham.

For days at a time, Telegin was gone on his mysterious errands, Nadia Nikolaevna stayed in the house to avoid Michael, and Michael and Maria sat alone in the sun. It was good to relax and do nothing for a change, and feel the warmth sink into one's body. Spring was at its height. The warmth even penetrated his leg, which lay well-wrapped on a cushion.

As he sat back with his eyes closed, Maria read aloud from her favorite edition of her favorite author, Hugo, translating the French into Russian as she went. It was one of the few things she had saved and been able to bring along. It was such a pleasure even to hold the volumes and feel the thick bindings and heavy paper. And the words and stories swept her out of the present, into a different world where things were right. The words were a way for her and Michael to communicate without speech.

"I love this," she said one day.

"Yes, it is fairly interesting. Too bad it's all nonsense."

"Who is your favorite author?"

"Marx, of course. Or is it Lenin?"

Her leg hung by the knee from her chaise longue and she lazily swung it back and forth. How incredibly smooth it was, smooth and full, and at the same time firm. As it reached his end of the arc, toes in the air, he caught her heel, removed her sandal and kissed her ankle.

She tried to pull it loose, but he held it lightly. "Please!" she said. "What are you doing?"

His lips were still at the scene of the assault. He looked at her without letting her foot go. "Isn't that obvious?" he said. "As you see, I'm kissing your ankle."

"Why?"

"I want to."

"Stop it!"

"No!"

342

He chuckled, the low, amused sound she knew so well. She shivered. Then he relaxed his grip and she pulled free.

The days passed and his leg grew stronger. He was now able to walk with difficulty with a cane. Maria hitched the horse to the carriage and they drove to various points in the neighborhood, to the town and to the river. It was pleasant sitting on the bank under the trees, on the shifting carpet of shade and sunlight, pleasant at any time of day. It was a broad river, so broad at this point that it could have been mistaken for a lake. Far away, at midstream, small boats sometimes passed silently, as in a mirage. Waterbugs darted. Fish rose. It was still. Minutes passed during which they comfortably said nothing, joined by a bond of silence against superficial lies they would have had to tell.

"How delicious it would be to swim," she said one morning.

The water lay before them absolutely still. Just overhead, a bird was singing, the notes very clear, the sound pleasant, the tempo rhythmic and very slow. The odor of grass after a rain was in the air. Her body, smooth and long, lay quite near his.

"Go ahead," Michael said.

Maria instantly was on guard. She had made a mistake. It was imperative that they remain distant. It would be dangerous to get too close. The enticing prospect of a swim had confused her.

"No, I don't think . . . ."

"Go ahead."

He put his hand on her shoulder, and slowly drew his fingers down her bare upper arm, past her elbow and then down the backs of her long fingers to their tips. He put his hand on her shoulder and began again. It was agonizing, unbearable. Yet she could not move her hand from its place, palm down on the ground between them. It was impossible even to shift it slightly. If only she could. If only she could take it completely away. It would be worth anything to escape this unbearable pain. Anything . . . .

"Go ahead."

She got up abruptly. "Perhaps I shall . . . ." She walked quickly to the water without turning around, taking her clothes off almost without stopping, her tingling arm now functioning normally. Her clothes fell to earth in a line behind her.

She walked out to hip level and dove in. It was cool, luxurious, like an embrace caressing her everywhere at once. She surfaced, dove again, surfaced and dove again, swimming with long, easy strokes, from time to time turning on her back.

Then she came out, walking toward him, leaving her clothes where they lay. She stopped at the next tree a few yards away and, reaching up, squeezed

343

the water from her hair. A branch was before her at the level of her breasts. The water was evaporating, but beads of it flashed on her skin. Her full, rounded belly swelled, giving proof of her early pregnancy. Her body was no longer the schoolgirl's he remembered. Now it was fully ripe and round. The flesh, like the meat of a peach, seemed about to burst with life. Her legs were long and firm. In her posture and the tilt of her head was a serene, unashamed, womanly self-confidence.

"Come here!" he said.

"No, peasant!"

"Come here, I say, brat!"

"And I say no!"

She put her hands behind her head and slowly lifted her black skirt of hair. It fell, cascading down her back and chest. She tossed her head.

"Chase me!" she called. "Catch me!" She turned and laughed. She looked at him over her shoulder. "If you can."

He chuckled. "Perhaps. Let's see."

She turned again, faced him, and walked closer, until she stood before him, silently. Slowly he reached out and took her ankle. Their eyes met.

"There. I've caught you."

"Yes. I'm caught."

Her ankle was on fire. Then she was on the mossy ground and in his arms. Her skin was tingling, burning, blazing. It was like the painful — but wonderful — sensation of long dormant taste buds suddenly aroused by food.

They stayed at the river until well after dark. Early the next morning they came back. They came back every morning. It was so good to lie absolutely still and naked, bodies touching from head to toe, or near each other in the sun on the sandy bank.

"Did your father own all this?" Michael asked one afternoon.

"Yes," said Maria. "Down to the river."

"Where is your father?"

"In the North. Oh, look! A boat!"

"I see."

"Where is it going?"

"I don't know."

Maria nervously knew Michael would return to the subject of her father. She had to think of something else to talk about.

"Your poor back," she said.

"Yes."

"Your scars are hideous."

"Yes. Aren't they?"

344

They were. Long, thin, white lines of scar tissue crossed his back. Maria touched them gingerly. They were hard, swelling ridges. And there were red splotches of different shades. The sight was repellent, but somehow enhanced his appeal.

"I know how you got them," she said. "From Golovin. I know everything. You would not take off your cap. My uncle told me. And you saved your father."

Michael was annoyed. The fact that Maria knew these things was embarrassing. Why was Orloff such a busybody?

"I'm embarrassed," said Michael. "I was stupid. Today I wouldn't take the rap."

"You're wrong," she said. "You shouldn't be embarrassed. You were noble."

Michael smiled wryly. "You're thinking of your own father. I understand. But, unfortunately, our fathers are not alike. For yours one could do anything easily and without regret. For yours you would want to do what I stupidly did for mine. And because they are different, the result would be different, too. You would not spend five years in prison. For instance, once in the factory, your father . . . ." Michael related an incident which illustrated her father's virtues.

Maria had known, of course, that for the pleasure of the past days a price would have to be paid. That was why she had been afraid to enjoy them. Michael's perfectly sincere words slashed her, his honest ignorance making the pain worse. He did not — and must not — know what he was doing. She felt intense emotion but pretended she did not. His talk, she told herself, was simply that — talk. But his voice went on, blindly cruel. If only she could stop it, or at least change the subject. If only she could stop the pain — tell the truth and at the same time lie.

"My leg is healing nicely," he said.

"I see that."

"You're a good nurse."

"Yes. Be sure to mention it to Ilyitch."

"I, too, take orders well. Very soon, I'll have to leave."

"I know."

"Come with me."

He said it gruffly, harshly, like an insult, proving how difficult it had been to say. And Maria at first could not believe he had. Yet, after the past few days, what else could she expect? Her surprise and shock were simply a stupid pretense. She was trying to conceal the fact that she had caused her own pain. But, at the same time, her surprise and shock were real. She hated

345

him. He was a fraud. Why could he not behave as he advised her to? He would not accept the fact that there was nothing between them, and could be nothing between them, but a meaningless affair. It was he who continually insisted on forcing her to say it. He was a hypocrite.

"Have you forgotten that I am married?" she said.

"Nonsense, comrade. This is emancipated Socialist Russia. Marriage is a Capitalist hangover. There is no objective need for it."

"And that I am bearing my husband's child?"

"That doesn't matter either. Another Capitalist hangover."

The last rein on her emotions broke. She felt herself approaching a state of panic. She realized she had to drive Michael away, finally, irreversibly, as she had tried, and failed, to do once before. They could not see each other again. She could not risk it. She could not bear it. They had to become enemies.

"Apparently you have misunderstood, comrade Voronov," she said. "I was afraid that might happen, but I assumed you had more sense. Unfortunately, I was wrong. Haven't you ever wondered why I *am* married to Cyril Modestovitch, and not to you? Or why I have always called you 'peasant?'

"The answer is that you *are* a peasant and always will be. You were a Tsarist peasant under Nicholas and you're a Socialist peasant under Lenin. A worker, a drone, an underling who humbly takes his extra rations. And I have no intention of ever being saddled by an underling.

"Or were you joking? Yes, surely you were. You must have been! Surely you can't seriously believe I would eagerly go with you from army post to machine shop to officers' mess, when by staying where I am, I will get back the things and position taken from my parents and me by you and your Bolsheviks! You can't possibly be that stupid. You can't! Why do you imagine Cyril Modestovitch and I are working with Marchenko?

"Apparently you have forgotten your own good advice, comrade Voronov. 'Trust no one and rely on no one.' Remember? That is why I find your references to my father particularly amusing. Like your own, he is a fool. He refuses to cooperate or even come here. He's too good for us since we have joined the Party. You're all the same, you see, no matter which side you're on.

"Really, Michael Fyodorovitch, I am very surprised. You talk sensibly, at least you did until today, but either you don't believe what you are saying, or you lack the insides to carry it out. Is that a Capitalist hangover, too?"

"So what we have been doing here for the past week is simply amusing ourselves. And that's all. Do you understand me now, comrade Voronov?"

A veil fell over Michael's face. His features hardened. His expression returned to normal.

346

"I see," he said. "Yes, I understand perfectly. Please excuse my unfortunate lapse. I don't know what came over me. You can be sure it will never happen again."

They boarded the carriage and silently returned to the house. While they were away, Telegin had returned, and with him was Kolodsky. They were sitting together drinking on the back porch — one slight and birdlike; the other large, ponderous and porcine. Indeed, Telegin had gotten even larger of late. He looked as if he would have difficulty simply walking, yet, curiously, he was unusually agile. His torso seemed to carry all his weight. His arms and legs were perfectly normal. On him they looked stunted, like pseudopodia rather than normal limbs.

"Come join us," he called, waving a bottle of champagne.

He poured out two more glasses. "A toast!" he said. "To the noblest idea ever conceived by the mind of man. To Communism!"

"I'll drink to that!" said Michael.

"You said it," said Maria, looking Michael in the eye.

Kolodsky drank, but did not join the toast. He was nervous and angry at finding his tormentor there. Why did Michael always turn up? Why was there never any way for Kolodsky to retaliate?

"Yes, my friends," said Telegin, "thanks to the inexhaustible genius of Marx and Lenin, the historically inevitable age of greatness has arrived."

"You seem more than usually pleased," said Maria.

"Business is good."

Michael raised his glass. "To comrade Marchenko."

"A great man!" said Kolodsky, slightly defiant.

"One of the greatest," Maria laughed bitterly.

Telegin chuckled and filled everyone's glass. "A splendid toast, Michael Fyodorovitch," he said. "Curiously appropriate."

"Why?"

"Kolodsky tells me you recently caused Marchenko some inconvenience."

"Yes, that's right. I did."

"What happened?" asked Maria.

"It seems our guest confiscated some state property belonging to Marchenko."

"And your guest is in lots of trouble," said Kolodsky.

Maria began to laugh a bit wildly, and the others watched. Telegin alone wasn't puzzled. Nadia Nikolaevna came out of the house and Telegin flamboyantly kissed her hand. She sat near him while he filled a glass, pursing her lips slightly at Michael to show her dislike.

"You'll want to join us," said Telegin. "We were just drinking to comrade Marchenko."

"This is probably the right time to thank you for your hospitality, Cyril Modestovitch," said Michael. "I have the unfortunate gift of offending people. Like Marchenko. I don't know why. You are the only person I haven't offended. And I'm taking care not to do so. I sense a growing friendship between us. Thank you. I am quite grateful. I've had such an interesting affair with your wife. May I have some more of that remarkable champagne?"

Nadia Nikolaevna's mouth was open, her lips forming a large ellipse. The lips of the bottle made a perfect circle, hanging open over Michael's glass, but Telegin's hand did not move and nothing came out. What sort of joke was this?

"As we all know, Michael Fyodorovitch has a rather disgusting sense of humor," said Maria. "Luckily he is a typical proletarian. He can do no wrong."

"Of course," said Telegin, beginning to enjoy the joke. "The cause is clearly the oppression he has suffered." His hand moved. The bottle lowered. The champagne began to rush to the mouth.

"She has such a charming strawberry birthmark on her thigh," said Michael. "Don't you agree, my dear Cyril Modestovitch?"

The bottle stopped. Telegin looked from Michael to Maria.

Maria covered her face with her hands. "Must you be so obtuse, Cyril Modestovitch?" she said. "Must you humiliate me again? It isn't like you. I am surprised. How clear must I make it? Yes, your guest forced me, as we went for a walk. There. Now I am exposed. Must I give you the details? If so, tell me, and I shall."

"Is this true?" Telegin said.

"Of course," said Michael. "Is something wrong?"

"You never should have allowed him to come here," said Maria. "You must order him to go. Now!"

"Order me?" said Michael. "That's amusing."

"I refuse to listen to this," said Nadia Nikolaevna. But nobody paid any attention to her and she did not move.

The thin man inside Telegin was getting ready to come out. Telegin felt him climbing up the layers of his psychology, knifing at Telegin's insides, on his face a cat-like grin. Telegin was angry, which surprised and annoyed him. Anger was unpleasantly *gauche*. Michael had taken something of his. Telegin had not known Maria had become so important. He looked at Michael. Their eyes met. Michael's face was perfectly calm, even friendly. He almost wore a smile. Perhaps that was the reason Telegin was afraid: Michael's behavior was so completely incongruent, which gave the conversation an eerie quality.

"Why?" asked Telegin.

"I felt like it," Michael said. "Surely you aren't annoyed, Cyril Modesto-vitch? But, my dear friend, I am dumbfounded. A bourgeois mistake as obvious as this is the last thing I would expect from a Communist of your quality. Surely you remember that marriage has been abolished. It was merely a Capitalist device to protect private property. That's right, isn't it, Kolodsky?"

"Sure it is."

"He's an animal," said Maria.

"Of course I am," said Michael. "We *all* are. Fill my glass!"

The glass in his extended hand was a challenge. Telegin chuckled. What else could he do? The thin man climbed petulantly down through his entrails. Telegin's hand moved up and forward. The mouth of the bottle descended. The champagne burst out and filled Michael's glass.

"We must try to understand," said Telegin. "Poor Michael Fyodorovitch has suffered so much. His actions are involuntary, caused by his childhood. Once again, the Capitalist system is to blame."

"I apologize, Cyril Modestovitch," said Michael. "I was wrong. You are a good Communist, after all. Nadia Nikolaevna, isn't your son-in-law a marvel of Communism?"

"I'm sure Cyril Modestovitch is better than many I know."

Maria rose abruptly and walked toward the house. Telegin called after her, but she did not stop, and he followed.

"You do not care for me at all," she said. "Why else would you talk like that?"

What Michael was trying to do was clear: to force Maria to leave Telegin. He did not know why they were together. She would not tell him. She could be as devious as he. Coldly, the words of an unloved wife came from her mouth. Real tears were in her eyes.

Telegin was surprised again. One of the things he had enjoyed about their arrangement was Maria's revulsion. Could it be that his fatal charm had overcome her?

He patted her hand. "I was leading him along. Tomorrow I'll send a telegram from town. Comrade Voronov will get his orders."

Telegin rose early the next morning to do so, but Michael had risen even earlier and was gone.

XLVII

Confusion ruled the land. There were lines and no lines. A town was Red and then White, then Red, then White. Adjoining towns were different colors and some were Green, opposed to both the others. Russia was a land of insanity.

The Reds were driven out and the Whites occupied the town near which Telegin and Maria were living. Maria had wanted to retreat with the Reds to be sure of continuing to get her father's letters, but Dolgorensky and Marchenko had told Telegin to stay, to see and hear and report what he could. And Telegin liked the arrangement very much. Denikin's forward units were steadily approaching Moscow and were already close to the city. The Whites vowed they would be in Moscow by autumn. If they won, Telegin would turn up on the White side. If not, he would remain a loyal Red agent. It made no difference which side won. He was safe either way.

In the elegant dining room of the old house, Telegin raised a glass brimming with champagne.

"Gentlemen!" he said. "To the one who is with us in spirit, whose memory we cherish and which drives us on. To the reason we are fighting and winning. To our beloved Emperor Nicholas II."

The White officers sprang to their feet and drank with fervor. "God save the monarchy!" someone shouted.

"Masha, play something!" said Telegin.

"Yes, Cyril Modestovitch. What?"

"Patriotic tunes, of course."

She went to the piano in the alcove and began to play. Telegin began to sing and the officers joined in.

"To you, gentlemen!" said Telegin, filling their glasses. "Our deliverers. May almighty God bless you! If only you could know what we have gone through here. The Reds . . . ."

He shrugged expressively and slumped in his chair. An officer with tears in his eyes patted his shoulder.

"We shall be in Moscow this fall," the officer said.

Lopatkin also was at the table. Maria had not seen him for months. He was serving as a cavalry captain with the Volunteers. Maria had been able only to warn him not to mention Stepan, and longed for later when they could talk alone. How disconcerting it was to see him singing with the others. She had never been able to think of poor, vague Vasya as a soldier.

At last the others left or went to their rooms. Lopatkin was alone with Telegin, Maria and her mother. But apparently he was not in the mood for talk, even though he was slightly drunk.

"Well? Tell us, tell us, Vasya! What has happened?" Maria said excitedly. "How is Petrograd?"

"Petrograd still exists. That is really all one can say."

"And when were you last there?" Telegin asked.

"Some months ago. For my last periodic stay with the Cheka." Lopatkin looked meaningfully at Maria.

"It is a crime against God that such an organization is allowed to exist," Telegin said.

"Did you happen to hear anything of my husband?" Nadia Nikolaevna hesitantly asked.

"Yes," Lopatkin said. "I saw him."

"Where?" both women asked at once. "What did he tell you? Did he look well?"

Lopatkin was puzzled. "Yes. At the time."

"And his mood?" asked Maria. "Was he fairly happy?"

"Happy? What does that mean?" Lopatkin asked. "I see your lips moving, Masha, and hear a sound, but I do not understand the word. And it would make no difference if I did, because there's no such thing.

"They had just asked him for the last time to run the factory. And for the last time, he had refused. He had found a way to beat them. They could not make him bend."

"It's about time someone put those Bolshevik frauds in their place," said Telegin.

"He organized our entire cell. He was everywhere. If something was needed, he somehow would get it — or make it. He could make anything. But you know that. I never saw anyone with so much mechanical ability. Unfortunately, I do not have that gift.

"But the most extraordinary thing was his manner. It seemed to give the others confidence. I know it did me. I never saw him so calm, even serene.

And this, as you may imagine, is not the easiest thing to manage."

Tears of joy filled Maria's eyes. She tried to speak but could not.

Lopatkin patted her hand. "Masha, I was with him just before he died. He spoke of you at length. He really did love you very much. He described so many amusing times, and things you had done, with such pleasure, such verve, that once or twice I almost laughed. In that place! I didn't, of course. But that's the way he made one feel.

"And the way he left us. Usually, as soon as they know, they begin to shake. Sometimes they lose control completely, even of their muscles, and must be dragged from the room, not screaming, not struggling, but simply unable. Even in the best, one sees some sign. But he! On his face was the expression of a medieval knight. And there was a smile, as if they — not he — were being defeated. And perhaps they were.

"Does this upset you, Masha? Nadia Nikolaevna? I'm sorry. I was afraid it might. I debated with myself whether to say it. Perhaps I was wrong. I had hoped it would bring comfort in the face of your great loss. I remember every detail about that morning. It was still dark when we heard them coming down the hall. They stood just outside the door. They always did . . . ."

Lopatkin's voice went on, slow and earnest. In it were good Russian words, all words whose meanings she knew, all grammatically arranged and properly pronounced. But now it was Maria's turn to misunderstand. Indeed, she understood nothing Lopatkin had said. She heard the words perfectly, but their individual meanings, put together, made no sense.

She stared at him dumbly. Obviously this was not some joke. No one in the world would make such a joke, especially not Vasya. Therefore, she simply had misunderstood. That was the only possible explanation. That was logic. After all, the expression on his face was vague. Indeed, for proof she had only to turn to the others. On their faces she would see the same perfectly normal expressions. She would know that they had understood and she had not. All that was necessary was to establish that he had not said what she thought. Obviously she was suffering from some strange mental lapse. Later, she would recall it as rather amusing. She would mention it. The others would laugh, especially her father. Her mother would gently chide her.

Slowly and mechanically, as if operated by gears and pulleys, she turned her head and looked at Telegin. His face was unfamiliar. On it was shock. Slowly and mechanically, she turned to her mother. Her face was blank, a reflection of Maria's own.

It was absolutely imperative to stay in control. If she lost control, it would add reality to what seemed to be happening.

"You were with him when he died?" she said mechanically.

"Yes, Masha," said Lopatkin, still oblivious.

"Where?"

"In the Gorokhovaya. Where else?"

"When?"

"I don't remember. Some months ago."

It happened that in her pocket was the last letter from her father. In fact, her hand had been around it all the time, absently. Now she realized what it was, drew it out and unfolded it slowly. She placed it carefully in Lopatkin's hand.

"But we received this letter from him only three weeks ago. We have been receiving letters from him for months."

Lopatkin looked at the letter stupidly. "I don't understand."

"Look at the letter," she said shortly. "Look at it, Vasya! Read it! Don't you see?"

She spoke brusquely, but she was pleading. It was as if the matter would be decided by Vasya's opinion and the letter he was holding were some sort of evidence, tangible proof of her father's existence. If only Vasya would read the letter and see what it was, rub the paper between his fingers, even crinkle it a bit, he would realize that what he was saying was nonsense. The letter proved her father was alive. Letters, after all, do not write themselves.

"Read it, Vasya!" she commanded. "You have received letters from my father in the past."

Lopatkin forced himself to read the letter. He looked at Telegin and Nadia Nikolaevna for help. They gave none. He knew that Maria wanted him to do or say something, and he wanted to do it or say it at once, but he had no idea what it was.

"Excuse me," he said. "Something is wrong. Masha, I was with him. I remember every detail. It was still dark . . . ."

Maria ripped the letter from his hand. Obviously, for whatever reason, he was refusing to understand. He was talking again, about what she did not know, but it made no difference because talk proved nothing. Letters did, and Maria had one.

She looked at the letter again herself. She rubbed it between her fingers as Vasya should have done. It was in her father's handwriting, of that there was no doubt. And although very short and consisting only of pleasantries, it was filled with figures of speech her father liked to use. She thought through the earlier letters they had received, all now upstairs in a drawer, and filled with recollections only her father could know.

Of course the letters were genuine! They could have been written by no one else. Any other theory was impossible.

The thought provoked a question, silly, yet annoying. She turned to Telegin, slowly, mechanically, the gears and pulleys soundless and smooth. She did not say anything. She simply looked. On her face was an expression he had never seen before — on her face or any other.

"Masha, I assure you!" he stuttered in a voice he did not know. "The letters are genuine, as far as I know. They have been delivered as I promised. What he says is nonsense."

The gears and pulleys operated again. Her head turned. In the darkness beyond the lamp at the far end of the room, a face appeared. An extraordinarily handsome face, topped with thick black hair like her own. Around the mouth and eyes which watched her was a suggestion of petulance. She knew the face quite well. And she knew its name. It was the face of the man who had once been her brother.

She said the name aloud: "Stepan."

The sound hung in the air, testifying to the truth of what Lopatkin had said. Who else but Stepan could have written the letters? Only a member of the family could know such details. Who else could so perfectly duplicate her father's handwriting?

So it had all been wasted. There had been no point. All her efforts had meant nothing. Her life was ruined, finished, stupidly and for no reason. The universe had inanely flung her in a ditch. Michael had been right all along. There was nothing but meaningless sacrifice, betrayal and frustration.

In the darkness where Stepan's had been, her father's face now appeared — keen, generous, supremely confident, creases of humor at the corners of the mouth.

She pressed her eyes shut, scalded with guilt and shame. How could she be so petty as to feel sorry for herself after what had happened to her father? She had not known she could be so small.

She rose.

Nadia Nikolaevna was staring at her, blank with horror. Lopatkin looked imploringly from her to the others, still completely mystified, still afraid that he was the cause of whatever had gone wrong. Telegin was nervously rubbing his hands.

"Where are you going?" he asked in a timorous voice.

"To Petrograd."

"To Petrograd?" said Nadia Nikolaevna mechanically.

"You can't do that," Telegin said.

"I'll leave in the morning. You will prepare the necessary papers, Cyril Modestovitch."

354

She went through the open doors into the next room, and began opening drawers in a chest.

"But you would have to cross the lines," said Telegin, following her closely. "The trains are impossible. And there is fighting in every town along the way. Isn't that right, Vasya?"

"Yes," he stammered. "That's right."

She opened a drawer and took out a case, and from it took a revolver her father had bought during his travels in the United States. It was imperative that she use her father's revolver.

"Vasya!" she called. "Please come here!" Lopatkin jumped up nervously and did. "Show me how to use this," she said.

Telegin waved his hand at her and pointed. "But . . . but you're pregnant."

She looked down at herself. "Yes, so I am." Her pregnancy now was very advanced and very obvious. "At least there's not much danger of rape."

For years as a dancer she had learned to study and respect her body, but now at the sight of it she felt intense revulsion, as if she were the victim of some humiliating disease. If only she could escape it. If only she could remove the ugly swelling within it.

She put the revolver in Lopatkin's hand.

"Show me!"

LXVIII

It has been said of course that everyone wants to kill his father. Still, it is not an easy thing to do. Few attempt it. Even fewer succeed.

Some people can be killed without complications. They need killing; their lives cry out for termination. One feels guilty if a chance is missed. To kill them is a public service and, more, a civic duty. Not to kill them is bad manners, at the least. One does it even if one is not in the mood.

Others need killing just as much; they are the majority, and propriety requires that some justification be presented: "I noticed that in raising the teacup, he did not properly extend his finger, so of course, et cetera"; or, again, "Coming in unexpectedly, I found her using my razor to shave her legs. You will find her body in the garden, Inspector, part of it, that is, et cetera."

But for killing one's father a somewhat more elaborate explanation is necessary, not because killing one's father is particularly wrong — these are, after all, modern times, times of challenge to outworn values, times of progressive, modern methods — but simply because the rarity of the achievement is bound to raise questions about how and why it was done.

The perpetrator may begin to wonder himself.

Stepan's explanation was that it simply hadn't happened. He had not been responsible, after all, for the original arrest. That had happened in the aftermath of the attempt on Lenin, and was compounded by his father's refusal to operate the factory. The fact that his father was in prison was not Stepan's fault.

What Stepan had done was just to play a little trick, a necessary little trick that had gotten out of hand. That was all. Even the idea had not been Stepan's, but Telegin's. Certainly Stepan had enjoyed it. Both Maria and his father had needed the trick. Stepan actually deserved their thanks.

All he had done was keep his father at Number Two Gorokhovaya after others had been released, others who had been arrested with his father. That was all. He had meant to release him later, after the lesson had been learned. Stepan could not have been expected to know that by doing this, he had made his release impossible. His death had been an accident. No one knows everything and has total power. Stepan, after all, did not run the Cheka. He was still only an ambitious official of middling rank. He had no way of knowing what his superiors might decide. He had no way of changing their decisions.

So all he had really done was to play a little trick.

That was all.

He had played a little trick and it had gotten out of hand.

Dolgorensky had been watching the affair, getting angrier and angrier. Had Danilov been released — "graduated," as Dolgorensky called it — with the others in his "class," Dolgorensky would gradually have forgotten about him. But Danilov's constant presence was a continual affront, "a deliberate insult to the Soviet power," Dolgorensky chuckled. It meant that Danilov was still refusing to cooperate, was a bad "student," that Marchenko was still unable to convince him. And the Food Trust was still on Dolgorensky's back about their damned agricultural machinery. The fools! Were they really so stupid that they believed what they said? Agricultural machinery, indeed! But they *were* saying it, which meant trouble for Dolgorensky. It meant that Danilov should be taught a lesson. Dolgorensky had simply stamped some papers.

On the next morning, as usual, Grodsky had opened the cell door, and just stood there picking his nose. This was so much better than throwing bombs. True, Dolgorensky had ordered that for hygienic reasons, Grodsky must bathe, but he was still perfectly free to pick his nose. And he now had a little power. He liked to wait and watch the faces before he called the morning's names, the names of those who would be liquidated. There was always such a laughable variety of droolings and tics. This morning he had only one name and he called it: "Danilov!" But there had been no drooling and no tic. To his regret, Danilov had just come to the door, as Lopatkin had a week before. Lopatkin could have had no idea he would just be interrogated and returned. Bourgeois were not supposed to behave like that, especially if they were as capitalistically bloated as Danilov, or as contemptibly vague as Lopatkin.

Stepan was in his office when Grodsky took his father away. Indeed, he had watched them leave the building through a window. He had known of Dolgorensky's decision soon after it had been made. He always tried, through Kolodsky, to know as much as possible. He could have tried to change it by persuading Dolgorensky he was succeeding with Danilov. Or he could simply

357

have replaced his father with somebody else, which happened all the time. Identity did not mean very much. Stepan himself had become someone else. Just the other day, a man scheduled to be taken had died in his cell and Grodsky had replaced him with the man nearest the door.

But such an act would have meant a certain risk. Why was Marchenko doing this for a "former person" such as Danilov? What was their relationship? Did comrade Marchenko's background require another look? Such questions would inevitably be asked in the atmosphere Stepan had helped create. Knowledge of a foreign language, possession of a page from a foreign newspaper, indeed, failure even for less than a second to meet an interrogator's glance, were officially accepted proofs of guilt. Stepan himself liked to say that he could establish guilt — bourgeois "blood" or even the possibility that a crime might be committed — simply with a long look into a man's eyes, where the slightest wavering was as good as a confession.

Of course, Stepan did not in any way fear taking risks. Certainly not. He relished it. It was part of his theory that history is determined by men of power and will such as he.

But, at the same time, man is simply a chip on the crest of history — a meaningless, powerless, comatose little chip. As a good Communist, Stepan knew that. Perhaps this curious incident had some historical significance. Perhaps it was meant to be. To interfere with it could well have meant interference with the inevitable, with history. And therefore with Communism. Perhaps Stepan's theory was completely wrong, a product of his egotistical refusal to admit he was a powerless little chip. Life was full of meaningless little incidents which determined history, and over which one had not the slightest control. Indeed, to interfere in any way would have meant surrender to the personal. And this, of course, was the basis of counter-revolution.

Furthermore, his father had been given a chance to release himself from custody. All he had had to do was agree to run the factory. Orloff himself had argued that he should do so. But to the very end, Danilov had stubbornly refused. Why should Stepan be punished for what his father had decided? Why should Stepan have to suffer after making the right choice? That would be obviously and grossly unfair — a violation of the "individual rights" his father loved. What was happening to his father was the result of his own stupid ideas. It had nothing to do with Stepan. It was the inevitable, unavoidable and predictable work of history. All Stepan had done was to play a little trick. That was all.

That was why, as Grodsky took away his father, Stepan had done nothing. Nothing but watch calmly from a window. That was why he had been

358

equally calm when told of Danilov's death. He had been executed along with some others, all "bloated Capitalist bloodsuckers." Since Communism is perfect, he had of course been guilty. Since Communism is perfect, he had of course been executed. Even ordinary sympathy would have been a sign of weakness — a personal element — and therefore a confession that Stepan had not yet achieved the perfect Communist morality.

That was why Stepan's current uneasiness had nothing to do with his father. Stepan was very sensitive. He could detect even a hint of injustice or criticism toward himself. He was uneasy because, surprisingly, there had been more of this lately than usual. Everywhere there were individuals who, jealous of his success, wanted to slight him. But because of his success, they were afraid to, so that their criticisms were perceptible only in a glance or intonation. That was happening all around him, he knew. And there was more to it than simple jealousy. The glances and intonations were accompanied by gloating smiles, the reason for which Kolodsky could not discover. So Stepan's uneasiness was identifiable yet vague, caused and at the same time causeless. But it obviously had nothing to do with his father.

Indeed, there was no reason why it should. Even in prison, his father had tried to hurt him. Stepan had planned to avoid him during his stay in the Gorokhovaya, so that Danilov would know only the name of the man in charge of his case. Yet Stepan had been asked to attend one of the interrogations conducted by Dolgorensky, and it had been impossible to refuse. What reason could he give? In fact, he had rather relished the coming scene as he walked toward the proper room along the corridor, remembering the scene long before in a different world, when his father had refused to advance the money Stepan had embezzled from the regiment. But he knew at the same time that his sudden appearance would inevitably produce a shock, which Dolgorensky would notice and wonder about even if his father tried to conceal it, notice even in an involuntary widening of the eyes; and that his father on the other hand might even expose him. With his hand on the knob, Stepan was still preparing counterattacks to these possible thrusts.

Yet his father had not given the slightest sign of recognition. Stepan had been relieved, of course. His shoulders, which he hadn't realized were hunched, had begun to relax slowly. Yet, at the same time, he had unexpectedly felt disappointed, almost cheated. For his father to have accused him, or even spoken, would have been an objective admission of their new relationship — and of Stepan's power, of the fact that Stepan no longer needed a few paltry rubles. He had looked his father straight in the eyes. This was normal. He always did it during his own interrogations. The look that came back not only did not contain a plea — a plea would have been too much to ask — and was not only impersonal, it was blank. Not simply as if Stepan were being ignored, but as if he were not really there and the eyes did not even see him.

Why had his father done this? Surely not to protect him. That could not be. The only possible explanation was that in his new and powerless situation, his father had chosen this as the only way he could show his contempt. As always, he was trying to hurt his son. It became important for Stepan to elicit a personal expression from him — even the slightest. A sign of recognition. The simple admission that Stepan *did* exist. He had unwisely conducted additional interrogations alone, and pointed out to his father that it was now safe to speak. But in answer to everything personal, Danilov remained silent. He had answered everything else as if Stepan were just another Chekist. In his voice was not even the trace of sarcasm for which Stepan would have settled. At the proper places he had called Stepan "comrade Marchenko," but did not emphasize the words as Stepan hoped he would. There was nothing.

And Stepan obviously could not mention the matter. He could not simply say, "Admit that you are my father, and I am your son." That would have been a defeat. It would have accomplished exactly the opposite of what he wanted. It was necessary that Danilov himself voluntarily say the words. Stepan did not know why he was surprised that his father had not. He had behaved exactly as Stepan knew he would. He always had. He had behaved exactly as Stepan knew he would when Orloff had brought the offer from the Food Trust. So had Orloff. Stepan had known Orloff would not come to see him, Marchenko, about the matter; that would have been a personal plea. His father and his uncle were so much alike.

Only when he mentioned Maria had Stepan known he was making progress. In the cold blue eyes he had seen a flicker, and he had followed it almost involuntarily, as a shark follows blood. He should have known Maria would be his father's weak spot. She always was. Danilov had always favored her, to Stepan's detriment. So he no longer tried to get his father to claim him. Instead, Stepan told him about his daughter.

"Surely you remember her, citizen Danilov," he had said. "Your daughter, Maria Ivanovna. A remarkable individual, isn't she? She is married, you know. Yes, to Cyril Modestovitch Telegin. Surely you remember him, too. He is also a most remarkable individual. Yes, your daughter did it to save you. That was the deal. Her sacrifice is so remarkably, so characteristically beautiful. She is probably enjoying it so much that she should thank you for the chance. And at the same time, it's trite. Don't you agree? It's happening so often these days, you see — all the fault of those nasty Reds. And not at all the way it happens on the stage.

"It's amusing — isn't it? — to imagine the reality of it. Not some melodramatic Italian literary conception. But the dull, dirty, daily reality of this remarkable individual, your daughter, being touched by the pudgy fingers of a man you both despise — just so that *you* can stay alive. Perhaps it's you who owe her thanks, after all. Her boring sacrifice is a success. You are alive, citizen Danilov, aren't you?"

In his father's eyes he had seen a flash. That was all. Conceivably there had been a movement of the mouth. He was not sure. But the flash had been enough. Stepan had smiled to ensure that his father should know he had seen it. It was all he needed. True, his father still refused to speak and had refused to discuss the arrangements for the letters, so that the arrangements had to be made by Kolodsky. But Stepan nevertheless had felt the warmth of victory. And he deserved it. His father should not have abused him so. His father should have given Stepan what he wanted. Now Stepan was sorry, but now it was too late.

He had enjoyed handling and reading the letters after his father had written them and before Kolodsky took them south. They reinforced his sense of victory. Letters, after all, reveal the writer's insides. Especially letters like these, filled with references only he and Maria could recognize. It was like holding his father's mind between his fingers. And as he read each one and handed it to Kolodsky, he was reminded again of Maria and Telegin's pudgy fingers, and of the fact that the letters kept them together. It was the funniest thing he had ever heard. The only thing funnier was the fact that his father knew all this, yet had no choice but to write the letters anyway.

That was why Stepan had been surprised when his father stopped and refused to write another letter, hoping that Maria would think him dead and would leave Telegin. Stepan had decided to write the letters himself, not because he was nervous about the result if they stopped arriving — not at all — but because he refused to give up the great pleasure they gave him. Indeed, composing them even heightened the pleasure. It took artistry to reproduce perfectly on paper a man's own mind in his own handwriting. Telegin would be impressed. What a pity Stepan could not tell him! As he wrote, he almost giggled at the thought of Maria reading.

On the other hand, after his father's death, the letters somehow almost convinced Stepan his father was alive — not that Stepan was uneasy about it. Not at all.

He was just finishing a letter now. It was a touching letter filled with humor, the kind his father liked so much. He folded it and went to look for Kolodsky. From the room next to his, two guards dragged a man into the corridor as he passed. He looked inside in time to see the officer at the desk slip something into his mouth. Like so many, he apparently needed cocaine to perform his duties. With a glance, Stepan had seen that he was already so narcotized he was not fully aware of his actions. Stepan did not know him — apparently he was rather new — but he was probably another of those who used euphemisms to describe what he was doing. In short, he was a weakling.

Stepan snorted. He had no need of cocaine or euphemisms. He had the courage to call things as they were. There was absolutely nothing to be uneasy about. He was a man of total will, after all — a man of steel.

XLIX

The Reds were pushing Denikin's forces back. Maria had crossed the lines and was in a Red-controlled town. In the hot, dead air, the red flag hung limp atop the station, as if waiting to be replaced again. Below, at the entrances, bunches of people milled about. And from inside the station came an incredible stench.

For a moment, Maria stood just outside, trying not to breathe, peering into the makeshift entrance broken through the wall. She was alone. She had refused to allow Telegin to see her off, and her mother still sat at home blank with horror. She was dressed in the oldest possible clothes, pockets filled with various supplies, and against her skin was the hard, metallic touch of the gun.

Her nose and lungs struggled to escape, but it was useless. She went in. It was dark and her eyes took time to adjust. When they did, she saw on her left an alcove, its floor covered with excrement. The walls, which had once been white, were peeling. And people were going in and out. In front of the alcove was a low, makeshift partition of crates, above which appeared the head of an old woman, her face impassive, her eyes vacant. This was not the way things were in old St. Petersburg. As she watched, something leaked from under the partition and approached her along a groove, and she moved quickly aside, flailing fingers hunting the wall. Someone cursed and shoved her into it, and she involuntarily sucked in lungfuls of stench. She remembered reading somewhere about people being frozen inside a glacier. This also was like being immobilized inside something solid. But it was hot, a dead heat in a lifeless air. The vast hall was packed with people, talking, gesticulating, running and colliding. The conversation seemed far away. She could even hear the buzzing of innumerable flies. Or was it the ringing in her ears?

Now she was in a line which did not move. Hours passed. Her feet began to hurt. She was accustomed to working on them for long periods, of course, but the unaccustomed weight pressed them down, especially at the high and delicate instep. She stood on one and then the other, resting them, which gave momentary relief. But the pain rose up her legs and her soles began to burn. She stamped them on the floor, which did no good. The only consolation was that many other victims were now behind her, which at least provided the illusion that she was making some progress.

She had to sit down immediately and did so in her place on the floor. The line at once began to move, she sprang up eagerly and it stopped. The line was so long that it was impossible to tell what had happened, if anything, and she sat again, having advanced no more than a few feet. Another hour passed. It was getting dark. At last she stood before a middle-aged man in a military tunic, who sat at a table calmly whittling.

"Your papers," he said tonelessly, without looking up.

Maria dug in her pocket and took them out. Here at least there would be no trouble. Telegin himself had prepared them. She held them out to the man in the tunic, a thick sheaf of documents and forms, signed, countersigned, stamped and marked.

He did not take them. She understood that she should put them on the table and did so, and he idly looked at the one on the top. He turned the others over with his knife, looking at each without interest, and when he had finished returned to his whittling.

"Your papers are not in order," he said.

"What?"

"Your papers are not in order."

"But that cannot be!"

Again he assured her that it could be and was, his voice toneless and mechanical, as he very carefully studied his whittling. And now for the first time, the man looked up, and Maria saw a reptilian gaze. His eyes were flat, yellow and metallic. Images were imprinted on the retinas and conveyed along the nerves to the brain. But, as in a lizard's eyes, there was absolutely no comprehension. And Maria realized that it would be pointless — even stupid — to continue trying to explain.

Someone shoved her. "Come on, citizen. We ain't got all night."

The lizard in the tunic gestured with his knife. She took her papers and stepped uncertainly off the line. Nearby at the gate, was a man in a ragged railroad uniform.

"Where is the station master's office, please?" she asked.

"I don't know," said the man. "That is not my job."

A train was standing at the platform. She did not know whether it was hers, but it was spitting steam and she became nervous.

"Is that the train to Petrograd?" she asked.

"I don't know."

She found the office herself and in it two men, one of whom wore a badge and the railroad uniform. The other was the usual uniformed Chekist. He came forward now with his left hand extended, the other carefully placed in his tunic, an obvious victim of the Napoleonic syndrome. He was very young. His mouth opened to form words, but before he could do so Maria placed her papers in his hand. He smiled and shuffled through them quickly.

"Hm. Yes," he said. "Your papers are quite in order." He handed them back. "Now, what is it you want?"

"Your man outside says they aren't."

The two men looked at each other and laughed. "Oh, I see," said the adolescent commissar. "You mean Vanka. Of course. You have fallen afoul of Socialist mathematics."

"I don't understand."

"You see, the man outside is completely illiterate."

"Illiterate?" asked Maria. "You mean he can't read?"

"Not a word," laughed the commissar. "Most illiterates can't."

"But how, then, can he read one's papers?" she sputtered.

The commissar was so puzzled he took his hand from his tunic. "He can't, of course."

"Then how can he tell whose papers are not in order?"

"This brings us to Socialist mathematics. You see, Vanka can't read, but he can count very well. Every day he selects two numbers and applies them to the 'former persons' in the line. Those chosen by the first have papers out of order. Those by the second are simply arrested. And you have been chosen. Socialist mathematics has caught you. Your papers are not in order. Socialism is so beautifully amusing and just."

"But suppose one's papers are really in order?" asked Maria. "You yourself just said mine are."

The commissar's hand returned to his tunic. He spoke in a patient, friendly voice, as if humoring a disobedient child.

"You see, if we say papers are not in order, then the papers are not in order. It's really that simple. And if you think for a minute, you will understand. How *could* papers be in order if we say they are not, since we are the ones who issue the papers?"

The commissar smiled with genuine warmth. He was perfectly serious. He was perfectly sane. He was intelligent. And he was pleasant. He talked like a cheerful university student.

"In your case, as in any other, I am going to apply the rule. I have said that your papers are in order, and therefore they are in order — because I have said so. Do you see now that you must be thankful for the rule?"

"Yes, comrade commissar, I do see that. Thank you."

"You are a bourgeoise, of course, but I see that you will soon present us with a new Soviet citizen, so it is important for you to realize not only that Socialism makes sense, but that it is so beautifully magnanimous." He took her papers and with a flourish made a mark.

"Then I may get on the train now?"

"Of course."

"When will it leave?"

"Precisely at eleven," said the station master. "You have thirty minutes."

Outside, the other man in the railroad uniform was still standing at the gate. Maria volunteered her papers, but he did not seem to care. She passed through onto the platform and into a large crowd. The passengers were not yet being allowed aboard. Chekists in uniform barred the way. An hour passed and then another. It was not quite as hot, but the stench was even worse, if possible.

A rumor came by that the train would not leave at all. She worked her way out of the crowd and went back to the gate.

"When will it leave?" she asked the man in the uniform.

"I don't know," he said. "That is not my job."

"What *is* your job?"

He smiled. "I don't know."

On the platform there was a roar. People were surging into the train. Hands were reaching up and grabbing. She fought her way through to the door of a boxcar, but her condition made it difficult to climb up and others were shoving her aside. Again and again she reached up without success. A foot accidentally but roughly hit her face. Another stepped on her hand in the same way.

"Help her up!" somebody said. "She's going to be a mother."

"So what!" said someone else. "Another mouth to feed."

A hand pulled her firmly aboard and at that moment the train lurched forward and began to move, leaving many would-be travellers on the platform, shaking others off.

In a minute the town was gone and the train was in open country. Maria was on her way to Petrograd.

L

It was remarkable what an effect just being naked had on a man, Stepan thought. One could work on a man for months and not produce results as good as by simply stripping his clothes off for a few hours. Why was that? Perhaps it was simply that a naked man feels humiliated. But why? Was it because clothes and uniforms are pretensions, men's attempt to appear better than they are, their attempt to conceal that they are hairless worms — so that when they are exposed they go all to pieces? Stepan could not conceive of himself doing such a thing. He had no such pretensions. He had nothing to conceal. He knew he was a hairless worm — and he was glad. He could have taken being stripped with a laugh.

But the three men before him now could not. They were suffering from bourgeois pretension. The man in the middle was tense and stiff, still resisting, but the fact that he was resisting showed he was already in the first stage, which was very acceptable after only four hours. The other two were beginning to disintegrate, their features twitching, their flesh quivering, their bodies about to go out of control, as if their bones had somehow been pulverized. How ugly the human body is, Stepan thought.

He nodded to Kolodsky.

"Fire!" Kolodsky yelled.

The squad of aiming soldiers did so. There was a puff of smoke and a boom, which echoed in the open air. The man in the middle lost control of his face, the muscles shivering, a tic at the left eye, the treatment revealing hidden weaknesses as always. The man on his right was lying face down, an arm hanging into the grave he had dug. The other man was on hands and knees, eyes fixed, staring stupidly at Stepan, who slowly strolled up.

"That is correct," said Stepan. "You are not dead. Since this is your first offense, the Cheka has decided to be magnanimous. But at the same time, we do have to teach you a lesson, don't we, so that you will really understand how wrong speculation is. Otherwise we would be shirking our duty to the people — to you. We would not deserve the thanks you pay us. We would be accessories to your crimes. For your own good, you must realize — not just be able to repeat, but understand, deep in your entrails — that the food on which you are profiting must be left with the Food Trust and that you have been stealing it from the people's mouths."

Kolodsky laughed into his tunic. He turned over with his boot the man who had fainted. The man on his hands and knees began to scream, calmly, regularly, in short, mechanical bursts, in a strange falsetto that belonged to someone else. He was a fat little man. He resembled a large beetle. Suddenly, with unexpected speed, he jumped into the grave. The screaming stopped. It was replaced by the sound of someone feverishly digging; the sound of someone feverishly eating. Stepan saw that he was eating the dirt in the fresh grave as fast as he could, loudly chewing and swallowing, with both hands shoving it into his mouth.

Remarkable! thought Stepan. That had never happened before. What did it mean? Would the psychiatrists know? How fascinating his work was. He would not change it for anything. He loved adjusting people to Socialism. He motioned to the soldiers to pull the man out. The thought of his father came unexpectedly to mind, and Stepan pictured him digging a grave, as the prisoners had just done. Stepan shrugged the thought off. It was stupid. Why should such a thing occur to him? He was a man of total will — a man of steel.

With difficulty, the soldiers got the madman out of the grave, his mouth and cheeks still stuffed with dirt, and returned him and the other two speculators to their cells. Stepan and Kolodsky went at once to his car. It was a remarkably beautiful day, a perfect day for a drive through the city. Stepan felt the glow of perfect health and satisfaction. Sooner or later, the city would be his. All other worms would wriggle for him.

They stopped at Stepan's rooms and went up. Tata was not there, which pleased him. Lately, he found her annoying. Her morose behavior and her flat, toneless voice were unpleasant, as unpleasant as the long periods in which she said nothing. She was not the old Tata. She had changed, in a way and for a reason he could not understand. He would have to do something about her. Her success as a Soviet artist was not worth his discomfort.

He threw Kolodsky a bottle and a corkscrew. "Open that."

"Certainly, comrade Marchenko," said Kolodsky, flattered by being in the confidence of so important a man.

While he did so, Stepan cut a large piece of cheese from a wheel recently sent him by Telegin. Stepan had a passion for cheese and this wheel was just right. Working with Telegin was the best thing he had ever done. Business would be better if it weren't for the damned speculators, but it was good.

LI

The boxcar was travelling slowly, which made the ride even rougher than usual. At least, incredibly, it was not very crowded. Almost everybody had gotten off at the last station. Only a tall old man had gotten on, so that there were now in the car, in addition, only a very young mute girl, whose name, Maria had learned, was the Princess Lobanovsky, along with her old woman, and some middle-aged women Maria could not figure out. She stretched, enjoying the room while she could. At the next station, she knew, another mob would swarm aboard. She leaned back on the straw and looked out through the open door at the passing plains.

Nothing moved. Nothing changed. And the same thing had been happening for days. The monotony and boredom totally paralyzed thought and action. Ordinarily she would have chafed and complained, but now, to her surprise, she was glad. The monotony and boredom made the trip so much easier to bear. They had a deadening effect, so that she seemed to herself to be in a state of suspension. That was why she was almost comfortable.

The tall old man had been watching her, and now he came over. "Excuse me, please," he said. "You look familiar. Do I?"

"No."

"I am sorry. I thought I knew you. I am Fyodor Pavlovitch Voronov."

Voronov looked much more than ten years older. The hair he had left was perfectly white. He licked his lips. His face was apologetic and obsequious. Maria found it difficult to believe he was Michael's father.

"May I know who you are?" he said.

"Yes. Maria Ivanovna Danilova."

"Of course. That is why you looked familiar. My son was employed by your father at one time."

"Yes. I know."

370

Voronov licked his lips. "How?"

"I read about it. It was a famous case."

Voronov sighed, extended his hands and let them fall. "Eh!"

"Yes," said Maria.

"Gone. All gone."

"Yes."

"We are all responsible, you know — all of us — you, me, all we 'liberals,' smug, condescending, omniscient, with our government appointments and endless carping. We are responsible for the destruction of Russia."

He was leaning forward and almost whispering, as if telling a secret. He enjoyed believing that he had destroyed Russia. It gave him a feeling of the efficacy he had always lacked. It so perfectly explained why he was ruined now.

"Not exactly," said Maria. "I'm not guilty. I was smug and condescending, but not a 'liberal.' I was a dancer. I took no interest in politics. I still don't."

"But that's exactly it!" he said excitedly. "You took no interest. You paved the way."

The train crawled slowly down the track. The dead plains slowly passed.

"Perhaps you are right," she said.

"We are all guilty, all of us. We have destroyed our country. We have destroyed Russia. We deserve whatever happens to us."

Voronov spoke loudly and began to sob. None of the women paid any attention. Such outbursts were a normal occurrence.

"Do you know why I permit myself the luxury of attacking you?" he asked. "Do you know what I am?"

"No, I don't."

"Ask me. Ask me what I am."

"What are you, Fyodor Pavlovitch?"

"You are looking at the biggest fraud in Russia. There are some who helped the Bolsheviks with money or protection because they believed that was the best way to make Russia a constitutional republic. They did not know what Bolshevism was about. The Bolsheviks used them — used them and laughed."

"Yes. My father. He gave them money."

"There are even those who have joined the Bolsheviks because they believed the same thing or something similar. They thought Bolshevism would be good for the workers. They sincerely thought it was humanitarian."

Yes, she thought. My uncle. Orloff was one of those.

"At least they acted from honesty and strength. They were sincere. I on the contrary acted from dishonesty and weakness. I was a hypocrite. I still am. I'm probably lying right now. And if I am, I don't even know it. I welcomed the Bolshevik coup. I hailed it. I agreed that the seizure of a few buildings in Petrograd by a few Bolsheviks was a 'revolution.' I was sorry, you see; sorry for the 'poor workers in the factories'; sorry for the 'poor peasants on the farms'; sorry for everyone; sorry for the world.

"But now I see that I didn't really give a damn about the workers and the peasants. I still don't. I never will. It isn't possible to feel sorry for a peasant. Have you ever smelled one? They never bathe. A whiff indoors can knock you down. How can one feel sorry for someone like that? Anyone who says he does is lying. I'm the only one I feel sorry about. Do you know why? Ask me."

"Why?"

"Because I am a failure, for God's sake! Can't you see that? Are you so obtuse? A complete, total, utter failure — a self-made failure. I wanted to believe that everyone else needed my pity; that everyone else was as petty and evasive as I — as big a failure. I wanted to believe that success was impossible, because that made it easier to be a failure. Now you know what my 'humanitarianism' was. Do you understand now why I call myself a fraud?"

"Yes, Fyodor Pavlovitch. I understand."

"In fact, for the remainder of whatever time we may spend together, I would appreciate it if you would address me not as 'Fyodor Pavlovitch,' but as 'Fraud.' The truth will give me a little pride."

"Let me think it over, Fyodor Pavlovitch."

"Perhaps you shouldn't. I don't deserve it. It was because of my puny, microcosmic, infinitesimal, small, mean, putrid, petty, stupid, rotten, contemptible emotions — it was because of them that our country was destroyed; because of my aimless, meaningless mind." Voronov began chuckling, which grew into a laugh. "For instance, do you know where I am going now?"

"No, Fyodor Pavlovitch."

"Ask me. Ask where I am going."

"Where are you going?"

"I don't know. I'm just — going. Most people have some purpose, some reason, for going. You do, I suppose?"

"Yes."

"Not me. I'm just going; without purpose, aim or point, like my whole life. I am going only to create the pretense that I do have a point; that I really am going somewhere. Do you understand?"

"Yes."

"I don't. But so what! It's all nonsense, anyway. I'm just babbling. I don't know what I'm saying. Why do you waste your time listening to me? There's nothing worse than an old fool."

"What else can I do, Fyodor Pavlovitch?"

"Ha, ha, yes, that's right. You're trapped. There's nothing else you can do. You have no choice. You must be assaulted by my puny emotions, whether you like it or not."

Voronov loudly began to cry. "No! It's impossible! Kick me off! I can't let you sit near me. It would compound the crime. I betrayed my own son! I sent him to prison! Do you know why?"

"Why, Fyodor Pavlovitch?"

"Because I am a coward — a rotten, sneaking, dirty coward. Yet he went willingly to save me."

"Yes. I know."

"Do you? How?"

"I knew him once."

"It is because of me that he is a Bolshevik."

"Yes."

"You admit it! Kick me off! Spit on me! I deserve it!"

"Do you know, Fyodor Pavlovitch, I seriously believe that the wheels on our boxcar are square. Observe the strange rise and fall of our bodies. Could that be possible? — or am I just mad?"

"Yes, it is strange. There can be no doubt."

"You reassure me, Fyodor Pavlovitch. Obviously it's the work of the Communists."

"Obviously. Thank you very much. I see you are pregnant. Forgive me for asking, but are you married?"

"Yes."

"Who is your husband?"

"Telegin."

"The writer?"

"Yes."

"Another disillusioned 'liberal.' "

"Not at all. He has never been happier. He is a Party member and a perfect Communist."

Voronov was flustered. He had made a faux pas. He did not answer and Maria said nothing more. They sat side by side in silence. The train rose and fell. Its forward progress seemed composed only of accidental lunges. It was hot. Maria was very hungry and wanted to eat, but was afraid to take out her food. She would willingly have shared a bit with her companion, but involuntarily was afraid even of him. To be seen eating, after all, could be very risky.

Hours passed. At last they were in a station in a nameless town, and then standing on a deserted siding. No one even bothered to go to the door and look out.

A soldier passed, torso framed in the door, picking his way along the cross ties. One of the women in the corner stiffened.

"It's him," she whispered.

"Are you sure?" said another.

"He's one of them, I tell you," she said pointing.

"She's right," said a third. "I recognize him, too."

The women leaped to their feet, rushed to the door and jumped out upon him. He turned his head and raised his arm to unsling his rifle, but before he could do so he was smashed to the tracks with a loud shout. Then he disappeared in a cloud of skirts.

Voronov shuffled to the door. "What new lunacy is this?"

One of the women had the rifle by the barrel, repeatedly raised it and smashed the butt to the ground, as if violently working a churn. The shouts between her feet turned to screams, then died. The other women were on their knees flailing their arms, but after a time they got up and continued with their feet. Voronov saw not a body, but a pulpy mass wrapped in a rag.

"Impossible!" he said softly. "It cannot be!"

The Princess Lobanovsky was beside him, also staring, ignoring the pleas of the old woman to come away. It was the first thing she had taken an interest in for months. Suddenly she began to talk, pounding upon the car wall for emphasis.

"Kill him!" she chanted. "Kill him! Kill him!"

Her words seemed to have a sobering effect. The women returned to normal and began to leave the corpse. Blind with tears, Voronov staggered back to Maria and sat down.

"Yes, kill!" he sobbed. "Kill us all. Kill Russia. Kill the world. Kill everything. Kill everybody."

LII

"Yes, it is good cognac, isn't it," said Dolgorensky, admiring his glass. "You will be particularly interested to learn that it comes from the stock of Danilov, the late industrialist."

"Why should that be of particular interest to me?" said Marchenko.

"Think and you will remember, comrade Danilov."

"So you know."

"Yes. Since you played that amusing trick on your sister."

"So you know everything."

"Yes, Kolodsky described it one day with relish. He admires you very much. But I'm puzzled. You seem disappointed."

"I am."

"I'm sorry. Your disappointment disappoints me. Did you really believe you could conceal your identity forever? From us? You of all people should know better than that."

Stepan began to chuckle. He realized the reason for the smirks he had been noticing. "My compliments. You're right, of course. But after all, 'What's in a name? A rose by any other name . . .' et cetera."

Dolgorensky filled Stepan's glass. "I appreciate that. Yours is one of the few opinions of any value. And how sweetly that is put. So true. So luscious. What a pity it conflicts with Marxism-Leninism and is wrong. What a pity Shakespeare couldn't know that. Unfortunately it isn't that simple, you see. I'm sorry. The time has again arrived when someone must be tried for speculation, and the decision has been made that your unfortunate background qualifies you perfectly for the role. Your last service to the Cheka you love will be to demonstrate once again our 'scientific affection for humanity,' and our 'painstaking zeal to protect the people' from the 'anti-social crime of speculation.' Even by punishing our own men. And, at the same time, you will prove that you aren't one of our own men at all, but a bourgeois adventurer who somehow wormed his way in. Faultless Marxism-Leninism, isn't it? Your trial will be a dramatic and instructive event, in the course of which you will confess and hear a lecture, and then you will be sent to Solovetsky for some years. Even you could not improve on that, Stepan Ivanovitch. Or could you? Please tell me. I value your opinion so much."

"But surely you can't believe and endorse this nonsense!"

Dolgorensky shook his head. "You disappoint me again, Stepan Ivanovitch. I am surprised. You are being silly, which is uncharacteristic. Of course I don't — which is why I've done nothing for months. I sincerely admire the way you do business. You inherit the talent from your father. Why should good food be wasted on stupid farmers? You deserve all the profit you can get.

"No, the villains of the piece are the 'liberals.' Why must we always be plagued by them? They're enough to make one believe in God. There are several varieties of this species, as you know. There are, for instance, those who know nothing of politics, but support us in the nonsensical belief that Communism has something to do with 'freedom' — as if there were such a thing. Your father, for instance. There are those who know Communism has nothing whatever to do with 'freedom,' who know that discipline is what the people need — but who believe they need it for their own good. The fanatics who secretly enjoy man's suffering; who actually believe what they read in Marx; who actually believe our nonsensical slogans. Who admire our efficiency but misunderstand our purpose. Who actually believe our purpose is to distribute free bread. That would be your uncle, of course.

"Then there is the vague, silly blabbermouth, who doesn't know what he believes but wants to be 'well liked'; the sheep who wants to be in fashion, wants to be sophisticated, intellectual, *au courant*; the 'independent thinker' who wants to be 'part of something big,' because it's 'so exciting.' There's no shortage of these, God help us. There's no sense wasting time on them.

"And finally there is the most contemptible type of all: the type who knows perfectly well what Communism is about, but refuses to admit it even to himself — especially to himself; the sneak, the pickpocket, the swindler who believes his own story and fights to the death any attempt to save him.

"Unfortunately we need this menagerie now. Perhaps we always will. Not even Communism is perfect, apparently. This is why we must periodically conduct these nonsensical charades. We must help the 'liberals' deceive themselves.

"I detest insincerity, Stepan Ivanovitch. I believe you know that. I detest hypocrisy. There is nothing I admire more than a man who knows what he wants and takes it. That is why I am sincerely sorry that you must be

376

sacrificed — especially to satisfy these various weaklings. I feel drawn to you. We are alike. You are that rarest thing in the Party. You are a true Communist."

Dolgorensky filled Stepan's glass again. "To you, Stepan Ivanovitch. And to Communism."

LIII

It was a hot day in the dead of summer. The train had stopped between stations in a field. They had no idea where they were. The locomotive had broken down and would need a day to be repaired. And Maria, the Princess Lobanovsky, and her old woman had taken advantage of the delay to leave the train and search for food.

At last they found a farmhouse and bought some milk, real milk, and even some bread, a few potatoes and some salt — after convincing the wary farmer that they were not Chekist spies.

"We're poor ourselves," the farmer had said. "We want no trouble with the Committees of the Poor."

Then they had escaped into the woods like thieves, searching for a safe place to devour the contraband. Suddenly there was a noise behind them in the trees. Somebody was following them. Maria turned and saw the foliage move. The princess and the old woman apparently had heard nothing.

They were moving at a normal pace, which was too fast for Maria. She was beginning to get tired. She would soon have to stop. She looked behind again and in a clear space saw a large, mangy old yellow dog, slowly trotting along in pursuit. There was nothing to worry about after all.

Then they came to a deserted shack and sat in the shade against one of the broken walls. Maria took a gulp of the milk and passed the crock along to the others and leaned back to savor the taste. She was very tired. She was having periodic abdominal cramps, but she had tried to ignore the pains.

Maria felt the old woman beside her stiffen. She opened her eyes. The dog was only a few feet away, watching them silently. His eyes were yellow circles, surrounded by red. His ribs protruded through ill-fitting skin. He was swaying. Like all three women, he was ravenous.

Oblivious as usual, the princess put the crock down. The dog came forward. A long, yellow tongue descended into the milk.

Maria sprang up with a roar of fury. But the dog did not retreat. A lid rose and a yellow eye stared at her, but the yellow tongue noisily continued slurping, coated with the precious milk. She grabbed the crock and raised it high, but the dog followed her and jumped for it as she backed up. She kicked at him, but he did not seem to notice. She picked up a rock and threw it harmlessly into the trees, and the dog wobbled into them after it. She sat down heavily against the wall, holding the crock safely beside her.

But in a moment the dog was back. Once again he stood quite near, swaying slightly, his yellow eyes fixed on them, his yellow tongue dangling. As before, he started forward. Maria threw another rock, this time trying to hit the dog. But she missed. As before, the rock went harmlessly into the trees. But this time the dog did not follow it. She threw another rock, but now he simply turned his head to watch it go. He would not let them alone until he had the milk.

Beside her was the old woman, rigid with fright. And beside the old woman was the Princess Lobanovsky, young, strong, and oblivious to what was happening.

Maria shoved her. "Drive him off!"

But the Princess Lobanovsky remained comatose. As always, she simply sat and looked. Maria slapped her and shook her forcefully. "Will you drive him off, damn you!"

There was no response. Maria ripped a loose board from the wall of the shack with difficulty. It was wide, but fairly light and easy to hold with two hands. Her stomach cramped again. Again she ignored it.

The dog advanced to the crock, and she swung the board from her knees with all her strength and hit him on the side of the head with a crash. He yelped and ran away. She could hear him crashing through the foliage, yelping as he went. She leaned on the board and listened for a long time until, at last, the sounds died.

Then she fell heavily on her back, gasping for breath. She had never been so tired. She could barely breathe. At last she was able to raise herself on her elbows, and the old woman came over and helped her up. They continued the long walk back to the train. It seemed that hours passed. The sun was low. They did not know how far they were from the train.

Suddenly she felt a piercing, overwhelming pain. So violent was it that it stopped her dead, snapped her head back, and wrenched her mouth open for a scream. But she was unable to produce a sound. She had not known such pain was possible. It was; now she knew that, but it could not be borne. If only she could die at once. It was as if every organ, tissue, and cell of her body was being individually tortured by a sadist dedicated to his purpose.

She managed to extend a hand and steady herself against a tree. After a few minutes the pain subsided, first to the point where it was merely excruciating, then to the level of bare tolerability, then finally it petered out. As it did so, her mind began working again, and Maria realized that her time had come.

She was afraid, and she was angry. The thing that was about to happen was inevitable — a reminder that she had been used and could do nothing about it. She resented the fact that even at this distance, and long after she had discovered the trick they had played on her, Stepan and Telegin still controlled her destiny, perhaps decisively. She could not prevent it. She did not even know where she was now. And there was no doctor.

She got up and hurried again after the princess, who was already some distance away. Under no circumstances must she miss the train. But after a time the pain struck again, doubling her up once more, crippling her. Once again it stopped and she slowly staggered along.

Exactly how long it was before it struck again, she did not know. The world was becoming vague. But this time when the pain began again, her legs became numb and she collapsed under the nearest tree. The sky, leaves and branches above were whirling. The old woman's face appeared, bending low. The toothless mouth formed a smile. She nodded and patted Maria's arm. Somehow she had gotten the princess to sit at Maria's head and hold her hands.

The pain came again and then again. Now she was able to scream. What a relief it was to do so with all her might. She screamed and screamed. With the energy that remained, she struggled to free her hands, but the princess held them as if she were a child. It was a relief too to be held so tight. She felt as if a huge weight were pressing down on her. Hours passed.

It was very dark. The moon was full, but little of its light filtered through the trees. What if I burst, Maria thought. What if I split open and don't come together again. It feels as if it is happening now.

She heard a slap. Nothing happened. Something was wrong. The old woman was having trouble with the cord. She put it in her mouth and chewed it, but her elderly, toothless gums were ineffective. She roughly shook the Princess Lobanovsky.

"Bite it!" the old woman shouted in her ear.

The princess surprisingly did as she was told. Her teeth easily cut the cord through. The old woman held something tiny and wet, covered by a wrinkled, shrivelled skin. Again there was a slap. And this time the thing howled. How remarkable, Maria thought. Will such a thing actually become human?

380

The old woman dried it with her skirt and looked it over. She wrapped it in the remains of a rag and held it out to Maria.

"No! No! Take it away," she said.

"What do you mean, *barinya?*" said the old woman.

"I'm rid of it," said Maria. "I don't want it."

The infant began to cry loudly.

"All right," said Maria. "I'm sorry. Give it to me."

With the old woman's help, Maria weakly sat against the tree. The baby wailed. She reached out and pulled it close. Without hesitation it began to feed, rhythmically pulling at the nipple, its tiny hands pushing at the breast. The bald head moved up and down, the eyes in the wizened face shut tight. The infant looked exactly like Telegin.

"Ugly little brute, isn't it," she muttered. "What is it?"

"God has given you a boy, *barinya.*"

Maria snorted. "God, did you say?"

There was a sound in the woods and Voronov came running up to them through the trees. "I heard a noise," he said. "Where have you been, Maria Ivanovna? What has happened? Oh . . . yes. Excuse me. I'm sorry."

He was embarrassed by what he saw. And he was very agitated. "You must hurry, Maria Ivanovna. The train . . . ."

The old woman scrambled to her feet. "Yes, *barinya*, you must hurry."

She hurried off with the food and the princess in tow. Bright with moonlight just beyond the trees was an open field leading to a rise. From beyond the rise came a train whistle.

"Come, Maria Ivanovna," Voronov urged. "You must hurry."

"I can't, Fyodor Pavlovitch. Look."

"But you must. Let me help you."

Voronov was becoming more and more agitated. "But Maria Ivanovna, they say the area is full of Greens."

"You need not stay, Fyodor Pavlovitch. There is no reason in the world why you should feel an obligation."

"Yes, yes, I know that, I don't. But . . . "

"No. I can't."

He put his hands to his head; he began to shake. The whistle blew again.

"I am going to leave you!" he shouted. "Do you know why?"

"Please, Fyodor Pavlovitch. Go if you must."

"Because, as I told you before, I am a snivelling, repulsive coward. Now do you see? I'm going to prove it."

"Please, Fyodor Pavlovitch, go!"

"But don't you understand? Please, Maria Ivanovna! Give me the only shred of pride that is possible to me. Say it! Condemn me as a fraud. Say you know I am a snivelling, repulsive coward."

"All right," she said wearily. "You are a snivelling, repulsive coward."

"Yes, yes, I am!" he shouted. "You're right!"

He punched his temples, turned, and ran, still shouting. "Thank you!" he yelled.

Now he was crossing the moonlit field, still shaking his fists and shouting, and still she could hear him clearly. "Strike me down!" he bawled. "I believe! Strike me down! Please! End my misery! What ludicrous, impossible joke is this?"

Then he was at the top of the rise and gone. A few minutes passed. The train whistled again and started, chugging loudly. Smoke rose from just behind the rise. Then it faded; the train whistled again and was gone. The silence rushed in like water in a whirlpool.

She was alone, more alone than she had ever been. Even with the toothless mouth still pulling at her breast, she was alone. She did not know where she was. She could barely even stand up. No one could help her. No one would ever know if she died here.

I can't do it, she thought. No one could. I simply can't go on.

LIV

Stepan expertly adjusted his face. It was difficult to do. He could not help smiling at what was to come. He smoothed his mouth with his hand, but could not stop smiling. He took off his cap, changed his mind and put it back on. Then he knocked.

The door opened, he stepped forward into the light and deferentially removed the cap, nervously but without ostentation, a worried expression on his face.

Katerina Nikolaevna stared. "Stepan? You're alive?"

"Yes, aunt," he said shyly. "I'm alive."

Katya clapped a hand to her head. "But ...." She looked pointlessly from side to side. "Petya!" she called.

Orloff came to the door and looked out. His eyes narrowed and then widened. "Stepan? Is it you?"

"Yes, uncle, it's I, Stepan Ivanovitch, your nephew."

"Well, come in, come in! Excuse me! Sit down!"

Stepan looked deftly around. It was plain, neat and austere, as he had expected, with some cheap furniture and many books. Stepan nervously twisted his cap. "Thank you, uncle. I am still not sure I was right to come. Perhaps I wasn't."

"Of course you were!" said Katya. "This is a miracle."

Orloff spread his hands. "But ...."

"Yes, uncle, it is rather confusing, even to me. Painful, in fact. Which is why I am here, to tell the truth. It's a dismal story. That's why I was reluctant to come."

"Well, tell it, Stepan, tell it!" Orloff said. "I see you are a Chekist officer. You are a Party member, then?"

"Certainly."

"Another pleasant surprise. But why then haven't we heard from you?"

"Yes, Stepan," said Katya. "We really should be angry."

"I'm sorry," said Stepan. "Perhaps I was wrong. I thought it best to stay away. You see, I have taken another name."

"What name?"

"Marchenko."

Orloff stood mute for a moment. "I begin to understand."

"You see, uncle, I was captured — not killed — in the offensive of '16. So I had time to think. I knew that you were a Party member, of course. And as a good monarchist, I strongly opposed you. That is the truth. It would be stupid to avoid. In fact, I had often denounced you in public. And I had seen Socialist material before, both at home and at the front — in fact my assistant in the Gorokhovaya is a man who once worked for my father. I once caught him in the trenches handing out such literature, which he doesn't remember.

"But at the prison camp, I began to read these pamphlets for the first time. I began to realize that the truth was just as the Party's leaflets said: that there was no good reason for the war at all, that we Russians had no reason to be fighting the Germans and vice versa, that the war was nothing but a conflict between forces to whom we were pawns, that the real villains were the Capitalist exploiters in all countries.

"I resented that, of course. We all did. I began to wonder — since they were right about the war — if the rest of what the Socialists said could be true. So I read widely, beginning with Hegel. I read Marx and Engels and Lenin. And I saw, of course, that the war was a product of our diseased Capitalist system — a symptom which would flare up again and again. I realized that the only solution was to destroy the system, to . . . . Uncle, aunt, suddenly I am embarrassed. How stupid I am. I have been lecturing you — of all people — on the virtues of Socialism. Forgive me, but I am trying to describe the growth of my thought."

"Of course, Stepan," said Orloff. "Go on."

"Unfortunately, uncle, we do not know each other well."

"That will be remedied."

"I am a man of strong feelings and strong convictions. I know you are, too. Once I had made those discoveries I could not rest. My conscience could be clear only if I acted appropriately — only if I joined the movement to destroy that system. In fact, uncle, I experienced what has been called a 'religious conversion' — I'm speaking metaphorically, of course."

"I understand perfectly," Orloff said.

"Yes," said Katerina Nikolaevna.

"I realized what a selfish, dissolute, pointless life I led — a succession of meaningless, empty pleasures — and I decided to change it before it was too late; change it abruptly and completely. And I began this new life in the traditional revolutionary way with a change of name. I would have preferred the name chosen by comrade Dzhugashvili, but of course he had already taken it. So I decided to become 'comrade Marchenko.' "

"It's interesting that my experience was almost exactly the same," said Orloff. "Except, of course, for the change of name."

"Unfortunately there are other differences, uncle. As you said, I have not come to see you. I am guilty. In the first romantic flush of my conversion I wanted to avoid even the hint of opportunism. Perhaps I did not trust myself not to try to profit from our relationship. The fact that you are my uncle made me uncomfortable. In my opinion, not enough Party members feel the same way. That is why I decided to avoid you. Then my father was arrested. I suppose you know my father is dead?"

"Yes."

"I wonder, uncle, whether you can imagine this situation not as an abstract idea, not as part of a popular romance, but as a plain set of facts that was happening to me. Here was my father in the Gorokhovaya — and I was the officer in charge of his case! He was not a bad man, you know."

"I know that. He contributed heavily to the Party. Unfortunately, like so many, he was not adaptable. He refused to try."

"He did what he thought was right. He was wrong, but he was a man one could respect. That's inexcusably bourgeois, I know."

"Not at all," said Orloff. "You're right."

"Call it weakness, uncle, and it probably was. But the truth is that as the days passed this problem devoured me. What could I do? I told myself that there must be a way out, all the while secretly aware that there wasn't. I developed the habit of walking in his corridor, of listening at his door. Yes, aunt, listening at his door. Only that barrier was between us, very thin and yet so thick. And through it I imagined I could hear him breathing. Day and night, I searched for some way to intercede."

Stepan jumped up and nervously walked around the room, his nervousness nicely balanced between ostentation and subtlety.

"I am sorry," he said coldly. "Please forgive this disgusting outburst. I am very embarrassed. I don't know what I'm saying."

Katya jumped up. "Don't be silly, Stepan." She drew him to his chair. He expertly rubbed his eyes.

"Uncle, the truth is that I thought then of coming to see you, of asking you to intercede. But I knew all along, of course, that I could not — that in fact I could do nothing. I knew you would refuse me, angrily, contemptuously, as you should — as I would have refused you — as a man whose

Socialist principles had failed to meet the test. I knew you would have said that the use of influence, of personalities, of family relationships, was impossible. That it was cheating, the very thing we had destroyed as part of Tsarism. Socialist justice would have to run its course."

"How remarkable," said Orloff. "Did you know I was at the Gorokhovaya to see him? To discuss a proposal from the Food Trust?"

"In the Cheka we know everything, uncle."

"He rejected it, of course. Even though it cost him his life."

"Yes," Stepan said. "He would."

"When I left him, I stood in the same corridor you mention, possibly in the same spot. It occurred to me that I could see comrade Marchenko, the officer in charge of his case. You see, Stepan, I too had a moment of weakness. But I didn't see you. I took the same course you did. When I left the building, by the way, I met your sister. She had been to see you, I assume?"

Stepan nervously lit a cigarette. How convenient! He had not known that. He rubbed his hands to show he was perspiring, the movement nicely balanced between ostentation and subtlety.

"I had not known that," he said. "She had. Yes." Stepan smiled. The moralists were right. It felt good to tell the truth.

"Strange that she didn't say anything to me," said Orloff.

"She had not seen you for years, uncle. She did not know you. You are a Red Army general. Perhaps she was afraid of you."

"Masha? Afraid of me?"

"She had just left my office. She had not known either, of course, that I am Marchenko. I remember that afternoon so well. She came into the room, walking slowly. She was afraid. I was looking out the window. I did not want to turn around. But I had to. In fact, I wanted to — more than anything else. I had not seen any member of my family for years. I had refused to see my father. I could not refuse my sister, too. I turned. And Masha saw my face.

"Uncle, like you I have been in war. I have seen the most intense emotions. But I have never seen anything so intense on a human face. Masha actually shook with relief. She had to reach for a desk to keep her balance.

"And then! Then, aunt! I had to deliberately turn her relief into despair. Almost as if I were toying with her, almost as if I were playing a joke. I tried to explain, but she could not understand. Unfortunately, she is not a Communist. She fell on her knees. She crawled. She prostrated herself. I could even feel her trembling as she tugged at my legs. My little sister pleading for her father — our father. And I had to refuse her."

Stepan covered his face and rose. Uncontrollably, his mouth tried to smile. Through his fingers, he saw a tear in his aunt's eye.

"What am I, uncle?" he shouted. "Am I a monster without human feelings? An incurable victim of Tsarism? Or am I just a weakling not good enough to be a Socialist? Tell me!"

With an obvious — but not ostentatious — effort, Stepan pulled himself together. "I am sorry," he said coldly. "This is unforgivable. You really should throw me out. Excuse me. I should not have come."

He took his cap and turned to go, but Orloff stopped him.

"You are so strict, Stepan," Orloff said.

"So are you, uncle."

"Yes, but you are strict in the wrong way. You see, Stepan, we are not simply making adjustments here. We are remaking the world — from the beginning. The hero of this greatest drama of all time is History — precise, unruffled, implacable, irresistible. And History's instrument is the Communist Party, the most perfect machine in this age of machines.

"In a venture of this magnitude there are problems and misfortunes. There are horrors. That is unfortunate. I wish it could be otherwise. But it is inevitable. Childbirth, they say, is not a pleasant experience. Unfortunately there is no other way to produce a child. And soon the pain of childbirth ends. The mother is happy; she has a child.

"Now compare today's horrors with the sweeping rightness of our goal. Idealism at last made practical. Justice finally embodied. And you and I are instruments of the instrument, Stepan. Think of it! The earth is pregnant with Communism and we are the doctors. We are being used by History. When we sign a document, issue a decree, make a plan — yes, and deal logically with our enemies — it isn't we who sign, decree, plan and deal logically, but History. History moves our arms as surely as a machine moves its pulleys. And the same applies as surely to the people who oppose us. They too, all of us, are part of this shattering drama.

"So you see, Stepan, you are too strict with yourself and at the same time not strict enough. What are our fleeting, puny, inconsequential emotions, our likes and dislikes, our personal problems, in comparison with all this? When the war ends and we can devote all our resources to the tasks of reconstruction, we will build a paradise — not after death in some imaginary place, but here on earth. After the wasteful, inefficient Capitalist system is destroyed, we will create an abundance that will make Croesus seem poor. The cause of oppression and war will be removed. Man will scientifically be made happy.

"No one has the right to prevent all this. No one is immune from the progress of History. We are all expendable. What happened to your father was

387

unfortunate, of course. But he did what he had to. As you said, he caused it himself. You are not to blame. You, too, did what you had to do. You would die just as well. I realize this is easier for me to say than for you to hear, but it is true."

"Thank you, uncle," Stepan said bitterly. "I'm reassured. Unfortunately, it no longer makes a difference."

"What do you mean?"

"They're kicking me out. My trial has been set."

"What?"

"Dolgorensky has found out who I really am. It's a matter of 'bad blood,' you see. He is even suspicious of you, uncle. He has accused me of speculation, which is ironic. I have confiscated more than anyone else."

"Dolgorensky is deliberately cruel," said Katya. "He enjoys it. He has always plotted against you, Petya. He is an embarrassment to the Party. He has no idea what Communism is."

Orloff was seething. Katya was right. Dolgorensky understood nothing but the rules and regulations. He never had. He had no understanding whatever of character. He was cruel, not because of duty but because he liked it. He was not a true Communist at all. Stepan had sacrificed everything for the Party, and now Dolgorensky was trying to destroy him. It was unjust. Stepan had earned the protection of the Party, whether Orloff was the one who gave it or not. Their relationship — by marriage — was irrelevant. Saving Stepan would be a service to the Party. Refusing to help him, in fact, would be disloyal to the Party.

"I'll take care of it," said Orloff.

"It's no use," said Stepan. "He has made up his mind."

"I know that," said Orloff. "So we will simply ignore him. Report to the Gorokhovaya as usual and continue your duties."

Stepan nodded, too overcome with emotion to speak. Orloff embraced him in a powerful hug.

"It's good to have you back, comrade Marchenko," Orloff said. "What Communism needs is more men like you."

LV

How long she had been walking she was not sure. Was it weeks or months? Or was it really only days? For a long time she had seen absolutely no one. The sun rose and set, rose and set, but it was as if time as a dimension had ceased to exist. Was she just imagining it all? Was she just the prisoner of a dream? Where was she going? She knew only that it was necessary to keep moving in a reasonably straight line, moving endlessly into eternity. She was doing so, the dust was rising around her boots, the brush bending, the mud sucking. But it seemed, at the same time, that she was overhead, watching and studying herself, small, pathetic, struggling, staggering, tottering and falling — apparently making little if any progress. What was the point? Was there a point? What kept the curious, pathetic thing moving?

The baby was no problem. She had made a sling and carried it on her back. But her breasts ached, the sensation dull, steady and throbbing.

She loosened the sling and put the child down. She selected a tree with a properly rough bark, and rubbed her back at the inaccessible point between her shoulders against it. That was the only place she could not reach the lice. What a pleasure it was to rub slowly and carefully at the spot. To think that only a few years ago, she had not even known there was such a pleasure. Perhaps there were still other pleasures she did not know about..

Slowly and carefully, she maneuvered her back across the bark. Where had she picked up the lice? From Voronov? From the old woman? Were they the gift of the Princess Lobanovsky? It was impossible to tell, of course, but without the lice, she would not have enjoyed rubbing her back against the tree. And she was enjoying it so much.

At length she had rubbed everywhere and sat down to rest. Something was crawling across her stomach. She dug through her clothes angrily and found it, bloated and dark, filled with her blood. Does this have any political significance, she wondered? It must. She squeezed it vengefully between her fingernails and it popped.

The infant began to cry. She shuddered, again aware of the pain in her breasts. She exposed the one that hurt less and gave it to the infant, who began to nurse. It was as if an animal were chewing madly at her nipple. Something was wrong. Drops of sweat appeared on her upper lip. The pain was so intense that it drew her head back, and she banged it repeatedly against the tree so the infant could take his fill.

But the child was not satisfied. He still cried as loudly as before. She squeezed the breast herself. Nothing happened; it was dry. She adjusted her clothes and got up, shouldered the infant and set off. She had to find milk immediately.

Again she was plodding through the dust. The day was hot. She felt slightly feverish. She knew only that she must lift her feet and put them down. Then there was a road. A woman passed going the other way, head bowed, also plodding on an errand of her own.

"How far to the nearest town?" Maria asked.

But the woman did not answer or even break stride. Head bowed, she plodded on as if Maria did not exist.

Then there was another road with troops and civilians going both ways. There were long lines of wagons and artillery. Which army it was, she did not know. And she didn't have the slightest interest in learning.

"Please," she said to various people. "Just a minute. Listen. Please!"

No one paid any attention. It was as if she were stupidly talking to the rocks in a rapid.

There was a camp some distance ahead, off the road in the trees, and she walked toward it. Hundreds of soldiers lounged about, talking, washing, chewing and spitting sunflower seeds. Some of them called to her. She did not hear a thing. Beyond the camp among some rocks at the point farthest away from the road, someone was cooking meat over a fire in a big pot. A cow, a real cow, was tethered to a tree. Maria had read about them. She had even seen a picture of one once. And sitting on a big rock beside the cow was a man milking it.

His strong hands moved up and down. Jets of milk spouted out. Maria could hear it pinging in the pail.

"Please give me some milk," she said.

He did not look up. "In exchange for what?"

"I have nothing."

"Then you'll get no milk."

His strong hands did not miss a stroke. The milk spouted out. The cow lazily flicked her tail.

"Please," she said. "My baby must have milk." She unslung the baby and held it out.

"There's nothing so special about your brat. Or anybody's. If not killed off, they turn into people. Ain't that right?"

Maria sank to her knees. "Please! Are you human?"

"Sure I am. That's why you'll get no milk."

"What army is this?"

"This is Yudenitch's crowd, it is."

"Which side are you on?"

"I don't know, really. Yudenitch, they say, is marching on Petrograd. Me, I'm on my side."

Maria began to cry loudly. She could no longer hold back the tears. It did not in the least humiliate her, as it would have a short time ago. "Oh, God!" she sobbed. "Oh, my God!"

The man looked up. Still he did not miss a stroke. He was young and strong, but his eyes were weak. The pupils were indistinct, the color was vague. The vision seemed normal, but they were eyes which never looked at anything very long or ever saw anything important.

"There is something you could give in exchange." He smiled.

"But there isn't, I tell you. I haven't a thing."

"Sure you do. We could have some fun."

"Fun?" The idea was too ridiculous. Surely he knew there was no such thing. "Can't you see I'm filthy? I'm full of lice."

The man grinned broadly. He was missing several teeth. He looked even more stupid than before. "So what?" he said. "Who isn't?"

"No," she said. "Absolutely not."

"Suit yourself. But you can't expect any milk without something to exchange. You're a *boorzhui*, ain't you? That's Capitalism."

Maria became aware of the hard, metallic pressure against her side. It was the long blue barrel of her father's gun. The man was again ignoring her. The milk was pinging in the pail.

"Perhaps you are right, comrade," she said.

She loosened her clothes and the man looked up. Again she saw the stupid grin.

Then his face fell. "What . . . what are you doing, citizen?"

She waved the gun. "Get out of here."

The man got up and moved away. Suddenly he had lost his self-assurance. "What are you doing?" he asked.

"I'm robbing you. That isn't Capitalism. It's Communism."

"Yes, citizen. You're right. It is."

"Now you get out of here. Run! Don't come back! If I see you around here again, I'll blow your head off. Any objections?"

"No, *barinya,* no! I'm glad to do it."

The man turned and ran. He did not miss a stride. He did not look back.

She reshouldered the infant and picked up the pail. It was already nicely heavy with milk. Then she ran off in the opposite direction, as fast as she could without spilling any, pail in one hand, gun in the other. She ran a long time, choking, stumbling.

Finally, she put the pail down and fell heavily to the ground on her knees, gasping for air. Then she removed the sling.

The baby was dead.

The baby had been dead for some time. It was already getting stiff. She put it carefully on the ground and stared at it. There had been no point to it all. It had all been a waste. Everything always was a waste. It was just another totally meaningless death, the sort that happened daily.

She picked up a dead branch and began to dig. It occurred to her with horror that the body might be eaten, so she dug as deeply as she could. Then she laid the baby down. She covered it with dirt and then with stones and branches.

She picked up the pail and drank some milk. It was good. The baby was lucky; it was dead. But Maria was unfortunately still alive. She returned the gun to its place against her skin.

Then she stood erect and turned back toward Petrograd, concentrating once again on moving toward her goal.

LVI

Stepan had never felt so well. His mood, in fact, surpassed exultation. A sense of well-being flooded him. It was almost as good as being drunk. He had been promoted shortly after Yudenitch's defeat. Only a few hours before, he had been told he would soon be transferred to Moscow.

The only thing that bothered him now was Tata. Lately, she had become so tiresome, so dull. It showed up clearly in her dancing. She had developed the annoying habit of staring at him — just staring. She disapproved of him, of course. She was such a bourgeoise. Stepan would have to send her away. He needed a gay and eager woman — a woman who would adore him as a god.

He went to the desk and switched on the light. What better way to end the day than to begin his next literary composition. He really did enjoy them. He suspected he was something of a literary artist. Perhaps they could be published — in the public interest. He would speak to Telegin when next they met.

"My dear Masha," he wrote, in his father's flowery, old-fashioned hand-writing. "The weather here is perfect."

How trite! he thought. Who cares about the weather? Perhaps his talent was really of a different sort. Perhaps the letters should be framed and hung in the Hermitage. He might even do a tour at the Commissariat of Finance, designing new issues of paper rubles. They too — backed by nothing — were forgeries of a sort. He laughed silently. He had to admit that that was not trite. He would have to remember to tell it to Telegin.

An idea of unusual interest occurred to him. An inspiration. So far he had been writing the letters straight. His purpose had been to establish their authenticity. But now that he had, why not begin some variations? Why not give Maria something to wonder about?

"I have been reading Marx again, Masha," he wrote, "and for the first time, I begin to see the truth of what he says. I have been wrong. Take, for instance, the labor theory of value. Masha, why don't you ... ?"

With mounting satisfaction, Stepan savored his work, the authenticity of the handwriting and the syntax, and now the interjection of Socialist philosophy. He had surpassed himself. He had actually played a joke within the joke. His artistry would impress even Telegin.

Of course, this did not surpass his visit to his uncle. What could? He had won by using Dolgorensky's knowledge of his true identity, coupled with his own perfect knowledge of Dolgorensky's and his uncle's personalities. Like the greatest of generals, he had turned his own weakness into a strength. He had turned his enemy's weapon into his own. How annoyed — and frustrated — Dolgorensky was.

True, the victory at his uncle's was more practical than what he was doing now. But, speaking artistically, what he was now doing compared very favorably. He added a few more lines to develop the idea, being careful not to overdo it. He studied the result. It was a work of genius.

A sense of power flooded him. His mind was an irresistible force, a locomotive rushing down blazing tracks, a bullet felling its target, a fist smashing a jaw. He was a man of total will — a man of steel.

If only he could know Maria's feelings as she read his lines. It was unsatisfying to have so small an audience, and furthermore, to be denied its applause. If only Maria could know the truth. If only she were here!

Suddenly he got the feeling that he was not alone. It was silly, of course, only the result of what he had been thinking, and he shrugged it off; but its effect was enough to ruin his concentration. He could not get the letter ended. He looked into the darkness beyond his desk, and saw nothing. He heard nothing — which made it impossible to understand why the hair on the back of his neck was bristling. It was nonsensical, of course; stupid, in fact; there was no reason for it. But to get the thing finished without wasting more time, he went to the wall and switched on the light.

Maria faced him from the other end of the room.

He started violently. Was this real? He pressed his eyelids together. It was. And the eeriness was compounded by the fact that she did not look alive. She sat in a chair and did not move. Her face was white and completely without expression. But her eyes were wide, bright and piercing. Her vision was strangely direct and concentrated, as if it had intensified and at the same time expanded. He knew it could not be, but she did not seem to blink.

A queasy smile appeared on Stepan's face. "Masha?" he asked. "Is that you?"

Maria rose slowly, mechanically. Her mouth opened and began to move. "Good evening, comrade Marchenko."

394

Stepan's smile became more secure. Maria's voice proved she was real. He was reassured. He began to take a step. This would be amusing, after all.

"Do not move, comrade Marchenko. Not even a little bit."

He was looking into the muzzle of a revolver. And as he watched, Maria cocked the hammer, as she had been shown.

Stepan stopped. "What is that, Masha?" he said.

"Do you know why I am here, comrade Marchenko?"

"Why do you call me 'comrade Marchenko'?"

"You *are* comrade Marchenko, aren't you?"

"Yes. Certainly. But . . . ."

"Do you know why I am here?"

"No, Masha. Of course not. How would I know that? But I'm glad you are."

"That is good to know. I am here because you murdered my father. Surely you remember him. This was his revolver."

Stepan stared at the muzzle like a victim hypnotized by a snake. Her voice came from behind it, metallic and slow.

"That's not true!" said Stepan. "That's unfair! You hurt me, Masha. There was nothing I could do."

She looked at the desk. "What were you writing?"

"That? Oh, that's nothing. A letter. That's all."

She went to the desk and picked it up. "Yes, I see. It is a letter." She threw it to him. "Read it, comrade Marchenko!"

"Masha — "

"Read it!"

Stepan hesitated, but Maria had already seen the letter. He read it through, mumbling and slow. "My dear Masha, the weather here is perfect . . . . "

The man of steel looked up at her. In the corner of his mouth he felt a twitch. It was invisible, he knew, but he could feel it.

"I wanted to protect you, Masha. I knew how upset you and Mama would be to know the truth . . . I thought . . . I wanted to shield you."

Stepan's voice slowly trailed off. It had made no impression on Maria. Her face was still and expressionless as before.

He became angry. What right had Maria to break in here like this? The world had changed. No longer could Maria bully him as she used to. What right had she to subject him to this game? Everyone was always trying to thwart him — carping, complaining, scheming behind his back. No one ever gave him a chance.

"Look here, Masha, I am a government official. Do you realize that? I am an officer of the Extraordinary Commission. You have no right to break in here like this. Now give me that gun before you get into trouble."

He made as if to step forward, but did not. She was smiling, smiling without malice, as if they shared some amusing joke.

"I'm willing to forget this, Masha. I promise!"

Suddenly the man of steel weakened. His body shook. His face twitched. He cried. His mouth was completely out of control.

"I couldn't help it, Masha. I'm innocent! There was nothing I could do. I tried. I begged them. They wouldn't listen. You don't know them. They almost got me, too, Masha. They're against me. They all are. They're rotten, Masha. They want me to fail. All I want is to make something of myself. No one ever gave me a chance. Masha, please. He was my father, too. I'm just as sorry as you are."

"That is good, comrade Marchenko. That is very good. I am very glad to hear that you are sorry. It is very good to know."

"Masha, please!" he shouted. "I am your brother!"

"You are mistaken, comrade Marchenko. My brother is dead. He was killed in the 1916 offensive. You are comrade Marchenko, a government official."

"Masha! Please!"

"Say it! Tell me who you are."

"I am comrade Marchenko . . . ."

"Yes. And therefore you cannot be my brother. You can't be two people at once. Isn't that right?"

"Yes."

"You are not my brother, are you?"

"No. I am not your brother."

"My brother is dead."

"Your brother is dead."

"Thank you, comrade Marchenko. You explain it very well."

"Masha, please! For the love of God . . . ."

The gun bucked. The barrel blazed. Blood appeared on comrade Marchenko's tunic. He looked down at it with curiosity and covered it with a hand, but the stain escaped around it and through his fingers. He looked up at Maria and shuffled forward a few feet. On his face was a peculiar smile.

His neck was extended. His lips were pursed. He was trying to say something. And at last he got it out.

"Mama . . . ."

Maria squeezed the trigger again. The bullet slammed comrade Marchenko into the wall, against the light switch. The lights went out. Just as they did so, she saw him fall. She took the lamp from the desk and looked for him.

She heard a tapping and found him behind the desk. The heel of his boot was twitching against the floor. His eyes were open. He was looking at her.

Comrade Marchenko was very dead.

Part VI
Michael Voronov

LVII

Orloff rubbed his temples. It would do no good. He knew that. But he did it anyway, which made him angry. His head ached. His eyes were burning. There was an unusually bad taste in his mouth. And he was tired, more tired than he had ever been before. Tired to the bone, but at the same time unable to sleep.

He was still suffering from the revelation of the truth about Stepan. Stepan had deliberately lied to him, deceived him. Stepan had used him to avoid the punishment he deserved. Stepan had committed the worst possible crime — a crime against the State. He had been a hypocrite, a speculator, an enemy of the people — pretending all the while to fight speculation. Dolgorensky unfortunately had been right about him. Perhaps there really was something to his theory of "bad blood." But how then would Orloff explain himself? His blood was just as "bad."

But Orloff refused to admit that he was even more depressed by his recent transfer to the Cheka. He refused to admit that he hated the work. It was necessary. He knew that. It was worthwhile. The fight against the speculators was going very well. As always, he had obeyed the Central Committee's orders without question. But while Michael had harshly applauded the change, as Orloff had expected, Orloff himself painfully missed the military life he loved.

Indeed, the Central Committee had assigned Orloff to investigate Stepan's murder and find his killer, which made Orloff even more uncomfortable. That, too, was necessary. Someone had defied the Party. But, although he knew it made no sense, Orloff felt that by conducting the investigation he was somehow siding with Stepan.

Why had his transfer to the Cheka been necessary? Was it because the corruption was worse than at any time under Nicholas? So bad that the Party proclaimed special "Party Weeks" to fight it? Was it because the Extraordinary Commission to Combat Speculation, Sabotage and Counter-Revolution was so corrupt itself that no one could be found within it to do the job? Were the Chekists using him as Stepan had? Using his reputation as a cloak behind which they were still stealing? Why were so many Chekists arrested, and then not only released but also rehired? Indeed, if, as Marx said, conditions create the society, then was the cause of the current corruption the conditions the Communists themselves had created? Was it possible that Communism was even more corrupt than the monarchy?

Such questions were, of course, nonsensical. He tried to put them from his mind. But as soon as he did so, the questions were back again.

Katya was sitting near him, talking. Orloff had always particularly enjoyed her voice — soft, husky, very low. But of late it was strained and harsh. He refused to listen, but she continued.

"The Tsarists were less hypocritical," Katya said.

"What does that mean?" Orloff asked.

Katya sighed. "Nothing, Petya."

"I want to know!"

"No, you don't. You weren't listening. You never do."

Orloff shrugged. Lately it was even unpleasant to touch her. When he did, he felt her tense. She had refused him for so long, he no longer made advances. He no longer even tried to talk about it.

They did not know it, but the so-called Revolution was beginning to "devour its own." They were already out of date. The Revolution had passed them by. They were both the sort that is the bane of every utopian — that is, impossible — movement when it has entered middle age: the sort that insists on living by the movement's principles, and thereby shows how impossible they are; the sort that becomes an embarrassment and reproach to those more pliable and "realistic." They were the sort of whom people say, "He was born too late."

The only thing Orloff was satisfied about lately was that he had helped Maria — as he had promised. She had left Telegin and returned to Petrograd. Orloff had gotten her a job in a Soviet bureau. From time to time he called to see if she was all right.

There was a knock and Orloff opened the door. It was Dolgorensky, grinning like a Cheshire cat.

"Good evening, comrades," Dolgorensky said. "Am I intruding?"

"No," said Orloff, to his own annoyance.

"That is good," said Dolgorensky. "I am glad. We so rarely see each other, Petya. Isn't that strange? After all, we work in the same building. Of course, we're both very busy. Being a Chekist isn't easy, is it? I don't mean to defame your glorious Red Army, but the Cheka is the real essence of Communism. Without the Cheka, Communism could not exist."

"Surely you're not here to explain the Cheka."

Dolgorensky snapped his fingers. "You're right. Thank you, Petya. You are such a perfect Communist — if I may say so without embarrassing you. That, of course, is why I admire you so.

"I am here to present your nephew's replacement. You will work together closely. I knew you would want us to come."

Orloff became aware that someone was standing behind Dolgorensky in the darkness.

"May we come in?" Dolgorensky asked.

"Of course," Orloff said, and stood aside. The figure came forward into the light. It was Golovin. He had not changed in the past six years. He seemed no older. His expression was the same. It was as if he had just come from the Siberian prison he used to patrol. Like Dolgorensky, he was smiling. The only change was that Golovin now wore the uniform of an officer in the Cheka.

"You know each other, I believe," said Dolgorensky. "Victor Karpovitch Golovin."

"So good to see you again," Golovin said.

He crossed the room to Katya, bowed before her, and sat down. Katya was frozen with horror.

"It is remarkable," he said. "You have not changed a bit. You're as charming as ever, Katerina Nikolaevna."

"Victor Karpovitch is a true Communist," Dolgorensky said. "One of the best. His help will be invaluable to you, Petya."

"You put me in a mood to reminisce," Golovin laughed. "Remember your attempts to escape, Peter Sergeievitch? Remember the time I caught you outside the wall? So much has changed since then, hasn't it?" He pointed at Katya. "You were cross with me when you came to visit. Do you remember, Katerina Nikolaevna?" He snapped his fingers. "How stupid of me! I embarrass you. Forgive me, please."

"Suddenly I realize why you are both so startled," said Dolgorensky. "In your good Communist minds is the logical question: How is it that a member of the Capitalist power structure, an oppressor, a lackey of the Imperialists — one of Bloody Nicholas's prison guards — how is it that such a man is now a Chekist officer?"

"I had no choice," Golovin said.

"Victor Karpovitch is a product of the best proletarian stock. He had been victimized just as much as his prisoners. The Capitalists had forced him to betray his class interests. Victor Karpovitch was not responsible. He was oppressed like everyone else."

"It was just as you told me yourself, Peter Sergeievitch."

"The Capitalists had trapped Victor Karpovitch in poverty. They forced him to become a prison guard to eat."

"You were right all along, Peter Sergeievitch," said Golovin.

"Then Victor Karpovitch saw the light."

"I had been a Communist all along and I didn't even know it."

"You should take pride, Petya," said Dolgorensky. "Another triumph added to your glorious Communist career."

"I shall be grateful to you always," said Golovin. "It was because of you that the Capitalists kicked me out."

Golovin and Dolgorensky exchanged a smile. It was even better than they had expected. Orloff's attempt to thwart Dolgorensky had been reversed. And he was finally paying well for having humiliated Golovin. Golovin had replaced Stepan completely. He had even taken Stepan's woman, Anna Andreevna, whom Golovin had first met long ago in Siberia. Yet he wondered if Katya had ever told Orloff the full truth.

They sat quite near each other and he stared at her, smiling slyly, like one conspirator to another. Her eyes glazed, she shuddered and bowed her head. And with a thrill that was almost sexual, he realized that she had told Orloff nothing.

Suddenly, Katya was very conscious of her body. The man who had raped her was staring at her, and Katya felt strangely naked, as if Golovin could see through her clothes. She could endure it only if she did not look at him. She sat still as death, staring at her lap, her knees pressed together tightly.

"There is, in fact, a second reason for our presence," said Dolgorensky. "The Central Committee has decided to conduct spontaneous demonstrations across Russia in your nephew's honor."

"Demonstrations?" Orloff heard himself say. "To honor Stepan?"

"I knew you would be pleased," said Dolgorensky. "I can well understand your emotion. I would feel the same. He was your relative by blood, wasn't he, Katya?"

"But how can this be?" Orloff asked.

"Yes, Petya, think of it!" Dolgorensky said. "The flags, the crowds, the speeches, the eulogies — and the hero's burial in the Kremlin wall."

"Stop it!" said Katya. "Either stop it, or get out!"

Dolgorensky's full, feminine lips pursed. People rarely spoke to him like that. And when they did, the words were usually their last. But this time, he was glad to hear them.

404

"Forgive me, Katya," he said. "I assumed you would understand. As you know — comrade Lenin has said it — we face serious problems during this period of Socialist reconstruction. There are countless rotten remnants of Capitalism. And until we develop the new Soviet man who will eliminate and prevent these problems, we unfortunately must use the man we have. Petya, isn't that right?

"The man we have is still infected with Capitalism and therefore demoralized. He is the worker refusing to produce simply because he must go hungry — unaware that it is objectively valuable that he go hungry. He is the small shopkeeper in the Alexandrovsky market, gouging out his so-called profit as usual by capitalizing on that hunger. He is the *kulak* in Tambov, rotten with the archaic passion for land, creating that hunger by withholding his grain, greedily demanding some trinkets in exchange.

"Such a man unfortunately needs constant inspiration. He needs periodic dramatic stimuli to activate his puny brain — somewhat as the bell activated Pavlov's dogs. Unfortunately the problem has not changed since Tiberius. And what better, more satisfying spectacle could there be than a mass demonstration for the murdered man — our self-sacrificing, ascetic, fallen comrade Marchenko. That young hero, that perfect example of the new Soviet man we are trying to create."

Orloff stared at him, still somewhat dazed. He could not understand. What was the point?

"But you yourself denounced Stepan," said Katya. "He was to be tried!"

Dolgorensky smiled. "Correct. And as you should remember, he was not tried because you interceded, Petya. But then he was alive. Now he is dead. The situation has changed. And as Leninists, we must be flexible and change with it. Then, we could have produced a trial proving that the lies told about the Cheka are lies; that we are working always to protect the people — to protect the Revolution; that Socialist justice is exactly that — justice. And that we apply it even to one of our own. But this — this is even better. It shows how right you were to intercede, Petya. Thank you.

"There is, in fact, still another benefit our fallen comrade will provide. And that will come when the murderer is tried. How is your investigation proceeding, Petya?"

"It is proceeding. There is still nothing new."

"Time is short, Petya. We must have this assassin. His trial will be public, giving our citizens and the world a good taste of the might and glory of Soviet justice. A touching pageant will be produced, starring the departed but living spirit of our fallen comrade, the perfect Soviet man — the perfect Chekist —

struck down by a vicious criminal. Using the Socialist principles of Dr. Pavlov, all the frustrations, irritations, hates and angers of those of our citizens who are less than perfect will be focused on the inhuman killer — exactly as the sun's rays are focused by a magnifying glass.

"That is why the Party has also decided that Marchenko's previous existence as your nephew did not happen. He was not your nephew. That is a lie. And there is nothing the Party hates more than lies. It was the truth when Marchenko was to be tried, but now that he is to be eulogized, it isn't. And therefore it must not be mentioned — by anyone to anyone. It might give the false impression that we in the Cheka are careless and allowed a bourgeois, a former officer, to penetrate our ranks. People might believe that our perfect Communist wasn't perfect, and this of course would be a totally false impression — a lie — exactly what the Party is fighting to destroy. So the man we bury in the wall will be simply Marchenko.

"Which reminds me, Petya, of why I am here. In my excitement, I had forgotten. Isn't that amusing? As good Communists, we should get to business, shouldn't we?" Dolgorensky unbuttoned his tunic. He smiled. His lush, feminine lips were unnaturally red.

"You see, comrades, the demonstrations will spontaneously erupt next week. We are organizing them now. Katya, you would be dumbfounded, if I may say so, by the preparation necessary to produce such spontaneous demonstrations. The orders must be sent to all chiefs of divisions. Why, the printing of the wall newspapers alone . . . . Katya, we will bring the country completely to a halt. All state employees will spontaneously volunteer to attend. It is fair to say, in fact, that the degree of spontaneity is determined by the amount of preparation. A completely spontaneous demonstration is one that has been completely prepared.

"The main demonstration of course will spontaneously erupt in Moscow, and there we need someone to deliver the eulogy, someone known to the country as a hero — someone with a stainless reputation for truth. Can there be any doubt, Petya, any doubt at all about whose name immediately jumps forth? I suggested you. And Ilyitch approved. There was no other choice. This is no time for false modesty, Petya. After all, we aren't going to mention it — because it simply isn't true — but, after all, he *was* your nephew. You *do* have emotions, as do we all, and you will be all the more effective, with the inner satisfaction of knowing that you are praising him.

"Remember, Petya, that it was because he was your nephew that you interceded and so beautifully proved me wrong."

Dolgorensky removed some papers from his tunic. "It was comrade Trotsky himself who suggested that, as a busy Chekist investigating

406

Marchenko's murder, you might find it tiresome to prepare a speech. So we've done it for you. Comrade Telegin wrote it, Lunacharsky's deputy. He volunteered. But, of course, you know him. He is married to your niece."

"Yes."

"I so enjoy family loyalty. Don't you, Victor Karpovitch?"

"I do."

Dolgorensky smiled and held out the papers. Golovin was smiling broadly, too. They had planned all this together carefully, Orloff knew. Dolgorensky refused to admit that Orloff had acted for the Party's good as always. Dolgorensky did not really care about the Party. He never had. He was interested only in indulging his whims. He was selfish. Orloff detested him. Selfishness was what he had been fighting for years. Selfishness had caused all the Tsarist corruption. Selfishness was causing all the trouble that remained. From the very beginning, years ago, Dolgorensky had resented anyone with more authority than he. He could not even bear being contradicted. He was a Communist simply because he wanted power. He gave no real loyalty even to Lenin. In his eyes now, Orloff saw the same intense irritation with which he used to discuss the Tsar. The smile on his prominent, feminine lips was the same — the same as always when he hurt someone. This time he was smiling because he had made an arrangement in which anything Orloff chose would be wrong. How true it was that, in battle, the successful general is the one who knows his enemy best, he thought.

"You cannot do it," said Katya. "Tell him you refuse!"

Orloff looked from Dolgorensky's threatening, anticipatory smile to the small sheaf of papers in his hand. They seemed to be nothing more than that; nothing more than a sheaf of papers.

"You seem to hesitate, Petya," Dolgorensky said. "There is nothing wrong, I hope?"

"No," said Orloff.

"You would not refuse an order from the Central Committee."

"Certainly not."

"Petya, the words will burn in your mouth like coals," Katya said.

"Your discipline has always been the envy of the Party," said Dolgorensky. "Hasn't it, Victor Karpovitch?"

"It has."

Orloff extended a hand and took the papers. It was nothing more than an ordinary sheaf of papers after all, papers on which Telegin had put some words. There was nothing to fear. There was no reason for Katya's unseemly display. Dolgorensky's schemes were beneath Orloff's attention.

Dolgorensky smiled. "We shall see you next week."

Dolgorensky and Golovin let themselves out. Orloff began to look through the papers. They contained nothing but the usual phrases, in Telegin's usual style: " . . . this young man . . . the perfect flower of Communist society . . . struck down by a vicious counterrevolutionary assassin . . . criminal oppressor of laboring masses thirsting for revenge."

And suddenly Orloff realized that these were words that would come from his mouth, heard by thousands of people. He could clearly see the cobblestones in Red Square, between which their upturned faces seemed to sprout like hundreds of thousands of unconscious, pink cabbages. How petty Dolgorensky and Golovin were! How childish! What did they hope to accomplish with such nonsense!

"Petya, are you going to do it?" Katya said.

"Yes."

"Are you going to demand that Golovin be removed?"

"Golovin has been appointed by the Party. He says he has seen the light, and the Party obviously believes him. I appreciate your sympathy, Katya. Very much. You are still angry about his behavior in Siberia. But, as he said, he had no choice. And I have no right to intrude my personal dislikes. You always took things too personally, Katya. You still do."

Katya stared at her lap for a long time. "I am so cold, Petya," she said. "I have refused you for years."

"Yes." He was puzzled. What did this mean?

"Shall I tell you why?"

"Yes, Katya. Please do."

Katya rose and walked slowly to the fire. She stared intently at Orloff for a moment, calmly, deliberately unfastening the buttons on her gown. Then, quickly, she let the gown fall from her shoulders to the floor. Orloff's eyes widened. He had not seen his own wife's naked body in years.

"Katya!"

She lowered her eyes and turned away. The light from the fire shone on her back. The initials VKG blazed on her skin.

"What happened?" Orloff whispered.

"Golovin raped me. Yes, that's right. Golovin poured vodka down my throat. Golovin dumped me outside town. It happened the night your friend Voronov escaped, after Voronov told me what had happened outside the wall. It happened because you were so perfectly impersonal. You were right to spare Golovin. He had no choice. It was Capitalism that forced him to do what he did. I remember feeling sorry for him at the time. Your decision must have been difficult, Petya. You wanted to be free. You missed me so much. I know that. But you were right. It was worth your additional

408

imprisonment. Golovin has become a good Party member, as you hoped. Compared with that, our continued separation did not mean a thing. Why, then, am I complaining, Petya? What is wrong with me? If I am just not good enough to be a Communist, say so."

Her words made no impression on him. He heard them, understood them, but felt nothing. "I didn't know," he heard himself say.

"Of course you didn't. You couldn't. It was stupid of me to bring it up. What's wrong with me?"

"Katya, wait. Listen to me."

"Yes, Petya, I know. 'We are involved in a historic enterprise which will transform the world. That is why we must sometimes do things we dislike. The world can be reconstructed only after it is destroyed. The measuring rod is the welfare of the Party.'

"I know all that. And I agree with it, Petya. You know that. I don't know why I'm behaving like this. I'm out of control. I want to behave properly, but I can't. Something I don't understand won't let me. That is why I must go away. I don't want to go, but I must. Why, Petya? Do you know? Nothing I say seems to make any sense."

"You are leaving me?" Orloff asked.

"No. No. Don't be silly. I simply must go away for a while. Isn't that stupid? I'm going mad."

Katya continued talking volubly, in a frenetic, disjointed, uncharacteristic way. Her voice painfully and unintelligibly slashed at Orloff's brain. If only she would stop. But she did not. Why was she doing this? She knew he was not at fault. She knew they both had to obey the same rules, that he was suffering as much as she. Yet Katya was blaming him. She was indulging her petty feelings, which he disliked. Her behavior reeked with bourgeois egotism. As she chattered on, she was the perfect picture of the spoiled *barinya.*

"Go then!" Orloff told her shortly.

Katya nodded. His answer had been inevitable, she knew. Even more inevitable than historical determinism. Hearing it made her strangely serene. It was something she could count on. The certainty of his words paradoxically drew her to him. And at the same time she was afraid. She was rushing to disaster and could not stop.

Orloff ordered a car and put Katya aboard. He had made the right decision, he knew, about her and about the speech. Katya would realize that and be back before long. His decision would be instructive. Katya would thank him. The only solution was to let her go now. If he had refused, the problem would have gotten worse.

As he stood at the window and watched her car go, he remembered an early morning in Siberia when, as on all visiting days, he was at the barred window studying the road. He had done that so many times, year after year. An hour or so would pass in this way, and then, far away, something would move. It would be Katya in a carriage coming from town. And year after year, on such days, he would watch for another hour as she approached.

It was one of those small recollections which for no great reason return years after, fleeting but as vivid as the original experience. Once again he saw in detail the barren road, the first faint movement, the approaching horse and carriage, and Katya's face. He remembered them all exactly as they were. The same quality of light was in the air, and the same damp smell. And once again he felt impatient. He wanted to see Katya so much.

Then he returned to 1920 and saw that the carriage had turned the corner and Katya was gone.

LVIII

The square was completely filled with people. One could not see the ground. There was no place to put any more feet. Indeed, those who could not enter were jammed into the adjoining streets, like the tentacles of some impossible monster. All government offices had been closed, as an inducement to Soviet employees to attend. Bands were playing. Every hand held a flag.

It was a completely successful spontaneous demonstration.

The various dignitaries and their guests stood in groups on the stand. Dolgorensky's sensuous lips were smiling. Beside him, Telegin's chubby face beamed. Telegin was overjoyed. Orloff would soon read the speech he had written. Maria stood not far away. Telegin had been trying without success to persuade her to come back. Now she was talking with Michael, whom Telegin hated.

"I'm told you are doing good Party work," Michael was saying.

"That's right," said Maria.

"Congratulations."

"Thank you."

They looked at each other coldly. They had been talking for fifteen minutes and had not yet exchanged a sincere word. Both believed they were glad they detested each other. They looked forward to such meetings, so they could tell each other so.

Telegin hated to be near Michael, but he joined them. "Masha," he said. "I must speak with you later."

"Must you, Cyril Modestovitch? Why?"

"In private."

"He says he must speak with me later," she told Michael.

"So I heard," said Michael. "Why?"

"He won't say."

"Won't he? Why? Why must you speak with her later, Cyril Modestovitch?"

Telegin smiled. How amusing! She was trying to humiliate him. She always had. That was why he wanted her. She knew perfectly well he wanted to ask her to come back. But she laughed at him in front of Voronov. She was not impressed by Telegin's growing power. She knew he no longer had to plead for anything – and did not care.

That was why it would be even better when he forced her to come back. He was one of the few who knew she had killed her brother. At the right time, he would remind her. Stepan dead was as good as Stepan alive.

"Let me think it over, Cyril Modestovitch," she said.

Smiling, almost laughing, she looked down at the crowd. Soon, she knew, Telegin would threaten to expose her. Why was Telegin so totally stupid? She looked at her uncle, who stood nearby. He, too, was stupid in a way. His eyes stared blankly at the crowd. A sheaf of papers was in his hands. He had brought her down from Petrograd, Maria believed, because – although he could not mention it – he knew Marchenko had been her brother. Orloff had thought it best that she be there and know nothing. What would he say if he found out she knew it all?

The bands began to play. A light breeze caught the flags. The entire world was festooned in red. Orloff came forward with his papers and looked down at the crowd. Strangely, they all seemed red-eyed and slack. They looked as if they were cattle packed too closely in a pen. Why? he wondered. Why the strange incongruence between the fanfare and their faces?

He looked at his papers and began to read: " . . . this young man . . . the perfect flower of Communist society . . . struck down by a vicious, counterrevolutionary assassin . . . criminal oppressor of the laboring masses, thirsting for revenge . . . I promise you, the Party promises you – he shall be avenged! . . . "

To his surprise, it was no trouble at all. The words came easily and fluently from his mouth – so easily that it was unnecessary to give them any thought.

Words and faces faded away. Once again it was 1906. Orloff stood at the head of a small room, badly lit by a few candles. Not a ray of daylight got in. A handful of men sat in the shadows.

No one moved. No one spoke. Orloff was gradually becoming annoyed. His body was tense – rigid in fact. Everyone waited. Everyone listened. From quite nearby, came the incongruous sound of children playing.

"You see?" Dolgorensky finally said. "There's something about him I distrust."

412

"There's something about everybody you distrust," said Orloff.

There was a familiar knock, the door opened and Plotkin came in.

"You're late," said Orloff.

"Sure I am," Plotkin said. "It isn't easy getting across town at this hour."

"All right. Let's get started." Orloff pointed to a drawing on the wall. "This is the Mutual Credit Bank on Fonarny Pereulok."

"How much?" Plotkin asked.

Orloff paused. "Two million rubles." From somewhere in the shadows a whistle came. "For living expenses you will be allowed the usual fifty kopecks a day," said Orloff.

"Fifty kopecks?" said Plotkin. "Surely you are joking!"

"No, I am not. Do you think it is too much, comrade?"

Plotkin became embarrassed. "Not at all. Not at all."

Orloff's finger again moved to the drawing. "You, Arkady Andreievitch, will place yourself here. You already know what you must do . . . . We have exactly six minutes in which to work . . . you, Plotkin, will place yourself here. You also know what you must do . . . it is imperative that the timing be absolutely perfect . . . you, Plotkin, will arrive exactly two minutes after we do . . . ."

To his surprise, it was no trouble at all. The words came easily and fluently from his mouth. Had anyone told him only a few years ago, that he, Peter Sergeievitch Orloff, an officer in the Imperial Russian Army, would soon be planning a bank robbery — which would bring him a total of fifty kopecks a day — he would have assumed that the teller was a dangerous lunatic. But the Revolution, after all, needed millions of rubles. Printing presses were needed to teach the people they were oppressed. A Revolution took a lot of preparation.

Then Telegin was shaking his hand. "Thank you so much, comrade general. Thank you so much. Such an honor to have you read my words."

Hands applauded. A band played. Once again it was 1920. It had all been so easy. He could not remember what he had thought there was to fear. He looked at the crowd again. They were standing as before, bodies sagging, faces blank, patiently waiting to be told to go. They obviously had not heard a word, proof that his meaningless speech had made no difference. No one was really interested in it. Yet, he could not help suddenly feeling very tired. It was, no doubt, the influence of the expression on the crowd's collective face.

And there was one in the crowd who was more interested than most. Far away among the faces, Katya watched. She had not wanted to come. She had planned not to come. But she had been drawn irresistibly. Unlike the others, she had heard every word. She had remembered many of Telegin's phrases. For her, too, it had not been as bad as she had feared. Petya had been right, as always. It had made no difference, after all. She knew she would be all right before long.

A signal was given, and the crowd, heads lowered, began to sing quietly. There was another signal. The crowd began to leave the square. The tentacles in the side streets disappeared, followed by the body oozing out. No one mentioned the ceremony. No one spoke at all.

LIX

Some just gave up. Some fought. Others joined. The most difficult thing of all was to remain unchanged. It was impossible. Maria's act, which in normal times would have caused a scandal, was now too ordinary even to be mentioned. Everyone had a story somewhat like hers. Fathers betrayed sons, mothers betrayed daughters, brothers betrayed brothers, and friends betrayed friends. Stepan's execution had not been a crime. It had been justice. The laws governing his sentence superseded those written by the lawyers. To have avoided it would have been a crime against her father. Maria felt numb, not because the thing had been done, but because it had been necessary.

Yet her new situation upset her far more. She had told her uncle only that she had left Telegin, and Orloff had asked no questions. He had become her protector; indeed, he seemed even more concerned about her after her aunt had left for Moscow. Maria did not know the reason for Katya's departure.

She knew that Orloff's new duties at the Cheka included finding Stepan's killer. It was as if she were being protected by a bear which at any moment might playfully smash her with a paw. Orloff believed, or so she thought, that she had never met "comrade Marchenko" and had not known who he really was. And he had known the truth about "Marchenko's" criminal activities, but had not revealed it. Indeed, she had seen and heard him make a speech in which he had eulogized "Marchenko." So it was impossible to know exactly what he would do. It was important to remember that a bear could be dangerous.

One of the greatest successes of the Communist system was complete abolition of the Capitalist problem of unemployment. All Soviet citizens were forced to work. Orloff personally issued her labor book and found her a job in the Food Trust.

Every day she went to the office. Every day she read the wall newspaper. Every day she attended meetings. Every day she listened to nonsense and dutifully passed it on. And every day the boredom attacked her. "Reality" had become, like sandpaper on wood, a force which smoothed her into conformity.

The office was a large room filled with people, all jabbering, gesticulating, and running as if they imagined it would speed their business up. But why anyone would imagine that, Maria could not guess. She stood behind a long table covered with papers. Next to her, another girl quickly came and went. Strangely, she did not seem bored at all. Could she be abnormal, or was it just a pretense? What was the girl supposed to be doing? Unlike Maria, she was dressed fairly well, including silk stockings and a trace of scent, undoubtedly gifts from some commissar for her favors.

"Typical Soviet 'secretary,' isn't she," said Marina Nikitovna.

"An archetype," said Maria.

"A slut is what she is."

Marina Nikitovna's dull, mousy hair was still drawn back in a bun. Her face was still pinched. She still wore rimless glasses. Her clothes looked like winding sheets draped on a cadaver. And she still felt the same seething deprivation and envy, the same boiling insult and injury. The Revolution had changed nothing for her at all — which increased her seething. She had been passed by and did not know it.

The one benefit she had was working near Maria. How good it was to see her reduced to Marina Nikitovna's own level, to see her feel what Marina Nikitovna felt, to see her become like Marina Nikitovna. That, after all, was the purpose of Communism.

Maria shuffled the papers around. She knew that they not only made no sense, but were meant to make no sense, and that nothing could be done to make them sensible. Yet she had a compulsive urge to try. The desire itself had an illusory effect, as if something were accomplished just by rearranging the nonsense.

"Oh, yes, the figure is mathematically exact, I assure you," an educated voice was saying in the crowd. "The average food ration contains only 60 per cent of the calories needed for survival."

Maria saw a small, bearded, professorial type briskly haranguing with an index finger.

"Take an ounce of salt fish, for instance." He counted out the caloric values of various types of foods, not angrily, not hungrily, but simply for the delight of demonstrating an arithmetic proof.

"But we are still alive," someone said.

"You misunderstand me. I am speaking statistically, of course."

The large, misshapen line flung forward, with the peristaltic action of an intestine, and someone new was disgorged before her. This time it was a fairly healthy, nondescript, middle-aged man. Without a word, he opened a well-wrapped package and took out a dead rat.

She drew back reflexively and then came forward. Nothing so interesting had ever happened there before.

"What is this?" she asked.

He looked at the rat as if puzzled. "It is a rat, your honor."

"Yes, yes, I see that. But what's the point?"

"I found the rat in a jar of jam, your honor. Issued on a card in a government store. The jam is still sticking to him. See?"

"Yes. Fascinating."

"The rat displaced its own weight in jam from the jar. Ain't that right, professor?"

"Most assuredly," said the bearded man. "That is a property of solid objects."

"So I want the rat weighed, and an authorization to be issued for that amount of jam."

"Do you seriously expect me to handle a rat?"

"If your honor prefers, I'll weigh it myself."

She looked into his eyes to see whether it was a joke, and saw that he was incapable of making one, which made the situation even funnier. She wanted to prolong it but could not imagine how. She pointed to the door of the chief of the section.

"Take your rat and go in there."

The man thanked her, repacked his rat and left. Before her now, with downcast eyes, stood an elderly woman, almost as tall as Maria herself. She seemed very fragile. There was something vaguely familiar about her.

"Yes?" said Maria very shortly.

"I would like a saucepan." The elderly woman did not look up. Her voice was apologetic, timorous.

"Are you aware of the proper procedure to get a saucepan?"

"No, comrade," the old woman said.

There was a roar from inside the office of the chief of the section, the door opened and the man with the rat came out with the assistance of the shiny toe of a boot. The door closed and he hurried down the hall. The old woman had not even turned to look.

Suddenly Maria realized that the woman before her was her former teacher, Natalia Stepanovna. Tata had said that Natalia Stepanovna had been coaching her. Maria had not seen her for more than a year, since the summer of 1918. It had been a painful meeting, punctuated with nervous exclamations, cruelly reminiscent of Maria's ruined career and wasted training, an unwanted echo of what might have been. But this — this was far worse. This could not be Natalia Stepanovna. Her large, maternal figure was gone. In its place was a brittle, inadequate container. Her hand rested upon the table. It was not the hand of Natalia Stepanovna, but a worn and wrinkled claw. Her fierce, imperious glare was gone. Her spirit had been sucked dry, as if by a gigantic leech.

Maria stared, dumb with horror, a horror tinged with embarrassment, as if she were deliberately spying on something private. Perhaps the shock would have been less if she had seen the change take place gradually, but seeing it like this was an abrupt reminder of all the things she had slowly become used to, and of the vanished world they had replaced; a world in which art and success had been possible.

Maria touched her own face. It occurred to her that she, too, had changed. Would the shock be as great for Natalia Stepanovna? Maria seriously wanted to know. If only Natalia Stepanova would look up. If only her head would tilt, as in the old days, and the imperious glare blaze down her nose.

Maria chose a meaningless piece of paper and shoved it roughly under Natalia Stepanovna's nose.

"Complete this form!" Maria said rudely. "It must be countersigned by three officials here. That will take you the whole day. On the next day, provided the form has been approved, you can exchange it for another, which allows you to go to the government store where samples are on exhibition and pick out by number the kind of saucepan you want. There you will get a coupon entitling you to buy it at the government cooperative in the district where you live.

"Then you find out what day saucepans are being sold, and buy one — if they haven't been sold out. I realize you *boorzhui* don't like standing in line, but keep going back until one is left. In a week or so, you should have your saucepan."

Natalia Stepanovna did not move. She did nothing. There was no indication that she had heard.

"Another perfect example of Soviet efficiency," said Maria.

"Yes."

"Do I detect a note of sarcasm in your voice?"

"No, comrade. I don't know what you mean."

"Well, then, what are you waiting for? Do you think I have all day? There are others waiting and they aren't as fancy as you."

Natalia Stepanovna made a bowl with her hands, a bowl of bones and wrinkled skin. "All I want is a saucepan," she said softly.

"What!" said Maria. "Are you arguing with me?"

Maria felt a flash of hope. The large head would now come up, the eyes flashing as of old, the tongue hurling sarcasm and insult. Hit me! thought Maria. Slap my face!

"No, comrade. I'm sorry," Natalia Stepanovna said softly. She absently took the paper and shuffled away, neck bent, eyes down, a shapeless figure in a shapeless coat.

Across the room, some commissar or other was smiling at Maria, to her dismay. He had completely misunderstood.

The girl with the scent and silk stockings was back. "Uppity *boorzhui* give you any trouble?" she asked. "Just look at the bloodsucking leech."

Maria swung blindly and hit her on the ear.

The girl shrieked. "Are you crazy?"

"You slut!" said Maria, as if she were going to do it again.

Marina Nikitovna had never enjoyed herself so much. "Is anything wrong?" she asked Maria.

The girl ran off holding her ear. Natalia Stepanovna went out the door. Blindly and stupidly, Maria took the next man in line, her mouth making the usual meaningless remarks, her hands moving meaningless papers as before.

Now she was glad that Natalia Stepanovna had not recognized her. If she had, it would have been even more painful than what had happened; not simply because Natalia Stepanovna would have been embarrassed to see Maria behind the counter and humiliated to be seen in this way by Maria, but because it would have reestablished a personal relationship, and there was nothing more painful than a personal relationship. Michael was right. The Communists were right. More and more, she was coming to see that. Nothing was more foolish and painful than intimacy. In one way or another, it always led to disappointment. It was best to avoid arousing one's emotions. Indeed, it was wise to blunt and eliminate one's emotions. It was best to avoid any personal desires. Only in that way could one avoid the stupidity of reality. She was beginning to realize how wrong she had been.

The day ended and she left the building. An automobile was parked at the curb. Was it just another commissar, or was someone being arrested? How strange it is, she thought, how amusing that the sight of an automobile presents only those two possibilities.

A hand appeared atop her shoulder. A voice spoke.

"Masha, I must speak with you. Please get in."

It was Telegin. Her husband appeared as prosperous as ever, perhaps even more so. His cheeks glowed with a curious health, like the workers shown on the Soviet posters. As always, he was fashionably dressed.

To her surprise she felt absolutely nothing. How comfortable that was. Only a short time ago, in this situation, she would have been overwhelmed by various emotions. Now her mind worked perfectly without their interference, observing, classifying, integrating and evaluating. But she felt absolutely nothing.

"All right," she said.

She got in, followed by Telegin, and the car immediately began to move. It was very new. It was very comfortable. There was a luxury about it she had not seen for some time.

"You did not wait to speak with me last week," he said.

"I did not wait to speak with you last week."

"Why not?"

"Let me see. I did not want to."

"A good reason," he chuckled.

"Isn't it?"

"Yes. Did you enjoy the ceremony?"

"Very much."

"I thought you had. Your uncle read my speech quite well."

"Of course he did. He's a Communist."

"As a fellow Communist, you must have been proud."

Maria laughed, without sarcasm or bitterness. Telegin's remark had been very funny. She laughed because she enjoyed it so much.

In some subtle but important way, she has changed, Telegin thought. It was interesting. She still did not like to play the game, like that late virtuoso, her brother Stepan. It was a change of a different sort. But Telegin did not know what sort of a change it was. He did not yet know whether it was good for him or not.

"It was amusing, was it not, Masha, to see Stepan immortalized?"

"Yes, wasn't it? Funniest thing I ever heard. One wonders why people say Communism is a bore."

"It was even funnier for us. We alone know the truth."

"Yes. That's true. Isn't it amusing that truth does not exist?"

"Forgive me, Masha. I had forgotten. You're right, of course. There's no such thing."

Telegin was beginning to enjoy himself. She was playing after all, in a mystifying but thoroughly original way.

Telegin's expression changed. His face became solemn. "Masha," he said, "your mother is dead. It was a sudden illness. The doctor never knew what it was. It was over very quickly. I did what I could."

"I'm sure you did, Cyril Modestovitch."

Maria felt absolutely nothing at all. Her mind efficiently registered the information, and thought back to the last time they had seen each other, at their country house in the south; back even to the imaginary times before 1917, when her mother had been a completely different person, a woman of silk, perfume and laughter. Maria saw all this inwardly in great detail, and was absolutely without emotion. What a marvelous relief that was. She was more and more pleased with her new psychology.

Telegin took her hand. She gave it. The evening was cold but, as usual, his hand was damp. She felt a large ring on one of the fingers. And from his body there came a French scent.

"You may be sure, Masha, that your secret is safe with me," he said. "After all, if I do not protect you, who will? I am all you have left. You're an orphan."

Maria did not answer. There was no expression on her face. It was as if she had not heard.

Telegin spread his hands. "You see, Masha, between those who share a secret such as ours, a bond is established. A powerful bond. A bond stronger even than blood. The conspirators are irrevocably drawn together. And the same situation happily applies to us, Masha.

"The bond which unites us is the secret itself. The closer we are, the safer the secret. Such a happy state of affairs. After all, Masha, we are so much in love. And the farther apart we are, the more in danger the secret — such an unhappy state of affairs. The longer the chain, the more weak links there are. This worries me, Masha. That's the truth. You know how concerned I have always been for your welfare.

"That is why I want you to come back to me."

Maria laughed again, in the same way. They were driving along the Neva now. People watched, mesmerized, as they passed. A ragged little boy held out a newspaper.

"Perhaps you should just turn me in," she said. Was she half serious? She was not sure, she was so exhausted. Perhaps she was.

How remarkable! Telegin thought. What a thorough change. She was playing well. What a refreshing contrast to her earlier naiveté.

Telegin adopted an indignant expression. "Absolutely not, Masha! What *can* you be thinking? I am angry, in fact. I take your suggestion as an insult — an insult to one so concerned about your welfare. I refuse to give you up, Masha. We are so much in love."

421

"It is your duty, Cyril Modestovitch — your Communist duty. Surely a Communist of your quality would not forget that."

He smiled. "Certainly not, Masha. Need you ask? I have had a difficult struggle — a storm of conscience. I deserve your sympathy. If our love were only slightly less intense, I might have done as you suggest. That is true. Nothing is more important than love, Masha."

"There is no need to threaten me, Cyril Modestovitch," she said.

Telegin adopted an innocent expression. "What do you mean?"

Only a short time ago, she would have demanded that Telegin end this charade, and admit clearly that what she said was true: that he was threatening her. But now she did not want that at all. She did not care. Indeed, she wanted Telegin to continue.

"Why do you want me? I have always wondered."

Telegin was startled. Sincerity was a tactic he did not often face. For a moment, he did not know what to say. Maria had always found him repulsive. Everyone had. No one had ever taken him seriously. No one could. He had always been so impossibly fat. But more and more, people were beginning to take him very seriously indeed. They were beginning to realize that Telegin was no joke. He was now Lunacharsky's deputy. Earlier, he had hated their revulsion, but now he welcomed it. It was proof of his efficacy, proof that he was very serious indeed. And Maria had found him more repulsive than anyone else.

He would have liked to tell her this but he could not. Saying it would prove he needed to, which would be humiliating. But he did not need to tell her. She would know. Telegin could communicate so much without seeming to. He was an expert.

He smiled and put a hand on her knee. "Something in your spirit calls to something in mine," he chuckled.

Maria did not move. She felt nothing, which was good. That was exactly what she wanted.

"That is good to hear. I was hoping you would say that. I want to come back. There is nothing in the world I want more."

"Splendid, Masha! Of course there isn't."

"I have been so confused, Cyril Modestovitch. Forgive me. At last I understand, with your help. You are so sleazy. You're the sleaziest person I know. And for years I have been deluded by the Capitalist lie that this is bad. But no more. At last I understand how admirable you are. Of course I'll come back to you! You could not keep me away. I want to be as close as possible to your perfect sleaziness."

"Splendid, Masha! Splendid!" he roared.

LX

Maria's reconciliation with Telegin annoyed Orloff. He would not say so, but he had been taking his job as her protector very seriously. Even more seriously, for some reason, since Katya had left. Indeed, he had gone about it almost as a mission. And now it was unnecessary. Orloff did not like Telegin. He never had. He was irritated by Telegin's success in the Party. For instance, Telegin had emerged unscathed from his relationship with Stepan. Why? Telegin obviously had nothing in common with Communism. He was such a perfect representative of the old regime, of everything the Party had fought against. He was sleazy. How could it be that the Party's interests now required that Orloff publicly read his words? Doing so had not been as bad as Orloff had expected, but the question continued to annoy him from time to time.

And he was disappointed with Maria. He had thought that, with his help, she was becoming a good Communist. But apparently he had been mistaken. She had suffered a relapse. Like so many others, she was more interested in silk stockings. Perhaps Maria should be given an important assignment. Perhaps her intelligence had been wasted as a clerk at the Food Trust.

"How is your English?" Telegin asked her one day.

"Adequate," said Maria.

"Good news. Your uncle has given you important Party work."

"That's good news, Cyril Modestovitch."

"Your uncle is an important man to satisfy and cultivate."

"My uncle is an important man to satisfy and cultivate."

"Your first task requires that you travel to Perm. You will leave in two days. The details will be explained to you there."

"As you wish, Cyril Modestovitch."

"There is one problem. Voronov has been assigned to head the operations in Perm."

"That's a problem, Cyril Modestovitch."

"I cannot understand his success in the Party. Why would your uncle advance this man? He has nothing in common with Communism."

"Not a thing."

"He's nothing but a stupid, illiterate peasant."

"How loathsome."

"Correct. He may very well try to attack you again."

"It is not impossible, Cyril Modestovitch."

"Unfortunately, he is your uncle's adjutant."

"Yes, Cyril Modestovitch."

"And your uncle is a very important man."

"Whatever you say. Whatever anyone says."

Telegin slapped his thigh and roared. Splendid! What a remarkable transformation. She understood. She understood everything.

Two days later, she sat in a train as it slowly left the station in Petrograd. She was completely alone in a comfortable coach, which somehow had been untouched by war and revolution. She looked out the window. Forlorn faces on the platform looked back, belonging to those who had been unable to squeeze into the cattle cars. She looked at them, felt absolutely nothing, and lit a cigarette.

The door opened and Michael came in, followed by another man and a woman. The man was small, bald, bearded and looked intelligent. The woman was young and stupid. She wore too many cosmetics, too much jewelry, too much perfume, and gaudy clothes. She was actively chewing sunflower seeds.

"Hello, peasant," said Maria.

"Hello, brat."

"And who are these other peasants?" she asked.

"Just a minute," said the girl. "Who are you calling a peasant?"

"That's Pushkin," said Michael, pointing to the man.

"Pushkin? Oh, dear. You have no poetic tendencies, I hope?"

"No, I'm a Soviet economist."

"And what does a Soviet economist do?"

"You'll laugh."

"Try me."

"The purpose of a Soviet economist is to destroy economics."

Maria laughed. "You're right. It's funny. What does it mean?"

"Nothing, really. That's the point. You'll understand when we get to Perm."

"He's dangerously sane, of course," said Michael. "There's nothing to fear. He'll be locked up. He's one of the bourgeois specialists we cannot do without."

424

"Is your work so complicated, then?" she asked.

"Inordinately."

The girl spat some seeds into her hand. "Just throw them on the floor," said Michael. The girl did so with relief.

"And what about this *barinya?*" asked Maria.

"I am a Soviet secretary," said the girl.

"A euphemism," said Michael. "Actually, she's my mistress. Her intense modesty makes her reticent."

"And what does a Soviet secretary do?"

"You'll laugh," said Michael, cutting the girl off.

"Try me," said Maria.

"A Soviet secretary destroys communication," he said.

Maria laughed. "You're right. It's funny."

The girl alternately colored and smiled, as the man without emotions expertly played on her emotions. She tried, but understood nothing of what was really being said.

Maria, too, felt absolutely nothing. That was good. She wanted to feel nothing. Michael had been so right all along. She marvelled at her beliefs of only a few years ago. How could anyone possibly be so naive? Had she had any emotions, Maria would have blushed. But she did not. She began to study her English phrase book.

Michael smiled with contempt. "What are you doing?"

"I am studying my English."

"Say something in English."

"Communism is a dirty fraud."

"What does it mean?"

"Long live Communism," she said in Russian.

"An original sentiment."

"Yes, isn't it? What are we going to Perm to do?"

Michael chuckled. "To put on a show. We are going to show some Americans through our new automobile plant."

"Since when do we have a new automobile plant?"

"We don't, of course. The idea is ridiculous. But the Party wants the Americans to think we do."

"Communism is a dirty fraud," she said.

"You will serve as guide and interpreter."

"How shall we convince them?"

"You will see."

"Communism is a firty draud," said the Soviet secretary. "Have I got that right?"

"Not exactly," said Maria. She laboriously taught the girl to say it. "Communism is a dirty fraud," the girl repeated.

Everything was ready when they got to Perm. The building selected had actually been a factory at one time, and now appeared to be producing automobiles. A few actually stood in the yard, along with some very large crates. An assembly line of sorts had been installed, along which travelled unrecognizable pieces of metal. And people in work clothes – all Chekists – hurried back and forth, hammering and tightening, as if trying to meet a schedule. But they were hammering and tightening nothing. It was all a charade. The "workers" were actors, smirking against their will.

Maria and a Communist engineer named Khrushlov met the Americans at the gate. They were representatives of some trade union or other. There were half a dozen, and what unusual people they were. They were well-fed and healthy. Their skin actually seemed to glow. As a result, they seemed childlike, an impression heightened by the fact that they continually smiled and shook hands. They actually enjoyed being where they were. Was that possible? It was as if they were infants, somehow grown to maturity, but still infants in adult clothes. Did all Americans look like this? Something was wrong. The Russians next to them looked shrivelled and small. The Russians were normal. The Americans were not.

Her English worked fairly well. She listened to the Americans' questions, relaying them to Khrushlov, who gave her the answers. The Americans were very curious, they wanted to know how everything worked, and everything's purpose, but they seemed to believe whatever she said. How naive they were. They were boys playing at being men. Apparently, "real life" did not exist in America. Under Khrushlov's expert handling, she recited production figures, distribution schedules and other things she did not understand. The Americans smiled with delight.

Walking slowly down the line, they passed Michael, who was playing a Soviet worker in the farce. He was polishing a piece of equipment with a rag. He smiled and nodded, deliberately overdoing it. She knew him so well. He was enjoying himself.

His Soviet "secretary" was busy at something else. She spat some sunflower seeds onto the floor, and the Americans interviewed her.

"Do you belong to a trade union?" one asked.

Maria relayed the question to the girl.

"The Russian Federated Soviet Republic has the best and freest of all trade unions," said Khrushlov.

"The Russian Federated Soviet Republic has the best and freest of all trade unions," the girl told Maria.

426

"The Russian Federated Soviet Republic has the best and freest of all trade unions," Maria told the Americans.

The Americans nodded, smiling warmly. Everything was as they had expected — as they had so much wanted it to be — in the glorious Russian Federated Soviet Republic. Why did those so-called "experts" at home spread such reactionary lies? Why didn't they come to Russia and hear the truth — from the mouths of the Russian workers themselves? It would hasten the day when Americans would enjoy the benefits of Socialism.

"And are you allowed paid maternity leave, *tovarisch?*"

Both women looked at Khrushlov. "Of course," he answered. "The Russian Federated Soviet Republic has the best and freest of all maternity leaves."

As Maria gave the answer, a sour expression appeared on the face of the American next to her. At last one of them had understood. Now, at last, this farce would be exposed.

"You see?" he said, to the man who had asked the question. "And we call ourselves a modern country!"

The Americans moved off in a miasma of good will. As they did so, the Soviet "secretary" raised her fist.

"Communism is a dirty fraud," she said loudly.

The Americans turned, nervous and confused, looked warily at each other and at the Soviet "secretary." Then the one interested in maternity leaves began to laugh. Surely the girl's remark had been a joke. Furthermore, it was proof of the great Socialist freedom! An American worker would not dare to denounce Capitalism as the dirty fraud it is. He would be fired and beaten by the boss's spies and goons.

The laughter seemed to work. The others joined in. The Soviet "secretary" joined in, too. And soon they were all laughing loudly and heartily. Khrushlov bent double. He could not stand up. Even Michael was smiling. Only Maria was not.

The Americans waved at the girl and went out. Such an amusing, unexpected joke! So thoroughly enjoyable! They got into their German touring car and drove off. As they did so, they looked back — at the imposing Soviet automobile factory, owned not by bloodsucking Capitalists but by workers. Unionized workers, some of whom stood before it now; workers with free maternity leaves, waving at them, along with the scholarly Soviet engineer and the tall, slender Soviet interpreter. What an idyllic scene. It was perfect. There would be so much to tell their fellow trade unionists at home. Then their German touring car turned the corner and they were gone.

"Did you see it, comrades?" Khrushlov yelled. "I couldn't have stood it another minute. I would have exploded like a shell."

Khrushlov was helpless. "They believed everything we told them. Everything! Have you ever in your life seen such fools?"

"Comrade Lenin is wrong!" someone yelled. "They'll not only sell us the rope we'll hang them with — they'll hang themselves!"

Everyone was laughing as hard as he could. It hurt so much they were hitting each other. Khrushlov tightly held his middle and gasped. His eyes were tearing. He could not speak. The Soviet "secretary" was howling.

"Stop it! Please!" she shrieked with laughter.

There was a roar. "And they say Woodrow Wilson's even dumber," someone yelled.

Michael looked at Maria coldly. He did not know that she had no emotions. He was relishing his belief that she found the incident painful.

"An excellent job," he said. "Your uncle will be pleased." He looked at his watch. "It's time to collect Pushkin and get back."

Michael, Maria and the Soviet "secretary" got into another car, and were driven across town to another factory. It was a printing plant. Metallic arms rose and fell, wafting huge sheets of something. The huge sheets were piling up. Inky men were tying bundles. Maria went to a press and saw that it was printing paper rubles. Each huge sheet was covered with them.

"Isn't it beautiful?" Pushkin said.

"It is," said Maria.

"Shall I tell you what you are looking at?"

"Please."

"The Soviet government, like all others, has bills to pay. So, like all others, it prints the paper it needs. That is what I am doing now. We are geniuses and magicians. We are creating money. This paper is money simply because we say it is.

"Unlike all others, however, the Soviet government is at the same time applying a theory so sophisticated, so brilliant and profound, that nothing like it has been imagined since the beginnings of the science — a theory compared with which the best ideas of Smith and Bastiat are — as you already suspect — childish ravings. Smith and Bastiat impressed themselves unduly. They were prisoners of their own systems. They bowed to reality. But we Communists are remaking reality. Do you know what you are looking at, comrade?"

"No."

Pushkin's voice rose in triumph. "We are printing what we need to pay our bills — and at the very same time, we are also printing enough to make it unnecessary. We are using money to destroy money. Isn't that brilliant?"

"I'm sure it is, comrade. What did you say?"

"Money, as you know, is the root of all evil, at best an unnecessary Capitalist invention. We are wiping it out the easiest way, simply by printing enough to make it worthless."

"People won't take it," said Maria.

"Of course they will! Russians are stupid. They're ignorant. They're cattle. They like standing in lines and in cattle cars. They'll kill anyone who won't let them."

Pushkin pulled a couple of sheets from the stack and shoved them at Maria and the Soviet secretary. "Here! Take some! Go ahead! It may come in handy. It has various important uses!"

Was he serious or simply sarcastic? A growing note of hysteria was in his voice. Maria looked dumbly at the paper in her hands. It was still wet and her fingers were stained with ink.

"Think nothing of it," Pushkin said. He whirled the sheets away. "I'll get you a dry batch."

He ran off and was back in a few minutes with two small packages, and gave one to each of the women. "A souvenir of your visit to Perm, comrades," he said.

Telegin met her at the station in Petrograd. He was in the best of humor, so good it could not be dissipated even by the sight of Michael. His hands waved, his pudgy fingers bulging around his rings. "Well?" he asked, when they were alone in his car.

"A great success, Cyril Modestovitch. We fooled everyone."

"Splendid!" said Telegin. "Splendid! The inspiring truth about our new Socialist automobile industry should be known. American workers, too, have the right to share our progress."

"In fact, they have no right not to," said Maria.

"Well said. How do you feel?"

"I don't, Cyril Modestovitch. I'm dead. So are you."

"Still, I have some interesting news," said Telegin.

"Oh?"

"You see? You're curious."

"What has happened, Cyril Modestovitch?"

Telegin chuckled and squeezed her knee. "You will be pleased to know, Masha, that your brother's murderer has been arrested."

"What?"

"Yes. Convenient, is it not? A relief, in fact. The truth is, Masha, that I have been very worried about you. But your uncle has come to the rescue as always."

"But who . . . who is it?"

"Oh. Yes. That's sad, Masha. Your brother's murderer was Tata Beresova. Surely you remember her. You were in the company together. She was a good dancer — almost as good as you. She had an original quality, a style. It is difficult to describe. Perhaps I am simply out of practice. It's a long time since I reviewed the ballet. We writers must keep in practice, too.

"In fact, I saw her dance not long ago. It's a shame. A waste. Why did she do this to herself? One shouldn't go around shooting commissars, should one? It seems — forgive me — that Tata was Stepan's mistress. Morals today have come to a sad pass. Apparently she shot him during a lover's spat. Poor Stepan was about to throw her out.

"So tragic, isn't it? Pathetic. Such a waste. No longer will Tata be a glorious Soviet artist. No longer will she help to build our glorious Soviet culture. This is, no doubt, what she will be thinking as the bullets begin to penetrate her flesh. But then it will be too late, Masha. It's too late now. Tata has betrayed the Party. The disease of egotism has claimed another victim.

"Which reminds me, Masha: Why do you insist on continuing your work in the Food Trust? It's important, of course. You like it, I know that. But you have no right to withhold your genius from the people. You owe it to the people to return to the company, and become the prima you were meant to be."

Maria felt an emotion. It was horribly painful. She sat quite still, which did no good. Telegin's words penetrated her consciousness like blows. She was burning up, and at the same time she was tired. Her eyelids felt like awnings. She could not keep them up.

Her uncle's face appeared before her, his cold blue eyes stared into hers. She shuddered. She was afraid. She was terrified. Her uncle disappeared and was replaced by a smiling Dolgorensky. "Your conception of guilt is quite naive," he was saying. Then she saw Michael, lips arched in the characteristic mocking smile. In it she saw the words, "You see?"

She did see. She saw at last. Michael had been so right all along. Once again she saw that everything was meaningless. Nothing had value. All of existence was a sour joke. Why had she taken so interminably long to under-stand?

The car was moving swiftly and easily. Many people whirled by outside. They must have been making the usual amount of noise, but Maria could not hear a thing. She knew Telegin was still talking because she saw his mouth move.

Telegin was right. What had happened was so sad. Maria felt so sorry for Tata. What a pity that there was nothing to be done. She wished there were.

If there were, she would do it. But, unfortunately, there was absolutely nothing. Tata had acted, and now she must pay. The Cheka did not make mistakes.

What a hypocrite I have become, she thought. How insincere. Such a fraud. Of course something can be done! Tata can be exonerated. I can confess.

Suddenly she was very angry. Hadn't she already done enough? How many such decisions would be forced on her? How long would this stupidity go on?

Relief crowded out the anger. She knew she would tell her uncle nothing. She was glad she was a hypocrite, glad she was a fraud. At last she was behaving properly. It was every man for himself. Everything else was a mirage. She was no better than anyone else. Why should she be? It had been stupid to think so. She was sorry for Tata, of course. They had been friends. But that didn't mean Maria should sacrifice herself. Tata had just been a victim of bad luck. Indeed, she had brought it on herself. She had gone back to Stepan. Why should Maria have to suffer because of Tata's stupidity?

Maria felt remarkably better. She had been overwhelmed by terror, but now it was completely gone. She was amazed at how easy the decision had been to make. She looked at Telegin and saw that it had never even occurred to him that she would make any other. He, too, was a fraud and hypocrite, of course. He was perfect. She envied him. She hoped one day she would be as good. And at the same time, he was the most genuine and natural person she knew. Even Michael was bitter about reality. Telegin, however, could imagine nothing else.

"You are right," she said. "Why should I deprive the people? I'll rejoin the company as you suggest."

"The people will thank you, Masha. You'll see."

"I suddenly feel remarkably well. I don't remember ever feeling better."

"You've changed, Masha. That's the truth. There is a development, a flowering. I don't know what to call it. But it's good."

"Cyril Modestovitch, there is no one in the world I would rather be with than you."

She leaned back against the cushions. They were very comfortable. She was enjoying the ride very much.

LXI

Orloff studied the reports on his desk. The workers had struck the Patronny and Trubotchny mills, the Baltiysky and Laferm factories, and had refused a government order to go back to work. They had issued a proclamation demanding "freedom." Martial law had been declared. Orloff had arrested the strikers as saboteurs, which immediately had led to more proclamations. Zinoviev had wired to Moscow for troops. But the same thing was happening there. And the farmers had risen in Tambov, Siberia, the Caucasus and Ukraine.

He looked out the windows. A regiment of troops was marching down the street on their way to the South to fight against Wrangel. Across the street were a sign which warned, "Who does not work, shall not eat!" and another urging a fight against corruption.

It could not be avoided. Something was seriously wrong. But what it was, he could not understand. They had gone by the book. Everything should have worked out as Marx had said. But it hadn't. The goal seemed to be deteriorating as they approached it. Orloff was beginning to feel doubt but fought it off. What was happening, he knew, was somehow temporary; an unpleasant phase that would soon pass. The dawn of the Revolution would be revived. Katya would come back. She had written recently to say only that she was still living in Moscow. Orloff wondered what she had been doing.

He sat again at the desk and picked up the next paper. It concerned one comrade Tatiana Alexandrovna Beresova, a People's Artist, accused of the murder of comrade Marchenko. At last he had solved that troublesome case. Kolodsky had remembered that Stepan was planning to break off with Tata. This had been her motive. Kolodsky had not realized how important that was. Tata loudly claimed to be innocent. They all did. Orloff was sick of it. Now there would be a carefully arranged trial, in which would be dramatized once again the career of the late hero, the greatness of Communism and the

432

criminality of its opponents. "Even in death, Marchenko serves Communism," Dolgorensky had chuckled. "Perhaps there is an afterlife, after all."

The door opened. Kolodsky came in. "Comrade Telegina to see you."

"All right. Send her in."

Maria would take his mind off his troubles. Indeed, he was always glad to see his niece. She was one of the few people he really liked. But this time there was something strange about her face as she came in and closed the door. It was pale, expressionless, like a mask — or like the face of someone already dead.

"Come in, Masha," he said. "Sit down."

Maria stood stiffly in the center of the room. "This is very difficult for me, comrade Orloff. Please do not make it more so."

Orloff frowned. "What do you mean?"

"I am here to explain the murder of my brother."

Orloff felt his blood stop. "What?"

"I said . . . ."

"Your brother died in a prison camp, Masha. He has been dead for three years."

"No, comrade general. He died in his apartment. He has been dead only four months. I killed him. Arrest me, comrade general! Release Tatiana Alexandrovna!"

She was irritating him and he gestured at his stack of papers with annoyance. "Masha, please! I know she is your friend. But I'm swamped with work. I have no time . . . ."

"Stepan was killed with an American revolver. It belonged to my father. You found it beside the body."

His mind was racing, but there was no escape. Maria was obviously telling the truth.

"So you knew Marchenko was your brother all along?"

"No. Only since I went to him to plead for my father."

"There was nothing Stepan could have done, Masha. There was nothing I could have done, either."

"Stepan was responsible for my father's death. It was Stepan who forced me to marry Telegin in order to keep my father alive. It was Stepan who sent me counterfeit letters from my father after his death. Stepan did nothing. That was how he killed my father. Stepan was responsible. I do not care what the Party says.

"An old friend who knew of my father's death came to visit. He told me the truth. I came to Petrograd. I killed Stepan. Here, for the record, is one of the letters. As you see, it is dated after my father's death. You have been looking for *me*, comrade general. And now you have found me."

Orloff looked at the letter. It was definitely real. He even recognized whose handwriting it was supposed to contain. He had received a few letters himself over the years from his late brother-in-law. The letter proved her claim, but he continued to study it. He did not want to continue the conversation.

"Why are you telling me this?" he asked.

Maria laughed sarcastically. "Because I am a fool."

Orloff's headache had returned, pushing his eyes slowly from their sockets. He rubbed them thoroughly. As always, it did no good. "You could have kept this to yourself," he said. "Why didn't you?"

"Forgive me, comrade general. I know the Cheka is never wrong."

"Masha! Stop it!"

"I am at your disposal, comrade general."

But Orloff did not answer. He did not look up. He did not move. He could not. He continued studying the letter until he saw nothing.

"All right," said Maria. "I'll be at home when you want me."

He heard the door open and close. Once again he was alone. He felt intense relief. He liked being alone. It was uncommunistic, he knew. But he always had liked being alone. And he had never liked it as much as he did now. Maria had finally gone. That was all he wanted. His lungs unhurriedly reached for air. His heart calmly pumped his blood. In the thin wall of his temples, he could feel the regular rhythm of his pulse. But his mind, happily, had stopped. It was blank. He idly picked up the paper bearing Tata's name. He looked at it. He understood nothing. But it crinkled loudly between his fingers.

And, to his horror, he began to think. He could not help it. Ignorance really is bliss, he thought. It would be so blissful not to know. The malaise he had felt recently seemed like luxury in comparison. If only it were possible not to make a decision at all. If only he could just forget the whole thing. But that, of course, would *be* a decision. Why had Maria decided to come here? Why hadn't she simply kept her mouth shut? Why had she passed this decision on to him? What was at stake here now was her physical survival. But she seemed to be driven by some foolish, antiquated sense of justice . . . .

He broke off suddenly and laughed aloud, a toneless, mocking laugh which was unlike him. It was as if he were the butt of his own practical joke. He was ashamed, an emotion which also was unlike him. He was being petty, thinking not of others but of himself. What about the innocent Tata? What about Maria, his own niece? The fact was that Maria *had* told him. He *did* know. What was he going to do about it?

He went again to the window and looked out. The gray, stolid buildings were still there, as were the signs glorifying work and the fight against corruption. Once again he was annoyed, without knowing why — which made it worse. A shabby, old-fashioned carriage with green and white trimmings was coming across the square. It was drawn by an equally shabby horse. Somehow it reminded him . . . .

It was 1907. He was standing in a doorway across from the Alexandrovsky Gardens. The carriage would be along soon on its way to the opera. In his pocket, his hand cupped the bomb. The plan was perfect. He would throw it and escape through the Gardens.

It was intensely cold. His breath was like smoke. He stamped his feet briskly but felt nothing. He could hear the sound but there was no sensation. He laughed silently. Perhaps when the carriage came by, he would be unable to move. Someone would find him frozen the next morning. At least he could be sure of the bomb. He had rigged it himself. Last week the new man had blown himself up. One had to expect that when dealing with amateurs.

Kolodsky came by as scheduled with the tray of cigarettes.

"Cigarettes, your honor?" Kolodsky said.

"A package of Doves," Orloff said.

Kolodsky handed the package over.

"How much?"

"One hundred kopecks, your honor."

"A hundred kopecks? It's too much. Who would pay it?"

"You should, your honor."

"In that case light one."

Kolodsky opened the package, took out a cigarette and lit it. He put the cigarette in Orloff's hand. Then he silently shuffled down the street.

So everything was going according to plan. There were only a few more minutes to wait. He wanted very much to draw some smoke, but that could easily disrupt the timing. This was an important cigarette. And, in fact, it was already dangerously short when he heard the bells. The carriage was coming up the street. He could clearly see the green and white trimming.

He waited. The cigarette was beginning to singe his fingers. But it was important that the carriage reach the right spot, as in rehearsal. When it did so, he took out the bomb and lit the fuse, and ran swiftly into the street toward it. The Grand Duke's face was framed in the window. Orloff's arm drew back to throw.

At that moment, he saw that the Grand Duchess was in the carriage, and on the seat across from her were the children. How had this happened? Dolgorensky had assured him the Grand Duke would be alone. She did not recognize him, of course. But she was the patroness of his former regiment. They had ridden together in several reviews. Now she looked at him quizzically, her lips pursed. The children were pointing at him and laughing.

Orloff's arm was still cocked to throw. Suddenly the Grand Duchess understood. Her eyes widened. Her lips formed the word "No!" She wrenched the children away from the window and threw herself upon them. The Grand Duke shouted. The driver looked around.

The carriage had passed. Orloff had made a decision. Now it was too late. The choice was made. He threw the bomb as far as he could into the Gardens. It lifted some wreckage with a hollow roar. He ran through the Gardens as scheduled. The carriage turned a corner and disappeared.

Dolgorensky was roughly pulling his sleeve. "Why didn't you throw it, damn you?" he yelled.

"The children."

"Damn the children!"

Once again it was 1920. Orloff was still looking down into the square. The carriage turned the corner and disappeared.

"You said he would be alone," he said flatly.

Orloff shook himself fully into the present and rubbed his eyes. Behind them his brain boiled with pain. It was as if, like an insect, he were being squeezed slowly between gigantic fingers, the pressure increasing as he struggled against it. How stupid it had been to remember all that. Why had he?

Once again he felt annoyance with Maria — she was clearly the cause — and immediately thrust it off. To feel it was a weakness, a self-reproach, and it was replaced by shame. Still, even that was preferable to the realization that the facts drew him to an obvious conclusion. He had given his word. He had promised her father he would protect her. He did not give his word easily. Yet he had given it easily, even gladly, to Danilov. Why had that promise produced such a conflict with the Party? Once again his mind was whisked away into the past, to the many good times he had spent in Danilov's company. He felt a nostalgic warmth for his late brother-in-law. He remembered his futile attempts to save him.

Indeed, the pleasure Orloff had drawn from the guardianship of his niece in recent months had now been compounded by the very confession which accused her. What Maria had done was so beautifully right. It could not be improved. It was exactly what Orloff would have done in her position. He, too, had been victimized by Stepan. Her actions shone with moral purity, as if calculated to appeal to the thing he valued most. He felt admiration — and at the same time he felt jealousy. What Maria had done — from her attempts

436

to free her father, to her present confession — was such a contrast to the staleness of the life he now lived. It demonstrated once again the truth that life was black and white and not gray. It reminded him of himself twenty years before. He sensed, without understanding, that her motive was related to his own motive for entering the Party.

How could it be that her actions were so clearly in conflict with the Party — and therefore wrong?

That was why even the shame of being petty enough, even for a moment, to blame her for his problem was preferable to the pain of knowing that he had one. She was wrong. She had murdered a Party member. And Orloff too was a Party member. He had also given his word to the Party. And what the Party did was right because the Party did it. That was precisely why Orloff had joined. A Party requiring less than complete dedication was for hypocrites. Anything worth doing should be done completely. Anything less was just amateur meddling. Only the Communist Party was right. That was an axiom requiring no investigation. Orloff's emotions about Maria's actions were totally irrelevant.

Indeed, the same personal factors which compelled him to one decision also compelled him equally to its opposite — because they *were* personal. They introduced an unscientific, subjective element into the affair. It was the personal factor which in every situation made things difficult to see. It was the personal factor which caused injustice. That was why it should be eliminated. That was why the Party had eliminated the Tsars. Personal wishes always made things stupid, picayune and dull. They had reduced the heroic to the pedestrian. The measure of the greatness or pettiness of a particular action was the amount of personal motive it contained. That perhaps was the great lesson of Communism. So the thing that was really driving him to one conclusion was the very fact that he wanted the other. It would be weakness, repulsive weakness, to violate a universal principle in favor of a whim.

Maria was wrong. She had killed a Party member. She was an enemy of the people. She must be condemned.

And yet . . . how could he be sure? Years ago he had obeyed the principle and spared Golovin; he had been wrong. Would he be wrong today if he condemned Maria? No one would condemn him if he spared her. Indeed, no one would know.

He laughed sarcastically. The degeneration he denounced in others had begun. He was even beginning to think like a bourgeois.

Stepan's face appeared in his mind, and then Telegin's. How could such people be members of the Party? What did it mean? Was there any explanation for it in Marx? Perhaps they, too, were simply hangovers from Capitalism. It was interesting to speculate . . . .

But he could not. The problem returned. It was intolerable. It could not be avoided. He had to make a decision. And he had never had a problem like it. He had made difficult decisions, but had always known what was right. He had never had a moral conflict. He had never done anything about which he later felt guilty. He was a man to whom everything was objective, scientific, usually settled by a directive from the Party. And now he had been forced into an impossible contradiction, forced to choose where choice was impossible, where the alternatives were as desirable as they were intolerable.

Hours passed. It had long been dark. He still stood unseeing at the window. Suddenly realizing this, he went to his desk and sat down. He had nothing in mind. His mind was still a blank. It was just something to do, creating the illusion that something was being done. Again he drummed on the desk, which also accomplished nothing.

Only a few inches away, on the far side of the desk, were the two heavy rubber stamps, each in its usual place on its heavily inked pad. Between them they decided who lived and who died, who stayed and who was sent away, who was freed and who was not. Indeed, their thick bodies and knobby, bulbous handles gave them the appearance of stocky little men on whom Orloff imagined faces and uniforms. It was as if the messages they conveyed were printed on the soles of their boots. And somehow — he did not know why; they were in their usual place and looked the same — somehow all this now struck Orloff as unusually strange. Indeed, these innocent devices now struck him as thoroughly extraordinary. As if for the first time, he realized that he, Orloff, just one man sitting in a room, somehow had power, absolute power, over millions of lives. He had even more power than Nicholas once had, and because of it millions were afraid.

He could exercise this power simply by choosing a stamp and pressing it on a paper. It was the most extraordinary thing he had ever heard of! For the first time he began to understand, really understand, that his fantasy about the stamps was another small evasion. The stamps, of course, decided nothing at all. He, Orloff, did all the deciding and each decision concerned a separate individual. It was as if he were stamping his heels on innumerable human bodies, transformed for the moment into sheets of paper on his desk.

A wisp of fear — an emotion Orloff never felt — rushed through him. Something was fearfully, crucially wrong. Just as suddenly, he threw the emotion off. It was absolutely imperative to keep control. There was nothing wrong. Nothing at all. All he had to do was make the proper decision.

In fact, he now saw clearly what he had to do. He looked calmly at the appropriate stamp, already sure it was the right decision. The fear had gone. He felt intense relief. Yet he could not reach across the desk and pick the stamp up.

Another hour passed. Or perhaps it was just a few minutes. He was not sure. Then he picked up the stamp. As usual, there was no trouble at all. It had been stupid to think there would be. It felt perfectly ordinary to the touch.

Orloff raised the stamp and brought it down. The proper orders were printed on the paper.

LXII

Telegin eased his bulk into a chair and looked around. Nothing had changed, which was good. He liked the decor. He was in one of his favorite places, and he was already mentally chewing the French delicacies he would order. Along with them, of course, he would have some wine, but he could not decide what it should be. Chateauneuf du Pape? St. Emilion? How wonderful it was to have such problems. His belly prodded the table edge with delight. It was good to get away, at least momentarily, from the endless herds of unbearably boring and smelly proletarians. How anyone could seriously believe them capable of enjoying a ballet was inconceivable. Indeed, their noxious influence had permeated even here. Especially here, he thought, as he looked around. For instance, those commissars talking too loudly to their wives who wore too much lipstick. Trying to prove they are as good as their betters. Trying to prove they belong in this place reserved for Party members. The grace and charm of the old days had not survived. The idea that they could appreciate the food here was ridiculous.

Still, they were better than the usual proletarians. This lot had at least bathed recently. Telegin began to relax. Things in general were going very well: his work, his pay, his relationship with Lunacharsky. Indeed, it had been one thing to be a ballet critic, even the most influential; it was another to wield the force of the government, the power to shape men's minds. And he wielded more and more of it very well. Communism was the ideal system, and he, Telegin, was the ideal Communist. At last he was living as a real intellectual should.

Michael had not arrived yet, which was good. Telegin was enjoying the anticipation so much. He was about to arrange another of the schemes for which he would be famous. It would be simple but effective. It would be devastating.

Kolodsky had come to see him in great excitement not long before.

440

Kolodsky had heard such an interesting thing eavesdropping outside Orloff's door. "Comrade Marchenko" had really been Stepan Danilov. Stepan had done nothing to save his own father, and had forged letters to his sister to prove their father was still alive. And his sister — Telegin's wife — had confessed to Orloff that, because of it, she had killed him. Kolodsky had been positive that Telegin would want to know.

There had been nothing threatening in Kolodsky's words or in his tone. Kolodsky was a worm. He would not dare to make a threat. And Telegin could crush him like a worm. Indeed, there was nothing in the situation he could threaten Telegin about. He had no reason to threaten Telegin, who had always treated him well, like the useful worm he was. He was telling this to Telegin simply because it was a secret, and because he hoped Telegin gratefully would use his growing power to advance him. Kolodsky was tired of being just a worm. For him, the Revolution had made no change. People still treated him like a worm. The commissars treated him like a worm, as had the Tsarists. On his face had been the usual, nervous, wheedling smile.

But, at the same time, the new situation was dangerous. It was obvious what Orloff would do about Maria. He was a fanatic. He would condemn her. The fact that she was his niece was less than irrelevant. He would condemn Maria *because* she was his niece.

Perhaps this would be bad for Telegin. After all, she was his wife. Perhaps he would lose his hard-won position — and even more. It was impossible to discuss anything with a fanatic. Orloff might condemn Telegin, too. He still resented the articles Telegin had written about him years before. Orloff would welcome this chance to hurt him. Perhaps it would be best to throw Maria out. The less there was between them, the better.

Indeed, Telegin reluctantly had been thinking this already. He did not like the new Maria. Until recently, she had rebuffed him because she felt disgust, but now she wanted him for the same reason. And the fact that she wanted him ruined her appeal. Telegin no longer felt desire. To want something so contemptible demeaned her. It proved that she deserved to get it. She had become a bore.

Telegin had decided to give her up. He would deliver her to Voronov and thus rid himself of all his problems. Voronov still wanted her, Telegin knew. They had probably been deceiving him all along. In this way, Telegin would even the score. And he would do so by using a unique weapon: the truth — not the whole truth, but part of it. His skill at this game was continually improving.

Now Michael was coming across the room. Telegin had called and suggested they meet. As usual, Michael's voice on the telephone had been insulting. But Telegin had known his curiosity would force him to come.

Michael sat down, filled a glass and drank. He looked at Telegin — looked *through* him. There was nothing on his face, not even a sarcastic smile, not even that recognition of Telegin's presence. It was as if Telegin did not exist and were not there, which would make his coming triumph even better. But minutes passed, and Michael said nothing, so Telegin raised his glass. "To the proletariat!"

"I'll drink to that," said Michael. "They're essential. Do you realize that if there were no proletariat we would have to invent one? If there were no proletariat there would be no Communist Party."

"True," said Telegin. "I had not realized." Troubled sincerity appeared on his face. "Your simple presence provokes the truth. You once said you hated hypocrisy. So do I, Michael Fyodorovitch. I mean that. Masha and I have been living lives of hypocrisy."

"Of course you have. You're frauds. We're all frauds. No one has ever been anything else."

Telegin nodded, crushed with guilt. "You're right. And the truth is painful, believe me. But at the same time you make it easy. It's the truth I'm here to tell. I have been insincere, Michael Fyodorovitch. I have made you suffer. But I could not help myself."

"Think nothing of it."

"Do you know who murdered comrade Marchenko?"

"Certainly. It was Tata Beresova. I arrested her myself, which proves her guilt."

"No, Michael Fyodorovitch. It was not Tata Beresova. I must reveal the truth. It will bring me relief. The real murderer is Masha — my wife!"

"That can't be true," said Michael, at last showing interest. "At the time, she was with you in the south."

"No," said Telegin. "She left soon after you did."

"Why?"

"Do you know who 'comrade Marchenko' really was?"

"Who was he?"

" 'Comrade Marchenko' was Maria's brother."

"Stepan?"

"Yes."

"That can't be true either. Her brother died in a German prison camp during the war. You are mistaken, Cyril Modestovitch."

"Am I?" A sly smile crossed Telegin's face. "Stepan was released soon after Brest-Litovsk. But he left his name behind, in the prison camp. Like so many sons of the bourgeoisie today — and who can blame them? — he refused to be denied the fruits of Socialism because of his father's bourgeois name. He took another name, the name of some nondescript private killed in some campaign. At the time, as you will remember, you were a fugitive. I believe you served together. What name did you use?"

Michael did not answer. He filled his glass and drank. Once again he saw Stepan as he had the last time — at the bridge.

"Stepan was an ambitious man," Telegin said. "And at the same time he was selfless. He had become a dedicated Socialist — dedicated to the public good. He wanted to serve the proletariat. He joined the Cheka. He became 'comrade Marchenko.' "

"Comrade Marchenko," said Michael.

"Yes."

A piece of the puzzle finally fitted in. Michael remembered Kolodsky and the freight car full of food. Kolodsky unknowingly had taken Stepan's orders. "Comrade Marchenko" — his boss — had been a bourgeois; the son of the man Kolodsky had hated.

"Stepan's father — your former employer — was arrested. The Food Trust offered his release if he would cooperate, but he refused. The workers were starving. They still are. They needed food. But in a spirit of revenge, Danilov egotistically refused to help them. Egotism is the basic cause of all problems. And by so doing, Danilov sealed his own doom. He destroyed himself. It was poetic justice.

"Stepan faced a painful moral conflict. He suffered intensely. I know; we were friends. On one hand was his personal duty to his father. On the other, his social duty to the people — to the Party. He chose the Party. He did not intervene. He could not. Painful though it was, he did his duty. He kept his word.

"I, too, suffered. It is painful even to recall. I wanted Maria. Can you blame me? Of course you can't. You want her, too. But she refused me. She laughed — and you can't blame her either. She was right, Michael Fyodorovitch. I am contemptible. I am a fraud. I don't deserve Maria Ivanovna. Indeed, look at me! I am repulsive! I am disgustingly fat! The thought of my bloated, pudgy body smothering Maria's makes me sick!

"But I, too, have feelings. I'm sensitive, in fact. You may not have thought so, Michael Fyodorovitch, but it's true. I. too, have hopes, aspirations and desires. People don't believe that, because I'm so fat. They laugh. Can you imagine the pain? And love is a madness. Don't the poets say that? Desire forces one to do things. I've done them. I admit it. All's fair in love and war.

"Stepan and I were friends. I've said that. I had lent him some money to pay a debt. I always try to help a friend. He listened to my problem. And he understood. We agreed that I would tell Masha she would get letters from her father, if she would come away with me.

"And she did, as you know. She's so fine! — too fine! She would have done anything — and did — to save her father. And I would have done the same — and did — to get her. Can you blame me? I'm human, too!"

All the pieces fell into place. Michael heard his own voice, heard it clearly, telling Maria about Stepan. He heard Maria's, harshly driving him away. Michael understood everything at last. It was horribly painful. He had never felt such pain.

"It worked," said Telegin, "but then Danilov destroyed himself. It was poetic justice. The authorities executed him. Why must the sins of the fathers be visited upon the sons?

"Stepan wanted to shield his mother and Maria. He, too, did something stupid because of love. He began to write the letters himself. Maria found out. Someone told her, someone who knew her father was dead. I don't know why, but she blamed Stepan. She came to Petrograd. She killed him. Was she wrong? I don't know."

Telegin filled his glass. He smiled. He had never felt such joy. Michael had not moved. He was staring at the table. But Telegin could see that that was because his emotions were so strong. At last Telegin had hurt him. He had finally drawn blood. At last he had penetrated that impassive face. Telegin felt contempt. He knew that Michael was in his power. He waited. He knew there was no need to rush.

"Why are you telling me this?" Michael asked after a while.

"Because Masha is suffering, Michael Fyodorovitch. She wants you. She has lost you. She has driven you away. I know everything, Michael Fyodorovitch. She has told me. You could not help yourselves. It was love. Go to her. Take her. Relieve my guilt and pain. We will both thank you. It will be a favor. I can no longer live with this hypocrisy. It is an insult to the Party."

"It is good of you to tell me," said Michael.

"It was good of you to come."

Michael could not concentrate. He could not think. He knew that what Telegin said was true. And he knew that he could not wait another minute.

"I'll go now," he said carefully, as if he were drunk.

"Yes," said Telegin. "I think you should."

Michael got up as in a trance, and walked slowly away. Telegin watched him, smiling with delight. It had taken years, but Telegin had finally beaten him. Everyone had a weak spot. The problem was to find it. Voronov had been reduced to a bunch of painful emotions. It would make him a better

Communist. Comrade Lunacharsky would be pleased. Telegin was the right man to supervise Soviet education.

"Michael Fyodorovitch! Come back!" he called in a stage whisper. And Michael did so, automatically, standing before Telegin as if hypnotized.

"Be assured that the truth is safe with me," Telegin said.

Michael nodded. "Yes. All right." Again he slowly walked away.

It was perfect. It would get even better. If only Stepan could be here. Telegin snapped his fingers. "Waiter!" he called.

LXIII

Maria poured a glass of vodka and gulped it down. Perhaps if she drank enough it would blot out reality. She lit a cigarette and leaned back in the comfortable chair. It was pleasant in the large but cozy room. Indeed, once again she was living very well. She had returned to the company. She was now a "Soviet artist," whatever that was. "From each according to his abilities, to each according to his needs." Communism made sense once you realized that none of the commissars really believed that stuff. It was just cleverly devised nonsense to deceive the proletariat.

She thought of Tata, who was still locked up. What was it like where Tata was? She shrugged and poured another glass of vodka. The temptation arose to blame Tata and she yielded to it, coasting luxuriously on a wave of resentment. But at the same time, she knew that it was her own fault, not Tata's. She had gone to her uncle out of momentary weakness. Her own egotism had betrayed her, as Orloff would have said. What right had she to think she was so important? What were her spurious values worth? She had failed Communism's sensible moral code. Had she been a true Communist she would have done nothing — and she wanted more than anything to be a true Communist.

Her uncle was one of those who really did believe the "ideology." He believed it all. Somewhere, somebody had to, she supposed. But why Orloff? He was by no means a stupid man. But he was naive. She had never understood him and did not now. There was no way of knowing what he would do next, except that soon she would hear a knock on the door and some Chekists would take her away. That was one thing she could be sure of. Perhaps Michael would make the arrest. That would be amusing and appropriate; so communistic.

It made no difference, of course. She felt nothing. She was already dead.

She looked around the room idly. Her glance fell on the set of Hugo in the bookcase near the fire. It was a weakness — part of the reason she was still not a perfect Communist. She should not have kept it. There was no place for Hugo in a world such as this.

She drew a volume from the shelf and greedily felt the binding, like a criminal indulging in a secret pleasure. It gave off a leathery, enjoyable aroma. There was an elegance about it which itself told the story of another, impossible world. It surprised her, but she was still so stupid she enjoyed it.

She opened the book. The pages had long yellowed. She saw that the volume was *Les Misérables.* Idly she turned the pages, not really reading — she almost knew the book by heart — but browsing from one familiar episode to another. Nothing had changed. Serene and irresistible as always, the prose crossed the page, elegant and sure, inexhaustibly powerful like an endless army of marching men in ranks of ideas. Maria vigorously shook her head. What nonsense! What stupidity! Could anybody seriously believe such stuff? Luckily, she was no longer taken in.

This volume, like the others, was full of engravings. One was between her fingers now, under the filmy paper protecting it. She lifted the paper and looked at it. It was a portrayal of the scene in which Cosette goes alone into the night to fill the water bucket, struggles to return with it, sees a hand suddenly descend and take it — and sees Jean Valjean towering above her. Impossible! thought Maria. So utterly childish!

Yet, to her surprise, she began to cry, calmly, without emotion. The tears fell quietly on the page, tears not just of frustration but of hopelessness. They were one of the few remaining luxuries that had not been declared counterrevolutionary. She enjoyed them without enjoyment, enjoyed involuntarily. Tears were so obviously a sign of weakness, so stupidly and undeniably feminine. And most important, so totally and laughably uncommunistic. Could one seriously conceive of Lenin . . . *in tears?* But there was nothing else she could do. She had no choice. Hugo, the master, had laughed. Her spurious Communist personality suddenly was gone; try as she might, she could not sustain the pretense.

"Oh," she said aloud. "Oh, my God, my God."

Suddenly she became aware that she was not alone. Someone was standing at her chair. Quickly and guiltily she rubbed her eyes. "What is it? she asked. "Who is that?"

At last they cleared and she could see. It was Michael.

"All right," she said. "Arrest me. Go ahead."

He lifted her, slowly, carefully. She was so light.

She tried to speak again, but could say nothing. Yet it made no difference, because Michael shook his head. "Don't talk."

447

He looked at his thumb on her upper arm. As before, the firm, tawny flesh around it billowed, the billow crested by an arc of light.

"Telegin told me everything," he said. "Why didn't you?"

"Everything?"

"Yes. At last it's all right."

She realized that once again there was something Michael did not know. But he would know soon enough. There was no need to tell him. What would happen would happen, and there was nothing either of them could do. The difference was that before she would have struggled with the fact; now she was resigned.

"Why would Telegin tell *you* everything?"

"I don't know. Does it matter? Do you really care?"

"I care. But it doesn't matter."

They both laughed in a way not often heard any more. They did not laugh defiantly, nor cynically, but quietly, intimately, for the simple pleasure of laughing together.

"We're going to escape," said Michael.

"Escape?" She said the word as if these were nonsense syllables and meaningless sounds — as if there were not, nor ever could be, such a concept. "Escape . . . to where?"

A globe was on the table near them. Michael spun it and stopped it with a finger. "To England? To America?"

"There's no such place. Anybody can make a globe and paint anything he likes on it. It doesn't really prove — "

Michael dug a hand in her thick black hair, pulled her to him and held her close.

LXIV

There was a knock and Orloff started, as if caught doing something wrong. He had been writing another letter to Katya. He had written many letters to Katya. He had never liked to write letters, but now something compelled him to write and write. And there seemed to be little point in it. Katya still had not replied. He knew her address in Moscow and nothing more. But he was writing not so much to ask about her as to tell her about himself, about personal details of no particular consequence — what he ordinarily described as trivia. He put the letter quickly and guiltily in a drawer. "What is it?" he said shortly.

The door opened and Michael came in.

"You sent for me, Peter Sergeievitch?"

"I . . . sent for you?"

"So Kolodsky tells me. Perhaps he is wrong."

Orloff squeezed his temples. "No. So I did."

During the last few months, his feeling for Michael had been changing. No longer did he feel the usual warmth and tolerant sympathy for one who does not know the truth. Now he felt a combination of anxiety and resentment. He did not know why. He had thought about it. He knew only that, until recently, he had always been glad to see Michael and now he was not. Perhaps part of it was the fact that Michael himself had somehow changed, especially in the last few days. No longer was Michael the dour, seething personality Orloff had twitted for years. There was about him now a serenity and a touch of humor. Indeed at this moment, for some reason, those qualities seemed unusually pronounced. Orloff was even more repelled. And he was annoyed by being repelled.

Since what he wanted least at the moment was to see Michael, who now approached him, he began poking through the papers on his desk. "Let me see," Orloff said.

Somehow he has changed, Michael thought. For the first time, Michael saw signs of age in his face. He had lost his color. His face was gray. Perhaps that was because he now spent so little time outdoors. But the usual alertness was also gone. It had been replaced by a vague sadness Michael had not seen there before, a sadness posing as fatigue. But why? Was the cause Katya's departure months before?

Somehow their psychologies had reversed. Now it was Orloff who seemed to be suffering from some wound. And now it was Michael who wanted to do something to salve it for the old friend he grudgingly admired so much. But, remarkably, the thing he wanted most to tell him, which also would have been the best medicine for him, was at the same time the last thing in the world he could tell him. It was too personal. If only Michael could communicate the truth without naming it. It was what Orloff wanted. He had said so for years.

"We have been together such a long time," Michael said.

"Yes," said Orloff shortly. "A long time."

Ordinarily, Orloff would have asked with mock sarcasm why Michael was saying this now. What was wrong, Michael wanted to know? He thought of asking, but he knew that would be a mistake.

"So much has changed," he said.

"Everything."

Orloff had always enjoyed talking with Michael. They were equals, and Orloff's equal was not easy to find. But now he found even this inconsequential conversation uncomfortable. He wanted to keep Michael at a distance. He wanted to tell Michael to shut up. But that would be irrational, which would make matters worse. There was nothing he could do but grimly listen and answer.

"Do you remember, Peter Sergeievitch, years ago, when you accused me of being a mindless brute?"

"Yes."

"You were right, of course. That's just what I was. An intelligent animal. That's all. I saw, saw clearly, but I didn't understand. And you used words like justice, truth and honor — even in the dust of the wool-cleaning machines. Do you remember? You said there really were such things, and I refused to listen. You said one day I would understand and tell you so.

"You were right. I escaped then, but was still in prison. I have been in prison all these years."

The change in Michael was even more pronounced. He was talking volubly, which was unlike him. His voice was lively. His face seemed to glow. What was behind it? But Michael was still talking, the words hurtling out, slashing savagely at Orloff's consciousness. He did not want to know, after all. He had to stop that voice at once.

He found what he was looking for and handed it to Michael.

"What's this?" asked Michael.

"An order for arrest."

It was a sheet of paper. On it was a name.

Michael read the name: Maria Ivanovna Telegina.

They looked at the paper between them for some time. It crinkled in Michael's fingers in the otherwise silent room.

"You know her, I believe?" Orloff said. "You stayed with the Telegins while recovering from your injury."

"Yes."

"She is my niece."

"Yes."

"It was she who murdered the late comrade Marchenko. Marchenko was her brother. He betrayed her. She killed him."

"Yes. I know."

"You know? How?"

"Telegin told me."

"Why would he do that?"

"He understands you better than I do. He's a rat deserting a sinking ship. And there's another reason."

"Which is?"

"I love her."

It was absolutely silent in the room, except for the crinkling of the fateful paper. The two men looked at each other. Orloff felt that some strange, grotesque doom was creeping in around him, and that there was absolutely nothing he could do but watch — watch himself perform like a puppet on a string.

"Peter Sergeievitch, I have never asked for anything, as you know," Michael said. "I do now. It is the only thing I will ever ask for. I ask that you destroy this paper and forget what is on it."

"That isn't possible," Orloff whispered.

"If I may paraphrase our leaders, what is one inconsequential bourgeoise to the Communist Party?"

"An innocent woman is in prison."

"That isn't my fault. It's yours. It's the Party's. You can release her. Say you made a mistake."

Orloff shook his head. "It can't be done."

"What must I do?"

"There's nothing."

"Must I beg? All right. I'm begging. I'm pleading. Spare this one woman, Peter Sergeievitch. Please!"

Orloff stared at him and instead saw Golovin. Had Katya pleaded with him as Michael was now pleading for Maria? Orloff saw Katya tottering dizzily on hands and knees. He heard Golovin's peculiar laugh. Golovin now sat in an office down the hall. He was one of the Communist Party's best members. Orloff had urged him to join long ago.

Guilt exploded within him like a shell. His skin burned as if turning on a spit. "Stop this nonsense!" Orloff said brusquely.

"You could do it easily. No one would know."

I am not responsible for what I say, Orloff thought. My mouth moves, but it is History that speaks. There is no such thing as freedom. There couldn't be. There shouldn't be. Freedom would be too much to bear.

"I would know," he said mechanically, as if from memory, realizing as he said it how stupidly melodramatic it was. "It would be a lie, a repudiation of law and justice. It would be an insult to everything we're fighting for."

"Law and justice?" Michael said bitterly. "Are you joking, Peter Sergeievitch? You must be. Law and justice . . . today, in Russia?"

Orloff hit him without warning across the mouth. A trickle of blood came from one of its corners.

"Thank you," said Michael. "At last we agree."

"I'm sorry," said Orloff. He took the paper from Michael's hand. "You have a personal interest. It would interfere." He went to the telephone, lifted it, and said into it, "Golovin."

"How appropriate," said Michael. "There will be a trial, I suppose?"

"Of course," said Orloff. "A commissar has been killed. The Party needs an instructive example."

"The Party is a fraud. Communism is a fraud. You're a fraud."

"Golovin? Yes," Orloff said into the telephone. "Come to my office." Orloff hung up.

"You will arrange for the release of citizeness Beresova," he told Michael. "But first you will sit down."

Michael looked at the pistol on Orloff's hip and did so. Orloff sat at his desk. Across it, within reach, stood the stamps like little men. Orloff got up and went to the window. A column of soldiers was marching to the station on their way to one or another front. They understood nothing and would understand less after Trotsky explained it. It was a cold day, cold and bleak.

Neither man spoke. They waited in silence for Golovin.

LXV

"Imagine my feelings, comrades," said Telegin, his voice confidential and at the same time hortatory. "Imagine my feelings, when I discovered that I had taken a gilded viper into my nest." He pointed a manicured finger at Maria, who calmly looked back.

"Look at her!" he shouted. "Don't you see? Imagine my feelings, comrades! Please!" His voice became even more confidential. "The feelings of a man who has fought and suffered for the Revolution."

He spread his hands, palms up. "I am a simple man, as most of you know. A man of strong and direct emotion. I believed it was possible to rehabilitate the daughter of an industrialist. That's the truth. You will think it stupid. And it was. My irresistible enthusiasm, my bottomless sympathy for humanity, my limitless love for the Revolution, my unshakeable loyalty to the Party, contributed — however indirectly — to the frightful event we are considering here. I am guilty, comrades! I am guilty!"

Telegin squeezed the back of a chair for support. He shook his head. "Comrades!" he whispered. "I was wrong. I confess it. It cannot be done. Do not be deceived by yourselves or anyone else. Do not be deceived as I was. If the root is bad, the tree will be bad, too. And by their fruits, ye shall know them, comrades!"

Telegin raised two pudgy fists. "Is it any wonder, comrades?" he bellowed. "Now do you see why I turned her in? Nothing is more important than the Party. Not even one's wife! That is why I asked for the honor of conducting her prosecution."

At the rear of the long room, behind the barrier, the crowd began to murmur. "You did right, comrade!" came a voice.

It was chilly in the room, but Telegin was damp with sweat. He was the center of attention. He had always known he was a star.

Kolodsky sat at the table nearby, nodding. He was impressed. He had been right to put his confidence in Telegin. Telegin was a good Party man and would advance him. It never hurt to know important people. Next to him sat Dolgorensky, lips pursed, eyebrows arched. He, too, was impressed. Telegin was a star. He would go very far in the Party. Kolodsky didn't understand anything. He never had.

Orloff appropriately was acting as head of the tribunal. Maria looked at him. Orloff looked back. There was no expression whatever on his face. Indeed, his face seemed incapable of expression, as if carved from hard wood by a beginner in a hurry. His head was perched on his rigid shoulders like a totem. They both knew that when it was over, Orloff would recommend "mercy" in prescribed fashion and send Maria north to one of the slave camps, where, along with all the others, she would keep the Soviet economy going.

Maria looked up. Michael sat above, in the first row of the gallery. Their glances met. His hands were around the railing, the knuckles squeezed white. She smiled calmly, the smile saying that nothing could be done, and that she was resigned to her fate.

But Michael did not return the smile. He had not wanted to come. Now that he had, he wanted to leave, but he couldn't. He did not want to see and hear it, but he had to.

Now Telegin was questioning Kolodsky.

"And you say the accused came to see comrade Marchenko?"

"She did. Yes."

"Why? What happened?"

"She threatened him. She demanded that Marchenko release a member of her family — a profiteer."

Kolodsky stepped down and was replaced by Dolgorensky.

"You knew comrade Marchenko personally, comrade commissar?"

"Very well, comrade prosecutor. We were good friends. It was one of the great privileges the Party has allowed me."

"And what sort of man was he, from your knowledge?"

"He was a fine specimen of the New Man the Party is creating, comrade prosecutor."

Telegin turned and stared at Maria, his hands on his substantial hips, a foot tapping the floor with exasperation.

"What is your defense?" Telegin screamed.

"I have no defense," Maria said softly.

"No defense?"

"No. I'm guilty. I killed him."

Michael rose abruptly, climbed the stairs and went out. He could not listen to any more. Maria's eyes followed him. Go home, she thought. Forget this. Nothing can be done. Goodbye.

Michael walked blindly through the streets. Crowds of drab, faceless people passed by. They respectfully got out of the way for him, because he was in uniform. They did not know that he, too, had no hope.

Hours passed. He did not know where he was. He was walking aimlessly, going nowhere. He stopped at a corner, in a daze. A hand reached up and pulled his sleeve. A voice spoke.

"Paper?" it said.

Michael looked down. It was Crestin-Galkov. They had not seen each other since the days of the 1916 offensive. They had not known each other very well. Indeed, the other did not recognize Michael. He had finally won his Cross. The ribbon shone on his tunic. But he had lost his legs. The stumps, ending just below the knees, were protected with leather. Crestin-Galkov stood before a stack of newspapers.

"How much?" asked Michael.

"Fifty thousand rubles."

Michael peeled off the appropriate bills, took the extended newspaper and walked off. He turned the nearest corner and threw the newspaper away. He did not want it. It was a fraud, like everything else, like the currency Pushkin had printed to pay for it.

Suddenly he stopped. He had an idea. It was crazy, but no crazier than anything else. Maria could be freed. It was possible. There was no chance at the trial, or while she was in her cell. There were too many guards and other prisoners. And nothing could be done once she was aboard the train. But between the cell and the train, there was a weakness. As always, when the time came, she would be marched under guard with some others through the streets. She would be in chains, but this would be the weakest link. It could be done if she were last in line.

Afterward, she would need papers — false, like everything else — and Michael knew exactly where to get them.

Kolodsky had been home only a few minutes when Michael got there. He was alone, but Michael nevertheless drew him aside, looked around and began talking through a hand. He was not good at theatrics, but he knew that with Kolodsky it was impossible to overdo.

"We are pleased with your testimony, comrade," he said.

"Thank you, Michael Fyodorovitch. There was nothing else to do."

"You have a good grasp of dialectics."

Kolodsky's pigeon breast swelled.

"I need your complete confidence," said Michael.

"You have it. What about?"

Michael pointed, his voice an explosive whisper, his finger an inch from Kolodsky's nose. "You have been selected to receive important information, and to perform important Party work — both of which must be kept absolutely confidential."

"I am glad you came to me, Michael Fyodorovitch. What is it?"

"A conspiracy has been discovered," Michael breathed.

"A conspiracy?" Kolodsky said the word with the excitement of a child. He was almost as surprised as he was happy. He had long thought that what he really wanted had passed him by.

"What sort of conspiracy?" he whispered.

"Once again I must caution you about the need for secrecy," said Michael. "This is not your usual bunch of speculators. This time we are dealing with foreign powers."

Kolodsky suppressed his joy with difficulty. "I understand perfectly, Michael Fyodorovitch. You will not be disappointed."

"What do you really know about Telegin's wife?"

"She is a Capitalist wrecker, a worm. She betrayed the Party."

"And did you also know that she is an American agent?"

Kolodsky whistled. "No wonder she speaks English so well."

"As our leaders have written, just before Capitalism collapses, it seems stronger than ever. It gathers its waning strength for a last blow. Its reptilian carcass thrashes about. It is already dead but doesn't know it. It makes a loud noise which, in fact, is a death rattle. And many Communists become confused and frightened. Unfortunately, they don't have your knowledge of Marxism. Indeed, there is good reason to be frightened: such a reptile can kill. At such times, even more Party vigilance is needed. Do you agree?"

"Completely."

"The tail of the reptile is thrashing about now. The Capitalists are preparing a final, dangerous blow. The existence of Socialist society is at stake. The Telegina is just one of many, you see. The horrifying but characteristic truth is that the British and the Americans have placed agents in every important bureau of our government. The railroads, the Food Trust, even the Cheka itself has been compromised."

"The Cheka itself! Incredible!"

"But not surprising. The Capitalist beasts will stop at nothing to destroy us."

"The swine!"

"These are the people the Telegina is conspiring with."

"But why was this not mentioned at the trial?"

456

Michael smiled. "You reassure me, Kolodsky. I see that we have chosen well. You instantly identify our problem. You see, we do not know who all these agents are. We must not move prematurely. If we do, we will never identify them."

"Yes, I see."

"Our problem is very complex, comrade. We know that her friends will try to free the Telegina on her way to corrective labor. They plan to attack the train. And it is unlikely, but they could succeed. They will have agents on board. We won't know them — until it is too late. They will attack the guards from front and rear. They are well-organized. They are in important places. They have access to every document. And the Telegina is very important to them. They must prevent her from exposing them.

"So we have decided to use this worm, comrade, as a worm should be used. We are fishing in a stream with the Telegina as bait. Sooner or later she will wriggle properly, and we shall have the fish we want. Don't you see the solution? It's obvious!"

Kolodsky became nervous. It *was* obvious, but he didn't see it. Perhaps Michael would change his mind.

"We cannot let these fish simply take her and run," said Michael. "At the moment she is the only bait we have. And if we do nothing, we may be sure they will. Somewhere on the way to Solovetsky they will take her — or kill her.

"But at the same time, we cannot make an official move. They are all around us. The most superficially zealous Chekist could be one. They would know our plan. They know everything. They would swim to the bottom and stay there before we know who they are.

"So there is only one solution. We ourselves must take her before she even gets to the station. We must unofficially take her from ourselves, and create the impression for her that we have been sent by her friends. Her friends will wonder, of course. They will even get uneasy. But since they won't know a thing they will do absolutely nothing. They will wait uneasily for word of what has happened.

"And they will find out. Because shortly thereafter, the Telegina will tell her 'rescuers' what we want to know."

"Brilliant, Michael Fyodorovitch! Brilliant!"

"Strictly by the book."

Kolodsky had resented Michael for years. Kolodsky himself had introduced Michael to the Party. And yet Michael, once a Party member, had advanced far beyond him. Indeed, Michael had treated him with contempt. It wasn't Kolodsky's fault that he was a puny little man. But now that resentment disappeared. Michael had chosen him for this assignment. Kolodsky would be promoted. He would win the recognition he had long deserved. No longer would his fellow Communists ignore him.

"What is my assignment, Michael Fyodorovitch?"

"A good question. And at the right time, you will be told. But now we need the proper papers for our guest."

"And for ourselves. Otherwise she would suspect."

"Correct! Good thinking! We have chosen well, after all. Has comrade Orloff returned to his office?"

"No, Michael Fyodorovitch. He was tired. He has gone home."

Michael smiled. "No, he hasn't. This is part of the plan — so we can get the papers. We need the government stamps on his desk. Comrade general Orloff has ordered that he is not to know anything of the plan himself. We are surrounded by enemies. One mistake would be enough."

Kolodsky chuckled and nodded vigorously. "It's perfect, Michael Fyodorovitch. Perfect! The Telegina will think we have joined the other side. She will actually believe we are her allies!"

"Exactly!"

LXVI

It was cold. Michael's breath hung in the air, threatening to congeal. He stood unnoticed at the rear of the darkened doorway. There was still no sign of dawn, and no sign of the prisoners. It was so cold that even the thieves and prostitutes wouldn't have been about — if they had existed. Of course, there no longer were such people; Communism had made them completely unnecessary. They were symptoms of the putrid disease of Capitalism. The frozen bodies found every morning were frauds. The theory said thieves could not exist — and so they didn't.

It was still. The streets were empty. The nearest police post was a few blocks away. Michael had seen half a dozen men warming their hands at the fire. And Kolodsky was ready around the corner with the bomb. He would be a problem later, of course, and Michael had not decided what to do with him. He had no opinion one way or the other about Kolodsky. No one had. But for now, he could not do without him. He would provide the needed diversion. Michael had thoroughly reconnoitered the area. This was the best place to make the rescue. It was the only place. And they would have only a few minutes. They must not miss.

He felt for the package containing the clothes. It was there. The papers crinkled in his pocket. And along his side, he felt the weight of the gun. Once again, he went over the plan. He had forgotten nothing. Nothing could be done about it now if he had.

A car came slowly down the street. It was a government car; there were no others. He shrank into the darkness in the building entrance and it turned the corner and left the street. He was already behaving like the fugitive he had been — and soon would be again. He was doing so quite naturally. He had always been a fugitive. The years since the Bolshevik coup had merely been an interruption. Once again he was escaping from the psychopathic engine of the state.

The sound of many feet came faintly into range, and with it the distant clink of chains. He had heard it many times, of course, but now for the first time it had a festive quality, like Christmas ornaments tinkling on a tree. Already he could see the two soldiers at the head of the column, the prisoners behind them in single file. It was another shipment of women to the north. Their heads were bent, faces covered, blindly plodding on and on. It was impossible to tell one from the other. They shuffled by silently like shadows on a wall, cloaked in their breath as in a cloud.

His mouth was dry. In spite of the cold, he began to sweat. The soldiers in the middle of the column were already passing.

Then, from the darkness of the doorway, he saw Maria. As he had arranged, she was last in line. Like the others, she was trying to keep warm, which was difficult in her ensemble of rags. But, unlike the others, her head was erect. Her face was calm. She remained untouched.

The tension mounted. She was very near, but he could do nothing. It was as if she were far away. In a second, she would pass. What had happened to Kolodsky? Suppose . . . .

Suddenly the bomb exploded. Kolodsky was right on time. Noise and the pungent smell of powder filled the air. The women bumped into each other and stopped, as if the column itself had shuddered. Michael lit and threw the smoke bombs. There was a hiss and an eye-smarting fog appeared. Women screamed and began to cough.

Maria was standing only a few feet away. But so was the rear guard of two soldiers, frozen with uncertainty. Nothing could be done if they stayed where they were. And they did not move. Minutes passed as they squinted warily through the smoke.

At the front of the column there was a shout, the soldiers stiffened and ran toward it. And as they did so, Michael stepped out and was immediately at Maria's side with a hand on her mouth. He lifted her with his other arm and they were quickly back in the protective darkness of the doorway. He put a finger to his lips and she nodded. He pointed the finger at her shackles and she nodded again.

They waited. The smoke was clearing. The soldiers ran back to the end of the column, and then past it, along with an officer, to the corner. The officer waved a pistol. They looked around. Then the soldiers resumed their places and the officer stepped into the smoke, walked toward the front of the line and disappeared. Minutes passed. Nothing happened. Maria and Michael looked at each other. The automobile that had passed earlier came back at great speed. A voice said something, ending with the word "prisoners." Someone began walking

460

slowly down the column. Then someone else followed, walking quickly.

"No, no, Shishkin!" said a voice. "There's no time for that. Get them to the station. We'll do it there."

"Move on!" a voice shouted. "Get these hags going!"

The chains and feet began moving again. The column was leaving. Like the tail of a great beast, its end flicked and was gone. Now there was little to worry about until the prisoners were counted at the station.

The carriage turned the corner as scheduled, and Michael hurried Maria into it along with the bag of clothes. Kolodsky was on the box, playing taxicab driver.

"I'm the one who yelled," he said over his shoulder.

"Very clever," said Michael. "You're making fools of these Communists."

Kolodsky chuckled. "Yes. Yes."

Maria looked at Michael, puzzled.

"Now for this Soviet jewelry," he said, ignoring her. He removed it easily with the clippers. It fell noisily in a pile on the floor. He handed her the bag of clothes. "Get into these," he said. "There's even cosmetics."

Maria did as she was told. The Soviet rags joined the chains on the floor.

"You know who we are, of course," Michael said. He cocked his head at Kolodsky's back and nodded.

"Of course," said Maria.

"You will come with us."

"Yes."

"Here are your papers. Put them away."

Kolodsky chuckled. "You are surprised to see us?"

Michael nodded.

"Yes," said Maria. "I had thought you were Communists."

"You never can be sure who your friends are," laughed Kolodsky.

Every sense taut and tingling, Michael settled down for the short ride, carefully watching Kolodsky's back. He had nothing at all against the man. He did not wish him ill. Indeed, even though Kolodsky did not know what he was doing, Michael felt grateful to him for doing it. But at a certain point, they would have to part. Somewhere Kolodsky would learn what he was doing, and he would be as angry then as he was cooperative now. Hopefully they could simply separate, Kolodsky still knowing nothing.

They arrived at the station without incident and in silence. Kolodsky abandoned the cab, their papers were examined and they were passed through.

Kolodsky winked at Maria. "You see what we are able to arrange?"

Before them was a Soviet train, half covered with people like a molting snake. Arms, legs and heads protruded, their owners otherwise lost to view. Voices roared. A shrieking child stood alone on the platform, no one paying the slightest attention. People scurried up and down trying to find someplace to light. Every few minutes, someone was disgorged and fell to the platform. Others surged to the vacated place.

But the three fugitives had no such trouble. Michael had cast himself as a commissar, Maria as his secretary and Kolodsky as his assistant. A commissar and his retinue, unlike the rabble, deserved a private compartment. They sat comfortably in one now, watching and waiting. There was nothing else to do, except think about the prisoners marching through the streets to the station.

Kolodsky was in the best of humors. Everything had been arranged. The station where they would get off had been selected, as well as the isolated "hideout" where they would take her.

What a strange little man Kolodsky was, she thought. Amusing, really. His nose was waggling, taking her scent. He had always done that. She knew that he was enjoying the reversal of their positions. But she felt no resentment. His enjoyment was natural. Even though their positions had been reversed, she felt sorry for him. She always had. There had always been something pathetic about him — there still was — a wheedling, nose-waggling desire to please.

But she did not know why he was helping her now. He had always been a Party member, one of the best. His mind had never contained a question. It was extraordinary. She refused to believe that he not only had left the Party but opposed it. She could not imagine why he had said what he had. Michael would explain it to her later. She knew only that she should say nothing. And that she was free. No one was bothering her. She was being left alone. Freedom was nothing more than that. Why, then, was it so difficult to get?

Suddenly she was hot, as if in a fever. She shuddered, visibly, and took out her papers, filled with apprehension and joy.

"They are real, aren't they?" she asked. "This is really happening. Everything's all right."

As she spoke, the door handle moved. Someone was coming in. Michael was immediately on his feet and the papers fell to the floor. Kolodsky gathered them up and returned them.

The door opened and another commissar was looking into Michael's face, trying to decide which of them was a bigger commissar.

"There's no room," said Michael, barring the way.

462

"Of course there is!" said the other shortly, beginning to push on Michael's arm.

Michael spoke softly, just loud enough to hear. "No."

The other commissar looked again, was satisfied and moved on. Michael closed the door and resumed his seat.

Kolodsky's expression had somehow changed. He sat stiffly with a nervous smile, nose drooping like a flag in dead air, as if he had seen something frightening.

And he had. He began to realize that everything Michael had told him was a lie, and that this entire operation was a fraud. Voronov had simply been using him, using him to save this girl who had always held him in such contempt. Voronov and the girl were making a fool of him. Why had he been too stupid to see that? Voronov, after all, had stayed with her and Telegin in the south. And there had been something between them. Why had Kolodsky not suspected anything? Especially since they were so alike. Michael, too, had always looked down on Kolodsky. He had never been a good Party man; always questioning, doubting, full of sarcasm. Behind their calm facades, they were laughing at him now as they always had, ridiculing his puny size and extraordinary nose. With difficulty, he kept invisible a passion to hurt them, to return the pain they had given him, to toy with them and then show he had known the truth all along. He felt a combination of self-contempt, anger and fear. For he realized that there would be ramifications to what was happening — to what he had been a part of. The problem wasn't simply that he was being betrayed. The thing had already gone too far to erase. There would be an investigation and he would be blamed with the others. He would lose his job, his Party membership, everything. As far as the Party would know, he was part of the plot. He had to get out of the compartment at once. He had to get help to arrest these traitors. If the train left with him on it, Kolodsky was as good as dead.

What he had seen was a word, a single word, among Maria's papers as they lay on the floor. The word was "Warsaw." And it proved that Voronov had never intended to get any information from her, that there was no information and there were no spies. Voronov was simply trying to take her out of the country.

Kolodsky cautiously scented the wind. Once again, with the departure of the commissar, it smelled quite calm. He sat very still: it was imperative that he do nothing to let Michael suspect. There was always the possibility of violence with Voronov, and Kolodsky was afraid of violence. It would be dangerous. He smiled nervously. His nose waggled. Slowly, calmly, he got up to go, and Michael quickly was at the door with him.

463

"Where are you going, Nikita Sergeievitch?" asked Michael.

"Just outside," said Kolodsky. "Wouldn't hurt to check around."

"Perhaps it would be safer for you to stay in here."

Kolodsky squeezed his arm. "Whatever we know will do us good. Our departure is delayed. Maybe something has gone wrong."

Michael was sincerely worried about Kolodsky. He wanted Kolodsky to stay out of trouble. And trouble was what he might find outside. There was no way of knowing whom Kolodsky might meet on the platform. There was nothing he could learn that they needed to know. But it was also important to avoid unnecessary conflict, to keep Kolodsky's confidence and not arouse suspicion. And all the while, since Michael had taken Maria from the column, they had not been free to talk, because of Kolodsky's presence. It would be not only pleasant but valuable for them to do so. In fact, the tension of this unnatural silence was unbearable. It could do no harm for Kolodsky to look quickly around the platform. It would be good to know when the train would depart.

"All right," said Michael.

Kolodsky opened the door and went out. His excitement was rising. In a moment he was walking quickly along the platform, oblivious to the babbling crowds around him. He was enjoying a new set of emotions. He was going to pay Michael and Maria back for years of superior remarks — and pay them both back at once. What right had they to think they were better than he? How surprised they would be when he confronted them later. Then he could show how superior he really was! Indeed, comrade general Orloff might well give him Michael's job. Didn't he deserve it? At great risk, Kolodsky had penetrated an anti-Party gang, played along and discovered their plans. Kolodsky was a Soviet hero. He would be honored. There would be parades. The fire inside him had become a conflagration.

He began to run.

*   *   *

"Are you sure?" the commander of the detachment asked.

"I counted them myself, comrade captain."

"That's what worries me," the commander said.

He grimaced. These peasants from God-knows-what jerkwater town! Can't even count. How could the Party hope to make Communists of them?

"Where are you from, Shishkin?" the commander asked.

"From Moscow, comrade captain."

"Moscow? . . . And did they teach you to count in Moscow?"

"Yes, comrade captain."

How irritating this Shishkin from Moscow was. Dumb as a brick wall and didn't even know it. The commander turned away with a sour expression and began counting the prisoners himself. They stood in the cold at the side of the station, like bales of old clothes waiting to be stacked, arranged in four rows as he had ordered. And even before he reached the last row, he saw an empty place at its end; saw that it would contain only forty-nine bales and that Shishkin was right. He finished counting and counted again, not because he expected a different result, but simply to delay thinking about the one he had. The result was the same.

"There are 199, Shishkin," he said. "You're one short."

"As I said, comrade captain. Maybe that was the purpose of the incident."

"Silence, you silly bastard. Of course that was the purpose of the incident."

"That's why I wanted to count them . . . ."

"Shut up!"

With virtuosity and gusto, the commander excoriated Shishkin, choosing from a rich storehouse of invective, raising doubts about his relatives and the legal relationship between his parents. There was no point in it, he knew, other than the fact that he enjoyed doing it, but he enjoyed doing it so much. He liked sticking his face into Shishkin's, and the fact that Shishkin could not pull his face away. He liked the sound of his voice bellowing curses. He liked feeling the cords in his neck stand out. But all along he knew he was accomplishing nothing, fruitlessly trying to keep reality at bay. He had been given 200 prisoners. The papers said so. And he knew as surely as Marx made red apples that the commander of the train would refuse to accept even one less than that number. In fact, in his place he would do the same. Without the exact number of prisoners, he could not get rid of them. The prisoners would imprison him like a set of chains. There would be an investigation and he would be blamed. He would lose his job. He himself would be locked up. True, he was now excoriating Shishkin. But he, after all, was the commander. Shishkin was not. That was why he had the right to excoriate him, and why Shishkin had to take it. And the realization that Shishkin would probably be ignored, while he, the commander, would be made to suffer, caused him to prolong and intensify the excoriation. Furthermore, Shishkin, as he had said, had suggested that the prisoners be counted immediately after the incident, at the scene. Had it been done, the commander now realized, the escapee conceivably could have been caught. And Shishkin would remember that the commander had refused. Shishkin would ruin his promising military career, all because of one lousy prisoner. Somehow it was Shishkin's fault. Shishkin must be made to suffer.

"You're as dumb as a brick wall!" the commander shouted.

At last he was silent, mouth still twitching, eyes staring stupidly, his body itching with sweat in spite of the cold. The excoriation had done no good. The problem was still there. Shishkin returned his look as unfazed as before. And the commander was out of ideas. For the first time, he saw himself as one of the prisoners, covered with rags held together with chains. Shishkin would be the captain and would excoriate him. Shishkin would take unfair advantage. If only the incident could be erased, as if it had never happened. But for that the commander would need to replace the prisoner.

At that moment he saw an odd little man running furtively along the building. "Here! You! Stop!" he shouted.

But the little man ran on as if he did not hear, and this aroused the commander even more.

"That little man, Shishkin!" he shouted. "Bring him here!"

"Certainly, comrade captain!" Shishkin said, and was back in a moment with the little man wriggling in his hand. What a strange little man he was. His eyes bulged in his small face. His prominent nose waggled at them both.

"Your papers," said the commander.

"Of course," said Kolodsky. "Excuse me. I did not hear. I am glad to see you, comrade captain."

"Are you?" said the commander, examining the papers. To his regret, they seemed to be in order.

"Name?" he said, with bored formality.

"Kolodsky, comrade captain. Nikita Sergeievitch Kolodsky."

The commander felt a thrill of joy. There was a different name on the papers.

He shook them at Kolodsky. "Whose papers are these?" he bellowed.

Kolodsky, in his excitement, had forgotten the discrepancy. Now he remembered. "They are mine, comrade captain."

"The names do not match."

"I know they don't. The papers are false. That is why I am glad to see you. You must come with me."

"Must we!" roared the commander. "Shishkin! You hear?"

"I hear, comrade captain."

"I am wearing civilian clothes for a reason," said Kolodsky. "I am a member . . . ."

"Silence!" the commander bellowed.

"Call general Orloff. He will . . . ."

466

Kolodsky was on the ground, dizzy, his face covered with blood.

"Not another word," bellowed the commander. "Not even one."

He fingered the false papers and began to chuckle. "Shishkin," he said. "Return prisoner number 200 to his place."

"But comrade captain," said Shishkin, "he is not a woman."

"Of course he's not a woman, you lout! What of it?"

"All the others — "

"Look, Shishkin!" bellowed the commander, handing him the transfer documents. "Did they teach you to read in Moscow? Do you see anything said about women here? All it says is 200 prisoners. Am I right?"

"You're right, comrade captain."

"Return the prisoner to his place. He has a long trip to take. If he escapes again, you will replace him."

Once again there was a full shipment of prisoners, and Shishkin was moving them out to be checked and loaded. Once again the commander was in his best mood, somewhere between euphoria and rage.

"Shishkin!" he bellowed. "You're as dumb as a brick wall!"

LXVII

Michael walked toward the head of the train, his feet noisily crunching the snow. It was a brilliant day, so bright it was hard to see. It had stopped snowing for a time. Far ahead, the tracks beckoned to a point on the horizon. But if they were simply to start walking, it would be an admission of guilt. Why would anyone leave the safety of the train for the uncertainty of the tracks when all he had to do was wait? Unless there were something he was trying to conceal? Maria could not bear the risk. She probably could not make it. If he had been alone, he would have set out long ago.

As he thought this, two figures came into view, far ahead on the other side of the tracks. Somewhere beyond the horizon they would find Poland — if they were not stopped and could walk that far.

Maria could not. But she could not wait either. Time was passing, in an unfamiliar and painful way. Time was what she needed most, and Michael had stolen as much of it as possible. That was why he had risked choosing the longer but less dangerous route to Poland, rather than the shorter but more common direction of the Baltic. And now the time so frugally collected was escaping, evaporating, disappearing, dwindling like an account being embezzled with the helpless knowledge of its owner.

Michael smashed his fist into the peeling paint on one of the coaches. Nothing could be done. The train lay in the snow like a large, black, dead reptile. It had inefficiently completed a sizeable part of the trip in the jerky, peristaltic manner of a snake. Then with a shudder, it had simply died. This could have been expected, of course, which was why no one had been surprised. Like much of the rolling stock in Russia, the locomotive was of elderly, unserviced, pre-war vintage. At the same time, however, the death was not a thing for which one could have planned. And now the corpse lay unmourned in the snow, on a plain far from anywhere.

For a few days, Michael had been trying everything possible. He had found the cause of the trouble in the locomotive and knew how to fix it, drawing on his long-forgotten days as a mechanic. But it was impossible to do so without tools and parts, and there were none. The policy was simply to operate the equipment until it stopped. And he had searched the surrounding countryside for horses — one good horse was all they would need — but, of course, everything resembling a horse had long since been commandeered or eaten.

Exactly why Kolodsky had not come back and what had happened to him, Michael did not know. But he knew for sure that as the minutes slipped implacably away, Orloff was implacably coming closer. Michael could clearly see his face. On it was the flat, impersonal expression of Communism. And the expression of an individual who has been betrayed.

Michael reached the locomotive, where the coarse aroma of *mahorka* filled the air. The engineer and fireman were smoking. But vile even as that cheap tobacco was, it could not obscure the even more pungent, penetrating odor of the burning bodies of the latest typhus victims. At that moment, some soldiers carrying the day's remains were disappearing over the hill above which the smoke hung in a haze. The train had died, and now the population which lived in its intestines was gradually thinning out.

The train commander was also in the cab. "Sickening, isn't it?" he said.

"Nauseating," said Michael.

"Most of them are prisoners, of course. There's not much air back there, you know."

"They don't deserve any," said Michael. "They stifled us for years."

"It saves us the trouble of feeding them. There's no shortage of good Communist bellies aboard which need the few supplies we've got."

Michael pointed up the tracks at the receding figures. "Those two . . . ."

The commander nodded. "My men, comrade commissar. Quite all right. The storm has ended, so I've sent them ahead to wire for an engine. We should be moving again in a few days."

Michael walked back along the other side of the train. So there was something to look forward to, after all. Perhaps it was the solution. He was reluctant to accept it, but at the moment there was nothing else to do. Now if a way could only be found to stop time while the days passed. He went into the proper coach and found Maria.

"You can smell it even in here," she said.

"Yes."

"And to think I used to complain about *mahorka.*"

"It does change one's perspective."

"Yes."

"Our comrade commander has sent someone ahead to wire for an engine. We'll probably be moving in a few days."

"Do we have a few days?"

"I don't know."

Suddenly she felt faintly dizzy and feverish. Perhaps the cause was fear. Or that hideous, inescapable smell. Or was it the inescapable hunger? She put a plate on the table before Michael. On it was a fish head and a slab of something masquerading as bread.

"You mean we're supposed to eat this stuff?" he said theatrically.

"Don't worry. You won't taste a thing."

"You aren't supposed to."

Grimacing with distaste, they began to chew, the moldy taste searing their mouths, the inescapable smell of death in the air. But they had to eat to stay alive.

A few days later as Michael was returning from the woods with some kindling, he saw a commotion at the head of the train. The train commander and two other officers he had never seen before were shouting at each other loudly, accompanied by the hoots and whistles of the engineer and the fireman.

The commander pounded a fist into a palm. "Those damned Poles!"

"What has happened?" Michael asked.

"Those damned Poles!" said the commander.

"The Poles are invading on a wide front," said one of the other officers. "Exactly what Pilsudski is after, we still don't know. But he is advancing with great speed."

"Why?" asked the commander. "We gave them freedom. We are their benefactors. Ingrates! Vermin! May God torture Pilsudski in hell, comrades. Pray for it!"

"And what does this mean for us?" asked Michael.

"You're to return at once along the tracks, comrade commissar."

"Without an engine?"

"You're to march. There are other men and wagons behind us."

Michael's glance followed the officers' two horses. That they were alive at all was a surprise. They seemed amazingly well-fed. A soldier had come up and was now walking away with them.

"Certainly," said Michael shortly. "It's the only decision. Let's get started."

He got down from the cab and walked back along the train. Defeat was closing in. To return as ordered was out of the question. They could not return. But the confusion which necessarily would accompany the Polish

470

"Afterward, we won't care."

"Not at all."

"Who will bury us?"

"I don't know. We're leaving."

"Now?"

"Yes. Get together as much as you can of that stuff you've been passing off as food. We can't carry much. We'll have to go on foot."

Maria nodded and began gathering the meager supplies. It was a pleasure to obey him, to yield to his will, which was even stronger than her own. Indeed, she drew strength from him. It was intoxicating. Perhaps that was why she felt so weak and dizzy.

In a few minutes they were ready. It was dark — there was no moon. The makeshift candles flickered on their stand. The moribund population of the dead train was settling down. It was quiet, except for the wind, which was now high. The windowpanes shook in their frames.

"I'll blow out the candles," said Michael, "which will make it dark between the coach and the snowbank. We only have to run that far. We'll drop under the coach first to look around. If the sentry is there, we'll wait until he passes."

He put a hand behind a candle and expanded his lungs. As he did so, they heard horses galloping, followed by loud shouts. Lights bobbed in the blackness. A mounted man rode by the window with a torch. Men were running along the train. The population was awake. The train itself seemed to come alive. Authoritative footsteps crunched the snow and then boomed into the coach itself. The door handle moved, the door opened and a tall, heavily dressed man came in.

It was Orloff.

Orloff had already been betrayed twice: by Michael who had arranged Maria's escape, and by Maria herself. He had discovered it simply by asking the commander of the prisoners' detachment about her — in an offhand way, to conceal his interest — and the terrified captain had blurted out the truth, blaming the escape on Shishkin. And what had made the betrayals possible was that twice he had surrendered to his weakness, indulged his meaningless emotions, put himself before the Party, ignored the Party's warning to avoid the personal. It was the personal, as Marxism taught, which was causing all the trouble. It was for personal reasons that he had asked the captain about Maria. Of course, he could just as well have concluded that it was because of his personal interest that he had learned of the escape; had he not asked that personal question, he could not have heard the answer. But he did not. He had surrendered to his weakness to ask about her, and Maria had already

advance would be an advantage. The interests and policies of the
sides, the reasons for the latest outbreak, indeed, even the sides th
merged in his mind and became less and less real. Michael's only desi
get Maria safely out. And time was running out.

Two soldiers passed, carrying a corpse on a door. Another corp
between two more soldiers.

It was Kolodsky.

Kolodsky must have been on the train all along. Why had
reappeared? Where had he come from? Where had he been? Was
another typhus victim? Michael uncomprehendingly watched h
disappear.

Two loud rifle shots crackled in the air. Michael heard a comm
the other side of the train, crawled under, and went toward it. A sol
propped against a tree. One of the officers Michael did not know was
him with the barrel of his revolver, calmly, methodically, shouting
while.

"He killed our horses," the officer shouted. "He killed our hors
son of a bitch shot our horses."

Indeed, the corpses lay near each other nearby. A crowd was
fighting over the remains. Someone was noisily severing one of the
large, elderly woman bent with a bayonet and ripped open the
horse's belly with ease. She pulled the incision apart and plung
hands inside, withdrew them streaming and handed something drip
a boy. She plunged her hands inside again. Eyes wild with fear an
the horse raised his head and tried unsuccessfully to get away. I
somehow still alive.

Michael took out his revolver and shot the horse. No one seer
notice. The officer was still beating the long-dead soldier. The crow
swirled around the horses. Michael walked away quickly. It was gettin;
The wind rose and it had begun to snow.

"What happened?" asked Maria when he came in.

"Nothing much. Somebody shot some horses."

"They'll eat them."

"I saw Kolodsky."

"Where has he been?"

"I don't know. He's dead."

"We're going to die too, aren't we?"

"Yes."

"When?"

"Soon enough. Until then, we'll act as if we weren't."

gone. She no longer needed his personal interest or sympathy. He had exposed himself with difficulty and had been rebuffed for his pains. Again he had been betrayed by the personal element, as when he had trusted Stepan. The personal element had to be stamped out. The perfect man — as he had said himself — was completely impersonal, simply a mechanical instrument of the Revolution. He wanted to say this to Michael and Maria. He wanted to hurt them, to make them suffer, to pay them back for their betrayals. But that, too, would only be personal. And Orloff had not come all this way for personal reasons. He had come to deal with two enemies of the Party. That was why he felt no emotion. That was why his face was impassive.

"Michael Fyodorovitch Voronov," he said. "You are under arrest."

"This is it," whispered Maria.

"Yes," Michael said.

"You will both come with me."

"No," said Michael. "We won't."

Orloff unsnapped his holster and drew his pistol. "Do not force me to use this, Michael Fyodorovitch."

Michael smiled. "You misunderstand as usual. I want you to use it. We have had enough. Enough of your 'trials,' your Party — and of you. We have had enough moralizing, Peter Sergeievitch. Kill us here. Now. Kill us yourself. It will finally square our accounts."

Once again, Michael had introduced the personal element and Orloff was repelled. Had he wanted to do as Michael asked, the personal element would have restrained him. But Orloff slowly realized that he did not want to do it. In fact, so opposed was it to his personal wish and so difficult would it have been to do, that it seemed to him he should do it, and that it would be right. It would be a test. It would prove how good a Communist he was.

He nodded. "All right."

His voice was hollow and expressionless. He cocked his pistol and aimed at them along the barrel. They were young, very young. He had not really noticed it before. They were standing close together. Michael's arm was around Maria's waist. They looked at him calmly, without fear, as if what he was about to do would have no great effect. He saw that, unlike him, they were untwisted and serene. And the disorientation he had been experiencing recently returned. In Maria's place he saw her father, and heard himself promising Danilov to protect her. Then he was again in the tunnel outside the prison camp, and Michael was urging him to kill Golovin.

Then he saw Katya's face. She was smiling at him, her lips parted, her prominent eyes perfectly confident, her bearing proud, even regal. On her arm was the basket in which she used to bring him food. And he realized that now was the proper time to do the job, to apply the science of Marxism-Leninism, finally to become a perfect instrument of the Revolution, at last to stamp out every trace of the personal. He pulled the trigger.

Nothing happened.

He pulled it again. Still there was nothing. Perhaps there was something wrong with his pistol. But there couldn't be. He had checked the pistol not long before. He concentrated carefully, squeezing the trigger forcefully. Still there was nothing. He looked from Maria and Michael to his forefinger. It was pressing with all its energy against the trigger guard. He had not been squeezing the trigger at all. Somehow, he had lost control of his nervous system.

His forefinger was pushing forward on the trigger guard, throbbing, vibrating, bloodless and white. He could not move it. Minute after minute passed. Icy sweat was running down his face. His rigid arm was getting tired, so painful that he began to enjoy it, as if it were a lance protruding from his side. Then his frigid face began to quiver. His burning arm began to shake.

His arm fell heavily at his side, the gun dangling uselessly in his hand. His head fell forward on his chest.

"Send her away," he whispered.

Michael nodded. "Go out," he said.

Without a word, Maria left.

Orloff's shoulders began to heave. His head hung heavily. He could not lift it. An unrecognizable sound came from his throat, reluctantly, involuntarily, as if squeezed out.

"It's all wrong," he said. "It always has been."

"Yes."

"It's worse than Tsarism."

"It is. Much worse."

"You tried to tell me. I wouldn't listen. Katya tried to tell me. I drove her away."

"You're not a true Communist. They're happy with the truth."

"Who is a true Communist?"

"Golovin. Telegin. Dolgorensky."

"But our theory . . . ."

" . . . is a fraud. It was meant to be a fraud."

"A lifetime," said Orloff. "My whole life."

The emotion of self-pity was new to him. He shuddered and tried to shake it off.

474

"Take two horses," he said. "Go now."

"What about you?"

"Forget about me. Take them. Go!"

Orloff heard the door open and close. He was alone.

"Yes," he said aloud. "What about me?"

LXVIII

Katya was not the analytical type. She was not introspective. She did not weigh and calculate. This did not mean that she was stupid. On the contrary, she was very bright. She could have calculated had she tried, but she did not. She did not want to. Her intelligence was of a different sort. She was completely without guile or nuances, completely forthright and direct. And she was singularly deficient in patience. Emotions roared up in her and she acted before she fully understood why. And this, of course, created problems. She did not always express her emotion. She could restrain it if she chose. She had waited in Siberia for Orloff for years. But, surging beneath the restraint, the emotion was there. Her quick, truthful, decisive manner had drawn Orloff to her many years before.

And that was also why she had left him in the wake of the violent distaste she felt for Orloff's agreement to eulogize Stepan. Lately she had been assailed by one violent emotion after another, all unpleasant, ranging from despair to disillusion to outrage. Until now, she had seen the Revolution somewhat at a distance. Now she was living in it, seeing it at close range. Not that anything unusual had happened. She had not particularly suffered. But before, she had been isolated because of her husband's position, and now she was living the life of an ordinary Soviet citizen. She had a small room. She ate in the communal kitchens. And with her labor book, she did compulsory labor in obedience to Soviet law. She had taken a job as assistant to the directress of one of the large nurseries recently established to make New Soviet Men out of the millions of Russian orphans.

The directress was Nastasya Lvovna Filipova, whom Katya had heard about, but had never met. Nastasya Lvovna was one of those for whom the Revolution had been perfect. Soon after the coup, she had kicked Filipov out. She still wore a tight tunic, and tugged at her ear constantly. But now she was the directress of an important Soviet institution.

"Our goal, quite simply, is to obliterate the personality," she had said.

"Obliterate the personality?" repeated Katya. "But why?"

"Personality is a function of the individual," said Nastasya Lvovna. "It is dangerous, unreliable and useless. It lends validity to the imaginary, erroneous concept of the individual — and therefore to what the bourgeois calls 'individual rights.' The victims of the notion could cause themselves trouble. It is our duty as the vanguard to protect them from themselves.

"Earlier systems tried to do this just by outlawing 'private property,' by replacing 'individual rights' with discipline. But they left the job undone. The desire for these things survived. We are the first to do the job completely, not with typical bourgeois oppression — but by manufacturing beings who have no such desires. We are building automatons, robots, constructed to serve. In the future, when surgery and genetics have been further developed, we shall combine those sciences with the manipulation of the environment. Until then, we must be satisfied with the latter alone. Even so, I think you will agree that we are having remarkable success. Some of the dirty little brutes housed here undoubtedly are the spawn of various Capitalist oppressors. We shall never know. But observe that after only a short application of our methods, their mothers would not know them. Is that not good reason to be inspired, Katerina Nikolaevna?"

"But you yourself have a very strong personality, comrade directress."

Nastasya Lvovna chuckled. "Quite true. Quite true." She tugged at her ear. "After all, someone must operate these robots and automatons. Some serve and some rule. Each of us has his or her place. That is the answer, my dear. Science and system. Have you noticed for instance that we allow our brats no toys?"

"Yes."

"Science and system, my dear. That's the answer. Our methods were devised by comrade Telegin himself. We must abolish pleasure because a man denied pleasure never knows he deserves it. And a man given pleasure always wants more. Pleasure is the bacillus that causes private property. No doubt you have already heard Peter Sergeievitch explain this."

"No. I haven't."

"I haven't seen him for years. You are separated, I assume, for some Party reason?"

"I would rather not discuss my personal life, Nastasya Lvovna."

Nastasya Lvovna chuckled. "Your *personal* life? There's no such thing. Surely you knew that! We owe the Party thanks. Personal lives are so puny and boring."

Katya rose, face burning, and left the office. Nastasya Lvovna chuckled at her.

What was it she had expected so many years ago? Katya tried to remember exactly, but could not. Words flitted without meaning through her mind: justice, liberty, freedom — they meant nothing. The Revolution itself, she realized, had only been a word. It, too, did not mean a thing. She told herself that she was generalizing falsely, but everywhere she went, the stories were the same.

And gradually, they began to change her because of the strong feelings they evoked. The repeated outrages had a narcotizing effect. To produce the same intensity of emotion required a stronger and stronger dose. For a minor outrage, she felt nothing at all. Intense emotions cannot be constantly maintained. Gradually she was becoming numb, neutral, impersonal. Soon she would be in perfect conformity with Telegin's theories as applied by Nastasya Lvovna.

The one pain that did not lessen was caused by the absence of Orloff. This separation was unlike his years in prison. That, although painful, had been understandable. And there had been an end in sight. But this, although necessary, was at the same time incomprehensible. It was as if a part of her body had painfully been removed. Why was it so? Must it be so? She knew that in this case, she could not be wrong. But suppose she were? Suppose the cause of the trouble was just her own blind impulsiveness? She wanted to rejoin him, but she could not. And the irreconcilable conflict was consuming her.

She went to the innumerable Communist meetings sponsored by various groups every night after work. Attendance was voluntary, of course — everyone said so — but absence created such a bad impression. Why would anyone *not* attend these meetings? It was common knowledge that they were conducted for the people's own good. What else would anyone do with his evenings? Night after night the meetings went on, every night, throughout Moscow and everywhere else, educating the beneficiaries in the complexities of Communism. Undoubtedly, because of her name, Katya could have stayed away; but she wanted to attend because it was the rule. She did not like the meetings at first, but she went.

Gradually, as with everything else, her opinion of the meetings changed. Perhaps they really weren't so bad. Perhaps if she gave them a chance, curbed her emotions, she would see that Petya was right. Perhaps, if she allowed them to, they would change her, reconcile her conflict and help her end this horrible loneliness. That, after all, was the purpose of the meetings: to bring Soviet citizens together in mutual understanding; to heal the divisions in Soviet society. For what egotistical, bourgeois reason had she come to believe

478

that she was more knowledgeable a Communist than comrades Telegin and Lunacharsky?

After a while, in a perverse way, she began to enjoy the meetings. At work, during the day, she looked forward to them. It wasn't really so bad being bored. Indeed, it was an advantage; somehow the meetings soothed and relaxed her. Her personal problems seemed less painful and important.

She was sitting in such a meeting now. How long had she been there? She could not remember. She was in a sort of daze. There were not many others in the room, about a dozen, and they too appeared comatose. Why were they there? What was the meeting about? Katya concentrated, but she could not remember. A few feet away, a young girl was talking, delivering some sort of lecture to the group. Katya could see her mouth moving, the edges of her teeth and her tongue darting in and out, her hand making accompanying gestures. But she could hear nothing. There was a steady, drowsy buzzing in her ears. Was that the girl's voice? If it was, why couldn't Katya distinguish any words? Or was it simply an inexplicable buzzing, not related to the unheard voice? The others appeared to hear nothing either. What in the world was the girl talking about? Did everyone else hear the buzz?

The girl finished abruptly and sat down. There was a pause, long enough anywhere else to be unsettling. No one moved. No one spoke. The buzzing had stopped. It had been the girl's voice, after all. Katya felt ashamed. She had been rude. She hadn't listened. The girl would be mortified to learn that she had been talking to herself. Next time, Katya would have to try harder.

"Very good," the discussion leader finally said. "Very helpful." His skin was perfectly smooth and pink. He smiled in a strangely babyish way. I am obedient, his smile said. I am lovable. Don't hurt me.

"Yes," said the others, vigorously nodding their heads. "Very helpful. Very good indeed. Remarkable grasp for so young a girl. Yes."

"Vasili Ignatievitch," said the discussion leader, "I believe you are to speak to us today."

"Yes," said Lopatkin. "That's right." He shuffled through some papers. Here was someone Katya could not figure out. Her simple presence seemed to make him nervous. He was not hostile, but he avoided her almost to the point of rudeness; she had no idea why. And this had been the case ever since she had joined the group. She did not know who Lopatkin was. She had never heard of him. But he knew perfectly well who she was. And he did not know how much she knew about "Marchenko"; whether she knew everything, or not. He did not want to find out. He did not want to discuss it. The subject made him nervous. Indeed, that was why he had left Petrograd for Moscow.

That was why Katya, a reminder of Petrograd, made him nervous, too.

Vague, mild, meandering as always, Lopatkin rose with his papers and began to address the group. "Why I Am Thankful To Comrade Trotsky," he read.

The discussion leader smiled. He could not help himself. The idea had been his. Its originality impressed him. Comrade Trotsky would be pleased, if he knew.

"The difficulty of this topic is the question of where to begin," said Lopatkin. "Innumerable answers come to mind, each as good as the next. We have so much to thank comrade Trotsky for. In fact, if there were no comrade Trotsky, God would have to invent him. If there were a God. Of course there isn't. The young lady explained that very well. Which is why we are doubly lucky to have comrade Trotsky. And that is also why, comrades, I hesitate to talk. Perhaps in my place you would choose a different reason, just as good. But no better, I am sure.

"You see, recently, in our Soviet office, a department of the glorious Red Army, the toilet was repaired. Comrades, I invite those of you who have never seen our phenomenon — the glorious Soviet spaciousness of the room, the glorious Soviet cleanliness of the tiles, the glorious operation of the Soviet plumbing — I invite you to enjoy this wonder yourselves, as guests of the glorious Red Army, as guests of comrade Trotsky himself.

"Of course, some of you may say, 'So what! Your toilet was repaired. So what!' But, comrades, I have saved the best for last. You see, on the door — inside — there is a lock. Do you begin to understand? And, periodically during the day, I go into the toilet — all quite natural, you see — and I turn the lock and I am *alone*. Do you see? Alone! Has any of you ever been alone? Perhaps you are unfamiliar with the state. A-l-o-n-e. It means to be somewhere with no one else present. It is quiet in the toilet, very still. And I stand there, perfectly quiet — and alone — and inside my head, I can hear myself think.

"Comrades, being alone is the greatest discovery since Marx. Try it! I never realized that until now. So intense is the pleasure that it is almost painful. One can't enjoy it too long at a time. One is driven to unlock and open the door and listen to the others talking outside. Comrades, believe me, it is better than cocaine — almost as good as a woman, in fact. Not as good, of course, but almost.

"And comrades, do you know what I tell myself silently in my mind, as I stand shuddering, quivering — and alone? Do you know what I tell myself every time? I say, 'God bless comrade Trotsky.' "

Lopatkin was finished. He folded his papers and sat down. Again there was a silence, as after the previous speaker. But this was different. Now there was a tension in the air, a warning. Something was wrong, something unspeakably frightening. True, Lopatkin had praised comrade Trotsky, done it effusively. But there was something wrong with the way he had done it, something threatening, something not properly educational or illuminating. Perhaps the problem was simply that they had heard what he said, which was unusual. Perhaps there was more. He had spoken in such a conversational, casual tone. But perhaps he had done so precisely because what he had said was so wrong. They looked at him and at each other, struggling hopelessly to understand, mouths opening and closing slightly, eyes blank, opaque, unseeing, like fish behind aquarium glass.

Then a huge factory worker, bald and bull-necked, rose — fists clenched, body rigid. "Outrageous!" he bellowed. "Insane! Counter-revolutionary!"

The discussion leader, like the others, had been struggling to understand whether there was anything wrong or not, whether or not Lopatkin should be praised. Now, at last, intelligence appeared in his eyes, and with it anxiety. He realized that as discussion leader he would have to make a scene. He would have to oppose somebody, another mind and will — and he could not. He could not move. He was lovable and obedient and afraid of being hurt.

"I am sorry. Excuse me. I do not understand," said Lopatkin, genuinely puzzled. Why would anyone call him counter-revolutionary, especially after he had praised comrade Trotsky so?

The girl who had preceded him began to cry loudly, in great, spasmodic sobs. The factory worker took two steps and smashed Lopatkin in the face. Lopatkin hit the wall and then the floor, his face bloody. The factory worker stood over him, fists shaking.

"Get up, you worm!" the factory worker said.

"I'm sorry," said Lopatkin, through the blood bubbling on his lips.

Suddenly, Katya felt a violent emotion. A sharp, intense pain was in her chest. Her hands were cold. She put them on her face and realized it was burning. Tears were cascading through her fingers. She felt so sorry for Lopatkin, sorrier than she had ever felt for anyone before. She was wracked with pity. She wanted to comfort this clumsy young man, to stroke his hair, soothe and reassure him. And to explain why what he had said was so wrong.

481

LXIX

The important thing about Gennady Arkadievitch was that the Revolution meant nothing to him one way or the other. It had not changed his life in even one respect. That is the only thing one can say. There had been a central government far off in Petrograd before; now there was another far off in Moscow. There always had been and always would be a central government, one not very different from the next. For hundreds of years, for no sensible reason, armies had fought on this ground to seize, to protect, to establish and to overthrow these central governments. All of which meant nothing to Gennady Arkadievitch. Soon the Communist central government would be overthrown by a new central government which, in turn, would be overthrown. That had always happened and always would. Before the Revolution, in one way or another, he had survived. And in one way or another he was surviving now. What did it matter what the armies continually fought about? Gennady Arkadievitch needed only a few mouthfuls of food, some clothing and shelter at night. That was all. He did not occupy too much space in the universe. To occupy too much space in the universe could be dangerous. He did not like tumult or excitement.

That was what worried him about the man on the wagon. During the last few days in which the new orders had been in effect, people coming down the road had usually behaved in one of two ways. They had begged: "No, comrade, why would you think I am trying to escape? I am a loyal citizen of the glorious Soviet fatherland. I am simply going to get some relatives made homeless by the Poles. Please let me pass." Or they had blustered: "Obviously you are unaware that you are talking to the cousin of a Soviet commissar."

But the man on the wagon did neither.

"Get out of the way," said the man on the wagon.

The sun was behind him and he was difficult to see. He was a tall man and he was standing erect. With him was a girl who was obviously ill. There was nothing else in the wagon. But the most unusual and therefore the most frightening thing was his tone of voice. It did not even convey a command. Calmly, without embellishment, it simply stated a fact: the fact that Gennady Arkadievitch was going to get out of the way. There was an eerie inappropriateness about it. The man on the wagon seemed not even to look at Gennady Arkadievitch. And in spite of the fact that the snow had stopped, at least momentarily, and that it was a sunny morning – or, perhaps, because of it – Gennady Arkadievitch began to shake.

"But excellency," said Gennady Arkadievitch, "the Poles! The road is closed, excellency." He pointed down the road toward the invisible Poles. He squinted up at the man on the wagon.

"You have seen our papers," said the man on the wagon.

"Oh, yes, excellency, your papers are fine," said Gennady Arkadievitch. "Your papers are perfectly in order, excellency."

Gennady Arkadievitch was becoming certain that something was about to happen. What it was, he did not know. But the man on the wagon was as still as a hand grenade from which some idiot has pulled the pin. And Gennady Arkadievitch knew that there was no way he could stop it; that some other, unknown idiot had been responsible. He licked his lips and looked over his shoulder at the hut some yards away. It was all one and the same to him whether the man on the wagon went forward or backward. Gennady Arkadievitch would eagerly have waved him by. But the commander in the hut was possibly watching. The commander would hold Gennady Arkadievitch responsible. There would be questions, accusations. He would lose his vodka ration, at the very least. He had never made a decision in his life and now he was being forced to make one. Why? He had never moved, never asked, never demanded, never tried, never succeeded – or even failed – and now reality was repaying him in this ungrateful way. Even doing nothing, his usual solution, was in this case a decision.

Gennady Arkadievitch began to plead. "Excellency, please...." He hunched his shoulders and showed his palms. They were empty, which proved his innocence.

The mouth of the man on the wagon moved. Again Gennady Arkadievitch heard the calm voice.

"You will get out of the way," said the man on the wagon, "and you will get out now."

Gennady Arkadievitch trembled, out of control. If only he could remove himself, completely, beyond memory. If only the man on the wagon would believe him. Gennady Arkadievitch reached into his coat and took out the orders from the center. Yes, that was what he needed. The orders from the center. They would prove not just that the road was closed, but that he, Gennady Arkadievitch, had had nothing to do with the decision. That he, too, was simply a victim, an insect stuck to a dissecting board with a pin.

Gennady Arkadievitch held the orders up. "Here, excellency, look for yourself. The orders from the center. The orders from the center, excellency, please!"

With great speed, the arm of the man on the wagon rose. Gennady Arkadievitch saw a whip. With great speed the arm descended. Gennady Arkadievitch felt a rivulet of fire cross his face. He staggered and fell backward in the snow. The orders from the center whirled away across it, inert, meaningless, proving nothing.

Michael cracked the whip again, this time over the horses' heads. He shouted. The horses sprang forward and were quickly going at good speed. Behind him, a loud voice was screaming, the voice of the man he had whipped into the snow. A door banged open. There was the slushy patter of many running feet, another voice shouted and bullets came pinging into the drifts all around him.

Then he was at the top of the ridge, over, and out of range. The horses were running fast and free. The guards would now go for their own horses, he knew, and would find that Michael had carefully dispersed them. He was in the clear. He looked at Maria. She sat on the bed of the wagon. She was smiling but her face was flushed, alive not just with excitement but with fever. They had managed to stay ahead of the Reds, at least so far. But the colorless, invisible enemy — typhus — had caught them. Maria needed a doctor at once.

Hour after hour passed. Michael's arm rose and fell. The whip cracked, biting at the air, goading the horses on and on. It was cold, but the sun on his face was hot. And before them, the icy plain stretched to the horizon and beyond — lonely, bare, as if they were the only people alive. They had with them only a little food and some almost worthless rubles. Nothing else. Michael had never been where they were going. If they arrived — and they would, they had to — they would have to begin at the very beginning. They would have to learn a new language. They would be exiles; homeless and without a country. And yet this was preferable to life in their native land. Perhaps they would again meet the Americans they had deceived. Would the Americans believe the truth?

On and on they went. Whip cracking. Hooves pounding. Wheels creaking. Snow crunching. Hour after hour. Through sunset, moonrise and late into the night. Finally Michael stopped reluctantly to rest. There was an abandoned shack some distance from the road and they used it. It was in fairly

484

good condition and would keep the weather out. They did not speak. They couldn't: they were too exhausted. They both fell asleep immediately.

Michael was awakened by the rising whistle of the wind. It was just getting light. And it was snowing. A gust whipped in his face as he stepped outside. There already had been a sizeable snow fall. The horses were standing in the lee of the shack, and he bridled one but it would not come out. He pulled it forward and it came a few feet, then fell to its knees and collapsed. There was another noisy gust and the corpse began to blend into the snow, not even needing to be shot. Michael put the other horse into the traces, loaded Maria into the wagon and they were off.

All day they went forward, at less than half the pace, the horse reluctantly spending itself, the snow gusting, the light dim. Maria was dizzy, burning with fever. Her skin sizzled, yet she was cold. Her mind flitted from thing to thing. Faces passed before her: her mother's, her father's, Orloff's, Stepan's. She could not concentrate. But there was no need to. If only the hideous movement would stop. More than anything else, she wanted to lie still.

Toward evening, the second horse gave out in the traces in the middle of the road. Michael shot him where he fell, undid the harness, came around the wagon and lifted Maria out. She was shaking her head with despair.

"What's wrong?" he asked.

"There's nothing left," she said. "I'm finished."

"No, you aren't."

"I can't go on."

"You don't have to. Leave it to me."

"But the horses. . . ."

"Forget the horses. I'm going to pull."

She shook her head crazily. "It can't be done."

At the side of the road there was a rocky place, protected from much of the wind and snow. He carried her over and put her there. Her lips were moving and he bent to hear.

"Leave me!" she was saying. "Leave me!"

"You're talking nonsense, comrade. Stop it."

"Without me you can make it. With me you can't. Please! Leave me! Just let me sleep."

He ignored her and stripped the wagon to nothing but a platform on wheels. He stripped the harness. The process took only a few minutes, but when he got back to the rocks, Maria was gone. The place where she had sat was still faintly visible. The snow was whirling. It was difficult to see, even a few feet. There were no footprints to tell which way she had gone. He ran some distance in one direction and saw nothing, then some distance in the other and jumped on a big rock. She was not far off and moving away with difficulty. Luckily, her dark clothes made her easy to see. As he watched, she fell and continued on hands and knees.

With a few long strides, he was beside her, and pulled her to her feet. "Do you realize how silly you look doing that?" he said.

"Have you been watching?"

"Yes."

Maria began pounding at him, frenetically but weakly, fluttering like a bird. "Brute! Beast! Savage! Peasant!"

In less than a minute, she was out of energy. Maria collapsed against his chest. He carried her to the wagon, laid her on it and tied her down. Again her lips were moving and she was whispering.

"Too tight, too tight," she said into his ear.

"No."

"Please!"

"Comrade, I'm sorry, but you just can't be trusted."

He got into the harness, adjusted it and pushed. The wagon's motive power had been reduced from eight legs to four to two. But grudgingly, reluctantly, the wheels began to turn. Again they were moving, this time even slower, but moving in the right direction. Periodically he untied her, got her up, brushed off all the snow, forced her to move, held her, warmed her, to keep the flickering life in her alive. The wind rose even higher and it was against him. Cascading snow slammed into his face. At first he squinted, trying to see through it. But he could see absolutely nothing, and it was easier not to try. Indeed, there was a piercing pain in both his eyes, and he closed them for long periods and staggered blindly on. It was important only to keep his feet moving. After a while, his feet lost all sensation. The strap around his forehead was like a jaw biting into his brain, gradually crushing and splintering his skull. From time to time, he tripped and fell.

Reality slipped away. He could see nothing. His eyelids were frizzy and sealed with snow. He could hear nothing, except for the whistling wind. He knew nothing. He remembered nothing. He was in a vacuum, a void in which reality did not exist. He did not know where he was going or why, or whether it was remotely possible to get there. He could not even be sure that there was such a thing as time and, if there were, how much time had passed. He was sure only of one thing: He had to keep moving and would keep moving forever through the void, pressing forever against the burning strap on his forehead, raising and lowering his insensible feet, staggering forward blindly through eternity.

When he awoke it was morning and he was leaning against a tree. The sun was shining. The snow had stopped. Before him was a town, a river, people. Beside him was a road clogged with refugees plunging past him toward the roofs and the water. Where they were, he did not know. Maria was at his feet, sitting against the tree, eyes closed, mouth slightly open. The fever was at its height. But the wagon was gone. What had happened? How had they gotten here without it? He struggled to understand, to remember; but he could not. He knew only that for some reason it was necessary to keep moving. He lifted Maria. She seemed very heavy. He stepped into the road and was swept away by the crowd, down the steep incline to the river and the town.

He could see, but somehow his eyes would not focus. And before them was a tangle of heads, wheels and other objects, turning, waving, running and colliding. He could hear, but only faintly, as if the shrieking, crying and bellowing were a long distance away. He lifted his feet and put them down, allowing himself to be propelled by the mob. His head fell uncontrollably back on his neck, tilting his face blindly to the sun. In a few minutes he had staggered down the hill and was moving with the others through the heart of the town. Buildings whirled. They seemed about to fall. Faces were in windows screaming. He put Maria down and leaned against a wall. Somebody was immediately pulling at his trousers, an officer in some strange uniform, who somehow had lost the use of his legs. His mouth was moving. Michael heard his voice. But the officer spoke no words. He simply made a sound. Blood was pouring from his mouth and nose. Michael's ears were ringing. He picked up Maria again and staggered on. Behind him, the officer drew his pistol and shot himself. The sound was lost in the general din. No one paid the slightest attention.

Then there was a beach. There was a river. There was a bridge. And from every street, people were pouring across the beach onto it. As Michael was about to leave the street, a machine gun began firing from above and behind them. The Reds were already on the bluff over the town. There was a shout and a wailing. The refugees already on the beach began to run, forcing themselves onto the bridge. Some fell. Others screamed.

"Come back! Come back!" someone gasped. "Help!" An arm rose from the beach, reaching. A head rose. Then they fell.

"It's hopeless," someone said. "We're trapped."

The refugees about to cross the beach stopped. Behind them in the streets, others still pressed forward, angrily trying to force their way through, unaware of what had happened.

Then the firing stopped, too. The beach was strewn with bodies.

487

Suddenly there was a scream so desperate, so fearful, so full of horror, that it clearly was heard even over that roar. It was so frightening, in fact, that the roar stopped.

"Papa! Papa!" the voice called. "Come back!"

A priest had been dislodged from the crowd and was wandering on the beach. A large crucifix on a chain shone on his breast. He was a huge, elderly man. And he was blind. Arms before him, he was staggering in circles, making no progress, tripping over the bodies, trying unsuccessfully to find the voice. It called again, but he continued as before. He was confused.

The Reds on the bluff began firing again. With one hand, the priest tightly seized the crucifix. Tiny tornadoes of sand flew all around him. His tall black hat flew off. Then a round caught him in the shoulder and he went down. Still holding the crucifix, he sat up with difficulty, eyes nothing but large, empty whites. He stared up at the machine gun, struggling to see. But he could not. Then the heavy bullets slammed him again to the ground and he was dead.

But the firing continued. The bullets smashed into the large, inert form. The Reds wanted not simply to kill him, but to eradicate him; to wipe him from memory; to destroy any evidence that he had ever existed. For several minutes they continued firing. And gradually, the proof disintegrated, until nothing was left but some bone and black cloth, a twisted crucifix and a wet mark in the sand. Yet the firing continued for a minute or two more.

Finally the firing stopped. There was complete silence, eerie in view of the huge, impatient crowd. Thousands of eyes stared, saw and disbelieved. Then there was a penetrating, raucous laugh. Far above, on the bluff, stood a man shaking a fist.

"Oh, my God!" said a soft voice in the crowd. "Oh, my God!"

"We're already dead," said another. "We're in hell."

The machine gun was empty, Michael knew. It would take a few seconds to reload. He picked up Maria and began staggering across the beach, picking his way between the bodies toward the bridge. He was already more than halfway there, and behind him the others were following close. He could already hear the water lapping at the pilings and the wet sand sucking as he lifted his feet. Then the machine gun began firing again, and around him there were screams and whirlpools in the sand. Once again people were falling.

There was a flash and an explosion and he dropped Maria and went down. His face was raw, bloody and burning. He could not see. He felt for Maria and straddled her on hands and knees, shielding her from the hail of bullets and bodies, one of which slammed into his back and slid off. Again he lifted her and got to his feet. He heard footsteps clattering on the wood of the bridge. He staggered toward them, blindly, unconsciously, his face blazing, chest heaving, arms and legs numb, mind and body out of control.

He had been stripped of everything, reduced to nothing. All that remained was his will to keep moving.

LXX

Orloff did not feel very well. His neck was stiff. His stomach was upset. He had just eaten without enjoyment at the station buffet, but he felt painfully hollow. In fact, he felt nauseated. The trouble was that he could not sleep. He had never before realized what a pleasure it was, and had never had any trouble enjoying it. But lately sleep had become a rare and unpleasant necessity. Hour after hour, he would lie in bed or pace the floor. And he had lost his enormous ability to concentrate. He would sit at his desk for hours trying to think. His manner had changed. No longer did he radiate the certainty of unarguable authority. He was nervous, diffident, insecure, as if afraid of being punished. And at the same time, he was regularly overcome by emotions, often contradictory and apparently causeless. In the halls of the Gorokhovaya, puzzled colleagues watched him pass.

But soon he would see Katya and would feel better. That was why he had come to Moscow. He no longer liked the town and had not been there for some time — not since he had made the speech. He would see Katya and they would get together again. He would tell Katya he had been wrong. He would tell Katya she had been right, although he still did not understand how. It would be a new experience. He looked forward to it. He had never before had to say he was wrong, until he had said it to Michael. He was still not used to saying it. He wanted to abase himself, which was also something new. He had been selfish about his principles. He had not thought of her. As always, he wanted to sacrifice.

Expressionless faces passed him in the street, on heads that protruded from castaway clothes, silent, remote, as in a dream. Orloff felt anxious. Perhaps something had happened to Katya. Perhaps she was ill. In the present situation, she would have been too proud to ask him for help.

He realized he was walking across Red Square. It was in Red Square that he had made the speech — on the very spot he was crossing now — to an audience of thousands of the same remote faces. Had they listened? Had they heard? Now they were passing, but paid him no attention. Were they deliberately ignoring him? What right had they to put on airs? No one was any better than anyone else. He flushed as he thought this. Such thoughts were beneath him. The fault had been his. No one else was to blame. It was the speech that had started the trouble. Or had it?

He found the right office and gave his name and hers. The Soviet receptionist wore too much makeup. It was caked heavily around her mouth. It was too red. Like so many insignificant things lately, it irritated rather than amused him. Indeed, lately he was always irritated to some extent. She smiled too coyly, too deferentially, which also repelled him.

Now someone was shaking his hand vigorously. It was Nastasya Lvovna, whom he did not recognize. "So good to see you, comrade general," she said. "Such a long time. So many battles. Perhaps you will stop by my office later to reminisce." Nastasya Lvovna looked at her watch, turned abruptly and was gone.

A door opened and Katya was coming down the hall. To his relief, he saw that she was smiling. She was radiant. Her eyes shone. Her arms were opening. And to his surprise, she kissed him passionately on the lips in view of the receptionist. It was unlike her. The receptionist smirked, revealing her missing teeth. Deep cracks furrowed her makeup. It annoyed him.

"So good, Petya, so wonderful," Katya was saying. "I knew it! I was just about to come to you!"

No longer was Katya calm and quiet. Now she was excitable, even effusive. She could not get the words out fast enough. They were clipped uncharacteristically. The end of each was devoured by the next. She spoke somewhat like Nastasya Lvovna.

"Petya!" she said, eyes brimming with joy. "You were so right! Thank you! I should have listened!"

There was a strange incongruity between her speech and her manner. She was mildly irritable, but did not seem to know it.

Puzzled, Orloff tried to move her down the hall where they could be alone. But she did not notice and would not move.

"I was being selfish, Petya, sinfully so," she said. "Don't you see? Somewhere over the years I had gone wrong. What right had I to make such demands? Especially after the Party had placed such confidence in us. For years I foolishly thought I was a good Party member, when all along I was putting my puny whims above it. I was playing at Communism, Petya. I was nothing but an insipid bourgeoise and didn't even know it. A fraud!

"But now, Petya, now you will be pleased. When I breathe now, I do so because Communism wills it. When I raise my arm, the reason is the same. I no longer have a separate existence. I am a tool, a cell, a limb of the Revolution. I am not even talking to you now. Communism is. I have been working at it, Petya. God knows, it has been painful! One resists, twisted by one's petty, personal feelings. We all do. But I learned from you, Petya, from your great example. I knew that the pain proved I was making progress. And the result! The bliss! To want nothing, hope nothing, feel nothing, be nothing — to surrender everything completely to the Party. To have the integrity not to hold back. Thank you, Petya, thank you! You are responsible! You get all the credit! You saved me. I am your creation. Petya, come live with us. We need you!"

"Us?"

"Yes. Our commune, Petya."

"Your . . . commune?"

"You would love Moscow. It is so exciting. Our leaders are all around us. This is the Party's heart. Do you hear it beating, Petya?"

He became aware that someone else was with them, a younger man, vaguely interested, vaguely present, simply vague.

"Petya, this is comrade Vasili Ignatievitch Lopatkin. A member of our commune," she said excitedly.

Comrade Lopatkin was vaguer than ever. He felt good, completely at peace. He had no resentments, no dislikes. He liked everything. He loved everybody. The problem of his misunderstanding in the discussion group had been solved. Nastasya Lvovna had explained his mistake. She had encouraged his and Katya's idea about the commune. Now everything was finally set right.

"Most gratified," he murmured, without looking at Orloff. "Heard so much. Been an admirer so long."

Tears of bliss were on Katya's face. "Oh, Petya, don't you see? At last I understand! At last I see what you wanted me to know!" She held up a book. Orloff had not noticed it. "Look, Petya. Engels. *Origin of the Family.*" She opened it and began to read: " '. . . It was the first form of the family to be based, not on natural, but on economic conditions — on the victory of private property over primitive, natural, communal property. The Greeks themselves put the matter quite frankly: the sole exclusive aims of monogamous marriage were to make the man supreme in the family, and to propagate, as the future heirs to his wealth, children indisputably his own . . . .'

"All must belong to all, Petya. Now I understand. You were reluctant to tell me. You were afraid I would suffer. You knew how stupidly rebellious I was. You didn't realize you were denying me peace. You were hurting me

492

with what you thought was kindness. I was your weakness. You catered to the ignorance of an insipid bourgeoise. You, Peter Sergeievitch Orloff, the perfect Communist! But I have been studying, Petya, as you see. For instance, it was comrade Lenin himself who said in his third *Letter From Afar* that 'if we do not tear women away from the deadening atmosphere of household and kitchen, then it is impossible to secure real freedom. It is impossible even to build democracy, let alone Socialism.'

"Petya, I am so happy. I have never been happier. Forgive me for having caused you so much pain. I was so stupid. I'm sorry."

Was this some sort of monstrous joke? Was it a silly attempt at sarcasm? But Katya was not only incapable of sarcasm, she did not know what it was. It had always been, and still was, alien to her. Katya always took everything literally.

He looked into her eyes. They were covered with a glaze, as if she were looking through a curtain of unawareness. She was looking at him, but her eyes did not appear to see. Her smile was fixed, her voice metallic, and it excitedly continued reciting quotations.

He turned abruptly, staggered away and began to run. Behind him, her voice mechanically called his name. Startled commissars stopped to stare. He brushed them aside. He had to get away.

Then he was standing at the entrance to Red Square. Before him the cobblestones stretched endlessly away, to the place where he had made the speech. Suddenly, he was very short of breath. He put a finger in his collar, but it was already quite loose. He was covered with sweat. An iron vise squeezed his chest.

The cobblestones were churning, like a sea in bad weather. Wave after wave of cobblestones approached, each wave higher than the last. The air was filled with them, rising and falling, blotting out the sun and the sky. Then they formed a pattern. They were whirling around him. He was standing at the bottom of a vortex of cobblestones. Indeed, everything else, everything in the world, was whirling around him as well. He could see nothing but a strange blur.

Orloff raised his arms. "Citizens!" he roared. "Comrades! I can't breathe!"

The Red Square rose in answer and pressed him flat. Voices babbled. Faceless heads were peering down. A hand tentatively reached for his collar. He saw and heard everything, but could not move.

An automobile horn blew with authority. An automobile door opened and closed. Heads turned. The crowd parted.

"What's all this?" asked an approaching voice.

Hands were under his arms and lifting. He was being propelled quickly through the crowd. The voice loudly cleared the way. Again the automobile door opened and closed. He was seated on the comfortable cushions of a limousine. The voice spoke shortly. The limousine began to move. A hand clapped him on the knee.

"So good to see you again," said the voice. "My regrets that it must be like this. I did not know your health was bad. How lucky it is that I happened along. You're working too hard. That's the trouble. You need a few weeks in a glorious Soviet sanitarium."

Orloff painfully turned his head. Telegin was seated next to him. The limousine was moving with difficulty through the crowd and Telegin abruptly lowered the window.

"Get out of the way, you louts!" he bawled. "Move!"

He raised the window and settled back comfortably on the cushions. His jowls were quivering.

"Trash! Garbage!" said Telegin. "Imagine being near enough to one of these creatures to smell him. I'm told they don't change their clothes all winter. I'd rather deal with African apes."

Telegin, on the contrary, was turned out perfectly, dressed in the latest London style. It seemed as if he had been swept up moments before from Whitehall and deposited a few moments later in Red Square. In that shabby setting, he looked very out of place. Indeed, he was bigger than ever. His massive middle permanently concealed his feet as in some pedestrian sort of eclipse. His jowls hung in dewlaps to his collar. He took a bottle from a car pocket and passed it to Orloff with a pudgy smile.

"Cognac. Drink! You will feel better."

Orloff did as he was told. As he lowered the bottle, he noticed for the first time that Dolgorensky and Golovin sat facing him.

"Congratulations on your promotion," said Dolgorensky.

"Yes," said Golovin. "I have always admired you so much."

"Forgive me," said Telegin. "I had not heard."

"Comrade general Orloff is now the Cheka's number two man," said Dolgorensky. "He is responsible only to comrade Felix himself. He has been properly rewarded for the skill with which he solved Marchenko's murder and smashed the conspiracy to free the murderer. Her escape was the fault of the general's treacherous former adjutant. Isn't that right, comrade general?"

Dolgorensky had never hated Orloff more. He, Dolgorensky, had deserved that promotion. Why did Orloff have such luck? He was soft, bourgeois; that was why he had fainted. The truth was he had botched the Marchenko affair. He had been promoted simply to conceal his failure.

494

"So pleasant, so nostalgic, to see you again," said Telegin. "It brings back fond memories of the day you read my words — *you* — reading my puny, paltry, inexpressive words — to such an audience in this very place. And at the same time, it brings sadness because the occasion was the funeral of your unfortunate nephew. Ah, well, 'The bitter with the sweet,' I always say. I, too, have suffered, comrade general. Your niece was my wife. But, then, the Revolution spares no one, does it? It shouldn't! So sad. Tragic, in fact. But inevitable. You have no idea how much I suffered in presenting the government's case. My own wife! Forgive me, comrade general; of course you do. Masha was your niece. But duty, the sternest taskmaster, called — a call you in particular will understand — calling me to rise above the puny pleasures of selfishness. Duty to the greatest of all Revolutions, led by our glorious leader, Lenin.

"We have all gladly sacrificed so much, comrade general, to build this best, this finest, this most humane, of all possible worlds. But imagine sacrificing one's own dear wife with the knowledge that I could have used trickery to save her. You will want to comfort me, I know, but I have recovered. Thank you. I accept. The personal has no place in the Revolution. 'You can't make an omelet without breaking eggs.' Catchy, isn't that? Who said it? Was it Robespierre?

"How opportune it is that we meet at this time, comrade general. I am just on my way to see comrade Trotsky, to explain the application of our commune program. Why don't you come along? You would be fascinated, I am sure. We are having amazing results in developing the proper Communist attitude. Comrade Lunacharsky thanked me just the other day in the name of the State.

"We have suffered so much together, comrade general. We are truly 'comrades in arms.' We have so much in common. We should see more of each other. I hope we will. You are such a perfect Communist, comrade general."

Orloff took another pull on the bottle, a long one. Some of the contents ran down his chin. His head hurt. He could not concentrate.

Telegin smiled. What a piece of luck! It would be an advantage to appear with Orloff before Lev Davidovitch. Lev Davidovitch would be impressed. Lev Davidovitch thought highly of Orloff. Lev Davidovitch would think highly of Telegin.

Then they were inside the Kremlin wall.

LXXI

It was very early on a summer morning. It was clear. It was cool. It would be a perfect day. The sun was rising. The dust in the road already hung in its rays. The birds and insects were loudly harmonizing. Eastern Europe was waking up.

Michael stepped into the saddle and rode slowly out of town. Far away, across the fields, he could see the roof of the hospital, near the road, on a steep hill. There was a breeze, and the crops rustled. The horse thudded softly in the dust. The smell of wet grass was in the air.

He was almost at the foot of the hill leading to the hospital. At one side of the road was a stand of corn, tall, green, ready to be picked. At the other was a canebrake, and behind it an orchard. He rode into the orchard and under a tree. It was a peach tree. Nearby were others, cherries and pears. He inhaled the aroma. He pulled a peach down. It came quickly, easily — it sprang into his hand — as if eager to fulfill its purpose. There was a worm on the peach and he brushed it away. The peach was magnificent; yellow, red, firm but soft, full, plump, pleading to be eaten.

He bit into the peach. His teeth sank easily into the yielding, orange meat. The nectar sprang out, thick and sweet, awakening his taste, filling his mouth. It ran down his chin and fell on his tunic. He did not wipe it off. He licked his lips and leaned back on the cantle, threw his head back and chewed very slowly. The long, thin scar on his cheek blazed like molten metal. The serenade of the birds and insects was at its peak.

He licked the pit clean and threw it away. It fell to earth, where it would father more. Peaches, pleasure and human life were possible.

Then he saw her. She was standing at the top of the hill, in front of the hospital, on the lawn. She was alone. And suddenly she rose up on her toes, back arched, torso forward, as if affixed to the prow of a schooner, fists raised high in a spontaneous, exuberant celebration of health. Her fists

496

opened, flowering, fingers reaching for the morning, reaching up, up for the sun.

He moved out from under the tree into the open and she saw him. She called him, clearly. He heard his name. She kicked off her shoes and began to run, her long, golden legs flashing, her hair a black mane. She sailed easily over a hedge. Then she was standing, smiling, lips parted, arms wide, reaching, waiting, waiting for him, suffused with a proud, inviolable splendor.

Michael Voronov took the reins. He put his feet in the stirrups. He squeezed the horse. He shouted and sat erect to the gallop. He thundered through the orchard toward her, yes, and peach, pear, cherry bursting, earth turning, day breaking, Michael Voronov sprang across the canebrake. He rang upon the road. He flashed across the sunrise.

Then he was rising, rising in the face of nations, over the heads of kings, beyond the reach of commissars, above the guilt of history; rising to the white swan, to the winged victory; rising to her, to the soundest heart, to the serenest conscience, to the greatest joy, to the highest virtue.

THE END